REDEMPTION

REDEMPTION

ELLE CHARLES

REDEMPTION

Copyright © Elle Charles 2022

Cover design by Rachelle Gould-Harris of Designs by Rachelle

www.designsbyrachelle.com

For all enquiries, please email: elle@ellecharles.com

www.ellecharles.com

ISBN: 9798800066562

First publication: 16 May 2022

First Edition

Contents

Prologue..1

Chapter 1 25

Chapter 2 35

Chapter 3 53

Chapter 4 59

Chapter 5 75

Chapter 6 87

Chapter 7 97

Chapter 8 113

Chapter 9 127

Chapter 10 141

Chapter 11 155

Chapter 12 165

Chapter 13 173

Chapter 14 187

Chapter 15 205

Chapter 16 213

Chapter 17 223

Chapter 18 229

Chapter 19 245

Chapter 20 259

Chapter 21 265

Chapter 22 273

Chapter 23 287

Chapter 24 295

Chapter 25 301

Chapter 26 307

Chapter 27 323

Chapter 28 335

Chapter 29 343

Chapter 30 355

Chapter 31 361

Chapter 32 367

Chapter 33 375

Chapter 34 391

Chapter 35 401

Chapter 36 411

Chapter 37 425

Chapter 38 433

Chapter 39 443

Chapter 40 453

Chapter 41 463

Author Note 471

Follow Elle...473

About the Author...475

Works by Elle Charles 477

Author Note

Redemption is the first of a duet within the series and ends on a cliffhanger. The concluding novel, Reparation, completes Jeremy and Evie's story and will be release in due course.

Redemption is a long, slow-burning, all-the-feels romance. It is the fifth instalment of the Fractured series and is a full-length novel.

Throughout the story, there is cross-referencing to events within the previous four books, and it is therefore crucial to have read the full series so far due to the story arc, the various character backgrounds, and their relationships.

Please be advised this novel contains descriptive scenes of sex, violence, and drug use.

Prologue

BRIGHT RIBBONS OF neon light illuminate the damp city streets for miles. The music is thumping, the crowds bustling. I gaze around with disinterest, the vibe of the night already wearing thin and grating on my last nerve. I inhale deeply on the cigarette lodged between my lips. The sharp shot of nicotine hits the back of my throat before its poison expands my lungs in a toxic cloud. Flicking the end on the ground, I grind it beneath my boot the same moment my pocket starts to vibrate.

I pull out my mobile and sigh at the screen. John Walker. A man I've known and respected from the age of thirteen. A man I've always looked up to as a father figure. And a man who equals staunch intervention of my less than desirable lifestyle choices.

My thumb hovers above the screen, moving between answer and end until I press red and slip it back into my pocket.

I lean back against the wall and take in the typical Friday night playing out before me. The area is heaving, and the queue from the nightclub opposite snakes down the street and around the corner. People flow from the clubs and pubs onto the pavement, adding to the drunk and disorderly chaos.

"Hey, man, how much?"

I swing my head to the side and look the young lad up and down. He can't be more than eighteen – *just* – and it's kids like these who plague my guilty conscience. But who am I to tell them to just say no? Yet as I stare at him, my internal morality duelling inside with my immorality as to whether or not I should sell to him, a long-forgotten memory quickly resurfaces. I remember when I was once a teenage, Friday night recreational user. *Once* being the operative word because those days of *once* are long gone. Once becomes twice, twice becomes thrice, and suddenly you're hooked. Still, I can't specifically recall when I went from being recreational to dependent. All I know is, in the space of less than twelve months, I'd become unrecognisable to myself.

"Depends on what you want," I eventually answer, immorality winning the battle.

"Well, what have you got?"

1

"Most things." I keep it vague because I trust no one. And it wouldn't be the first time the police have used kids in a sting to gain convictions in their attempt to clean up the streets.

The lad grins – the foolish git – and removes a wad of notes from his pocket along with a few condoms and his debit card. I observe his clumsy, inebriated movements. It would be so easy to fleece him of his cash. But of everything I am and everything I am deemed to be, I'm not a thief. Druggie, supplier, unintended bringer of death – *maybe* - but never a thief.

"What does twenty quid buy me?"

I slip my hand inside the bag strapped across my torso and produce three different packets. Holding them close to my hip, out of sight of prying eyes, the kid weighs them up until he taps his finger on the bag of coke.

"You've taken this before, right?" I hold the bag back before I hand it over, my morality refusing defeat so easily. The kid rolls his eyes and nods, disconcerted. I inconspicuously shake my head and exchange it for cash because he's on an unknown path of destruction along with the rest of the weekend users. It's a path I know well. I once walked it. I now live it. And one day, I know it will devour me completely.

"Nice doing business, man," the kid says and walks away.

"You fucking idiot," I breathe out, although I'm unsure which of us I'm referring to as my mobile vibrates again. Retrieving it for the fourth time tonight, the caller piques my attention, and I swipe the screen.

"Rem?" The Yorkshire drawl of Dominic Archer fills my ear before I can even say hello.

"Hey, how are you doing?"

"John's been trying to call you," he replies, not bothering to reciprocate my greeting. "Have you spoken to him?"

"No." I furrow my brow, speculating what the urgent urgency is.

Dom sighs, agitated. "Well, I suggest you make that call asap, lad."

"Yeah, I will, but I'm busy right now. I'll call him later," I reply half-heartedly. Knowing my luck, he'll just want to impart his latest lecture on my varying and illegal ways of earning an income. I know what I'm doing is wrong. I don't need him to spell it out to me. *Again.*

"No, Jeremy, now! For once in your life, quit peddling your fucking filth and do as you're told!" Dom demands. "And I appreciate I'd be better off talking to a brick wall, but just for the record, you need to stop that shit before you get caught and banged up. The Blacks have got you in far too deep, and you need to get as far away from them while you still can!" Then he hangs up.

"For fuck sake!" I grit out under my breath. Glancing at my watch, it's almost midnight. I look around at the intoxicated revellers and mentally calculate how much gear I've shifted tonight. I haven't been as busy as I am most nights, but my trade is swings and roundabouts, and I can't exactly advertise my nefarious services in the classifieds or online, can I?

I scroll through the missed call log, pick out one of John's many unanswered calls during the last hour or so and dial.

"You rang?" I ask when he picks up.

"Where are you?" His tone is harsh and unwavering, taking me back.

"Hello, J, it's nice to hear from you," I quip sarcastically. "What's wrong with you all tonight? Dom's just given me an earful too!" I'm being flippant, but honestly, I really couldn't care less.

"Cut the mouth, Rem. I haven't got time for this. Where are you?"

"I'm in town," I reply with a sigh.

"Is Deacon with you?"

I narrow my eyes – he never asks about Deacon. *Ever.* "No, I don't know where he is. Why?"

John's redundant sigh fills my eardrum. "You're not lying to protect him, are you?"

My face screws up at his furtive insinuation. "John, what are you talking about?" I ask in confusion. "I've not seen him since this morning."

"I'm on my way up to Manchester. Something happened tonight." His voice turns solemn, raising the hairs on the back of my neck.

"What?" I impatiently wave a prospective purchaser away, suddenly caring a lot more than I did moments ago.

"Charlie was repeatedly raped and beaten in Sloan's digs tonight," he says without equivocation, but the charged emotion in his tone is undisguisable.

"What?" I ask again in disbelief, my voice faltering, my eyes beginning to sting. Charlotte Black, Sloan and Deacon's half-sister is like my own sister, and she's just fourteen years old. "No, you don't think Deacon is capable of-"

"Oh, I think he's more than capable," John cuts me off. "I think he's willing. I think he's able, and I think he'd enjoy it, too."

"No, no, no. Not Charlie," I say because he'd never do that to his own flesh and blood. I know he hates Sloan in a way that is unfathomable, but he's never said anything about Charlotte. "John, you're wrong; he wouldn't."

"No. I. Am. Not!" he shouts. "You go home tonight and before you start injecting that fucking shit into your veins, ask him. Look into his eyes when he replies, and then you call me and tell me that I'm wrong! And another thing now that I've finally managed to get you on the blower after all these months, you need to get clean, Jeremy. You need to get clean and sober, and you need to get away from the Blacks. They're poison!"

"John-" I start to no avail.

"No, you listen up and listen good. You keep in Franklin's pocket; you're doomed, sunshine. In case you've forgotten, let me re-jog your memory. You've got a family down here who love you. A girl up there who loves you – a girl that they've also managed to get addicted."

I grind my jaw. I don't have the heart to tell him the truth on that one.

"What will it take for you to get on the wagon? One of your customers dying? Your girl dying? Think long and hard about the life you're living, Jeremy. The path you've chosen only leads to one place – death. And it will break my fucking heart if the day ever comes that I have to stand at your grave when they put you in the ground prematurely!"

The line suddenly goes dead, and I lower the phone and stare at it. A hundred different scenarios fight for supremacy inside my head, but only one is winning. I swipe the screen with my thumb again and press call.

"Yeah?" Deacon answers on the third ring. I narrow my eyes because he sounds uncharacteristically cheerful.

"You at home?" The suspicion in my query is apparent, but he doesn't pick up on it.

"Yeah."

"Okay, I'm done for tonight. I'll see you in thirty minutes." I hang up and slip it back into my pocket. Zipping up my jacket, one of my regulars approaches me with a twenty in his hand.

"I'm out!" I announce and walk the other way.

"Come on, man, I need a hit." He grabs hold of my arm, causing me to stop.

"I said *I'm out*, arsehole!" I shrug him off and continue to walk. "I'm out," I whisper, but I'm not out, not really. And I'll never be truly out until I'm laid out. John's right because one day, I fear it *will* be prematurely on a mortuary slab.

"Deacon?" I slam the front door behind me. "Deek?"

"In here!" he shouts back as faint giggles float over the atmosphere.

I dump the supply bag on the hallway floor and open the living room door. The room is a mess. Granted, we don't live in the lap of luxury, but it's not squalid either. However, tonight it seems Deacon has himself a little party. Lager cans and takeaway containers litter the carpet, while the coffee table has become a makeshift cutting bench.

I narrow my eyes as he guides a rolled-up note over a line on the table and snorts it back heavily. My sight drifts from him to the half-naked, half-cut woman straddling his leg.

"Where were you tonight?" I fail to keep the undisclosed accusation from my tone again.

"Out!" He pinches his nose and wipes the back of his hand under it. "God, this shit's good!"

"Where?"

"What the fuck is this?" He throws his arm up, hitting the girl's cheek and knocking her to the floor in the process.

"Something happened tonight, and I need to know where you were."

"Fine! We were in a bar watching the football, weren't we?" He elbows the girl's shoulder as she scrambles to her knees at his feet.

"Erm, yeah?" She answers his question with a question, completely oblivious. Whether that's intoxication or otherwise, I don't know.

"So, you weren't anywhere near Sloan's gaff?"

"No! Why the fuck would I want to see that prick? He's too close for comfort. What happened? Did his place get robbed?" he asks sarcastically, and something flashes in his eyes. I stare into them for a beat, unsure what to make of it.

"Something like that," I murmur, since something did get robbed – a young girl's virtue, but not only that, her trust and her future, too.

I bend down and remove a bag of H from the table and toss down tonight's takings. "I'm going to bed. Is Em here?"

"Yeah, she was here when I got back, sticking all the proceeds in her veins as usual. You need to warn that bitch that I'm going to start charging for her consumption. It's not normal."

My brows peak because no, it's not, and that's something else I've never admitted the truth about, either. Nothing further is said, and I shut the door behind me and jog up the stairs.

Opening my bedroom door, the landing light cascades over the sleeping silhouette of Emma Shaw, the first and - probably - the only woman I'll ever love. I knew it from the first moment I ever saw her. Approaching slowly, I lean down and press a kiss to her lips while simultaneously pressing two fingers to her throat to check for a pulse. It's morbid, but it has to be done, considering her penchant for overindulgence is becoming out of control.

Satisfied with the slow reverberation in her jugular, I pull out my phone. There's another missed call from John, but right now, I just want to wash away everything that I've learned tonight.

Steam fills the bathroom while I strip off my clothes. Ducking under the flow, I stare at the partially mouldy grouting and press my forehead to the tiles. I close my eyes, my thoughts consumed by Charlotte and what she must be going through right now. I sigh wearily. I know I need to call John, and it's a call I don't want to make. I asked the question, and I got the answer. I don't know if Deacon's lying, but I can't call the woman half-naked in the living room a liar either.

I turn off the shower, wrap a towel around my hips and stand in front of the mirror. I run my hand over my face, wondering when my appearance became so gaunt and shallow. Once upon a time, I was called handsome. The last time being the night I enticed a beautiful woman into my bed – a bed in which she still resides frequently. But the measure of the man I am will never be calculated on my looks. It will be calculated on what I do with my life, the direction it turns, and what happens after. Only I have no idea what tomorrow holds, never mind next week or next month.

I turn off the light and close the bathroom door ajar. Passing Deacon's partially open door, the girl from downstairs is now naked, flat on her back, her limbs spread, her wrists tied to the headboard spindles. The bed rocks hard, and the combined grunts and moans grow louder until she whimpers like she's in pain.

"Deek, please, it hurts. St-" Her pleading is in vain when he backhands her, and she shuts up. I linger for a moment, wondering if I should stop him. It wouldn't be the first time he's gotten rough with one of his many and varied conquests, and I've had to step in. Some of them like it, others – like this one – not so much. More often than not, I tend to leave them because they're grown women, and it's not my place to tell them what they should and shouldn't be doing. God knows I'm no paradigm of virtue of what's right or wrong.

I close my bedroom door, drop the towel on the floor and reach for the tattered old belt on top of the dresser. Slipping the leather through the buckle, I yank it tighter around my arm and grab the teaspoon and the sachet of H the same moment my phone starts to slide across the top.

John.

"Shit," I grit out and grab my phone. "Hey, is she okay?"

"No, she's not okay. Did you do what I asked?"

"Yeah. I asked him, and he said he was in a bar with some girl he's brought back here."

"And you believe him?" he asks sceptically.

"John," I sigh. "I've got no reason not to believe him!" I keep my anger in check for the sake of the woman asleep just a few feet away.

He chortles, unimpressed. "You really are a dumb bastard! Stop shooting up, lift the blinkers and see him for what he really is! Rem, I'm warning you again, you need to get out fast. Nothing good will ever come of the life you're living with their involvement. They're fucking toxic. Why can't you see it?" Then, for the second time tonight, he hangs up.

I toss the phone on the floor in anger and clench the small bag in my hand. Tossing that to the floor, too, my appetite for perpetual chemical bliss gone, I unravel the makeshift tourniquet and climb into bed.

I stare up at the ceiling as a thin arm slides over my chest and fingers stroke my nipple. "Hey."

"Go back to sleep, babe," I tell her, and she sighs content.

"Is Mandy still here?" she asks drowsily.

"Mandy?" I keep up the pretence, although I presume that's the woman Deacon is currently screwing.

"Yeah, she came over this afternoon while Deacon was out," she replies, ensnaring my attention completely.

"Has he been out all day?"

7

"Hmm, hmm."

"What time did he get back?" I stroke her arm tenderly, lulling her into a false sense of security.

"I don't know. A couple of hours ago. Why?"

"Nothing," I tell the ceiling in the dark because my reasons for believing him have just diminished.

And the blinkers have finally started to lift.

THREE MONTHS LATER...

THE HAZY AFTERNOON sun streams through the window, bathing the skyline with a warm summery glow.

I clench one end of the belt between my teeth and the other end in my hand as I puncture the inside of my wrist. Slowly, methodically, I press down the end of the needle. I fall back on the bed, the empty syringe still lodged in my hand. The high kicks in instantly, and euphoric bliss begins to wash over me.

The sensation courses through my veins, blurring the edges of my already imperfect, damaged world. Within minutes, my body is floating, soaring higher into the heavens. But I know, in the deep recesses of my brain, this chemical high I continually chase is as far removed from heaven as one can get. Still, I'm enslaved by addiction. Compelled and bound until it begins to wane, and I repeat the process. Again, and again, and again.

There is no end to this perdition until it is *the end*.

"Jer?" My name is a husky whisper, tumbling from the lips of the love of my life. "Jeremy?"

"Yeah?" I reply as a slender leg glides across my abdomen, and Em smiles down at me seductively, straddling my groin while her long hair fans over my chest.

I run my hands down her bare flesh and palm her hips as she slowly rocks back and forth. I groan, but unfortunately, her efforts are in vain because attempting to stimulate me when I'm this far gone is near impossible.

I cradle her beautiful face, remembering when her cheeks were full and coloured by good health. Now, just like me, she is what was once fashionably termed *heroin chic*. Her skin is a sickly pallor colour, her cheeks are hollowed out, and her body is visibly bony. Deacon often jokes that he might use her as a model to gain more custom from the image-obsessed who only care about being thin and looking good.

"I love you, Jer."

"I love you, too," I reply as she leans down and peppers my face with kisses. My hands roam up her back, and my fingers trace the unnatural divots of her spine. Even in my drug-induced state, I know this isn't good.

Day by day, she gets skinnier and skinner and more dependent. Dependent on alcohol, dependent on drugs. Dependent on me to supply her with both. In the last few months, her well-being has declined further. These days, the rare times she is sober, she always says I brightened her world the day we met. But what she refuses to see is that I darkened hers. And if we carry on like this, I may inadvertently end it, too.

"How do you feel?" The question slurs over my tongue. When I first started taking, I couldn't string two words together. Now, a full-blown addict – one who hits up daily to maintain the extreme hedonistic pleasure that only my drug of choice can provide - I can still engage in simple conversation. *Just.*

"Okay, but I need you," she replies, but she doesn't need me, not really. She needs what I can give her. As anticipated, her small hand manipulates mine open, and she removes the needle and unravels the belt from my bicep.

My body rocks momentarily as she climbs off me and drops to the floor. She riffles through the paraphernalia on the chest of drawers and goes about preparing her next fix. She brushes her long, mousy blonde hair away from her face as she concentrates, insofar as she can, considering she's still coming down from the last fix just a few hours ago.

As I observe, my peak level having just been reached, I wonder if this is what I look like. The lowest of the low. The scourge of society, scrambling around the floor, the only thought of poisoning my bloodstream and getting high and out of control.

"You want?" she asks, snapping me out of the thoughts.

"No," I reply, and her incredibly beautiful features fall. I drop my head back onto the pillow and silently admit the blunt truth that has eaten away at me these last few months, but one I've never confessed. And that truth is I don't want to be like this anymore. I don't want to live a life where the first and last thing I think of every day is where my next hit is coming from. It took me a long time to admit it, but I'm an addict, one who's desperate to stop. Sadly, two addicts in a relationship render my intentions futile because we're not on the same page. Because whereas I may have inadvertently made her an addict, she has inadvertently made me an enabler.

I stare up at the ceiling as the clatter of the teaspoon, and the soft flick of a lighter resounds. Minutes later, the feminine moan I know so well fills the room. I close my eyes, falling deeper into bliss as Em's breathing becomes more intense until a gasp of ecstasy floats up from the floor.

"Baby, come back to bed," I murmur, my eyes closed while the faint, pained sound of my name seeps into my subconscious.

"*Jeremy...*"

The room is in complete darkness when I wake. The moon shines, gently illuminating the deathly silent atmosphere inside.

"Em?"

I drag my hand over the bed, but she isn't there. Scrubbing my hands over my face, my skin is sticky, perspired, and I'm in desperate need of a shower.

"Em?" I call again, still receiving no response. I reach over and flick the bedside lamp on.

As I rub my eyes and sit up, I glance around and find her curled up in a ball on the floor. I throw my legs over the side of the bed and move the two steps towards her.

"Come on, baby. You need to get into bed. It's late." I reach down and gently push her shoulder. Just like she didn't reply, this time, she doesn't move. I shake her again, this time with more vigour, and she rolls over under the force.

My eyes amplify as they scan her rigid, prone frame. Horror fills me while realisation hits. My eyes take in the empty needle still clenched in her hand, the wide-eyed, pained look on her face, and the protruding veins.

"Em? Em!" I drop to my knees and take her in my arms. "Baby, wake up!" I shake her hard, but she is cold and unresponsive, and I know it's too late. "Come on, baby, open your eyes for me! Open your fucking eyes!" As I tussle with her lifeless body to grab my phone, the bedroom door slams open.

"What the hell? It's three in the morning, dickhead!" Deacon spits out. My eyes meet his, and sheer panic consumes his usually hard, emotionless face. "Please tell me that stupid bitch hasn't OD'ed! And please tell me you haven't called the fucking police yet?" I sit frozen in shock, amazed by his callousness. I know he can be a heartless bastard. He's proven it on more than one occasion, but this takes the cake.

"She needs a fucking ambulance, Deek. Here!" I throw my phone on the bed. "Call them!"

"No!"

"She needs help!" But before I can't say anything further, he rips off his t-shirt and begins to quickly collect up all the incriminating evidence scattered around the room in it.

"She doesn't need help; she's fucking dead! We'll call the police when this place is cleaned up. We'll put her in bed and tell them you woke up and found her like that. Leave the needle in her hand. It looks suspicious if they don't find it. Now, drop the bitch and help me!" He rips open the wardrobe door and reaches for the supply bag. The supply bag that he insists stays in my room, no doubt to ensure I take the fall if we ever get raided.

Tears fog my eyes and stream down my cheeks. I hold Em tight, wishing she would wake up, but I know it's a dream that will never materialise. I know I'll never hear her laugh again, or the way her eyes light up when she's happy, or the way she's the only colour in a room of black and white. I'll never know what it feels like to move inside her again or feel the closest thing to heaven when she just smiles.

But the most painful realisation of all is that I've finally done what I feared – I've killed her. Granted, I didn't give her the needle. I didn't shoot it into her vein, but I did supply her. If it wasn't for me, she'd still be shrouded by light. She'd live a long life. Now, she'll just be forever young.

"Remy!" Deek breaks through my procrastination. "You better fucking help me because you know who her father is, right? If that bastard turns up here tonight and finds her dead with all this evidence, you and I will be facing a long stretch for manslaughter. That's if he doesn't get to us first. Now, drop her and get that shit flushed." He points to the teaspoon on the drawers, still holding a hit. "I'll explain to my dad. He'll understand."

I stay where I am until Em is ripped from my arms, and Deacon throws her body onto the bed.

"Son of a bitch!" I get to my feet in a rage and charge at him. I punch him across the cheek, but he grabs me by the throat and whips his knife from the back of his jeans.

"Fucking listen!" He traces the knife tip from my temple to my cheek. "There's nothing we can do for her. She's gone, but when the police show up and find all this, we're gone, too. You think you can survive prison? An addict like you?" He loosens his hold and steps back. "Now, I'm going to drive all this stuff over to one of my dad's dealers, and you call the police. Tell them you woke up and she was dead beside you. If they ask, tell them she got *you* hooked. Understand?"

I stare into his black eyes, seeing the vile truth behind them. He really doesn't care about anyone but himself.

"Tell me you understand, Jeremy!"

I nod slowly. I understand, all right. I understand that I finally need to do whatever it takes to leave this life of misery and dependency behind. Because if I don't, I will share her fate.

John was right; dying is what it takes. I just never thought it would be my girl who succumbed to the darkness.

Deacon collects the t-shirt and the bag and slams the door behind him. I crawl onto the bed and cradle Em. The agonising sound of my tortured wail fills the room. My scream is damned and in vain. Holding her close, stroking her hair, my heart is truly broken. My single reason for living is no longer here with me, and now I officially have no one.

Long minutes tick by until I grab my phone and dial nine nine nine. I end the call and close my eyes. A few minutes feels like a few hours until blue lights and emergency sirens fill the street.

I press my lips to the cold skin of Emma Shaw and vow to get clean. I've promised it for the last year, but it has never materialised. Before I left London, my mother warned me I would end up dead. She feared the next call she received regarding my welfare would be one to inform her of my passing. Right now, I know she's right. And I also wish I was dead because my world has just become darker than it ever was.

But little do I know, the worst of my darkest and deadliest demeanours is yet to come.

NINE MONTHS LATER...

"GET UP, ARSEHOLE!" Deacon's irate tone rips through my hearing like a ball and chain.

"Leave me alone!" I roll over on the bed and grab the pillow – Em's pillow – and inhale her long-diminished scent. Clutching it tightly, I pretend it's the woman who died mere feet away. But it's not, and during that time, I've managed to fall further down the destructive rabbit hole.

"For God's sake!" The foot of the bed jerks, and the duvet is dragged away, followed by the pillow. "Do we have to do this every day?" he asks, devoid of emotion. "The silly bitch is dead, and she's never coming back. Get used to it!"

I roll over again and block him out. After all these months, I've become particularly proficient in selective hearing. Namely, selectively blocking *him* out of *my* hearing. Especially when the conversation involves Emma Shaw.

"Come on, get up! We've got business to attend to." He opens the wardrobe door and lifts out the holdall containing every class A drug illegally flooding the streets of Britain.

"Business?" I query, rolling back over, my high from a few hours ago now ebbing away.

"Yeah, so get cleaned up. Make sure you put on another shirt. That one stinks." He throws a small packet of pure H at me before striding out of the door. I snatch it up like it is gold dust, and I should because it isn't the cut-up crap that Franklin has me flogging every night to anyone who doesn't give a damn if they see tomorrow.

Ten minutes later, the familiar bliss subdues any lucid thought and tugs me back into that palliative place I'm dying to escape from but doomed to stay confined in.

The bedroom door slams open again, rebounding off the wall behind it. Deacon leans on the frame. "Change of plan. We're going to a party instead."

"A party?" My response is slurred, but it's the best thing he's suggested in months.

I clamber off the bed, pull the dirty t-shirt over my head and reach for a clean one on the stack of creased clothing on the floor. My body lurches to one side, and I slap my hand on the wall before I lose my balance completely.

"Here." He tosses me a couple of prepared needles and a packet of cable ties. "Put those in your pocket."

I stare down at them. The little voice in my intoxicated brain is querying why we would need cable ties at a party. Drugs, I understand, but cable ties? Unable to comprehend it, I pocket the stuff and follow him out.

The motion of the car is constant as I close my eyes and slouch in the passenger seat.

For the last nine months, my mind has played on constant loop, recalling the night my beautiful angel finally surrendered to the darkness I created within her. A part of me wants it to stop because it's too painful to continually relive the moment I felt her cold skin touch mine. But the other part of me, the moral part, wants it to continue. To remind me over and over because it's a punishment I deserve. And ultimately, the reckoning I might face one day.

The car jerks to a stop, throwing me forward into the dash, and, unfortunately, sobers me slightly. "Where are we?" I rub my eyes and look around at the rundown, unkempt council houses lining either side of the street.

"Hell," Deacon replies without hesitation and gets out of the car. Opening my door, even in my woozy state, he isn't wrong. "Come on."

The fresh night air filters through my nostrils, sobering me further. I continue to follow behind Deacon, who's striding toward a house with purpose. I take in the façade, wishing I hadn't shot up earlier and came here with a clear head because who knows what waits on the other side.

"Hey, have you seen Ian?" Deacon asks some guy leaning inside the doorway with a drunk woman on his arm.

"Yeah, he's somewhere inside. Hey, you got anything on you tonight?"

Suddenly my brain decides to gain focus. I start to reach for my pocket, but Deacon notices my action and stops me.

"No, I'm not here for business tonight. Just pleasure."

I can feel my brow furrow. If we're not here for business, then why are my pockets bulging with full syringes and a random pack of plastic ties?

"Okay, I'll catch up with you during the week."

"Sure." Deacon slaps the man's shoulder and jerks his chin for me to enter.

My feet carry me deeper into the house. The small living room is packed. Various bodies in various states of undress are hanging off every piece of furniture. I yawn as I glance around, and my sight catches the picture of a young family of three on the fireplace. I step closer and stare at it, recalling a similar picture on my mother's wall back home, taken many years before my father walked out and never came back.

I cast aside that unfortunate memory because it's the first of my many disappointments. I turn to find Deacon, standing in a doorway that leads to an equally small kitchen. As I edge closer, I dawdle because the man he's talking to looks ashen. Deacon continues to speak to him, but the man shakes his head and firmly says no.

"Rem, this is Ian." Deacon knocks back a bottle of ale while I try to focus on the man that looks vaguely familiar. I can't remember where I've seen him before, but if Deacon knows him, he's probably one of Franklin's many dealers.

"Hey," I greet, my voice normal, my high starting to flounder. These days, I'm finding I need to hit up more frequently to sustain that feeling of debauched perfection. I fidget and scope out the surroundings again, needing something to maintain my fading state. I spy the bottle of gin on the table and grab it. Downing a large mouthful, the liquid cuts a sharp path down my throat. I swallow another shot and listen with disinterest to the conversation being carried on between Deacon and Ian behind me.

"You owe us two grand. Where is it?" Deacon hisses, and I catch sight of Ian, who looks terrified.

"I haven't got it. I'll get it to you, though. Every penny."

"And how are you going to do that, arsehole? I know you've been using when you should've been selling. The numbers don't tally, Petersen. Dad wants his money now, and so do I!" Deacon grabs Ian's shirt and pulls him forward.

"I'm sorry, Deek. I haven't got it! I'm sorry." Ian's voice trembles.

Deacon drops his head down and sighs. "That's not what I want to hear. Lucky for you, we both know the other ways I take payment. *Again.* Didn't you learn anything the other night? You might as well just pimp the little bitch out permanently. You clearly don't give a fuck about her. Look at what you allow her to live in, you piece of shit!" He throws his hand out towards the room in general. I have no idea what's going on between them, and I don't want to know. I'm in far deeper than I care to be with no feasible way out. I don't need whatever shit they're talking about coming back on me.

"No, I can't. No more!" Ian pleads, but Deacon grabs him by the back of the neck and forces him out of the room.

15

I knock back another mouthful of gin and slump onto the battered old sofa. The music blares through the room, and time ticks by slowly. The bottle slips from my hand and tumbles across the floor. As I bend to pick it up, a needle falls from my pocket. Snagging it between my fingers, its potency calls to me like a siren.

A cold shiver runs down my spine because all the promises I made to get clean will always be null and void. Regardless of the numerous weekly calls I've had with John, Sloan, and everyone else who still gives a toss about me, I'm an addict. And I can't stop, irrespective of how much I'm dying to.

I make fast work of shrugging out of my jacket, lodge my forearm between my knees and flex my fisted hand down. Holding up the needle, checking for air bubbles – although it's redundant since all it does is delay the inevitable – I sink the tip into my skin and penetrate my abused vein. The liquid drains from the tube into my bloodstream quickly, and my body returns to that place it is so attuned with.

I slump back into the sofa, riding the wave through the storm of loud music, copulating couples, and general chaos until somebody hits the back of my skull.

"Rem?" Deacon moves around the sofa, with Ian following behind sheepishly. He grabs hold of me and stands me up. My legs wobble beneath me, unable to gain stability until he steadies my stance.

"Where have you been?"

"Around. I've got a job for you. Pass me the stuff."

I fumble with my jacket, but his frustration is evident as he digs into my pocket for the ties and the needles.

"Where's the other one?" He shakes me before he pushes me forward. "Come on!"

My hand grips the bannister as I sway past the bodies obstructing passage up the stairs. Reaching the landing, numerous moans leak from the bedrooms, and I glance across the landing to see a couple openly having sex. I squeeze my eyes, unsure if it's reality or just imagination.

"Wait here," Deacon says as he enters a room with Ian and the door slams shut. I curl into the wall behind me. I watch people move up and down the stairs and in and out of the bedrooms.

My head snaps up when commotion leaks from inside the room. I place my hand on the door handle, but it opens unexpectedly, and I step back.

Ian gives me a grave expression and momentarily glances over his shoulder. I follow his line of sight just in time to see Deacon toss someone down on the bed.

"Promise me," Ian says, closing the door. "Promise me you won't hurt her too!"

I shake my head. I have no idea what he's talking about. "I'm not hurting anyone. I can barely stand or think straight," I mumble incoherently, rubbing my eyes, just wanting to go to sleep.

Ian nods, but his face tells me he is far from mollified. "I need to make a call. Don't let him go too far."

I narrow my eyes. I still have no idea what he's talking about. I slouch back down the wall and rest my forehead on my palm, desperate to feel wild oblivion. The sounds from inside the room intensify. I've no idea how long Deacon has been in there or how long we've even been inside this house tonight.

"You little fucking bitch! What did I tell you?" Deacon's shout seeps through the closed door, and I stare at it. Something isn't right here; I've felt it all night. This isn't just some party.

I force myself up as the cries of a terrified female ring out. I loiter, unsure what to do until the faint but familiar sound of flesh hitting flesh infuses my ears.

In all the times I've heard him fucking around with the cheap tarts he often brings home, it's never sounded like this.

I grip the handle tentatively again, debating woozily what I might be interrupting when a pained, gurgled scream resounds.

I throw open the door, and a shudder runs through me when Deacon smashes his fist over the girl's face. Her whimpering dies instantly, and her erratic breathing begins to even out.

Deacon turns around and grins like the devil. "Here," he says with a sneer and throws the cable ties at me. "Put them on. She likes it rough."

His statement resonates over and over like an echo, and I look at the plastic in my hands. My brain clouds over, and I slowly approach and pull one out. Fastening her wrists to the bed head, I drop them on the floor and look over her skinny naked frame and then her face. This is the girl in the picture downstairs. Nausea in my stomach is instantaneous, and I step back the same moment Deacon flicks the last needle and jabs it into her neck.

Clarity hits me like a bucket of ice-cold water, and I stumble back. The girl whimpers, and horror fills me. I scrub my hand over my

17

head in shame and absolute shock. I edge out of the room like a coward. Slamming the door behind me, I loathe myself for what I've just unwittingly become a part of. My head lulls against the wall behind me, and I slam it back repeatedly. Every vile grunt coming from the room is now a reminder of what I've done while I sit here helpless, plagued by my guilt.

I close my eyes, praying for redemption, when a barrage of feet thuds up the stairs. I raise my head and look ahead as Sloan barrels towards me. He grabs my head hard in his hands, and his eyes narrow in anger, revulsion and contempt. Letting me go, I drop my head in shame, and my body begins to shake. Sloan's eyes glaze over venomously, and in a split second, his arm swings up and his fist lands on my face, forcing my head to swing to the side.

The pain is negligible because my insides feel like they are eviscerating when John appears behind him. He gives me a glare of 'I told you so', then pulls me aside before he boots the door open.

Comprehending there's nothing I can do, I clutch my face and stagger to the top of the stairs as they enter the room, and all holy hell breaks loose. Gripping the bannister, I fight through the horde of bodies and push my way outside.

The cold snap of night assaults me, and I stagger towards the Walker Security transit van. Resting against it, my head in pieces, my sanity shattered, feet beat hard on the pavement. I watch Deacon abandon his car on the street, and he runs from the house at speed with Tommy following until he eventually becomes one with the darkness and he's gone.

I slump down against a rear wheel, but I know I should be doing the same. Running, hiding, disappearing indefinitely.

Hurried strides approach, and I drag myself up. Sloan advances towards me with the broken girl bundled up in a dirty, bloodied sheet in his arms.

"I'm sorry, I'm sorry, I'm sorry," I repeat, begging for vindication. My pleas are in vain and ignored as Tommy and Stuart give me hard, unforgiving looks and open the rear doors.

"Get those blankets…" Sloan says, pretending I'm not just five feet away from him.

Consumed by my own self-hatred, I kick the tyre and bang my head against the side of the van, listening to them fight to save her life inside.

The sound of shouting followed by a woman's terrified cry pierces my ears. I move around the vehicle, too cowardly to look inside and witness the aftermath of what I have assisted in, to see John knock out Ian on the doorstep.

"She's your fucking daughter, you heartless bastard!" John's distinctive boom carries over the fraught atmosphere. I loiter on the spot, aware I should be anywhere but here right now.

John strides towards me with determination, his face depicting his unadulterated fury.

"I'm sorry. I didn't know... I didn't know!" I whimper, but my words are in vain because my actions will never be forgotten nor forgiven.

His eyes darken, and he growls. Moving swiftly, he smashes his fist over my face, and I fall to the ground, terrified, as he stands over me.

"I fucking warned you!" He drags me up by my collar. "I suggest you get the fuck out of here! Leave! Get yourself clean, and then come back and say you're sorry! Right now, it isn't fucking good enough!" He pushes me back, and for once, I'm going to do the right thing and listen to him.

My body is heavy, my heart is broken, as I move further and further away from the house until I too, am devoured by the impenetrable, murky night.

Running through the streets, the sound of sirens beckoning, my lungs are ready to explode. My body, finally coming down from the chemical high, is ready to give up, and my head, still in that place of seeing my so-called best friend do that to a young, defenceless girl, is consumed by the image. An image I shall carry with me to the grave. One that shall plague me in this life, right into the afterlife, and beyond into purgatory.

With the adrenaline of fear and loathing pushing me to carry on, every street that passes darkens my thoughts further. How could I have been so fucking stupid? Why did I trust the son of a bitch? Both John and Dom warned me, and *I knew*. I knew in my heart something wasn't right tonight. I knew, and still, I did nothing.

Making a running jump towards a six-foot fence, I scramble over. I inch around the side of the dark, silent house, slide down the wall and rest my head on my knees. My body shakes from the cold, harsh reality in which I have played a demonic hand in.

Tonight, I assisted in ruining a young girl's life. I involuntarily assisted in systematic rape. I might not have perpetrated the crime, but I'm guilty by action, if not association.

Lifting my head, I hit my skull back on the house wall until the pain reverberates in my forehead. But it's not enough. Nothing I do for penance ever will be.

The night replays in perfect detail behind my eyes. Each painful vision digs its claws in and refuses to disperse. The house, the stairs, the room... The broken girl in a bloodied sheet, with bloodied, torn wrists that I gave to her. My tears for an innocent girl begin to flow. I wallow, but it's worthless because they will continue to assault me until I cannot think of them anymore. And I will carry them with me until the day I am no more.

My lids drop in capitulation, the gravitas of my actions heavy on my conscience, and I pray for forgiveness. For redemption. First, for a girl I allowed to die, and second, for a girl I'll never see again.

THE COLD NIP of morning and the accompanying birdsong wakes me. I rub the sleep from my eyes and look around. I'm still in the garden of the house I took refuge in last night. Stretching out, I force myself back over the fence and look up and down the street cautiously.

Dawn is breaking through the partially darkened sky above. Rotating my shoulders, the stiffening side effects of sleeping on paving slabs is unforgiving, but I deserve every painful pull of my muscles. Truthfully, I deserve so much fucking more.

I walk with no purpose until I reach home. *Home*, it's now a dirty word. The sanctuary of the diseased, a place I bed down and get high.

I pat down my pockets, unable to find my keys until I remember I didn't bring them out last night. Trying the handle, it's still locked, which means Deacon didn't return last night, either.

Removing my jacket, I look around the unkempt garden and pick up the large brick that has been propping open the garden gate since we moved in. I wrap it in my jacket, then smash the side window and climb through.

I brush off the shards of glass and dart upstairs to my room. I grab my duffle bag, gather up the pile of clothes on the floor and stuff them inside. Ripping open the drawer, I pull out the few keepsakes I possess and the pictures of Emma. I wrap the frame in a couple of t-shirts and shove it inside, followed by some more loose snaps.

Morning has fully broken, and I run back down the stairs and into the living room. I upend the sofa and rip open the crudely sewn up sacking on the bottom. I fumble around inside until I find the stash that Deacon doesn't know about. Retrieving the bags of ecstasy, illegal highs, and the money that costs lives, I stare at them. After last night, this money represents everything I want to escape from. But unfortunately, escaping costs money, and this is the only income I have.

As I clutch the rolls of tens and twenties, I open the bags of powder and tablets. Kicking open the toilet door, I lift the lid. I should have done this long ago. I wish I *had* done this long ago. Last night was just the pinnacle. Aside from Em, who knows how many lives I've destroyed - through drugs or otherwise - in the time I've been living in this city. Two and counting – that's if you don't include my own. With a mixed sense of relief and anxiety, I flush the toilet, and my only source of revenue drains away.

I look around the deserted hallway for the last time. With nothing further left for me here now, I climb through the window, right myself and look up at the house with disdain. I head towards the city centre, but I don't know where I'm going, although eventually, I will have to face hell. I need to make reparations for my actions. I need redemption to cleanse my soul.

My feet refuse to carry me any further, and I take respite in a bus shelter and stare at the building opposite. My knee shakes incessantly as I light up a cigarette. Taking a deep pull on it, I work myself up to confess my sins. Flipping my mobile in my hand, I dial John's number.

"Hey," he answers.

"I'm sorry," I whisper.

"Rem, where are you?"

"How's the girl?" I query, still staring at the building.

"How do you think? She was lucky, if that's what you can call what she's lived through. Where are you?" A siren resounds from the rear of the building, and a police car speeds onto the street. "Jeremy, don't!" John shouts down the line - he knows exactly where I am.

"I need to atone for my sins, J," I tell him pitifully, taking a final drag on the cig before dying it out under my boot. "I need to right the wrongs I've done. I need to confess, about Em, the drugs, the dealing, the girl…"

"You'll serve hard time. They'll give you multiple sentences. You won't survive."

"I know, but it's nothing in comparison to the life sentence I assisted in creating last night. Forgive me, John. Tell Sloan that I'm sorry." I hang up and concentrate on my courage.

An hour later, still sitting at the bus stop, my phone ringing relentlessly - courtesy of John, and now Sloan - a police van pulls up. A scuffle ensues when they drag out a man who's screaming, violently protesting his innocence. Looking at him, he's also a product of a failed system. He's someone I never wanted to become. But for all my ill-gotten gains and mistakes, I'm just like him. John's right: I'd never survive prison. As streetwise as I like to think I am, I'm not tough. I'll fight for what I love, regardless of whether I can win or not, but when push comes to shove, I take the easy option. The first being selling drugs when I gave up finding a half-decent job. The second, when I became hooked on said drugs when I just wanted to feel numb for a while.

Clutching the wad of cash in my pocket, I hail down a taxi, slide inside, and watch life carry on obliviously.

"Seven fifty, mate," the driver says, decelerating outside the train station.

"Cheers, keep the change." I pass him a tenner and climb out.

My eyes work over the departure boards in the midst of chaos. With a one-way ticket in hand, I sit on the platform and wait for the train to arrive. Pulling out my phone, I bypass the calls from John, find who I'm looking for and press call.

"Archer," Dominic answers on the second ring.

"Hi," I greet, not really knowing how to ask my request.

"Rem, where are you? J's going out of his mind that you're going to turn yourself in."

"I was... I should. God, I fucked up, Dom. I knew. I knew something wasn't right."

He lets out a resigned huff. "Yeah, you knew what he was, but you couldn't have known last night was going to happen."

"But I should have! After Charlie and Em-"

"What's done is done. You can't change it now. Jeremy, where are you?" His tone softens, revealing his concern.

"At the train station." I inhale deeply, daring the words to leave my mouth. "Dom, I need a favour," I start, praying he will accommodate it. "A big one."

"Go on," he replies, seemingly aware of what I'm going to ask.

"I need to get clean. For good. I want you to help me." I suck in a fearful breath, terrified he will refuse. It's a lot to ask of him, and he doesn't owe me anything.

The line stays quiet for long minutes until he inhales. "If we do this, Jeremy, you do it cold turkey. No methadone, no substitutes. You can't get clean from one addiction by becoming hooked on another. Because with your personality, that's precisely what will happen."

I stare up at the sky and bite my lip in fear because he's far from wrong. My entire life, I've been addicted to something, and when my current compulsion stopped hitting the right spot, I'd move on to something else.

"Agreed," I finally reply, bracing myself for the excruciating withdrawal symptoms I'm going to be experiencing before nightfall. "I'll see you in an hour or so."

"You're making the right choice. I'll see you soon." Dom hangs up, and I stare at my phone then dial John.

"Thank God!" he grits out with relief. "Where are you?"

"Victoria station."

"Good, I'm still up here. I'll come and get you."

"No, I can't face any of you right now. I'll keep this number, let you know how I'm doing, but I can't come back. Not yet. My mother is so disappointed in me that she can barely stand the sight of me, and Sloan and the guys probably hate me."

"No, Jeremy, that's not true," he soothes.

"I'll speak to you soon." I pause. He deserves more than that from me. "I always looked up to you like you were my father."

He sighs deeply. "I know you do. Look, I respect what you're saying, but if you need anything, anything at all, you know who to ring."

"I already did, and that's where I'm headed. I'm going to get clean, J, I swear. I love you, all of you, and I'm sorry." I hang up and slip it into my pocket. I rest back, absorbing the static sounds of the station and wait for the train to take me from a life of nothing to start a new life of nothing.

Closing my eyes, my body and mind are still heavy. One thought, in particular, weighing them down. One day, I need a young girl to forgive me for destroying her life. I don't know how I will ever find her again, but one day I have to try. An innocent girl is already dead because of me. I loved her, and I killed her with kindness through the

ELLE CHARLES

act of supply and demand. I can't have another dying because of my actions too.

Inside, I want redemption, but I know I don't deserve it. And just like last night, running is the only way I'm going to survive. Yet last night isn't the only reason why I will spend my life in proverbial chains, constantly looking over my shoulder. Nine months ago, I was forewarned there was an invisible target on my back by an inconsolable, grieving father.

Still, running and finding a way to redeem myself has got to be better than the alternative of rotting in a prison cell, fearing whether or not I will get shanked and killed today.

In truth, I once believed I was one of the good guys, but now I know differently. My soul has been marked by my actions. And if there is one thing I am blatantly aware of, it's that when my time eventually comes, I know there's a special place in hell for men like me.

Chapter 1

"REMY, YOU CAN'T avoid me forever. If I have to drive my arse up there, you're not going to like the end result. Call me back ASAP! If you don't, tomorrow I'll hunt you down!"

The irate tone of Sloan Foster fills the room until the machine automatically stops recording and a short beep resounds. I reach over the desk from my reclined, uncomfortable position and hit delete.

Picking up my mug, the rhythmic tap of the morning rain pelting against the windowpane grounds me. I swallow a mouthful of bitter, tepid coffee and stare out over the dark, dreary skyline and contemplate.

As I set down the mug, I catch sight of the small picture on the desk and pick it up. Staring at the vibrant, healthy girl behind the glass - the way I always remember her now - I recall the three painful events, the dark days on my calendar that changed my life beyond recognition nine years ago. It started with the brutal assault of Charlotte Emerson, Sloan's sister, at the hands of her other brother, Deacon Black. And it ended with the equally brutal assault of Kara Petersen, who, through nefarious contacts and a very simple twist of fate, is now Sloan's girlfriend, and she also suffered unimaginable cruelty at the hands of the same man.

But ultimately, the event that has really shaped who I am is the death of the girl in the picture.

Emma Shaw.

I inhale deeply and swipe my calloused thumb over the face of the only woman I've ever loved. "I miss you," I whisper, feeling the unshed tears in my eyes sting. In truth, she will always be the cross I bear, my biggest regret in life.

Now, at the age of twenty-nine, I'm finally what I've always wanted to be - clean and sober. And I have been for the last eight years. It took a long time to get here, and I'd be lying if I said I still didn't crave it, because there's no such thing as a recovering or ex-drug addict. The same way there's not really any such thing as an ex-drinker or an ex-smoker because when you've had a taste for it, you always remember what it felt like to drown in your drug of choice. In my heart, I will always be an addict, and every day is a constant

25

struggle to stay on the right path. I confess, some days, I just want to fall back into the mindless, disconnected bliss I would feel when I chased the dragon.

In some ways, life was easier back then. Wake up, get high, sell, sleep. Rinse and repeat.

But an easy life is not an enduring life, and I vividly remember the day I walked out of the train station and found Dominic waiting for me on double yellows, uncaring he was obstructing the flow of traffic. He wasn't lying when he said I would have to do it cold turkey. That very same night, I begged for my own passing. If someone had told me years ago - when I was smoking cannabis while promising my mother I'd never dabble with the harder stuff - that what I would experience would be akin to death, I'd have thought twice before plunging that first syringe into my unsuspecting vein.

Still, as Dom says, you can't change the past. Or cause and effect, which seems to be his life mantra.

Trapped in morbid thought, the landline starts to blare again. I place the picture down and silence the infernal sound.

He's really grating my last nerve with his non-stop calls for the last few days. I know why he's ringing, but I'm not sure I can do what he's asking of me.

From the many conversations I've had with Dom, I know tomorrow night Sloan is going to announce his impending marriage to Kara. In reality, she's always been his, the same way he's always been hers. Right from the very first moment he laid eyes on her, weeks before the night she was assaulted – not that she's aware of it. But it's hard for me because while he has every reason in the world to celebrate: success, love, the woman he's secretly lived and breathed for nine years finally his in the truest sense of the word, I can only commiserate and wonder what might've been if I hadn't delved down the wrong rabbit hole.

Scrubbing my hand over my face in conflicted frustration, my fingertip absentmindedly drags along the raised scar that now runs from the corner of my eye to my lip. The newest - and only visible - scar I've got to show for the life of nothing that I've lived for the last decade. Except this scar is significant in ways it shouldn't be because it's the scar Deacon gave me for my betrayal of him and for my protection of Kara.

Movement outside piques my attention, and the door slams open to reveal an extremely annoyed Dominic Archer. He strides in, in all his unyielding glory, throws the suit bag over his arm on the cabinet and picks up the phone. With an unimpressed brow, he holds the handset to his ear, his expression one of infuriation.

"He'll call you back." Then he hangs up. Typical Dom - short and sweet.

I shake my head in disgust and cross my arms over my chest as I lob my feet on the desk. "Why the hell did you tell him that?" The caustic question rolls off my tongue venomously.

Dom folds himself into the chair and steadies his unwavering glare on me. "Because it's the truth. You and I both know you wouldn't miss one of the biggest nights of his life, irrespective of what that deluded brain of yours keeps telling you. And trust me, it is fucking deluded!"

I huff and gaze up at the ceiling. "No, it's realistic, is what it is," I counter because the last time I saw Sloan and Kara was just a few weeks ago when I finally confessed the heinous, horrific part I played in her life. It was the first time I've ever spoken of that night to anyone but Dom and whoever was present back then. I've always said the day I had to re-tell it, I would do it only once. I'll never forget the way she looked at me. It was far worse than the day in the flat all those months ago when I betrayed her trust again and brought John up here to force her hand. I deserved the hatred she spewed at me...and the scorching coffee she threw at me. But witnessing that devastation take over her fragile features again, seeing the strong girl I respect so much fall apart through my words in front of people who were, until then, unaware of my actions, was my undoing. After she fled my apartment in tears, I fled back up here. And I've not spoken to any of them since.

My fingers drift over my scar again, and the sensation of Deacon's knife piercing my skin and my subsequent wail resounds silently in my ears. For the last ten months, every time I've relived that moment, it feels like it's happening again right now. It's a phantom burn that never stops. My eyes slide back to Dom, who observes my action closely.

"You told her the truth weeks ago," he states, verbalising my thoughts. "We've been through this. You can't keep running when it gets hard."

"I know, but I don't know if I'll ever be able to make it right between us," I admit, sensing myself starting to open up for the second time in eight years. "Every time I look at her wrists, I'm reminded of what I did. Likewise, every time she looks at my face, she's reminded of the sacrifice I made to save her. We both carry our scars openly, and yet we both refuse to talk about how they came to be."

"Cause and effect." Dom shrugs and stands. "Like I said before, you can't change the past. We all have things that we hide. And for good reason. Do you think I like looking in the mirror and seeing what I am behind the mask? I've done shit that will turn your stomach." He walks to the door and stops. "You've fucked up and made monumental mistakes, but you're one of the good guys, Jeremy," he says, still with his back to me. "Not many men would take a blade to the face to save the life of an innocent. Call him, then get your arse back down there and be at his side for the biggest night of his life. You'll regret it if you don't."

The door slams shut, and yet again, I'm left with my beleaguered thoughts. I pick up the phone and turn it in my hand. Over the last nine years, I've done everything in my power to redeem myself for my actions back then. Even going as far as jeopardising my hard-earned sobriety and getting back in with the Blacks to ensure Sloan could keep tabs on them for Kara's sake. I shake my head because that proved to be futile as it did almost fatal. For her and me.

I pace the room before pausing in front of the large window and dial. The ringing tone deepens in my ear as I wait for him to pick up.

"Dom?" Sloan's mixed British-American twang answers.

"Wrong arsehole, half-brit," I reply, throwing some light on my call.

Sloan inhales with a sigh of contentment. "You're right – you are an arsehole. But since you're family and I love you, I'll just have to deal with it."

A grin pulls on my cheeks and slap my hand high on the window and lean into it. Sloan remains quiet, obviously expecting me to break the ice.

"I'll be leaving shortly. I just need to sort some things out before I go." But the only thing I really need to do is go home, pack a bag, and put the alarm on.

"Good. I'm glad Dom managed to talk some sense into you."

"He didn't, but we all have to do things we don't want to. How's Kara?"

"She's good. Completely unaware of my plans for tomorrow, of course," he says, amused because he does like to keep her in the dark.

And speaking of all things dark... "Does she hate me? Has she said anything lately?" I ask quietly, definitely not wanting to hear the answer.

"No, she doesn't hate you. She's confused and conflicted, and she tries to hide it, but she doesn't have a hateful bone in her body, regardless of how often she lashes out and pisses everyone off. And she has every right to. She knows you inadvertently hurt her, but she also knows you saved her, hence the conflict."

I inhale sharply because what she doesn't know is that while I couldn't save her the first time around, the second time, I couldn't save myself. But ultimately, the woman I should have saved has been lying six feet under for the past nine years. She doesn't know that either, and I dread the day I have to tell her. It's not any of her business, but it was a pivotal part of my swift decline into oblivion. Charlie's rape set the wheels in motion, but Em's death was the catalyst for everything that came after.

"Rem, stop overthinking it," Sloan says, realising I'm dwelling. "We could talk about this over and over, and the outcome would never change. For any of us. You've got more lives than a stray cat, and this is a second chance to do something right at long last. To finally have the semblance of a life you deserve."

"Yeah..." I breathe out, disheartened. "Yeah, you're right. Look, I'll drop by in the morning to see you."

Sloan clears his throat. The sound of his footsteps and a door closing amplifies over the line, indicating he doesn't want inquisitive ears eavesdropping. "Actually, I won't be here. I'm going to be driving up north."

I jerk my head back in surprise. "Why?" I ask suspiciously.

"Because I need answers to questions, and I need permission from the mother of the bride to marry her daughter."

My mouth falls open in shock. "You are fucking kidding, right? Do you honestly think it's safe driving up to Manchester? Dom and Kieran haven't heard anything about the Blacks or Ian Petersen's whereabouts."

"I know. That's why I'm bringing John and Stuart with me."

I don't respond, but I do roll my eyes. John, I understand, but I'm at a loss as to what Doc could do if the Blacks get wind of the unwanted visitors in their neck of the woods. While John is army trained, battle hard, and thoroughly competent in hand-to-hand combat, the best Doc could do is stab them with a needle and run the other way in his scrubs. I grimace, having unknowingly compared the good doc to myself in some respects. Because that's what I formerly did and still do now: I cut and run.

"Stop worrying, Jeremy. I'm driving straight up, asking my questions, then driving straight back down. Apparently, I won't have time for sightseeing since John has drafted a strategic schedule. Not to mention his love/hate affair with the M25 and M6 respectively." He laughs to himself, but I'm far from amused. He has no idea the ramifications of his being anywhere near Manchester will do if Franklin or, God forbid, Deacon unexpectedly cross his path.

I shake my head, still completely in despair but thankful he isn't going off half-cocked on his own - which is normally his way. "Well, in that case, I'll see you tomorrow night. Spare a dance with your beloved for me."

"I will," he says with a content chuckle. "A short one."

"Before you go, is this a full black-tie gig?"

"Yeah," he replies mockingly. "Dare I ask if you have a tux?"

"Yes, you can, and no, I don't. Unlike you, my current and previous professions don't require a flamboyant, rigid dress code," I retort facetiously because why on earth he thinks that someone like me has a tuxedo in his wardrobe is entirely beyond my comprehension. If I didn't know him as well as I do, I'd swear he's exhibiting signs of premature dementia.

"Good job I've pre-empted that then, isn't it? See Dom. He's got what you need. Speaking of which, dare I ask how he is?"

I puff down the line. "He's an arsehole, Sloan. He's always been an arsehole, and he *will* always be an arsehole. To be honest, as the days pass by, you remind me of him more and more!"

"There's nothing wrong with liking and exerting control."

"There is when it makes you narrow-minded and clouds your judgement."

Sloan gasps. "Is that what you really think of me?"

I grin wickedly since he can't see me. "I think the real question is, what do you think of yourself? Better yet, ask Kara. I'm positive she'll have a few choice words regarding your overbearing possessiveness."

"Fuck you, arsehole!"

I laugh. "Hmm, tempting, but I'm not that desperate, darling. I'll see you tomorrow." He hangs up, and I cradle the phone against my neck.

Caught up in my ever-turning thoughts, my eyes roam the room until they fix on the suit bag draped haphazardly over the filing cabinet. I amble over and unzip it. My fingers caress the black material, the crisp white shirt, and the bowtie hanging around the hanger hook. Zipping it back up, I slip my phone and wallet into my pocket and snatch up my car keys.

I hesitate whether I should rap my knuckles on the slightly open door and instead pop my head around it. Dominic is sitting with his head in his hands, staring down intently. Every now and then, he does this, but the man is nothing but secretive, and he always covers up what has him enthralled. I push the door back fully, the same instant his head rises from the papers in front of him. I stride quickly across the room, determined to find out what has him looking so pent-up while he faffs around, trying to throw a wad of paper over the top. Rather unsuccessfully, it should be noted.

"Julia Emerson." The words flow from my mouth with realisation as I catch the partially covered picture of a woman who is pretty much my second mother. And a woman who, with the assistance of the man in front of me, orchestrated her own fake death to ensure she would be free of Franklin Black forever. "What are you doing?" I toss my accusation out there.

"John said she's adamant she's coming to the wedding, and I have to make it happen."

I nod, unsurprised. No mother would want to miss her child's nuptials, especially considering the tangled, twisted web which has brought it together.

"Wait a minute, what wedding? He hasn't even asked her yet!" I reply. Dom's head drops to the side, and he raises his brows. "For fuck sake! He's already arranged it, hasn't he?" I shake my head and chortle in disbelief. Although I shouldn't expect anything less. "Well, I guess I must attend now, if only to see Kara's reaction to the whole affair."

I reach over and disturb the stack of paper Dom lobbed down and realise the file in front of him is full of pictures and reports. Dated documents, detailed daily movements, coffee mornings, shopping sprees, events. All of a woman currently residing thousands of miles away in New York.

"What the hell is this?"

"It's nothing," Dom replies quickly, collecting up the papers and closing the file. I lift my brows, feeling my forehead crease. He's lying, and my look confirms I'm aware of it.

Dom growls, rubs his eyes with his finger and thumb and throws his hands on his hips. "Have you ever wanted someone so much it makes you mindless?"

I scoff because he's preaching to the choir. "Yeah, every day, and she's buried in a Lancashire cemetery." I place the suit bag over the back of the chair. "Dom, as far as I'm concerned, I've not seen any of this. But for every little piece of advice you've ever given me, right now, I'm going to return it. Sooner rather than later, I think we're all aware this business with the Blacks is going to blow up. One day, Jules will be able to walk the streets of England again and not fear retaliation from Franklin. Now that Sloan and Kara have finally got their act together, we know it's a given. But irrespective of what happens in the future, you cannot start something with her whenever the opportunity finally presents itself. Sloan will go after you like a rabid dog if you so much as sniff near his mother, and John-"

"Will not give a shit!"

I grind my jaw because he's right. John probably won't care. Not to say that he won't have an opinion - he will. But he served in the army with Dom, he's aware of the man's integrity and morals, so in that regard, J will probably be fine with it. What he won't be fine with, however, is if Dom starts something with Jules while still hitting up the bars for cheap one-night stands and irrevocably breaks her heart.

"Are we done?" he asks, eyes wide with annoyance.

"Yeah," I reply because there's no point in even talking about it. Aside from knowing his name, the woman wouldn't be able to pick him out in a crowd. "Thanks for the tux, by the way." I lay the bag over my arm. "And the Lexus. I promise I'll give it back to you someday."

Dom's expression turns from vexed to relaxed in an instant. "Thank Sloan. He's the one who bought it and had it delivered here for you last week."

"Last week?"

He nods. "You don't belong up here, son. Your home is down there with your family. That said, there's always a place for you here. And keep the car; I don't need it." I try to hide my smirk, but the man does adore his ostentatious Maserati. For some, a swanky Lexus would be a step up. For him, it's absolutely a step-down. He rises and moves around the desk as hurried, thumping steps canter across the corridor outside.

"Sorry, am I disturbing a romantic moment? Would you like me to come back later?" Kieran Hyde, Dom's number two, queries with amusement as he fills the doorway and vanquishes the air in the room with every step he takes further inside. At six foot four, with muscles the size of boulders and blond hair that would put a Nordic warrior to shame, he's a formidable presence. That is until he opens his mouth, and his thick scouse accent makes an unexpected appearance. "There's something that you, particularly," he turns to me and tosses a newspaper down on the desk, "need to see."

Dom and I both lean in at the exact moment to see what has the man-mountain so excited. An unseen force levies a direct, winded punch to my gut seeing Edward Shaw's name splashed over the front page in large capitals.

"My, my, my, how the mighty have fallen," Dom comments with a touch of glee. "Just when I thought the day was off to a terrible start. Corruption never pays, boys."

"You would know, boss," K retorts, earning himself the middle finger and a grin.

I shoot them both a glare from the corner of my eye for their flippancy while I work fleetingly through the front-page article of the regional Manchester paper.

"I think it might be safe to assume that the target on your back might finally be fading." Kieran slaps me on the back, probably on the same spot Edward Shaw's invisible knife might critically impale if he ever got within a few feet of me. I give him a half-smile, but I'm aware that target is still shining brightly, just waiting for the man to hit the bullseye one day.

"I think it's dangerous to assume anything." I jab my finger on the face staring up at me. "All this recent development does is give him more impetus than ever now that the law isn't behind him. He hasn't got anything left to lose anymore. He's been found corrupt, but there's nothing here to say he's going to do time because of it."

But I, of all people, have no ground to get on my moral high horse because inside a cell with bars arming the windows and three-inch-thick steel doors is definitely where I belong.

"Do you still think he's gunning for you?" Kieran asks thoughtfully, crossing his arms over his chest, his face contorted in contemplation.

"Let me ask you this. If your only child died and the man you hold responsible is still living and breathing and walking free, what would you do?"

Kieran inhales deeply and shakes his head. "I've said it a hundred times. It wasn't your fault the girl died. However, I'll put some feelers out on Shaw and keep you updated if I hear anything."

"Thanks, appreciate it." I nod as he looks at my arm.

"You finally talked to boy wonder?" he asks, referring to Sloan.

"Yeah," I confirm.

"Are you coming back?"

I shrug because who knows. I might be back in a couple of days. It might be a couple of months. It might be never.

Kieran's arm comes around my shoulder in a man hug. "Well, I for one, will miss you. You never know, I might be calling you to get back up here when I can't corral Dom's arse in line."

"Thanks, but you might be on your own there." I grin and turn to Dom, who waves me off.

"I'll walk you out."

Moving down the corridor, both men at my rear, I glance back into my office. "Forgot something." I stride towards the desk and snatch up the picture of Em. Dom gives me a tight smile and pats my shoulder.

Outside, I throw my stuff into the back and slam the door. I reach over and shake Dom's hand. "Thanks for everything."

He nods. "Remember, straight and narrow, clean and sober."

"That's the plan." I open the door and slide inside.

"If you need anything, you just have to call," K offers, then walks backwards.

I reach for the door handle but stop. "Kieran? You still didn't answer my question. What would you do?"

"You want the truth?" I nod. "I'd rip his heart out," he replies with a pained expression, daring to say what he really thinks aloud. While I appreciate his honesty, my sanity would have preferred he stayed mute on the subject.

I close the door and turn the key in the ignition. The two imposing men stand sentry while I pull away from the kerb and drive down the street.

As they become smaller and smaller in my rearview, Kieran's frank admission resonates inside my head. *I'd rip his heart out.* Rubbing my hand across my chest, it's clear my back isn't the only target Edward Shaw will be aiming for if the opportunity ever arises.

Chapter 2

"SHIT!" I HISS as the burglar alarm activates. I quickly tap in the code – twice, since the first attempt was wrong – and the noise ceases immediately. I transfer the picture frame in my hand into my back pocket, drop the holdall on the floor along with the suit bag, and lock the door behind me.

The stale, unaired scent of the flat I haven't stepped foot inside of in weeks infuses my nostrils. The last time I was here was when I confessed to Kara the horrific part I had played in her past. I should feel cleansed that I've unburdened my soul of that long-overdue admission, but I don't. I feel disgusted, and every time I look in the mirror, I see what I once was, a traitor, a double-crosser, a turncoat, a liar. Take your pick, they're all the same, and there's only so long I can blame my decline into oblivion on drugs, regardless if that was the initial cause.

I place my keys on the console table and pad down the narrow hallway. Entering the kitchen, I open the fridge and pull out a bottle of ale and a long out-of-date pint of milk that has congealed. I dump the milk, unopened, in the bin because even I'm not man enough to open it and uncap my bottle.

I walk back the way I came, grab the suit bag and carry it into the bedroom. Laying it on the bed, I glance at the top of the wardrobe and reach for the shoebox containing the only pair of leather brogues I possess. Ones I rarely wear, specifically bought for events like this. Lifting it down, my hand dislodges the box next to it that I rarely open, the one housing pictures of Emma at a time when she was healthy and vibrant, beautiful in my arms when I was also all of those things. I push the box back and inhale deeply. I don't want to think about her, but how can I not? I leave the dress shoes on the bed and close the door behind me.

In the living room, the sunlight streams through the undrawn blinds, and I open the patio door to let some air in.

I loiter on the small balcony, absorbing the varied sounds of the city seeping up from below and beyond. I remove Em's picture from my pocket, put it on the small table, then drop into one of the two chairs.

Knocking back a mouthful of ale, I lean down to the upturned terracotta plant pot, lift it with my finger in the drainage hole, and find the packet of cigarettes and lighter I keep out here. It really is a disgusting habit, and luckily for me, I'm bizarrely not addicted to nicotine. With my compulsive personality, it should be a given, but I never have been. I can take it or leave it. The rare days I do fancy one, it's for nothing more than boredom. Or something to accompany my procrastination. Like now.

I slide the patio door across, flick the lighter, and the end glows red. Blowing out a smoke ring, it evaporates on the atmosphere as my sight fixes on Em, smiling at me behind the glass. Taking another drag of the cig, I blow out the smoke slowly. It drifts away on the breeze while my thoughts drift back to the day a strong, level-headed girl wedged herself into my life.

TEN YEARS AGO...

I STRIKE THROUGH the classified ad for construction labourers and apprentices. Tapping the pen on the next advert down, this one for bricklayers, I immediately cross that out too. Doing a quick skim of the other ads, they are all for trained, skilled positions. Unfortunately, the only thing I'm trained in is fucking up – more often than not, these days - and the only skill I possess is touting the Blacks wares all over the city and managing not to get caught and banged up. It wasn't a rash decision that made me approach Franklin for a 'job'; it was a financial one. I confess I don't particularly like my current income stream, but I also don't want to starve and sleep rough, either. I guess I'm learning there is a certain truth coined in the term 'beggars can't be choosers'.

I pick up my glass and down the last dregs of lager. Reaching into my pocket for my wallet, I wave over the bartender for another.

"Any luck?" He gestures to the local recruitment paper, and I pass him a tenner.

"No. I guess the economic shift is hitting hard at all angles. This place is pretty dead for a Saturday afternoon." I jerk my head back towards the half-empty establishment behind me, which I expected to be livelier since it is derby day, and the pre-match build-up has already started.

He hands over my change and leans on the bar. "It's like this every day. Used to be a time when this place, along with the rest of the bars in the area, would be full of office suits or footy fans from midday until closing. Now, since everyone is fearful of being made redundant, unable to pay their way and living on the poverty line, they stay at home and drink."

I nod, concurring, since the only reason why I'm sitting here, drinking away money I can honestly ill afford to, is the fact that Deacon – my friend and housemate – is currently entertaining, for lack of a better word, his latest, easiest conquest.

"It's shit at the moment, but I hope you find something, mate."

"Yeah, thanks," I reply as a gaggle of girls walk in and line up along the bar next to me. I glance down at the next ad for a roofer and huff as I strike through it. Every week for the last few months I've endured this torture. All the same jobs are advertised week in week out, and week after week, I inevitably strike through them because I don't fit the criteria. Seriously, when my school careers adviser gave me the lecture on having a respectable trade, I really should've listened. But my fifteen-year-old self was already fed up with school, so the prospect of going to college to further educate myself in plumbing, carpentry, or construction was not appealing. Now I'm paying the price.

"How about that one?" A pale pink-tipped finger taps an ad for television walk-on parts and models. My shoulders shake in silent laughter until the sound escapes my throat. "What's so funny?" The unidentified female asks innocently.

I hitch my brow and glance at her from the corner of my eye. Her long blonde hair is tucked behind her ear, while the other side falls in a shiny veil over her shoulder. Intrigued, I rotate my arse on the stool to get a better look. My laugh diminishes when mesmerising, ice blue eyes meet mine, and fuck me if this girl isn't just the perfect specimen of the female form. I'm not a saint. I've met a lot of beautiful girls; I've slept with a few of them, but in this moment, they all fade in comparison to this beauty before me.

I continue to stare, completely unashamed, completely entranced. From her small, perfectly proportioned nose to her naturally full, pink lips, complemented by her flawless, minimally made-up porcelain skin. My eyes continue their descent. Down her slender neck to the swell of her small breasts, over the defined curve of her waist and flare of her hips, all the way down her shapely thighs to her feet.

My eyes repeat the process in reverse, silently approving of the black high heels, dark, tight jeans and black tight top, until those stunning blues ensnare me, holding me hostage. She stares back, and I'd like to think she's as affected by me as I am by her, but I very much doubt it. Girls like her don't look at guys like me.

"Em?" Her head turns slowly towards one of the other girls. "What do you want?"

"A G and T, please." She licks her bottom lip, and my body responds in *base instinct at her action, wondering what it would feel like to kiss and bite that lip myself.*

"Two G and T's, a rum and Coke, a dry white wine, and a Peroni, please," the other girl requests.

I pick up my lager, needing something to take the edge off the instantaneous heat I'm experiencing - since I can't exactly get high in a public place - when the barman slaps both hands back on the bar, and his eyes drift over them.

"ID, all of you."

I smirk while a chorus of unhappy females chime out their ages in succession, along with the injustice and humiliation of being ID'ed at their age. The barman stands his ground as three driver's licences and two passports are shoved under his nose. Satisfied, he reaches for the glasses.

Picking up my pint, I fix my gaze back on the paper when that pink-tipped finger taps on the ad again.

"So, are you considering it?"

I smile, unable to do anything else, and furrow my brow. "A TV walk-on? What is that?" I scrunch my nose up since I don't have a clue.

She grins and tucks the other side of her hair behind her ear. "You know, you sit in the background in a pub or a bar." She waves her hand behind her. "And drink a beer." She nods at my glass. "And you repeat it however many times until the actors get the scene right. You'd be perfect."

"Thanks for the suggestion, but I don't think that's the vocation for me." I knock back another mouthful and set the glass down.

"What about the modelling gig?"

Her G and T is placed in front of her, and she pops the straw into her mouth. She sucks on it, and the liquid in the glass decreases steadily as her incredibly kissable lips move unconsciously up and down the plastic. The action is barely noticeable, but God do I notice, and unfortunately, it gets my vivid and somewhat filthy imagination worked up, visualising other things she could be sucking on. My blood drains to my waist and causes an immediate, unwanted reaction that I'm glad she can't see.

"I don't think I'm cut out to be a model either," I answer gruffly.

"Really?" she replies in astonishment. "But you're handsome and se-"

She quickly snaps her head away, and I lean back to see the shocked expression of her friend next to her, who cannot believe she has just said that, and the other girl grins, also averting her eyes.

Turning back around, I smile. Yeah, she's affected all right, and I'm not one to pass up an opportunity. Not when it's beautiful and blatantly interested. Not to mention, I haven't felt a prominent spark towards anyone like this in ages, maybe never, even.

"Sorry, I didn't quite catch that." I feign deafness. *When she starts to fuss with her hair until it's hanging as a silken barrier between us, I slide my hand over the bar and stroke my finger the length of her hand. My action is only meant to be an innocent gesture, but it causes her to jolt in surprise, and a spark of electricity shots up my limb.*

Eventually, she turns. Her lips are pursed together in embarrassment, and her cheeks are crimson. Her beautiful blues can barely look at me as she fails to find something to fix her mortified gaze on.

"Sorry, what did you say?" I press again, desperate to hear her say those words out loud.

Her eyes close in resignation, the beautiful thick lashes fanning the delicate skin beneath them. "I said you're handsome."

"And?" I query with a fake vagueness.

"Sexy," she whispers, pursing those beautiful lips again. I smile, taking advantage of the moment since she still has her eyes closed.

"Thank you," I whisper back, and her tense features soften. "Coming from a beautiful girl like you, that means a lot."

Her eyes slowly open, and she covers her face with her hand, still embarrassed, but her resulting smile is blinding. "Thanks."

"What's your name?"

"Emma Shaw. My friends call me Em."

"It's nice to meet you, Emma Shaw. I'm Jeremy James, but I get called a variety of names: Remy, Rem, Jer. Take your pick."

She laughs, and her discomfort withers away. "It's nice to meet you, Jeremy James. You're not from around here, are you?"

"No, I'm a London boy through and through. It's the accent that gives it away, isn't it?" I'm grinning, pathetically enraptured by this beautiful, chatty girl, who, if she knew the truth about me, would already be running in the opposite direction.

"Actually, it isn't the lack of a Mancunian accent, it's the coat." She gives said coat the once over, and I look down at myself, wondering what's wrong with it. "You can always spot a southerner a mile away. Do you want to know how?" *She picks up her drink and sucks that damn straw again.*

I stare into those playful blue orbs and nod, desperate to hear anything come out of her luscious mouth. Honestly, she could talk absolute shit for hours, and I'd sit here, absorb it all and recite it word perfect later.

"Well, you see..." She moves close enough that the faint aroma of whatever shampoo or hair product she uses permeates my nostrils. "When the months start to turn a little nippier, and the temperature drops, say, September, northerners put on a jumper or a light jacket." *She sets down her drink and shows me the ridiculously thin, pneumonia-inducing jacket looped*

through the straps of her bag. "Southerners, on the other hand, put on a thick jumper and the heaviest coat they possess and complain it's cold." Her fingers slide along the hem of my thick, quilted winter coat and give it a spirited tug. "That's how you can tell."

I down the rest of my drink and look around the still half-empty bar. Out of all the patrons in the premises, I'm the only one wearing a thick coat, but granted, it was cold this morning. Obviously, I'm not going to admit that and expose my tender southern inadequacies. I bring my eyes back to her, and she beams knowingly, proud of her demonstrable abilities. The sound of slurping punctures the companionable silence between us, and I eye the glass she has now drained completely. I look down at my own, the same moment one of the other girls slips off her stool.

"Em, are you ready to hit the next bar?"

Emma's face falls a little, and she turns her head towards her friend but still has one eye on me.

"Actually, I think I might stay here for a bit, if you don't mind?" She gives me a look, one which asks if that's also okay with me. The side of my mouth hitches triumphantly, and I wink.

Her friend, however, is unimpressed. "Actually, yes, I do mind! The pub crawl was your idea. We didn't even want to come in here. Oh, whatever! Come on, everyone. Emma is staying apparently!" The girl grabs her things and strides out of the bar. The rest of the group follows behind her, each bestowing Emma a death glare.

I glance back at the door to see the small gathering of girls gesturing, probably bitching about being ditched. "Maybe you should go with your friends," I suggest because they are far better for her than I am - regardless that they do appear to be the backstabbing kind.

"No." Emma gives me a steely glare. "She's just pissed off because she found out her boyfriend cheated on her last week. I'm actually glad I met you because now I won't have to listen to her get drunk and cry over him all night. Again."

I gasp. "So, you were just using me?" It's been a while since I've flirted, but I'm thoroughly enjoying this.

"Why, of course!" She smiles broadly, participating in the game, raising the stakes.

"Now I understand why you called me handsome and sexy. It was all just a ploy to escape. My God, I think I might be offended." I keep my expression neutral, not wanting to run her off completely. Truth be told, I want her to stay.

Emma's cheeks turn pink again, and she trains her eyes on the bar. I grin at her half-arsed attempt at lying about her true thoughts.

"Right," I murmur, still trying to sound serious. "Well, if I bought you another drink, would you, maybe, reconsider your evaluation of me?"

Her head darts up, and she shuffles closer. "Maybe...handsome." Her eyes capture mine. They are filled with something I can't quite put my finger on, not that I'm an expert in the complexities of the female mind, but still, there's something there. Something possibly taking root for both of us.

"Is that a yes?" I press her softly, wanting to hear the confirmation, just to ensure I'm not imagining that a beautiful young woman is taking a genuine interest in me for something other than what I can illegally supply.

Emma smiles again. "Yes, I'd love to stay and have another drink with you."

"Another G and T?"

"Erm..." She focuses the bottles behind the bar. "How about we do some shots?"

I laugh singularly as I glance at the clock mounted on the wall beside the brass bell. "No, I think it's far too early for that."

"Oh, come on, it'll be fun!"

"I'll tell you what, how about we have another drink, maybe order some food, and then we can revisit the shots suggestion later?" Or not at all. "Sound good?" I stroke the back of her hand in supplication, praying she agrees. If so much as one shot snakes its way down my throat, she's going to see me for what I truly am. For me, shots - unless monitored - equal total oblivion. Because the instant my body starts to feel limber and the potency of the alcohol begins to kick in and clouds my judgement, I will, without fail, reach for a needle.

Still, in this moment, in the presence of a girl I barely know, I feel like I can go one night without hitting up. It's the first time in months I've felt like this. I only wish every day could be like this, but my obsessive, uncontrollable personality won't permit it.

"So, drinks and dinner... This is almost like a date."

My train of thought brakes sharply as her moderately correct assumption weaves through my ears and embeds in my grey matter. I fix my attention back on her as her fingers tangle with mine, and she squeezes.

"Almost," she whispers.

I stare at our hands and remain stock still, realising that's what she wants. The reason why she first approached me. She wants a date. With me. Shit! In the space of thirty minutes, I've gone from being single to laying the initial foundations of a possible relationship.

The sounds of the bar - some more augmented than others - fill the void of silence. I mentally run through the ramifications of what the imminent future might entail with this girl. While the idea might be premature, the *reality may not be.*

Suddenly, her fingers extract themselves from mine, and I snap out of it as she shoulders her bag. "I'm sorry, that was presumptuous. I think I better go."

"No, wait!" I grab her then ease off because I don't want to upset her any more than I already have. She looks downbeat, waiting for me to say something. "I'm sorry. I was just thinking."

"It's okay. I didn't mean to be so blunt and obvious. It was nice meeting you." She quickly strides to the door, and I slide off the stool and spin her around.

"I don't want you to leave." The statement is out of my mouth before my brain can process it. "Stay. Please." My tone is soft and very truthful. The last thing I want is for her to walk out of that door with anyone but me. She stares up at me, and even in her heels, she's still a good foot shorter than I am. I slowly lead her back to the bar, and she observes attentively as I fold up the newspaper.

"I thought we were staying."

I shake my head. "How about an early dinner?"

She presses her lips together, and her cheeks contort in contemplation as her mouth pouts from side to side. "As in a date? A real one?"

I laugh, unable to hold it in. She isn't backward in coming forward, that's for sure. I nod, making her smile victoriously. "Yes!" she hisses in delight, drawing out the S. "I'd love to. Thank you."

"No," I murmur, my hand acting of its own volition and reaching for her hair. "I should be thanking you." I tuck the thick lock of stunning blonde back behind her ear, and she blushes.

"Why?"

"No reason." Although I could spout off a few reprehensible ones without even needing to think about it. "I just need to-" I halt mid-sentence and instead jerk my head towards the sign for the gent's, unsure if she will get embarrassed by my saying I need to take a piss. Women are weird like that sometimes.

"Okay." She clambers back up onto the stool and flips the paper over as I stride away and push open the toilet door.

A few minutes later, I zip up my jeans. I move away from the urinals and wash my hands. Removing my phone from my pocket, I tap on Deek's name and wait for him to pick up.

"Hey," he greets, garbled. I quickly move to the door and open it slightly to see if anyone else might venture in.

"I can't do any business tonight."

"Why? You out on the pull?"

"*No, the streets are crawling with police.*" I lie, very proficiently, since I haven't seen one bobby all afternoon. But, yes, I have indeed pulled.

"*Ah fuck, I forgot it's match day. Yeah, no worries, Dad'll be fine with it. Pick up a curry on your way back.*" He sniffs long and hard down the receiver, and I realise I'm probably better off staying well away for now if he's already doing lines.

"*Actually, I thought I might stay out. Catch a film.*"

Deek snorts. "*What? Are you trying to be a normal, upstanding member of society?*"

"*Something like that.*" My hand wavers on the door handle, and I watch from the gap as Emma concentrates on her phone, waiting for me.

"*Fuck, okay. I'll see you later, man.*"

"*Yeah.*" I end the call, let the door close, and slip my mobile back into my pocket. Pulling out my wallet, I thumb through the tens and twenties – rent, food, and drug money – to see how much I have. I'm satisfied it's enough to buy a decent dinner, but if not, the credit card with the balance that always seems to go up and never down will be making an appearance instead.

As I straighten myself up, my eyes flick to the vending machine on the wall. I stare at it and debate whether I might be tempting fate to assume that Emma will want more than dinner with me this evening. It's been a while since I've had sex. The last time was a girl in a club who dragged me up a small alleyway that was already littered with used condoms some three months ago.

I shake my head. I can't do that to her. That, being screwing and using her. I harden my resolve and look back at my reflection in the mirror. Truthfully, regardless of my despicable and immoral employment status and my personal inability to just say no, I really am a nice guy, a good guy. I don't lead women on. I don't make outlandish promises to get them naked, and I don't push for more than they are willing to give. And I'm not about to start deviating from that path now.

Striding back out of the gents, determined to show Emma the good guy I truly am this evening, she spins around on the stool. "*I thought you'd got lost!*" she flirts sarcastically.

"*Really? Funny you didn't care enough to come and find me.*" I flirt back, enjoying her easy teasing.

"*Ew, I wasn't about to come looking for you in the dirty boys' toilets.*" She slips down from the stool, and I hold out my hand.

"*Touché,*" I say with a smile as she slides her hand in mine, and we head out of the bar.

"SO, WHAT DO you fancy?" Emma asks, distracted as we pass numerous restaurants. *My first reaction is to say 'you', but I keep my mouth shut. I think we're both aware there is a mutual attraction here. If there wasn't, she wouldn't have pushed so hard, and in return, I would have let her walk away when she had the chance.*

"I can eat anything. I'm not fussy. You pick somewhere." And with those words, I pray she doesn't want a Michelin starred dining experience tonight. *"How about this place?"* I suggest gently tugging her towards the contemporary bar and grill, which is a step or two up from bog-standard pub grub. *She bites her lip and then, rather grudgingly, turns to the menu board just outside the door. The prices aren't too bad - in my opinion - and I can definitely swing it without skipping the rent and getting further into debt.*

"Let's look somewhere else," she says and attempts to walk the other way.

"Em, what's wrong?" I query delicately, using her nickname for the first time. *Her fingers fidget at her mouth, and she starts to mumble.* *"I'm sorry, I didn't get that."*

"I can't afford it." Her words are laced with humiliation, but I thank God I've been blessed with the company of someone who doesn't expect me to fine wine and dine them. *"I've only got thirty quid left to get me to and from uni and work until payday in two weeks. I don't want you paying an exorbitant amount of money for dinner when I'm the one who came on to you."*

An uncontrollable urge wells inside, and without further thought, I manipulate her into my arms and hold her. Long minutes pass until she eventually peers up at me. Her beautiful, intoxicating eyes ensnare me again, and before I can even stop it, I cradle her face tenderly, dip my head down and press my mouth to hers.

A fire sparks the moment her soft lips move tentatively against mine, and I cup her face. I thread my fingers through the silky strands of hair at her nape and press my thumbs ever so slightly into her cheekbones. The kiss becomes more frantic, and she grips my back hard, her fingers digging in through the three layers I'm wearing, while her mouth fights against mine, pushing for more. She presses her chest forward, and I swallow her blissful, tortured moan, never having enjoyed kissing so much before.

"Sorry, sir, a table for two?" And the moment is obliterated.

I reluctantly pull away from the luscious mouth I've wanted to kiss for the last hour and acknowledge the waiter, who is definitely in the wrong place at the wrong time. Or, maybe for us, the right place at the right time. Who knows what would have happened if he hadn't have broken the spell.

I lift a hand from Em's face and raise one finger. *"Can you give us a minute?"* The waiter agrees and goes back inside.

"We can go somewhere cheaper. I don't mind, Jeremy."

I smile. I was completely enthralled, and now I'm wholly impressed by her low maintenance and how considerate she's being. "Let's go inside. This is a nice place for a first date."

"Okay," she replies contritely and lifts up on her toes to kiss me again.

"And, if you're lucky," I say, holding the door open. "I might even let you order the cheapest thing on the menu!"

"SO, I HAVE a confession."

I glance at a very relaxed Emma, circling her finger around the rim of the wine glass. We are currently on bottle number two, and both of us are feeling the effects. I've accepted that I will be paying on the credit card, and I've accepted that it's more than worth it. This has been the best night of my life, hands down, without a doubt.

It's been two hours since we manhandled each other on the pavement, and numerous couples have already been and gone as we have sat here, eating and talking. We have chatted through a range of topics, from our favourite foods, films, music, and TV programmes. I have found out she is eighteen, an only child, currently at uni, studying English Lit and working part-time in a high street clothes store. She has found out I am nineteen, also an only child, currently working in sales and distribution, but looking to expand my horizons into something more productive, preferably not TV or modelling work. I'm not proud of the fact I'm consciously lying to her. My earlier assumption of our mutual attraction being very real is no longer an assumption. The last few hours of being in this girl's company have proven that I'm facing a very real, terrifying risk of falling hard and fast for her. It has also confirmed that I might finally have a reason to get clean. I only hope when I do have to tell her – because I know I shall since you can't just turn off addiction – that she understands.

"What's that?" I finally ask, raising the glass to my mouth.

She laughs in that boozy, giggly way girls do. "I did suggest the bar crawl. I promised we would only be there for one drink." Her eyes are wild, and I wonder what she's expecting my reaction will be in her moderately drunken mind.

"Well, I figured you did since your friend had no reason to lie, but why didn't you leave with them?" I don't need to ask the question. I know she stayed for me, and I'm very grateful for that.

"Leaving would have ruined my best-laid plan." She pouts and bats her lashes. "You see, they didn't want to go into that bar, but I did." She steadies her gaze on me from across the table. "Because I saw you as we were walking past." She glides her hand through the space between us.

I lean back in my seat, amazed that she selfishly orchestrated it just to meet me. She has just gone up yet another notch in my book. *"You went in there for me?"* My voice is strained, shocked that she's risked her friendships to hook up.

"Yeah...for you. Shall we get out of here?"

I nod, a bit far gone on reality, and indicate to the waiter milling around – probably dying to get rid of us – for the bill. He slaps the black leather wallet on the table, and I don't even bother looking at the total and pass him my card.

Ten minutes later, we're back on the pavement in the same spot we were before. It's just gone ten, and the streets are rowdier now with the two sides of the city's football fans.

"It's late. Let's get a taxi. I'll take you home." I slide my arm around her back, noting she's shivering in the thin, shiny thing she calls a jacket.

"Jer, I can't. If my dad sees me in this state, he'll kill me."

"Weren't you already getting drunk with your girls before I scuppered those plans?" I remind her gently.

"Yes, but I was meant to be staying at Zoe's house. I can't exactly go there now after I blew her off." She gabbles on until, as expected, the words I dread finally emit her mouth. *"Can I come home with you?"*

I hold in the pained groan rising in my throat. Truthfully, I'd rather she didn't. Not because her home is probably a million times nicer than my rented hovel, but because Deacon will be there. I don't want him getting any ideas about her and the reason why she might be staying. It wouldn't be the first time he has tried something with a couple of my one-night stands after the event has occurred between us.

"Please, I promise I won't try anything!" she pleads desperately, and I bite back my laugh because I should be the one reassuring her of that.

"Let me just make a call." I glide my arm around her waist and tap away on my phone.

"Hey," Deek answers on the second ring.

"Are you still at home?"

"Nah, I'm at a party. I'll be gone all night. Are you going home?"

"Yeah. I was just wondering if you still wanted any food." The deception rolls off my tongue easily. *"But I guess not. I'll see you sometime tomorrow."*

"Yeah, later." He hangs up, and I put my phone away.

"Come on, let's go." I tighten my arm around her as we dash towards the taxi rank. Climbing inside, she nuzzles next to me, and before we have even made it out of the city centre, she's already half asleep.

I gently guide her out of the taxi and close the door. Leading her to the house, I hold her firmly while I unlock the door and wave her inside. She's dead on her feet, but she's perking up a little in the new surroundings she's found herself in.

"How many people do you live with?"

"Just the two of us, but Deacon's out for the night." I lock the front door and move in front of her to quickly glance into the living room. My eyes scan fervently, making sure Deek hasn't left out anything that could end whatever this is between us before it even begins. "Can I get you a drink? A glass of water?"

"No, I'm fine. I'd really like to go to bed, though." My body responds immediately to that suggestion. She gives me an innocent look, but I've seen it plenty of times before, and there's not one iota of innocence in it.

"Em…" I rub my hands over the tops of her arms. "It wasn't my intention to bring you back here. It wasn't even my intention to meet you. So, please, don't do that."

"Do what?" She bats her lashes, again her implication far from innocent.

"That! I won't take advantage of you. I'm not that kind of guy. Look, you can sleep in my room, and I'll sleep down here."

She suddenly looks repentant, realising the awkward position she's put me in. "No, please. We can share a bed. I promise I won't touch you."

I chortle singularly. "That, I fail to believe, but I'm going to hold you to it." I lead her upstairs, and she takes in the surroundings of my rented house. It isn't great, but it was the best of a bad bunch.

I flick on the bedside lamp, and she takes in the fairly barren room, consisting of a double bed, a wardrobe, a chest of drawers and a bedside table. I don't have much, and none of it's particularly amazing to look at. I leave her to look around as I open the drawer and pull out a t-shirt for her to wear.

"The bathroom is the second door down." I put the shirt on the bed, expecting her to take it and run to the other room. Instead, she begins to get undressed in front of me. Again, failing to keep her promise of not doing that.

As she starts to lift her top, I swear to God, she's going to fucking kill me before this night is through. Some men would consider this a blessing from heaven to have a beautiful girl throwing herself at him. Right now, all I'm experiencing is hell. Pure, unadulterated hell.

"I'll be back in a minute." I all but run into the bathroom because she's more intoxicating than drugs have ever been. Closing the door, I bang my head against it, seriously considering the abrupt need to take a very cold shower. Except, if I do, I run the real possibility of her joining me. I shift and drop my forehead heavily towards the bathroom mirror and finally accept that either way, I'm utterly screwed in this situation.

I pull the light cord off, having finally worked up the courage to re-enter *my bedroom. I close the door and find Em already snuggled under the duvet. I turn off the bedside lamp, strip down to my boxers, and slide into the other side. I stare at the ceiling, cursing anything and everything because this is torture I don't need. Usually, when put in a situation I'm uncomfortable with, I get high. Sadly, I can't do that tonight.*

"Jer?"

"Em, please go to sleep," I request in a strained tone. The bed moves, and her arm snakes its way over my chest. I jolt as her flesh connects with mine, and for all my good intentions, I give in and roll over to face her. Even in the dark room, I can still make out her features perfectly.

"Thank you for letting me stay. I'm sorry if I've made you feel uncomfortable."

I lift my hand to her face and tenderly stroke her cheek. "It's okay. I just don't want you thinking I got the wrong impression. That I expect payment of some kind for tonight."

Her lips part slightly and curve. "No, I didn't think that at all. But honestly, I wish you would." *Her hand comes over mine, and she slowly moves my fingers to her mouth. She lightly kisses each fingertip, forcing me to decide what exactly will happen between us tonight because it's clear something is going to. I know I have tread carefully. That I have to be the one to decide since she will probably let me do whatever I want. She's made that much clear. Still, I can't find it in my heart to be that man, to take that proffered advantage.*

"Just so you know, I want to see you again, and I think you want to see me, too."

"Yes. Yes, I do."

"So, tell me how far you're willing to go?" *I ask softly.*

She shuffles closer, and I realise she hasn't bothered with the t-shirt I left out for her when her bare breast grazes my arm. Her nose runs the length of mine, and her tongue swipes over my bottom lip. I quickly slide my arm under her and press her against me. This is playing with fire, and everything ignites, like petrol being thrown on a flame. My mouth slams against hers, and she drags her fingers through my hair, forcing me closer. My tongue slides between her lips and duels with hers. I slip one hand between us and roll a taut, distended nipple, causing her to buck harder. I stretch my hand under her further until I reach her arse – thankfully, she has kept her knickers on - and rub rhythmically.

"Oh, God! I could come like this," *she exclaims, practically breathless.*

Fuck.

I'm unable to get enough of her as I manipulate her where I want her. I adjust my hand from behind the top of her thigh to her arse and squeeze. She moans incoherently, her fingers tightening in my hair, not comprehending that's just making me more mindless and rabid. My hand is so close to heaven that I could easily slide my fingers up there, but instead, I pull her over me. This is purely for my own selfishness, considering I'm still not so far gone that I'm willing to have full-blown sex with her, but just so I can feel the way her nipples graze my chest and her swollen core heating my thigh.

Her mouth becomes more ardent until she breaks away with a molten glint in her eye. Her hand slowly works down my chest until she is rubbing the hard-on I'm fighting hard against.

"Em...no. No condom."

"I've got an implant," she retorts, her hand pulling the fabric away to feel my dangerously aroused flesh.

I shake my head. It isn't the fear of giving her STIs since I always use a condom. It's the fear that maybe one of the needles I've injected with might not have been as sterile as I thought. I can't do that to her. I can't pretend that isn't a possibility.

"No, not tonight," I say through gritted teeth. I push her away slightly, and she gives me a dejected look. I scoot myself up the bed until my back is against the headboard, and I pull her back over me. "Use me, ride me, but I won't be inside you like that tonight."

I mollify her easily, and she presses her mouth back to mine. Within minutes all is forgotten, and she rubs her core against mine. The sensation is electrifying, powerful, and I fight the urge to rip off her flimsy knickers and sink into her wonderful depths. I work my mouth down her neck and sit my hands on her rib cage. I manipulate her back in order to allow myself unfettered access to her chest. My mouth captures one perfect, beautiful nipple, and I suck reverently, enjoying the way it feels in my mouth, on my tongue, between my lips. She grips my shoulder for support, mewling and thrashing. I lower her back down and slap my hands on her hips, controlling the rotation, grinding her swollen centre against my equally swollen groin.

"God, you feel so hard, so good." Her words come out husky, and I know she isn't far away.

"Can I touch you?" I ask and circle my finger on her pubic bone, ready to give her something. Her eyes flicker, revealing the ecstasy she is luxuriating in, and she nods, understanding precisely how I'm going to touch her.

I move my hand further over the fabric covering her until my finger slides up and down her centre. The material is already moist, and it takes every ounce of willpower not to do more. I continue to stroke until I reach her clit, and then I play relentlessly.

"I want you inside me, Jer," she whimpers, trying to manoeuvre my hand, but I don't budge because what she doesn't understand is that I won't be able to stop there. To feel that delicious wet heat she's creating... I'd be in her in a heartbeat.

"Not tonight," I repeat again, amazed by my own control. She presses down harder on my hand, then takes her own initiative and grabs my aching dick and starts to pump. The sensation is too much. The feeling of my fingers so close to her wet flesh, her hand and the cotton covering me generating sublime friction with each ministration, and the grunts and moans we're both emitting. I slide my fingers just inside, grab her nape and pull her back towards me. Her small breasts slide over the fine hair peppering my chest, and it's just one more sensation to take us both over.

My mouth slams over hers, and I pillage without due care, working my fingers tirelessly between her legs. Her hand presses against my shoulder, and she pulls back. Her head tips up, and she cries out and careens over the edge. I observe her raw reaction, loving the way she looks. Beautiful, uninhibited. Fucked.

Minutes later, she slides her hand from my shoulder to the side of my neck. Her face is a picture of post-pleasure, her skin perspired, her cheeks flushed. Her hand pumps me solidly, over and over, as she kisses me with open eyes, waiting for the inevitable.

It doesn't take long, and within seconds the pressure building detonates. I growl out, completely floored by the orgasm exploding in my abdomen. I hold on to her tight, feeling a strange, unexpected vulnerability wash over me.

She plants her head against my chest and starts to laugh. I gently pull her back, and she gazes at me with nothing but respect.

"What?" I query softly, stroking her damp hair.

"I didn't keep my promise. You'll soon realise I'm not very good at that." She kisses me, and I laugh in disbelief because she got what she wanted, but I got so much more. I got the realisation of knowing that sex, penetrative or not, is so much better with someone you care about. That's something I've never had before. "You were right, Jer."

"About?"

"You are a good guy. You didn't take advantage."

"That's debatable."

I kiss her forehead and shuffle down the bed, adjusting her with me. My thoughts are plagued with the desperate need to clean up - or at least change my boxers. Soft mounds of flesh press against my chest, and nimble fingers draw delicate shapes over my skin. Any further rancid thoughts of sleeping in my own body fluids are eliminated when Em presses a lingering kiss to my nipple and finally settles down.

Eventually, my eyes close, and I sleep the most peaceful, dreamless sleep I've had in a long time.

I BREATHE OUT, open my eyes and stare at the horizon. The sun is starting to set, and the beautiful memory of the day we met fades away.

Until I lost her, it was always my favourite. The one that always pushed to the forefront of my mind whenever her name was spoken. Still, in the end, the only memory I remember now is the one where I screamed her name in vain and rocked her lifeless body on the bed in which we shared so many amazing moments.

I rub my thumb over her picture. Even after nine years, sometimes, I still expect her to walk through the door or call out my name.

"You warned me," I murmur, lighting up another cig. "You warned me, and I should have listened." I inhale deeply as my hand shakes. My mind rewinds, remembering how she always said she couldn't keep promises.

She didn't lie.

And it wasn't long after our first date that I'd find out just how true her statement was.

Chapter 3

I FOLD DOWN the starchy collar and adjust the bowtie I've managed to fasten correctly with the aid of Google. Sliding on the waistcoat, I straighten up and step away from the full-length mirror on the back of the wardrobe door. Tugging my sleeve cuffs, I'm surprised by my uncharacteristic reflection. The look is impeccable, sleek and defined. And entirely out of place on me. Feeling somewhat uncomfortable, my eyes work from the bottom up. From the black trousers, shiny black leather belt, waistcoat, and crisp white shirt, I've got to admit Sloan did well when he ordered this. It's done precisely what he anticipated – it's made a silk purse from a sow's ear.

And it's turned me into an unlikely gentleman for the evening.

I run my hand through my hair, which is in dire need of a trim. It's longer than it has been in months, to the point where it's starting to curl at the ends and annoy me. I really should have got it cut this morning, but I was still in the mindset of not giving a toss. Now, in comparison to everything else being immaculately presented from the neck down, I probably shouldn't have dismissed it so quickly.

I continue to evaluate my appearance - something I rarely do - and realise how far I've come. The last time I stood in front of a mirror and really looked at myself, was just before Dom locked me in a sparse room with a boarded-up window, a bare mattress, a bucket, and nothing I could self-harm with. It was the night I feared. Before leaving me to suffer on the long hard road of withdrawal and survival, he grabbed me by the nape and forced me to look at myself properly for the first time in two years.

I was shocked. I hadn't appreciated just how far I'd let myself go.

At only twenty, I was the epitome of drug chic. I was the person you crossed the street to avoid. My skin was almost grey, my cheeks were sunken, and my eyes were dull, lifeless, even. My body was gaunt, emaciated through overindulgence of drugs and very little sustenance by way of actual vitamins and nutrients. Truthfully, up until that point, I didn't give a shit if I lived or died. Everything I had ever loved had been taken away from me. I had a grieving father vying for my blood and a duplicitous best friend who aggressively encouraged my usage to hide who he truly was.

And the only way I could forget any of it was to close my door and flood my veins.

When I look back on those days now, I can hardly believe I was that man. Now, having achieved eight, nearly nine years of living relatively clean under my belt, if you didn't know me, you wouldn't be able to reconcile me with who I once was. While I still possess the faint tell-tale incision marks on my arms, particularly on the inside of my elbows, I'm a picture of health, and I actively shy away from anything that could steer me back down the rabbit hole.

My body is now strong and healthy since Kieran made it his mission to keep me on the straight and narrow, and he dragged my reluctant arse to the gym most mornings when I was living in Leeds. He made a grand statement of my OCD needing something to latch on to, and in turn, I swapped the rush of a chemical high for the rush of natural endorphins.

I'm back to being the man that Emma had considered handsome. But even she was wrong because I was in the clutches of addiction when we first met, and physically, I'm far better now than I was then. The only real visible difference between then and now is the scar that Deacon happily carved into my face.

My finger automatically drifts to my temple, and I exhale, wondering what she would make of it. Whether or not she would still consider me handsome is anyone's guess, but even when she witnessed the real me for the first time, she still saw the good. I did everything I could to make her see there was no future with me, but she refused to walk away, believing she could eventually fix me.

Unable to deal with the psychological repercussions of the ubiquitous memory of that terrible day, I mentally drag it back into the dark, untouched recesses of my brain. I cover my face with my hand as a watery film coats my eyes and threatens to unravel my sanity. Trapped inside the authentic memory, my mobile rings from the floor where it's currently charging.

As I remove the cable, the screen glows brightly with Devlin's name until it stops. Rubbing my finger and thumb over my jaw, it starts to ring again.

"Yeah?" I answer, devoid of any demonstrative tone.

"Are you nearly ready?" he asks.

"Yeah, I was about to call a taxi," I lie, since a part of me is still trying to psyche myself up to do this.

"Don't bother. We're just pulling up outside." Then he hangs up.

I stride to the window and glance down at the street to see Devlin, Simon, and Tommy clambering out of a taxi, all suited and booted. I shake my head, wondering whose grand idea of divine intervention it was that they felt the need to come over here and escort me just to ensure I would attend tonight.

But I know damn well who suggested this: John. And if I thought he wouldn't already be thoroughly engrossed with the lovely Marie Dawson, I'd call him on it.

I stride out of the bedroom as the intercom system beeps, and I press the button for the main entrance. Fastening my watch and positioning the shiny square cuff links, an almighty bang thuds against the door.

"Open up! Police raid!" Simon shouts, probably loud enough for the other three flat owners on this floor to hear, not to mention those living above and below me.

"For fuck sake!" I rip open the door, grab Si by his jacket and haul him inside.

"Hey, watch the suit!" He slips out of my grip to smooth his jacket in a noble fashion.

"Screw the suit! If you pull another stunt like that, you'll be getting buried in it!" I motion my hand for Tommy and Dev to get inside.

"It was a joke, arsehole," Si retorts as I slam the door shut.

"Yeah? Well, it wasn't funny. You may not appreciate this, but other people are living in this building. And they probably won't share your warped sense of humour, either."

Simon huffs and puffs something sounding a little like 'sorry', and then he slinks down the hallway and into the kitchen.

A hand suddenly slaps my back, and I jump. "Hey, calm down. He's just being Si. What's wrong with you?" Tommy asks.

"Nothing." I pinch the bridge of my nose in frustration. "Everything... Look, I'll apologise, don't worry." I sigh, but the way the sound emits my throat, anyone would think I have the weight of the world pressing down on my shoulders.

Tommy nods, unimpressed and follows in Si's direction. I fold my arms over my chest and lean back against the hallway wall and look up to the ceiling. Steadying my gaze on the intermittent red flashing light of the smoke alarm, Dev moves into my line of sight.

"Are you sure you're okay?"

I drop my chin to my chest. "I'm fine, but being back here..."

Dev's expression constricts, but no further words are needed because we both remember the last time we were all here in this apartment together.

"I spoke to uncle J and Dom after you left." He places his hand on my shoulder. "They told me everything, including what happened to the girl in Manchester."

I huff in disgust and anger and lightly bang my skull against the wall. "They had no right."

"No, they had *every* right." He throws a sideways glance down the hallway. I follow his gaze to Tommy and Si, necking my non-alcoholic beer as they approach. "You've not exactly covered yourself in glory, son, but we all forgive you."

"Why did you never tell us?" Tommy queries sympathetically.

I shrug. "I never wanted anyone's sympathy, so what difference would it have made?"

"True, but why did you never tell Kara?" he asks, addressing the very valid point I have ruminated over since Sloan told me she was finally an integral part of his life.

"Because I didn't want her to forgive me out of misplaced empathy! We can talk about this until the end of time. What if Em hadn't have died, would I still have been at that party? If I was sober that night, would have I still gone out with Deacon? I don't know. None of us does. Regardless, Em's dead and Kara will probably never forgive me. She made that much clear when she walked out of that door!" I throw my arm out. My temper is rising higher and higher, and it's not anger directed at these men - my friends, my brothers - it's directed at myself because there are so many things I could have done differently. Maybe the outcome would still be the same, or maybe my conscience would be less haunted by events I'm partially guilty of if life had been different and my choices had been better.

"You know, little lady carries an awful lot of emotional baggage, but as far as forgiveness goes, I think she might surprise you," Dev says.

"Thanks for the vote of confidence, but I'd be an idiot to believe that she ever will. She holds a mean grudge. Ask her father," I comment sarcastically.

Dev huffs. "You are *nothing* like her father!" he spits out, almost hateful.

"No," I reply emotionless. "I'm just the man who tied her to her bed and allowed her to be violated against her will. Some would say we are one in the same." On that, I stride into the living room and open the door and slide it shut. Retrieving my cigs from under the plant pot, I light one up and inhale deeply as the door slides open.

"Fuck, that's rank! Go stand over there." Dev points to the other side of the deck.

"It's the lesser of three evils, and it's my balcony, arsehole." I grin and blow a smoke ring at him. "Did John send you over tonight?"

"No. Sloan."

The silence between us grows uncomfortable until the door slides again, and Tommy and Simon join us.

"Kara will forgive you," Tommy says.

"It's not all entirely her," I admit quietly. "The root of my fears stem from the night Deacon raped Charlie. I refused to see what was there. Then Em overdosed not long after. Did they tell you how I held her cold, lifeless body until the ambulance arrived? How her father told me I was marked when he arrived on the scene and said I would always be dead man walking until I am no more?" I query, wondering just how much John and Dom shared with them respectively. "I constantly live in the past because I'm aware I don't really have a future."

"That's bullshit," Si mutters. I die the cig out on the side of the plant pot and flick the end over the balcony into the communal garden below. "You know, you can piss me off like no one else can, but I love you. Even when I had to listen to what you did to little lady, I still loved you. And I always will. But tonight, you need to start learning to live again."

I rotate and glare at them. "I am living."

"No, you're existing," Tommy wades in. "The same way Sloan and Kara were both just existing until they found each other again. The three of you share a murky, entwined past. I know I was there *that night*, but I wasn't, not really. This is about you three. Sloan's already forgiven you, Kara will definitely forgive you, but the real question is, when will you start forgiving yourself?"

I stare at the trio and gradually allow the possibility of living versus existing to finally become a reality. In all honesty, for the last nine years since Em died, I haven't dared to enter another relationship. Notwithstanding the one night stands I had both before, and after her, no one has ever piqued my interest the way a wayward girl in a dingy Manchester bar did. Maybe she set the bar too high, or maybe-

A phone rings and removes me from my procrastination. Tommy brings it to his ear as he steps back inside. "Yeah, we're on our way."

Si slides the door open and tugs on my arm. "Sorry about the police raid jibe. It sounded good in the lift."

I shake my head and pull him in for a hug. "If I wasn't so pissed off at life, I would've probably seen the funny side, too. I didn't mean what I said. I love you, man." I let him go and step back inside as he slides the door across and locks it.

"Oh, and speaking of funny sides, nice dickie bow!" Si laughs and runs his hand over his short hair.

My hand rises instantly as my eyes take in the three black ties they're all wearing.

"It makes you look almost respectable," Tommy pitches in, and I show him the finger. "Pray, good sir, where did you get it?"

"Sloan."

"Figures," he replies, amused.

"It took me thirty minutes to perfect this bastard!"

Dev chuckles and scratches his cheek. "And it'll take you less than thirty seconds to remove it."

Thirty seconds later, the dickie bow unravelled in my hand, I fish out the only black tie I own and slide it around my neck. Tossing down the redundant bowtie, I slip into my dinner jacket and flick off the hallway light. Tommy taps in the alarm code and locks my door.

Approaching the waiting taxi, I nudge the Windsor knot into place at my throat and bob down to get inside.

"You look beautiful, Cinderella." Simon kisses my cheek. Tommy and Dev snigger, sitting across from us as the hackney cab pulls away from the kerb. "Just remember, you have until midnight to start living. Otherwise, the carriage will turn back into a pumpkin."

I eyeball him and furrow my brow. I don't even want to know why he's quoting Disney. "One day, Si, you might start taking life more seriously."

"Nah, I think you take life seriously enough for all of us, Rem."

I face the front and grin because I can't argue with that. Except in present company, aside from Tommy, no one else really knows what it's like to lose someone in the most tragic of circumstances. But with all the things that my hands have done and my eyes have seen, I don't know how to live flippantly or easily.

Except after hunting out Kara tonight and getting the lay of the land straight from the horse's mouth, I'm finally going to try.

Chapter 4

THE TAXI STOPS down the street from the Emerson Hotel. The road is packed, prohibiting further passage. I fondly remember these chaotic scenes from events when I was younger, and Jules would bring me along with Sloan and Charlie. Usually, we would just end up in the penthouse suite, playing dress-up and sitting in front of the large windows overlooking the city, gazing at the lights twinkling, gorging ourselves on pop and crisps.

Getting out of the taxi, that unwelcome sensation of not fitting in returns tenfold. I stay behind the other three as we reach the hotel steps. Casting my sight over the attendees, they are dressed in their best and are ready to cut loose the only way rich people think is acceptable. Honestly, they think they are a cut above the rest, untouchable to the great unwashed. But personally, I'd rather slum it in a dingy club than live it up with the affluent and influential in their fake society.

"Here." Dev passes me an invite. I study it in all its gold leaf, ostentatious, cardboard glory while advancing the steps one at a time in a line that is twenty deep in front of us. As we get closer, I swear hives are starting to break out, and I twitch, unable to get comfortable. I glance behind me when a guffaw of fake laughter ensues, and my sight is unexpectedly drawn to the other side of the street as a man - who I swear could be Ian Petersen, Kara's AWOL father - watches from the shadows.

My feet continue to move as I continue to eyeball the figure until my concentration is distracted.

"Sir?" I face one of the security guards manning the entrance. "Arms out." Doing as requested, he waves a handheld scanner over my body in a fluid motion. The moment he looks at my face, his eyes are instantly drawn to the scar, and he visibly baulks. Typical, although no longer surprising. This is the reaction of everyone who sees it for the first time because people are frightened of what they don't know. "Invite?" I hand over the card, and he studies it – for far longer than he has any other - until he gives it back, still unconvinced.

I pass through the doors being held open by the hotel's concierge and gaze around the congested foyer. Even with my six-foot-two height, I'm failing to spot anyone until the dirty blond head of Doctor Stuart Andrews and his girlfriend Sophie Morgan move through the foyer. I affix my sight on them and spot Sloan walking away with James, the reception manager, while Sophie sidles up to a brunette who can only be Kara.

I hesitate to move forward, which seems to have been a constant occurrence in my life for the last decade. I've never moved forward; I've just remained static, existing, but not living - as I've already been informed this evening.

"You can't avoid her forever, sunshine." Si bumps his arm to mine before barrelling his way through the throng just in time to divest Kara of her jacket.

As everyone gravitates into the ballroom, she bobs up and down on her tiptoes, trying to locate Sloan. My eyes work the space, and aside from the few random women who are giving me interested looks - since the scar doesn't only just attract negative attention - I take the opportunity to get my apologies over with now. I take a deep breath, and my feet move quickly.

"He's right over there," I say softly behind her. She pivots instantly and steps back. Her eyes widen, God knows what she's thinking, and she gives me a once over before glancing behind me. I observe intently until she steps closer and reaches out.

"I'm sor-"

I close my eyes and simultaneously mouth *no* to silence her. She should never have to apologise to me for anything. I've never expected it, and I never want to hear it. Just behind her, Sloan waves in a beckoning motion.

"He's waiting for you. Nine years and counting, I think he's waited long enough. Go."

Kara starts to turn, but something stops her. Then she does something I wouldn't expect in a million years - she wraps her arms around me.

"Thank you. For everything." Her words are barely a whisper, but they have just changed the status quo. Still, this is the first step in gaining her forgiveness and, hopefully, my future redemption.

She eventually releases me, but yet again, she completely surprises me when she slides her arm through my mine. I guide her through the crowded space towards Sloan. Stopping a couple of feet away from him, he smiles. For the first time, I realise what Tommy said on my balcony is right. This is about forgiveness between the three of us. Enlightened, with potential optimism swamping my soul, I lift her hand and kiss the back of it.

"Save a dance for me, Kara," I request politely before I turn away.

"I will," she confirms as I make my way through the crowd with a contented smile she will never see.

Passing the horde of bodies, a young woman walks straight into my path. I reach out and grab her before she goes arse over tit, and her small hands press against my chest to steady herself.

"I'm sorry," she says fretfully, gathering up the length of lace that orchestrated her tumble in one hand.

"Are you okay?" I lift my hand to hers to extract it from my person, and a long-forgotten sensation slithers through my veins. It's the feeling of euphoria that drugs could never replicate. It's the rare sensation of being touched by another and experiencing the prominent frisson of attraction at a level you don't feel with everyone.

The woman lifts her head to reveal her crimson cheeks, but her expression never falters when she looks at my face. "I'm fine. Thank you." She stares straight into my eyes, not giving my scar a second glance. Now that, for me, is incredibly thought-provoking because she's the first person to see beyond the obvious and unavoidable.

"Evelyn!" a man shouts some ten feet away. Her eyes close in annoyance, and she purses her lips.

"I'm sorry," she mumbles. Her hand drops from my chest, and she walks towards the man who has just called her. I stare after her, wondering who she is, while the man, who is likely her father – or her sugar daddy – grabs hold of her wrist and drags her away.

Standing in the ballroom doorway, still wondering what the hell has just happened, I lean against the ornate architrave and observe the living. While I can't see the girl who made me feel things I haven't in almost a decade, I do chuckle when I see Stuart and Sophie are already on the champers, while Tommy, Devlin, and Simon are congregated around a table, laughing. Charlie Emerson and her fella, Jake Evans – another of John and Dom's prodigies – are floating around, meeting and greeting. This is also her legacy too, after all.

My gaze drifts to Marie Dawson, Kara's mother, for want of a better status, as she smiles and chats away with a besuited gent. Watching her, having witnessed the way she is with Kara, makes me feel guilty. I haven't spoken to my own mother for a while. Months, even. Our relationship was rocky for many years, then I hopped on a train north, and it became non-existent. During my stretch in Manchester, I think I spoke to her maybe a handful of times, more to let her know I was still alive and kicking rather than to engage in general chatter.

After leaving Manchester for Leeds and living with Dom for the best part of eight years - until Sloan dragged me back into the fold due to Deacon's unwanted return - I spoke to her on the days that mattered; birthdays, Christmas, New Year's, Mother's Day. I need to call her. I need to make amends for being a shitty son and virtually abandoning her for years. As far as blood relatives go, she's all I've got since I'm an only child, and my father deserted us before I even reached double figures.

"Dare I ask?" a deep rumble comes from behind me.

I turn abruptly. My mind is pulled back into the here and now as John slides up next to me and passes me a lager.

"It's low alcohol," he says, but it doesn't need any clarification. This is the second of my three evils. Drugs being the first, tobacco being the third. Unlike the drugs, but just like the smoking, I'm not addicted. Still, I'm aware of how easily that could change if given a chance. In all honesty, if someone gave me a hit right now, I'd be back down that rabbit hole before midnight strikes.

"Rem?"

"Just thinking." I swallow a mouthful.

"Thinking is a dangerous activity for you, sunshine." He lifts the glass of red wine to his lips.

"Everything is dangerous for me, J. I should come with a warning: hazardous to health, may result in death." I don't mean for it to sound funny, but it evidently comes out that way when he laughs heartily.

"Well, in that case, you need to spell out the dangers to the pretty little miss over there." He inconspicuously nods to a dark-haired girl – the same one who piqued my interest, not to mention raised my blood pressure - who is now scrutinising me with blatant curiosity. "Although, let's be honest, you wouldn't dare approach her, so I guess there's no danger there, is there?" He nudges my arm, and I realise he's goading me, pushing me into the land of the living again, just like the triumvirate of clowns did earlier.

"It's the scar," I say, necking the bottle. "It attracts a lot of unwanted attention, like flies on shit." I wave the bottle nonchalantly but feel crap for saying it. After all, she didn't seem to give two hoots. The funny dies when John grabs my arm and spins me around. "Right, you listen up and listen good. You're not shit, Jeremy. You're a good guy who made mistakes. It could happen to anyone. I stand by what I said all those years ago. It would break my heart if anything happened to you. Dom's tried for years to get you out of that shell you've surrounded yourself in, and it hasn't worked. Now I'm telling you, you get your head out of your arse and live your life properly. To the full, every day. Death is something we all have in common, irrespective of colour, race, or wealth, and you've experienced it first-hand already."

"John-"

"She-" he cuts me off and jerks his chin back to the girl still observing inconspicuously, "isn't the only woman to have taken an interest in you this evening, and you've only been here half an hour! Regardless of that scar, you're still a handsome guy, and many a woman has noticed." He runs his hand over his face, exasperated. "Go strike up a conversation with one of them, let yourself forget for just one night. But whatever you do, don't do a Sloan of old and take anything home and fuck it because it momentarily replaces the one that got away-" He stops abruptly, remembering she didn't get away. She died. "Jeremy?"

"I hear you!" He pats my shoulder then heads to the table where the rest of our unrelated, familial group are sitting.

Intrigued, I glance back at the girl. J's right: she is a pretty little miss. All dark hair, dark eyes, with an aura of mystery surrounding her. My fingers reach up, and I intentionally touch my scar, drawing her attention to it again. In return, she gives me a small smile. It's shy, unassuming, and outrageously flirtatious in the most demure way imaginable. And it surprises and pleases me in equal measure.

I push off from the door frame and cut a path through the other guests. Perching myself against the bar on the other side of the room, far away from my interfering family, I order another low alcohol lager. I knock back a mouthful the moment the barman slides it over, and a throat clears behind me. I turn to find myself in the sights of a woman, maybe mid to late fifties, with far too much hair and makeup and nowhere near enough clothing, giving me the most audacious, wanton smile.

"Evening," she greets sultry and claims the stool next to me. It's almost laughable, but I manage to keep a straight face.

"Hi," I reply bluntly and bestow my drink with more interest than her.

"Are you on your own tonight?" Her hand moves slowly over the surface, and I assess her fingers.

"Yes, but I'm sure your husband will be looking for you." As I've said before, I'm many things, but a marriage wrecker is not one of them.

She laughs, feigning shock, and puts her hand on her chest, making an unnecessary display of her leathery cleavage. "I'm recently divorced."

"Really?" I counter unimpressed. She might see me as a bit of rough for the night, but I see through her. She's probably nothing more than an overindulged housewife with a rich husband, experiencing a bit of boredom or lack of sex, who whores herself out to numerous bits on the side. I reach out and grip her ring finger hard. "This rather fresh indentation proves otherwise. I suggest you find your husband and stop trifling with men you don't know," I say forcefully. With that, I pick up my bottle again. She huffs, but in the corner of my eye, I witness the wedding ring being slid back on her finger.

I sigh heavily. This is a new fucked up version of hell, even for me. Considering I've made amends with Kara – sort of – I wonder if anyone would miss me if I just slipped away now? Pondering my thoughts, the stool next to me shifts, and pretty little miss makes herself comfortable.

"Hi," she greets politely, then requests a small glass of white wine.

My downcast eyes absorb her, from her nude heels, up her legs, one crossed over the other, to her slim frame adorned in a black lace, knee-length dress. There's no excess skin on display aside from a slight hint of chest - not cleavage - from the moderately cut round neck and her toned arms.

"Would you like another?" The confidence radiates off her. Her eyes hold mine, and it feels like history is repeating itself as I stare into them. This time, blue eyes are replaced by hazel, and blonde is replaced by brunette.

"Sure." I nod. "I'm Jeremy James. It's nice to meet you properly." I hold out my hand.

"Evelyn Blake. Hello, again." She laughs shyly and slips her hand into mine. I inhale sharply, comprehending what I felt in the foyer was not imagination. For the second time in my life, and for the second time in the last forty-five minutes, I feel that spark, that attraction. In the last eight years, I've had a few women warm my sheets, but I didn't feel a morsel of what Em made me feel.

Until now.

Evelyn turns back to the barman, requests another of 'whatever he's having' and shuffles back around. She studies the room, and it's more than obvious she's just as uncomfortable as I am. I watch discreetly when her eyes land on the man who called her in the foyer earlier, and her body tenses.

"Would you like to move to one of the tables?" I point to one obscured by dim lighting and a floor to ceiling marble pillar. She agrees, palpably relieved. I slide out my leg and stand as she struggles and almost loses her balance. I move without even thinking and place my hand on the small of her back to stop her from almost taking another tumble. Instinctively, I glance up to find my nosy family all watching me with surprise. My first reaction would be to tell them to fuck off, but since I'm trying to make a good impression here, I just flip them the finger instead.

I guide her towards the empty table in the corner and pull out a chair for her.

"Thank you."

I grin to myself as she sits down, and I glance back at the nosy sods. When she is settled, I remove my jacket and hang it over the back of the chair. She gazes at me with an intensity I can't put into words until she reaches down and slips off her shoes. Her toes are tipped with black polish, a stark contrast to the nude shade gracing her fingernails. She raises the wine glass to her lips and takes a sip, and again my mind goes into overdrive.

"So, I haven't seen you at these events before." She sets down the glass, turns her body entirely to mine, crosses one knee over the other again and folds her hands in her lap. It's all very prim and proper.

"No, I've just moved back down here. A friend charmed me into coming tonight." I take another swig of my bottle

"Really?" She smiles, accentuating her natural, flawless beauty, and it's positively breathtaking. "Who's your friend?"

"Sloan Foster." I look in the direction of the rabble.

"Oh. My dad is a client, but he's also on the board of directors of Emerson and Foster."

A cold chill envelops my spine in instant realisation. That is the last thing I wanted to hear. Unfortunately, I'm aware of the board of directors. The only Blake on the board is Andrew. He has been for a number of years, and he's not one of Sloan's favourite people.

"Do you work for Mr Foster?" she asks keenly, encouraging further conversation.

"Sort of." Which is not a lie since Sloan has his fingers in a lot of pies. One being John's company, Walker Security, another being Dominic's shady agency, as he likes to call it. Others being this hotel, the Emerson family legacy, and the clubs he owns. The man is gifted at making money and equally gifted at seeing off the competition.

"That sounds ominous."

I laugh. "So it should. It's my way of saying I'm currently unemployed, but in the past, I have worked for him. What do you do?"

"I'm at uni."

Uni?

I stare at her, trying to work out her age. Minimum is eighteen, but she definitely isn't older than the mid-twenties. A part of me is hoping she says a number in those mid-twenties.

"Uni?" I reply, feigning surprise, gritting my teeth. I'm sure the look I'm wearing is unintentionally sinister, judging the subtle change in her expression. "What are you studying?" I smile reassuringly and put the bottle to my lips.

"Business management. I'm only in my first year."

"First year? How old are you?"

"Nineteen," she replies, her eyelids blinking anxiously. "I took a gap year."

Fuck! That means she really *is* just a girl. Granted, she's an adult, a woman in her own right. Old enough to drink, vote, buy a house. But, fuck, she's so young. Far too young to be blatantly flirting and attempting to get involved with someone like me. I'm pushing thirty with nothing to show for it.

"Wow," I breathe out and polish off the last of my lager. Words fail me. I don't know what to say. I expected it but thinking it and hearing it are two different things. Sadly, I realise I probably need to let her down gently. Or at least deviate her from whatever romantic idea she may have swimming around her head.

"Evelyn-"

"Evie," she corrects tersely, almost like she knows what I'm going to say.

I sigh. "Evie, I think you're a lovely young woman. I really do." I start diplomatically since I can't imagine she'll be impressed being called a girl. "But I'm ten years older than you."

Her eyes fix on the table and stay trained on the ivory linen. Her head moves, and she starts to look around, but even from here, there's a glassiness forming in her eyes.

"I'm sorry, please excuse me." She stands, scraping the chair back.

I reach out and grab her. "No, wait." I inhale sharply, my lungs expanding so fast it physically hurts. Her eyes meet mine, and she looks down at my hand on hers and her lips part.

"Look, it isn't your age I have a problem with-"

"Really? Your reaction says otherwise," she counters and straightens her shoulders, showing she's far wiser than her tender years.

Truthfully, it was one of the first things I noticed at the bar. It was how she brazenly took the advantage and approached me. It was how she conducted herself and made the first move. Her confidence, her self-awareness, it all just adds to the package, and I'm not sure if I can't not succumb to it. My personality has always been addictive, and I fear she may be next on a long list that has already been and gone before her.

My head is in turmoil. I like this girl, and I think she may even like me. If she didn't, she wouldn't have approached me. She sure as hell wouldn't have accepted my invitation to sit here.

"Okay, fine. I'll admit your age is a little concerning."

My hand is still latched tightly onto hers, but I know myself. If I wasn't remotely interested, I'd have already let her go, but for some reason, I can't. It's not because she ignites the blood in my veins; it's something else. It's the way she looked at me in the foyer. She saw past the scar and saw the real me. She saw me when no one else ever really has.

Except for one.

"Please don't leave," I request softly. With her fingers still linked in mine, she sits, this time next to me as opposed to opposite me. She confidently picks up her wine and takes a sip, waiting for me to say something.

I glance around the room, mentally evaluating the couples present and whether a ten-year age gap is so bad. Marie is four years old than John. Charlie and Jake also share a four-year age gap, as do Kara and Sloan. Oliver, Sloan's dad, was a decade older than Jules, and she wasn't much older than Evie when they met.

Still trying to justify it, my eyes cut to the dance floor, and I catch Sloan twirling Kara around, both laughing, undeniably in love without a care in the world. No one exists for them right now but each other. They are finally living, and while I may be rashly judging where this is going, I know I must endeavour to do the same. I have to because if I don't, I might as well be six feet under alongside Em.

"Let's start again." I turn back to Evie. I reach out my other hand and enfold hers between mine. "Yes, I have an issue with the age gap. It's not for any other reason than at twenty-nine, I will naturally want different things than you currently do."

"Really?" Her chin lifts defiantly, daring me to spell out those differences. I'm not going to play because a game of words will always be just that, and people change their wants and needs on a daily basis.

"Yes. Please don't be impertinent. I'm only trying to be honest. But considering you're the only girl – sorry, woman – to ever look at this," I drag a finger over my face, "and not recoil, maybe I'm dismissing this too hastily."

She slowly grins, and I'm about to throw caution to the wind and ask for her number when she starts to fidget, and her smile evaporates. The action is unexpected, and I don't understand the sudden change until someone approaches in my peripheral vision. Timidly, she looks up at him and pushes her glass in front of me. The man's brows lift in annoyance, and he turns his hardened glare on me, not missing the scar across my cheek.

"Evelyn? Are you finished monopolising this *gentleman's* time?"

My eyes narrow in disgust. How he accentuates *gentleman* indicates he thinks I'm anything but. I train my eyes on Evie, silently begging her to defy him and stay. But I know she won't. She's clearly a good girl - the way she pushed the wine glass towards me proves it.

"Evelyn?" he probes firmly again. "I want you to meet Baron Maxwell-Clarke's son."

Her face falls in dismay, but she nods in consent. "Okay, Dad. I'll be there in a minute."

He gives me another undignified stare. His eyes remain fixed on my temple until his lips form a sneer, and he eventually strides away.

Evie stands and moves around the table. "I'm sorry. He shouldn't have spoken to you like that," she says, showing she's intelligent enough to recognise his subtle insult.

"It's fine. With this decorating my good looks, I'm used to it," I joke, attempting to put her at ease. Instead, she blushes.

"You are good looking," she says quietly. "But you shouldn't have to get used to it. Honestly, he looks down at everyone, including me." And in a split second, I see something in her that I recognise in myself - someone vying for acceptance, trying to please. Still unable to fit in.

She turns away, and I follow her line of sight to her father, who is waiting with a lad roughly her age, staring in our direction. "I'm sorry. I better go."

I move closer to her and lightly hold her shoulders. "Don't be. I need to seek someone out for a dance anyway. I'm on a promise."

Her shoulders stiffen, and her head tilts back. "Oh, a…girlfriend?"

I shake my head. "No, Sloan's fiancée."

She visible relaxes and leans forward. "Well, we can't have you breaking that, can we?" She laughs, and I reciprocate.

"Definitely not." I lift her hand and kiss the back of it. Sliding my arm around the small of her back, I grab my jacket and slowly walk her towards her father. "It was nice meeting you, Evie."

"And you," she whispers. "Maybe I'll see you later?" Her dark, penetrating gaze ensnares mine, and I nod, enraptured, forgetting the age gap entirely.

"Sure. Come and find me. I'll take you for a spin around the dance floor, but don't expect anything worthy of Strictly. The best I can do is not let my two left feet trip over each other."

She places her hand on her chest and laughs at my very candid confession regarding my dancing abilities.

"Evelyn!" Andrew Blake hisses, and she rolls her eyes and pouts 'bye'.

I drop my arm from her waist and walk towards the table where Kara is sitting with Stuart. Halfway to the dance floor, I snag two bottles of ale off the waiter's tray and blatantly look back. Evie is still watching me, albeit she's also pretending to listen to the boy her father is evidently trying to foist upon her. She bequeaths me a beaming smile, and for the first time tonight, a calm slowly creeps through my soul, and I don't feel so much at war with myself.

Reaching the table, I tap Doc's shoulder and hand him a bottle as he watches Sloan and Sophie on the dance floor. I pitch my brow when Soph drags Sloan, and he attempts to drag her back.

"You can guess who wears the trousers in our relationship!" Doc laughs and knocks back the ale. I don't dare tell him that all women wear the trousers in a relationship. Although I fear he may find Sophie doesn't just wear the trousers, but the whole three-piece suit.

"My dance card is almost full," I tell Kara and make a gesture of glancing at a small group of women for emphasis. I don't wait for her response. Instead, I stride onto the dance floor before I have second thoughts. I can't dance, at all, but this is for her, and if I have to dance like a prat to gain reciprocity, I will. She slowly makes her way over to me, but my eyes turn to slits as a woman – one I vaguely recognise as Sloan's ex – slams her hand on Kara's shoulder. Kara's head drops down, and it's more than apparent she's the victim of an unprovoked attack.

I dart my head up and spot Sloan, still dragging Sophie along. I stride hastily towards them and snag his arm.

"Thank fuck! At least someone has decided to rescue me at last!" he exclaims with a smile while Sophie gasps dramatically.

"Hardly! The only person who needs rescuing right now is your future wife from that dastardly ex-bitch of yours!"

Sloan's head shoots up. His irises are almost black as he looks around the room. He strides over the dance floor with Soph and me in tow. He gently passes her off to Doc, and I wait with them as he approaches a table and speaks to one of the men getting tanked at it. The man starts to rise, but Sloan unequivocally bangs his fist down and stalks back to us.

I grind my jaw as the woman continues to belittle Kara by throwing herself at Sloan. That is until Sloan walks Kara to the front of the room, and after a few minutes of banter, he finally announces their engagement to rapturous applause.

"Dance, Rem?" Charlie wraps her arms around me from behind.

"No." I throw my head to the side and laugh.

"But you used to dance with me all the time upstairs when we were young!" She gives me the pet lip.

"Yes, I was young and stupid, and the answer is still no!"

"Fine, I'll make Jake dance with me instead." She digs her elbow into my side – something she also did when we were kids – and turns on her heel. Following her example, I head back to the bar.

"Same as before?" the bloke asks, and I nod.

"Cheers." The cold liquid chills my throat, and considering the shit that has already gone down this evening, it's heavenly. I guess if there's one thing tonight has made me grateful for, it's that I don't have any mental exes running around, ready to sabotage any future relationships. It's a poor thought, but it doesn't make it any less true. I rotate and lean back against the bar. Now consumed with disinterest, I'm ready to call it a night. I've done what they asked - I've shown up. Finishing off my drink, I slide the empty bottle back to the bartender.

"Another?"

"No, thanks," I say as I spot Evie with the same kid from earlier. She looks thoroughly engrossed by whatever he's saying, and while an imminent sadness ensues, it's the right thing. I'm too old for her, not to mention I wasn't joking when I told John I was hazardous to health. I don't need another woman falling for me, trying to fix me when you can't fix the unfixable.

I slacken my tie and start walking towards John, who is in deep conversation with Dev. As I continue my stroll, J sees me and kicks out a chair.

"Having a good night?" His brows lift.

"It's been interesting," is all I commit to because it hasn't been boring, that's for sure.

"Very interesting for you, it seems." He drops his chin to his chest and swings his head towards Evie.

"What do you know of her?"

"She's the apple of Daddy's eye. Why do you ask? *Interested?*"

I shuffle, uncomfortable as uncle and nephew both eyeball me. "Just wondering."

"For crying out loud, get over there and talk to her," Dev throws his opinion into the ring.

"She's nineteen!" I offer up in defence.

"And? She's legally an adult. Not a thing Daddy can do about it."

"Oh, I beg to differ."

John laughs. "So do I. It all looked very cosy earlier."

"You're all nosy bastards." I laugh.

"Sorry to interrupt." We all look up as James moves in front of the table, wearing a worried expression.

"What's wrong?" John asks him, immediately on high alert.

"An Ian Petersen just walked into the building."

John's up in an instant. "Where is he?" James points to the foyer, just in time to see Sloan running out.

"Dev," John starts as we all walk across the room. "Keep an eye on the door. If he's here, the Blacks may not be too far away." Dev nods and diverts off to the foyer.

"James, where have they gone?"

"The conference suite," he replies, and John gives me a look. My stride matches J's as we reach the room where raised voices are leaking from inside. "James, don't let anyone anywhere near here."

I throw the door open as Kara screams and vents. I look from her to John, then stand behind Ian. "Franklin's going to kill me," he says, practically incoherent.

My mind rewinds to the night I first met Kara. Even in my hazy state, I remember Ian was snivelling and begging then, too.

"I told him no," he says over and over.

"What do you mean?" John asks, and the man slouches in the seat when he looks at him.

I step forward and glare at Ian. "Last year, he finally said no to the bastard. You were too late in growing a backbone. Where is he? Where's Franklin?" I demand.

"I don't know."

Ian's pitiful response makes me see red, and I grab him by the throat and slam him into the wall behind us. "You're lying! Where the fuck is he?" I drill my eyes into him until Kara gets in front of me. "Kara, move!"

She shakes her head insubordinately. I find her resolve commendable, but she can't possibly forgive him. In turn, I have to wonder if she really forgives me.

When she still refuses to budge, it takes everything I have to let him go. I step back and glare at her. "Why are you protecting him? He fucking destroyed you!"

And I'm just a two-faced cunt because I also assisted in that destruction.

"I know!" she screams, throwing her hands in the air. Sloan quickly wraps himself around her and points his finger for Ian to sit back down.

I lean against the wall while Kara finally faces off with her father. It hurts to hear some of it, and every time she asks why, Ian turns the tables, trying to make her feel guilty. Every now and again, I catch John's infuriated expression. He's obviously feeling the same way I am. I listen, absorbing every word, hating every new piece of information I shouldn't be in receipt of until Ian turns around and addresses John.

"I'm the one who called you eight years ago, but it doesn't matter because I'm dead now." Ian begins to get up, but Sloan forces him back down and leaves the room.

The tension emanating is thick as we wait for him to return. Time, yet again, rewinds inside my head, and I remember being outside her bedroom door and Ian saying he needed to make a call. Back then, I wasn't in a fit state to question why Sloan and John had just turned up out of the blue. Or how they knew they would need Doc's assistance. I just accepted it for what it was. Now it all makes sense.

The door swings open, and before it has even shut, Sloan throws a thick envelope on the table. I spear J with a scowl. Money will not help this situation. If I thought it would, I'd have begged Sloan years ago for a few hundred grand to buy off Edward Shaw.

Sloan leans over the table and glares. "You take that, and you don't come back. Ever." Ian's hand slowly slides over the top, and he fists the envelope tight. Then, without so much as a second glance at his daughter, he shuffles out.

"James, back door," Sloan says, pointing to Ian. He wraps his arm around Kara as we make the long walk from the conference rooms, down the staff corridor nearest to reception, and deeper into the bowels of the building.

I loiter, long after Sloan and Kara have left with John, watching as Ian sits in the alleyway with his head down. I don't know what to say to him because if it wasn't for him and the cruel twist of fate that joins us all together in ways unimaginable, I wouldn't be here watching him.

Making my decision, I slam the door shut because any words of wisdom I have will fall on deaf ears. I slouch against the wall and take a breath. The reality hits hard. I appreciate I was lucky. I escaped the Blacks clutches, and I've managed to stay clean for almost nine years. If I hadn't, I'd be facing Ian Petersen's fate right now - a life of nothing and no real future.

I stride back down the staff corridor and turn off towards the ballroom. Most of the guests are still present, downing free booze, but I finally decide to call it a night.

The frigid air hits me as soon as I step outside. I look up and down the street, wondering if I'll be able to hail a taxi when my eyes latch onto Evie Blake. Holding her jacket tightly around herself, she slides into a limo and closes the door. I pull out my phone, swipe the screen and bring it to my ear.

"Did it all go well?" Dom queries.

"Depends on what your definition of 'well' is," I reply. "Ian Petersen showed up, and Sloan foolishly paid him off. Thankfully, there's no sign of the Blacks. Oh, and I met a girl."

"Really? I know I should be asking about Petersen, but I'm more interested in this female whom you see fit to mention."

I smirk. I knew that would grab his attention more than anything else. "I need you to find out everything you can on Andrew Blake, his wife, and his daughter, Evelyn."

"I see. Out of curiosity, what has brought about this uncharacteristic change? For the last eight years, all you've done is plunge deeper into yourself. Why her? Why is she suddenly so different?"

I inhale deeply. I can't hide from Dom. He's seen me at my lowest. He cleaned up my sick and shit when I was going through withdrawal. There's nothing about me that is a mystery to him.

"She saw beyond the scar," I confess quietly. "She saw *me.*"

Dom's steady breathing maintains, but I know he'll be shocked by my sudden change of heart regarding getting involved with anyone.

"I'll email everything across now," he eventually replies. "Unlike you, I'm aware of all the players before the game begins."

"I wouldn't expect anything less. Thanks," I reply and hang up.

I stare intently at the limo as it moves slowly down the street. Eventually, Evie Blake becomes red lights on the landscape, but hopefully, she will not be a distant memory.

My phone vibrates in my hand, and I swipe through the numerous emails Dom has sent until I see the one with her mobile number. I smile to myself, slip my phone into my breast pocket and walk off into the night.

Chapter 5

APPLYING THE HANDBRAKE, the engine idles under the bonnet. I gaze intently at the house six doors down on the other side of the street. My eyes flick to the dashboard clock, indicating it is almost seven. I stretch out, insofar as I can, wondering what time she leaves for work these days. When I was in my teens, she was out of the door any time between seven and eight and sometimes wouldn't be home until six.

It's been almost a month since I returned. During that time, I've debated whether my mother would welcome me or even be happy to see me. Granted, our relationship isn't as caustic as it once was, but I can't expect her to greet me with open arms considering the emotional hell I've put her through for years. Years when she begged me to stop smoking weed, when she begged me never to put a needle into my vein. Years when she begged me to sort out my life before it killed me.

I rub my hand over my chest. A dull ache overpowers my heart, recalling the almighty arguments and fights we used to have. Until the day she finally stopped fighting. She made it very clear that if I wasn't going to fight for my own existence, then she would stop expending her energy on a losing battle. The words I volleyed at her in response rush back to haunt me. It wasn't the first time I told her I hated her, but it was the first time I told her that I wished she was dead. It was the drugs talking, but I've regretted those words ever since. I squeeze my eyes tight, embattled by all the fucked-up shit I did. Back then, I never saw it through her eyes – a mother trying to save her son – and in all honestly, I probably never will.

Now older and wiser, having experienced the consequences of drugs and, subsequently, drug-related death first-hand, my respect for her is immeasurable.

Time ticks by slowly as I sit and wait. My mind delves in and out of the past, and snippets of days gone by rise to the surface. In-between being equally plagued by my past actions and shaking off my guilt, faces of her neighbours, the small-minded, judgemental people I remember well, gradually begin to emerge from their homes, ready for the start of the working day. Unlike them, I have nowhere of importance I need to be. I'm still jobless, although thankfully not homeless, but my funds are dwindling, which means I'm going to be kissing someone else's arse today, too.

I glance at the clock again, ready to give up hope, when the front door opens. As my mother hefts her large work bag over her shoulder and locks the door, I step out of the car. The slam of my door captures her attention, and she slowly rotates - clearly detecting something that is ingrained in all parents whenever their children are near - and she stares at me, practically in shock. Even from this distance, I recognise the pain and disbelief on her face. At fifty-five, April James looks her age, but she also looks tired and beaten. And I know I'm the ultimate cause of that.

I put one foot in front of the other, but she raises her hand, and I halt mid-step, not wanting to cause her any more undue distress. She clicks the lock for her car and climbs inside. I stand motionless as she reverses out of the driveway and slowly drives towards me. The car stops, and the window winds down.

"Not now, Jeremy. I'm late," she mutters, barely able to look at me. As a district nurse in a relatively small village with an ageing populace, she's probably busy with morning appointments and home visits. I guess I should have called ahead, but I also didn't want to give her an excuse not to see me. There are things that I need to say, things that I should have confessed years ago.

"I'll be back around three," she says before the window slides back up, and she carries on down the street.

I watch after her while that rampant feeling of desolation floods my chest again. For the best part of fifteen years, she tried talking to me. And the first and only day I've ever tried talking to her, she brushes me aside. Of course, I don't blame her because if I were in her shoes, I'd do the same.

There's no doubt in my mind my mum loves me. She's said it often enough during the handful of calls we've had, but I know she doesn't trust me. Unlike some addicts, I never ransacked the house of its possessions and pawned them. Likewise, I never fleeced her purse for cash, but I did constantly lie regarding the truth of my usage and how I obtained the money to pay for it. And that is the biggest obstacle between us because trust is everything to my mother. While I'm not the first James man to let her down, I should have been an unlikely candidate. Her trust in me should never have been something she needed to question.

I sigh heavily and climb back into my car. Refusing to reflect on it any further, I text Sloan. Turning the ignition, I belt up and put it into gear. Five minutes later, ringing blares throughout the car, and I tap the button on the dash panel.

"Hi," I greet and brake at a pelican crossing for the two elderly dears to cross.

"Hey, what's up?" Sloan asks casually.

"Have you got any free time today?"

"No, I've got a board meeting starting in ten minutes. It could go on all day and well into the night," he replies flatly, but since I know how much the other men like to squabble and argue over the most inconsequential of matters, I can understand his lack of enthusiasm. "Why?"

"I need a favour."

"Well, I intend to stop for lunch around one, so come over then."

"Sure, I'll see you later. Thanks." I press the button to end the call and drive back into the city, silently praying my afternoon doesn't go from bad to worse.

MY GLOVED FIST smashes the bag hard, and the satisfied sound of it hitting the worn leather reverberates through the clamour for the umpteenth time. After a few more hits, having worked some of my pent-up aggravation out of my system this morning, I step back with my hands on my hips. Lifting my head, I stare around at the other occupants and divest myself of the worn boxing gloves.

I swallow large mouthfuls of water and crane my neck from side to side to work out the tension. En-route to the cardio area, I drop the gloves on the floor, sit my bottle in the holder and toss the towel over the front of the treadmill.

Turning up the speed and gradient, before long, my feet are pounding against the machine, my body screaming at me to slow down, but I can't. This is my current addiction of choice and one I will happily indulge in until my body is on the verge of collapse.

In the last three weeks, I think I've spent more time in this building than I have in my own flat. Granted, there's nothing in my home to maintain my interest and subdue my compulsions, and that's critical for me to stay on the right path since I'm jobless at the moment. At least here, my lonely mind can't wander. Here, my brain is occupied, my body is active, and my hands aren't hitching for something I fought so hard to be clean of.

Thirty minutes later, the machine gradually slows down and switches to cool-down mode. My heart is pounding, and my muscles are aching, but as always, I feel alive. Wiping the towel over my sweat covered face, chest and arms, I gulp down the rest of my water and begin to stretch out my legs.

I look around mid-stretch, the premises has thinned out over the last few hours, and now there are only a handful of people milling around. Picking up my towel and gloves, I toss them over my shoulder and note the time as I amble into the changing room.

My hand fixes on the tiles as I drop my head forward. The hot water streams down my back, momentarily soothing my overworked body. Washing the perspiration from my skin and hair, I turn off the shower, wrap the towel around my waist and move back into the changing room.

Forty minutes later, I reverse my car into a space in Emerson and Foster's underground car park next to Sloan's Aston and step out, mindful of scratching his baby. Taking the lift to the reception suite, I find Gloria, Sloan's long-standing PA, fussing with a stack of papers and huffing and puffing in annoyance.

"Good afternoon, Gloria. I hope he's paying you well to pander to his minions." I wink.

"I do it for the love of the job, Jeremy," she says with a feigned smile. "But he pays handsomely, too! Sloan said you would be coming over. You've got good timing since he's just stopped for lunch." She approaches with the documents in her arms. "Would you mind?"

"Of course not." I take the stack while she retrieves a plate loaded with sandwiches from behind her desk. Walking down the corridor, the rooms divided only by glass; I catch sight of various board members dallying around a table laden with food, waiting for Sloan to call them back into the meeting. My eyes latch onto Andrew Blake, whose head shoots up the moment he sees me. His eyes narrow, and I hold his haughty stare, but it's nothing in comparison to what I've experienced already in my three decades of life.

"So, a little birdy tells me that you had a *dalliance* with Evie Blake at the last Emerson event."

I pause and slide my eyes to Gloria, who's wearing a mischievous grin. It really isn't like her to gossip. Christ knows over the years she's seen and heard things in this office that will stay within its walls, so I can only assume who told her. "That girl has a big mouth," I reply with a friendly, inquisitive smile.

"That she has, but she also has a heart of gold."

I chuckle and agree wholeheartedly. While she does have a heart of gold, Sophie Morgan is also garrulous beyond reason. She never knows when to shut her trap, and she just says what she thinks without thinking about it.

Gloria pauses before she enters the boardroom and smiles. "Evie is a lovely girl. I appreciate you probably think she's too young, but she's got a wise head on her shoulders. I think it would be a real shame if yo-"

"Gloria," I rudely interrupt because I don't need someone else harassing me about something that's never going to come to fruition.

For the last three weeks, I've had John and Dev breathing down my neck about her. Needless to say, I haven't called her. After looking at all the information Dom sent, I thought it better to leave it be. She's young, intelligent, and deserves far better than anything I could ever offer.

Gloria bestows me a coy look, then taps on the door and pushes it open. I place the papers on the end of the large table, then move to Sloan, who's standing in front of the window, gazing out over the city.

"Coffee, gentlemen?" Gloria asks, back in PA mode as she places the plate on the table.

"Please," Sloan replies. "And lace it with some sedatives. I'm going to fucking need it," he finishes on a sigh.

"Not for me. Thanks, Gloria."

The door closes, and I turn back to Sloan, who crosses his arms over his chest and lets out a long-drawn-out breath.

"Want to trade places?"

"No," I reply, amused. "It's tough at the top, but I have to tell you it isn't any better at the bottom either." Sloan rolls his eyes. "How's married life treating you?"

"It's fantastic," he says, absentmindedly turning his wedding band. I smile at the small, inconspicuous action, but his response and his overall body language are not the same. I decide not to query it because it has nothing to do with his wife or the life he has chosen that's pissing him off right now; it's the men in the other room. From the moment he took over as CEO at the age of twenty-one, they have belittled him, berated him, and generally just annoyed the hell out of him. Yet because of him, they are richer than they could ever have imagined, but still, they don't acknowledge that. It's hard being king.

The door opens, and Gloria re-enters, carrying Sloan's coffee. She sets it down on the table, along with two bottles of water and promptly leaves.

"What did you need to see me about?" He breaks the silence and drops down into one of the chairs. He gives me a knowingly look, already aware what I'm going to ask.

"I need a job." I pull out the seat next to him and sit. "I was wondering if the manager's position at the club is still vacant."

Sloan raises the mug to his lips and grimaces. "You know, I love that woman, but her coffee is like rocket fuel," he says and drops the mug down and pushes it away. I smile, but I won't be the little birdy who gives her that little piece of information. "The job's still yours, Rem. I didn't fill it from the last time you absconded because I knew you'd be back." He pulls over the plate and picks up one of the four triangles of sandwiches.

"Thanks, I appreciate it."

The silence devours, and I reach out for a sandwich as the door opens tentatively.

"Sorry, gents, but they're getting anxious out there," Gloria says.

"Tell them they can wait!" he snaps. "Sorry, Gloria."

The door closes again, and I reach across the table for the bottles. Putting one in front of Sloan, I open the other. My eyes catch sight of the documents, and I slide one over.

"Are they fighting again?" I ask curiously because, without a doubt, Sloan's business ethic is second to none. It's just a shame that the men he has been in command of for the last seven years still refuse to agree on anything.

"Yes, which means I won't be going home until midnight, at best." He runs his hand through his hair in exasperation.

I put the paper down and raise my brows. "At least you have someone to go home to."

Sloan gives me a sad look. "Do you want me to tell Kara about Emma?" I begin to open my mouth, but he stops me. "It's your story to tell, but I just thought it might be easier coming from me."

"Look, I appreciate the gesture, but I'd rather you didn't. I don't want her forgiving me out of misplaced sympathy for past poor choices. I'll tell her eventually, but not yet."

"Okay. Have you heard anything more about Edward Shaw?" He picks up another sandwich.

I shake my head. "No. Nothing since he was caught double-dealing. Dom and Kieran haven't heard anything either."

"Let me know if you do."

"Sloan, you can't buy off everyone to ensure an easy life." I wave my hand flippantly because Edward Shaw isn't Ian Petersen. No amount of money in the world will ever cloud the moment he came face to face with his daughter's lifeless, irregular veined body.

Sloan shrugs his shoulders and uncaps his water. "No, but I can buy off everyone to ensure the people I love stay living. I accept you won't ask me for money to deal with him. If I thought you would, I'd have handed it over years ago without question. But seriously, if you ever need it, it's yours."

I stand abruptly and brush off the breadcrumbs. This conversation is pointless. "Look, I need to go. I'll be in the club from tomorrow, if that's okay? I've got something that I need to do this afternoon."

Sloan levels his gaze on me. There's a hint of distrust in his expression, and I can't decipher whether he thinks I'm veering back down the wrong path. The Black path.

"Before you ask, I'm going to see my mum. I went this morning, but she was running late."

His expression turns from distrust to disquiet. "Is it the first time you've seen her since you came back?"

"Yeah." I shuffle anxiously. "Actually, it's the first time I've seen her in nine years," I admit the disgraceful truth, but he already knows. We grew up together; went to school together. While his mum lived in one of the biggest mansions in the area, I lived in the village neighbouring it. He knows all too well that my relationship with my mum went downhill from the moment my father turned his back on us. Then it disintegrated completely when I started using.

"It's time I told her everything. She doesn't know any of it."

"She'll understand," he says and pats my shoulder.

I shake my head. "No, she won't. But I can't clear my guilty conscience if I don't ever talk about it." A light tap on the door draws my attention. "I'll see you later."

I exit the boardroom, and Sloan follows me out. He bypasses the men all waiting around the door as they enter, and he follows me back down the corridor. I automatically slow my stride when I spot

Evie in one of the rooms with her father. I twist around and share an ominous look with Sloan.

"He treats her like shit," he begins. "She can't seem to do anything right in his eyes. She's nothing more than a commodity. He constantly talks about marrying her off to some Baron's offspring. Andrew Blake cares about money and status, and his daughter is just a means to an end to get closer to both."

I inhale, vexed. "Why are you telling me this? What do you expect me to do about it?"

"Nothing." Sloan edges back, his hands up in yield. "Absolutely nothing. Just know, the only time I've ever seen her smile properly is when she was with you." He pivots on his heels and strides back into the conference room.

I twist and catch sight of Evie's vacant, disinterested stance as her father literally talks down to her. I don't need to hear the conversation to know his words are disparaging. Her expression and his demeanour confirm it.

A throat clears, and Gloria approaches. She follows my line of sight into the room. "Sophie wasn't the little birdy who told me." She raises her brows at the conference room, and I huff. I have no idea what they all expect of me – what *she* would expect of me - if given a chance to explore what could become of this.

Gloria slips her arm through mine and pats my forearm as she guides me away from the room. Moments later, the disgruntled tone of Andrew Blake fills the silence.

"I want you at dinner tonight. No ifs, no buts. Understood?"

"Yes, Dad," Evie's despondent voice - which has consumed a few of my dreams these last few weeks - replies.

I rotate on the spot, bringing Gloria with me and face off against the man. For some unknown reason, he doesn't like me. Seeing as he also doesn't know me, I concede it's the scar that he finds worrying and repulsive. But given Sloan's admission regarding the man's love of money and connections and how he will use his own flesh and blood to secure both, I also have to throw the fact that I'm not wealthy or influential into the ring too.

Surprisingly uncaring what he thinks of me, and since I currently have Gloria by my side, I throw caution to the wind – something I should have done the night I first met Evie.

"Hello, Evelyn." Her name rolls off my tongue in a tone that implicates more than a general salutation. Gloria picks up on it instantly, and she drops her arm from mine, then reaches up and plants a polite kiss on my cheek.

"Take a chance," she whispers before clearing her throat. "Well, it's been lovely seeing you, Jeremy." The overemphasis in her tone ripples around the space, and I smile at her cunning. "Don't leave it too long next time."

"I won't," I reply with a charming smile and kiss the back of her hand. She then scurries towards Andrew and ushers him back into the boardroom.

"Go home, Evelyn. Now!" Andrew orders, infuriated, as Gloria starts walking faster until she all but shoves him inside the room and closes the door. She huffs and disappears off into another room.

Evie turns from the boardroom and smiles at me. "Hi. It's nice to see you again."

My eyes trail over her. Today she's dressed more casually, but she still has the same pull she did all those nights ago. I'd also be lying if I said she hadn't featured in one or two of my more *detailed* fantasies.

"And you." I smile and check the time. I still have a few hours to kill until I have to make the trip back to see my mother, but this is an opportunity I don't want to miss. "Have you had lunch yet?"

She smiles shyly, causing all kinds of turmoil to furrow in my gut, and she shakes her head. "No, but I can't." She inconspicuously glances back to the boardroom door.

I admire her conviction. She still is, and always will be, a good girl. Definitely far too good for me. "Can I walk you out instead then?"

"Sure," she replies. "I'd like that." I wave my hand towards the door, and she strolls off in front of me.

"So, how have you been?" I ask when the lift stops two floors down.

"Good. I've been bogged down with uni, but other than that, I'm okay. You?"

"The same as before." The doors close, and I step back until my spine is moulding against the brass bar running the interior.

"I'm sorry, by the way," she says unexpectedly, drawing my attention back to her.

"For what?" I subtly shake my head, misunderstanding.

She tucks a stray chunk of hair behind her ear and smiles. "For not coming to find you later at the event. For making you uncomfortable about my age."

I wave her words away. "You didn't. I just have some things that I'm going through at the moment. It's not you; it's me."

She chortles. "That's so clinched."

I shrug. "Maybe, but it is the truth. And yes, your age did-"

She gives me a coy flick of her brows.

"Okay, *does*, make me slightly uncomfortable."

She seems deep in thought. "Only slightly?" Her body sways towards mine, and I realise maybe she isn't that good after all.

I grin. "Yes, only slightly," I confirm, while silently conceding to myself I rather do enjoy her easy company. I also acknowledge that being in such close proximity to her today has proven her initial allure wasn't a fluke and evidently isn't going to go away any time soon.

The lift pings, and we step off at the ground floor. I focus on the way her hips and backside sway in the tight jeans she's wearing. A multitude of images run through my head, and I shift uncomfortable with my own thoughts, imagining all the ways I could peel them off her and get her under me.

She dallies in the busy lobby and turns around. "Why are you here today?"

I shove my hands in my pockets to adjust the uncomfortable tightening in my jeans. "I needed to see Sloan about something." I intentionally omit the part regarding my newly employed status.

"You're close?" she asks as a phone beeps.

"Hmm, we grew up together."

"Oh, right, I didn't realise just how close you are." She swipes her phone and studies the screen with narrow eyes. She reverts into herself instantly and averts her gaze elsewhere. A thick silence descends between us. I don't make my observation known because I don't want to frighten her off, but there's something there that is very odd and worrying.

"Why were you here today?" I ask, and she gives me a nervous look.

"Oh, my dad took my phone by mistake this morning. I had an early lecture, so I thought I'd pick it up on my way home. Speaking of which, I need to go." She rotates and looks hesitantly towards the revolving doors.

"Would you like a lift? My car's downstairs." *Please say yes,* I think, while my body starts to twitch prematurely at her unknown response.

She shakes her head and shoulders her bag higher. "No, it's okay. I can get the Tube."

I breathe out heavily. "Evie, what's wrong?"

"Nothing," she answers far too quickly, but it doesn't take a mind reader to know. It's her father. Most likely checking up on her to make sure she's fulfilling his orders.

"Look, regardless of my slight discomfort regarding your age, I like you, and I think you may even like me. I'd like to see you again."

She purses her lips in contemplation and nods. I rattle off my number, and she taps it into her phone and slips it into her bag.

"Thank you for walking me out." She stretches up on her toes, and her soft lips tentatively press against my cheekbone the exact moment her fingertip gently traces my scar. Awareness sears every nerve and cell under her unexpected, tender touch, and I fight against the desire and desperation to grab her and pull her closer. She settles back down and smiles at me. "I'll call you."

Once again, I watch her walk away. Those delectable hips and arse sway invitingly. I exhale heavily. I'm playing with fire in this dangerous game I've just become a willing participant in. Logically, I know I need to stay away from her. Yet after seeing her today, I know, unequivocally, that is no longer an option because Evelyn Blake may become my latest addiction.

Chapter 6

A YAWN ESCAPES my throat as I roll my shoulders and rub my eyes. After nearly two hours of waiting, it's almost four, and Mum still isn't back yet. Although she said three, it's hardly surprising considering this was pretty much routine when I was growing up.

I climb out of the car and stride across the street. Loitering on the pavement, I scrutinise the house judiciously. A part of me is thankful it's exactly the same as it was the last time I was here. From the red, painted front door to the blinds still in situ at the windows. Warm familiarity washes over me, and a handful of fond memories rise from the void. My eyes skim over the small, half paved front garden and are instantly drawn to the rose bushes we planted together when I was younger. They are almost spent for the season, but I will never forget the deep reds and burnished oranges whenever they were in full bloom.

I continue up the driveway and reach around the top of the back-garden gate to flick the latch. It swings open, and I step onto the decking and stare in disbelief at the overgrown lawn that has gone to seed and the weed riddled flower beds that Mum was always so proud of.

Anguish floods me instantly. I sit down in one of the patio chairs with my head in my hands. I've been reckless and uncaring, and it's clear she's been struggling for a while. Throughout the sporadic handful of calls we've shared over the last decade, she's never once asked me for anything. Likewise, I've never once enquired as to how she was coping since she never indicated that she was finding life hard. I should have known better than to think she would ever ask me for anything. The harsh reality is that I couldn't even look after myself most days. Many times, I believed I was impervious to anything.

"I thought I'd find you back here, kiddo."

I turn around as Mum closes the gate, carefully places her bags down near the doorstep and sits in the chair next to me. Although she is on my left – my good, unmarked side - I place my hand over my mutilated cheek, holding back the inevitable.

"Sorry, I didn't mean to intrude," I apologise, gazing up at the dark clouds rapidly approaching on the horizon.

"You didn't, and this will always be your home. You know, when you were younger, you would always come out here to think."

"I remember." I allow my focus to drift to the conifer trees lining the boundary. The branches rustle as the breeze picks up, and I close my eyes, reminiscing on the countless hours I would sit in this exact spot and listen. Years ago, I used it to block out the collective screaming and shouting courtesy of my parents. Then, after my father left, it was an aid to block out my mother's crying. Years later, when she was apparently all cried out, I would sit here and debate whether I should light up the spliff in my pocket. When the fight was lost, and the drugs started to overpower my mental will, I would sit here and get high and off my head.

But today, I'm not going to do any of those things. Today, I'm going to finally give my mother the truth she once begged me for. And pray to God she finds it in her heart to eventually forgive me because if she doesn't, it may prove to be the definitive tipping point that takes me back over the edge.

Fingertips stroke the back of my hand, and I lock eyes with Mum. She inhales a long, redundant breath.

"I remember too, and that's why I never sit out here anymore. Some days I can't even bear to look at it. So much so, one of the neighbour's boys comes round and tidies up once a month, and I keep the blinds shut." She tilts her head back to the patio doors that lead into the dining room. "Whenever anyone has asked why I've never had the courage to tell them the truth."

My knee shakes incessantly, and I temple my hands over my nose and mouth, waiting for her unspoken truth. "And what's that?" I query when she doesn't commit to it further.

"That I carry far too many guilty memories of allowing my son to sit here and destroy his life."

I rock back and slap my hands on my thighs. "You didn't allow me to do anything."

"But I didn't do anything to intervene, either."

"You did as much as you could." I shake my head incredulously. "And in hindsight, what would you have done differently? There wasn't anything you could do. I guess you could have told me to say no. Lock me in my room. Well, you tried those numerous times if my frazzled brain remembers correctly. In retrospect, knowing now what

I didn't then, there wasn't anything you could have said or done to deviate me from the path I choose."

"But you did it, you got clean, and you have been for years. Something drastic must have happened for you to change and succeed."

"Yeah, it did," I breathe out and gaze up at the sky. Light rain droplets begin to fall in rapid succession until a slow, building rumble of thunder roars through the heavens.

"Let's go inside." Mum holds out her hand. Consciously keeping her on my good side, I grasp it firmly and rub my thumb over hers.

"You used to do that when you were little."

"I remember," I reply again, although I know I'll probably be saying that a lot in the coming hours. Remembering isn't the issue; forgetting is.

I bend down and pick up her bags as she unlocks the door. It opens only a few inches, and she turns the key in the security chain.

"You really need to put a deadbolt on the gate. That latch is just calling for trouble."

"I've thought about it," she begins. "But there's nothing to steal. And if kids want to get in and torch the grass, they'd be doing me a favour." She walks down the hallway, removing her jacket as she goes.

I inhale deeply at her humourless retort, but I can't find the words to respond. There's a valid point to her logic, but it isn't the grass that concerns me. It's the house that is my mother's home. The thought of anything happening to her is just too much to bear.

"Drink?" she asks as she strolls back in and fills the kettle.

I look around the kitchen and step into the adjoining dining room. Again, they haven't changed in the eleven years I've been gone. Whether she has kept them the same due to familiarity or financial reasons, who knows. I also have no right to ask.

"Jeremy?"

"A weak coffee's fine, thanks."

Mum pauses in front of the cupboard, practically in shock. "A weak coffee? I would've thought you'd want something stronger."

I round the dining table, ensuring I keep my right cheek out of sight. For now. "I like to keep a clear head these days. I try to avoid anything that could cause me to relapse."

She lifts down two mugs. "Understandable. How long have you been clean now?"

"Nearly nine years," I reply quietly, peering into the living room. An exhale, barely a whisper tickles my nape. I turn abruptly to find her behind me, and I instantly cover my cheek.

"That's amazing. I'm proud of you." She smiles then turns back to the kitchen as the kettle starts to boil. "Go on in. I'll be a minute."

I move into the living room and look around. Just like everything else, it's still the same, with the exception of the sofa.

"Here you go." Mum places the mug on the table. The deluge outside is gaining momentum, and rain runs down the windows as the room gradually darkens.

I shrug out of my jacket, drape it over the sofa arm and sit down. Mum raises her coffee to her lips, studying my appearance thoughtfully.

"You look well. Far better than I expected, if I'm honest. So, how long have you been back?"

I grimace. I really don't want to confess the truth, but I can't lie. "A month."

Mum's mug hits the table hard, and I'm thankful I didn't tell her this is my second return in the space of a year.

"A month? A goddamn month!"

"Mum, I di-" Her finger points straight at my face, silencing me immediately.

"Every day for the last eleven years, each time the phone has rung, I've braced myself for the worst. And each time when it wasn't a call to confirm you were either in accident and emergency overdosed or in the morgue dead, I've been grateful that someone up there is watching over you. I knew you would never, ever come running back here with open arms, but a month, Jeremy!" She rubs her forehead, but her wild eyes never leave mine.

"Mam." My adopted northern twang makes a rare appearance. "I'm sorry, I didn't think." Except I did think. I thought long and hard, and I thought the door would be shut in my face. "I don't want to fight with you. I'm sorry I didn't come over the moment I came back, but I've had a lot of shit on my plate lately."

She chortles. "And what the hell do you think I've had on mine? I've been dealing with your shit for fifteen years. Notwithstanding the fear of answering the phone, how about the fear of answering the door in case it was someone you owed drug money to? You have no idea the hell you've put me through all these years, and you know why? Because you weren't here to witness it! If you want my sympathy, kiddo, you may be waiting a long time."

"Ma-"

"No! I need to say all these things. I need to say them because I've bottled them up for so long they now consume me. You have no idea what it was like to watch you drown in your demons. The drugs, the dealing – don't think I don't know about that! You had half the kids in the village hooked by the time you left. I could handle being avoided like the plague and talked about behind my back. I could handle it when I heard the *unfit mother* whispers following everywhere I went. I could even handle it when the surgery fired me because of you. Guilty by association was the justification if I remember rightly."

"Mam, I'm sor-"

"But the worst thing you ever did to me - aside from wishing me dead - was leaving me. Your actions left me childless, friendless, and almost homeless when I fell behind on the mortgage. I appreciate you've had it hard, but it hasn't exactly been easy for me, either."

I stare down at my feet. There's not a damn thing I can say. I never realised how the ramifications of my actions would affect her in all the ways she's just confessed. If I had known... I still wouldn't have done anything differently. I was selfish, self-absorbed, and arrogant. When I was still living here, I wasn't a full-blown addiction, but I was well on my way. At the height of my addiction, I only cared about where my next fix was coming from, and I would have sold anything I could to get it, including my mother.

A tear stings my eye, falling from my duct, down my cheek. "I failed you. I wish I was a better son. That you could look at me and feel proud. I didn't come over sooner because I couldn't stand the thought of you being still so disappointed in me." I stand and pick up my jacket. "I think it might be best if I go...and not come back." I stride with determination towards the back door, but a sharp tug on my elbow pulls me back.

"Jeremy, no! For once in your life, stop running away." Mum spins me around and cradles my cheeks. "You're my son. My only child and I will always love you. I didn't care what people in the village thought of me. I was already a failure to them because I couldn't keep my husband happy." Her thumbs swipe away the tears staining my cheeks. "What hurt me the most was that I knew, deep inside, you weren't the boy they were all claiming you were. They called you the devil. They said you were a monster."

"But I am. *I am* a monster," I tell her, unable to disguise the desperation in my tone. "The things I've done…"

"No, sweetheart." Her hands clench either side of my face. "You were misguided, easily led by that horrible, despicable Deacon kid, but you were never a mon-" Her confession stops mid-sentence as her finger rubs over the scar. I've done my best to disguise it from her, intentionally positioning myself so that she would have to stay on my left. I couldn't hide it forever, but I wish I hadn't finally decided to get my hair cut last week.

"Oh, my God!" She forcibly turns my face and stares frantically at my temple. "Oh, my God! My beautiful boy! Who did this to you?" She lets go of my face and wraps her arms around my back. I hold her tight. Her fingers dig into the divots of my spine, creating a tender sting in her concerned motherly hold.

"There are things I need to tell you, Mum. Important things. I don't know where to start." I carefully pull away from her and brush my fingers under her eyes to wipe her tears. She continues to stare, shocked at the dark pink jagged blemish marring my once perfect face.

"You can start by telling me who did this," she says, determined to get the truth out of me. Whether I tell her now or later doesn't really matter, but I can't plunge her deeper into my ongoing mess.

"I can't."

Her hands drop, and she steps back. "Can't or won't?"

"Both." I can't put her through the pain of hearing how I got this because I know my mother, and she will press for every detail. I also can't put her through the anguish of knowing there might still be more to come until I gain my redemption.

"Fine!" She turns back towards the kitchen, and I glance at my jacket, wondering if now is the perfect time to cut and run. A moment later, she returns with her work bag in hand. "Sit." With a resigned sigh, I park my arse on the sofa as she rummages in her bag. "Since I'm not stupid, and I'm a trained nurse, I would say this scar is less than a year old." She lifts her brow in rhetorical query.

"Correct," I confirm miserably.

"The original stitches clearly left a lot to be desired."

I grind my jaws. My idea of a fun time was not the night Kieran stitched me up - a few hours after Kara kicked me out of Dom's decrepit bolthole - while I poured whisky down my neck to blot out the agony.

"So did the anaesthetic," I murmur, sounding amused but mentally far from it.

Her hands suspend in mid-air, and she gives me an unimpressed grimace. "That's not funny, kiddo. Nothing about this is."

"Trust me, *I know*. I wasn't laughing," I say gravely.

She sits back, crosses one leg over the over and folds her arms over her chest. "Are you going to tell me these important things, or are you just going to avoid that too?"

I take a breath, lean forward, and rest my elbows on my knees. I fist one hand over the other in front of my mouth and stare at the family picture on the fire surround. "You said I'm not a monster, but I am. The things I did after I left here will prove you're wrong. Girls got hurt because of me, Mum."

"Jeremy…"

I shake my head. "A girl died because of me." I close my eyes as her upset gasp drifts over me. My stomach recoils, and the putrid taste of acid invades my throat.

"Darling, what are you saying? Did you…" She breathes out, open-mouthed. In the corner of my eye, I can see her disgust, clearly thinking the worst of me.

"Do you remember Charlotte Black?"

"Hmm," she murmurs. "Do you still see her?"

"Yeah, Sloan, too. He got married recently."

"Oh," she replies, dejected.

"Don't be offended that you didn't get an invite. It was an incredibly small affair. However, we're deviating," I say as the thunder and lightning grow stronger and the rain teems down the windows. It's fitting, considering the storm of words she will have to deal with next.

"Jeremy, where are you going with all this? What have Charlotte and Sloan got to do with it?"

I turn to face her properly. "Everything. When I was living in Manchester, Deacon attacked Charlotte. Brutally. Sexually." Mum's horrified gasp conceals the tension. I hold up my hand because the more questions she asks, the longer this will take. "Everyone warned me. You, Sloan, John. You all tried to tell me what he was, but I didn't see it until it was too late. I was almost at the height of my addiction, but that isn't what put me over the edge. Months earlier, I met a girl.

A beautiful girl. Emma. She was my life. She didn't know I was on drugs when we first met, and even when she did find out, she believed she could save me. Assist me in getting and staying clean. And I tried, for months, I really did. But it was all in vain because, in turn, she became an addict too. Except whereas I was still looking for a way out, she was getting in deeper. She initially claimed she needed to feel mellow to deal with uni until she dropped out and spent every moment with Deacon and me."

I stand, pull my wallet out of my pocket and sit back down. I remove the picture of Em and pass it to her. "One night, I was high, and I passed out while she was injecting. She died, curled up in a ball. She still had the needle in her hand. I held her in my arms, but she wouldn't wake up!" I squeeze my eyes to stall my tears, but it's impossible. They tumble over my cheeks easily and in rapid succession.

"Oh, Jeremy. It wasn't your fault!" Mum forces me back into her arms.

"If she had never met me, she would still be here. That's a fact." I curl further into her and lay my head on her shoulder.

"No, no, no. She chose to start using. The same way you did, and it could have taken you the same way it has taken her. If anything, the blame lies with that bastard Black. If it wasn't for him, you'd never have started using. He did that to you, and he did that to her, too. You didn't kill her; he did." Unfortunately, I can't agree with her on that point.

"After Em's death, I fell further, deeper. I didn't want to live. The only thing I cared about was numbing the pain. Months after her death, I did something despicable. Evil. I hurt a girl. It was unintentional, but I still did it." I inhale deeply at my mother's concerned expression. I stare into her eyes, never removing my gaze as I tell her of the repercussions of Em's death. The words flow from my mouth, a part of me desperate to finally air them and rid myself of at least one burden I've carried for the last decade. "And I closed the door, and I left her with him," I say eventually, before finishing my sad, sordid story. My body shakes feverishly, the shivers far worse than those I went through in that godforsaken room.

"The morning after, I made a vow to finally get clean. But for years, those three events have haunted me. Charlie has never held me accountable, and Emma can't exactly forgive me. But eighteen months ago, I got my chance at forgiveness with Kara, the girl I tied down. Through a random twist of fate, she met Sloan again through a set of bizarre circumstances that Deacon inadvertently orchestrated." I absentmindedly stroke my scar. "She's now his wife, but none of it has boded well for me. I'm still wallowing in misery, wondering 'what if'."

Mum presses back, and her fingers stroke the scar. "Deacon did this to you, didn't he?"

I close my eyes, but all I can see is the glint of the blade coming closer. It's quickly followed by the sharp, unbearable piercing of my flesh and the excruciating drag of the knife's edge cutting through my skin.

"Jeremy, answer me!" She shakes me hard.

"Yes." My confession is a whisper. "I'm sorry I failed you."

"Failed me?" she replies, confused.

"If it wasn't for my weakness, you wouldn't have lost your job, your friends, almost this house," I confess, offering her an apology a decade or so too late. I blamed her for everything growing up, even when it wasn't her fault.

She sighs. "And if it wasn't for *my* failings, my inability to see what was in front of me until it was too late, you'd have never ended up the way you did in the first place," she counters.

I furrow my brow. "I think we'll have to agree to disagree there."

"True, but I think it's safe to say we both have many failings and weaknesses to atone for." She exhales, and the sound of relief fills the room. "Have you got any plans for dinner?"

I shake my head. "Nope, just me and the microwave."

"How about you stay. We can have our first family meal together in-" Her eyes and nose scrunch up. "What has it been? Ten, fifteen years?" she asks, honestly unable to recall the last time we sat down to eat together.

"Longer," I tell her.

She smiles and motions for me to get up. "We've had our ups and downs, kiddo, but always remember this is your home. Yes, we've had our fights and blazing arguments, but I'd never turn you away. Now, we can either go and buy a Marks' two can dine offer, or we can march into the local and show all those two-faced arseholes who wrote us off just how handsome, amazing and grounded my son is now."

I baulk. The thought is enough to bring me out in hives. "How about a quick pint and then a trip to M and S?" I suggest, reaching the perfect compromise.

"Good idea," she agrees and walks out of the living room. I follow sedately, listening to the rustle of her retrieving her bag.

Outside, she holds her jacket over her head, and we laugh as we dash for my car. Inside, I start the engine and make eye contact with one of the neighbours I never bothered to learn the name of, and Mum grabs my hand.

"Ignore them, all of them! I love you, kiddo. I'm glad you've finally come home."

"Me too, Mum. Me too."

As I pull away, a glaringly obvious thought occurs to me. For years I've avoided this place, but I never thought declaring and unburdening myself of my past transgressions would bring us closer, but strangely and thankfully, it has.

Chapter 7

THE THUMPING BASE of the nineties dancehall classic reverberates around the small office as I finish reconciling the latest invoices to land on my desk.

I lean back in the chair and swing my feet upon the top and take a swig of my non-alcoholic lager. Extending my arm out, I tilt the security monitor recording the interior of the premises with the bottleneck. As I scan the screen, thankful nobody is shaking the place up tonight, the phone rings. I glance at the LCD panel with indifference before picking it up.

"Problems?" I ask vigilantly. I confess the last few weeks have been a baptism of fire for me. They have tested my limits. From the usual drunks, fighting over whose round it is, or who is hitting on whose girl, to the pushers who think they can make an easy sale. Fortunately for me, but unfortunately for them, I've not only seen it all, but I've done it all too, and now I can spot them a mile away.

"Depends on whether or not you want them to be your problem," Paul, one of tonight's security, replies dryly. I lean closer to the monitor and switch it to the external feed. Zooming in on the front of house, I sigh with relief because one of these days, I'm going to get an expected guest I really don't want.

"Unfortunately, they will always be my problem. I'm coming down and reiterate the damn dress code!" I say, blinded by Park's bright white trainers. I hang up, but not before I hear Paul verbally face off with Simon regarding his choice of footwear.

I push up from the seat and grab a handful of VIP passes from the drawer. Catching my reflection in the one-way glass overlooking the club, the light illuminates my scar to perfection, adding a slightly rough touch to my all-black attire of turtleneck sweater and fitted dress trousers. This is my work getup, not because Sloan demands it, but because it allows me to observe unobtrusively, to blend seamlessly into the background of handbags and glad rags. Unlike the patrons downstairs paying through the nose to even get a foot through the door, I'm not here to be seen.

Striding through the club, my eyes roam over the VIP area with its plush, comfortable seating and intimate feel to the vast dance floor. I always wondered why Sloan bought this place years ago, but tonight, like most nights, proves why; it makes money effortlessly. The financials confirm the entry fee alone covers more than the majority of the running costs, maintenance and wages.

"Hey, boss, you might need a coat. It's chilly out there," Vicky shouts from her desk at the cloakroom.

"It's fine. I'm just collecting the inbreds!" I shout sarcastically.

"Oh, is Foxy here?"

"No!"

"That means yes!" she sing-songs. "Tell him I'll find him later." She overemphasises her wink, then proceeds to swap coats for tickets and entrance for cash.

I roll my eyes and chuckle, thoroughly entertained, while weaving between the bodies entering the premises. Stepping outside, I tap Paul on the shoulder. He turns and jerks his head towards Tommy, Simon, and Kieran.

"What the hell are you doing here?" I ask K.

He hefts me up in a full-body lift, and I grunt when his bulky arms compress my middle. I swear, if he doesn't drop in me in five seconds, I'm going to start experiencing asphyxiation. My feet kick and flail, trying to find solid ground, and I pull back when he kisses my cheek.

"Cheap and cheerful, here-" he refers to Simon and Tom, making me laugh "-said they were coming tonight, so I thought I'd tag along and see you. That, and Dom ordered me to come down here while John's out of town." He grins, constricting me further in his arms, and finally drops me back on the pavement. "Are you going for the full Johnny Cash look?" he asks as I straighten my sweater. "You clean up well, you handsome git! Now, are you going to let us in? We keep saying yes, but your man here keeps saying no." His face drops and saddens, and he juts out an exaggerated pet lip. He looks like an oversized toddler sulking.

"Now that's just pathetic." I motion for Paul to let them in. The man stands aside while Craig, the second bouncer, inches closer.

"Fortunately for us, we don't have any wheel trims here, but no nicking the glasses now!" he goads Kieran playfully, erroneously stereotyping all Liverpudlian's the world over.

"Oh, very fucking funny, arsehole. Can't tell you how many times I've heard that before!"

"Sorry? What was that?" Craig fires back, his hand to his ear. "I'm surprised anyone can understand a word of what you're saying half the time. Just out of interest, what is a pan of scouse?"

"Piss off, you cockney git, or you'll get a pan of my mam's finest offering over your head!" Kieran counters.

"Typical gobshite arsehole. I bet you're a Kopite, aren't you?" Craig continues to prod the bear, exposing his teeth in a playfully smile.

"Oh, shit!" Tommy murmurs while Si practically chokes on his tongue, disbelieving the burly bloke has dared to go there.

Kieran feigns horrified and pretends to spit at Craig's feet. "Fuck you, that's a dirty word! Blue all the way! Toffee until I die!" He pumps his fist in front of his heart. "I bet a Londoner twat like you is a Man United fan! Dirty fucking Liverpool? Blasphemous!" He continues to chunter, but the rest of his disgusted statement lingers on the air as he ambles his ridiculously large frame into the building.

I laugh as *'insulting cockney bastard'*, *'Man U fan who's never been to Manchester'*, and *'I bench press you for fun'* drift towards us. I turn to Craig. "You know, he could crack your skull with one hand."

He shrugs and laughs. "Yeah, probably. Tell him I'll buy him a drink later! I quite like my face how it is." I slap his back in jest and turn back to the stairs inside.

"Here." I hold out the VIP passes to Si, Tommy, and Kieran while the sound of possible affray seeps into my ears. I glance back to the entrance just in time to see Paul and Craig restraining a rowdy group. "Go in. I'll be there in a minute."

I saunter back to the door and stand beside security. The lads in the group kicking up a fuss bestow me questioning stares, but it isn't me they are suspicious of; it's the scar.

"Your choice, boss," Craig says in a bored tone, having witnessed and dealt with this scene a thousand times before.

I give each member of the group a stern, assessing glare. "ID?"

"Oh, come on, man!" one of them says exasperated, throwing his hands in the air. "I'm twenty, for crying out loud!"

I point to the Challenge 25 sign behind me and shrug. "ID?" I level my gaze on him. After a few moments, he huffs, pulls out his wallet and shows me his driver's licence. "Now that wasn't so hard, was it?" I cajole, and the rest of them grudgingly produce their ID.

"Can we come in now?" the cocky little sod asks.

I roll my eyes and consciously rub my scar. "Listen up, fellas. As the manager of this establishment, I'm going to do you the courtesy of letting you in rather than embarrass you in front of your ladies." I tip my head towards the girls in minuscule dresses, freezing their arses off behind them. "Don't give me a reason to kick you all out. Keep it clean and respectful. I catch one whiff of a fight or anything that displeases me, and you're out. All of you, and I won't give a shit who started it. Okay?" They all nod, and I wave my hand towards the door. A multitude of 'thanks' come from behind them as the girls in their group totter along in their heels.

"I'll keep an eye on them," I tell Craig and Paul before I stride back inside. Taking the stairs two at a time, I gaze around the club, attempting to locate my unexpected guests in the sea of dancers and drinkers. The place is wall to wall tonight – the same way it is every night – but there's no mistaking the robust form of the man who has slammed me into a gym mat countless times at seven in the morning when he's forced me to spar with him.

Striding across the room, Tommy waves me over from his stance at the bar. "What are you having?" I ask him.

"A Peroni? Si, K, what do you want?" Tommy asks them. The other two give me their choices, and I walk around to the back of the bar and flip the top and enter. Grabbing the three bottles, I uncap them and pass them over.

"Give us a minute," I tell them and call over the next to be served in the growing queue. As my good luck would have it, my newest friend from outside gives me a grin.

"I thought you were the manager?" he asks cockily. *Again.*

"I am. Come here." I crook my finger, and he leans forward. "I was once a twenty-year-old arsehole, too. Thought I knew it all. The reality? I knew nothing." I intentionally drag my finger down my face, drawing his attention. "Now, what can I get you?" He straightens his shoulders and reels off the long list of drinks for his friends.

Turning back to the bar, I grab the bottles and glasses. "Cassie, can you do me a few cocktails?" I ask one of my bartenders.

"Sure, boss," she replies with a smile.

"So," the lad starts hesitantly. "That scar's a Glasgow smile, right?"

"Hmm. Half of one, anyway." I proceed to line up the bottles in front of him, and the rest of his group close in.

"Were you conscious?" another asks in fascination.

I laugh dryly because, at the time, I really wish I wasn't. "Unfortunately."

"Fuck, man. I bet that hurt!" The lad bristles and touches his own cheek.

I roll my eyes and chortle singularly in the din of voices and music. "You have no idea," I breathe to myself.

"How did you get it?" the first kid queries as he picks up a bottle.

I place the last drink on the bar and lean into it. "Russian roulette. I picked red. Black won." I force a grin at my double edge connotation. Obviously, they have no idea what I'm talking about, but Black did win. The same way the Blacks always win.

"Hey, I'm sorry for being a dickhead outside. How much?" He unzips his wallet.

I snap out of my reminiscing. "On the house. Call it a goodwill gesture."

He looks startled. "Okay, thanks." He holds out his hand, and I shake it with respect.

"Although," Kieran pitches in from the side of the bar. "If his goodwill gesture is thrown back in his face tonight, I'll be throwing you against the nearest wall. You won't like the way I deliver civil justice. Got it?"

The lad holds out his hand to Kieran, who shakes it. "Got it." He turns back to me and lifts his drink in gesticulation.

I edge around the back of the bar, syphon myself a pint of Coke and duck back under. Claiming a stool, Kieran snags the one next to me and glances around.

"I see cheap and cheerful are already checking out the talent," he comments after a beat and swings his head to the dance floor where the aforementioned twosome are clearly gauging the women present. "Dom said this place pays for itself, but I didn't expect it to be this busy. Shit music, though."

"It's like this every night," I say, knocking back a mouthful of pop. "And it's hits of the nineties and noughties. It's nostalgic."

"No, it's shit. It was shit back then, and it's still shit now. Not to mention half the kids here are too young to remember, or they weren't even born."

I grimace at the depressing thought, not that I remember much of the nineties, but still, I won't argue with the big guy. "Do you want another?" I motion to his half-empty bottle.

"Sure, but first, is there somewhere private we can talk?"

My partially mellow mood ebbs away, and I make the mistake of staring into his eyes. Holding his gaze, we're both aware there's only one discussion that requires complete privacy. I inhale deeply and nod with reluctance as I slide off the stool.

"Yeah, the office." I walk a determined path around the perimeter of the dance floor and up the stairs with K hot on my heels. The door slams shut, and I wait in front of the window, watching the uninhibited and carefree living their lives.

"How's the girl? Dom told me that she lost her best friend recently." K edges close in my outlying vision.

"Hmm, Samantha. She never regained consciousness from the battering Deacon gave her. Kara blames herself." I sigh redundantly. I'm shouldering some of that blame, too. I should have tried harder. I should have made the stupid girl see sense. Still, I didn't lie to Kara when I told her that I tried to help Sam. I did, but she just wouldn't listen. She thought she could handle Deacon. She thought that his obsession with Kara was all mouth and bluster. It's distasteful, but fortunately for her, at least she won't be here for the final show, whenever that may be. However, it may pan out.

"I heard she lost her dad last week, too."

"Yeah," I murmur. "Killed himself using money that Sloan slipped to him at the last event."

He shakes his head in astonishment. "Dom didn't tell me that part. She's had it pretty rough lately."

"Ever turning circles."

"Are the bizzies going to investigate Sloan?"

I shrug. "I don't know, but you can't arrest someone for handing over money. It's not like Sloan gave him the drugs." I grimace and shift, extremely uncomfortable with the reality of this conversation. "To be honest, I've tried to stay out of it. I've got enough of my own problems. I don't need theirs on top."

K snorts. "Their problems *are* your problems, son. They've *always* been your problems. Ever turning circles."

"Touché," I concur and gulp a large mouthful of Coke.

"How long are they staying up in Manchester?"

"No idea, but Petersen's funeral was yesterday. I guess it depends on how long Kara wants to stay. Regardless of the less than capable skills of her mother, she's still her mother, and she needs her. They need each other."

"Speaking of mothers," K queries. "Have you spoken to yours recently?"

I sigh in agitation and scrub my hand over my face. "Yes, actually. Look, we both know you didn't come down here on command to talk about Kara's mother or mine, so say whatever you've got to say. You don't need to butter me up and give me false hope."

He turns and leans against the glass. "I've heard a few rumblings out of Manchester and Liverpool."

"The Blacks?" I ask, hopeful. But if it was the Blacks, he wouldn't be here, irrespective that Dom and John probably used that as an excuse to get him down here. I know Kieran, and I know it would take more than an off-the-cuff remark about Franklin or Deacon to get him to travel two hundred miles to a city he abhors.

K drops his head and looks over his shoulder at the club below. His rare silence speaks volumes.

"Shaw," I breathe out when he doesn't respond. I follow his line of sight to the VIP area.

"Word on the street is that he's sold his house and is in the process of offloading his assets." He gives me a cold, sympathetic look. "There's a price on your head, son."

A chill shiver drifts down my spine, cooling every nerve in its wake. "Nothing new there - there's always been a price on my head." I sound uncaring, but I do care. Between the death of Samantha Jones, having finally succumbed to the injuries Deacon inflicted for her assistance in helping me to liberate Kara from a fate surely worse than death, and Ian Petersen's probable, intentional overdose, this last month has put a lot of things into perspective for me. I never let it in, but one day, I hoped to grow old. To live a long, substantial life. Now I fear I may indeed die young.

"Now isn't the time for flippancy, Jer. All I know is it's big, and Dom is countering whatever Shaw is offering. Just be vigilant and cautious. Don't leave yourself exposed. Trust no one."

I nod slowly, barely moving, but my stomach somersaults. It's not surprising. I'm a debt that still needs to be repaid, but hearing it is more than sobering. I jolt in shock when K taps my shoulder.

"Let's stop the morbid talk and have a drink. I may even impress the ladies with some of my more electrifying moves!" He snickers, then his face drops with a mixture of intrigue and concern, and he presses his nose to the glass. "Jesus, has he been spiked?"

I narrow my eyes and stride to the monitor. Flipping through the security feeds, I zoom in on the dance floor and spot Tommy's striking red hair instantly. Next to him, Simon shows off some of *his* electrifying dance moves.

"Is he having a seizure?" Kieran asks, dumbfounded, still watching the show.

I chuckle. "Nope, that's just his dancing style. Now you see why we don't let him out often. Give him a few drinks, and he's in Saturday Night Fever."

"Or Grease!"

I laugh with him, turn off the monitor and walk to the door. "Let's go get that drink. Then I want to see *your* dancing style."

"I'll show you mine if you show me yours, baby!" K bats his eyelashes at me.

"I'm not that easy!" I counter. I lock the door and follow him down the stairs.

"Shit, I guess that means I'm not sleeping at yours tonight then?"

"Playing the poverty card isn't becoming. We both know *you* can more than afford a decent hotel room. Call Sloan for a room at the Emerson. Live it up in five-star luxury for the night. I'm sure he'll give you one of the penthouse suites."

He stops, and I walk into the back of fifteen stone of solid muscle. As I rub my chest from the impact, he pulls out his phone and starts to text away. I move around him and make my way towards Tommy and Simon, who have now relocated to the VIP.

Gems of sarcasm linger unspoken on my tongue when I see Si's exhausted slump, but I play it safe and leave them unaired. Especially when I note either cheap or cheerful has already got a round in. Picking up the bottle of non-alcoholic lager, I take a swig as K throws himself down and grins.

"Who's Laura?"

I instantly glance at Tommy because I know he likes her even though he'll never admit it. "She's one half of the hotel's reception management. Why?"

"John just arranged a room for me. When I called her, I asked if she would provide me with a complimentary robe, slippers, and toiletries. She said she would be on duty and personally organise them. Is she pretty?"

My eyes flick to Tommy, who scowls. "Yeah, she's very pretty. Naturally beautiful, really." I'm rubbing the man's nose in it, but I'm not lying. "She's so high-" I raise my hand up. "Slender but curved where it matters. She's exceptionally sweet and very single, I believe."

"Jer, don't," Tommy's stern unimpressed tone invades my ears.

"Don't what?" I eyeball him hard. He doesn't counter, just shakes his head. "Tom, if you like the girl, tell her. Get over to the hotel and ask her out. If not, Vicky said she'll find you tonight. A little advice? You all go on about how *I* need to start living, but maybe you all need to, too."

Tommy drains the last of his beer and slams down the bottle.

"Drink?" I lighten the mood.

"Sure, get me a Jägerbomb," Si requests, whereas Kieran and Tommy ask for the same again.

"Come on, then." I hold my hand out to Si. "Pony up, boys. No free booze or women tonight."

"Christ, you sound like Sloan!" Si says, insulted, and waves a fiver at me like a strip club punter.

"Forget it." I stand and make my way to the bar. Slipping under the top, I pull out the two bottles, pour a shot of Jägermeister into a Red Bull, and syphon another Coke.

"Do you want some help?" Cassie asks. I decline with a smile. I lodge a bottle between each arm and my chest and a glass in either hand. "I'll let you out." She holds up the top for me to exit.

Moving through the mass of people, the combined scents of liquor, tobacco, perfume, and body odour assaults my nostrils. Heading towards my destination, my eyes firmly on the drinks, I turn to avoid a possible collision with a very boisterous, drunk woman blocking my path and come face to face with the woman who promised to call but hasn't.

"Hi!" Evie greets in surprise. Her tone and demeanour are a complete contrast from our previous meeting.

I smile, immediately liking this relaxed, unguarded side of her. It's a side I haven't been fortunate enough to witness until now. Whether it's a little booze in her system giving her some Dutch courage or she really is pleased to see me, I have no idea. Either way, I don't give a shit. I've been waiting for her call for the last month to no avail. But now that I finally have her here, I'm not going to let her escape for a third time.

"Hi." I give her a coy grin. "Is your phone broken?" I query light-heartedly, starting the seduction. It's been a long time since I've had to work for it, but for her, I'd walk over hot coals. Why? I have no idea. All I know is that I can't get her out of my head.

Evie's face twists in misperception, considering my question, and she furrows her brow. She opens her mouth but doesn't get time to speak.

"You haven't called," I clarify, taking in her little black dress.

Her confused expression morphs into a mortified smile, and she bites her lip and glances down. "I didn't know what to say," she mumbles.

The corner of my mouth curves, and I move my arm slowly and tip her chin up with the rim of the glass. Her eyes met mine, and I breathe in and smile. "You say 'hi'."

She reciprocates my playful expression and softly touches my forearm. "Would you like a hand?" Her eyes flit between the four drinks, and I nod. She carefully removes the two bottles lodged between my arms and chest and walks in synch with me to the VIP.

"Evie, this is Tommy and Simon." I introduce them as I put the drinks down and push them in front of the guys. "You may recognise them from some of the events you've attended."

Evie nods. "Yes, I remember you both from the last one. Hello," she greets, and they each grin.

"And this is Kieran."

"Hi, sweetheart. How are you doing?" he asks her with no airs or graces. To him, everyone is a friend until you cross him, and then you become his enemy, making his surname of Hyde fitting.

"I'm good." She fidgets as the three men eye her with intrigue.

"Who are you here with tonight?" I ask and take a sip of Coke.

She looks over her shoulder to three girls standing next to Derek, the bouncer on the VIP section, who is denying them entry. "My friends. Holly," she points to one of them, "Sarah and Caroline," she indicates to the other two.

I put down my drink, grab the rest of the passes from the table and place my hand on the small of her back. Leading her towards her friends, she gives me tiny, discreet glances, and even under the strobe lighting, I recognise the fresh, rosy tint colouring her cheeks.

"Evening, ladies," I greet her friends. "Put these on. Compliments of the manager."

"You?" one of them asks, and I wink. "Thanks! Do we get free drinks, too?"

I laugh. "No, but you do get a comfy chair for when those start to hurt!" I pull a face at the six-inch spiked heels she's wearing. Why women do this to themselves is beyond comprehension. "Derek, ensure one of the tables is reserved for them."

"You got it." He moves aside. The threesome titter between themselves excitedly as Evie turns to me.

"You didn't have to do that but thank you. They'll be bending my ear about this for weeks to come."

I chortle. "Not a problem. Come and find me later. You can say *hi* over a dance."

She flushes and nods before joining her trio of friends, who are now seated at a table not too far from where my trio are.

"Derek?" The man turns and edges towards me. "Can you ask Cassie to bring a bottle of Moët over to them?" He immediately adjusts his earpiece and microphone and shows me his back.

I jerk my head towards the bar as Cassie presses the earbud and retrieves a bottle from the fridge. Striding back to the table, I drop my phone down and do my best to circumvent the fascinated stares of three sets of eyeballs. I turn to the table Evie and her girls are occupying just in time to see Cassie approach with the bottle of fizz. Evie's eyes broaden as Cassie's mouth moves, and she turns to me, and I quickly look away, hopeful I haven't been caught. Girly squeals drift faintly over the atmosphere as the cork pops. I smile rhetorically, feeling all kinds of weirdness gripping my sanity. I reach for my pop and look up as I gulp down a mouthful.

"Go on, say it," I encourage the noisy sods.

"I think Jeremy might have a girlfriend," Kieran mocks. He runs his hand through his blond hair and bats his lashes again.

I place my drink down, failing to hide my grin and sit back. "That's a deranged look you're wearing, K." I laugh with one eye on the girls, who are toasting and clinking their champagne flutes together.

"Seriously, I think she's quite sweet," he comments. "I know she's young, but she clearly likes you. I say go for it." I hold his knowing gaze. Undoubtedly, Dom has spoken to him about the information I asked for concerning her.

"Are those her friends?" Si eyes them inquisitively.

Never breaking the unspoken connection with Kieran, I rock my head repeatedly in confirmation. "Yep," I say as K jerks his head in silent demand for me to get my arse over there.

"I'll tell you what, I'll take one – or three - for the team, so you can get her alone." Si stands and puffs out his chest with pride, but I grab his arm and drag him back down.

"There'll be no taking of anything. I want her to make the first move. Something is holding her back, and I want her to come to me with no force or pressure. Let's just see how it plays out for now. She knows what she has to do."

"Fine. Another drink?" he asks.

"Are you actually buying?"

"Yeah, since you've just spent fifty quid on something that may not materialise. I can't have you skinning yourself in case it does turn in your favour, and she wants breakfast in the morning. If she does, call me, I know a cheap, greasy spoon near you." With that, he strolls off to the bar.

I nudge K. "Is he cheap or cheerful?"

"What do you think?"

Cheap!

I grin, and from the corner of my eye, I spot the quartet of girls slinking off to dance when the heavy opening beat of *George Michael's Killer/Papa was a Rolling Stone* fills the club.

Tommy snaps his fingers in front of my face, reclaiming my attention. "Are you really serious about starting something with her?"

I inhale deeply, audibly. "Yeah. Yeah, I am. I haven't felt this way since Em. I've indulged in one-night stands and cheap dates, and it's not enough anymore. I've been so scared of regressing for the last eight years that I've forgotten how to live. And I'm not the only one. Maybe you should get over to the hotel and start living, too."

Tommy pulls out his phone and taps away. A few minutes and a resounding beep later, he puts on his jacket. "Right, I'm off."

"To see sweet Laura?" Kieran queries while Si sets another round of drinks on the table.

Tommy leans down to him. "A gentleman never tells."

Kieran snorts. "Well, you ginger, are no gentleman. Now spill!" Tommy flips him the finger and strides away. "I might see you later tonight then," he calls after him. "Or maybe tomorrow!"

"Ah, more for me!" Si says with zeal, sliding Tommy's abandoned drink towards him. He polishes off the shot then chases it down with some ale.

I lift the bottle of non-alcoholic lager to my lips, thankful Si made his own decision on what to get me. Honestly, I dare not calculate how much caffeine and carbonated liquid is roiling around my stomach. I haven't drunk as much fizzy pop as I have tonight in a long time.

Downing half the bottle in one, my phone vibrates on the table. I slide it over with my finger, and my smirk materialises as Evie's name appears on a new text. Opening the message, one word is all it takes.

Hi.

I stand abruptly and scan the dance floor, praying I see her between the bodies, the lights, and the general clamour.

"Problems?" Kieran asks.

"No." I shake my head, finally spotting her staring right at me. "She just made the first move."

Kieran twists in his seat and stretches his up. "I know it's been a while for you, Romeo, but you *never* keep a lady waiting. Park and I will keep the table warm until you return."

"Screw that, scouser. Tommy's probably gone to hook up with Laura, and this one's about to hook up with little miss over there," he exclaims, using the name that John bestowed upon her the night of the event, which means they've all been gossiping in the office. "If you think I'm sitting here with you, you have another thing coming. Let's go grab a piece of tonight's action." Simon runs his hand over his virtually non-existent hair and flicks up his shirt collar. "Just do us a favour, don't open your mouth."

"Oh, you're a funny git!" Kieran nudges him to move, putting more bite into his tone than usual. "Could say the same thing about your dance moves!"

I watch them stride away, then cut through the VIP to the DJ. "Hey, Gareth. Do us a favour and play this next," I ask, scrolling through the night's playlist on the laptop beside him, and stop on my request.

"No, I've just played gorgeous George. I was about to play Faithless. You know it gets the crowd going, which means more money in the tills for you."

"Don't care. I want to give the late, great man another airing. You can play them after. Come on, I'll pay you to play it."

"You're already paying me, Jer. Tell me why you want it, and I'll consider it," he says as the current song nears its end.

I point to Evie, who's still watching me. "I want to dance with that girl."

Gareth gives me a pointed look and quirks his pierced brow. "Fine. Anything for love, right? I'll even set the lights in time with it." He taps the laptop screen and sets my request.

I slap him on the back. "The best DJ in London!" I head to the dance floor as the lights begin to dim.

As requested, *The Strangest Thing '97* begins to emanate from the speakers, and I sidle behind Evie. I trail my fingertips in a barely-there touch up her forearms, and she gasps and jolts her head around.

"Hi," I whisper as the beat of the song kicks in.

"Hi," she replies and begins to turn.

"No. I want to dance with you. Just like this." I grip her rib cage and encourage her to move.

She grins confidently at me from over her shoulder, but I can feel a revealing shiver ripple through her. The first verse fills the floor, and Evie sways, finding her rhythm. I capture a faint linger of perfume mixed with her unique scent. It's heady and sublime, and I feel drunk in just a few moments of her company.

I lift my head, my nose gliding through the long, silky strands of her hair and see Simon and Kieran dancing with her friends. K winks and twirls two of the girls around, one in either hand.

Reverting my concentration on Evie, I glide my hands from her ribs to her taut waist. Her hips rock from side to side, then back and forth, causing her rear to rub intermittently against my groin. The tightening in my abdomen is obscene, not to mention the blood rushing to my dick. When I asked her to dance with me like this, it was purely because I'm a shit dancer. Now I'm relieved she agreed because at least she won't see the growing erection I'm sporting that has one resolute mission – to get inside her.

Evie continues to move, rubbing up in front of me. Whether she feels my hard-on, I don't know. She hasn't given any indication she has, but fuck if I won't be walking off this dance floor in discomfort. Lost in dirty thoughts, her hands enter the mix, and she glides them up and down the side of my hips and thighs. I breathe heavily against her, and she sways harder. Her movements cause her hair to brush against my forearms, and the scent of her unleashes more unbridled desires within me.

And all of it combined is absolutely killing me.

Without warning, I spin her around, and she presses her hands against my chest. She slowly peers down with a satisfied smile – the first indication she is aware of what she's doing and what she's inadvertently accomplished - then she stares up at my mouth. I quickly glance over the top of her head. Si and Kieran are still very much engaged with her friends and are paying no never mind to us. I capture her determined stare again and tangle my hand in the hair at her nape.

"Kiss me, Jeremy," she whispers and breathes heavily in anticipation. The strobe lights flash across her face and chest, and I witness the flare of her irises and the heaving swell of her breasts. Unable to fight her allure much longer, I claim her mouth. Soft, uncertain strokes turn hard and demanding within seconds. Her fingers dig firmly into my deltoids, holding me in place, while she lashes her tongue against mine in a steady, sensual assault.

I gradually move from her luscious mouth to her jaw. Peppering her with kisses, I dip lower and press my face into the curve of her shoulder. Her faint, delicate scent sends another direct message to my betraying appendage, which hardens impossibly further. I press my eager lips to the slender column of her neck, and her cheek slides against my scar as she lifts her head instinctively, giving me additional, unfettered access. The content sigh against my ear is all it takes. I kiss her again, swiping my tongue over her skin, tasting her, wanting to devour her.

Christ, this is dangerous. She's more intoxicating than any drug I've ever taken. She could make me lose control without even exerting any energy.

I squeeze my eyes in clear recognition. The power she has over me is extraordinary and breathtaking. This sensation is unparalleled, unprecedented, and unbridled. Before tonight, I was positive I hadn't felt this way since Em, but I was wrong. Without obliterating her memory and what we shared, the truth is what this girl makes me feel, even Em couldn't. And I want more. A lot more.

"Jeremy…" Evie's breathy murmur catapults my mind back into the present. I look up when she pulls back, uncertain. "I'm sorry, I-" I press my thumb to her mouth to silence any regret she may now be experiencing and give her a reassuring smile.

The song is just finishing, and I lean in and glide my lips over hers again. Her hand grazes my face, and she tenderly traces my scar.

"I have a confession," I mumble against her mouth, cradling her face.

"What?" she mumbles back, her hands now firmly on my back.

I kiss her again and pull away. "I can't dance."

She tosses her head aside on a laugh. "That's okay. Your amazing kisses make up for it." She bites her lip, and her fingertips massage the muscles lining my spine. "I like you, Jeremy James of the sad eyes. I mean, I *really* like you."

I don't reply because what I'm feeling for her right now, I can't find the right words to do it justice. I slide my arm around her waist and start to guide her to her friends, but she stops me.

"Have I said something wrong?" Her concern is palpable.

"No." I turn her to face me. "I really, *really* like you too, Evelyn Blake. And I *really* wish I could stay on this dance floor, tangled up with you all night."

Her eyes gleam, and she purses her lips together in contemplation. "When do you finish?"

"Midnight. Why?"

She shrugs and pouts mischievously. "I'll see you later," she says coyly. She touches her lips to my scar again, then slips out of my hold and moves back to her friends. One of them wraps her arms around her and whispers in her ear. The expression of giddy excitement graces Evie's stunning features until her mouth opens, and a surprised look ensues when *Insomnia* starts. The crowd moves in, and her face is finally obscured by the raising of hands with the pulsing beat of one of the greatest dance anthems of all time.

Striding through the club, the music pumping out of every speaker, bouncing off every wall, I can assimilate because I fear with Evie there may be no release, no peace, and definitely no cease for my mental rationale with her in my life.

Chapter 8

THE FAINT ELECTRONIC hum of the air conditioning intersperses with the music seeping through the walls as I rub my eyes and glance at the time on the screen. Stretching my neck from side to side, I pace to the window and press my forehead to the cool glass. The shuddering beats continue to reverberate through me as I maintain my stance and observe the revellers still partying the night away. My gaze drifts to the dance floor, and the picture consuming my mind's eye from just a few hours ago clings with ferocity. The memory of Evie's soft lips, how she felt in my arms, and the way her body moved with mine, is a memory I will relive over and over. One I shall remember when the nights are cold and lonely.

Touching my palm to the glass, I pinpoint the precise spot I last saw her before she slid on her jacket and left with her friends, taking Simon and Kieran with them. She didn't say goodbye – not that I expected her to – but after leaving her earlier, I stood in front of this window and watched her. And that was the biggest mistake I've made regarding her so far. Because the more I watched, the more I wanted. So much so, I fear she could, beyond doubt, become my newest, unhealthy obsession. Except, I confess it's not a fear, it's a fact, and I already feel it in my gut.

An incessant buzzing at my hip breaks my deep, meaningful thoughts, and I whip out my phone. Sliding my thumb over the screen, I crane my neck, somewhat in shock but thoroughly impressed.

Hi.

I grin at the simple, understated, yet implicit message. She's making the first move.

Again.

My thumb swipes over reply, and I begin to tap out a response. I don't have a clue what to say, but I'm spared the colossal intellectual effort when another message lights up the screen.

It's midnight Jeremy James of the sad eyes.

Jeremy James of the sad eyes…? My so-called sad eyes narrow then amplify, wondering what's going on. From four weeks of radio silence to a night of a hell of a lot more than just technological communication, now this.

I press my thumb to the screen and delete my original line of text. Two new, half-arsed sentences later, another message appears.

I'm waiting...

I tighten my fist around the phone as a knock raps on the door, and someone depresses the handle. Tossing my phone on the desk, I unlock the door and open it.

"Finally! I was wondering what else I'd have to do to get you to either respond," Evie waves her phone, "or come out."

She steps closer, wearing a gorgeous but nervous smile. Taking a chance, I slide my arm around the small of her back and pull her inside. She yelps in excitement, and I study her for a few moments, judging which influence she is currently drunk on – alcohol or me.

"Did I tell you how much I really, *really* like you?" I ask, identifying she's still very much sober. Her lips purse together, and I slide my arm under her arse and hoist her up.

"Yes," she replies evenly. Her eyes are dark and desirous, and she presses her breasts to my chest. "But I'd prefer it if you showed me again." Her small bag slips from her shoulder the instant she wraps her legs around my hips. Her hands grip either side of my face, her fingers tracing my scar tenderly, and she smashes her mouth to mine.

Yet again, fierce desire spreads through me like a raging wildfire. It scorches every carnal cell, igniting my heated blood further, hardening me in places that still desperately want inside her.

"Evie…" Her name tumbles from lips, but I'm not beneath begging if this is what it feels like to have just a little taste. Manipulating her further up my front, I begin to lose my grip on the fabric of her dress. I adjust my hands to ensure she's supported and secure until my fingers unintentionally stroke the very private place where her thighs and backside meet. I mentally berate myself, but the determination to slide her silky little shorts aside and plunge my fingers deep is far too strong for even my steadfast will to resist. But resist I shall.

"Oh, that feels nice," she whispers, shocking me as she wiggles against my hand.

Deprived of rational thought, I carry her to the desk and sit her on the top. I step back and rub my jaw in heavy contemplation. I've waited for this moment for weeks - probably from the first night I ever saw her. But now I've finally got her here, I realise she deserves more. Better than *this*. With each rumination, her eyes sadden unexpectedly, wearing a forlorn expression I can't put into words. I'm about to open my mouth and ask her to come home with me when she glances around and begins to adjust her clothing in obvious distress.

"Oh God, Jeremy, I'm sorry," she rushes out, reading me completely wrong, and starts to shuffle off the desk.

"Sweetheart, stop." I delicately grab her shoulders. Her beautiful, soulful eyes ensnare mine, and I'm gone. Honestly, it's all it takes. And all it would take to get her to lie back and spread her legs would be a few simple words of fake promises, but I can't. She may have made the first move, and granted, this show of brazenness might have hammered home what she really wants, but I know she's not a slut. Dominic dug deep, far deeper than I imagined he could. "I don't want you to be sorry."

"But I am," she whispers. "I just want you to want me."

Pride explodes within me, and I kneel in front of her, unknowingly giving her all the power. Holding her thighs in either hand, I rub circles over her soft, shivering flesh. "I *do* want you. I want you so much. For the last few hours, I've been unable to think of anything else. But not like this. You deserve better than this." *Better than me.* But a man doesn't choose a woman, a woman chooses a man, and it's evident she has chosen me.

She nods, but disappointment still plagues her stunning face. "I think I should go." She slides off the desk, straightens herself up and moves past me. The skin of her forearm grazes mine, and I reach back and coil my fingers around her wrist.

"I don't want you to," I confess, capturing her eyes. She tentatively moves back and enfolds her hand in mine. "Come home with me." The words are out there before I can take them back, but I have no regret saying them because they're true.

"I'd like that." She stretches up on her tiptoes and kisses me.

My hands find her shoulders, and I push her back. "Although, if you don't stop doing that, we're not going to make it out of this room." I chuckle lightly, but the more she keeps on pushing, the more I'm going to take - and it's going to reach the point where I'm not going to be able to stop.

"I'd like that, too." She bites her lip. Her shy expression mingles with her growing red cheeks while the excited sensation in my belly flourishes further.

Guiding her to the door, her palm tight against mine, I flick off the light. We walk hand in hand through the club - which is still busy but not as full to capacity as it was earlier – when an afterthought occurs to me. It's been a while since I've done this. Well over a year, if not two. I don't know what I'm expecting tonight. Honestly, I'd be happy just to hold her, but I can't take the risk that this may go further than that. However, considering all the implications and Evie's less than subtle inferences that this seems to be heading a certain way, I'd rather be prepared.

I pause in the corridor which leads to the toilets. "I'll just be a moment."

"Okay," she replies quietly.

An unexpected sense of déjà vu strikes as I stride towards the gents, my hand already in my pocket, pulling out my wallet. Unzipping it, I shake out the change and, thank Christ, there are more than a few stray pounds lurking in there.

Feeding the coins into the machine, I'm impressed it's actually working and glad I won't have to make a special trip to the nearest twenty-four-hour supermarket and risk embarrassing Evie.

I retrieve the three-pack of condoms that have dispensed and debate. I know I don't have any at home due to my self-imposed abstinence, which is something I need to rectify, but how many will be required tonight, I can't say. A few moments later, my wallet six pounds lighter but six condoms heavier, I venture back out to Evie, who beams beautifully as I approach.

"Ready?" The word tumbles from my mouth with ease.

"I can't wait," she replies with honest fortitude and entwines her fingers in mine.

I lead her through the hustle and bustle of the club, then through the staff door that leads to the alley where my car is parked. Holding the passenger door open, I observe her graceful movements as she climbs inside and gets comfortable. I close the door and linger beside it for a minute, gathering my thoughts. Walking around the bonnet, my stomach is in knots, eagerly anticipating every amazing moment that may pass between us before morning breaks on the horizon and steals her away.

Driving through the city, merry revellers fill the pavements and spill onto the streets, calling it a night. So many memories come flooding back. Memories of when I would be taking advantage of their inebriated inability to string two words together and their reckless abandonment of self-preservation. Around about now, the old me would be scoring illicit sales left and right, lining my pockets with blood money. Except I'm not that man anymore. That man is now buried deep in the murky side of my soul that I dare not venture to wade through again.

A soft, tentative touch on my knee drags me out of my procrastination, and I glance from the windscreen.

"Are you okay?" Evie asks with a hint of worry.

I smile. "Fine. I'm just thinking about things...life...you... Tonight."

"Are you having second thoughts?"

I drop a hand from the steering wheel and squeeze hers on my knee. I then slide my fingers between hers and grip them. "No," I reply honestly, sensing the faint trace of goosebumps prickling her soft flesh. "Are you?"

"No," she whispers shyly.

"Good, because tonight's been the best night of my life for a long time. So far."

"Really?" she asks incredulously.

I nod. "Really." I lift our conjoined hands to my lips and kiss the back of hers. Returning her hand to my knee, I shift gears and accelerate.

The streetlights flash in intervals as I speed home. I slow down at the security gates, tap in the code, and wait for them to open. Cutting the engine in my designated space, I get out and stride around to the passenger side. Opening the door, I hold out my hand, wondering if *she* might have had second thoughts. That thought is eliminated when her fingers slide across my palm, and she gracefully climbs out and stands tall in front of me. She closes the door, and her anxious eyes study my face.

"Now I'm nervous," she confesses and drops her head slightly.

I slip my arm around her back and tip up her chin. "So am I." I placate her with a delicate kiss designed to pacify her worry and mine.

I hold her close as we ride up to the flat that Dominic kindly paid for when I originally returned months ago. Granted, Sloan pays me handsomely to manage his club, but irrespective of outward appearances, I really don't have two pennies to rub together. I guess you could say I'm living a champagne lifestyle on a lemonade budget, courtesy of my wealthy friends.

Unlocking my door, I flick on the light and motion for Evie to enter. She steps inside cautiously and looks around the narrow, nondescript hallway. I tap in the alarm code as she removes her jacket and hangs it on the coat rack.

"Would you like a drink?" I ask, completely out of touch on how to initiate a one-night stand.

"Sure. What have you got?"

"Non-alcoholic lager or water," I offer, waiting to see if she will question it.

"You don't drink?"

"I do occasionally, but I don't really keep stock of anything harder than that in the flat."

"Why?"

I raise my brows and shake my head, unable to verbalise my usual line of *it's one of my three evils*. "I just don't." It's not that I don't want to tell her; it's that I'm ashamed of what she will think. And because it will raise further questions that I really don't want to have to confess this soon.

Her eyes reveal her curiosity, but she doesn't probe further. "Water's fine. Thank you."

I trace my fingers over her jawline before I enter the kitchen. Pouring two glasses of water, I grip them tight as I venture back into the living room to find her in front of the balcony doors.

"This is an amazing view," she murmurs, transfixed on the twinkling skyline.

"It is," I reply, referring to the woman, not the vista, and pass her a glass. Unlocking the doors, I step outside. I set my glass down and drop into one of the chairs. Evie takes a sip of her water, places it down and leans on the railing to admire the landscape.

My eyes roam, from the tips of her black stiletto heels, up her very shapely legs, over her perfectly rounded rear, all the way to the long silky hair blowing in the night breeze. My blood boils at the beautiful sight in front of me, and I shift in the chair. My groin hardens and lengthens, and without thinking, I gently palm my crotch.

"Want a hand?"

My head shoots up as she steps closer. I should feel ashamed that I'm completely perving over her, and she's just caught me attempting to relieve myself, but I can't as she stands above me with a genuine smile on her face; her eyes focused on where my guilty hand currently rests.

"I-I-"

She puts her finger over my lips, silencing my apology, then stretches her leg over my lap and sits astride my thighs. My hands instantly find her hips, and I tug her closer. Her centre compacts nicely with mine. She brings her hands around my shoulders and links her fingers at my nape. Seconds turn into minutes as we sit in silence, staring at each other until she rotates her pelvis. My hands slide down around her backside, and I knead her supple flesh when she rocks once more. Soft lips taste mine, and I'm helpless to do anything other than respond.

"Evie…" I breathe out, my shaft pulsing, ready to tear through the fabric separating us. My mouth slams unforgivingly against hers while my fingers dig into her skin and manipulate her position on my lap. Moving her fluidly, rhythmically, our cores rub relentlessly, tightening everything further beyond belief.

"Fuck, sweetheart, you feel good," I get out between frantic kisses.

"So do you." She grinds harder. "Touch me, Jeremy. I want you to."

"Hold on." I bury my face in her neck, sucking and licking reverently. Her fingernails cut into my shoulders, and I spread my legs out in a sudden action, causing her to bounce and giggle. Gritting my teeth, I slide my probing palms under her shorts.

"God, your fingers are so cold!" Her body clenches while I rub circles, closer and closer to her hot flesh. I then tentatively stroke a fold, and she shudders once more.

"Jeremy…" Her pleasurable sigh ripples through my ear while her mouth assails mine. I drop my head back as she begins to unbuckle my belt. Her small hands work frantically until she has me unzipped. A snap of cold air chills my front the moment she pulls my turtleneck up my torso and over my head. She smiles gloriously, a combination of pre-orgasmic bliss and something else, and I wish I had more time to consider it, but I don't. Taking the initiative, she gyrates on my hand while slipping hers into my boxers and clamping her palm around my length.

I hesitantly run my fingers along her intimate shape, still somewhat uncertain, but knowing all too well this is what she wants.

"Tell me what you want, sweetheart," I urge because I have not, and will not, ever take advantage, regardless of the unspoken consent currently being acted out between us.

My question hangs ominously in the ether as her other hand joins mine between her legs, and she positions my fingers at her entrance, stroking herself in the process. "Slide them inside me, Jeremy," she finally confirms, already growing breathless.

Sensing the thread my sanity is precariously dangling from becoming weaker and weaker, I grip her wrist and bring her fingers to my mouth. Devouring the maddening taste of her, I can't hold back any longer. I plunge a finger inside her fiery heat; she's hot, wet, and so fucking ready. Sliding in and out, grazing her swollen clit, her hand pumps my rock-hard length simultaneously, and my balls tighten up in heavenly anticipation.

The city is still alive in the distance as Evie moans, and the beautiful sound echoes in the dark night surrounding us. I lodge my mouth over hers, swallowing her welcome whimpers so my neighbours won't hear. Working each other towards the edge of the sensual precipice, my tongue invades her mouth, exploring and savouring every millimetre. Her tongue lavishes mine while our hips continue to chase each other's touch.

"Jeremy!" She eventually gasps and pulls back. Her eyes are closed tight in concentration, and I know she's close. Easing a second finger inside, I gently stretch her and continue to rub my thumb over her swollen nub, determined to make her mindless. Her eyelids flutter open in surprise, and she gives me a determined gaze. "I'm close, so close." She propels herself back and forth on my hand while she compresses hers around my length and pumps harder.

"Don't stop, sweetheart." I lift my hips off the chair, working her harder. I sink my teeth into the crook of her neck and suck. Within seconds, she's moaning and writhing, constricting my fingers inside her, and it's fucking fantastic.

"Oh, God! Oh, God!" She comes with such ferocity that I don't ever want her to stop. She's stunning like this: flushed, wanton, and thoroughly turned on.

Within seconds, my abdomen explodes, and I groan out as powerful pleasure tears through me, granting me momentary relief. As the sensation gradually wanes, I slide one hand through her hair and cradle the side of her head. Without shame, she stares into my eyes, breathing heavily and mewling as her orgasm carries on and on. Witnessing it, I feel so proud that I want to beat my chest in triumph.

"Fuck, you're beautiful," I tell her, watching her eyes widen and her brow furrow, running through a multitude of unspoken emotions.

"So are you." She smiles beautifully, unknowingly adding more allure to her potency. I frame my hands on her face and study her. Her cheeks are perspired and glowing, her eyes gleaming. "Stop staring! You're making me uncomfortable!"

I chuckle. "I can't help it; you're phenomenal." She fails to hide her grin and instead kisses my scar to hide her embarrassment.

Her hips finally ease down, and she flails against me, still holding my dick. Her thumb rubs across my bulbous head, and I shudder at the sensitivity. I wrap my arms around her, having experienced something so remarkable and potent that I want to rejoice in the moment.

"Are you okay?" The words leave my throat with concern since she's been quiet for far too long. I pray she doesn't regret what we've just shared because I want more, a lot more. And I want it all before the sun rises.

Evie presses her forehead to mine and peppers my face with kisses. "I feel incredible. I never knew it could be like this."

"Like what?" I tip my head back to look at her.

"Amazing like this. I've read about all-consuming sex and orgasms, but I've never experienced them. I never thought I would."

A terrible thought occurs to me, and it's clear that Dom's info is far from fact. It's downright fucking wrong!

Evie, completely perceptible and aware, gives me a grin. "In case you're wondering, I don't normally do this."

"Do what?"

"You're my first."

"Your first, what?" I ask, almost fearful. Considering her statement of never having experienced orgasms and sex, I don't mind if I'm her first in the biblical sense, but anyone's first time deserves more than an alleged one-night stand. Granted, for me, it was never my intention, but she doesn't know that. *Yet.*

She laughs, interpreting my worried expression perfectly. "No, not that! I'm not a virgin," she confesses, and my face falls. One minute, I'm terrified she is, the next, I'm flaming jealous she isn't and that someone else has already been here before me. "I've been with two boys. One was my first when I was seventeen – *big* mistake - and

the other was my uni boyfriend – *huge* mistake - until he dumped me six months ago. What I meant was, you're my first one-night stand."
I nod, relieved, thankful. "No, I'm not." Her eyes cross in misunderstanding. "This isn't a one-night stand," I clarify. "For me, this is the beginning." She pouts and opens her mouth. "I admit," I press my finger to her lips. "I'm still a little concerned about our age difference, but I think we have something special starting here. I'm not willing to let it go for the sake of a number that doesn't really mean anything. Are you?"
She shakes her head. "No. I want to see where this goes. I don't want to throw away something that could be amazing." She then rests her cheek on my bare chest and draws circles around my nipple. Her eyelids flutter against my pecs, and I nudge her gently.
"Let's go inside, sweetheart. It's late, and I need a shower. I have six hours of nightclub to wash off, plus I smell like a brewery."
She extracts her hand from my shorts and gives it a look. "Lead the way," she says, forcing me to stand. I lock the doors and watch her shimmy out of her dress in the living room. I kick off my shoes, drop my trousers and walk out of them. Evie gives me cheeky glances as she slinks down the hallway, unclipping her bra with an arm around her breasts.
I laugh at her innocent - or maybe not so innocent - striptease, but hell, I'm liking this game immensely. I grudgingly stop for a second as I pull off my socks and toss them aside.
"I think we've gone beyond shy and reserved tonight, don't you?" I query playfully as I fish the condoms from my trouser pocket.
She stops with a shrug and grips the top of the sexy little shorts covering her delectable backside. I must confess, I didn't fully appreciate them when I had my hands inside them, making her come. But seeing them now, and the way the lace and satin mould over her flesh, I make a mental note to buy her as many pairs as she wants.
Lost in thought, my eyes lift just in time to see her naked bum disappear into the bathroom as said sexy little shorts hit me in the face. Screwing them up in my hand, I enter the bathroom and toss them into the laundry basket.
I loiter, admiring the extraordinary outline of the amazing woman steaming up my oversized shower cubicle. I tap the glass, and she opens the door. My stare is hard and brooding, scanning every inch of her body, knowing I have every dirty intention of kissing, licking, sucking, and fucking it. My eyes drift from her apex to her tits.

Outside, I didn't get the chance to feel her nipples on my tongue, and that's something I plan to rectify right now.

"Are you coming?" She cocks her head and juts out a leg, exposing the luscious flesh hidden between her thighs. I slide my shorts off and toss them at her.

"Hmm, inside you...in about ten minutes, sweetheart." Ripping open the condom wrapper, I begin to palm my semi-hard shaft. Her eyes focus, and her lips part seductively, observing the way I take myself in hand. Sliding the condom on, I hurry inside the same moment she throws my shorts onto the shower base. My large hands grip her small waist, and I pin her against the wall.

"So forceful!" she chides, licking her lips, grinning with excitement.

I wiggle my brows and allow my mouth to descend. Gliding my hands up her waist, I enclose a wet breast in one hand. Her tits are true perfection. Unblemished, porcelain flesh, tipped with a blushing pink areola and nipple. They are the perfect handful and are currently begging for my attention. But considering her admission regarding the two previous mistakes and what little experience she has, I'm going to take my time with them. I bend slightly until her nipples are in my eye line, then tenderly squeeze, earning myself a wanton whimper. Grinning to myself, I purse my lips and blow softly, earning another welcome sound of gratification. I finally gaze up into her expectant eyes. Wide, brown pools mentally devour me with their look of longing and anticipation. Never breaking contact, I take her luscious peak into my mouth and suck reverently.

"Oh, Jeremy..."

I concentrate on the expression clouding her features as her nipple stiffens further on my tongue. She licks her bottom lip before clenching it between her teeth, and I draw mine and graze them up and down her small tip. Fingernails dig into my shoulders, and she presses her head back as I continue to lap at her nipple and roll the other between my finger and thumb. Even under the steam and hot flow of water, her body shivers, pleasing me immensely.

"Like that?" I ask, desperate to hear her breathy response.

"Yes..." Her hazy eyes focus on mine. She cradles the back of my head, holding me in place, guiding me. "More."

I lightly sink my teeth into her taut tip again, this time intentionally marking her. She hisses beautifully, her fingertips finding my scar, and she begins to rub her thighs together where she stands. I grin and slowly slide my hand down her abdomen, my finger drawing circles over her swollen core.

"Jeremy…"

My name rolls off her tongue in desperation. My body, stiff in all the right places, jerks in base response, and I know I can't wait much longer, having already experienced what it feels like to be inside her.

"That's so good!" she exclaims, rotating her hips, pushing her centre deeper into my touch. Sinking my fingers inside her again, her gasps of delight ring in my ears as she finally reaches her peak. Her expression is exquisite, and I gaze at her in exaltation, unbelieving someone up there has given me this. Given me her.

I memorise every little look and sound. The way her eyes squeeze whilst she trembles through her high, the way she bites her lip before they part, and her husky moan washing over my face. I gradually ease down and bestow one last kiss to her red, distended nipple before claiming her mouth.

"God, how I want you." The words flow from my mouth, and she gives me a naughty smile.

"Good, but now it's my turn," she says, then abruptly pushes me back and slides down the wall.

I dare not look as her soft mouth - that I've gotten to know so well tonight – lightly touches the tip of my shaft. I shudder. As much as I want her mouth on me, cocooning me, swallowing me, it's too much right now. I stroke her cheek, tilt her face up and shake my head.

"Later, sweetheart." I cup her chin in both hands and gently manipulate her back up. She kisses a line from my navel to neck, and reaffirms her hand with my dick.

I feel out of control as I watch her lift a slender leg and hook it around my hip. The sound of the water hitting the shower base does nothing to hide my desire, and I groan when she guides me to her opening. Finally, having reached the point of no return, she grips my backside in readiness. We stare into each other's eyes, the unspoken moment lingering as I position my hands – one above her head, the other under her right thigh, securing her – then slide inside her.

Holy fuck!

She feels magnificent surrounding my dick. She's primed to perfection, and the reality of claiming her at long last is even better than I could've imagined. Honestly, it's going to take everything I have not to rut into her with reckless abandon. Adjusting her leg so her heel is tight under my arse, I piston my hips back and forth.

"Oh God!" she moans loudly. Her core tightens around me, causing me to shift again, which in turn causes her to moan again. I hold back the groan in my throat, and instead, tip up her chin.

"Okay?" I query since I'm not a bastard who will fuck a woman who isn't comfortable.

Her heavy eyes shine, and her chest heaves as she nods repeatedly. "I feel fantastic. More, Jeremy, please." I grin, adjust my stance and the hand on her thigh, and give her what she's asked for.

My groans and her moans consume the small space as I plunge in and out. The friction between us is maddening as my wet flesh slides against hers. Every movement, from the touch of a hand to a chaste kiss, to the slightest graze of fine hair, is amplified. Intoxicated by this intense connection, I grab hold of her other leg and elevate her around my hips.

"Hold my shoulders, sweetheart," I say, and she quickly wraps her arms around me. Happy she's secure, I propel my hips harder. Each thrust presses her spine into the tiles, and she yelps in response. "Sorry."

"Don't be. You feel wonderful. Harder," she urges, and I alter my arms around her back to minimise the discomfort.

Screwing her mindlessly, each thrust is welcomed by her tight sheath and rouses me further until she constricts my dick and compresses her thighs around me.

"Oh, God!" she cries out, resting her skull on the wall and arching her back. My body shatters again in direct effect to her release. The combined guttural sounds fill the room, and I cease all movement and just watch as she rides the wave from high to low again.

"You're a vision when you come, sweetheart." I brush the wet hair from her face and kiss her forehead.

She purses her lips together and brings her hand over her eyes. "Oh God, I'm so embarrassed!"

I lower her hand and hold her chin between my finger and thumb, ensuring she can't turn away. "Evie, you're stunning like this."

"Like what?"

"Flushed, wanton; thoroughly turned on, and enjoying every minute of it," I repeat some of my earlier thoughts plus some new ones. "And soon, there won't be a place on you that I haven't kissed or caressed. I'm going to trace every inch of you with my tongue. I'm going to kiss every patch of flesh. And I'm going to learn every sound you make when I'm inside you."

A slow smile spreads across her cheeks, and she sucks on her bottom lip. "Sounds amazing," she whispers. "When do we start?"

I toss my head back, simultaneously surprised and shocked by her admission. But God, if she hasn't just said the words I've longed to hear. I place her down and move her under the shower.

"Tomorrow. It's late, sweetheart. Let's get cleaned up and go to bed." I remove the condom, tie it off, and open the door to toss it in the bin. As I shift under the spray, she places her hands on my chest and gives me a flirty smile.

"What if I said I'm not tired?"

Chapter 9

"EMMA...WHY? WHY? You promised!"

My body jolts upright as memories from a time gone by viciously drag me from my slumber. My heart beats uncontrollably, and I scrub my hands over my face in frustration. Blowing out my breath, I reach for my phone. I sigh superfluously, flicking the screen. It's only just six in the morning. While it's not uncommon for me to be awake at this time - I'm a light sleeper, always have been, even when I've been working late - it is unusual for me to be shocked back to consciousness by dreams of the past.

By dreams of unintentional, broken promises.

By dreams of premature death.

It's a sad truth, considering the effect it has had on me, but aside from the daydream I had on the balcony weeks ago of our first meeting, I've rarely dreamed about Emma for years.

I rub my eyes, experiencing acute agitation when a soft, feminine murmur rouses my attention. I shift carefully and gently run my fingertips down Evie's beautiful face. My stomach sinks, and I pray she didn't hear me call out another woman's name. If she did, she wouldn't understand. She will naturally jump to impossible conclusions, and I'm not prepared to divulge the truth this early in our relationship. Nor am I about to explain that she can't compete with the dead because that, in itself, presents a further set of assumptions that are detrimental to any longevity we may have.

Propping my head on my hand, my elbow sinks into the mattress. Studying her, I'm amazed that someone as beautiful as this girl - who, regardless of what I've said previously, is definitely far too young for me - finds me appealing. I'm also amazed she's still here. Last night, or more accurately, this morning, after working each other into a mindless stupor, I expected to find her gone when I woke up. I know I told her this was more than a one-night stand for me, but whether she genuinely believes it, I don't know.

In all fairness, I'm probably doing her a disservice by questioning her judgement, but when she made the first move last night, I realised, for once in my life, someone finally sees me as something more than the monster I'd allowed myself to become years ago.

She sees me for who I am… Scar and all.

And that is absolutely terrifying.

But regardless, in my heart, something is telling me this is the wrong time to encourage this budding relationship because I know the pitiful existence I ran away from is just waiting to find me again. I know when it does, my litany of poorly executed past decisions will ensure the gates of hell will one day welcome me with open arms and hold me in fiery purgatory as penance.

Now, I pray that if time is on our side, Evie doesn't become an innocent bystander who eventually gets burnt because of it.

Consumed by the untold, unforgettable misery, I trace my thumb over her bottom lip. She stirs, mumbles incoherently, then rolls over. Even in the dusky room, I can still make out her smooth skin, the dip of her waist and flared curve of her hip. I hover my hand over her, dying to touch her, to taste her again. Just to have another moment of true goodness and beauty to remember before she wakes up and decides whether she still wants to see me again.

My hand retreats of its own accord, and I prudently climb out of bed and pull out a pair of clean boxers. Sliding them on and adjusting myself, I look back, wishing I could be the good man she deserves. Except that may never be because any good woman who manages to stick around for the long haul will eventually see who I really am underneath the handsome face and honed body.

Em saw it… And it killed her.

Softly closing the bedroom door, I linger outside. After long minutes of stillness pass by, satisfied I haven't disturbed her, I quickly use the bathroom. A few minutes later, I quietly pad down the hallway, picking up our hastily discarded clothing as I go.

Throwing open the balcony door, the cold, early morning air chills me to the bone. My eyes scan the decking until I find my sweater. Dragging it over my head, I slide the door across, slump into the chair and retrieve my cigs and lighter from under the pot. The first drag of nicotine makes me lightheaded since it's been a while. I always say once I've finished a packet, I won't buy anymore. But once you've had the taste for it, it never fully dissipates. Hence, why I know there's no such thing as *ex* anything. Exhaling leisurely, the smoke evaporates on the atmosphere and the door opens, startling me.

"Sorry, I didn't mean to scare you," Evie apologises as she slides the door back. I hide my smile, seeing her wearing one of my t-shirts

– a sure sign she's been rooting through my things. I don't mind; the things I hide aren't physical. She moves to the railing and leans back against it. "I didn't realise you smoked."

I glance at the cigarette in my hand before I stub it out on the plant pot. "I don't, not really. Not anymore."

"Oh no, I don't mind."

My brows lift, and I glean from her expression she probably does. "It's not a regular habit, but every now and again, I just need one."

Her lips purse in contemplation, and she looks over her shoulder as the faint shrill of sirens disrupts the peaceful dawn. "Such as waking up and finding your one-night stand still in your bed?" Her tone is playful, but hell, if it doesn't pique my attention. "Or finding said one-night stand wearing your t-shirt?"

I stand abruptly and move closer. I skim my fingers down her forearm, until I snag her wrist and pull her into me. Chest to chest, she stares, firm and unwavering, probably wondering how I will react.

"I told you, you're not a one-night stand." I cradle her cheeks while my thumbs repeatedly brush over her temples. "Besides, I like you in my t-shirt," I whisper as an afterthought. Her eyelids droop in bliss, and she moves her head slightly, chasing my touch. She shuffles closer until her thighs press against mine.

"You mean that? You're not just saying it?"

"Which part?" I query, amused.

"You know which part!"

My lips upturn and I shake my head in affirmation. "I don't make false promises. I meant every word, sweetheart." I tilt her chin and devour her lips. Her arms wrap around me, and even through the two thin layers of clothing, her erect nipples tease my chest. "Cold?" I reluctantly break us apart.

"A little." She fidgets with the t-shirt hem at her mid-thigh.

"Let's go back to bed," I offer. Her eyes shine in anticipation, and she licks her bottom lip suggestively, one of her tells I recognise from last night. I lock the door behind us before she hastily drags me through the living room and down the hallway.

I kick the bedroom door shut and switch on the light as she stands next to the bed. She blinks as the room illuminates, but unlike last night, I want to see her. All of her. She notes my divided concentration and crooks her finger for me to come hither.

"Take it off." She nods at my sweater.

"Now, who's being forceful?" I toss her comment from last night back at her.

She grins as she ties her dark, messy hair up on top of her head. "Maybe I just know what I want." She confidently walks towards me and slides my jumper halfway up my torso. "I know a good thing when I see it."

I lift my arms as she stretches up and removes my jumper. "Really? Too much of a good thing can be bad," I tell her as she deposits it somewhere on the floor. Her eyes glide up my body, and she holds my gaze while her lips explore my chest.

"You're wrong," she murmurs, and I yank the t-shirt from her body.

Her hands fidget as she stands naked in front of me. I can see her worry instantly because there's a huge difference in being naked and lost in the moment, to being naked and allowing someone to see you in such a conscious fashion.

"Too much of a good thing is never bad." Her words are a whisper, and she steps forward when I do. I want her to finish whatever is on her mind, but I also want to start what's on mine. "It might be too soon to confess this, but you're all I've thought about since the event. I honestly don't think I'll ever get enough of you. I want it all, Jeremy, and I want all of you. I want to feel so consumed by you that I can't breathe."

Her words set my blood alight, and I shift until she's in my arms. Laying her down on the bed, she curves a leg around my thigh and arches her body.

"Evie… I want you too, sweetheart." I smash my lips to hers and hoist her leg higher on my hip until the softness between her legs presses against my flesh. My mouth devours unforgivingly, desperate to consume her, desperate to prove her confession isn't in vain. "I want every inch of you…in every way possible."

She touches my temple, deliberately grazing my scar. "I want you inside me." She pushes me back with renewed self-assurance. "I want you to make love to me."

I chuckle at her flightiness, grasp her ankles, and drag her closer. Crawling on my knees, I drape myself over her and place one hand at the side of her head. I gently take her chin between my finger and thumb and manipulate her to expose her slender neck. Working my lips meticulously over her throat, her body ripples from head to toe as I suck and lick, unable to satisfy my need to taste her.

"What are you doing?" she asks, her tone laced with desire, the vibration reverberating over my lips.

"I'm keeping a promise. I'm going to trace every inch of you with my tongue. I'm going to kiss every patch of flesh." I recant the promises I made last night. "What do you like?" I ask, beginning the start of the physical onslaught of sensation.

She shifts and releases a breathy moan. "My previous experiences weren't amazing." She gasps and gyrates her centre to mine. "I mean the actual sex was okay, but..." She trails off, and her face turns bright red. "I never managed to... I never came with either. They just couldn't get me there, I guess."

"Bullshit! Did they come?" She nods singularly. "Then they just couldn't be arsed to satisfy you!" And that just pisses me off even more that some men only care about themselves rather than worship the woman who has seen fit to allow them the privilege of being with her. Of being inside her. Of sharing something so sacred.

Evie's hands dig into my shoulders, and she sighs, diverting my thoughts back to her. "Jeremy-"

"Do you want to play?" I cut her off.

"What? Like cuffs, whips, and vibrators?" Her cheeks turn a darker shade of pink.

I shake my head. "No, I'm not into that. I mean, try out a few positions, see what you like, what you don't. I can be more than accommodating, and if you want to try cuffs and whips and bring a vibrator in, I'm sure I can improvise, but not today."

She laughs, mortified, and burrows her face into my chest. "No cuffs or whips...yet, but yeah, I'd like to *improvise* with you."

I eye her inquisitively, wondering where she will draw the line. I circle my fingers just inside her opening, and she gasps and automatically moves with me. Obviously, after last night we're both already in agreement that *here* is absolutely fine.

"That's so sensitive, so incredible."

"Good. Here?" I brush my thumb over her mouth, and she licks the pad, then slips it between her lips.

Her eyes skate down to my groin. "Yeah, I want it there." My dick jerks in immediate response, already stiff and raring for some of that.

I reluctantly extract my thumb and lean in and kiss her. Her tongue confidently breaches my mouth and lashes against mine. I groan when her small hand sheaths my length without notice, squeezing and pumping painfully slow, assisting in getting me off. I rock back on my haunches and bring her up with me. She yelps in surprise and folds her arms around my shoulders, curling her nails into my flesh, creating a pleasurable bite.

I growl, unexpectedly turned on by it and stroke down her back, memorising every contour. Manipulating my palms further around her backside, I slide my fingers cautiously between her cheeks. Her hold relaxes instantly, and she rests back. Her beautiful, enquiring eyes capture mine, and her lips part in seduction.

"Here?" I ask heavily, my breathing staccato, lodging in my throat. My fingers rub delicately up and down, stimulating her in a place she probably never expected.

"Maybe," she breathes out, biting her lip.

"Maybe?" I repeat, surprised, shocked from her intoxication, but sobering from her candid confession. I jolt when she suddenly rubs the tip of my shaft.

"Hmm, maybe. I trust you, Jeremy."

With those few softly spoken words, she has just claimed the power. Whereas she trusts me to take care of her, I don't know if I fully trust myself. I'd never intentionally hurt her, but sometimes, some things are out of your control. Sometimes, some things are unavoidable.

"Provided we can do it face to face, I trust you to take care of me like that." Her soft tone overrules my internal strife, and a variety of positions run through my head. But the dream of her spread out in offering for me, my body impaling hers in such an unspeakable but amazing manner, while I fuck her with my fingers, and burrow my face between her beautiful breasts, is enough to make me come.

Maybe the imaginary cuffs and vibrator she queried would come in very handy.

"Whatever you want, sweetheart, whenever you want. There's no rush here." Because there really isn't. I would never push anyone to do something they don't want to do on the proviso the relationship needs it or because I expect or demand it.

I carefully lay her down, her spine sinking into the softness of the duvet and remain on my haunches. "Beautiful," I whisper.

She bestows me a cheeky smile as she bends a leg back to her chest. I nod, impressed, and make a mental note to test her flexibility as she points it ramrod straight to the ceiling, brings it down to my dick, gives it a wiggle, then walks her toes up to my chest, tipping my chin, before finally dropping it back on to the bed.

"How long can you hold that position?" I query, acrobatic ideas forming.

"Long enough. Care to find out?"

I quirk my brow at her evasive response, but it is left simmering on the backburner as she spreads her leg wide to the side and grips the sheets keenly, giving me a spectacular view of her most intimate place. The resplendent sight of her like this, unguarded and unveiled, is breathtaking.

I lean down and kiss her again, gradually guiding my lips down her front. My shaft throbs as I take a rigid peak into my mouth, and she arches, pushing her chest up, allowing me more. Licking her areola, she convulses when I take it whole in my mouth and rubs herself on my thigh. I give her a little nip, and she jerks again with a gasp. I grin, lower my mouth from her chest and move down her stomach. I look up inconspicuously. Her eyes are fluttering with pleasure while her mouth parts, and she sighs happily.

Kneeling before her, I spread her legs and drape one over my shoulder. She gives me an apprehensive look, and I wonder if either of her previous two lovers had ever pleased her like this. Pausing at her belly button, I rim my tongue around it, preparing her for what I plan next. She writhes under me, her concern obliterated, and it emboldens me further. I continue my descent. Finally, I reach her pubic bone and press my lips to her centre.

"Jeremy," she whispers. Her worry is clear, and I lift my head and rub the leg currently positioned over my shoulder.

"I swear I won't hurt you. If this makes you uncomfortable-"

"No," she says, shaking her head. "I want you to, but it's just...no one's ever kissed me there."

"Never?" I smile externally, but internally, I want to beat her exes into bloody oblivion for never satisfying her like this. I inhale, regain my control, and kiss her inner thigh. She squirms in response. "How about we take it slow and build up to it?"

She agrees, but her nervousness is still apparent as she chews her lip and returns her hands to clench the sheets again.

"Close your eyes, sweetheart, and just feel."

When she does as requested, I dip back down and toy my finger over her flesh. She's already slick and prepped, and my control is skating on thin ice. The thought that I will be the first man to have ever put my tongue here is creating such powerful motivation in me,

I don't know how much longer I can refrain from sliding in and tasting her properly.

Her leg rubs up and down the back of my shoulder while I tease her clit with deliberate, unhurried circles. My thumb slides up and down, and I ease a finger into her core and rotate it. She breathes deeply, curling her toes into my skin and lifts her hips off the bed. Her body arches up and down repeatedly, pushing and pulling against my ministration. Pumping my finger in and out, using my thumb to stimulate her, her hands slide down her body, and she massages the insides of her thighs, and it's the sexiest fucking thing I've ever seen. She's almost there, and I grind my teeth together, determined not to come in my boxers the moment she falls over the edge and allows me to witness the most magnificent sight on earth.

"Jeremy, please," she whimpers, begging for release.

I continue the pressure with my thumb, knowing it will test her resolve not to let go. "I want you to come on my tongue," I say, gliding my eyes up her body. "Hold yourself up on your elbows. I want you to see how much I'm going to enjoy you like this."

"Oh…" she breathes out, balancing herself perfectly.

I gently reposition her leg on my shoulder and press her other down onto the mattress using the side of her knee. My dick throbs at the unobscured sight of heaven as I descend to her centre and run my nose over her length. She continues to breathe heavily. I slowly swipe my tongue over her moist flesh, and she judders and throws her head back in response.

"Oh… Oh!"

I bury my face between her legs, inhale her unique scent, then pierce her core with my tongue. Thrusting it in and out, she becomes wetter and wetter, and I can't harness my control.

"That's amazing. Don't stop!"

I slip her leg from my shoulder and spread her out under me. Holding her shaky thighs, in my peripheral vision, I can see her massaging her tits.

"Fuck!" I hiss while she rocks her hips up and down. Maintaining my worship of her, alternating between thrusting my tongue and sucking her swollen slit, I can feel her tighten up. She rolls her body with each touch and brings her hands down to my head, forcing me deeper into her. Her eyes flutter open and closed, but they never retreat from mine. She's watching, just as I wanted.

"Jeremy!"

My name, breathless on her lips, encourages me, and I slam my hands between her thighs and add my fingers, increasing the pressure with each stroke. As I continue to taste her reverently, her breathing intensifies further until she tilts her shoulders back.

"Oh, God. Oh, God! I'm-I'm-" she cries out, her centre compressing around me. I slow from a thrust to a lick, easing her down.

Eventually, she drops her chin to her chest and smiles at me. She looks fucked. Literally. Between last night and this morning, she's only had a few hours' sleep, but I'm not ready to end this. Not now, probably not ever.

I sit up on my haunches and draw her forward. She slides her hand around my head and kisses me hard. Pulling back, she tentatively tracks the tip of her tongue over her lip.

"You taste incredible, but you feel even better." Her eyes avert in embarrassment, but I grip her chin and smile. "Don't get shy on me now, sweetheart. Not when we've already agreed on whips, cuffs, vibrators, and your gorgeous, delectable rear." I hold the back of her neck and kiss her humbly. She walks on her knees until they are on either side of my thighs. My engorged head slides between her swollen folds, and I grind my teeth when she reaches down and manipulates it to her opening.

"Condom." I halt her wrist. From the six I bought last night, there are two left.

"I'm on the pill," she replies, teasing her finger around the circumference of my tip, trying to persuade me. "I want to feel you inside me, Jeremy. I want to feel you the way you've just felt me."

I run my fingers through her messy, tied up hair and force her to look at me. "We need to be safe and sensible." I know I'm definitely clean, and I know she probably is, too, but I have to keep my head here. I'm not reckless anymore, and I won't start again now. "Sweetheart, please. I told you, this is the beginning for me. We'll have plenty more days and nights of being inside each other, and I do expect to have them unsheathed."

"I just want to feel your skin inside mine. To feel your silky, hard flesh," she says, pumping my length. "To feel you fill me when you come."

Fuck! If I wasn't already on the verge of exploding, that has definitely done it.

"Condom, sweetheart." I reinforce my stance, amazed at my own tenacity. Evie reluctantly reaches back and picks one up from the bedside cabinet. Without further dispute, she tears it open and rolls it over me. I hiss out the moment her warm fingers massage my balls.

"You feel incredible, so hard, so big." She quickly climbs onto my lap, guides me where she wants me and slides down my shaft. I gasp out and grip her hips. "So full and strong..." Her thoughts are broken as the radio begins to play, indicating it is half six. She starts to lean back to turn it off, but I stop her.

"Leave it on. I like this song," I confirm while the hauntingly beautiful *Cannonball* fills the room.

She clenches my nape, gazing into my eyes as she rotates her pelvis painfully slow on mine. She slides up and down intermittently, and my body penetrates hers deeper, proving that a different type of heaven certainly exists for men like me.

I bring my hands to her rib cage and bury my face in her breasts, savouring the small valley in-between. Sitting my hands on her shoulder blades for support, she rocks back and forth, riding me to the point of insanity. I attempt to lift up my hips, but she clenches her thighs and tuts.

"It's my turn to make you lose control!"

I gaze at her, wondering where my innocent, shy thing has gone. Except, I can't say I'm sad to see this change. I don't want a submissive woman who won't do what she wants, irrespective of her experience. I want her to take control. I want her to say what she wants in bed.

"Fuck me, sweetheart," I tell her and grab her arse. Accepting the incentive, she finds her natural rhythm and style, riding me both hard and soft. Taking me to the brink and hauling me back, over and over, until she clamps her body down, and I finally fall over the proverbial edge and roar out my release, bringing her with me.

With my breathing finally evening out and my body relaxing, I throw one arm above my head on the pillow and slide the other beneath Evie. Long minutes pass by, but she makes no attempt to move, regardless that we can both feel me becoming flaccid inside her. I palm her cheeks and move the damp hair from her face. "I need to take care of this." I carefully lift her aside and stride naked into the bathroom to deal with the condom. A few minutes later, I slip back into bed and roll her onto me.

I run my hand through her hair, absorbing the way it feels between my fingers. I sigh contently when she rests her chin on my chest, her wide, mesmerising eyes fixed on me, seeing me. I'm thoroughly interested as to what she will do when she smirks and wriggles, seamlessly aligning our bodies.

No words are spoken as she presses her soft, compliant mouth to my chest, and her wayward hand glides upwards. I already know its trajectory, but I do nothing to stop its ascension. Seconds feel like minutes, and then she cautiously caresses my temple.

"How did you get this?" she finally asks, and I close my eyes momentarily. Her unintentional dirty query lingers on the atmosphere, ringing in my head like sudden tinnitus.

I tighten my arm around her in a protective action, pretending that if I hold her securely, the invisible evil surrounding me won't physically touch her.

"It's a long story," I murmur, trying to concoct an alternative version of events to circumvent the truth. Irrespective of the veracity of whatever line I feed her, I'm not lying; the story is long, and it's still not over. It's also painful and ugly, and I don't want to subject her to its brutality. I want a side of her to remain in ignorance, far, far away from the darker, murkier side of life.

"I didn't mean to pry-"

"You're not," I cut her off. "It's still just a very raw, recent memory for me." I study her expression while I twirl a lock of her dark hair around my finger.

She inhales a brave breath, her fingertip stilling on my cheek. "How recent?"

I close my eyes in resignation. If I want to keep her in my life, I have to give her something. "Ten months." When I open my eyes, hers are struggling to keep the wetness at bay. "Don't cry for me, beautiful." I glide my thumb under her lashes to collect her fallen tears. She shakes her head and begins to open her mouth, but I silence her before the first word is out. "We can't change the past. We can only learn from it."

"I know. I just wish it hadn't happened to you. However, it happened," she whispers and shuffles in my arms. "What time is it?"

"Around seven. Do you want to go home?" I ask, the reality hitting me in the gut like a fatal bullet.

"I don't want to, but I have to."

I kiss her while simultaneously manipulating her into my arms and then carry her into the bathroom. I drop her on her feet in front of the basin and pass her a new, unopened toothbrush. "A toothbrush is a very significant step forward in any relationship. I don't give these to just anybody, you know. I expect it to be used – by you – more than once."

Evie flushes pink and holds the brush to her bare chest. "Okay."

A LITTLE AFTER eight o'clock, the engine purrs as I drive through the streets. The early morning sunshine, lingering low in the sky, lights the way. The roads are quieter this time on a Saturday morning, and that just irritates me since it means I'll reach the Blake's house quicker than I'd like.

I kerb crawl to a stop and look over the upper-class mini-mansion, complete with faux Tudor frontage finishing its appearance. Christ, I'm ready to break out in hives. It's the real-life bricks and mortar version of goddamn Mordor.

Partially hidden behind mature conifer trees, with a pair of robust wooden gates and a state-of-the-art security system, I can't help but wonder if they are locking themselves in or locking the bad elements out.

The birds sing in the tree canopy overhead as I get out and open the passenger door. I hold out my hand for Evie and pull her into me the second she stands.

"Last night was extraordinary. *You* are extraordinary. I meant what I said. I want more than one night. I want tomorrow, and the day after, and the day after that… You get the picture."

"I do." She reaches up on her heels, holds my jaw between her finger and thumb and re-acquaints our mouths. With every second that ticks by, the harder it becomes to let her go. But let her go, I must.

"If you keep that up, I'm going to throw you back in the car, take you home and constantly have my way with you. I may never let you leave," I tell her as I straighten up her appearance.

She grips the lapels of my jacket. "Don't make promises you can't keep, Mr James, because I think we're both aware I'd like that."

I chortle at her brazenness. Still, I'm at a loss how to respond. From her initial hesitancy last night to her sudden confidence now, there has been a definite shift in her mindset. Whether forged during sleep, when her heart beat next to mine, or she wants to nurture our budding relationship during its infancy, I'll take whatever she will give.

"Are you working tonight?" she asks, diverting the conversation with ease.

"Yeah, but tomorrow I'm doing the day shift. I'll be finished around five. Why?"

"Well, I need to use my new toothbrush again, and I also seem to have lost a really good pair of knickers somewhere in your flat that I need to retrieve."

With both hands on her waist, I force her closer. "How about we barter? Your knickers in exchange for dinner?"

Her arms curl over my shoulders, and she gives me a chaste kiss. "You can't barter with something that's already a foregone conclusion."

"True. Well, how about dinner in potential exchange for your heart?" I cup her cheek, and she leans into it. Her eyes close, and she inhales before opening them again.

"It may require further consideration of time, but there's a very strong possibility that that's already a foregone conclusion, too." With that, her mouth captures mine again, and this time it's anything but chaste. Breaking away, she smiles before it slowly falls. Try as she might to hide it, that look is there again, the one from the event and then again at the office. It's a sadness concealed by confidence, and it pains me to witness it. "Oh, happy days," she mutters dryly, her eyes focused behind me.

Placing a protecting arm on her back, I rotate her around and come face to face with Andrew Blake, who is collecting this morning's paper from the in-set post box on the brick gate column. I maintain a dignified stance as I hold his daughter – my woman – with the passion of a man ready to fight for what's his.

"One last goodbye kiss?" Her beautiful eyes take on a scheming glint.

I grunt, splaying my hands wide over her waist and pull her close. Grazing them up her sides, conscious of the extra pair of eyes on us, I cup her face and brush my thumbs over her cheeks soothingly. My lips touch hers, very prim and proper. She stretches up, thrusts her tongue into my mouth and takes it to the next level. Long minutes tick by, and she moans, satisfied, and drops back down on her heels.

"I'll see you tomorrow," she says cockily.

"That was disobedient, but I can't wait."

She slowly pivots on her heel and walks towards her father. He doesn't so much as blink in her direction. Instead, he levels his disapproving, steadfast glare on me. I swear, if I was less of the man that I am, unconfident in my own skin, it would slay me where I stand. As it is, I've met and dealt with far scarier and far seedier characters than him.

I grin and wink at Evie as she turns back from the front door and waves. The gates creak and start to rotate back into position, and the last thing I see is the devious, hate-filled glare of Andrew Blake.

Jogging back to my car, I slide inside and stare up at the house. I was wrong all those weeks ago. I was fooling myself into believing that this mesmerising young woman was not old enough, or mature enough, to know her own mind or to mentally satisfy mine. In truth, she knows me better than I know myself, and maybe therein lies a new problem.

My entire life has been plagued by OCD and addiction. From toy cars to video games as a child to weed in my early teens. Then finally, in my late teens, the hard stuff I'd been using recreationally until it imploded in my face.

But of all my addictions, Evelyn Blake may prove to be the deadliest and most seductive by far.

Chapter 10

MY CURIOUS EYES work over my current surroundings, documenting the small, uninviting office with hidden interest. With its typically cold, clinical appearance, scuffed and aged painted walls, and faded, generic repo print of Van Gogh's Sunflowers, it's an unambiguous dissimilarity to the man I know.

I continue to observe whilst the clatter of metal drawers opening and closing and glass clinking together resounds in my ears.

I lazily avert my stare and spy the small picture of the good doc and his girlfriend, Sophie Morgan. Their attire confirms this is one of many taken during Sloan and Kara's recent wedding reception. A funny moment spikes, recalling the expression on the photographer's face when he found himself at a loss as to what to do due to the newlyweds doing a *disappearing act*, minutes after walking into the room. Eventually, he resorted to filling his memory cards with pictures of the well-heeled rabble, the hotel guests, and even some of the staff who were told to get merry on free food and booze. I grin in recollection. It was definitely one of the better days and nights I've had where one of my three evils was available in abundance.

Studying the picture, Sophie is her usual glamorous self, polished and coiffured to the nines. In contrast, Doc's tired and overworked appearance was the result of a long, unforgiving shift in an NHS A&E department. Not that it matters to him. The man is nothing if not dedicated to the profession he dreamed of being a part of from a young age.

Born into money with a stiff upper lip and a silver spoon in his mouth – something he never talks about – he could have chosen the easy option without a guilty conscience. He could have worked in the private sector, catering to those with enough money to pay for an operation that they would normally be waiting months for or one they wouldn't usually be eligible for. Instead, he chooses to remain with the NHS. His honest belief that he can help make a difference in a system that is intermittently broken and in need of a radical overall that may never come.

"We'll have the results back in a few days. When were you last tested?" The question slices through my rambling thoughts the same instant a rubber tube flies in front of my face and lands on the desk with a low thud.

I touch it tentatively and sigh as recognition and familiarity comes calling. Back in the day, my tourniquet of choice was always crude, fashioned from whatever I could lay my hands on; string, shoelaces, ripped fabric, belts. Even cling film. Anything that could assist meant anything goes.

"Rem?"

"A year, maybe eighteen months," I reply, distracted. Staring down at the rubber in my hands, it feels like an old friend has come to visit… Or finally, come home.

My muscle memory is shocked back into the past, and I'm consciously mindful these kinds of emotions are exceptionally dangerous. For such a long time, my aversion of talking about that period of my life was fundamental in ensuring I didn't fall off the wagon. If I didn't speak about it, it meant I didn't have time to reminisce on the feeling of euphoria I would perpetually chase. For years, this mentality of intentional ignorance has served me well. But just touching this innocent length of rubber has verified the simplest thing can drag me back into a place and time I feared would eventually kill me.

"Fuck it," I whisper under my breath, grab the tube, and tie it on. With one end between my teeth, I yank the other in my hand. I inhale sharply as the accustomed yet dormant sensation of constriction emanates around my bicep. Thumping the inside of my forearm, from my elbow to my wrist, teasing my veins to come out and play, I look up. "What?" I tilt my brow at Doc's wide-eyed disbelief. "Stuart, I think it's time to acknowledge that I'm more practised in vein detection and needle insertion than you are."

His mouth falls open. "I'm a doctor!" he says with defensive, horrified pride. He sits down, grabs my arm, and removes my perfectly acceptable tourniquet. It triggers a hiss to escape my throat as blood rushes through my limb again. "I'm trained in the professional extraction of bodily fluids, hygiene and care." Punctuating each word firmly, he continues to spear me with his unmistakable, pissed off glare.

I raise my brows and school my expression. "Yes, and I'm a former addict, trained in the art of hitting up every two to three hours at my peak in dirty, unsterile conditions. Trust me, care and hygiene

142

are overrated. Now, chuck that back and allow me to re-demonstrate."

Sadly, Doc doesn't throw it back. Instead, he re-wraps it around my arm and pulls, *hard*. Far harder than I did, that's for sure.

"Jesus Christ!" I flex my muscles insofar as the constriction allows. "Do you treat all your patients this way?"

"Only the ones I like," he replies dryly.

"You know, you may be a doctor, but your bedside manner is severely bleeding lacking, my friend. Even high, I was gentler than you!" I stretch my arm flat over his desk, mildly concerned at the numbness now setting in. "Hurry up. You're cutting off my circulation here!"

"Good!" Stuart cocks a brow. His unimpressed glare slowly transforms into a grin, and he laughs heartily. "Honestly, I'm surprised you even remember half of what you did back then. In my experience, most former addicts claim they don't."

I snort singularly. "Well, I think you'll find a fair few of them are liars. That, or they're too ashamed to. Depends on the individual. Either way, I remember." I turn away as he picks up one of the needles and presses his thumb over my vein. "I remember everything." I clench my fist, feeling my own anger and shame.

The silence and tension swathes around the small office, chilling me to the bone, vanquishing my ability to breathe until Doc knocks my knee with his.

"It wasn't your fault," he murmurs, averting his eyes back to the vial, watching it turn red.

I simultaneously fake a smile and roll my eyes because *it was*. Of course, I don't voice it. Voicing it means there'll be intervention darkening my door in the shape of John Walker and, possibly, Dominic Archer. As much as I love them both, I really don't want either breathing down my neck at the moment.

"I think we'll agree to disagree in that regard."

Without further explanation, Stuart's eyes tilt up, and the sadness consuming them is apparent. It isn't just my life; the trials and tribulations of a former addict, it's what it ultimately culminated in – Emma's premature death and Kara's unpardonable rape. Granted, Doc never knew Emma, but he did witness the aftermath of what Kara went through. He witnessed me at my lowest when I ran from the scene of one of the most despicable, heinous crimes that a man could ever inflict upon a woman. He also witnessed my escape from a seedy existence when I cowardly ran into the night and didn't look back.

Doc's mobile starts to ring, and whereas I glance across the desk, he doesn't even acknowledge it. His focus remains fixed on my arm as he withdraws the needle. My eyes flit back to his phone as it blares again, but a second scratch of a needle reclaims my attention, and I gaze over the top of his dirty blond hair as he extracts more blood.

"How's life with Sophie treating you?" I change the subject to something easy because my former life is a depressing topic of contention I'd rather not pick apart and scrutinise. Instead, I would rather laugh over the reality of his unexpected domestic bliss with Sloan's garrulous, spontaneous PA, whom he is ridiculously in love with.

"Very well, actually," he says, somewhat suspiciously, as he labels up my samples. I don't push it, but I don't need to when he freely elaborates. "She's definitely mellowed in recent weeks. She's no longer on edge... Well, no more so than she normally is. I think having Kara back has played a major part in that. Not to mention, she's constantly dropping hints about marriage now that Sloan's finally got his ring on it."

"Feeling the pressure, Doc?" I ask sarcastically as he reaches for another vial. "Flipping heck, how much are you planning on taking? Be kind and leave me some, yeah?"

Stuart chuckles. A moment later, he slides the needle free, tapes a gauze pad to my skin and finally removes the tourniquet from my arm. "To answer your question, yes and no. Yes, because in reality, Sloan has known Kara for a long time." His eyes meet mine in recognition because haven't we all. "Some marriages don't last half as long as his obsession has. And no, because I do want to get married and have kids."

"With Soph?" The question tumbles from my mouth thoughtlessly. I have no right to ask, but a part of me – the part that is finally ready to settle down - is oddly curious as to what makes *the one*. "Sorry, I-"

"Rem, it's fine, and yes, with Soph. But we haven't been together long, and everything needs to be done in order. I guess I'm a traditionalist and quite old fashioned like that."

"Sloan and J would say you're dragging your feet." I attempt to stifle my yawn, but it's no use, and it just comes out even louder than usual.

Doc pulls an enquiring face. "Sloan and J would railroad a vicar to get their way. Besides, John has no right to talk. If he thinks he wears the trousers in his relationship, he hasn't been paying attention, has he?"

I nod in concurrence as my mouth emits another yawn.

"Did something, *or someone,* keep you awake last night?" Stuart cocks his brow.

I rub the impending tiredness from my eyes. "I was working the late shift, but I'm currently functioning on about three hours sleep since my neighbours decided to have a domestic again this morning and the walls are paper-thin. Seriously, they either need a marriage counsellor or a divorce solicitor."

"Oh," he replies, intrigued but unconvinced. "I just thought *something else* might have been working you late into the night."

I chortle and shake my head. "God, you're all nosy bastards! I'm surprised *you* have time to gossip."

"Very true, I don't…but the missus does." He smirks, thinking he's fooling me, but he really isn't.

I pull a face in pretend disgust. "Isn't your relationship like ships that pass in the night? You spend more time here than you do at home!" I'm goading him, and his easy smile and nonchalant shrug confirm he's unoffended.

"Also very true. Some of us have to cover sickness. Some of us have been on shift for sixteen hours."

"Is that allowed?" The shock in my tone is undisguisable.

He shrugs again. "Does it matter? If I go home, people may die." He rakes his hand through his hair. "It isn't ideal, it isn't perfect, and some days I just want to hide in a dark room and go to sleep, but I knew what I signed up for, Rem. It's hard, but I have to believe I make a difference, otherwise what's the point?" His phone beeps again, and he reaches over the desk and picks it up. He rubs his eyes with his finger and thumb while his subsequent sigh ripples through the small space. Seeing his demeanour change in a split second makes me realise that in reality, considering no one depends on me to save them, my life is easy in comparison.

"Does it ever stop?" I ask, directing my eyes to his phone.

"No. If it isn't texts, it's calls. If it's not calls, it's emails. It never stops because life doesn't stop. Well, it does, eventually, but…" His voice drifts into silence, and he chuckles and grins as he taps away.

"Are you working this afternoon?" he queries, still concentrating on his phone.

"No, I'm off today."

He levels me with a conspiratorial, toothy smile, and I wish I could take back the last few seconds because I now have an inkling that I'm about to be coerced.

"So there's nowhere urgent you need to be?"

I narrow my eyes. "No," I reply shrewdly. He's fishing, and we both know it.

"Excellent!" He haphazardly stuffs his personal effects into his bag. "For once, that wasn't work." He shakes the phone with a gleeful smile. "We've got a lunch date. Foster's buying, and since this-" he thumbs towards himself "-nosy bastard is not only tired, mentally exhausted, hungry, and carless today, you're driving. I'll even buy you a non-alcohol pint as payment."

I sigh unintentionally, but my prediction of being coerced wasn't wrong. If I didn't know any better, I'd say this little set-up was deliberate since I've been avoiding Sloan for days. I've kept a low profile for no other reason than I don't want to discuss Manchester. I don't want to know if he came face to face with either of the Blacks. I just want to forget. I want to forget that house and street exist entirely, along with the memories that thinking about them invokes. I'm also confident that if I asked Kara her true thoughts, she would concur without a second thought.

"I just need to tie up with a colleague and hand over a few things, and then I'm all yours!" Doc winks, seemingly finding a second wind. He slings his bag over his shoulder, slides a chunky wad of medical files under his arm, then darts out of the door towards the nurse's station.

I loiter in the middle of the ward corridor, watching his cheeky interaction and gossiping with the nurses when my mobile chimes. Fishing it from my jacket, I roll my eyes at the typical Foster one-liner.

Told you you can't avoid me forever!

I scoff and type my own typical one-liner retort.

Dickhead!

"Ready?" Doc ambles towards me. He eyes my mobile inquisitively, failing to hide his telling smile. "Evie?"

I throw my hands in the air. "You just couldn't resist, could you?" I pick up my pace and stride towards the lifts, leaving him jogging after me.

"Hell, no! I've got a woman at home thirsty for knowledge, mate. If I tell her I've seen you today and not asked, I'll suffer later."

I huff and jab my finger into the lift button. "So, you want every little detail so that Soph won't withhold sexual favours?"

Stuart cocks his brow. "Rem, as perceptively aforementioned *by you*, I see these walls more than I do the ones in my own home. Trust me, I won't be suffering through lack of sex. I'll be suffering because she'll open her mouth and won't shut up!"

I snigger, recognising his unfortunate predicament as the lift doors close. "You're right - you will be suffering. That mouth of hers takes no prisoners and knows no bounds."

From the corner of my eye, he nods. "You have no idea."

"And you still want to marry her?" I ask comically.

He grins to himself. "Hmm. Her bark really is worse than her bite...but she does have a beautiful mouth." He runs his fingers through his hair and sighs content. "And her tongue can be wicked vicious..."

"Sharing isn't caring, Doc." I rock back on my heels and furrow my forehead at him.

"True." He shrugs. "But you're not a nosy bastard, so I know my confession is safe."

The doors slide open, and I stride out behind him. I shake my head because it's safe to say I'm not going to be able to look at Sophie - or more precisely, her mouth – the same way again and not think it is beautiful or vicious.

Although I'm sure my interpretation will be far less innocent than Doc's is.

THE DISTINCT AND customary aroma of ale seeps into my sinuses, replacing the inimitable, toxic stench of cigarettes from the smoking shelter. I inhale inconspicuously. Two of my three evils smell quite good... Even more so when you deny yourself them.

Stuart's head rises, and he yawns, revealing his now bloodshot eyes. I swear the man is going to fall down if he doesn't sit down. On the way over here, his second wind started to wane. I'm already anticipating having to drive him home, heft his arse into his house and tuck him into bed before the afternoon is through.

Inside the pub, I look around. The lunchtime regulars are taking up every inch of available space as expected. My sight is instantly drawn to the back of the premises, where the rabble are sitting, making more noise than usual.

I gently elbow Doc in the ribs, gaining his attention and simultaneously dragging him back to consciousness. "I'll get you a coffee. Wholemeal ploughman's?" I ask, more out of politeness than inquiry since I already know his preferred sandwich.

"Sure," he replies on a yawn, then leaves me at the bar to order lunch and to get another round in on Sloan's tab.

A few minutes later, with a numbered wooden spoon sticking out of my back pocket, my hands carrying a scalding hot coffee and a very tame lemonade, I inch closer to the table.

Sloan is holding court at one end, his iPad and mobile on either side of him, one beeping, the other ringing. John is sitting opposite, his posture completely contrary to Sloan's, as he crosses one leg over his knee, knocks back a mouthful of his half pint and flicks the page of today's financials. In between them, Tommy and Doc have their backs to me, whereas Simon and Jake are watching my every move.

I place the triple espresso down in front of Doc, and he immediately proceeds to dump three sugars into it.

I clear my throat, and Sloan looks up, his expression sombre and tired. "I see the king is holding court with his courtiers," I comment with a gentry accent.

He sighs with half a grin. "More like the minions and the jester." He glances at Simon, who produces a toothy grin. I smile at him, but his pride is odd in the face of an apparent put-down.

"That's right, boys." Si straightens his collar. "Entertainment value is priceless. You may laugh at me more than you laugh with me, but I know you've always got me."

Murmurs of agreement ripple around the table. I remove the wooden spoon still languishing in my back pocket when a hand on my shoulder startles me. I spin around without hesitation.

Dev steps back and holds his hands up. "It's just me. For crying out loud."

I crane my neck from side to side, scan the pub and then turn to Sloan, who gives me a pointed look, clearly wondering how I'm going to react as to the unknown location of his wife. I twist the spoon in my hand and then point it between Dev's eyes.

"*Where* is your charge?"

"Calm down, she's lunching with Jules and Marie at the hotel and then they're going shopping," he says, as John moves behind him and takes the spoon from me, protecting his nephew.

John settles himself back down and kicks out the chair closest to him. He then focuses on the paper again.

"Really?" I furrow my brow in disbelief. If there is one thing I know about Kara, she hates shopping. When she holed herself in Dom's flat, she bought only the necessities to get by. She didn't march around the shops to get them either.

John chortles, lowering his paper. "Kara will be looking for a way to escape, but Marie tells tales – that woman loves shopping. She just pretends she doesn't because Kara can't abide by it."

"Chicken salad?" the waitress asks, holding two plates.

"That's me," I reply and exchange the plate for the spoon.

"And the Ploughman's?"

Stuart's finger waves to the heavens, and she smiles at him. "Oh, thank you." He says with renewed enthusiasm and grabs the sandwich as soon as the young woman walks away. Upon first bite, his eyes close, and I swear he looks almost orgasmic – not that I'd know what that particular expression looks like on him, but this is what I would imagine. *Unfortunately.*

"Rem, how do you feel about babysitting?"

I lift my eyes to Sloan's, my mouth open, exposing a masticated mouthful. "Come again?" My tone sounds gormless, but that's because it is. What do I know about kids or babysitting? I'm an only child.

"I've been in touch with the local councils regarding loaning out the club for events for the city's children's homes. Music, food, games and dancing. I've even thought about getting in some local artists to teach them painting and arts and crafts type of things."

I raise my right brow slowly, the motion tugging on my scar. I take another bite of my sandwich to stall my cynical tongue.

Simon flat out laughs. "You're kidding, yeah?"

Sloan's unimpressed stare catches mine, and he addresses Si. "No, I'm very serious. I have the money and connections to make a difference in these kids' lives. Returning to Manchester and that house... It made me realise that it's about time I started giving something back."

I catch Sloan's eyes again, and silent pride fills me. My gaze automatically locks on to John's, who is smiling at his pseudo son, and he nods silently. In truth, everyone at this table has learnt a lot about themselves in the last year. And it's all down to one man's love and passion for a girl he could never forget.

"Shit!" Simon's curse destroys the touching moment. "Love and marriage have really done a number on you. This is the reality, gents. You have been warned!" he exclaims with exasperation, earning himself a slap on the back from an amused John.

"Finished?" Sloan glares at him.

"Not quite. Seriously, Foster, are you vying for a knighthood?" Si gives him a concerned look. "Because if you are, you're going about it all wrong. You do know you can just buy one like the rest of the dodgy millionaires do?"

A low whistle ripples around our group. I smirk at Tom, shaking his head due to the absurdity of the conversation. I listen intently as I pop a chip in my mouth. My eyes flick to Stuart, wondering if he's hit the deck yet, but luckily for me, he's still awake – just.

"So, you never answered me. What do you think?" Sloan reaches over and grabs a handful of chips from my plate.

I shrug. "I think it's a great idea. Honestly, if I had something to do when I was a kid, maybe I wouldn't have gone off the rails and got hooked."

The hush over the table is immediate, spreading like wildfire, like a disease, destroying and infecting everything in its wake, tainting all verbal conversion and silent thought.

I subtly grind my teeth, hating their aversion of talking about my past - *our past*, I guess. And maybe that makes me a hypocrite because I also hate talking about it, but eventually, we need to talk about it because it's the only way some of us will ever find closure.

"However, someone else will have to take charge." I reluctantly return Sloan's confused expression. "Police checks, Sloan. I doubt anyone would want a reformed sinner like me supervising and shaping the impressionable minds of vulnerable children."

He shakes his head in dismay. "You don't have a record for anything, Rem. There's nothing documented about your past," he states, very matter of fact, as my phone beeps.

"No..." I begin, distracted by the text from Evie. "But *I* know. Would you trust me with your future offspring?"

"Yes, because I trust you with everything, including my life and my wife's," he replies, giving me the greatest endorsement anyone ever could.

I study him, unable to form words at the ultimate validation he has just bestowed. Instead, I pick up my pint of lemonade and drain half the glass as my phone beeps again. I swipe my finger across the screen and baulk as I read the simple requests that are akin to what could be my premature death.

A drawn-out yawn emanates, and I glance at Doc, who is rubbing his eyes but has now perked up again, giving me a wicked smile. "Evie?"

"Oh, for Pete's sake! I'm never going to hear the end of this, am I?" I shake my head. "Don't you guys have anything better to do than stick your noses in my business?"

"No!" the collective male chorus sings in unison, followed by chortles and laughs and clinking of glasses.

"Fuck my life! While you're all so bent out of shape about my love life, you need to ask the fantastic Mr Fox over there what he's doing with your hotel receptionist." I point to Sloan, who's still smiling, until my words register.

"Wait! What? What are you doing with Laura?" His head whips around to Tom, who smirks.

"Why? Don't like being outfoxed? Get it? *Outfoxed?*"

"Unfortunately," Sloan deadpans in response, his hand now covering his face in dismay. "However, spill, now!"

Tommy shakes his head in bewilderment. "Sloan, she's your employee, not your little sister. I don't have to *spill* anything. Besides, you of all people should know that a gentleman never tells!"

Sloan's mouth drops open, his expression aghast. I scoff and clear my throat.

"I think we established just a few weeks ago that you, ginger, are no gentleman!" I say in my best, or possibly worst, scouse accent, channelling Kieran's statement from the club not so long back.

Tommy slaps his hand on the table and hoots. "And you, Jeremy James, are also no gentleman. You're just a scally with nine lives!" he counters, also in his best scouse.

I murmur in amusement. He has a point. "Hmm, but I think I might be down to five or six by now." My mobile illuminates again, and I rub my chin in contemplation.

"Text tennis or avoidance?" John asks, leaning into me.

I grimace. "Maybe a bit of both."

"Trouble in paradise?"

"What's up, Rem?" Jake finally comes out of his quiet, contemplative state. I pull a face, and the tendons in my neck stretch in protest while my cheek begins to itch. I frown, but I do nothing to hide it because this is monumental and not something I expected to have to indulge in this soon.

"Rem?" Jake presses.

"I've been invited to dinner at the Blakes'." Silence blankets the table yet again.

"When?" John's tone obliterates the quiet.

I exhale slowly. "Tonight. Shit," I whisper because things are turning serious. After only a few weeks together, this feels too soon. I look up to find everyone giving me a variety of questionable expressions.

"She doesn't believe in taking her time, does she?" Si states, and I shake my head.

"You're serious? You're going to break bread with the enemy?" Devlin asks, spreading some light, but yes, yes, I really am. "That's sacrilege!"

My worry wanes a little, and I chuckle, but I know the Foster/Walker opinions on Andrew Blake. He's *interesting* to them, but to me, the man is just plain dangerous.

"You sound sanctimonious, D," I retort and finish off my pop.

He scoffs. "And you're a glutton for punishment!"

My head concurs while swallowing the fizz in my throat. "I think you may be right. Either way, I will be breaking bread with Andy Blake tonight. Hopefully, if all goes well, it won't result in broken bones."

"It will if you do anything to offend his wife's father," John says.

"Why? Who's her dad?" I ask as a gentle yawn resounds next to me.

John leans forward and winks. "He's very *interesting*, but I'll tell you later. I think you might have your hands full today." He tips his head towards Stuart, whose head has just lolled against my shoulder.

"For crying out loud! I knew I'd end up hefting his arse home," I grouse. "Anyone want to help here?" I ask, and they all look down. Bastards. "Fine, but the next time one of you needs favour…" I fix my eyes on Sloan, who has requested my services this lunchtime. "The answer will be no."

Sloan flips his devices over on the table. "Fine." He moves around and grabs Stuart under one arm while I take the other.

"Christ," Sloan mutters as we stumble through the beer garden with the tired, exhausted doc. The other pub patrons watching probably think he's drunk. "What do they feed them in that hospital canteen?"

"Steroids!" Our sniggers are full blow chortles by the time we reach my car.

"Are you going to be okay getting him into his house?"

"Sure. I'll dump him on the sofa and wake him up a bit."

"Okay." He slaps my shoulder. "And what J said? We do need to discuss it with you later."

"Why not now?" I query, opening my door.

"Because we are not our family. Remember that. I'll see you."

"Yeah." I watch him return to the rabble. I climb inside my car and turn the ignition, wondering what his parting shot is supposed to mean. After all, no one can be worse than Andrew Blake.

Can they?

Chapter 11

THE SMOOTH, COMFORTING drone of the engine rumbles beneath me before I turn off the ignition and remove the key.

I slacken the tie around my neck, the invisible constriction making it hard to breathe. Tonight, I'm dressed to impress in the only decent suit I possess. It's one that makes an appearance at events, dinners, weddings, and funerals. It's also safe to say that if the Blacks or Edward Shaw get their way, I may even be buried in it one day. I roll my shoulders in consternation. Even thinking about either of those scenarios is too close for comfort.

I admit I don't particularly like donning the penguin suit, but this is for Evie. Financially, I may not be able to give her everything another man could, but what I will not do is humiliate her by wearing jeans and a t-shirt to meet her parents. Dressing respectably is a small price to pay for a little reciprocity and acceptance.

I climb out of the car and adjust my jacket. I'm sweating like a pig on its way to the butchers. It's not lost on me that that might be more metaphorically correct than I'm currently aware, especially if I rub Andrew Blake the wrong way. It's also not lost on me that I probably already have.

Pushing the dismal thought aside, I tug my sleeves, straighten my jacket, and press my shoulders back. With my head high, I stride confidently towards the large gates that conceal the Blake residence from the rest of the world. I lift my finger to the intercom button, but the creak of metal and wood resonates, and they begin to separate.

I tentatively move forward before I see Evie at the front door. She runs towards me barefoot, with a huge, illuminating smile on her face. I'm utterly mesmerised, unable to turn away, as her black, sleeveless, V-neck dress moves at her ribs while the calf-length skirt billows around her legs. She looks beautiful and classy, and once again, I wonder what I've done to deserve her.

With only a few feet separating us, she throws herself at me in a full body slam, and I catch her effortlessly. "I've missed you!" She coils herself around me, her limbs clinging to me like an exotic vine. Her scent, mixed with a delicate floral fragrance, infuses my nostrils, dosing me with a natural high.

"I can tell," I reply coolly, stealing a polite kiss. I chuckle against her mouth when she presses her lips to mine. My good intentions of making an impression will be wasted if Andrew Blake walks out here and sees us like this.

"Evie," I mumble. "I dressed in my best, but this behaviour will ensure your parents will see me at my worst." I slide my hand across her cheek, adoring the way they are flushed with a healthy, pink tint, not to mention the utterly naïve way she's pouting, trying to come across as innocent.

With a sultry smirk, she slowly slides down my front and steps back. Observing my appearance thoughtfully, she presses her palms to my chest, intentionally thumbing my nipples through two layers of material.

"You look great."

I sigh content, but that doesn't tell me anything of relevance. "Am I overdressed?"

"No, but I do like a sexy man in a suit. Trust me, you exude it like no one else I've ever met." She presses up on her toes again and places a single kiss on my temple.

My smile is undisguisable, and I enfold her arm in mine. I stroke the back of her hand continually as we walk up the garden path and into the house. She closes the door behind us, the echo drifting over the vast, open hallway, while I subtly check out my new, unfamiliar surroundings, the same way I always do.

"Come on, Mum's dying to meet you!" She tugs me down the hallway and veers us into a room where a woman – her mother, presumably – is on the phone with her back to us.

"I'll call you back, darling. Our guest has arrived." She pauses, listening. "No, he's Evie's new boyfriend! I've been bending her ear to meet him for weeks, and she's finally relented, but you know what she's like! Anyway, ciao until tomorrow!"

I cast a fleeting sideways glance at Evie, whose blush is unmistakable. Finally, after all the bluster of ending the call, Mrs Blake spins around, and it's clear my presence is a revelation. Seeing the man who has caught her daughter's undeniable attention, Mrs Blake's smile slowly vanishes as she scrutinises me from the feet up. Her expression disintegrates further with each inch until she appears positively horrified upon witnessing the state of my face. Maybe she wishes she hadn't bent her daughter's ear so much to finally meet me, after all.

"Mum, this is Jeremy," Evie announces, loud and cheery, lifting the sombre mood that has blanketed the room. I glance down at our linked hands and smile at her ignorant bliss of the current situation and thick atmosphere.

"It's lovely to meet you, Mrs Blake." I break the ice first since she is apparently speechless.

Mrs Blake's eyes lift, exposing an unexpected coldness lingering inside them. She smiles, equally cold, and reluctantly holds out her hand. "And you, Mr James. Evelyn hasn't talked about anyone or anything else for weeks," she says with a grudging tone.

"Mum, stop talking!" Evie admonishes, mortified. I stroke my thumb across the top of her hand again to comfort her. "Sorry, she wasn't supposed to divulge that." I grin, loving that she's extremely embarrassed, and I decide to score some brownie points.

"She's your mum. She's allowed to say whatever she likes." Evie makes a tutting sound while I catch the slight approving lip curve of her mum. I clench her fingers, and she reciprocates as a door opens and closes somewhere in the house, and footsteps echo in the hallway.

As each step resonates closer, Evie's conduct and disposition alter from frisky and flexible to serious and stiff. I inconspicuously grind my jaw, but all this does is tell me Daddy's home.

I risk a look at Mrs Blake, who is compressing her lips, looking intermittently between her daughter and the door. Sadly, her expression isn't a conciliatory one; it's one of anticipation, wickedly awaiting the outcome of her husband's reaction to the less than desirable man in her kitchen.

"Cathy?" The recognisable, exacting tone of Andrew Blake enters the room a few seconds before the man himself does. His purposeful stride fails him the moment we make eye contact, and I tip my head by way of greeting.

"Good evening, Mr Blake," I formally address him since we are very much aware of each other by now.

"Hi, Dad." Evie kisses his cheek. "You remember Jeremy?"

Andy moves around the central island in the kitchen and pours himself a large glass of red wine from the bottle proffered by his wife. He brings the glass to his lips, takes a sip, and kisses her. Placing the glass down, he levels his gaze on me again. His hands fidget, and he, rather subconsciously, twists the ring on his finger.

"Why, yes, of course. We met at the event. How have you been, Jack?"

I bristle uncomfortably, already pre-empting the way this evening is going to play out. "I'm very well, sir, but my name is Jeremy."

Andy runs his hand through his hair, flicks his brows and smirks. "Sorry, my mistake… Josh."

I chortle in disgust, making no attempt to hide it as Evie steps in front of me and slaps both fisted hands down on the marble top. "Dad, his name is Jeremy! Je-re-my!" she emphasises, furious. "Stop being so rude. Your ploy won't work." She then reclaims her place by my side and links our fingers, making a show of the action by raising them to her chest. I want to ask what she meant by ploy, but at the same time, I want to punch the air and beat my chest to show my dominance, and the fact his daughter has atypically – for him – pledged her allegiance and taken him down a peg or two.

Andy breathes heavily through his nose, then downs the rest of the wine. He slams the glass down on the worktop and levels me with a glare. Honestly, every time I've met him, he tends to wear the same expression - antagonistic, unimpressed, reviled, and disgusted. As ever, a single, vicious look from him should shrivel my testicles to peanuts and bring about immediate, acute impotency. But it doesn't because he's just a rich man playing hard arse.

The atmosphere thickens once more, and I watch as he pours himself another drink, plus a secondary glass. He approaches, offering me the olive branch of a seriously expensive glass of red.

"Please accept my apologies, *Jeremy*. Let us toast the start of this *fledgling* relationship," he says sarcastically. I take the glass, but I don't think twice before I set it down and push it away. Andy's eyes crinkle knowingly, and he gives a slight 'I told you so' look to his wife.

"You don't like red, *Jeremy*?"

"No, I-"

"We've got white, champagne, cava, or spirits, if you prefer."

I wave my hand, feeling a little cornered. "Sorry, no, I'm driving," I say, using the easy but honest option.

Mrs Blake gasps and lets out a small laugh. "My goodness, a small glass socially is perfectly acceptable. Plus, the delicious meal our chef prepared will assist in lining your stomach. I do it all the time." I give her an incredulous look that confirms I'm not surprised to hear that at all.

"I'm sorry, Mrs Blake, but I'm-"

"For God's sake, will you both just stop! Please?" Evie pleads. Her tone breaks my heart as she raises her white flag in my invisible corner in a show of solidarity of what we're trying to build together, clearly against the odds. "He's already told you; he's driving. Besides, he doesn't really drink." Upon hearing that, two unwanted sets of eyes focus on me.

I set my jaw and square off my shoulders, now thoroughly pissed off. I'm not pissed off at Evie. I'm pissed off at Andy fucking Blake's attempt to show me in a bad light. Granted, the blinding innocent glow that's been shining on me for years will eventually fade, but until then, I'd rather enjoy what this incredible young woman is going to bestow upon me. And when the time comes, and that penetrable darkness possibly consumes me again, I'll get down on my hands and knees and beg for forgiveness.

"Do you want him intoxicated, three sheets to the wind, driving me home tonight?"

I give Evie a double glance and desperately try to hide my triumphant smile.

"Sorry, what do you mean? This is your home," her mother counters with a reproachful and now slightly slurred tone.

Evie shakes her head. Her incensed exhale is indicative she's now as annoyed as I am and low on patience. "Mum, you know what I mean! I already told you I was planning on staying with Jeremy tonight. Now can we please sit down to eat since Dad's finally here? We wouldn't want our chef's expensive creation to spoil now, would we?"

I want to divert my eyes, but I give the Blakes' an apologetic smile as Evie leads me by the hand through the house. "I would give you the tour, but…" She lets out a redundant huff and shakes her head. "I'm sorry if they humiliated you. They shouldn't have treated you like that." She slouches back against the wall, utterly defeated.

I move closer and practically pin her against it. I grip the sides of her face and smooth my thumbs over her cheeks. Her hands grip my hips, and she moans in approval. "I know they don't really like me." She starts to shake her head and her lips part. I press a thumb over them to quell whatever lie she's going to protect them with. They're her parents, after all. "It's okay. They don't know me yet." I add quickly because one day, she may find herself having to choose a side. It wouldn't be of my making; it would be theirs, or more specifically, her father's. "Let's give it a few months. I'm sure it will get better." I feed her yet another lie because I know it won't.

"Okay." She reaches up and kisses me, deepening it with each movement of her lips. I push her back, and she pouts.

"I'm sure whatever naughty ideas you have running around your head can wait for a few hours."

She tuts again, still pouting. "True, but what if *I* can't?"

Yet again, I have to wonder what I've done to deserve this woman. I hesitate in response, but I need to suggest something, or dinner will be a long, uncomfortable affair. More so than it already is.

"How about a short tour of the house?"

Evie's eyes twinkle. "Short, as in my bedroom?" My mouth drops open, but the sexual tension between us is vanquished.

"Evie, we're ready for dinner!"

"Saved by mother," I murmur.

Evie smirks, and sadly, I now realise that's something she has inherited from her dad. "Lucky for you. But lucky for me, nothing will save you tonight." She begins to turn away, but I grab her arm and haul her back. Smashing my mouth over hers, she runs her hand down my arse, squeezing, inciting my body to respond.

"I'm already beyond saving, sweetheart, but tonight, I want to worship every inch of you. I want to lick every crevice and curve. I want to hear you call my name in a variety of tones I've already heard. I want to fuck you until you beg me to stop. Then after, I'm going to make love to you until we both pass out."

Evie straightens up and puts on a serious face. She smooths my hair and fastens my jacket, hiding my partial erection. Grabbing my hand, she leads me towards the dining room. "One hour, eat quick, ignore all conversation. The sooner we're finished here, the sooner I can get you under me."

I pull her to a stop. "Two hours, savour dinner, indulge in a little conversation. Then I can savour and indulge while *you* are under *me!*"

"Very presumptuous! But we'll see, won't we?"

"Oh, we certainly shall!"

"DINNER WAS FABULOUS. Thank you, Mrs Blake." I take a sip of water as Evie's leg kicks mine under the table again.

Three hours on from my initial, unwarranted treatment at the hands of the Blakes', dinner has actually been quite pleasant. Mrs

Blake has been attentive and made easy, if not slightly, drunken conversation. Andy, however, has just acted like an unassuming arsehole. Each word that has passed through his lips has been laced with deceit and innuendo. Evie, on the other hand, has grown more agitated as the evening has gone on. Needless to say, it's clear she's desperate to get out of here and enact her request of getting me under her.

"Thank you, Jeremy, but unfortunately, I can't take the credit. Oh, and please, it's Cathy," she says. "Would you like another drink? A coffee, maybe?"

"Actually, Mum, it's getting quite late, and Jeremy's working an early shift tomorrow." Evie lies – far too proficiently, I note. I rise the same moment she does, and her parents follow suit. Imparting further lies to gain our emancipation, she rushes out of the room with her mum to collect her bag from upstairs, leaving me with Andy for the first time this evening.

"I'll wait by the door for Evie but thank you for your hospitality tonight." I hold out my hand, which he refuses to take. I leave the room because what's the point in trying anymore. I rock back and forth on my heels and affix my eyes on the staircase. I silently groan as Andy swaggers towards me from the kitchen, another glass of wine in one hand, the other in his pocket. As we face off, time feels relative. A few seconds feels like a few hours until he takes a large mouthful, quite possibly his fifth or sixth glass tonight, and opens and closes his mouth.

"There's clearly something on your mind. I'm thick-skinned. I'm sure I can take it."

He chuckles darkly. "Oh, I'm sure someone like you can. You know, *Jamie*, I'm a tolerant man. I can tolerable the intolerable," he says, repeating a phrase that Sloan has used over the years. "But I would make the most of it while you can because it won't last."

I narrow my eyes and crease my brow. "I beg your pardon?"

He shakes his head, pointing his glass at me. "In time, hopefully, sooner rather than later, she'll see you for what you really are."

I grind my jaws. "And what, *exactly*, am I?" But I know exactly what I am, as does he, apparently. He knows I'm a former addict, and more fool him if he doesn't. Although if he does indeed know, he evidently hasn't informed Evie.

"Don't make me spell it out, *Jack!*"

"Spell what out, *Andrew?*"

He steps forward, a malicious darkness in his eyes. "You act big and tough with Foster and Walker behind you, but I wonder how you acted when-"

"Sorry I took so long," Evie says, running down the stairs, making a perfectly timed appearance. I take the holdall from her hands and slide her close.

"It's okay, sweetheart. Your dad and I were just talking sports."

"Urgh, let's get out of here! Goodnight, Dad." She doesn't kiss him goodnight and instead drags me out of the house. I open the passenger door and wave my hand. Her eyes linger over a tiny Fiat parked on the drive, then she slides inside. I fold myself into the passenger side, noting her attention is still on the tiny toy of a car.

Thirty minutes later, I reverse into my assigned space and cut the engine. Evie looks from left to right, and I wonder what she's thinking since she's been down here plenty of times before.

"Is this the only parking space you have?"

"No, I've got two." I thumb to the one on my left. "It only gets used if someone visits. Why?" I think I know why, but I still want to hear it.

"I love to drive, but I don't get to drive a lot since parking is really expensive. Then there's the congestion zone charge. Well, I just thought that sometimes I could drive myself over, and if I decided to stay when you were at work..." She shrugs, and I tip her chin.

"I'd love to come home and find you waiting for me. I'll get a permit sorted and a key cut for you. Now, we need to get inside because you've made me horny as fuck, and I want to worship you until the sun comes up since I'm not working, you little liar. However, you threw down a challenge that I would be under you, and as much I as I want to feel you beneath me, I really want to watch you ride me."

I climb out, slam the door, and jog around the bonnet as Evie hefts her bag out. I take it from her, click the car remote, and throw my arm around her shoulder. The sexual tension inside the lift is palpable. I pass her the key outside the flat door, and she unlocks it and steps inside.

The moment I cross the threshold, her eager mouth is on mine. In between our combined moans and gasps, I quickly rid myself of my jacket, and she unbuttons my shirt. Pulling it from my trousers, she flicks open my belt and trouser fastener and gives me a hesitant, innocent look. With one hand on the back of her head, I move my other to cover hers and guide them to my rock-hard shaft. I encourage her to rub me over my boxers before her inquisitive fingers slip beneath my waistband, and she begins to stroke me.

"Fuck, sweetheart!" I groan. Grabbing hold of her hips, I lift her up around mine. Pure, crazy lust takes over, and I adjust my hands until one hand slides under her tiny shorts and finds her opening. I plunge my fingers in and out while my thumb massages her. She's hot and wet, and I can't wait to lay her down, spread her out and slide inside.

"Oh, God!" she gasps, pure ecstasy spreading over her face. She fusses with her dress and pulls one side down to expose her beautiful tit. She rolls her nipple between her fingers, and it hardens perfectly. I lean forward and give it a long lick, loving the way her head lulls back and her core tenses around my fingers. My eager mouth can't get enough, and I take it whole and suck. She squirms, whimpering, tensing, pushing forward, pulling back. Shit, she's close.

"Evie…"

"Oh, God. It hurts so good. I ache so bad…I need it so much. I need to-to… Oh, God! Please!"

I slowly stop sucking and meet her gaze, unable to comprehend her gasping, illogical rambling. Her eyes are glazed, and I love the way she looks pre-orgasm. Her hands reach down, and she starts to push down my boxers.

"I need you inside me. Please, Jeremy," she begs, and I quickly move her, pull down her boy shorts and then mine. I step back a little, and she slouches her shoulders on the wall as I gather her dress between us. My eyes cross as I position myself at her opening and stare into her eyes. "Please, I'm aching for you!"

Her legs tighten around my hips, and I enter her in a forceful thrust. "Fuck!" I hiss as her tight, hot walls welcome me, surrounding me with heat, inducing me to lose all control in her embrace.

Evie sighs, and the sound of relief is so loud in my ears. My body is on fire, ready to explode for this woman. I lift her higher and plunge in and out, finding a comfortable rhythm. My mouth claims her nipple again, and I stare into her stunning eyes. Her hands find my face, and she brazenly strokes my scar as I continue to thrust. I watch with determination as she finally reaches her peak and her mouth parts, and she licks her lips, then cries out her release.

"Jeremy!" she breathes heavily and presses her thumb to my mouth. I taste the pad then suck it between my lips. "Come inside me." I internally groan. We haven't used a condom, and I honestly couldn't pull out now even if I wanted to. This is the first time we haven't used protection, and it's absolutely amazing.

Evie's chest thrusts up, causing her tits to bounce and a pink tip to catch the light. My fingers dig into her hips as the explosion in my gut takes place, and the release I'm desperate for finally arrives. I groan, the sound echoing throughout the small hallway as I continue to rotate my hips. Evie looks positively euphoric while rapture rushes through me.

Eventually, my hips slow and Evie's tensing stops. I lift my head, and she presses hers back and laughs. I bury my face in her neck and lick the soft column of skin. I hold her securely and tap in the alarm code. I awkwardly walk the few steps to the bedroom and lay her on the bed. She gently massages my semi-hard shaft, and it reacts eagerly. I'm not ashamed to say my dick is a slut and will probably never refuse. However, my body has survived years of substance abuse, and some days, I feel far older than my years.

"Let's get you cleaned up, sweetheart. It's late, and I'm tired and-"

Evie's finger shuts me up, and she cranes her neck and kisses me. "Shush, if you're tired, you can just lay there, and I'll do all the work. I'll ride you into insanity until you're mindless and enraptured. I promised that you would be under me, and you should know I *always* keep my promises."

My eyes roll in blissful anticipation as she pushes me onto my back and swings her leg astride me. I feel almost out of control as she slides her sinfully sexy body down my front and lowers herself onto my excited, straining length. Her hips rock with amazing precision as I penetrate deep inside her.

As she continues to ride me, I dare to close my eyes. After everything that's happened in my past, I pray I can finally believe in promises.

Especially hers.

Chapter 12

MY FEET SLAP on the wood as I pace up and down the length of the balcony. I grin at my phone, unsure how to respond to Evie's text of *I have a surprise for you x*, since I'm still raw all these years later from the last woman who made me similar promises. Although, I'm positive Evie's recent confession of always keeping her promises will prove more robust and reliable than Emma's ever did.

Pocketing my mobile, I lean against the railing, coffee in one hand, cig in the other. Inhaling another lungful of poison, I concede it's easier to reflect in retrospect. It's easy to look back with the beauty of hindsight and knowledge. What isn't easy, however, is forgetting. Or failing to see the signs that I, of all people, should have picked up on sooner than I did.

The mid-morning hustle and bustle of the city in the distance and the sporadic sirens disturb the calm, transporting me back to a time more turbulent and uncertain.

I HAVE A surprise waiting for you!!!

I cast my eye around my current place of business - loitering on a corner, which gives me a perfect line of sight to leg it if I see the police sniffing around – and wonder if I should cut out early to find out what Em's surprise is.

As I quickly tap out my reply, a fight between two drunks breaks out across the street. I glance left to right because if the two dickheads continue, they may not be the only ones getting arrested tonight. They will draw attention to not only me but also those touting illegal tickets and other random shit being sold. Securing my hand over my bag of tricks, I scroll through my phone log and press Deacon's name. Waiting for him to pick up, the two-man punch up has now grown into a ten-man brawl.

"Hey, what's up?" he finally answers.

"A fight just broke out. I'm on my way back," I tell him as sirens approach in the distance.

"Sensible, and your girl's here again."

Again? "What?" I ask because I've told her not to come around when I'm not there.

Deacon grunts. "Yeah, complaining about uni as usual. I gave her a little something to shut her up."

I narrow my eyes as I pick up my pace, but really, I just want to stop and question him. "What kind of little something?" I query.

"Don't worry, just a bit of weed, nothing hard. I'll see you soon!" he says ecstatically before hanging up.

I stare at the phone, disbelieving what's just happened. Since her first meeting with Deacon and his less than subtle insinuations, there's a reason I've kept her away if I'm not there, and this is why. I knew if she was alone and vulnerable, it wouldn't be long before he plied her with booze and drugs, starting her off easy before seducing her with the harder stuff. I've seen it before, and I guess you could say I'm one of his perfect products. I hope he isn't lying about just giving her some weed. She's too good for this life, and I never wanted her to get involved with me in the first place, and definitely not like this now. I would be devastated if anything happened to her due to my lifestyle.

I walk faster and arrive home in the record time of twenty minutes. Closing the garden gate, two of Deek's more colourful acquaintances are dallying by the front door. "Hey," one greets, and I wave him off because I'm shit with names, more so now than ever.

I cautiously enter the house, wary about what I may find. The music coming from the living room is loud, and I'm surprised he manages to throw these impromptu parties and not have the police shut them down. It just further validates my belief that he has the neighbours in his pockets, probably slipping them a hit or two to keep them quiet.

I jog upstairs to my bedroom and hide the bag in the back of the wardrobe and toss a load of dirty washing over it. Closing the door, I pivot around, noting for the first time the empty room. Although why I thought Em would be up here waiting for me with a party in full swing downstairs is a stupid idea, especially if Deacon is passing out free gear. I slouch back against the wardrobe door, recalling the time I was in the same position, and he offered me an escapism when I was around twelve or thirteen.

I gradually forget the mistimed memory and rub my eyes with my finger and thumb, wondering how I'm going to stop this wheel from turning.

I push off the wardrobe and venture back downstairs. I reluctantly enter the living room to find Deek sitting on the sofa arm. Em is next to him, hanging on his every word. I observe them as she lifts the spliff to her lips, and I ponder what number it is. It's clear it isn't little something number one. I should know.

"This is my personal Jesus." Deacon holds up a syringe, singing along to the song in the background. "I've told you before; it could be yours too. It'll take off the edge, ease your pain, make you feel invincible." He touches her leg, and I see red.

"Em?" I call forcefully and glare at the deceitful bastard.

"Jer!" Em scrambles up from the sofa, forgetting all about Deacon, much to his visible anger, and she wraps herself around me. With her hands manipulating my face, she proceeds to claim kisses in her giggly, high mess. "I missed you!"

"I missed you too, darling," I reply, hating the fact she's in this state. In normal circumstances, she would never allow herself to be so unimpeded in company she doesn't know.

"And we know that you missed me!" Deacon stands with his arms outstretched, ensuring all eyes are on him. He acts like the big man, thinking these people are his friends who respect him, but in truth, they aren't, and some can barely tolerate him, let alone respect him. He flings his arms around both of us, and Em giggles again, gracefully accepting the new roll-up he's just magically retrieved from his pocket.

"Share?" She smiles at me, wiggling the joint in her hand.

I wink for good effect. "Sure, but let me get a drink first. Want one?"

"I'll have a rum and Coke!" I press my lips to her forehead and carefully sit her back on the sofa.

I pad out of the room and into the kitchen. Again, more people occupy the space, and the thick cloud of nicotine sits on the atmosphere, making it hard to breathe. Grabbing a can of Coke from the fridge, I open the back door and slam it behind me.

I light up a cig and pace the weed riddled patio. I stare at the overgrown grass, failing to collect my volatile thoughts. Each one is more damaging than the last, but the crux of my issues is that I'm tired. I'm tired of this. I'm tired of pretending to be sociable. Tired of agreeing with everything Deacon says to keep the peace. Tired of being worried about getting banged up. And I'm really fucking tired of sitting around and getting high. But at the top of my non-exhaustive list is that I'm finally tired of being tired.

Knocking back the Coke and taking a last drag on the cig, I toss the can in the bin and stomp the cig out. Back inside, I carry Em's drink in one hand and a couple of bottles of water in the other. I enter the living room, but she's nowhere in sight.

"She's gone upstairs. Have a good night," Deek says, full of unknown insinuation, studying a syringe with a smug expression I can't pinpoint.

I close the living room door and head up the stairs. Thankfully, it's far less crowded up here, just a few people sitting on the stairs chatting. I tentatively open my door and breathe a silent sigh of relief at the sight of Em draped across the bed in just her underwear. Her head lifts as I place down the can and bottles, and she bestows me a sultry smile.

"Lock the door," she orders and clambers to her knees. There's something different about her, but I do as the lady requests and then turn around. She is now in front of me, and without warning, she begins to unbutton my shirt. "God, I'm so hot." She fans herself as she drops to her knees, peering up at me. Wordlessly, she unfastens my jeans and pushes them down enough until my dick springs free.

I gasp the moment she wraps her hand around me and moves roughly up and down my length. "Easy, slower," I request, and she pouts. "Gently," I murmur. I study her, still trying to decipher the sudden change, but all thought and worry are obliterated as her warm, wet mouth cocoons me.

"Oh shit!" I exclaim and let the door support me as she leads me into madness. I automatically cradle her head, slowly guiding her. Her hands grab my arse, and she lightly scrapes her teeth over me. "Fuck!" I hiss, becoming mindless as she continues to bring me closer to the edge. "Baby, I'm going to come," I warn her. Moments later, with her hot, sinful mouth still surrounding me, I finally release. My groans and grunts fill the room, and I watch her slowly withdraw and swipe her tongue over my head.

I lift her up, and she bites her lip. "I'm so horny. God, I want you!" She starts to tear at my clothing until my shirt is on the floor and I'm walking out of my jeans and boxers. I paw at her bra strap until that is gone, leaving her in her knickers. Em wraps herself around me, and I support under her bum as I move us to the bed.

"Baby, this is going to be so, so amazing! A new experience," she says, and my forehead furrows in query, but she kisses away my latent fears. My calves touch the mattress, and I lay her down. I hook my fingers on her underwear hem and deftly remove them before I stand.

I grin when she shuffles up and then crosses one leg over the other, but it's the sexist thing I've ever seen. I bend back down and grab her ankles. I climb in between them and slowly kiss up her thighs, alternating my attention.

"Jer, more!" she moans and shifts her legs. I reach up and circle her centre, loving how she writhes under me. I continue to press my lips to her soft thighs and squint when I note a small, red mark near her apex. I rub my finger over it but am distracted by her hand lowering. I hold it back, determined to have her come in my mouth before she assists with the endeavour. I tentatively lick, getting her used to me being down here before I lightly suck her clit. Her rapturous moans ring louder, and her body moves in time with my ministration, chasing more.

"Inside me," she begs as my tongue breaches her opening. Circling it inside, her feet glide the length of my back, and she cries out

I smirk against her, proud of my achievement, even more so when I'm sober enough to witness it, and I glide up her front. Kissing her taut, beautiful nipples, I stroke my dick and position him at her entrance. Eager focus to sultry gaze, she nods and closes her eyes as I slide inside.

"That's the best feeling in the world. The way you complete me." Her arms move above her head, and it suddenly seems as though she far away, but just as quickly, she's back again.

I carefully thrust, giving her time to acclimatise, before I go hard because between needing a drink, the need to get high, and the fact she's just had her mouth on me, I'm ready to explode.

My hips piston, surging in and out, and I kiss her and stroke her temples. "Okay?" I ask because she's slightly inebriated and more unrestrained than ever, and in the last few months, there's no way she would have sex while there was anyone other than Deek under the roof.

"Fantastic!" She grips my shoulders.

My long, resolute thrusts build in succession until my body begs for release again. Em manipulates and rolls me over. I gaze at her in all her wild beauty as she takes charge and works herself on me. Her head is thrown back, and I grip her hips as she pulsates on my shaft.

"Come for me, Jer!" she commands, and it feels like the catalyst to induce my body to give in. Mere seconds pass until my balls throb and finally release. I roar out, and she moves her hips harder, bringing me to completion.

Em's cries combine with mine, and it's beautiful. Eventually, spent and tired, she lowers herself down my front, her warm, perspired skin covering mine.

Time passes until I'm flaccid, and she's practically asleep. "Let's get you cleaned up." She grumbles as I attempt to remove the duvet while she simultaneously tucks herself back in. Her eyes flutter open, and I kiss her forehead and place my hand over her heart. "Go back to sleep, sweetheart. I'll sort you out."

"Hmm." She shifts closer. "I feel so mellow and nice. I love you, Jeremy."

I smile, although I know I shouldn't. She doesn't need further encouragement to smoke weed with Deek when I'm not here. "That's the cannabis talking."

"Hmm," she murmurs again, totally blissful. "And then some." Her wayward hand drifts, and I halt that endeavour.

"Sweetheart, will you do something for me?"

"Yeah."

"I don't want you alone with Deacon."

"Why? He's fun," she replies sleepily. I grimace in the darkness because she wouldn't be saying that if she knew the real him. The true bastard him.

"Just promise me that you'll be careful. He's not a fun, nice guy at times.

"Okay," she whispers while moving to get comfortable.

"And I want you to promise me that you won't take anything harder than a bit of spliff."

"Ah-ah," she replies more drowsily than before. I swear if I didn't know her any better, I'd claim she was coming down from something.

I stare at the far wall, listening while her breathing slows and a soft snore emanates. My mobile vibrates from my jeans, and I stealthily slide out of bed to retrieve it. I flick the screen, and the vibrating starts again, confirming it's Em's. Dropping my phone onto the chest of drawers, I grab her bag and sit it on the windowsill. I dig around inside in a bid to stop the constant vibrating until my finger touches upon something very familiar. I reach in, and my stomach metaphorically drops in horror. I don't need to see it to know what it is.

I lift the syringe out of her bag and hold it up to the streetlight filtering into the room. I cross back to the bed and pick up my phone. Adjusting the duvet, I expose Em's leg and turn on the phone torch and guide it up her limb. There at the very top is the offending mark. It all makes sense. Em's secret visits here, her friendliness with Deek, the way he was studying the syringe earlier... There are probably a hundred other things I could put my finger on if I thought hard enough about it, but right now, all I can think about is her betrayal and his assistance.

Anger builds inside me, and I stride out of the bedroom into the bathroom. Pulling on the cord, the light blinds and sobers me instantly. I glare at the full syringe – Deek's preferred 'gift' for the weak and unsuspecting – and wonder how much she has injected over the course of today, or even over the course of her visits, wondering if this is the first time and if she allowed Deek to do it or if he instructed her to... God, the more I think about it, the more worked up I feel. Taking a breath, I glare at the syringe and squeeze it in my hand.

"Emma!" I scream at my reflection, guilt already consuming me that the cycle is continuing. "Why? Why? You promised!"

I OPEN MY eyes and exhale. The clarity of the memory is still crystal clear and still the biggest, most regretful surprise she could have ever given me. I look down. The cig in my hand is now just a stick of ash, ready to fall with the tiniest provocation. I toss the end over the balcony and blow out my breath.

That day I saw it before I even knew what *it* was. I saw the puncture mark. And she knew it, too, because even high, she diverted my curious attention. I'll never know how long her coming to the house had been going on for or how much gear Deacon had plied her with. But I know this was the start of the beginning of the end.

And the start of the untimely demise of the girl I loved.

Chapter 13

I SHUT OFF the water, grab the towel from the top of the glass shower door and wrap it around my hips. I slide my arm over the mirror and rub my finger and thumb across my jaw contemplatively.

It's been a while since I've shaved, and my whiskers have now passed the itchy-scratchy stage, and I've currently got a full beard growing in. Pulling funny faces, debating whether or not to remove it, I grab my trimmer and razor. I hesitate because Evie loves it. She thinks it makes me look sophisticated. When I told the guys this last week, they said she would think the same if I was covered in dog shit and flies. Obviously, it was a huge mistake to share the love, but they're probably right. She is very biased in her judgement of me, and I'm not ashamed to admit that. She's going to be disappointed when she sees it gone, but it can be so uncomfortable at times. Besides, it will grow back...eventually. And she may forgive me...eventually.

I turn on the trimmer, and the electronic buzz fills the room. The first drag up my skin is a relief, and I watch my hair fill the basin.

With my face now smooth and fuzz-free, I tilt my head up and study my new reflection of old. Regardless of how irritating the beard was getting, it was perfect for covering the obvious.

Still wrapped in only a towel, I stride down the hallway. I stop at the open living room door and watch, intrigued, as Evie paces up and down my small living room. This new, unspoken living arrangement has become quite the norm between us these last few weeks, ever since I gave her a key and the car park code.

Slowly but surely, her time here has become longer and more frequent. The tiny toy she calls a car is parked downstairs more often than not - even when she isn't staying - so that she has an excuse to come over. Even Andy Blake has resorted to either calling the landline or the club to track her down when she refuses to pick up his calls on her mobile. Needless to say, he's never said it, but it's obvious he's pretty fucking annoyed. And it's even more obvious he's probably calling me all the names under the sun and then some for the alleged *corruption* of his daughter.

But in truth, she came to me that way, and I wouldn't have her any way else.

I lean against the door frame and lull my head. I smile as she bites her lip and scrunches her features up in frustration. Her head moves from side to side, wafting her long, dark hair in the same direction. The pen she's clutching taps the notepad in her other hand until she lets out an indignant huff and tosses them down.

I list to the left. I raise my foot when the door moves and the hinges squeak, and she spins around. "Sorry."

Her cheeks are bright red in mortification. "How long have you been standing there?"

I shrug as she approaches. "Not long. The studying not going so well?" I query delicately because I didn't go to uni, so I can't compare, counsel, or offer her any guidance. I barely just scraped by with a few good GCSEs in high school. What the hell do I know about BAs and MAs? The school of hard knocks, however? That I'm exceptionally educated in.

"It's okay. I just find it so maddening because it's not what I want to do. Although I'm not really sure what I want to do, and that's the problem. My dad told me in no uncertain terms that it was either business or law and that he wouldn't pay for anything else. So I'm kind of stuck."

My mouth opens in shock, and I chortle in repugnance. "That's fucked-up, sweetheart!" The words tumble unfiltered from my mouth. I've been careful not to bad mouth him, and all my hard work has just gone to pot. "Sorry, I just meant-"

She waves her hand. "No, it is fucked-up." She presses her fingers to my naked sternum. "I'm not stupid. By taking a course he approves of and him paying for it means he will always have some control over me. He's always been like this. For my GCSEs, he chose my subjects." She closes her eyes, almost painfully, and rests her cheek against my chest. "I don't love business management, but I don't hate it, either. I should be happy he's paying for my education and that I'll have the privilege of leaving uni without the noose of thirty grand of debt hanging invisibly around my neck before I even find a job."

I sigh. "Darling, his paying isn't a privilege; it's what parents should do if they can afford it." I run my hand through her silky hair, attempting to comfort her. "Still, what would *you* rather do?" She looks up from my chest. There's desire burning in her eyes. Whatever her ideal vocation is, I'm adamant that that dream has been shot down in flames so many times she probably dares not to mention or even whisper it any longer.

"Hey, you've shaved! That's sacrilege!"

"And you're changing the subject, but yes, I've shaved."

Her eyes darken, and her bottom lip juts out. "But I liked it." She stretches up on her tip tops and repeatedly brushes the side of her cheek against mine. "I like this too, but there's nothing quite like the feel of-" She stops abruptly and stares down my stomach.

"Sweetheart?" I query.

In the short time we've been together, I've learnt that she has this personality quirk where she's so passionate about what she's saying - whether it be something mundane, such as a ham sandwich, or breathlessly trying to explain what she wants – but she then realises at the last minute and stops herself. *Every. Single. Time.* Again, I have to wonder how many times her voice has been muted for that action to have become so automatic.

I lean back and tilt her chin up. The stunning pink hue staining her cheeks has me piqued. "Nothing quite like?" I repeat, hoping she will finish it.

Her eyes flutter shut, and she exhales. "Like when your bristly cheeks graze over my boobs. Or when they scratch over my nipples. Or when you're between my thighs, tasting me there, my skin abraded by it...it turns me on immensely."

I release the breath I didn't know I was holding, immensely turned on myself, with my length now standing to attention beneath the towel. "Tonight, I'm going to do all those things, and maybe you'll learn to love it smooth again."

She smiles, her eyes full of mischief and wanton anticipation. "Rough or smooth, I'll love it however you want to give it to me. Better still, why don't you give it to me right now." On that, she yanks away the towel, takes me in hand and slowly pumps. Her mouth covers mine, and I wrap my arm around her back as my hips move involuntarily under her touch. Our kisses become frantic, and the urge to rip her clothes off and take her on my living room floor is a very real possibility.

"Darling," I murmur, my body subconsciously aware that I don't have a lot of time to get off, get ready and get gone when her mouth leaves mine, and she drops to her knees. I gaze down at her in wonder, watching the woman I'm positive I'm in love with wrap her lips around me. Her luscious mouth works me from root to tip. Her hands grip either side of my arse, and it takes all I have not to grab her face and control her delicate, almost graceful, movements.

"Evie!" I call out and tap her cheek - our agreed sign for when I'm close. Except, instead of withdrawing – which she does eighty per cent of the time – she grips my rear harder. Her inquisitive fingers slide in between, proving the entire onslaught of sensation to be too much. She sucks more vigorously until I release, and she moans in satisfied response.

My head falls back, experiencing perfect euphoria as I empty myself of everything, including all the pent-up emotions of the last few months. I rub my hand lovingly through her hair until she finally extracts herself from me.

I open my eyes and dip my chin to find her still genuflected in front of me, her hands on her thighs, looking perfectly innocent and submissive. Admittedly, that's not really my thing, but I won't lie; it's a damn powerful sensation to see her like this.

"Jeremy, I lo-" I place my finger over her beautiful, blushing lips. I know she loves me, and I'm absolutely positive I love her, but I don't want her declaration when she's still on her knees after I've had my dick down her throat. I slide my hands around her chin and neck and gently encourage her up.

"I'm sorry, I thought you felt the same." Her voice wobbles beautifully.

I smile and rub my thumbs just under her lobes. "I do, but I don't want you saying it while you're still kneeling."

She blushes and tries to turn away, but I refuse her request and grip her more firmly. "I want you saying it when I'm inside you, making love to you. When the sensation is so deep and strong, that it transcends everything else." She nods and blushes more fiercely, and I touch my forehead to hers. "Thank you for taking care of me. I promise I'll repay the favour tonight."

"I didn't do it to keep score. I did it because I wanted to. Now, you're going to be late for work," she orders and walks me back into the bedroom. We both instantly look over the bed at the sex crumpled sheets that are still in the same state they were when we left them a few hours ago. "And the sooner you leave, the sooner you can come home to me."

She spins around, riffles through a drawer and tosses a pair of boxers at me. I watch dumbfounded because the idea of home with

Evie is more than a passing thought. "Earth to Jeremy!" Fingers click, and her arm wafts in front of me.

I blink a couple of times. "Sorry, I'm just...somewhere nice." My lips curve, and my somewhere nice remains as Evie perches herself on the bed and watches me get dressed. "Remember to keep the door alarm on, and I should be back around three, not that you'll be awake." I slide my arm around her waist and tug her towards me.

"I might be!" Her wayward hands grip my shoulders, and her fingers dig in, testing.

I chuckle at her presumption. "No, sweetheart, you won't." Her head inclines from side to side until she reluctantly nods. I slide on my jacket, pocket my keys, wallet, and phone, and she walks me to the door.

"Remember the alarm," I reiterate because I can't take chances with her safety. Granted, when she first started to stay over, I didn't set it in case she wanted to leave, but since it's obvious she has no intention of going anywhere, it's something I insist on. "And remember to eat something." This is another thing I've found I've had to reiterate. Otherwise, she becomes so consumed in what she's doing she forgets.

"I'll probably order a pizza," she says, rolling her eyes.

"Good, but set the alarm before and after it arrives."

This time she openly huffs her irritation. "You have such paranoia and OCD, Jeremy James of the sad eyes."

"Yes, I have, but tonight it's amplified because you'll be here alone."

"And I'll be completely fine! I think I'm going to study a little longer, but it feels like a lost cause right now. So, that means I'll try but will give up miserably, demolish my pizza when it arrives, watch some crap TV and fall asleep. Then I'll dream of your smooth cheeks rubbing my thighs until you come home tonight and turn my dream into reality." I open my mouth, but she beats me to it. "All with the alarm on! Happy?"

"Very." I grin since she's just said all the right things. "Do you know what happens to wayward, insubordinate girls?"

Her smirk grows craftier, participating in the game. "No, but you can show me that tonight, too."

I bend down and kiss her. "Are you're sure you don't want to come and meet the girls? Honestly, you'll like them."

She looks uncomfortable again. "No, I really need to *try* to study. Now, go. I promise I will alarm the door."

With one last kiss, I cross the threshold. Her scent lingers on me as I edge down the corridor to the lifts and wait for one to arrive.

"Jeremy?" Evie's muted call draws me back. I tip my chin to my girl curled against the architrave. "I'll leave a light on."

I LOITER IN the darkest corner of the club, a bottle of non-alcoholic lager in hand, watching my makeshift family let loose. The music is pulsating with some current crap that just becomes unforgettable background noise after a while.

I rest the bottleneck against my lips, ready to down another mouthful – for all the good it will do me since it's clearly not going to get me sloshed – but the sight of brother and sister twirling around the dance floor makes me smile. I laugh rhetorically when Charlie attempts to lead Sloan, and he tries - and fails - to regain control of the situation. Watching them, a tiny flicker of days gone by seeps into my head, remembering those long, hot summer days when we would play together. Charlie was only a baby, Franklin Black had yet to turn their colourful world dark, and Deacon had yet to get me secretly hooked on drugs.

I sigh, feeling so much older than my twenty-nine years. Tilting my head back, I scan the club and spot Kara and Sophie in the opposite corner. But whereas I'm aiming to remain incognito, they're simply avoiding the crowds – or at least Kara is. Sophie, who is always so in tune with her, undoubtedly assists with that unspoken truth.

I push off the wall and do a lap of the premises. Retrieving the radio from the back of my belt, I clear my throat. "Status update?" I request before the responding static crackle and Craig's cockney drawl replies.

"The latest update is, there is no update. Nothing interesting tonight. God, I'm so fucking bored. *I'm* considering shaking something up so that *I* have something to do. It's fucking chilly out here, too!"

I snigger, and although I shouldn't find it amusing, I do. "I'll bring you a coffee."

"Knight in shining armour, Rem." I chuckle, locating one of the staff to get the doormen a hot drink.

On my second lap, seeing nothing is still not shaking the place up, and the interior is just as quiet as the exterior, I glance across to the bar. While the entry queue may not be snaking around the street tonight, the bar is struggling with demand.

I roll up my sleeves on my way, ready to serve and be hospitable when a familiar "excuse me?" comes from the end of the bar. I've maintained my avoidance of her for months now because I'm a coward, and I fear what she may say if put in a corner and provoked. Her words would be spoken in defence, but an element of truth would linger in them. Sadly, that's the part I don't think I can face. Still, she's my best friend's wife, and the only way these two will ever be apart is in death. I can't exactly keep up the charade for the next thirty or forty years, depending on what other unresolved aspects of my life may happen along the way.

As I approach, Kara is wholly immersed in thought, smiling to herself. I pause and watch because it's a look I've never witnessed before, and it gives me hope that if she can move on – in a sense – then so can I. Her head drops, and she twists her wedding ring. I take the opportunity to find an advantage and casually but cautiously nudge her shoulder.

I step back instantly, distinguishing her returning gasp of shock and the fact she looks ready to swing for me.

"What can I get you?" I ask, inducing her expression to soften in recognition. A moment passes between us until she glances over the bottles with a grin.

"A triple vodka and a double rum – in the same glass!" Her eyes light up the moment her lips curve. She nods at me encouragingly, as if that's going to sway me into mixing her bizarre request. Instead, I laugh, unable to contain it. We both know it's never going to happen, and no amount of smiling, nodding, or eyelash action is going to change that.

In the corner of my eye, Sloan approaches with his finger over his mouth for me to keep quiet. Except, as far as these two are concerned, they're so connected with each other on a mental, emotional, and visceral level that they can sense the other's presence, and Kara's slight adjustment confirms it.

I avert my gaze to the empty bottle in front of me as Sloan whispers in his wife's ear, then he slaps me on the back and slips behind the bar.

"A triple vodka and a double rum – in the same glass, for your lady, and I'll have another." I hold up the bottle to show him what non-alcoholic offering I'm knocking back when Mark, the bartender, advances towards us.

"Sorry, sir, you-" Mark stops, realising the owner can pretty much do whatever he likes. Sloan grins and waves in acknowledgement, then demonstrates his best, or quite possibly his worst, attempt at tending bar.

With my elbow on the top, I rest my jaw against my fist and watch Sloan syphon a pint of lemonade. He sets my fresh bottle and his wife's drink down in front of her. She smiles gloriously at him, and he glides his finger down her chest.

"Your triple vodka and double rum, in the same glass."

Kara looks at the glass aghast, but in good spirits, she pulls out a twenty and slides it over the bar. I laugh again, but I know where I'm not wanted, so I grab my bottle and become one with the crowd. A thought occurs to me, and I pause and turn back. Sloan and Kara are walking through the club, his front to her back, his arm around her stomach as they enter the VIP section.

I watch inconspicuously, wondering if I look like that when I'm with Evie. A lovestruck fool, hopelessly devoted, undeniably in love. Most times, I certainly feel that way. My thoughts drift back to my woman, and I pull out my mobile and send her a quick *how's it going?* text. Her reply is almost immediate with a picture of her closed books and a simple one-liner: *Fabulous!*

I laugh aloud, wishing I could experience that fabulous with her tonight. *Remember to eat!* I send as a presence lingers near me.

"Evie?"

"Yes," I grind out, my tone lacking annoyance as Doc falls into my line of sight. I lean on the wall leading to the toilets as he shoots the breeze with me. "One day, you guys will stop wanting to live vicariously through me!" I comment in jest, and he laughs.

"Not likely. I'll live vicariously through anyone who allows me to, considering everyone's life is more interesting than mine at the moment." He necks a mouthful of ale, and I give him a questioning glance as Kara hurries into the ladies with Sloan strolling casually behind.

"Running like the wind! She's seen the light at last, half-brit!" Doc chuckles, causing Sloan to roughhouse him. I grin. It's been a long time since the atmosphere around our original, rag-tag group has felt so light and airy.

"No room to talk!" Sloan retorts as Sophie darts into the toilets, almost body slamming Kara, who is on her way out.

"Sorry, chick!" Soph calls out.

Kara's hands whip up in yield, and she turns to me. "Can I use the office?"

"Sure, what's up?" I ask as we walk across the VIP.

"A private number has been calling, and someone finally left a message."

I nod to myself as we head up the stairs to the office. Kara is still listening to the message, with Sloan directly behind her. Entering the room, Kara dashes to my desk and scribbles down a number.

"Baby?" Sloan's call fills the room as I stand at the window, pretending I'm overseeing the club floor and am anywhere but here.

"Hi, this is Kara Petersen..."

I selectively block her out, thankful for a diversion as my phone vibrates. Retrieving it from my pocket, I swipe the notification and smile at the half-eaten pizza on my living room floor and the simple question of *happy?* below it.

"Very," I murmur as I type the word, followed by *save me a slice.* I await her response when Kara's "my husband and I have an engagement this evening" floods my eardrums.

My phone buzzes again, and I lift my hand. I'm satisfied Evie has replied but somewhat annoyed it's getting quite late, and she has to be knackered and needing precious sleep. Swiping the screen again, I hold in my chortle at her response.

What's it worth?

I quickly type a single thumb response.

Me any way you want me

My fleeting moment of forgetfulness and joy is transitory as Kara's concerned tone cuts through my distraction.

"I haven't heard anything in months."

I lower my phone and turn to Sloan, who is also looking at me. Sliding it into my pocket, needing to focus completely on the moment, I edge closer.

A thousand scenarios race through my head, cluttering every cell, infusing fear into the places I've not scratched the surface of in a lifetime. I snap out of it the instant Kara's tone wobbles and finally threatens to break when Sloan asks what's happening.

"They've arrested him. Deacon. He attacked a woman..." She doesn't finish, but Sloan takes the phone. I automatically hold out my hand to offer support, and a part of me needing hers, but she moves to the window that overlooks the club.

I shift in the opposite direction, lean against the wall and watch the live security feed on the monitors. Right now, I wish something, or someone, would kick off because anything has to be better than being in this room.

"How long can you hold him?" Sloan queries, and I pretend not to be listening because if they hold Deacon, at some point in the next twenty-four hours, they'll be coming for me. Even if I wasn't guilty by action, I am by association, and I've always wondered when this day would come. It was never a question of *if*, but *when*. Now it appears *when* has finally arrived.

My stomach is doing somersaults, and queasiness threatens to escape my gut. I finally risk looking up when Sloan ends the call, and the verbal push and pull between husband and wife captures my attention.

"This time tomorrow, he'll commence rotting in hell at Her Majesty's pleasure for a very long time."

The bile rises in my throat because I will, too. Except it won't just be rotting, it will also be surviving. I'll have to watch my back every day. The first and last things I'll think of will be whether this is the last time I shall wake up or if it's the last time I shall go to sleep. I'll run the risk of getting beaten or possibly shanked. My name will be dragged through the mud. I'll no longer be Jeremy James. I'll be a number in a system. But to those in the system with me, I'll be called a rapist or a nonce. I'll be called things that are simply not true.

And maybe the only way to ensure I come out of this breathing on the other side is to see if I can cut some sort of deal with the CPS; confess, and face whatever fate the system sees fit to give me. I'm not ashamed to say I'll sell out the Blacks and request solitary confinement if it means I'll live to see the end.

I catch Kara's distressed expression because we both know what I'm thinking. The worry is probably written all over my face.

"Jeremy..."

I smile sadly and raise my palm. "This needs to be done. I've been running from it for nearly ten years. I'm tired of being devoured by the guilt. Of my every thought being consumed by it. I'm not running anymore. I need to be held accountable for what I did. Maybe I'll get my redemption after all."

Kara approaches, her look overwhelmed, and she kisses my cheek. "You've always had it. I was just never strong enough to say it." Then she moves back to her husband.

"I need to make arrangements for certain things. I'll leave a wallet in the drawer for you to execute." I open the desk drawer and begin to remove the few personal documents I keep in there that I've never taken home. "I'll be here in the morning with Marie. Goodnight, honey," I tell Kara, whose expression is still forlorn.

Sloan, on the other, looks furious and his jaw works, realising I've already given up on my freedom before the fight has begun. He bends over the desk and whispers, "I'll get the best criminal legal team. You're not going down for the life that that bastard dragged you into."

"Sloan, I'm guilty, and your wife is still suffering because of it."

He lets out a quiet huff. "And how do you think she'll be if you go down for five to ten? Tomorrow I'll make some calls, okay?"

My heart is breaking, overflowing with love and pain. I rise from the desk and embrace him in a long, brotherly hug. Terrified my composure will break, I wish them goodnight and lock the office door behind them.

I slouch back down at the desk and remove my phone from my pocket. Evie's reply from my last message is still waiting to be read, and I swipe it open, making my eyes instantly sting.

You can't barter with a foregone conclusion!

Tears fills my eyes, and an emotional sensation snaps in my chest. The only foregone conclusion that is absolute is that tomorrow, I will likely be locked up in a cell, awaiting a fate I've feared for a decade.

Recently, for the first time in years, I've allowed myself to hope. Hope for life, hope for love, hope for a future with a young woman who accepts me for who I am.

Now I fear my hope has been in vain.

THE ALARM BEGINS to beep when I open the door and swear as I disarm it. The flat is in darkness aside from the living room lamp – Evie's version of leaving a light on. I open the bedroom door, and she stirs but doesn't wake. I watch her for long minutes, wishing my life could have been different. Cursing the choices I made all those years ago, wishing I knew then what I know now.

A part of me also wishes I hadn't been so fucking honourable in my declaration of turning myself in. I have to, not because it's constantly eating away at me, but because Kara and Charlie both deserve justice for what he did. If I had paid more attention to Deacon than I had to the drugs he supplied me with, his evil depravation might never have touched them.

It's been hours since I've learned what my possible fate may be, and it's yet to sink in properly. It's bizarre, but what I plan to do in the next twelve hours doesn't feel real yet. I just wish I had longer. It's sod's law that I finally have someone to live for, but my liberty will be sacrificed imminently, proving anything can be taken away in the blink of an eye.

Evie shuffles in her sleep and murmurs. I want to hold and comfort her, kiss and make love to her, and fulfil the promise I made. But above all of that, I want to tell her how much I love her. I had my chance earlier this evening, and now it's lost. I may never get the chance again.

I close the door and pace through the flat. I fish a stray notepad and pen from the kitchen drawer and grab a bottle of water, suddenly berating myself for not possessing a bottle of spirit for medicinal purposes or for easing the effects of looming incarceration.

I open the balcony door and flick on the light. The small space illuminates, and I slump into a chair, retrieve my cigs, and light one up. Inhaling the toxic vapour, I swig back a mouthful of water. The pen between my fingers rests on the paper as I ruminate. I need to let her down easy, although I wish I didn't have to let her down at all. If I had my way, I'd bundle her up, throw her in the car and drive her far, far away, the same way I did when Kara asked me to help her last year.

Taking another drag of the cigarette, I start to write. It probably won't make any sense considering my thoughts are a jumbled mass of contradictions right now, but I hope it gets the validity of my confession across.

I've already written one for each of the guys, plus one for Charlie, Marie, and Kara, and left them in the drawer at the club, but this one is private. The things I have to say are for her alone.

As I light up another cig, the glowing ember emits a minute warmth. I watch the stick burn with each inhalation, but everything in my life has already gone up in smoke, burnt to cinders and turned to ash.

And whereas Kara's nightmare may finally be ending, mine is only just beginning.

Chapter 14

I STARE UP at the ceiling, one arm over my bare chest, the other above my head on the pillow.

I'm still awake as the day gradually steals the night. As expected, I haven't slept. I've counted every hour grudgingly while I await my fate and the consequences that may be long-suffering and not just for me.

Evie's delicate nasal breathing has been a constant comfort, accompanying my restlessness and unforgiving anxiety. Whereas fear has been my unwanted companion, plaguing my conscience from the moment I laid my head.

Lost in a world of invisible pain, visualising one possibly fatal nightmare morph into another inside my mind's eye, a murmur resounds, vanquishing further assumption. I crane my neck left, inhale a sharp breath and study Evie. Asleep on her right, her palms are tucked under her cheek in hidden pray. I smile at her childlike pose of the foetal position. I don't know if she knows she sleeps like that, and I don't have the heart to tell her. Then again, I sleep light as my subconscious is aware something may come in the night, so maybe her position is to subconsciously protect herself, too. I don't know.

Yet regardless of how she sleeps, she's a beautiful vision of innocence. And I pray by the end of today I'm not the one who will be responsible for its unholy destruction and broken essence when she learns what type of man she let into her heart.

I sigh wearily, completely frustrated with my current situation. I see beyond the woman warming my sheets and back into the dark, murky past that entwines with an equally dark, conceivable future.

"You're staring," a beautiful whisper I'll never tire of hearing penetrates my psyche. Regaining focus, Evie's fluttering lashes and partially parted lips fill my line of sight. This is fast becoming the best way to wake up, proving there are still new addictions to be had in my world.

Her soft fingers trace along the divots of my stomach muscles, and she bequeaths me a sleepy grin. "Morning, I didn't hear you come home last night."

I smile, loving that she considers this flat – and hopefully me – home. I'd be lying if I said that wasn't also another something else that is fast becoming addictive.

"Hi," I whisper because words fail me. I could tell her that I didn't want to wake her. I could tell her I stood and watched her sleep. Or I could tell her the truth – that I sat on the balcony until only a few hours ago, when dawn shimmered on the horizon, writing words that once she reads will ensure she despises me before night follows the day.

I could, but I don't.

Instead, I bequeath her a lazy grin, feeling the tug on my marred cheek, and manipulate her wayward hand to my mouth. She sighs in contentment as I kiss each pad of her fingers until her lashes flutter, and I take the opportunity to gain supremacy.

"Hey!" she exclaims when I roll her over and cage her beneath me. Cradling the side of her face, my thumb strokes her cheek repeatedly. I continue to stare, praying to all that is good and holy for the world to stop turning and allow us to live suspended in time in this perfect moment. But I'm more than aware we don't always get what we want, so this perfect moment will just become another memory.

"Jeremy, what's wrong?" Her worried tone is something I've rarely heard these last few months. I shake my head because the true question is, what isn't wrong. Without rejoinder or inference, I hold her and press my lips to hers. She moans into my mouth, her hands gripping my shoulders, guiding me where she wants me.

Time passes as I fall into the moment and further into this woman than I already am.

With our lips tasting and our tongues forever learning, I let out an involuntary groan when her calf rubs up and down my thigh. I shuffle onto my knees, support her back and pull her to me. With my fingers at her nape and my thumb manipulating her chin up, I lick and kiss down her neck until I reach her chest.

"Arms up," I request hoarsely.

She complies immediately, and I slip the cotton camisole over her head. She leans back, resting on her arms. Her perky tits catch the light perfectly, highlighting her taut nipples.

"You're beautiful," I tell her without thinking since I'm feeling somewhat dazed, but my subconscious knows it may not see this sight again for a very long time.

"So are you, scars and all, Jeremy James of the sad eyes," she says, repeating her favourite line for me. She shivers and sucks in her bottom lip. She bestows me a heavily hooded look, completely unashamed in her partially nude state. I lean forward and take a nipple into my mouth, delighting in the shape and texture I know so well.

"Oh!" she breathes out. Her subsequent sighs and delicate upper body ripples fuel my desire, and I suck harder, wanting to mark her so that she knows she belongs to me. Alternating from one to the other, I eventually kiss a path up her neck and claim her mouth. She moans with abandon as I lavish my tongue against hers and roll her already distended rosy peaks between my fingers.

"Oh, God!" Her hips spring off the bed, slamming into mine. The friction is all it takes to set me off, and I force her back until her spine melds into the mattress. "I'm yours, Jeremy. Take me." She squirms, her fingers teasing her breasts, before running down her stomach to the hem of her shorts and to her centre. "I want you inside me."

Her words, and the breathless honesty of them, sends a frisson of fire flowing down my spine to my abdomen. Smashing my mouth back over hers, thrusting my tongue inside, showing wordlessly what I plan to do with something else, I swell further in anticipation and excitement.

"I want you, Evelyn. I want you so much that if I told you, it would frighten you," I say gruffly, reaching for her shorts and yanking them down along with her underwear.

My eyes transfix on hers as I lob the last of her clothing across the room. She stares completely unabashed. "Tell me."

The fire inside stokes higher, and I sit back on my thighs and observe at her. Again, I need to put this memory in my mental vault since I don't know when I'll see her again. Her dark hair is fanned out over the pillow, her eyes are wide, shiny from stimulation, while her lips are red and stunningly swollen from being kissed.

"I want to kiss you until you can't breathe." I lean down and kiss her again, so hard and fervent, only stopping when I feel her becoming breathless, driving the point home. I smirk victoriously as she regains her composure, and a light dusting of crimson spreads down her neck, drawing my eyes back to her perfect chest.

I crawly slowly down her body, my tongue dragging a wet path from her neck to the gap between her breasts. "I want to suck on your tits until your nipples are so raw and tender that you beg me to stop."

She releases a sharp breath, automatically bringing one hand to her breast and rubbing her thighs together. I hold her turned-on gaze and blow gently over her chest before taking a breast in my mouth and making good on my promise.

"Oh fuck!" she spits out, very unladylike. She writhes beneath me as I suck her harder than I have before. My free hand finds her other tit, and I repeatedly roll the tip between my fingers, loving how aroused she is. Her hands on my head force me closer.

"Good?" I ask, knowing the question will add additional vibration and sensation.

"More!" she demands, encouraging my mouth to love with such vigour, I have to force myself to stop for fear I may unintentionally make her sore.

Reluctantly extracting myself, I glance up to where the annoyed huffing and puffing is emanating to find her dark, fiery eyes glaring daggers at me. Never removing my gaze from hers, I move lower, my lips gliding down her flat stomach over her belly button to her abdomen. Thankfully, her annoyance wanes, and she's now making appreciative keening noises.

I shift her beneath me and grab her undulating hips. I lovingly tongue her hipbones and slide my hand around her backside to adjust her leg until it's resting over my shoulder. I stroke my finger down her pubic bone, skirt around her centre and slide it down over her nub to her entrance then between her cheeks.

She gasps in shock. I entwine my fingers in hers, squeezing them, silently conveying that she has nothing to worry about.

Once she has relaxed again, I blow over her centre, earning myself an inviting hip roll and blissful sigh. My actions are languid and tender, calculated and deliberate. This is probably the last time we will ever be together, so I need as much as I can get.

"I want this." I swipe my tongue over her. "I want to slide inside and fuck you until you can't take no more." Another lick. "I want to taste you until you tell me to stop." And another. "I want to make love to you until the end of my days." With one last kiss, I sit up on my knees and ease a finger inside. Her heat envelops me, and she automatically parts her legs wider. Inserting another, her walls clamp down, making me wish I'd have just slid into her instead. She was already wet and worked up; we didn't need any foreplay. However, I'm not a selfish bastard. Well, not all the time.

"Yes!" she finally says between gritted teeth, riding my hand. "I want you inside me." I ease my fingers free, much to her vocal disdain.

I quickly slide on a condom and position myself over her. Her hands hold my face as she stretches up and kisses me. Her eyes focus the instant I slide inside in a fluid, unhurried motion. Still lost in those beautiful, fathomless pools, I'm aware she isn't particularly impressed with my speed this morning. She may want a quick, hard fuck, but I don't. Obviously, I can't explain my reasons, but I want to make love to her slow and tender. I want to memorise every touch and look, every gasp and moan. I want her mindless by the time it ends because then she won't question why, and I won't have to fabricate another lie.

Still inside her, I adjust her lithe limbs around my thighs and cradle her to me. Sliding a pillow under her back and shoulders, she gives me a lazy, enraptured smile. With her body elevated perfectly, I slide out and thrust back in. Our eyes stare deep into each others. Our bodies move in tandem. Our hearts beat to the same frantic pulse.

Her legs wrap around my hips, assisting to control the action. Her hands smooth over my chest, circling my flat nipples. Her pelvis rolls up to mine sinuously, and she squeezes me deep.

"What's going on here?" she asks suspiciously, short of breath, arching her hips.

"I'm making love to you, Evelyn," I reply simply, omitting my true reason since this is likely to be the last time I get to experience being inside her.

Her arms reach for me, and I press forward. Plunging back and forth, my abdomen is on fire, and a fleeting thought confirms that this could be the closest I may ever get to heaven on earth.

A groan escapes me when she tilts her hips again and crushes her thighs around my arse. My body thrums and pulses, confirming I'm minutes, maybe seconds, away from exploding. She continues to squeeze and release, her actions consistent with the way she's internally gripping me until she shudders and cries out.

"Jeremy!"

My orgasm finally peaks, and our combined breathing is hot and heavy until the fire dies to a smoulder. I press my perspired forehead to hers, loving the way her warm breath fans my face, assisting in cooling me off. God knows I need it right now.

"What time is it?" Her downturned eyes gradually meet mine.

"Early." I take a guess. I hold her tight and allow my lips to drift over the beautiful column of her neck. Her skin is soft and inviting, assisting further in my body relaxing. Gripping her cheeks, I lean back to study her face. Memorising every line and divot, every flaw and curve, I smile and kiss her again.

"You're acting weird this morning." She grazes her thumbs over my eyelids in a tender motion. "Maybe one day, you'll confess the truth and sadness behind these eyes."

"My truths are the stuff of nightmares."

Her lips curl, and she holds me closer. "Good job I'm not afraid of things that lurk in the shadows or go bump in the night." She laughs beautifully, and I force myself to emulate her playfulness under duress because it's either laugh or cry. In the foreseeable future, I think I'll be doing more of one than the other.

"You should be," I whisper, barely audible. She pulls forward, a questioning look in her eyes. Placating her curiosity with another kiss, I feel myself turning flaccid. I slide away, much to her one huff protest and pick her up. Carrying her into the bathroom, I turn on the shower and hold my hand under the flow until the water is hot enough. She sighs as I carefully stand her under the spray.

"Are you not joining me?" She pouts beautifully, and I furrow my brow.

"There's something I need to take care of first." I turn around and divest myself of the used condom, then knot up the pedal bin bag to dispose of it when I leave this morning.

Stepping into the shower, she pounces. I grin when she squeezes a handful of gel into her palms, rubs them together and forces me to turn around. Closing my eyes, she starts at my shoulders then shifts down my back. The lemon scent mingles with the steam, filling the space. I brace my hand on the wall and close my eyes when I feel her wet skin slide over mine as she moves down my arse to my legs. Long minutes pass until a small tap on my cheek startles me, and she gazes up with dark, mysterious eyes.

"Thank you," I tell her involuntarily. What I'm thanking her for, I have no idea. It could be everything, it could be nothing, but it's definitely for unknowingly giving me another perfect memory.

"Well, you always take care of me, and sometimes, I want to take care of you. That's what you do when you lo-" she stops abruptly, blushing furiously, and quickly turns around. My body clenches in anger because *I know*.

That's what you do when you love someone.
She didn't have to say it because I'm already aware of how she feels. I'd be lying if I said I didn't feel it too. Sadly, right place, wrong time. But what I wouldn't give to hear her say those words to me as a free man who isn't facing a sentence for a life he regrets.

Internally hating myself more with every second that passes, I take a moment to memorise the way the water drenches her hair. The way it sluices down her back in rippling waves, washing over the double dimples that join her spine to her hips, glistening over her pert backside and down her legs.

A multitude of thoughts fight each other inside my overwhelmed, overstimulated mind, but this morning was an exercise in both futility and longevity.

Every movement, every touch, and every kiss was methodically catalogued. Each carefully contained in the dark recesses of my brain, so when I'm cold and lonely, or frightened and alone, sharing a tiny cell with someone I don't know from Adam, I can reminisce on these last twenty-four hours, and remember what if felt like to be loved.

PULLING ON MY jeans, the whirr of the hairdryer and Evie's nonsensical humming fill the flat. "Breakfast?" I call over the din, feeling the despondency harden in my chest. She motions affirmatively before tossing her hair over to dry the underside. Grabbing a shirt from the wardrobe, I slide it over my shoulders. I leave it unfastened as I lovingly stroke my fingers down her arm and depart.

I stand sentry in front of the balcony doors, surveying the sky, waiting for the kettle to boil. Murky, grey clouds are gathering overhead, but a ray of sunshine threatens to break through the dire morning. With one hand braced on the glass, I study the 'Dear John please forgive me' letter in my other.

When I initially composed these last night, my ramblings were a riot of muddled words. That much is true just from reading them back a few minutes ago, but nonetheless, these are my truths. Honesty that both my mother and Evie deserve. But whereas my mother will probably find it in herself to excuse my transgressions since forgiveness is ingrained in the majority of women from the moment they hold their child for the first time, I know Evie – someone who has no responsibilities to me - will not. The truths I've written in her letter are confessions my mum has already heard and pardoned me of. I can only pray Evie sees past the blackness and despair and realises the powerful hold the drugs and the Blacks had on me back then. It was painful to divulge the truth, but she needs to know because no one can hide forever.

"Jeremy?"

"In here." I stuff the letters in my pocket and spin around. Evie grins, practically skips the length of the living room and launches herself into my arms.

"I could get used to this." I curl an arm around her back, and she presses her lips to my scar.

"Good. I want you to, then maybe you'll see no reason to let me go." Her cheeks flush crimson, and she slides down my front and toddles off into the kitchen. My mind relays her words over and over because I will let her go - sooner than she expects.

I lean against the kitchen door and watch as she makes two coffees and a few rounds of toast. The faint buzz of my mobile floats on the atmosphere, and I look over my shoulder to see the screen fade to black from where it's charging on the lamp table.

"What's happening at the club today?"

I amble towards her. Her body is resting languidly against the worktop, and she lifts a slice of buttered toast to her lips.

"It's…" I begin until I remember I've not actually told her. "Oh, Sloan's letting out the premises for disadvantaged and vulnerable kids. It's a mix of stuff, games, music, crafts and the like."

She's clearly impressed. "He's generous."

I nod, more for myself. "You have no idea." His generosity stretches far and wide. So far and wide, in fact, he's going to forsake his wife's mentality and use his generosity to try to keep me out of prison when I really do need to reap what I've sown.

She picks up another slice, and I open wide as she teases it into my mouth, happy when I take a bite.

"So, you're going to be painting faces, dancing, and playing pass the parcel?" Her wayward hands find my chest. She inhales, her eyes closing, almost like she's drugged. I should know, after all.

I chortle, blanking out the image. "No, I'm going to confine myself to the office."

"Want some company?"

"I'd love some, but I've got a meeting at two with Sloan."

"Meeting with the boss? Scary!"

Yes, absolutely terrifying. "Possibly."

"Shame. I guess between kids and the big boss, you probably won't have time for me." Her bottom lip sticks out dramatically, but she's smiling, so I know it's all pretend. "I'll collect my things and go home." She presses her lips to my cheek and slinks towards the bedroom.

"You can stay, if you want." My phone then buzzes. *Kara calling.* "Hey," I answer. "Are you and Marie on your way over already?" God, I didn't expect them this bloody early.

"No, I was actually calling to see if she was with you. She hasn't come into the office yet."

Torrents of rain are falling outside, making it even more dismal than it already was. "I'm still at home. She might already be at the club. I gave her a set of keys the other day. Come and pick me up, I'm not going to be needing my car today." I squeeze my eyes shut and respire sharply, wishing I could take that back. "Kara, I didn't mean it like that." I feel like shit, and she probably does too.

"I know you didn't." Her reply is barely audible. "We'll be there soon."

"Okay, I'll be waiting, honey." I hold my mobile to my chest, terrified of what's going to come to pass. I glance towards the hallway when Evie remerges from the bedroom, her holdall in hand.

"Walk me to my car, good sir? I can't have your neighbours thinking this is the walk of shame again, can I?" She winks, and I burst out laughing. If that's the case, she's walking in shame most nights.

"Most certainly not, beautiful lady." I grab my things, bolt the balcony doors, alarm the flat, and lock up. We ride down to the basement in silence. The unspoken truth of what else is happening today has my heart in proverbial chains.

"I'll miss you," she says, dumping her bag on the passenger seat. She then kisses me, and I reciprocate with sadness in my soul, dying to confirm her statement carries my weight than she knows. As the kiss turns scorching and breathless on both sides, she eventually pulls away. "I'll call you." She sounds slightly winded, and it's just another memory I will remember for eternity. Climbing into her car, she reverses out and away.

I stride out of the car park through the manicured, communal garden, and rain droplets pepper my face and hair. I wait on the kerb, my gaze locked on the street, knowing the direct route Evie takes home. Turning my mobile in my pocket, I batten down the compulsion to call her. I've spent a lifetime fighting my inner demons, OCD, and various other addictions, and Evie should have been easy in comparison. But she has proven the most challenging yet most consistent thing in my life these last few months.

An unmistakable rumble reaches my ears. The engine growl grows louder and louder until Sloan's Aston rounds the corner and crawls to a stop. I'm not sexist, but I rein in my surprise seeing Kara behind the wheel of a car far too powerful for her. I walk around to the driver's side and open the door. I wordlessly jerk my head to the back, and she unbuckles and scrambles between the seats. I chuck my phone onto the centre console, slide in, and start her up.

I groan again as the car pulls against the snail's pace we're travelling at, wanting to go faster than the five miles per hour we're currently doing. I bite my tongue when the car in front slams on the brakes for no apparent reason. *Again.* I press my foot against to accelerator, allowing the engine to growl in response, gaining a finger flip from the driver.

The morning rush hour – or any hour in this city – is seriously testing my mental endurance. Traffic is stop/start, bumper to bumper. While Sloan's dream machine is highly responsive to the slightest touch, I doubt he will want it returned in need of new brake pads and discs, if he's lucky. Plus, considering the prick in front is just annoying me now, and with my already dire mood, there's a chance the wanker is going to get over two hundred grand's worth of luxury motor rammed up his arse if he isn't careful.

A short time later, I overtake the arsehole in front and pick up some speed. A phone buzzes, and Dev and I pick ours up while Kara digs around in her bag. Screw the ban - it's the least of my problems today. What's another year or two for flouting it, considering I'm going down for a long time anyway.

"Finally!" Kara exclaims, her expression relieved in the rearview, and she clutches her phone.

The rain has abated by the time I park next to Marie's Mercedes in the alleyway at the side of the club. I climb out, and Kara and Dev follow my stride towards the staff entrance.

The heavy fire door slams shut, the sound reverberating off the walls. I turn on the lights as we pass, and the floodlights illuminate every inch of the main room. I stare around with unease and a feeling in my gut that I haven't felt in months, not since I last saw Deacon.

My eyes fix curiously on the handbag at the end of the bar. It can only belong to Marie. I walk around the bar and remove a few bottles of water from the fridge while Kara's call echoes.

"She might be in the ladies," Dev says, clearing the four-foot-high bar with a one-handed jump.

I smirk as Kara berates him then turns to me. "Jeremy?"

"Yeah, honey?" I place down two bottles and open the third.

"Can you start getting the tables and chairs down and set them out in rows? There's about fifty or so kids, so just do what you can."

I laugh and take another gulp. "Sure."

My eyes remain fixed on Kara until she disappears. I set my half-empty bottle back on the bar and nudge Dev. "Fancy a trip to the cellar?"

The man huffs in disappointment, his cheeks expanding in displeasure. "No fucking way. Have you got a torch?"

"No, electricity," I quip and furrow my brow. "What is it with you and dark spaces?" I've noticed this in the past with him, but I've never dared to raise it since I imagine war will change even the strongest of men.

"It's nothing." He shakes his head.

"No, it's something, Dev, and it's got a clinical name. PTSD."

He huffs. "What do you know about it?" His tone is vicious, but that's just the pent-up anger talking.

"More than you realise." I tug his elbow and make him face me. "I held a dead woman in my arms for an hour after she OD'ed in my bedroom with drugs I was meant to be selling." Dev closes his eyes in pain. It's only recently they found out about that sordid side of my life. His mouth opens, but I shake my head. "Have you never been to see anyone about it?"

"No." His reply is sharp, quick, and very uncomfortable as he pushes open the fire door that leads to the staff corridor and jogs down the stairs to the basement. I watch him stride with purpose, clearly not wishing to elaborate on such a detrimental and undiagnosed issue any further. His or mine, for that fact.

I loiter for a few, fully aware there's not a single person in our ragtag familial group who is whole or balanced. Okay, that's a lie. Marie is probably the most put together and sane out of all of us. Still, when one hurts, we all hurt.

"Key, sunshine?" Dev calls out. I descend the steps two at a time and advance on him. I push open the cellar door and slip the wad of keys into my front pocket. The stale, dank odour penetrates my nostrils immediately, and I scrunch my nose in response.

"Gentlemen first." I smirk at Dev, my hand cutting through the atmosphere.

He returns my grin. "That's right, sunshine, because you are no gentleman," he says in scouse. "Fuck my life. I hate this shit!" His teeth sound as tightly clenched as his fists. "Let's get this over and done with, and the next time anyone asks me for a favour, you can all fly! Dark spaces... Smelly fucking cellars... Spiders..." he continues chuntering.

I flick on the lights and snigger, half amused, half concerned, as he continues effing and blinding, reluctantly edging deeper into the room. Granted, it's no longer dark, but it isn't silencing him yet.

I tap his elbow and nod to the rear corner where a ton of old retro wooden and metal school chairs are stacked.

"I think the last time I sat on chairs like this was over twenty years ago," Dev says, sounding less depressed and more nostalgic.

"You and me both," I reply as a strange, unidentifiable sound floats into the room. It sounds like...scratching. "Do you hear that?"

Dev's head snaps up, and he cranes his neck, attempting to gain clarity. "Kara, we're in here!"

A whistle then grows louder and louder until a maniacal laugh we've both had the displeasure of hearing before fills the room. My eyes bulge in terror the same instant Dev's do, and we both sprint for the door as the devil incarnate himself blocks it.

"Lucky, lucky! The turncoat cunt and the useless army twat! I couldn't have planned this better if I'd tried. We'll call it fate, shall we? No? Fine. We'll call it a means to an end, starting with Sloan's whore wife!"

The anger gaining momentum in my throat comes out in a roar, and I lunge for him, only forcing myself to stop when he casually reveals the knife he's had since we were kids. I baulk as he lifts it directly in front of my eye and makes a tsk sound.

"An eye for an eye? Or a scar for a scar?" He shrugs, then his leg lifts and plants his boot in my stomach. The impact of the kick knocks the wind out of me, throwing me back. My hands flounder to grasp at something, anything, for leverage, but the sharp strike to the back of my head from an unknown object triggers an instantaneous sickness, and I finally hit the floor in a dazed heap.

"Son of a bitch!" Dev hisses. From the corner of my disorientated, unfocused eye, he launches himself at Deacon. Deacon moves quickly, thrashing his weapon in front of him. In truth, he's never used his fists for anything other than battering frightened young women who are less inclined or too immobilised to fight back. He's always used a weapon – *this weapon*. The weapon his dad gave him. The weapon he gloated about threatening Sloan with when we were teens.

The weapon he used to rape and terrorise defenceless girls.

I attempt to push up from the floor, but my head is spinning, and I can feel the rotation of the earth. A grunt redirects my attention to the men fighting, and I focus on Dev performing a series of kicks and punches until he jumps back as the tip of Deacon's blade slices through his t-shirt. The lack of red tainting the material confirms he's not injured. However, in this inhospitable place, his own weapons – his limbs – have no room to gain traction or manoeuvre.

The blade glints under the lights, and Deacon flicks it, momentarily blinding Dev, gaining himself the upper hand. Everything then moves in the wrong direction, and I watch on in shock and fear as Deacon brings the handle down hard on Dev's head, knocking him out instantly. The balance of power shifts when an unconscious Dev hits the floor.

Deacon straightens; his expression is jubilant. He slides the knife back under his coat and pierces me with his deadly gaze. "This is on you, Jer." He jerks his head to Dev's lifeless form. "You killed Em. You could've stopped Charlie's attack, and you were more than compliant in Kara's-"

"I never fucking touched her!" I roar, my head spinning.

"No, you just drugged her and handcuffed her. You could've killed her. My point, Jeremy, is that you are not the hero in this story. You're the villain." He sneers, exposing every ounce of evil deceit I refused to see for so long. "Now, I've got more pressing matters to deal with, namely, Sloan's whore."

"NO!"

The cellar door slams shut, and the outside bolt is slid into place. His footsteps retreat until they are no more. I grab the back of my head, needing to move. I've failed her enough already. I can't fail her again. She needs me more than she will ever know.

I crawl across the floor, press two fingers to Dev's jugular and bend down. I emit a sigh of relief when a steady beat and an exhale of breath waft in my ear. I pull back to get a better look at him. The only visible injury is the cut on his forehead, which is still bleeding steadily. I rip a length off his shirt and fasten it around his head the best I can. Carefully twisting him onto his side, it's not quite the recovery position, but at least he won't choke on his tongue or something.

I fight back the retreating dizziness and drag myself up from the floor. I need to get out of here – not for me, but for Kara and, more than likely, Marie. It's all so clear to see now, and I pray he hasn't done to her what he has to so many before.

Forgoing the faint nausea, I take stock of the room. Unable to identify anything to assist escape, I eye the cellar hatch door that leads up to the street. I've still got the keys, but there's an anti-theft chain securing it on the other side to deter would-be thieves.

Imminent defeat overwhelms me. My redemption was two steps forward, now it's three steps back. Now Kara is out there alone, with him. *Again.* She may not survive.

On that thought, my resolve hardens. I scan the room again for anything I might be able to break out with. Dev murmurs, and my attention moves from him to the chair just behind him.

I scramble towards it, closing my eyes, fighting against the light-headedness, and pick it up. It feels sturdy enough, and by our own admission, they have to be at least twenty years old, if not more. Let's hope the adage of *they don't make them like they used to* is actually true. Although it was made to last, I doubt it was made with the intention of breaking and entering. But one can hope, I pray, dashing back to the door.

I grip the rear legs tightly and direct the chair back towards the small glass window reinforced with wire mesh. The impact takes me by surprise, and the wood back bounces off the pane and splits in two, only having made a minuscule dent in the safety glass.

I tighten my hands again, draw back, and put all my weight and might behind the hit. Then another, and another, until I growl in frustration and throw the chair to the other side of the room.

"Why, why, FUCKING WHY?" I scream at the door and proceed to use my fists. Adrenaline spurs me on with each impact of my bare knuckles on the glass, replacing the searing pain of cut flesh with sheer determination. I'm not making any further inroads into breaking the pane completely – there's a reason why these old glass windows are wired – but if I can make the hole big enough, I might be able to find something to cut the mesh and reach my hand around to unlock the bolt. Or at least that's what I'm making myself believe.

With the fantasy of freedom flowing, I continue levying hit after hit to the glass. The pain intensifies with each one, and I'm not so much as making the hole bigger than I am cutting up both sets of knuckles beyond recognition.

Eventually, the stinging becomes too much, and I press my forehead to the door, kicking it repeatedly in frustration because I've done it again. I've left her alone and offered her up to a monster. History is finally coming full circle.

The revelation proverbially assaults my psyche, and I slide down the door and rest my head in my hands. Back then, I could blame the drugs. Now? Now, I can only blame my complacency. Now, she will truly hate me forever. A red-hot tear trickles down my cheek as a faint scream echoes through the building. I'm up in a shot, and I press my face to the hole in the glass. A mixture of noises invades my ears, but the most prevalent is that of crying and running.

"Devlin? Jeremy? Please, somebody, help me!"

Relief overcomes me. "Kara?" I call back, but aware she may not hear me. I rush to the discarded chair from earlier, pick it up, and bang it against the door repeatedly. "KARA?" I scream at the top of my lungs until the reverberation of footsteps accompanied by the frightened resonances of a terrified female nears.

Steps stop outside the door, and the squeak of the bolt is like a chorus of angels singing. I stand back as the door is thrown open, then I grab Kara's shoulders, not giving a toss if she hates it.

"He's here! Marie...Oh, God..." Her expression is one of terror. "Where's Dev?" Her eyes lower, then widen, spying him on the floor. "Dev?" She drops to her knees. Conducting a quick assessment, her hand grazes the flannel tourniquet I fashioned in a moment of panic. She then stands and looks around the room grimly.

"He'll be fine, Kara, but you won't." Cautiously, she moves as far away from me as the space will allow, confusing me.

"Jeremy, no, please don't!"

I furrow my brow. A cold chill instantly runs through me, the instant realisation dawns. She thinks I'm with *him*. That I've probably been planning this all along. Son of a bitch! I grind my jaw as my eyes flit around the room again. I grab the sweeping brush propped against the wall, lodge my foot on the head and force the handle off. I reach for her, still not giving a shit, and dig into my pocket for the car keys and stuff them in her hand.

"When we get back upstairs, I want you to run. I want you to get in the car and drive. I mean it! You don't fucking stop!" I slam my lips to her forehead.

"Thank you," she says in a weird tone, but I know what she's really thanking me for.

"Redemption, remember?"

As we exit the cellar, the familiar scratching from earlier drifts over the tense atmosphere.

"Kara…"

My shoulders straighten as Deacon calls her out. Gripping the stick in my hand, I grab her elbow forcibly and drag her through the maze of back corridors. She wavers but doesn't give up. I retrieve the club keys and slip the ring over my finger, one eye on our escape, the other on the keys as I find the one I want.

I open the door that leads back to the club floor. Kara turns hesitantly, the car keys in her hand.

The door! Now! I mouth with conviction, indicating where I need her to go but fearing she won't. My fears are unfounded when she begins to move until she sees something.

"Kara!" I bellow as she slides across the floor in the opposite direction and trusses Marie into her arms. Completely unbelievable. Yet I can believe it because Marie is as good as her mother, and she will sacrifice herself for those she loves.

"Oh, isn't this sweet, sweets!"

I spin around instantly, the tone grating on me. Deacon fills the doorway, his typical malevolent smirk in place. I turn the stick in my hand and point it at him. "You and me, bastard! Let's fucking end this!" My words are powerful because I'm not afraid of dying, not anymore. However, only one of us will be walking out of here, and I'm going to ensure it's me, even if they add pre-meditated manslaughter to the list of charges currently growing against me.

"With pleasure!" Deacon opens his arms in a Jesus like stance.

I growl and run at him full pelt, raising the stick high and slamming it down on the fucker's shoulder. He sways but doesn't fall. I lift my arm and continue to thrash at him until the wood hits the floor when he steps back, and it cracks and splinters on impact. I toss the other end down the precise moment a punch to my temple knocks the wind out of me. I regain composure quickly and fist my hand to return the favour.

My fists are fucked as I take on the guy who was once my best friend. Extracts from years past flood my mind. They play like an untold story, at long last showing me everything he did that would guarantee I'd exist in misery until the day I fail to exist no more.

I feel rejuvenated, fuelled by the long-awaited insight, and my hands fly. Moving faster, harder, and I defy the pain radiating from my knuckles.

But all good things must come to an end, and I feel my strength slipping away the longer this goes on. I'm not a fighter; I'm a brawler and not a very prolific or experienced one either. I pray my stamina holds until Kara has managed to get herself and Marie out.

On that thought, I turn, and that is my ruin as Deacon lands a solid, powerful hit to the side of my head, instigating the dizziness to return tenfold in retaliation. I sway and hit the deck.

Seconds later, a gut-wrenching scream bounces off the walls, and I lift my head just in time to see Marie fall to the floor. Deacon has a death grip on Kara and is battering her face. "When I'm done with you, you'll be in a fucking box! Let the cunt sit at your grave and mourn you!"

Unexpected determination and clarity washes over me. I'm not like him. I'm not evil. I'm not a monster, not really, regardless of what I say when I'm hurting. I was just an addicted kid who made a mistake. That mistake was trusting him.

"Get the fuck away from her!" My thunder of abhorrence ripples around the vast space. Enduring the biliousness, I force myself up.

In a moment of selflessness, or maybe madness, since my body is already feeling the day's effects, I swing at him. I slam into him, and we both go flying over the chairs, ensuring every muscle feels further discomfort. Fate is clearly watching my back when I land on top of him. In my mind's eye, all I can see is our past, and my fists do the talking as I bring blow upon blow down upon him.

Deacon grins through bloodied teeth. "That's it, Jer, embrace the hatred! And when I'm done here with you and her, I want you to think about all the things I'm going to do to the little slut you have in your flat! I bet that bitch likes it rough, too!"

I drag him up from the floor, hold his neck in one hand and pound him with the other. I shift slightly, and he brings a knee to my side and takes the advantage when he pummels my scarred cheek.

My face feels like it's about to explode, and my body is silently telling me it's over, that we can't do this much longer. My energy is draining away second by second, and I drop to my knees, deplete and beat. Catching my breath, Deacon kneels in front of me. I steel myself the best I can because this is it, and I wonder how it will finally end for me.

Deacon's black, dead eyes ensnare mine, and he grips my chin. I force my eyes to stay open as he tilts my jaw. Three thoughts swarm inside my mind: my mother, Kara, and Evie.

Always Evie.

My lips curve at the vision of her this morning as I wait for the knife tip to penetrate my neck. My eyes close of their own accord, my body rejoicing in the memory. My reprieve is transient before the blade finally breaches my skin. My eyes widen as the tip slides down my unblemished cheek. The pain is indescribable, a fire burning wild, cutting a scorching path through my flesh.

I grind my jaw and sway, a woozy weakness taking over. My body finally signs off, and I grab my face, then hit the deck.

"I'll see you in hell after Shaw's found you, you son of a bitch!"

Deacon's taunt and the unknown pain radiating in my gut over and over are the last things I remember as my subconscious takes control.

And once again, my world is black.

Chapter 15

THE FAINT AND somewhat comforting sounds of beeps, clicks, and gentle whirring are vociferous, confirming precisely where I am.

My body begins to regain consciousness, and I murmur and swallow hard, fighting the compulsion to throw up. An aftereffect of being put under general anaesthetic, I guess. My lips and mouth are dry, arid, like the desert. If I didn't know any different, I'd be convinced I had consumed sandpaper. Sadly, I do know different.

Desperate for some water, I part my lips, but the unavoidable pain of newly stitched flesh engulfs my face, ensuring I groan incessantly. Raising my hand to my cheek, all I can feel is bandages which means it's going to be bad.

Really fucking bad.

"The stiches are dissolvable. In a few weeks, they'll be gone." A recognisable voice interposes the silence.

I swing my head, causing the burning tightness in my face to stretch, and pain spreads like fuel on a naked flame.

Doc leans against the wall, just inside the door. His grim expression says it all. "How do you feel?"

"Like shit, how do you think?" My reply is riddled with sarcasm, although my tone is despondent, surprisingly void of any bitter emotion.

Stuart's mouth starts to open, but I shoot him a glare of disdain. Averting my gaze, my fingers caress the gauze dressing, reminding me why I'm lying here cut up again. There's nothing anyone can say to make this right. I should be thankful; it could have been worse – the rat bastard could have slit my throat and killed me.

"Stuart, where's Kara? Marie and Dev?" I ask, jack-knifing up from the bed. I ignore the soreness still radiating in my cheek from talking and start to swing my legs over the side in an attempt to stand, but the pain in my side now starts to flare up.

"Calm down." Doc flattens his palm against my chest and forces me back down. "They're all fine. Well, as fine as can be expected, all things considered." He drags the chair closer to the bed and sits down.

"What do you mean? What happened?"

Stuart's grim expression takes on a whole new meaning. "He almost killed her, Rem. Another minute longer, she would have been dead. What do you remember?"

"Everything. Nothing." I scrub my hand over my face, accidentally snagging at the bandage. I hiss and glare at him again. "Get this fucking shit off me before I rip it off!"

His jaw grinds, but he reaches for a pair of gloves. "This might sting," he says, transferring to the edge of the bed.

I chortle. "I'll pass your bedside manner tips on to Kieran when I next see him." Doc rolls his eyes, but my arsehole attitude is far from diminished by his glare. I've got plenty to be angry about right now.

He slowly peels away the bandage and gives me a pointed look, wanting to hear what I remember.

I sigh. "We were fighting. My body was weakening with each hit until I couldn't take any more. My knees hit the floor, and Deacon stood over me. There was a moment where I thought he was going to slit my throat." I bristle and shake my head, causing the dressing to remove completely in Doc's hand. "Instead, he decided to give me this. I remember pain in my side when I was down…"

"Hmm, it appears that he kicked the shit out of you as you laid unconscious. You were lucky," he says, and I chortle again.

"Yeah, lucky I'm not dead. Unlucky, I'm now just the monster I feared. I've even got the dual scars for authenticity." Doc's brows lift, but he doesn't understand. None of them do. "Speaking of the rat bastard, where is he?" I look towards the door. In the time I've been awake, I haven't seen anything resembling security or police outside. If Deacon's in custody, I would expect him to be crowing to anyone who will listen, which means the police will be coming for me soon.

"He's dead."

"What?" I ask in disbelief.

"After he knocked you out, he went after Kara. Strictly between us, Marie seems to think Kara was ready to accept her fate and sacrifice herself for those she loves, including you. The armed response unit pumped him full of bullets. He was gone before he even hit the floor." He sneers, disgusted, and I frown in misunderstanding. "The chaplain gave him the last rights, but he's going to need more than that where he's going."

I nod in silence, concurring the truth – there is no redemption in hell. I turn to the window and inadvertently touch my newest scar. From touch alone, it feels almost identical to the other side.

"What about me?" I ask quietly.

"What about you?" Stuart's tone is confused, but again, he doesn't understand. He's a man of medicine, not law.

"Nothing. I just…" I just don't know. In theory, I'm free. Only those closest to me will ever know what I did all those years ago, and they won't go running to the police. I should be feeling elation and relief, but all I feel is guilt. Guilt that justice will never prevail.

"Look, Rem." Stuart stands and disposes of the gloves in the bin. "It's not going to be easy, but in time this will just be another nightmare." He reaches down and gives me a brotherly hug, then heads to the door. "Oh, while I remember, your mobile has been buzzing like it's going out of fashion. I'll be back with your release forms in a few hours. See you later."

I pick up my phone from the bedside table and swipe the screen. There's a mass of messages, both pre and post-assault, but the one that's shining brightly amongst the rest is the one from Evie.

I flick the message open and groan at her request for a family dinner. *Again.*

I swallow hard. My throat is dry, and I inhale a rueful breath. Whatever my reply, it's going to be lies because I can't have her seeing me like this. She'll demand answers – if she's not running for the hills before she opens her mouth, that is – of which she is more than entitled to considering our relationship status, but I just can't.

I tap out a response, claiming I'm covering sickness at the club tonight. Hopefully, Sloan has kept today's incident concealed. I guess I'll know soon enough whether it has made the local news.

I shuffle back down the bed and gaze out of the window. My heart is full, yet it feels hollow because I'm conflicted. Now more than ever. I finally have a chance to live my life, to experience things I once suppressed, never to be thought of or imagined otherwise. Still, someone has to be held accountable. Someone has to ensure justice triumphs. It won't be an act of self-righteousness; just the right thing to do.

My heart is heavy with emotion, and long minutes pass by. Tracking the movement of the clouds outside, my solitude is pierced when footsteps enter the room and my body rocks as someone sits on the bed. I grudgingly turn around and come face to face with the woman I failed again.

I can't muster a smile right now, considering even the slightest movement is painful, but it seems Kara can't either, if her sorrowful eyes and pursed lips are any indication.

"I'm sorry, Kara. We didn't realise he was in the building until…" She shakes her head, and I shut up.

"We all knew it would eventually come to this. It had to, but he's gone now."

Gone. Along with any chance of fairness. "I've been thinking about it, and I'm still going to turn myself in to the police, tell them what I did and live with the consequences."

"No, I don't want you to," she replies, looking to Sloan then back again. "As far as I'm concerned, it's finally over. You, inside, prolongs it. And it means my suffering continues, as will yours, and I can't live with that." Her trust and conviction are to be respected and admired, but I can't live with the consequences now.

"Kara…"

"No. You've been living with the consequences of it for nine years. It's done!" Salty tears sting my eyes as fully-fledged ones fill Kara's, and she leaves the room.

"Sloan, you've got to talk to her, make her see this is the only way!" I beg, knowing he hates it as a ruckus comes from outside.

"No, Rem, I respect my wife's decision. As much as we're all entwined together in ways unimaginable, it's her life, her memories… Ultimately, it will always be her choice. She could have had you put away months ago, but she didn't. What does that tell you?"

"Sloan-"

"I love you like a brother, but you're wrong about this." He shakes his head as he walks out and slams the door behind him.

THE DAY IS long and laborious, filled with unwanted visitors - namely, Tom, Si and Devlin, who, thankfully, is up and about and sporting a nasty cut to his head but is pretty much unaffected - until night creeps in.

I scratch the pen over the form, signing myself out, and toss them on the bed next to the NHS gown I woke up in. Sliding on my jacket, the door opens.

"Hey," John greets, looking more exhausted than I've ever seen him before.

"Hi," I reply cautiously. The man has been through the wringer today, so who knows where his head is at.

I follow him as he picks up my papers, scans them and puts them back down and moves around the bed. "How are you?"

"Fine. I'm sorry I couldn't protect Marie, John. Honestly, we didn't know-" He presses his finger to my lips.

"I know." His finger lifts and hovers over my fresh scar before pulling back, thinking better of it. "Marie's asleep. Come on, I'll give you a lift home. We need to talk."

I follow him out of the room. Talking is the last thing I want to do since he knows my next move.

"How is she?" I ask as we drive in silence. I'm aware of the internal conflict, but he's the one who said we should talk. "J, I'm not Sloan, and I won't be telling him."

He sighs, resigned. "She's not good. I told Kara she was fine because I didn't want to add more stress on them, but Marie's not in a good place. I also don't think it's because of what happened. It's deeper, older than that. Stuart's given me the name of a shrink. I said I'd try, but I won't hold my breath. Trying isn't going to be enough."

I don't comment since it would be an insult to. Marie is the most mentally stable and emotionally strong of all of us. Her life hasn't been tainted by evil like ours has. Or at least ten minutes ago, I wouldn't have thought so.

"She'll get better, John," I say and hold his gaze as my phone rings, and *Evie* fills the screen.

John gives me a knowing sideways glance and rubs his eyes. "When are you leaving?"

"ASAP," I confirm; there's no point in lying. "Once I've packed a bag, I'm gone."

"Why?"

"Why? Because Kara and Sloan want to forgive and forget, but we all know some things are never best forgotten."

He brings the car to a stop and taps in the code at the security gates to the flats. "And what about little miss?" he queries, using his nickname for Evie. He pulls into the empty bay next to mine, and relief spreads through me that Evie has decided to stay away tonight.

I climb out of the car and stride towards the lift. John is hot on my heels, and he spins me around as the doors open, and he pushes me inside.

"I asked you a question. I expect an answer!"

"What about her?" I fire back. The tension is thick, heaving with my anger and fear.

"You finally have a reason to live! Why the fuck are you throwing it away?" he shouts.

"I'm not!" I grab him by the shoulders and push him against the wall. Every emotion concerning Evie that I've bottled up for the last twenty-four hours explodes, and my resolve dies. I drop my head to his shoulder and allow my pain to flow.

"She's the rightest thing I've ever had in my life. She fits here-" I touch my chest "-perfectly. But look at me. This isn't a fairy-tale. It isn't Beauty and the Beast, and I'm not the unlikely fucking hero!"

The lift dings, and J wraps his arm around my shoulder and guides me home. Unlocking the door, he taps in my alarm code, and I pad into the bedroom and begin throwing stuff into a bag.

"John?" I call out.

"Yeah?" He pops his head around the architrave.

"Evie still has some stuff here. She has a key and access downstairs. Can you ensure she always has that? I get the feeling things aren't right at home. She's never said as much, but it's just a niggle. I'd like to know she has somewhere she can come to if she needs to." John nods, his eyes fixed on the perfume bottle on the dresser.

I reach into my pocket and remove the letters I've been carrying around with me since last night. "Can you give that to her for me?"

"Sure. Just answer me one question honestly." I tip my chin. "Do you love her?"

"That's not a simple question."

"Tough. Do you?"

"Yeah, I love her. Don't ask me why. We're a bit chalk and cheese, but loving her is as natural and instinctual as breathing. The same as the air in my lungs or the blood in my veins."

"Okay, I'll check on her...make sure she gets this." He waves the letter. "Where are you going?"

"Leeds. Where else?" He nods, already aware of my impending move. "If you need me, I'll come back, but I just need..."

"To get right in your own head?" he finishes for me.

"Something like that." I pick up the bag and wait for him to join me.

"I respect your decision, but I still think it's a mistake."

"Maybe." I shrug. "But she deserves better than a second chance, scarred up thug."

John's expression is thunderous as we board the lift, and he looks ready to hit me. "I'm not listening to this shit!" He stares at the floor, and we ride down the lift in silence. The tension is as palpable as it was on the journey up.

John waits by his car and watches me throw my bag into the back of mine. He wraps me in his arms and holds me. "Take care of yourself, son."

"I will." I break away from him and get into my car, glad my windows have dark tinting so he can't see my distress. I slowly reverse out. Looking in my rearview, John is still watching me, and I finally drive away.

THE MOON SHINES brightly as I pull up three hours later. Grabbing my bag and the supermarket carrier from the back, I jog up the stairs into the flat I haven't lived in for months.

I flick on the lights, and my eyes work the space. It has that distinctive, unlived musty smell, and my eyes do a good job of intentionally avoiding the layer of dust covering everything.

I drop my holdall on the living room floor and palm my mobile. I have intentionally avoided looking at it, but I can't avoid it forever.

I turn on the stereo, something to fill the lonely void, and enter the kitchen. Again, in bright light, it's long overdue a clean, but tonight I don't give a shit. Tonight, I just want to drown my sorrows and forget. Removing the bottle of gin from the carrier, I open the door to the cabinet and locate the cigs and lighter I stash at the top.

I place the bottle on the table and open the window. Lighting up a fag, I inhale deeply. The nicotine hits my throat in a vaporous cloud, fogging my tumultuous thoughts. I inadvertently start to hum to *Snow Patrol's Run*. It's appropriate because that's what I've done again. My life has come full circle – twice. One day I need to stop running, but that will only be a possibility when there's nothing – or no one – left to run from.

I neck the gin straight from the bottle, all the while my mobile vibrates for the hundredth time. Daring to look at it, I press the notifications, and the message from Evie is glaring at me, spelling out home truths I can't bear right now.

You've left???? My god you lied to me and I believed you! You lied to me you don't love me. If you did you wouldn't have left me with no explanation or goodbye. How dare you use me and discard me like nothing. I hate you Jeremy James!! I hate you!!!!

I scream in frustration and anger and throw the phone across the room. I bring the bottle back to my lips, swallowing as much as I can in the shortest space of time.

The clock changes from ten, to eleven, to just after one in the morning. During the last few hours of my drunken stupor, I've experienced every emotion I can verbalise.

The faint click of the door lock seeps into my gin infused brain, and I lift my head as Dom enters. "I expected to see you at mine hours ago," he says, until he recognises I'm pissed out of my head. "What the hell are you doing?" He takes away my bottle, causing me two types of pain.

"I'm trying to forget. I've destroyed her. I've destroyed me. I've fucked it up big time!"

"What?"

"I loved her, and she loved me. Now she hates me."

"Who?" Dom asks, annoyed.

"Evelyn Blake, a beautiful woman who saw past this." I haphazardly throw my hand to my face – drawing Dom's attention to my newest addition. He crouches next to me and tilts my chin, examining the damage.

"John called, but he didn't tell me." He throws his arm around my shoulder, pulling me close. "I'm sorry, son."

"I've got a full Glasgow smile now, Dom!" I puff out my chest, but the realisation breaks me and my body slumps because even I'm repulsed by my appearance now. The tears behind my eyes fall, and I wipe them quickly. "I'm sorry. Men don't cry."

Dom sighs. "But we do. We hurt, too." He manipulates my head, and I slide further down the wall. Curled in a ball with my head resting on his thigh, I stare into nothingness.

"I'll let you drown your sorrows tonight, but tomorrow, you turn it around and keep it around." His words are background noise in comparison to the pain ravishing my heart. The truth is tomorrow, Evie will still hate me from two hundred miles away, and I'll still be repulsed by my own appearance.

Finally, becoming the monster I never truly believed I was, I fall into a boozy darkness.

And I pray never to wake up.

Chapter 16

"GIVE IT SOME welly, Remy lad!" Kieran hollers, raising his padded hand for me to strike. In the corner of my eye, the disapproving looks from the other patrons at K's overzealous, loudmouth antics this morning are identifiable. He's being more obnoxious than usual, which isn't a hard feat for him, to be honest.

"Shut up. Your accent is distracting everyone!" I grin, baiting him. I bare my teeth as my feet move in perfect unison with the rest of my body, and I build my rhythm, punching right to left, hook and jab.

"That's it, lad! More power! You're killing it, son, killing it!"

"For God's sake!" I throw another punch, then step back. Sweat drips down my back, a faint line trickling down my spine, distracting and irritating me more than my brash scally sparring partner. I toss down my gloves, pick up my water and gulp down whatever is remaining. The clock ticks over eight o'clock, and the gym has started to fill up with people getting a workout in before they start work. I knock back another mouthful and scan the free weights area, recognising various faces.

"While you're procrastinating, as usual, I'm going to hit up the punch bag," Kieran says.

I nod and walk to the window where I can watch life carry on and steady my breathing. Kieran hasn't seemed to realise, or if he has, he hasn't mentioned it, but today is the first anniversary of my second scar.

My reflection flashes back at me, and I trace the blemished skin but drop my hand before anyone can question it. It's no longer red, inflamed or sore, and although it has healed visually, it still feels numb when I shave - almost like someone else is shaving me. It's a bizarre feeling. Kieran and Dominic are both adamant I've got some nerve damage or severed endings, but who knows. I never bothered to see a doctor when the stitches finally started to drop out. Instead, I went to see Doctor Kieran again, and the man sorted out the more stubborn ones with a few shots of Dom's good whisky and a pair of tweezers soaked in saline. Unlike the first time, I was suddenly quite content that I was lacking sensation and intoxicated on one of my three evils.

I rest against the window with one arm. Assailed by memories, including those that painfully convey the truth that another part of my life that's also lacking sensation is my love life. I'm not ashamed to say my poor dick hasn't seen any action since Evie, and even my hand is now tired of being acquainted with the pathetic prick.

Good times all around.

But good times are not meant to be steeped in misery and self-loathing, and that's all I've felt and actively sought since I left London in my rear-view twelve months ago.

Upon reflection, I can't say my choice was the right one - John was right about that. I should have stayed, explained the agonising truth to Evie, and endeavoured to build some semblance of a stable life for myself at long last, whether she still wanted me or not.

Instead, I've regressed to existing. Repeating the dull, monotonous grind, day in, day out, very likely until my days are no more. I've also regressed to living like a hermit again, refusing even the simplest of contact from anyone outside the Leeds outer ring road.

And it's apparent the majority have finally got the message.

In the beginning, my mobile was ringing and vibrating like there was no tomorrow. I couldn't turn the bloody thing on without having at least twenty or thirty texts and voicemails of varying requests, silly anecdotes, or faux threats from Sloan, John, Jake, et al. Even the women took note and upped the guilt trip. Whilst I read and listened, entangled in a variety of emotional intrigue, amusement, and sadness, they went in one ear and out the other because there are only two people I wanted to hear from. My mum, who, regardless that I've physically abandoned her again – her take on my latest bout of absconding – I've kept in touch regularly, unlike before.

The other is Evie. *Always Evie.*

But unlike my mum, as much as it pains me, I've had to sever all contact and let her go. Initially, she would text and call unremittingly. Gradually, her contact went from a few calls and texts per day to once or twice per month now, if I'm lucky. It kills me that she's given up, but this is what I wanted... No, this is what I created. I did this to her. *To us.* And everything I ever wanted with her, every sacred, secret dream I allowed myself to believe could be a possibility I will never have. Heck, I'll consider myself fortunate if she even acknowledges me if I ever see her again.

A part of me – the masochistic part - hopes the lack of contact means she's moved on. That she's found someone who can give her everything she needs, wants, and desires. The emotional part of me doesn't want her dwelling on the past, but the selfish part of me hopes that none of the above is correct. I appreciate that makes me a hypocritical bastard since I've never been able to heed my own advice.

The reality now is that my life is no different here than it would've been had I stayed there. I'm miserable and alone, craving a love that will never be mine again. All because of a friendship choice I made as a foolish teen.

Now that decision and its subsequent fallout will haunt me for the rest of my life.

I rub my cheek absentmindedly, tracing the abraded skin. They say the first cut is the deepest, but it's the second that is the most painful and detrimental. And it's the one that has cut through to the very heart of me.

The heart that belongs to *her*.

I inhale a shaky breath and lightly bang my head on the windowpane. "For Christ's sake," I mutter rhetorically. My melancholy side is prevailing this morning, cogitating on the morbid life I've twisted into shape.

I glance over my shoulder at Kieran powering his fists into a bag. His grunts float over the general hum of the gym floor, and I walk towards him, stopping to replenish my water bottle.

"Hi."

I flick my eyes up from the machine to the woman smiling at me. Her eyes scan my face, from one cheek to the other and rather than repulsed, she's blatantly intrigued.

"I'm Claire. Nice to meet you," she greets, edging closer.

My hackles rise, but I go with hospitable. "Jeremy. And you." There's no emotion in my tone. I quickly offer my hand, shake hers, then pull mine back.

I screw the lid onto my bottle and glance over Claire's head at Kieran, who's making gestures to construct conversation. I grudgingly look back at Claire, still smiling with intent. Don't get me wrong, she's pretty, some would probably say stunning, with her fake tan, fake nails, dyed blonde hair and absurdly plastered face, but she just isn't doing it for me. Even if I was genuinely interested, she still wouldn't do it for me.

"So," she begins, "I've seen you here for a while now. I was wondering if you fancy grabbing a coffee or something after we've finished?"

My eyes narrow immediately in response, and I scrub my hand over my forehead to hide my scowl. The alarm bells are going off inside my head. The fact that she's noticed me, but I've never noticed her – and trust me, I make it my mission to know who's around me these days – is discomforting. Likewise, her overemphasised use of *'we've'*. The last thing I need is to ruin my hardboiled sanity by engaging this woman in further conversation or anything else.

Dropping my hand, I force a smile, which probably appears more of a glower if her reaction is anything to go by. "It really is nice to meet you, Claire, but I'm not looking for *anything* at the moment."

She pulls her neck back and purses her lips. "It's just coffee." She laughs disingenuously, in protest and defence, and wraps her hand around my wrist, which means we can add pushy and passive-aggressive to the shortlist of her unattractive qualities.

"It's never just coffee," I reply and shake her the fuck off me. I'm ready to walk away, but her pouty, hands on hips stance goads me. Silly woman doesn't realise I've lived in this world. I've walked streets she can only imagine. I've done things she can only ever dream of. I've seen things that have mentally fucked even *me* up. I've witnessed the living, both the rich and the poor, at the top, the bottom, and everywhere in between, performing dishonourable acts for desperate, degenerate gains. And I've met girls like her, the ones who carry a sense of entitlement that they can do or take whatever they want because a handful of randy men call them gorgeous.

"I'm not interested." I hold her gaze as she absorbs what I've just said. Her face falls, and I can see the defensive wall erect within seconds. Instead of waiting for her vitriolic response, which will just waste more of my time, I turn on my heel.

"Who's the fit bird staring daggers at you?" Kieran asks when I'm in earshot, fists going hammer and nail at the punch bag.

"Just some woman who likes a bit of rough." I down another mouthful of water.

K's fists drop in front of him. He rips off a glove and rubs the towel around his neck over his nape. "You're not rough, lad."

I smile gushingly, causing him to copy. "K, you're sweet, but my face doesn't concur."

"Your face is fucking stunning, my friend. I'd do you if I was that way inclined." He grabs my bottle and chugs down half of it. "We done for today?"

I nod. "We're definitely done." I follow him to the changing room and remove my towel and toiletries from the locker.

The hot water beats down on my back as I stand under the shower, my arms braced on either side of the frosted glass.

"So, out with it then. What did you say to her out there?" K's question seeps from the next cubicle, over the flow of water and my discerning hearing.

"You're a nosey sod!"

"And I'm still waiting."

"Fine. I said I wasn't interested."

"You fucking blind?"

I chortle. "No, but you clearly are. Her type of beauty is ugly."

"We'll agree to disagree there, lad."

I grin. His roving eye tends to get him into trouble. I duck my head under the water and rinse out the shampoo. "Besides, the woman I want I can't have," I confess thoughtfully, the emotion in my tone intensifying but thankfully obscured by the din.

The curtain is pulled back abruptly, and Kieran stands there, naked as the day he was born. "Bullshit! You're just being an obstinate twat. Have you even tried to call her?"

I run my hands over my head to remove the excess water, turn off the shower, and wrap the towel around my hips. "No." I head into the changing room. Dumping my pile of sweaty gym gear into a bag, I stuff it inside my sports holdall.

"What about her texts?" He grips my chin, causing all eyes in the changing room to watch the show. Some are entirely enraptured, amused by the antics of the loudmouth scouse and the apparent cockney rebel. Others are uncomfortable and avert their gaze elsewhere.

I slam down the bag. "She stopped texting-"

"Don't! Aside from being a sulky, obstinate twat, don't be a liar, too. I know she still texts you a few times a month."

I narrow my eyes and give him a *how the hell do you know* glare.

K shrugs. "Holly told me."

"Holly?" I repeat, trying to recall which of Evie's friends she is. I can feel my face pull taut in concentration. I hope he will assume I'm incensed when secretly, I'm intrigued. In truth, it isn't much to give credence to, and most young women tend to be rambunctious in their retelling of a story, but if Evie's mentioned it to one of her friends, at least I know she's still thinking about me.

I unravel the towel from my hips and start to get dressed. I'm buttoning up my jeans when a sodden towel whips my back.

"Are you not at all interested in how I know?" Kieran rubs the towel through his hair, drops it on the bench, then combs his fingers through the damp lengths.

"No, but she's too young for you." The words tumble out before I can stop them, and I mentally cringe. Christ, I sound like Sloan when he rattles off his half-arsed threats to Jake – not that he has room to talk. Nor I, for that matter.

Kieran's bellowing laugh pulls me out of myself and fills the changing room, causing a few to flinch again. "Hello pot, meet kettle! Not only is he a sulky, obstinate twat, but he's also a contradictory one, too!" he goads, pulling his jeans on.

I want to fight my corner and tell him he's wrong, but I can't because he's right. I'm being unfairly two-faced, pure in my hypocrisy. Holly is the same age as Evie, and yes, Kieran is a few years older than me, but they're both consenting adults.

I sigh, eying him. "Sorry. I had a difficult time accepting Evie's age in the beginning."

Kieran nods lazily. "You still do, by the sound of it." He tugs on a t-shirt and picks up his phone and sports bag. "My offer still stands, you handsome git." He kisses my cheek and slaps my arse. The changing room befalls into near silence again, and the only prominent sound is K's chuckle as he taps away on his phone.

"What's up?" I zip up my bag and follow him.

"The boss has an unwanted visitor."

My head jerks up, and the way Kieran's jubilant expression withers tells me all the colour must have drained from my cheeks.

"Shit. Not *that* kind of visitor!" He grins, elbowing me in the ribs. "Well, maybe…" he adds thoughtfully.

I don't probe further, and he doesn't tell. These men are my friends, my allies, my family. They've dragged me from the dark side more times than I care to remember. They would protect me until the end, if need be.

On the way out, I stop by the water machine to top up my bottle. I casually glance around and catch sight of Claire, bent against the lateral pull machine, flirting up a storm with someone else. Relief rushes through me that I won't be finding ways to dodge her in the future and that someone finds her type of ugly beautiful. Don't misconstrue, she isn't ugly in the slightest, but true beauty, both inside and out, doesn't require acceptance. It's unassuming and bashful, and to every man on the planet, it has a name.

Mine is Evelyn Blake.

And until she declares she doesn't want to breathe the same air as me, she will always be my true beauty.

I SLAM THE car door behind me and press the remote to close the yard gates. This building, much like John's back in London, is old, decrepit, and monitored like Fort Knox.

A clap of thunder crashes above, adding to the torrents of rain, making for a miserable day ahead. Walking across the tarmac, puddles forming in some parts, glistening black and reflecting in others, only Kieran's Rover and Dom's Maserati are present. I breathe a sigh of relief that the unwanted visitor has already left.

The main door closes behind me, and Kieran and I head straight for Dom's office. The sounds of familiar, irate voices stop me in my tracks. I raise my brow in question at K, who just shakes his head. Great frigging help he is.

"All I'm saying is you need to find the *right* one, not *any* one!"

I close my eyes and frown as John's statement of conviction reaches my ears. I have a feeling I'm going to be put on the spot if I walk in there, and that's not a place I want to be.

"What? Like you have? *Found the right one?*" Dom replies, and something slams down. "Is *she* the right one, J?" Dom's question is coy and suspicious, insinuating things he never has before regarding Marie.

I push the door open, but the men inside are too busy inclining over the desk posturing at each other, practically nose to nose, to have even noticed me.

"What the hell is that supposed to mean?" John slams his fist down, and everything bounces then settles again.

"Nothing!" Dom growls. A flash of something is there but disappears from his face before J spots it.

I clear my throat before this becomes more heated than it already is, and two heads turn, adorning glowering expressions. John rears back to his full height and approaches me with all the grace of a raging bull. Worked up, his eyes are wild, his breathing is erratic.

"I'll be in your office." He stomps out, slamming doors as he goes. *Lucky fucking me!*

This day is getting better and better with each second that passes, and it's only just gone nine o'clock.

My teeth are on edge, and I grind my jaw. Dom's potent, unwavering stare would eviscerate most on the spot, but fortunately for me, I've been both the cause and the recipient many times. I'm also abundantly aware this is the look he wears when he's being forced to listen to something he doesn't want to hear. Surprisingly, he has no issue shoving his unwanted opinions down our throats from time to time.

I edge closer to the desk and note the file he has out. My brow quirks. "Does he know?"

He shrugs. "Possibly, who cares. Look, do me a favour, go home, and take *that*," he points towards my office, "with you."

I groan, unable to judge the lesser of two evils. If I refuse, I'll receive the full hairdryer effect when Dom's temper finally reaches boiling point, and I become the outlet for his anger. If I side with John, I'll just inadvertently agree to have him micromanage my life again to some degree from afar. I stare at the floor, praying to find the silver lining in this sorry situation.

"Jeremy!" I flinch, rocked from my stupor by Dom's frustrated shout.

"Yes, all right!" I turn on my heel. "For God's sake!" I mutter on my way out.

"No, Jer, you'll need more than God if you don't get *him* out of here ASAP!"

I slam the door behind me and hesitate in the corridor. I grin, a thought occurs to me. Never in my life would John have become my silver lining. I chuckle then enter my office.

John spins around from the window, his arms folded over his chest. "What's tickled your fancy?"

"Nothing." I shrug, and he raises a brow.

"You know, I thought he would've started to mellow in his old age," he observes, causing my smile to broaden, considering Dom isn't that much older than he is. Collecting myself, I shift uneasily as John's eyes affix on my cheek. "Jeremy, I-"

"Don't," I reply in frustration and pinch my nose. "Look, he's teetering on the edge in there, and I have specific orders to get *you* out of here."

"Hmm, I could have sworn he said, 'take *that* with you'. Maybe I'm hearing things…"

I snigger at his quickness. "Whatever. What the hell did you say to him to set him off anyway?"

"Not much. We just chatted about handbags and glad rags. Oh, and his penchant for pointless, brain dead, dolly birds. Luckily for you, I don't have anywhere else to be, so I'll tell you more on the way," he says, flouncing out of the door.

Lucky fucking me, indeed.

Chapter 17

"SO, WHAT ARE you doing up here?" I open the fridge. "Business?" I add casually for conversation, passing him a bottle of water and a glass as he looks around the flat.

"No, I'm here to take you home."

I lift my head to the heavens and close my eyes. "Well, you've wasted your time because I'm not coming back."

He tuts. "That's what you think, sunshine," he retorts and knocks back a large gulp of water.

"Seriously, J, I'm not coming back!" I reaffirm my position for all the good it will do me. It sounds weak even to my ears.

"This is familiar," John deadpans, observing the living room again, particularly where I'm perched on the sideboard, putting as much distance between us as the small space will allow.

"What is?"

He shrugs. "Oh, just travelling two hundred miles to drag you wayward kids back to where you all belong. This feels like déjà vu."

I purse my lips and silently concur. Last year, he was trying to convince another wayward kid to come home. "Did Kara put you up to this?" I wonder if she's finally repaying the favour for my involvement in that event.

He smirks. "No. She offered, but I figured we could save ourselves another potential scalding incident. Nevertheless, this little expedition has cost me Marie time." He falls silent again and glances at the floor. Obviously, Marie is now a touchy topic of contention, and that's not a good sign.

"How is she?" I ask because she didn't deserve what Deacon did to her. Likewise, neither did the rest of us.

"Come home and see for yourself."

I sigh loudly. "I already told you, I'm not-"

"Coming back, I know! You sound like a broken record, for fuck sake!"

"Good. And if I keep saying it, maybe it'll penetrate your thick skull! For fuck sake, indeed!" His brows lift, impressed. It isn't often I stand my ground with him, but by God, the man can piss me off like no other.

"I thought Dom would have beaten the mouthy little bastard out of you by now."

"Keeps him on his toes." I nod, albeit reluctantly, but I'm unoffended. "And your observation is incorrect. According to K, I'm a sulky, obstinate, contradictory twat."

John grins. "I could have told you that years ago. No doubt your mum probably has."

Now it's my turn to grin. "Hmm, but her language was polite and flowery, and then she offered me a cup of tea and a digestive." I tilt my mug of tea in response and bring it to my lips. John pushes off the sofa and approaches with a cautious gait. His cheery demeanour vanishes and his smile drains away with each step.

"I'm sorry." He cradles my face between his palms, his thumbs tracing the length of the blemishes. "I don't know what to say to make this right."

I shake my head, both in an attempt to extract him from my person and in answer, but he's having none of it. "You can't. There's nothing that can be said or done to change this."

He nods, grudgingly, tenderly examining my newest scar. "But if I-"

"It's not your fault. If it makes you feel any better, it could've been a lot worse. There was a moment when I feared he was going to slit my throat instead."

John blanches in shock. "Nothing about this situation will make me feel any better, especially that." He scrubs his hand over his face, looking ten years older in the last ten seconds. "It's been a year to the day, and I've got Marie down there drowning in nightmares. She likes to think I don't know, but I do. Kara's still carrying the weight of the world on her shoulders that the rat bastard finally hurt those she loves. Charlie doesn't comment because she doesn't want to remember that time. And Sloan... He just wants his wife and his sister to be able to close their eyes and not see the horrors they've lived through." He shakes his head, practically in tears. "And then there's you, hiding away up here, dwelling on life's elements that we can't change. God knows if I could've taken your place, I would have. I swear to God, I would."

Tears prick my eyes. It's clear he's secretly living with everyone else's hurt as well as his own, and it's obvious no one has noticed how much he's also suffering. I twist my head and ease out of his hold. I take a cursory glance at the clock, disheartened it's only now ten.

"Rem, we need to talk."

No, we bloody don't. Especially if this talk is what I think it is. I head into the kitchen to halt his enquiries for as long as I can.

"John, where's your car?" I call back.

A tapping ensues, and I turn to find him inside the small galley kitchen, his fingers rapping on the architrave. I suddenly feel claustrophobic. There's not enough space in here for two men of our sizes.

"Nice subject change and I'll play ball. For now. My car is in London, where we both should be. I got the train for a change."

I furrow my brow but can't stop my grin from forming. "The train? You don't do public transport."

"No, but as much as I do enjoy the beautiful scenic misery of the M1, the last time I was on it, I gained points on my licence. It was an emergency! They didn't even give me ten miles grace!"

I smirk. "Yes, they did…but you were doing over a hundred."

"Needs must, sunshine. And now we're back to the topic you don't want to talk about." He suddenly saddens, and his eyes cast over my cheeks again. "Jeremy, you need to stop running." I open my mouth, but he lifts his hand. "Tell me something true about your life here. Something good that you have here that you don't have in London. Something that has made this last year worth it."

I grind my jaw; he's placing me in a tight spot. I want to scream and shout and punch something, namely him, because I have fuck all here, and he knows it. "John, stop-"

"No, you need to get your arse home. You need to fall on your sword and right your wrongs. Years ago, I accepted the worst thing I ever did was keep Sloan from Kara when I knew where she was. I will not allow history to repeat itself!" The last word is a roar, and he turns on his heel, snatches up his jacket and slams the door behind him.

I take a breath and stride to the living room window, expecting to see him escaping into the distance. Instead, he's pacing up and down the small communal garden that the elderly residents tend and cultivate for everyone's enjoyment. I steel my spine. He's come all this way to see me; the least I can do is talk and talk honestly.

I grab my jacket on my way out and lock the door. Jogging down the stairs, one of my neighbours smiles in acknowledgement.

"Morning."

"Morning," I reply and hold the door open for him. I zip up my jacket and stride towards John, sitting on a memorial bench, gazing at the ground. His chin tips inconspicuously when I sit.

"You were right...about everything. I should have stayed and spoken the truth. I should have told Evie about Deacon, the lifestyle, the drugs, Emma... I know there are things she's hiding. I didn't push it, but... But maybe we're not supposed to be together." I sigh. "Two wrongs don't make a right, do they?"

He shakes his head. "That's all conjecture, but who knows. You could be happy trying."

"Possibly, but I can't imagine after reading my letter it would have left any doubt in her mind as to who and what I really am." I stare ahead, wondering how much she must hate me now.

John holds up the envelope addressed to Evie, still sealed and now very crumpled. "After you'd gone that night, I went over to her house and told her you'd left. It was the right thing to do, but I never gave this to her. Nothing good was ever going to come out of whatever you wrote in here. This isn't who you are now. It was never who you were, not really."

I take the letter and turn it in between my fingers. "You wanted a true, honest evaluation of my life here? Well, honestly, I'm terrified. When K said Dom had a visitor, my first thought was Shaw. I wake up every day wondering if it will be my last. Wondering if today will be the day he finally does as he vowed and finishes me off completely." John's eyes lock on mine. They are filled with worry and torment. "And it's exhausting, John. I'm thirty, and I have no real life to speak of. I get up, go to the gym, work, and then come home. Lather, rinse and repeat. I have nothing, and I, having been living in isolation for all this time, means I've not been there when you've needed me, and I've probably missed out on so much with Ev-" I stop myself. He doesn't need to see how pathetic I am.

John wraps his arm around my shoulder and pulls me close in comfort. His compassion and empathy for my self-inflicted punishment is enviable, especially when others would have just washed their hands of me long ago.

"I've been trying to convince myself she's better off without me." Sadly, I don't know what to think anymore. Conjecture and speculation have never boded well for anyone. "Tell me what I should do."

"I can't." His voice sounds distant. "But I do know this. If you want her back, you're going to have to work for it."

I scrub my hand over my face. Life was easier high. "How?"

"Purge."

"Purge?" I'm not following.

"Tell her everything."

"Everything? Are you high?" I ask, now really wishing I was.

"No. Are you channelling parrot? Yes, everything... Eventually. I can guarantee if you unload everything on her all at once, you won't see her again."

"Thanks. That fills me with so much confidence. You have no idea."

His lips quirk in my side view as he continues. "And the first thing you need to purge is the truth behind those scars." He nods at my cheek.

"No-"

"Well, you can't hide them, sunshine, so you might as well get it over and done with. And if, after the event, she's running for the hills and no longer wants you... Well, I need you. A job at WS."

"Jesus, I'm not that hard up!"

"I beg to differ!"

My mouth falls open, and I scratch my chin in contemplation. "Yeah, well, I'm sure Kara will be ecstatic to see me every day. She may have forgiven me, but a daily dose might prove too much."

He scoffs. "You're wrong about that, sunshine. Besides, she quit. Just upped and left in the middle of the day. Sloan got a piece of my mind, and the little arsehole just laughed. Can you believe that?"

I smile and slope my head to the precipitation laden skies. "I can. I'm more shocked that you can't. So, Kara's departure basically means you have a vacancy for a tea lady? Girl... *Boy* Friday? General skivvy?" The sarcasm rolls off my tongue with glee.

"Hmm, and don't forget the sandwich run at lunch." He winks, patting my knee.

"God, how desperate do you think I am?" I laugh and elbow his side playfully, aware of the unspoken agreement of my new position at WS. A crack of thunder darkens the sky further, changing from a few droplets to a torrential downpour within a matter of seconds. John's steps fall in line with mine as we leg it back inside, both now dripping wet.

ELLE CHARLES

"When are you going back to London?" I ask, shedding my jacket and shaking off the water.

Copying my action, he pulls a face and gives me a smug look. "How quickly can you get packed? M is expecting me by midnight." He climbs the stairs two at a time to my flat.

"Jesus, fuck. Are you deaf? I told you; I'm not coming back."

"Yes, you are, you little hypocrite."

"No, I'm not, you arsehole!"

"Yes, you are!" His voice echoes off the stairwell walls. "I'm going to repatriate your arse back down south if it's the last thing I do today!"

I slouch against the wall, staring up as his steps grow faint. Pulling out my phone, I hit the speed dial.

"Jeremy?" Dom answers immediately. "Are you going home at last?"

I shake my head; the man knows me better than I know myself. "Yeah. Third time lucky, maybe."

"You're up and down more times than a bleeding yo-yo." His sigh seeps over the line. "But I'm glad," he says, genuinely pleased. "You need them, and they need you. As ever, if you need anything other than what they can supply, you know where I am."

"Always. Thanks, Dom."

"Get J to give us a call. I'll speak to you later, lad."

I hang up before he does and press my skull into the wall and stare at the ceiling.

"Rem?" John's call reverberates through the building. I push off the wall and stride up the flights of stairs.

Deep in thought, I'd like to claim my heart and mind are in turmoil, but they're not. The cold, hard truth is, I'm ambivalent about going back. My life is nothing here but tattered remnants of a life lived on the edge for close to two decades. But now, the edges are slowly knitting back together and trying to finally form some semblance of a life from the carnage.

Not so long ago, I was desperately grasping the cliff edge, fearful of the crash and burn at the bottom. Now, I'd be willing to make that leap if it meant I had another chance with her. My life has come full circle thrice, but only she can decide if this is when the wheel finally stops turning.

Chapter 18

I ROLL MY shoulders and slacken the perfectly presented bowtie, currently causing a constricting sensation around my neck.

"Stop fidgeting!"

Clutching one end, I toss a dark look over my shoulder at Marie, who is a petite vision in a black gown which is definitely not her usual work attire.

"Shouldn't you be there by now? Arranging the hors d'oeuvres and stale petit fours?"

She grins, having accepted the long-running joke that her catering service is shit. On the contrary, these days, her name is synonymous with decadence and excellence, only offering the very best.

"It's Nicki's show tonight, darling."

"Which means Dev is going to become prolific in mastering the art of the disappearing act," I say, and she winks.

"Well, I don't care. I have no intention of picking up the slack. I'm there in body only."

"And what a body it is," John exclaims as he sneaks up behind her and glides his hands around her waist.

I turn away, feeling like a voyeuristic third wheel as they whisper sweet nothings to each other. Although throughout all of it, I really wish I could forget J's promise of *manhandling her things* later. It doesn't take a genius to decipher that statement. I clear my throat, earning myself John's best death glare.

"My woman, my house, my rules!" The landline rings, and he reaches for the handset. "Thanks." He puts the phone back down and fastens his dinner jacket. "The car's outside."

Offering Marie my arm, I escort her out. John then proceeds to turn on the internal and external cameras. He sets the alarm, activates the lights, and carries out what other security rituals he has going on these days in his attempt to protect and preserve whatever little sanity Marie still has left intact.

"Nervous?" she asks, pulling me from my mental ramblings, misinterpreting that my pensive expression is one borne of possibly seeing Evie again.

"I'm fine." I guide her to the limo and open the door, but she hesitates.

"I'm *fine*, too. And that's how I know you're not." She smooths my lapels and produces a smile that doesn't reach her eyes. She's right; I'm about as far from *fine* as she is.

"Marie…"

"You look extremely handsome." Her lips purse and I note her conflict. I glance down and gently take her hand in mine, my thumbs caressing one of the scars Deacon inflicted upon her. I raise her hand to my cheek, and her fingertips tentatively glide the length of the mark he inflicted upon me.

"Sometimes the memory hurts more than the reality," I murmur, and her eyes glisten. "It gets better, M. I swear to you it does." I pull her tight into my arms, and her body shakes slightly, fighting against her inner heartbreak. It pains me to see such a strong woman reduced to a shadow of her former self.

Determined steps halt a short distance away, and I look up to see John, wearing an anxious expression. He forces a smile and gently slides his hand over M's shoulder and down her arm.

"Angel?"

Marie edges back, head down, looking uncomfortable. "I'm sorry," she whispers, wiping the tears from her eyes.

I shake my head. "You're still beautiful, M. You're strong and fearless, and the rat bastard didn't take that away, and he'll never get the chance again."

She smiles - the first genuine smile I've witnessed since I've been back. "So are you. And if Evie can't see beyond the exterior once more, then she isn't the girl I thought she was, and she thoroughly doesn't deserve you." She then climbs into the car. John squeezes my arm and follows.

I CHEW ON my nails nervously and gaze out of the window. I'm seeing, but not really. The city is cloaked in darkness as each hour passes. The time when the troubled and down and out, or spirited and carefree, come out to play. I remember it well. Observing it from the other side, of course. The time when I had my finger on the pulse and one hand in my pocket, just in case.

As I recline deeper into the plush leather, my eyes tracking someone staggering until I can't see her anymore, I can honestly say I'd rather be at home, wallowing in my misery, than attending this function tonight. But, as John has already mentioned in the last week or so, I'm a special case. *Special* meaning he doesn't trust me not to fall off the wagon and throw myself into the pit of destruction and devastation again if left to my own devices. He's right, of course, because historically, when life turns murky, that's precisely what I do.

My own devices prove to be infallible after a while, and I, in turn, grow invincible with them. But sadly, none of it is good for my mentality.

"Angel, I'm just concern-"

"Darling, stop!" Marie hisses, distracting me from my reverie of mundane thoughts.

I keep my eyes trained on the window, but in the reflection, John and Marie continue to talk quietly. Albeit sometimes heatedly. Every now and again, the frustration in John's tone at M's short, curt answers is identifiable. Whether Marie has picked up on this particular tell in the time they have been together, I don't know, but for those of us who know him well, it's hard not to miss.

The comforting drone of the engine lessens under the tension, and I blink, still unimpressed with my current surroundings for the evening. I guess it's too late to slip out of one door while John and Marie exit the other.

Beams of light illuminate the ornate exterior of the Emerson Hotel. The last time I was here, at an event not too dissimilar to this one, was the night I first met Evie. I inhale deeply, unprepared for the emotional massacre that awaits inside. Except, I'm mentally battering myself for nothing.

"*Jeremy?*" My name is faint, almost inaudible against the thoughts going haywire inside my head.

During the past six weeks of my repatriation back to London, back to normality, and back to familial civilisation – if I can call it that – I've not heard a peep from her. I would've expected at least a text or two considering Sloan, by his own, overzealous admission, personally informed Andrew Blake I was back in town, but even that titbit of news hasn't been forthcoming. Either that, or it hasn't filtered down to Evie. Either way, I've had radio silence.

"*Jeremy?*"

It doesn't matter, though, because I have it on very good authority she isn't attending tonight. Granted, this information has come from Kieran via Evie's mate Holly, so who the hell knows. All I do know is I'm beating myself up for nothing.

My eyes flit over the entrance, or more specifically, the security manning the door, recalling the way they visually judged me the last time. It's like déjà vu, and I dread to think what they will think of-

"Remy!" John's boom is akin to an electric shock, jolting me back to the here and now.

"What? Sorry," I mutter sheepishly.

John gives me an exasperated glare. "Are you waiting for an invitation, sunshine?" His eyes jerk to the door, and mine follow to find the driver standing outside holding it open.

"Sorry," I apologise again and climb out. Straightening my jacket, I trail behind John and Marie towards the entrance.

The gentle breeze of this hot, August evening warms my skin. I think back to this time last year when someone else was gentle, hot, and warming my skin.

"Have you got your invite?" John asks. I remove the thick, embossed invitation from my inner pocket, and I wave it at him.

After more than ten minutes of being knocked from pillar to post in the hustle and bustle of people rushing to get inside, John practically growls. "It would have been quicker using the tradesman's entrance!"

I smirk; he's not wrong. We're not the type of men to have airs and graces. We like breakfast at a cheap, greasy spoon and ale from a bottle. The majority of the men waiting in line with us want à la carte dining and a glass of Dom Perignon in a lead crystal flute.

Marie sighs. "Very true, but it's not every day I get to see it from the other side. Indulge me, darling. Please."

John rolls his eyes in disgust at her reasonable request. "Fine, but you owe me. I could be enjoying a glass of champagne right now."

She sniggers. "What? That cheap stuff the tight little sod of an owner serves? You'd be better off drinking the dirty dishwater!"

In shock, I turn to John, who, like me, is fighting hard to contain his laughter until neither of us can suppress it any longer. I bellow out, my eyes watering uncontrollably, and cover my mouth as fellow patrons give us looks of pure disdain.

Hello, obscenely wealthy, meet the great unwashed!

"For Christ's sake, M, shut up!" I chide friskily, but she just smiles and shrugs, then hands their invitations to security.

"Don't you talk to my wife like that!"

"I'm not your wife!"

"Fine! You can politely inform Sloan that your wife-"

"I'm not his wife!" Marie says, cutting me off, and I roll my eyes.

"-told all and sundry he serves up shit!"

"Invite, sir?"

I look at the man and pass over my card with a curious purse of my lips, wondering how he will react. His eyes flit from one cheek to another, his expression one of pity.

A slight nudge to my side diverts my attention to Marie. "Come on, handsome. Let's see if we can raid the penthouse for Sloan's stash of the good stuff!" She presses her lips to my scar and enters.

"Hey, get your hands off my wife!" John says, amused. Unfortunately, I have no witty response because *she* kissed *me*. Platonically, I might add for transparency.

"I told you, I'm not your bloody wife, Walker!" Marie's retort is loud and clear, and John chunters as he strides towards her.

I rub my forehead with my finger and thumb. Deep breaths, that will work. Except it won't. If I laugh, I'll encourage her and annoy him. Likewise, if I school my reaction, it will sadden her and still annoy him.

Looking at the guard, I roll my eyes. "Thanks," I say, and he smiles and passes the card back.

"I'd say have a nice night, but I think good luck might be more appropriate with those two."

"You have no idea." I slip the card back inside my jacket and move through the bodies congregating in the foyer. I stand head and shoulders above most, giving me a better vantage point. Gazing over the crowd, my feet carry me into the ballroom, towards the table where Sloan is talking animatedly with Jake.

"Champagne?" a waitress asks.

"No, thank you," I reply, distracted.

"No? Shame, it's the good stuff I hear, not that cheap plonk the tight owner serves up! Anyway, if you don't want a drink, how about a dance later before my card is full?"

I squint as the tone shifts from terrible cockney to faint Manc. I glance down and smile instantly as Kara loiters next to me with two glasses of - what I hope - is the good stuff. This is the first time I've seen her since I've been back, and she looks well. Very well, in fact, and that makes me happy in ways I can't describe.

"I didn't recognise your voice. You sound practically southern," I tell her, then take the glass she has offered.

"Nah, not quite!" Her demeanour is playful. She stretches up on her toes and wraps her free arm around my back, imparting a chaste hug. It's awkward and uncomfortable on both sides, but it's progress. I release my arm and look down at the glass she has given me.

"I lied. Yours is low alcohol. Definitely *not* the good stuff," she says and takes a sip of hers.

I smile; she didn't need to do that. I'm not averse to drinking, and I can and do, but in settings such as these, where reining myself in might prove impossible, it's better not to dance with the devil.

"And what's yours?" I query at the pale liquid. My eyes slowly move down her front, wondering...

"Sparkling water with a touch of lime cordial." Her brow raises.

"Sounds...refreshing." I grin, and she reciprocates, subconsciously touching her stomach – as expected.

"It is. Anyway, a toast to..." She pulls a face, thinking.

"Redemption." No thinking necessary.

"That debt has already been redeemed," she counters thoughtfully.

I knock back the fizz and place it on the waiter's tray, who's working the space. "Debatable...but I'll take it." Kara smiles, but it's clear she isn't happy that I'm still trying to procure salvation from her. "May I escort a lady to dinner?"

"Yes, of course. I'll be sure to tell you if I see my husband, and you can make a run for it!"

I snicker at her quick-thinking sarcasm. We both know running from her significant other isn't an option. Trust me, I've tried and failed. We both have. Kara places her empty glass on a nearby table and links her arm in mine. We make our way through the room, towards the table where John and Marie are now taking their seats, alongside Charlie and Jake, and Sloan, of course.

From some twenty feet away, Sloan sprints towards us. His wife, already aware of his intentions, steps back just in time for him to lift me in a hug.

"Put me down, you silly sod!"

My feet touch the ground the instant my back is slapped in jest. I pull away, and his overjoyed expression falters marginally. I have to remember this is the first time he's seen me since the day he took his wife home from the hospital in the aftermath of the final assault.

"Don't." I pre-empt it before it can leave his mouth. I'm fed up of hearing apologies, of hearing guilt. I chose this life, and in turn, I chose the consequences; personal regrets be damned.

Sloan tugs his wife into his side and slides his other arm around my shoulder. His grip is tight, unwavering, ensuring I won't abscond tonight. Just for clarity, if I didn't want to hightail it out of here when I was still in the car, I really do now.

"A toast!" he announces, and Kara and I glance at each other, and she purses her lips. I wink. Our toast can be our secret if that's what she wants. "To family!" He then pours a bottle of what I know is the very good stuff and passes it to me.

"It's still one of my three evils," I comment as he tops up the rest of the glasses. He gives me a sheepish expression, and I scan the tabletop. Not a low-alcohol beer, soft drink, or a poxy bottle of water in sight. Not even Kara's fizzy lime cordial is present, meaning *she* might be keeping *him* in the dark. For once... Possible, but unlikely.

"I'm going get a drink...or five," I announce, unintentionally haughty, somewhat miffed, or maybe I'm just effed off in general.

"Rem, there's something I need to tell-"

I wave my hand at Sloan, effectively shushing him, then make a beeline for the bar. With my focus resolute and my steely determination fixed, a man staggers in front of me, blocking my path. Too late for me to deflect, his body hits mine at full impact, and I grab him before he goes down. He shrugs out of my hold and manages to right himself. Between the shock of the impact and the scent of hard liquor emanating from him, it takes him over the edge, and he falls back into another member of his group.

"What the hell?" he shouts.

"My apologies," I offer, although he should learn to use his eyes...and his self-control since the whisky stench is oozing fiercely.

The man straightens himself. He's vaguely familiar, but I can't recall from where. He tugs on his lapels and lifts his head, all high and mighty.

"Someone needs to tell Foster they've let the low class, mutilated criminals inside!"

I glower and seethe, seeing red. My fist flexes of its own volition, ready to pummel the cocky git into submission.

"Piers, don't. Just apologise and leave it." A timid tone rises from the group and induces my hand to relax because I know that voice, in all its different guises and physical states.

"No, I will not! *He* should be apologising to *me!*"

"I beg your pardon?" I fold my arms over my chest, taking on a more menacing stance. I pretend to step forward, and he instinctively steps back. "I thought so. All mouth and no action."

"Come on, sweetheart. I don't want you polluted by this man's presence any longer!" He's embarrassed, and I would be, too – creating a scene for no reason whatsoever and unable to back it up. Intrigue gets the better of me, and I shift a few steps just in time to see a hand slide around the idiot's arm, and its owner finally makes themself known.

Evie.

I maintain a neutral countenance, but I'm shocked to see her, considering my good authority has turned out to be anything but. She inches forward, and it's like a punch to my gut when she stares at me with cold indifference. The light that once shone brightly in her eyes when we were together has definitely died out. But I did this. Not only did I abandon her, but I've also emotionally scarred her, too.

Murmurs of fear and curiosity drift, and I turn to find some of the other guests watching. A short, feminine gasp rings in my eardrums, and I consciously touch my face, realising Evie has finally seen what I wish I could keep hidden. In my peripheral vision, she's staring at my cheek in absolute shock, and I feel my skin heat under her long-awaited yet unwanted presence.

"Stand back, Evelyn. Somebody call security and get this *person* out of here!" Piers pushes her back, much to her displeasure. I want to throttle him and tell him to remove his hands from what's mine. But she's no longer mine, and I have to remind myself of that now.

With one eye on the woman I want so desperately – who's here with another man - I catch Sloan, who's evidently no longer taking any chances when it comes to those he loves being caught in a showdown, barrelling over.

"Is there a problem, gentlemen?" he asks, taking his place by my side in this fracas.

"Foster, this *gentleman-*"

"Walked into me. It was an innocent mishap – on your part - which seems to have caused great offence when no real foul has been committed." I eye Sloan, who nods inconspicuously. "Clearly, money buys a multitude of things, yet it can't buy manners." I stare at Evie. "Or class." And she visible shrinks in humiliation.

"Pray tell, what would a thug like you know about class?" Piers asks, eying my scars.

Sloan steps forward, his expression grave. "Far more than you. Now, if you continue to make this unwelcome scene and insult my closest friend, you'll find yourself on the street. I suggest you walk away or face permanent expulsion from my establishment."

"I think you need to reconsider your friends, Foster."

"And patrons, it seems." Sloan tips his head. "*Pray tell,* maybe you should ask your *date* about my friends." I cringe because that's unfair and uncalled for. It's low, especially for him.

Chastened and mortified, Piers arsehole turns to Evie, who's conflicted. "Come on, darling. I just hope this degenerate's pollution doesn't linger on you!" He grabs her arm hard and drags her across the ballroom like a mangy dog. Like something he couldn't care less about. Truthfully, if I wasn't furious before, I am now!

"Sloan, I wish you hadn't have brought her into it."

He gives me a sceptical look. "She's already in it, Rem. The sooner she realises that, the better."

I huff out, but he's right. "Maybe I should go," I suggest because I can sense myself itching for a fight. I don't fight often, but by God, I need something to take my anger out on.

And he's standing at the other side of the ballroom.

And his name is *Piers.*

"Nonsense! He's just a spoilt little rich bastard who doesn't like being told no. He just needs someone to put him in his place."

I quirk my brow, wondering if he realises what's just left his mouth. "Takes one to know one, right?"

He grins and slaps my back. "Indeed, it does. I have no shame in confessing my beloved is well versed in keeping me in my place. However, all hilarity aside, I need you to stay because I want to see how little Piers reacts when Evie can no longer ignore the chemistry and magnetism between you, and she gravitates back to where she belongs. I doubt he will see it like that, but I guess once he finds out just how *filthy* and *polluted* you've already made her, he won't be too bothered. Cheap women and gold-diggers are a sure thing at these events. He'll find someone to warm his bed tonight."

A passing waiter stops, and Sloan takes a glass of fizz and passes me a bottle of water.

"Thank you," I acknowledge. "You would know all about cheap dates and gold-diggers." I knock back some water to cool me down.

"Why, yes, of course. My beloved knows I wasn't a saint, but she also knows she's the only one for me. I waited the best part of a decade for her, and I'd do it all over again if I had to. Anyway..." A slow smile spreads across his face. "A bet." He stares directly at the opposite side of the room. "By the end of the night, I bet Evelyn Blake is back in your arms."

I inhale, maybe a little too overly confident in my ability to reclaim what's mine. Although after a year of desertion, it might take more than a wink and a smile. "Tonight might be pushing it, but I think that might already be a given."

Sloan nods. "Okay, then. I bet at some point tonight poncey Piers explodes again, and I shall have great pleasure in booting the pretentious little wanker from my hotel once and for all!"

I snort. "I think that might already be a given, too. Something else, Sloan, something bigger."

"Fine!" He shrugs. "This time next year, you'll be committed to her."

I snigger into my hand. "I think it might be safer to assume that this time next year, I might be dead." Sloan grimaces, and rather than reply, he motions for the waiter.

"Boss?"

"Would you mind replenishing my table with a variety of non-alcoholic beverages, please, Ed?" The lad agrees and moves to the bar behind us.

"No more cheap fizz?"

He grins and straightens his shoulders. "Nope. I've got to stay sober for the big showdown later. It's about time someone else's life was more entertaining than mine."

My eyes, like heat-seeking missiles, instinctively find Evie, who is still watching me, until she turns away.

Sloan forcibly slaps my shoulder and strides back towards our table. I loiter for a minute before following him. However, I don't want to be entertaining; I just want quiet contentment.

But most of all, I just want her.

THE ASININE, BRAIN numbing conversation is never-ending, becoming more ludicrous by the minute with every mouthful of wine that passes the owner's loose lips, from this table to the next. I pick up my glass of Coke, having called time on the non-alcoholic lager hours ago. Although, I can't say having a stomach full of carbonated pop is doing me any favours, either.

From the relative safety of the table, my gaze automatically reverts to Evie. I've been unable to resist the temptation to stare at her all night, and now I'm not even trying to hide it. The delightful Piers has noticed me, and he's noticed her, reciprocating.

And he's not impressed.

But then again, neither am I.

Until this evening, my moral compass told me I should leave her alone. Allow her to get on with her life and find someone who doesn't carry as much baggage as I do, but seeing her has done me in. The unbidden memory of us together was dragged kicking and screaming back to the surface, and I don't think I'm the only one either. She's trying her hardest to pretend I'm not here, that I no longer exist in her world, but her eyes keep finding mine, beckoning me like a siren. I just wish she would walk over here because I know it will cause war if I walk over there.

I drain the pint glass of Coke and slide it into the middle of the table, having just finished off the small offering of soft drinks. Everyone is smiling and laughing, and while I'm happy for them, I just wish I could be happy for myself.

"Ladies, gentlemen, thank you for an entertaining evening, but I'm off." I shift the chair back and move around the table to shake hands and kiss cheeks. As I button my dinner jacket, I glance back at Evie, who is expressing an unexpected look of panic. I turn on my heel because this is personal torture I don't need. I'm many things, a masochist being top of the current list, but I must stop this. I need to stamp out this pain because if I don't, she will eventually repay the favour and break me instead. Although I think she already has since I've spent the last four hours watching her hang on the arm of another man who just wants her for window dressing. With a clenched jaw, I've also tolerated watching him drag her around the dance floor, almost viciously, ignoring her apparent protests but ensuring he catches my eye while doing it.

Add all that to what I was already feeling, and I *still* need something to take my anger out on.

And that *something* is still called *Piers double-barrel twat Maxwell-Clarke!*

I push the chair back under the table, pocket my phone, and impart my goodbyes.

Outside, the night air washes over my face, creating a sublime cooling sensation. I tilt my head to the sky, pondering whether there's rain forecast tonight. My only decent pair of leather dress shoes click as I idly descend the hotel steps, having already decided to walk home. It's not that far, but far enough that I might walk through the door with a better understanding of what my future may hold now.

"JEREMY!" My name is a desperate cry from lips I've longed to feel against mine again for a year. I steel my spine, bracing myself for whatever she has to say. She's had hours – no, months – to consider it, so I don't believe I'll be left with any ambiguity as to where I stand.

I spin around as she scurries towards me. With my hands in my trouser pockets, I wait for her to air whatever is inside her head.

"What can I do for you, Evelyn?" I keep my tone impartial because all I want is to hold her and kiss her and take her back to my bed and never let her leave. But that's not who and what we are anymore.

"*Evelyn?*" she repeats in disgust. "I'm *Evie* to you."

I close my eyes in provocation, hating what I'm about to say. "No. Tonight has proven you're nothing to me. You're another man's woman now, and I don't break up relationships or take other men's women. Go back inside, Evelyn. It's cold." I turn on my heel and descend the stairs.

"Don't you fucking walk away from me!" she screams.

I halt instantly. Murmurings of discontent swirl around us, from the bunch of suits smoking to the social climbers reapplying their make-up - trying to catch one of the suits' eyes. Evie gathers up the hem of her dress and follows until she's up in my face, standing the same height on the step above. My attention is caught by the guard from earlier, speaking into his radio, but it's drawn back when a finger jabs my chest. I grab her wrist when she does it again, only to see a bruise forming.

My gaze is on fire. "Did *he* do this?" I ask rhetorically.

She rips her hand back. "You've made it perfectly clear that you don't want me, so why do you care?"

I grind my jaw. "I do ca-"

"No, you don't! People who care don't leave, Jeremy!"

Staring into her pained eyes, she isn't defeated yet. As heartbreaking as it is, I can't go through this again. She belongs to someone else now, and even though I've hurt her, I can't allow her to do the same to me. In truth, I won't survive. I'll revert back into the darkness that owned and consumed me for years. I can't go there again. If I do, it *will* eventually kill me.

Evie studies me, and her eyes fix on the newest scar. She tentatively reaches out, and her finger ghosts over it. I curl my fingers around her wrist, mindful not to press too hard or cause her any further discomfort.

"Oh, God. I can't even begin to imagine." Her voice quietens, and she softly presses her palm into my cheek. The urge to lean into her and never leave is profound. Movement in the doorway reveals Sloan and John are now watching our pitiful reunion.

"I'm so sor-"

"Get off your high horse, Evie!" I move her hand away from me. "You were slumming it from the start. I was just a bit of rough to have fun with. We both knew that. You'd never have looked twice at me if Daddy had approved. I know it's hard to hear, but instead of ignoring this, maybe I should go back inside and tell your arsehole boyfriend all the ways I've already *polluted* you. Maybe we should have a drink and compare notes!"

Fire ignites in my face as she slaps me. Quite rightly, too. My mother would do far worse if she heard me. I've been intentionally rude, trying to make her hate me like she should. Trying to hide my own hurt.

She shuffles back in shock, her hand at her mouth, realising she's just hit me across my newest scar. "Oh, God, I'm sorry!"

"So am I. I'm sorry for all of it." I turn on my heel again, and Evie's hand captures mine.

"You're wrong, you know. I don't need nor want Daddy's approval. Just so you know, it was never my intention to just be here for a good time. It was always my intention to be here for a long time."

"How long?" I ask against my better judgement. She deserves more than I can give, and yet I just keep pulling her back, like a puppet on a string.

"For however long you wanted me. But maybe now that you think you're disfigured and unattractive, your views on how the world sees you are skewered and biased."

I chortle. "Skewered? Honestly, when you look at me, tell me you don't see only this... These!" I amend grudgingly, pointing to my face.

"It doesn't matter what I see because it's clear you've already given up. Maybe I need to finally be honest with myself and comprehend that maybe *you* only wanted *me* for a good time." She turns and drops her head down. "I refuse to grovel and fight for a man who clearly doesn't want or think as highly of me as I do of him. A man who doesn't believe himself worthy of having love or anything more." She then walks back up the stairs, stopping when Sloan blocks her path.

With her words ringing in my ears, my feet carry me into the night. The midnight hour passes as I kill time, roaming with no real destination. The constant buzz from my pocket indicates I'm not alone, but I can wait until tomorrow for John to rip me a new one for treating a good woman like crap.

The day is breaking as I finally board the lift and press the button for my floor. I lean against the wall, hating myself for every little piece of hatred I spewed tonight. It has played on loop, taunting me, haunting me, ensuring I cannot forget. It was a defence mechanism to protect myself, yet all it did was annihilate a woman who, apparently, still loves me.

The lift dings and the doors slide open. I halt in my tracks. Evie is sitting with her back to my door, still wearing her ballgown. Her appearance is now dishevelled. Her dress is torn in places, her hair is falling loose from its intricate style, and her make-up is smeared, especially around her eyes. Every nerve ending under my skin vibrates because this is more than just crying over me. This has something to do with *him*.

She clambers up, hesitant to look at me. I tip her chin and rub my thumb under her eye, noting a round red mark forming on her cheek. I look down at her wrist again and back up. "I won't ask again. Did Piers double-barrel twat do this to you?" She nods, appeasing me, unknowingly giving me more fuel for the fire that is slowly stoking.

Opening my door, I deactivate the alarm and hold out my hand for her to enter. It's a small action, offering her an olive branch. Except, I'm aware I'm not only just opening the door to my home again. I'm figuratively opening the door securing my heart again.

I close the door, and Evie produces the key I gave her last year from her clutch and locks it behind us. She gives me a tiny smile, and I reciprocate, admiring the fact she still has enough respect for me that she didn't just let herself in. Not that I would have minded, of course, but still.

Every cell is on edge, and I flick on the lights as I go. I slide back the patio door blinds and turn around. Evie is running her hand over every surface, almost like she's pulling back the past, remembering the many moments we shared in this place.

"What are you doing here, darling?"

"I talked to Sloan after you left."

I scoff involuntarily. Figures he couldn't keep his nose out. He just wants everyone to be as happy and settled as he is, but that isn't always on the cards for the rest of us.

"He told me things that now make sense. When I asked him why I should come here, when you refused any kind of communication with me for a year, you know what he said?" I lift my brow, intrigued as to what shit left his mouth. "He said mentally and emotionally I was already here. I've always been here. Physically, I just needed to follow again. So, I did. I followed my heart, but in hindsight, I fear that maybe pointless because you've seemingly misplaced yours."

Tears prick my eyes, and I fight to keep them hidden as she approaches cautiously. She presses her hand to my cheek again and stares into my eyes. "Tell me you don't want me, Jeremy. Tell me you don't love me. Tell me anything but just tell me the truth. You owe me that much."

I inhale a shaky breath and slide my arm around her waist, pulling her closer until we're only inches apart. "The truth is I do want you. I'll always want you. I love you like I've never loved another. That morning before I left, I wish I'd told you that, told you all the things I was feeling. I loved you before, I loved you during, and I still love you now. In the time I was gone, you were all I thought about. The emotional debts I owe you, I'd spend a lifetime repaying if you'd allow me." I pull her forward and press my lips to hers. It's unsure and tentative, but it feels like coming home.

"More!" Evie moans, controlling the motion, and I allow her to take the lead. As much as I want to hold her and never let go, I don't want her thinking I'm taking advantage. After the shit I threw at her tonight, I owe her this, and I'm grateful that she's giving me the second chance I know I don't deserve.

Time moves slowly, and minutes feel like hours in her embrace. She eventually makes a noise I know well, too well, then moves back and presses her hand to her lips in breathless uncertainty.

Compulsion compels me, drives me, and I drag her back, mindful of her already battered wrists. I cradle her face between my hands, my thumbs stroking her cheeks.

"We need to talk, Jeremy," she says with a sigh, and I nod. "No, I mean really talk. About us, and you, and why you left." Her finger runs the length of the new scar. "And this. *This* most of all, because I know *this* is the core of your problems." A tear falls from her eye. "Until you let this go, you will never really let me in."

"We'll talk about it, all of it, but it's late – well, early - and I'd rather we discuss how we move forward, or finally say goodbye, after the disaster that is tonight has worn off." She yawns and drops her hand from my face to my chest. "You can sleep in the bed. I'll take the sofa."

"You don't have to. It's not like we haven't shared a bed before."

"True, but you belong to another man now."

"Oh, for God flaming sake! What will it take to get through to you? I'm not with Piers!" she cries indignantly, throwing her hands up.

"Does he know that?"

She doesn't answer and instead just rolls her eyes in disgust. Flouncing off in a huff, she slams the bedroom door behind her. I chuckle rhetorically, but I can't refute that that spark, that undeniable chemistry we've had from the word go, hasn't died. If anything, it's stronger than ever. But while the current status quo between us still remains, something has changed. I identify it as hope, but I guess, for now, it's better not to make more of it than it currently is.

Except, from the moment I laid eyes on a woman who was far too young for me, at an event like tonight, my assertions were simple because she gave me the only real hope I'd known for a long time.

Opening the patio door, I step onto the balcony, snag my cigarettes and light one up. I stare as far as my eye can see. The burnished orange horizon swallows the night and brings with it a new day. A day in which a new chapter will finally begin, and I'll either be with her or without her.

Yet, regardless of what happens tomorrow, she's still an addiction. A beautiful, unguarded sickness that has weaved its way into my soul. A sickness for which there is no medical cure and no way of eradicating it from my obsessed heart.

Chapter 19

THE SOUNDS OF the city stirring drifts in through the partially open patio door, adding life to the light as it gradually swallows the dark. I yawn and rub my eyes. Sleep has evaded me, and I've grudgingly seen every hour come and go.

I turn over, unable to find a satisfactory comfort level for my six-foot-two frame on the small two-seater sofa. It creaks in protest beneath me, and I curse for the umpteenth time for being so chivalrous and gentlemanly.

I finally concede defeat and swing my legs to the floor, wondering why I bothered to torture myself in the first place. I already knew from the moment I allowed Evie back in that sleep wouldn't be forthcoming - not with her sleeping less than fifty feet away.

Vaulting upright from the sofa, a rush of blood to the head induces me to sway. I slam my hand on the sofa arm to steady myself, and every bone joint clicks while every muscle contracts. I slant my head left to right, working out the stiffness.

"God, that hurts," I whisper.

I stretch out my arms, then run my fingers through my hair as I pad silently down the hallway to the bathroom. I pause instinctively outside the bedroom door. It's so quiet you could hear a pin drop. But the splendid sound of silence this morning is a blessing because the longer she's comatose to the world, the longer I have to process exactly what I'm going to say to her. With that thought weighing heavy on my heart, I turn on the light and close the door behind me.

A few minutes later, I stare at my reflection as I dry my hands. Tipping my chin up, I study my face from one side to the other under the stark, shaving light. A faint rustle of movement stirs from the bedroom – the only advantage of the walls being paper thin – and I glance back at the mirror.

My fingers curl the rim of the basin tight as I lean forward and drop my head. This morning the stakes are high, too high, perhaps. It's safe to say that a few misinterpreted words will either make or break us. But of all the things that I must do this morning, the one thing I can't do is break her. Mentally or emotionally.

Not again.

Except it's easier said than done, and I fear whatever comes to pass before this bleak day is through may become a defining moment in my life. Feasibly more so than some that have come before it.

Opening the door, Evie is loitering in the hallway. She shifts uncomfortably, then mumbles. It's low and incoherent, and rather than think she's cursing me, I chalk it up to an apology instead.

As we attempt to skirt around each other in the doorway, I successfully conceal my immense pleasure at her attire. My t-shirt, working double-time as a nightie, does nothing to hide her, and my eyes betray me as they make swift work of admiring her soft, feminine curves once more.

"I'm sorry. I didn't-"

I shake my head. "It's all yours. Look, I'll make us some coffee, and then we can talk."

She nods imperceptibly. "I'll be a few minutes," she says after a long pause, then commences to pass me. Her bare forearm brushes mine, kindling a spark, igniting the dormant frissons of sexual yearning I've spent months wishing I could ignore.

The bathroom door closes, and I stare at it for a beat before I turn and put the key in the lock and turn off the alarm. I'm preparing for all eventualities, except I can't prepare myself to be broken-hearted before this morning has been and gone.

Stepping into the bedroom, I pull on a pair of jogging bottoms and a hoodie. As I zip up, my eyes fall on the crumpled bed and the ruined ballgown draped across the bottom. Caressing it between my fingers, the flush of water resonates through the walls, and I drop it back down and head into the kitchen.

The steam rises as the kettle finally clicks off. Pouring water into the mugs, I give them a quick stir and a dash of milk as a deliberate sniff derives from the doorway. I turn around and smile at Evie. She tentatively approaches and reaches for a mug.

Nursing it to her chest, I realise she's not only nabbed a t-shirt but now a sweater and a pair of jogging bottoms that have seen better days. The side of my mouth curls as she walks into the living room, and the material gathers in ripples at her ankles. Grabbing my mug, I follow to find her on the balcony, watching the sun ascend on the horizon.

Her head turns ever so slightly, acknowledging my presence as I close the door ajar. I sit in my usual seat, contemplating whether to light one up.

"You can smoke; I don't mind," she says, reading my undecided mind. The atmosphere is tangible, solidifying the distance between us. I reach for the packet and lighter and leave them on the table, just in case.

"You know what I missed the most when you left?" She breaks the terse silence. My brow furrows, and I'm suddenly voiceless. I desperately want to hear the answer, but I don't know if I can take it. "This. Perfect moments like this. Whether it was just watching TV or having breakfast together. Just perfect moments when I wasn't expected to act a certain way, or talk a certain way, or try to be someone that I'm not. You gave me perfect... Then you took it away without an explanation or even a goodbye."

I close my eyes in discomfort because she's right. I did take it away, and I did it deliberately. I removed myself from her life when I should have stayed and fought for what mattered.

Lost in procrastination, a soft palm cups my cheek, and equally soft fingers run the length of my scar. But unlike last night, this morning, I fall into her touch, wanting it to soothe me, to assure me. To set me free. Opening my eyes, Evie's sad pools reflect back.

"Tell me about *this*," she says, her thumb still stroking the newest scar. Her expressive features maintain their composure, neither hiding nor revealing anything, but I know she was shocked to see *this*. *This* which isn't the only cause of my leaving, but which culminated in it. Still, she was right when she said that *this* was the core of my problems. But today, regrettably, she's going to find out that *this* isn't the worst of them.

I gaze over the city vista, my mind furiously filtering through the misdemeanours of my past. A shiver snakes its way up my spine, and I crane my head, my eyes fixed on the rising sun. A new day equals a new way to fuck up.

"Jeremy?" I link her fingers in mine and squeeze tight.

"After *this*," I dare to touch my cheek, "I needed cessation."

She shakes her head in despair. "From what? From me?"

"From everything. My life is a cautionary tale I rarely tell, not even to those who already know and have lived through it with me." My eyes dare to find hers, and she gives me an encouraging nod. "My past is a painful story of two halves. Two halves I try hard not to dwell on but always fail miserably because they have shaped my present and, ultimately, my future."

"Two halves? I don't understand." Her face contorts, and I look away in shame.

Taking a breath, I finally purge. "I was an addict, on hard drugs, hellbent on self-destruction... There's me during the drugs, and there's me after the drugs. Two halves of the same fucked-up person." I risk a look back. "The dependent and the non-dependent," I emphasise. "You once asked me why I don't keep alcohol here. That's why. It's one of my three evils. Drugs, booze, and cigs, in that order," I say and pick up the packet still on the table, figuring I might as well light one up. I have no doubt she'll be gathering up her things in the next ten minutes and running like the wind. May as well start the stupor now, and at least that way, John, Sloan and Stuart might have a chance to pull me back from the brink before nightfall.

"Why didn't you tell me?"

I huff, and the smoke emits my mouth in a small cloud. "If our roles were reversed, would you?" She visible cringes. "Precisely."

"But you just said it yourself; you're an ex-addict."

I shake my head. "No, I didn't, but you're right; I no longer use drugs. Either way, there's no such thing as an ex-addict. Once you've had the taste for it..." I shrug. It's nonchalant and appears uncaring, but it's the only way I can currently disconnect myself from her curiosity. Besides, there's only so much of my addicted tale I can tell without implication.

Evie wraps her arms around herself. She gazes over the city skyline, then paces to the opposite side of the small balcony and slides down the wall separating us from the neighbours. "What does your past have to do with your scars?"

"Everything." I take a deep drag on the cig and blow out the smoke. "The man who gave me them was the one who showed me the door to decadent indulgence." I meet her gaze. She doesn't look disgusted, just intrigued.

For now, at least.

"Start at the beginning, Jeremy. I need to understand."

Inhaling deeply, I remove the cigarette from my mouth and die it out on the terracotta pot. I hold up the tab end and study it thoughtfully, remembering. "The first time I started smoking, I was twelve. A wild child, going through my rebellious stage," I emphasise, pulling a face. "I just wanted to belong. Naturally, for someone with my compulsive issues... I've got OCD. Undiagnosed, but..." I tilt my head and give her a knowing grin, and she smiles.

"So, eventually, when tobacco wasn't quite hitting the spot, I turned to marijuana. Before I knew it, I was snorting and injecting H, and I was addicted. I wasn't only using; I was selling, too. Deacon, my best friend, someone I looked upon as a brother, enabled me. He kept me high when the lows came calling. He kept me dependent for his own gain."

I stare into the distance while my mouth emits the shameful, appalling things I did from twelve to twenty-one when I was at my peak of chemical enslavement.

"Truthfully, considering that I'd sold my soul to the devil years before I even realised it, I'd have auctioned off my mother to the highest bidder to get high. Then one day, I realised I needed to get clean. I was finally at the stage where I was tired of feeling out of control, but every time I tried, I was drawn back in by the people around me."

"Jeremy..." I glance at Evie, shaking her head, pity swarming her pretty face. I turn away. I don't want her sympathy because it won't last. By the end of this, I want her to tell me that she still loves me, but she won't. And I won't blame her for that.

"In the months before I eventually got clean, numerous *incidents* occurred. It was a pivotal point in my life that finally made me see through him. A decade of friendship was gone in the blink of an eye. But in tragedy, I was reborn," I whisper, still ashamed of what that tragedy is.

The chair moves beside me, and my knee shakes as Evie sits next to me, her hand reaching for mine. "What happened to cause such a change?"

I look her straight in the eye. "Someone died. Someone he also assisted in their addiction." I drop my head down because that's on me, and I'm shitting the day she finds out – if she stays. Not to mention, it was my unknowing and unfortunate assistance in his attack on a young Kara, but it was Emma's death that took me over the edge.

"Oh, my God," she murmurs, shocked.

An uncomfortable silence emanates between us, and I find myself fidgeting, my OCD dying for distraction.

"Up until last year, I hadn't seen him for years. Then he did something I disagreed with, and I began to right the wrongs I had contributed to when I was off my head and unhinged. He didn't appreciate my altruism, and he gave me *this*." I point to my right cheek. "Then, almost a year later, I sacrificed myself again, and in return, he gave me *this*." I point to my other cheek and eyeball her hard, the deathly silence growing between us.

"And that's why you left," she states softly.

"I couldn't have you seeing me like that. How could I have even explained it then?"

"Jeremy, I'm seeing you now. And your confession then wouldn't have been any different than it is now." She reaches for my arm and slides my sleeve up. Her eyes scan over my skin, obviously looking for needle marks or drug lesions. "You don't have any tell-tale signs."

"No, I was smart, if you can call it that. I didn't pierce the same place repeatedly." If anything, I'm lucky the memories are not physical, just mental, but they still haunt me every time I close my eyes.

"This is a lot to process." Her beautiful eyes search mine, seeking further answers and clarification.

"You should leave and never come back." My words are harsh, but their delivery is soft. I'm merely stating facts. "Underneath the surface, my world is a dark place. A place of nightmares and monsters."

Evie's hand sits atop of mine, and she slides our fingers together and grips tight. "No, not when I finally have you back. I admit, it's a shock to hear, but I don't know what I expected."

I sigh. "I understand, but you need to know. Look, the key's in the door." She gives me a puzzled look. "You walked in of your own free will, and if you feel this is the end for us, you can leave of your own free will, too. I won't hold you back. I won't beg you to stay. Although it will kill me to watch you go, knowing it's the last time."

She wrings her hands together. "If I ask you an honest question, will you give me an honest answer?"

"It depends on the question." I'm not being evasive intentionally, but I won't make false promises.

"You've buried so much of your past, but I need to know. I need to be sure that whatever you're protecting isn't going to come back on me."

"It won't. It's over," I tell her, circumventing the truth and the conclusion of the most recent event.

"Will he come back? This Deacon?"

"No," I reply, and she frowns.

"Are you sure? How do you know?"

"Because he's dead. The Met pumped him full of bullets until he ceased breathing." Which was the only good thing to rise in the wake of what happened that day.

"What?" she shrieks, horrified.

"Sweetheart, please." I lower my voice, aware it's still only early, and my neighbours might be able to hear everything. She purses her lips together, seemingly abashed. She glances into the distance again. I gaze down at our hands as she circles her thumb over the top of mine.

"So, what's the second?"

My head snaps around, and I gift her with my confused gaze. "Sorry?"

"You said it was a story of two halves. You've told me about the first half, the dependent half. So, what about the non-dependent half? You said last year you started to right your wrongs."

She trains her expectant look on me, and I feel myself shrink back in the chair, wishing for the first time in a long time that hell's gate would open up and just swallow me whole right now. Fuck redemption. Rotting in purgatory might be easier on my sanity.

"Jeremy?" she whispers, worried.

I mentally debate, holding her stare. Realistically, keeping her in the dark for the foreseeable is crucial since any admission is detrimental to Kara and Sloan. Granted, it didn't work out too well for Sloan when he originally tried to keep Kara in the dark, but in the end, it has proven to be an episode that has made them stronger.

I reach around and stroke Evie's chin, causing a stunning blush to stain her cheeks in the morning light. "There's so much that I need to confess, things I need to purge myself of, but there are other people involved. I want to tell you, I do. It's just-"

"I understand," she says, completely compliant, her tone amicable.

The silence slowly creeps back in, and it's comforting in a bizarre way. The traffic resounding from the city is growing, and I look back to the living room, seeing it's almost eight o'clock.

"Every day that I was gone, I missed you. You were the first thing I thought of on a morning and the last thing on a night." The words tumble from my lips. She pushes up from her chair and gives me a subdued smile. Dropping herself onto my lap, her arms wrap around my neck.

"I missed you, too. If I didn't think there was a chance, I wouldn't be here now."

I cradle her chin and exhale, relieved. "I know, but darling, I have nothing to offer you," I confess. She stares deep into my eyes, without so much as a glimmer of disgust or dismay. "I'm a whipping boy for a security company that flies too close to the wind. I'm living a champagne lifestyle on a lemonade budget. This flat, the car, they both belong to a mate." I could go on and on, forever trying to get a reaction from her, but nothing is working. "Regardless that I don't have two pennies to rub together," I mutter as she gives me an incredulous look of disbelief. "Okay, so I'm not exactly destitute and starving, and I get paid better than I should. However, whereas my financial debt might be zero, my emotional debt... Well, I'm drowning in it."

"None of that matters."

"Yes, it does."

"Fine. We might be square peg, round hole," she says with a smile. "But we fit, Jeremy James of the sad eyes. From our first meeting to our first argument last night, our attraction is fierce. Undeniable. And our chemistry is scorching and off-the-charts."

"True," I reply, circling my thumbs over her cheeks.

"Besides, I have no room to judge. My dad considers me nothing more than chattel to be whored off to the wealthiest pervert who can raise his social status and pad out his bank account. He's been trying to pair me off with someone influential for years."

"Piers prick?" I begin, but she shakes her head. "We're going to talk about him eventually."

Her palm caresses my cheek again, and she leans closer. "I know." She squirms in discomfort. "He made me feel cheap and worthless," she admits shamefully.

"Have I ever made you feel like that?" I ask apprehensively.

She strokes her finger over my scar. "No."

"If I ever do, I want you to put me in my place. I don't want you mulling it over in silence."

"Okay." Her hot breath fans my cheek before her mouth ascends.

I fall into her embrace. Her kisses feel like searing heat, each one marking me, branding me, claiming me as hers. As I crack an eye open, hers ensnare mine, leaving no doubt in my mind that I'm wrong in my assumption. This isn't unknowing; it's very intentional - she's reaffirming her place in my life, in my head, and most definitely in my heart.

"Sweetheart," I murmur into her mouth.

Her hands tighten around my neck, and she shifts on my lap, straddling her legs around me. "Jeremy," she replies breathless but undeterred. Her seeking hands glide down my front until her fingers are digging into my waistband.

"Wait!" I pull back, grab her wrist, and she gasps. I instantly let go and hold my hands up in yield as she fists hers at her mouth.

I gently lower them, twist around her bruised arm and bring it to my lips. "I despised having to watch you with him last night." I press kisses over the dark spots. "Watching him touch you and grab you. And when he dragged you across that fuc-"

"Shush." She taps my cheek, clearing my enraged thoughts. She brings my hand to her mouth and kisses my knuckles. "I could say the same about you." She gives me a curious look.

I furrow my brow. "What about me?" I play along when there's no need. I know what she's insinuating.

She tuts. "Well, has there been anyone since you left? Since me?"

Triumphant fire ignites in my chest, and I want to punch the air again. "No," I reply, gaining myself a sceptical scoff. "Honestly. Over the last year, all I've had is a dextrous hand and a very active, debauched imagination."

Her cheeks glow crimson again, and she turns shy. "About me?"

I laugh. "Yes, each and every one of them."

A weird silence descends, and I'm fearful to ask, but I know I have to. I also know I have to accept whatever confession she has and make peace with it because I instigated it. Her fingers drift over my face, almost like she has a compulsion to touch my scars, and I stare deep into her dark, expressive orbs.

"You?" I finally dare to ask, and she looks down. A sign of guilt, perhaps?

She shakes her head. "I've not been with anyone since you, either. Not even Piers Baron double-barrel twat or whatever it is you call him!" She giggles.

The relief is overwhelming knowing she's still mine, and I laugh with her, although I know I shouldn't. "Don't call him that, darling."

"You do!" She glares with a grin.

"Yes, but I'm just a rogue with a filthy mouth, and you're a lady."

She slides her hands back around my shoulders and massages my nape. I groan, enjoying her tender touch. "Well, we have a problem then," she says seductively, applying further pressure. "You see, this lady loves your filthy mouth. And your dextrous hands. And most definitely your active, debauched imagination. But most of all, this lady just loves you. I loved you before you left me, and I still love you now." Her head drops, and I tilt her chin back up. "I've frequently wondered if I had told you more often, would you have still gone, or would you have-"

I cut off her train of thought with a kiss. Fuck being polite. I can't take it anymore. I grip under her backside as I stand, and her hold on my neck hardens.

With her mouth devouring mine, I stride into the living room with her coiled around me. She squirms as my fingers knead her bum, and I put her down on the sofa. She stands, wiggles out of the jogging pants and removes the hoodie and t-shirt in one fluid motion, leaving her in just a tiny pair of knickers.

"If you want me..." She leaves the unfinished sentence hanging between us and dashes from the living room. I chase after her, grateful there aren't many places to hide in this flat. I throw open the bedroom door, and she spins around to reveal her innocent expression. I shake my head as I grab hold of her and toss her on the bed. I kiss up from her ankles, teasing myself more than her. My mouth is on hers in an instant, taking what I need and giving her what she wants. Her hands roam my arse, and she pushes down my shorts before I kick them off.

Her legs spread beneath me, and the intense heat of her core is electrifying against my dick, which is stiff and ready, frantic to get inside her and let go. She reaches a hand between us and strokes me from root to tip, over and over, making me harder than I ever thought possible.

"I want you inside me, Jeremy James. I want you to fuck me hard and long and never, ever stop."

"Fuck, I want that, too!" I groan.

The combination of her words and actions are getting me off more powerfully than ever before. I move from her lips to her breasts, and my body throbs as I suck a nipple into my mouth, and it pebbles on my tongue. Every moan and cry she emits makes me more determined to give her what she wants, and my hand rakes down her body until it reaches satin. Rubbing my finger over the skimpy material, I pull back from sucking her tit and marvel as she grinds her pelvis in time with my hand.

I shove the flimsy barrier sideways and press a finger inside. She gasps, and her eyes glint beautifully. I smile, then tease her by adding pressure to her swollen core, and she lets go further with each circle of my eager thumb.

"Oh, God!" She rotates her hips, chasing the prize. "I've missed this with you so much," she breathes aloud. Her hands cradle my face. "I need more, so much more. Please."

And I'm gone.

I instantly remove my finger from her hot centre and drag down her knickers. She parts her legs further, inviting me into heaven on earth. She levitates herself on her elbows and glances down with dark, desirous eyes. As I align myself at her opening, she manipulates the position by digging her heel into my arse to force me closer while pushing forward on her arms.

The sensation of her body enveloping mine is intense, as is the hot, wet heat, holding me deep inside. Yet I know it won't last. I've dreamt of being inside her for months, and now that it's finally a reality again, I fear I may come quicker than desired.

"You feel excellent, babe." I groan with each arch of her spine until her core throbs when I'm fully seated at the hilt. Evie's face is a vision of pure unadulterated bliss, and she maintains eye contact as I grab her hip, retreat, then thrust back in again. Her hips move fluidly, sinuously with mine, finding our unique rhythm again.

It feels like time halts as I stare into her eyes, peering up innocently from under me. I hold her knees out and watch as my dick plunges in and out. Her body is hot and tight, and she puts me over the edge when she licks her finger and moves it down her body.

"Are you nearly there?" I ask, pounding into her as she rubs her clit, adding to the pressure I already feel inside her. I admit, I love making her come, but watching her touch herself makes me mindless. Screw my right hand. This is pure porn just for me.

"Almost!" She clamps her muscles around me, and I explode deep within her. She smiles victoriously, still rotating her hips. Moments later, she cries out – a sound I'm more than conversant with – and her body convulses from top to toe in an amazing wave.

Our speed eventually slows, and I run my fingers through her damp, tangled hair while our perspired bodies slide against each other. "Let's get you cleaned up, darling."

The hot water steams up the small bathroom as we cleanse each other. My body is betraying me all over again as my semi-hard shaft maintains its uncomfortable state, absolutely approving of the beautiful, naked female who has declared - in no uncertain terms –

that she wants a future with me, regardless that I can offer her jack shit.

A chortle escapes my throat, and she looks up, squeezing the excess water from her hair. "What's so funny?"

"I was just thinking about the future."

"And that's funny?"

I quirk my brow. "For me, it's hilarious." I pull her close, and her breasts graze my chest while my length skims her abdomen. "It just occurred to me that until you came along, I wasn't even sure I had one. And if I did, it was what you made me believe it could be."

She reaches up on her tiptoes and places a gentle yet smouldering kiss on my nipple. A torrent of powerful emotions consumes me, and I hold her tight into my side and kiss her crown. Relativity becomes relevant, as just a few minutes feels like a few hours until she stretches her arm around me and turns off the water.

Dripping all over the floor, I grab a clean bath sheet from the cabinet. Evie finishes squeezing the water from her hair. With a cheeky grin and crook of my finger, she pouts and sashays towards me.

I shake the towel out and throw it around her back, tugging on the ends to draw her closer.

"This is nice," she murmurs, stroking from my Adam's Apple to my collarbone. I reach behind me and grab another towel for her hair and one for myself. Fastening mine around my hips, I cradle the side of her head, mesmerised, enchanted, entirely in love with her.

"Yeah, it is nice." I lean down and lift her into my arms.

"What are you doing?" she asks with equal amounts of uncertainty and amusement.

I kiss her temple. "Taking care of you. The way I should've been for the last year. Let me do this, please." She nods as emotion streaks over her face, and she rests her head on my shoulder.

Half an hour later, she rolls up the ankles of a clean pair of jogging pants and knots one of my shirts at her waist. "How do I look?" she asks, tying up her damp hair.

"Beautiful. Always." I reach for her. "Come on, I'll drive you home. Your parents are probably wondering where you are."

She scoffs and picks up the tattered gown off the bed. "Hardly! My dad will think I've spent the night being *polluted* by Piers. He's probably elated at the thought of the connection. Probably hopes I tell him that I'm pregnant next month!"

I cradle her face and press my lips together. "Did that twat hurt you last night?" I finally ask. She squirms, thoroughly uncomfortable, but I hold firm on her cheeks. "I need to know."

She sighs in resignation. "He wasn't impressed that I was paying more attention to you than him. When we left, he got *handsy* in the limo, resulting in this." She lifts the dress with one finger.

"Define *handsy*," I request because the bastard is going to lose one if he's so much as touched her in a way that incenses me, more so than he already has.

"He *tried*, okay?" she confirms, annoyed. "He tried, and I fought him off."

I wrap my arms around her. Time passes, and I press her back and stare into her eyes. "I love you, Evelyn Blake. I have no assertions or illusions about us and trust me when I say I want you. I know I've hurt you, and for that, I'm truly sorry, but I still want to explore what the future may hold for us."

She presses her finger over my mouth and smiles gloriously. "I want that, too. Just promise me, if you feel the need to leave again, you don't leave me wondering why for months and months."

"I promise I won't. Also, always know you have a place here. If you want to stay, you can. You have your own key, and can come and go as you please again. You don't need to ask. Okay?"

"Thank you." She presses her small hands onto my chest and looks down at the dress. "Would you mind getting rid of this for me?"

"Sure," I whisper. I wrap my arm around her shoulder and lead her out.

DRIVING THROUGH THE streets, I glance over at Evie. The sunlight illuminates her porcelain skin and dark beauty to perfection, and I can't help but gloat at what a lucky bastard I am. Lucky, because I have an amazing, selfless woman in my life, but also because I've been given a second chance.

Pulling up outside the Blake residence is like déjà vu. I get out of the car, my sight trained on the house, and as expected, the gates begin to part. I open Evie's door and offer her my hand. She pulls up the jogging pants she borrowed from me as she exits and then presses close and lovingly stares into my eyes. I stroke my finger over her cheek, and her chin rests on the heel of my palm. All the while, the electric buzz of the gates resounds in the background.

"You free tomorrow?" I ask, and she nods enthusiastically. "Good. I want to take you out tomorrow night. A date. The first of a new chapter for us."

"I'd like that," she whispers, then touches her lips to mine. I keep her chin tipped up, leaving her with a kiss that leaves no uncertainty as to where we currently stand.

"Evelyn!" her father shouts indignantly.

"For God's sake!" she mumbles into my mouth, and I lick her lip just before she breaks our union. "I'll see you tomorrow."

I entwine my fingers with hers, resisting letting her go. "Are you going to be okay?" She nods again, then grudgingly turns and walks towards the house. I watch as she approaches her dad, and he has an obvious word with her. She subtly glances back with a smile and a wink, and I grin and throw Andrew Blake an ostentatious salute. He glares, not even attempting to hide it, and then the gates start to close.

Climbing back into my car, I instinctively look up at the house to find Evie waving from a large upstairs window, and I reciprocate. I grudgingly start the engine and pull off from the kerb. With my foot on the accelerator, my destination nowhere, the truth that has crystallised inside my head is a revelation.

The truth is, this woman gives me hope. A reason to believe the pain is worth it. A reason to carry on and fight to be a part of the world – her world. I always thought Kara granting me forgiveness was my path to salvation, but it's not. For me, Evie is true enlightenment. She is the guiding light waiting at the end of my path of purgatory and into redemption.

Chapter 20

THE THIN, SLIVER of smoke rises from the tip of the cigarette lodged between my teeth. I hold my phone up and re-read Sloan's latest warning message for the umpteenth time.

It's been five months since the event in which Evie found herself back inside my arms. Since then, life has been good, simple and easy. These days, she's virtually living with me again - which is a topic of contention for *some* we don't talk about - and we've fallen back into that effortless rhythm of love. Whilst she can be a little standoffish in terms of being around the rabble, which I believe is more deep-seated than John and Dom give her credit for, my mother is utterly besotted with her to the point I've already been threatened with the removal of body parts if I so much as cause a single tear to emit her eyes.

Unfortunately, during that time, I've also received daily cryptic messages from Sloan with references to dark clouds, grim reapers, unwanted attention, and various other anecdotes regarding my current squeeze – or rather my current squeeze's familial connections. Anyone would think with a heavily pregnant wife – who's *just* given birth, I might add – to fuss over, he would be focusing his happily ever after efforts elsewhere. But no, low and behold, he still feels the need to interfere in my life.

Regardless, forewarned is forearmed, and I need all the assistance I can get.

I toss my phone onto the old wooden picnic table in the yard which houses Walker Security, rub my hands together and zip up my jacket. Inhaling deeply, enjoying the hit of nicotine at the back of my throat, I grab the carrier containing the tattered ball gown Evie requested I get rid of. After hesitating what to do with it, I've kept it in the boot of my car. I know I can't keep it, but likewise, every time I see it, it reaffirms my hatred for Piers double-barrel twat, and the fact he thought he could touch – no, hurt - what is mine.

And she's always been mine, even when she wasn't.

With my lungs inflating with another blast of poison, I remove the cigarette from my lips and hold it between my finger and thumb. I debate whether or not to toss it on the dress, but then I remember cigs aren't cheap, and that bastard doesn't deserve more than he's already taken. As I inhale deeply again, I also need to remember that tobacco is still one of my three evils, and I'm falling back into the category of being a full-time smoker, not the recreational user I claim to be.

"That's a dirty habit, sunshine!" John appears from the side of the building, telling me what I already know. He removes the stick from my lips, throws it on the ground, and extinguishes it under his foot.

"Don't worry, I'm not smoking the hard stuff," I jest, causing him to eyeball me hard.

"That's not funny, but you better make sure you don't. Because if you do, I'll be in the next cell doing hard time alongside you. If I ever find you injecting, smoking, or snorting that shit again, I will put you down. Do not fuck up what you have with that girl."

I gaze down at the cracked tarmac where my confiscated cig end is now lying, dead and compacted. "I won't, but daddy dearest might do it for me." I'm not overexaggerating when I say it's safe to assume Andrew Blake isn't happy my shadow is darkening their door again. He made it abundantly clear the morning after the night before when I dropped Evie home all those months ago what he thought of me when Sloan texted to inform me of the man's interest in the *thug* she is infatuated with. He's also made it crystal clear the handful of times I've been invited to dinner since. He hasn't said it, but I know he wishes his daughter had hooked her star elsewhere.

And that star is called Piers!

The aristocratic arsehole whose family can raise the social, economic, and general profile of Andrew Blake and his disillusions of magnificence and status. Regardless, however hard you try to cover shit you want to conceal, it's always there, simmering beneath the surface. The chequered, interesting world of the Blakes is something they have fought hard to hide. Even from their daughter, I believe. But one day, if push comes to shove, and they make her choose, I will ensure they fall hard.

"Daddy dearest is aware there are certain battles he can't win, and this is one of them." J gives me a knowing look. "What are you doing out here anyway?" He reaches into the bag and removes the dress. "Evie's Christmas frock?" he queries sarcastically, his eyes crossing at the torn chiffon. "Was it fancy dress? Halloween might be a more appropriate outing for this, such as the bride of Dracula? Wife of Scarface?" He grins.

I shake my head gravely in an attempt to suppress my laugh. "I wish. Piers Maxwell-Clarke attempted to rape her in this the night we got back together. She asked me to get rid of it."

John drops it instantaneously, almost like it's coated in poison. "Jesus, Rem, that was aeons ago! Are you telling me you've been driving around with it for this all this time?"

I shrug. "I didn't know what to do with it, and every time I open the boot, it makes me remember more than just that night. John, is this my penance that the woman I love was almost violated the same way Charlie and Kara were? Is it a twisted type of retribution coming back to haunt me?"

John's sigh fills the silent void, and his hand grabs my shoulder. "Your actions were foolish, possibly dishonourable, but they were carried out by an addict who wasn't truly all there at the time."

I clench my fists. It's painful to remember those days. "I told her."

John's hand tightens. "You told her *what...and when?*"

"When we got back together. I told her I was an addict. I told her in a circumvented way about Deacon. I told her how our friendship had died. I mentioned no names, so in theory, I told her no lies, but I'm still lying."

I turn to look at J as he manipulates me closer. "Let it go, Rem. Please, for all that is holy, let it go."

I nod, unable to verbalise. Instead, I slide off the table, grab the matches and pluck one from the box, ready to drop it on the dress. Conscious the fabric will go up like a rocket under a naked flame, I inch back.

"Wait." John blows out the match. "I've got a better idea." He walks away, returning minutes later, petrol can in one hand, the other dragging an old oil drum. "A new year, a new start."

"Christ, you've lost your goddamn mind!" I exclaim, eyes frantic, looking for adequate cover.

He deposits the dress into the barrel and douses it with petrol. "No, but when the council and fire brigade show up and give me another lecture about smoke control, clean air, health and safety, blah, blah, blah, I'm going to claim diminished responsibility and tell them my woman's driven me to it." With a wicked gleam in his eye, he gives me a maniacal smile. Baring his teeth, he strikes the match and drops it into the drum. As anticipated, the flames shoot to the sky immediately. John laughs feverishly as he climbs up and sits on the picnic table, and watches the fire dance in front of us.

"So, what are your plans for the little bastard when you see him again?"

I stare into the distance, my mind delighting in all the suffering I plan for Piers. But sadly, I cannot. Because to dole out merited justice for his actions is hypocritical. If he deserves to suffer, there's no doubt in my mind I need to serve the same sentence. "I don't know." I fix my gaze on the ground. "Have you heard from Sloan?" I deliberately change the conversation.

"Yeah, he took Kara and Oliver home this morning. They're both doing well."

I smile because he deserves every happiness in the world, but that's what happens when you refuse to give up or be drawn into seeing something someone else's way. "I'm guessing Marie will be spending the night over there, doting on her first grandchild."

John's head moves from side to side. "No, she's working."

"Really?" I ask, practically dumbstruck.

"Really. It isn't for my insistence or lack of trying to get her to spend the night with me. She keeps promising me one day New Year's Eve will be mine, but I doubt it ever will."

"She's just busy. You know she's likes to micromanage."

He gives me a pitying stare. "No, it's more than that. She's distant. I noticed it last year and again this last week. There's a side of her that just becomes untouchable, hardened to the world. She looks like she's ready to burst into tears at any given moment over the tiniest of inconsequentialities." He scrubs his hand over his cropped hair. "There's no build-up to it. It's just there, *bang*! Last year, it continued for weeks afterwards, and I imagine this year will be the same."

"Have you tried talking to her, as opposed to talking down to her?"

He looks disgruntled. "I don't talk down!"

I smile like a Cheshire cat. "Yeah, you do. To us, anyway."

His pleasant demeanour fades into sadness, highlighted by the flames still chasing the oxygen skyward. "I've done nothing but talk, and she's done nothing but listen. It's a toss-up on who has the most self-preservation and conviction these days."

I force a smile for good measure, but I feel his pain because eighteen months on, he's still suffering and trying to hold it all together. I reach across and wrap my arm around his shoulder.

"It'll get better."

"You don't know that, son."

"No, I don't, but it can't get much worse, can it?" The atmosphere thickens as the heat circulates in front of us.

"So, considering I'm being abandoned, will I be seeing you and little miss tonight?"

I close my eyes in contention and drag my finger and thumb over my lids. "No." I shake my head grudgingly. "Tonight, unfortunately, I'm invited to the Blake's annual New Year's soirée." Of course, I would've preferred to spend the evening with John or even at the hotel, indulging in copious amounts of pop while sitting on the sidelines watching the celebration sober. Hell, even hiding from Sophie gobshite Morgan and her incessant need to dance all night is more appealing than spending an evening gracing the snake pit.

"Sounds wonderful," he replies flatly.

I chortle. "Any event for Andy Blake to social climb and get shitfaced. Take me back to the simple years."

"I'm surprised you remember the simple years."

"Touché." The heat radiates from the rim of the old drum while the flames lick the sides, chasing oxygen. My lips curve. There's something majestic about fire. It's deeply ingrained, going back to a time when it really was the simple years.

"Oh, and to make matters worse, it *is* fancy dress," I mutter.

John practically chokes on his laughter. "What are you going as?" he asks with a cocky grin. "The devil? A werewolf? Wereman? I guess you're already halfway there with that facial monstrosity."

"Very funny." I subconsciously scratch my scruff. I've been growing a beard back in since Evie likes it, and also because it assists in disguising my scars. "Are you going to the hotel's bash tonight?" He shakes his head no. "Well, what are you doing?"

"Dom's on his way down. Business, apparently. God knows what, I haven't asked. I find it best not to get too heavily entangled in his shady shit!" His brows lift, and I quirk my lips. I've had first-hand experience in Dom's dodgy dealings. Some of it I'd never even speak about, let alone acknowledge my participation.

"How long is he staying?"

J shrugs. "Pick a number. You know he breaks out in hives if he's forced to be away from his beloved Yorkshire for longer than a day."

I let out an undignified snort. "Very true. I'm guessing it's going to be a heavy night. Still, it's already going to be better than mine."

He nudges me, and I hold his concerned expression. "I'm picking Jules up from the airport in the morning, so I'm only going to have a few. Look, when you've had enough suffering at the Blakes, give us a call, and you can ring in the new year with two arseholes instead of one!"

My lips curve defiantly, but I don't utter a word. Instead, I just stare hypnotised at the flames still dancing in front of us until the yard gates open and the raucous rabble return.

Chapter 21

THE MOON SHINES in the twilight as I slowly glide the car into the kerb and cut the engine. I swing my head towards the imposing property, currently decorated in hundreds of tiny sparkling lights, and bring my hand to my mouth and chew my fingernail.

"*Jeremy?*"

My tentativeness has grown on the drive over, and the desire to twist the key and slam my foot to the floor is potent. So potent, in fact, my hand moves of its own volition and lingers at the side of the steering wheel column.

"*Jeremy?*"

Yet Evie is determined to play happy families tonight and prove her parents, or more precisely, her father, actually like me and-

"Jeremy?" Evie's clipped tone throws me off the train of thought, leading me down tracks that are anything but just. "You're zoning out again, Jeremy James of the sad eyes." She reaches up and traces her finger over my cheek. "Next time you go somewhere nice, take me with you."

I cup her delicate jaw and lean over the handbrake. "Always." She meets me halfway and claims my mouth. The movement of her soft lips controlling the intensity heats my blood. It consumes every fibre and cell, weaving its magic through my veins, enchanting all sanity and reason. I profess this new trickery is intoxicating, a natural hallucinogenic I can't seem to get enough of.

"Evie," I breathe out, prepared to drag her over my knee, until a sharp beam of light illuminates the car interior, and the bewitching sensation dies a slow death as I look up.

I keep my hand on her cheek and caress it slowly, deliberately, while Andrew Blake stares in disgust. His hand grips the steering wheel tight, no doubt wishing it was the neck of the *thug* his daughter is infatuated with and currently mauling her in public - albeit under the cloak of darkness.

"For God's sake!" Evie releases her seat belt. I grin shamelessly as she slides out and adjusts the little red dress she's wearing. All the while, her father, who has failed to notice his daughter is currently dressed like a Christmas tart since he's too engrossed watching me, is probably wishing his glare would eviscerate me instantly.

Oh, well, his fantasies will never be founded.

I continue to grin wolfishly as Evie winks at me, then purposely sashays around the front of the car and opens my door. "Did I tell you how much I love this incredibly sexy dress?" I climb out and paw the material at her hip, desperate to feel more.

"Hmm, maybe once or twice." She bats my hand aside, so I inch closer.

"Well, make it thrice."

"I will. And if you're a good boy and play nice tonight, I might even let you take it off me later. Call it a belated Christmas gift."

"Perfect incentive," I whisper, shifting from foot to foot since her words are having an inappropriate effect. In the corner of my eye, Andy's unimpressed expression is identifiable a mile away.

"Are you okay?" Evie asks, diverting my attention back to her. I take her hand and allow her to guide us across the pavement.

"Fine," I lie and stroke my thumb over hers. She bequeaths me a heart-stopping expression and shuffles closer into my side.

An ominous presence induces me to take a cursory glance over my shoulder. Andy is now a few steps behind, still wearing that impenetrable glare as we pass the dancing Santa and his reindeer staked along the path.

"Mum goes all out every year." Evie jabs the decoration and laughs when it rebounds back. "You missed it last year." My smile disintegrates, and I dare not look at her. Her amusement turns to anguish, and her lip quivers. "I'm sor-"

"Don't be sorry for being honest. I'm here now, and I'm not going anywhere again. New year, new start. Okay?" She sucks in her bottom lip, and I bend down and soothe her worry with a gentle kiss until a cough resonates from behind.

"Hi, Dad. Happy New Year."

"Hi, darling, and you," he says, then stabs me with his glare again. "Jeremy."

"Andrew," I reply, emulating his acidic tone. He straightens up, attempting to appear taller, but the man is still a few inches shorter than me, and I've faced off against far worse than his type in the past.

He strides with determination into the house, and Evie sighs redundantly beside me. "He takes some getting used to," she says, defending him. "He can be a little frosty, but he likes you really."

I tense my jaw to stop it from hitting the floor. Sometimes her naivety is adorable, and part of me never wants her to lose the ability to see the good in people even when it's not there. Still, she probably doesn't even realise that she's leading me like a sacrificial lamb to the slaughter, and she's doing it with a smile on her face. But regardless, I'd sacrifice everything for her, and while that realisation should be terrifying, it's not. It's pacifying, and I know it's because a part of me - the chaotic, nomadic part - has finally found peace and acceptance. Nonetheless, for the first time ever, it doesn't stop me from feeling like I'm entering the lion's den.

Inside the house, the music carries over the atmosphere and clusters of people gather in corners, laughing and joking, or deep in conversation. I inconspicuously glance up the stairs, and a ripple of anxiety runs down my spine and through my limbs because this feels far too familiar of a time in the past I want to forget ever existed.

"Hello, darling!"

Evie gasps and runs the length of the hallway towards her mum, who is waiting, arms wide, in the kitchen doorway. I follow on and stop a few feet away, allowing mother and daughter their moment.

"Good evening, Mrs Blake. Happy New Year. Thank you for inviting me," I greet cordially. I have nothing against the woman, and to be fair, she's always been more than welcoming to me whenever I've been here these last few months.

"Thank you, Jeremy. Happy New Year to you, too. And I've told you before; it's Cathy." Her words are genuine, and she reaches over and kisses my cheek. When she pulls back, she stares at my scar with indifference. "That looks better, less sore." She smiles. Again, it's honest and warm. "Now, if you don't mind, I need to play the good hostess and mingle."

"It'll take more than mingling to make you a good hostess." Andy Blake's scornful sneer fills the room, and the three of us turn simultaneously. The smile Cathy is emitting doesn't quite reach her eyes, and it makes me wonder if it's not only me who has a problem with her husband. "You've had twenty-five years to perfect it, and you still can't get it right. But what did I expect marrying a-a-" He huffs. "Send out the hired help. That's what I pay them for!"

In my peripheral vision, Evie visibly shrinks on the spot, and I instantly move towards her. "It's okay," I whisper, humiliated for the Blake women. "Let's get a drink, sweetheart." She acquiesces, pressing her lips together in uneasy contemplation while I press my palm to the small of her back.

"Thought you didn't drink, Jamison?" Andy quips, arrogant as you like. I glare at the vindictive sod over my shoulder. Yet in order to keep the peace, because my adoration for the man's daughter is worth more than the temptation to smack the bastard, I don't justify his baiting with a response.

Instead, I continue to move through the house, Evie's hand snug in mine as she charms and delights the guests and, unfortunately, shows me off.

RAPTUROUS, FEMININE LAUGHTER resounds in the orangery. I twirl my girl around, having found our own spot and a little piece of tranquillity away from everyone else and their morbid fascination with the newcomer. As patient as I am, there are only so many times even *I* can bear making idle chit chat about my appearance. When Evie noticed I was growing ever more frustrated with each passing question, she concocted far-flung, blustering stories from parachute jumping to rock climbing.

The only good thing to come out of such an intrusive evening is that I've managed to avoid any further run-ins with Andy.

The New Year countdown and the popping of corks echoes from the rest of the house. I turn Evie back out of the spin, and she laughs on the return trip, making me remember our age difference for the first time in months. She slams back into me, her front compressed tight to mine. Her palms sit on my chest, and she peers up lovingly.

"I love you, Jeremy James," she says, "Happy New Year."

I rub my hands up and down her back. "I love you too, darling. Let's go home and start *this year* off right."

"Perfect suggestion," she says, yawning loudly.

"Tired?" She shakes her head no but nods at the same time. "Maybe we'll start off right tomorrow instead."

"It is tomorrow." She slides her arm around my waist and rests her head on my shoulder. "I just want to say goodbye to Mum." I tip up her chin and kiss her, then pat her backside before she totters away on her five-inch heels.

Killing time, I venture into the kitchen and eye the obscene amount of empty and half-full champagne bottles on the island and grab a bottle of water from the fridge. While I stare out of the window, watching the clouds create dark shadows when they obscure the moon, steps enter. I sigh in irritation and reluctantly turn around, aware of who it is on an instinctive level.

Andy swaggers towards me, downing whatever is left in his glass. Unable to walk in a straight line, it's indicative he's had more than enough booze this evening for both of us. I twist off the cap and gulp back a mouthful of water, keeping my sight trained on him. He says nothing as he blindly reaches for a bottle of plonk on the island and pours himself another glass. He puts it back down and starts to twist the ring on his finger. I can't work out if it's an act of annoyance or a nervous tell.

Long, awkward minutes pass until his sudden intake of breath disrupts the silence and confirms he is finally going to say something. However, I'll be damned if I allow him to rip another strip off me for entertainment.

"Look, let's not pretend. You don't like me. You probably dislike the fact that-"

"Dislike is such a pathetic word, isn't it?" he cuts me off. "No, Jeremy, it's not that I *dislike* you. It's much more simplistic than that. The truth is, I *despise* you. And I *despise* the fact my foolish, idiotic daughter thinks you hang the moon and stars."

I maintain my stance, irrespective his statement has unveiled his true colours. Any advancement I thought might exist disappears in an instant, and the ambience thickens further between us, creating an invisible, simmering tension. I roll my shoulders and take a breath.

"Regardless of what you think of me, your *dislike* isn't because of the scars on my face. It's because my face doesn't fit, full stop. I doubt you'd approve of anyone who doesn't have money or connections. That's the real issue you have me; the fact there's nothing I have that you can use to your advantage." My hand tightens around the bottle, and I inconspicuously grind my teeth. He smirks with satisfaction, then downs his remaining wine. His expression is thoughtful, calculating, cruel.

"Oh, I wouldn't quite put it like that. There are plenty of things about you I can use to my advantage, Jonathan." A menacing icy blast envelops my spine. The thought of being at a disadvantage with this man is enough to put the fear of God into me.

"However," he refills his glass again, "unlike some, I have patience in abundance. Enough that I can even tolerate you. The true definition of intolerable, as I've said before." He knocks back another large mouthful and sways towards me. "Just don't use her too much." He stares at the glass thoughtfully. "I doubt the Baron will want the world to know his future daughter-in-law has already been fucked, tainted, and defiled by a thug!"

My temper spikes in disgust and unadulterated anger, and my fist clenches, ready to beat the bastard. "My God, have you heard yourself? This is your daughter you're talking about! And thug? What exactly do you think I do?"

He gives me a blasé stare. It's not lost on me that I could grow money, and he still wouldn't care because money doesn't come with a title – gentry does.

"Well, if you aren't aware, I work in security and formerly nightclub management. Both establishments owned by Sloan Foster." I don't usually name drop, but he also has business connections with Sloan, so there's not a damn thing he can say about that.

Yet, sadly, it seems there is.

"Let's just say I'm well aware of your former profession and the consequences that came with it. And they weren't security and management!"

"What the hell is that supposed to mean?" I slam the bottle down, and he closes the few inches between us until the intoxicating scent of red wine washes over me.

"It means I possess all the keys. It means I'm holding all the cards, and it means you need to watch your back because I own you, Jeremy James. Much the same way Franklin Black did a decade ago. When he controlled you like a pet dog! You remember those times, don't you?"

I hide my horror and discomfort because he's waiting for me to retort and refute it. Yet a part of me is in unimaginable shock. He wasn't lying. He does have an advantage. *A big one.* One that carries repercussions for more than just me.

"Hit a nerve?" he goads gleefully. He opens the fridge door and peers inside while I continue to gather my wits about me. "Speaking of hitting a nerve..." his muffled tone emanates over the tense atmosphere. "Maybe we should talk about Edward Shaw."

My ears prick up, and my entire body straightens instantly. "What did you say?" My hand slams down on the cold marble surface as he leans back and closes the fridge door.

He grins, and it's almost evil in its appearance. He holds up a can of Coke and gives it a slight shake. "I said, are you sure you don't want one more?"

"That's not what you said!" I fire back.

"No?" he mutters, feigning, furrowing his brow for show. "Well, what did I say, *Jeremy?*"

"Jeremy?"

I glower at him as the soft call of my name drifts into the kitchen. "In here!" I reply, hoping my tone doesn't reveal my fearful, diminishing mental state.

"Hey, are you ready to leave?" Evie's cheery tone sweeps through the room. Still, it can't eliminate the untainted hatred growing with each passing second between her father and me.

"Sure," I reply. She kisses him goodnight and then leads me through the house. My sight remains fixed on Andy, following a couple of steps behind. Evie opens the front door, and the chilly night causes a sharp pain to seep into my scars, an unfortunate side effect I've become accustomed to over the last few years as the months have grown colder.

"Jeremy?" Andy shouts the instant I reach my car, and I rotate grudgingly. "Are you sure you don't want one more?" His smile is triumphant. A victorious smile. A winner's smile. "No? Well, happy New Year. May it be prosperous and befitting!"

I don't indulge him with a response or parting civility. I just hold his sight until he eventually grows bored and slams the door behind him.

"What was that about?" Evie asks after I climb into the car.

"Nothing, sweetheart." I kiss the back of her hand.

She sighs and pulls the seat belt across herself. "Sorry if he gave you a hard time tonight."

"He didn't," I lie and twist the key. A slight flurry of relief overcomes me, yet my nerves are frayed and fraught while my sanity is very much on the edge of reason.

As the streetlamps pass intermittently, I concede I was wrong. His advantage is no longer a big one. It's absolutely cataclysmic.

And it couldn't have come at a worst time.

Never mind that long, fulfilling life I thought I might finally have a chance at. If Edward Shaw is aware of where I am... Well, there's a very genuine and worrying possibility that I won't live to see next week.

MY BODY JOLTS, shocking me awake. With my hand on my chest, the memory of old fades along with the lessening of my heart rate. I turn to Evie, sprawled out beside me, still sleeping soundly, unaffected by my sudden awakening. I exhale and rub my eyes. In my current mental state, I know I'll never be able to nod back off, so I slide out of bed and tiptoe out of the room.

I pace up and down the small balcony, a fresh mug of coffee in one hand, my mobile in the other. I drop myself into one of the chairs and remove a cigarette from the packet under the pot – the pot I keep promising not to replenish but always do.

Lighting up the smoke, I debate who I'm going to ring. Neither are going to respond kindly to my three o'clock wake-up call, but John and Dom have both gone to bat for me many times over the years to ensure I can live an easy life. The least I can do is let them know the ante has just been upped, and the possible fallout could have repercussions for all of us.

I scroll down the phone list and press call. "Hi, Happy New Year," I say as soon as J answers. "Sorry, did I wake you?" I add sheepishly.

"No, you didn't. I'm reading, waiting for Marie to come home."

I sigh. His problems are far worse than mine at the moment, and I really don't want to drag him into my shit again, but sadly, I no longer have a choice.

"Happy new year to you, too. How was the shindig?" he asks on a yawn.

"Interesting," I reply with an edge, using his favourite Blake synonym.

His quick nasal inhale resonates over the line. "More so than usual?"

"You could say that. Is Dom still down here?"

"Hmm hmm, he's at the hotel. Now explain *interesting*." His tone is sharp, leaving no room for dallying.

"Andrew Blake knows *things* he shouldn't. He knows *names* he shouldn't." I take another drag on the cig and blow it out with a wobbly breath. "John, I won't lie; I could have a very serious problem developing here."

"How serious?"

"Deadly."

Chapter 22

I ROLL THE stiffness from my shoulders as I drive through the city streets. I brake at a red light and squint through my aviators as the sun is exposed by the clouds overhead. The colours are vivid, glorious. But regardless of nature's spectacular beauty, right now, I should still be in bed, pressed up against another beauty, breathing in the scent of her hair, revelling in the warmth of her skin, holding her close, keeping her safe, protecting her from harm.

But I'm not.

Unfortunately, after my three o'clock confession, sleep eluded me. So instead, I sat on my balcony, wrapped in a throw, drinking enough black coffee to keep me wired until spring. And to top it off, my throat is now scratchy since my recreational smoker side burned through twenty cigs in provoking procrastination.

I turn the car into the private underground car park of Emerson and Foster and tap in the security code. I reverse into the last space marked *CEO*, joining the gathering of high-end motors. Strolling to the lift, I scan the assembly of luxurious vehicles - a Range Rover, a Maserati, an Aston Martin, and now my Lexus.

"The war council is in session," I mutter, amused, but this isn't a meeting of the minds over a beer or two. This is a strategy meeting on how to ensure I don't find myself within the grasp of a man still seeking possible vengeance a decade on.

With my phone in hand, I press the lift call button, then scroll through my phone book and hit dial. "I'm here," I announce as the doors part before me.

"I'll be waiting upstairs," Sloan replies and hangs up.

A few minutes later, the doors slide back to reveal the empty reception suite. Then again, it is New Year's Day, and this meeting is highly covert. I smirk on my approach to the small section of comfy leather sofas where Sloan is lounging. He yawns loudly, looking uncharacteristically tired and dog rough.

"Keeping you awake, Dad?" I query sarcastically. He practically vaults up with a huge, exhausted smile on his face. His happiness is infectious, and I drag him into a hug and slap his back, truly over the moon for him. "Congratulations, mate. You deserve *him*. You deserve *her*."

Whereas I'm tight with all these guys, Dom and John are very much father figures, but this man is my best friend. He's fought my corner from us being boys to men, right until the day our worlds figuratively stopped turning for the best part of a decade. We've existed in each other's lives from different ends of the spectrum for over twenty years. Some of those years we've got on like a house on fire, some of them we couldn't bear to be in the same room. But just like he's always been cheering on my side, there's nothing I wouldn't do for him. I've never said it, but I hope in his heart he knows that.

"God, Rem, he's beautiful," Sloan says, stepping back. A glassiness coats his eyes, and he sighs in awe. "He's got this dark hair." He touches his own. "And I can't see it yet, but I hope he's got my beloved's eyes." He quickly wipes away a tear. "Fuck, I'm crying."

I chortle. "I won't tell, but the best men always do." I nudge him playfully, and he comes over pensive and thoughtful.

"I wish the same for you one day. Who knows, one day may have already started."

I maintain my unpolished, outwardly veneer because I'm not living in a fairy-tale, and this time yesterday, I would've agreed. Today, however, I know my relationship with Evie carries an expiration date I'm not privy to. I used to think it would be because she eventually grew bored or found another more exciting and into the same things she is. But, considering why we're all here and the thinly veiled threats levelled at me last night, that day may come faster than anticipated.

Nevertheless, when our termination does transpire, I'm not ashamed to say I don't know how I'll mend my broken heart without potentially turning to an old friend for relief from the pain. The day the inevitable happens will be the day my sobriety is tested to the full. It will be another defining point in my life, where I either go out with the intention of polluting my bloodstream, or the day I say enough, and learn to live cleanly with the consequences of my actions.

Two raised voices I know well drift from the boardroom. The mixture of harsh words and insults indicates J and Dom are pissed off with each other. This has been simmering for a while, and there are clearly some underlying issues unresolved between them. Although what could possibly have occurred since John left him at the hotel and now is mystifying. I pitch my brow at Sloan, who rolls his eyes and yawns again.

"Apparently, Dom introduced himself to Marie last night. Well, per se, anyway." He yawns again.

Fuck!

I frown and scoff. "'Per se?' Either he did, or he didn't. There's no *per se* about it."

Sloan shrugs and opens his mouth. I quickly put my hand over it because it's a silent truth that yawning has a knock-on effect, and I need to be as wide awake as possible to spill my guts this morning.

"Irrespective of what he did or didn't do, he's got John's back up."

"I'm not surprised." I look towards the room. "John need not worry. Dom isn't interested in Marie like that." I shake my head as the voices reach fever pitch. I expect the argument to have escalated into a full-on brawl when I enter.

Sloan tugs on my elbow. "What do you mean, 'like that'?"

"Romantically." I shrug but regret it as soon as it's out there. I turn as naturally as possible, pull a face, and mouth *'fuck!'*.

Sloan moves in front of me. "What? Has he finally stopped pulling the brain-dead dolly birds?" He's gleeful and bizarrely, now very awake.

"Forget it," I mutter because I highly doubt he will be so enthusiastic if he knew the truth. I mean, I'm not even sure if it is true. I'm merely guessing. But if it is... Well, regardless, Sloan will be very wide awake indeed. But if anyone could give Dom tips on how not to be a whore while yearning for someone from afar, it's him.

Maybe if, or when the shit hits the fan, these two may find common ground somewhere. Laughably that prospect is right up there with Edward Shaw inviting me to dinner to regale old stories and share a toast for our combined love of his fallen daughter.

The voices grow louder as I saunter down the corridor with Sloan in tow, who's reverted back to yawning. I stop where the glass wall begins to see John and Dom, both wide-eyed and bushy-tailed, facing off over the table in the large conference room. I tap on the glass, drawing their attention. Throwing the door open with pizzazz, two sets of eyes spear me.

"Good morning, gentlemen!" I greet with overexuberance, but I'm mentally irritated having to be here. Two corresponding greetings fill the hallow, and I stride to the tea trolley and lift the jug. "Is Gloria here? Who made this?"

"I did!" Sloan answers haughtily, and I grin back at John. "Boy Friday?" I suggest sarcastically, causing John and Dom to laugh, albeit reluctantly in the current strained environment. "I'm sure his beloved would be in agreement."

"Very funny!" Sloan walks towards the vast windows, holding a dainty cup and saucer. I pour myself two tiny cups of black coffee, sans the civilised saucers, and pull out one of the many vacant chairs at the table.

I lift a cup to my lips and glance between Dom and John. Their identical annoyed, fidgety demeanours pique my playful side, and it's entertaining they're so pissed off with each other over something so little. I doubt Dom just waltzed up to Marie and announced who he really was.

"What did he say that was so bad?" I ask John, but stare at Dom.

"Ask the interfering git!"

I roll my eyes. I've been in the crossfire with these two many times over the years, and it's usually over nothing.

"Dom?"

He shrugs nonchalantly. "He doesn't like his missus talking to other men!"

"Does anyone want a digestive?" Sloan waves a packet of biscuits, bored. "There's some shortcake, too!" I snigger and put my hand over my mouth, but John's death glare stakes me before he levels it back on Dom. "Custard cream?"

"Screw your custard cream!" J says to Sloan, then glares at Dom again. "I warned you not to go anywhere near her! You know there are enough nightmares ensuring things go bump in the night at my house already, I don't need anything further adding to it, yet you did just that," he says, practically resigned.

"As I have already said, I didn't say anything, just asked her name," Dom replies in his defence.

"I didn't give you permission to ask her anything!" John counters in his.

"She doesn't need your permission!" Dom hisses. "Besides, she was diverted with other matters," he adds suspiciously and meets my eyes.

"Oh, for God's sake! I've heard this twenty times already in the last hour!" Sloan slumps further in his seat, biscuits lined up before him. "Can you save this pissing contest for later, and can we discuss the real reason why we're all sitting here?"

John and Dom both grunt in unison but can't disagree his logic.

"No Kieran at this secret rendezvous?" I attempt to ease the unnecessary tension.

Dom shakes his head. "He's had a heavy night on Merseyside."

"I bet that was messy." I laugh and wonder if I should call him on my way home.

"You would know."

I grin. "Hardly, D. The dragon already had me. I wouldn't know a good night on the sauce if it slapped me in the face."

"Gentlemen! I appreciate this might seem like a good time to catch up, and it might have escaped your notice, but I have a day-old child who I would like to go home to, so please, what, exactly, did Edward Shaw say back in the day?" Sloan queries, his calm demeanour coming undone.

"When? After I met his daughter, thus fucking up her life, or after I actually fucked up her life and killed her?" My words are mercenary, and I sound like a heartless prick, but this is the only way I can talk about it without it controlling my emotions more than it already does.

Sloan slaps the wood. "For crying out loud! You didn't kill her, Rem. She. Killed. Herself! You can say what you like, but those are facts, regardless of who that shit belonged to. She injected it; she, unfortunately, died because of it."

"Semantics," I whisper. "They were my drugs, my needles."

"Rem, I'm not going to argue with you. A girl died unnecessarily. Look, let's just get to the heart of the issue. You may as well start at the beginning and tell us everything. It's not like I have anything better to do – I'm only a new father!" he reiterates.

J snorts. "Well, you *don't* have anything better. Your wife kicked you out this morning, so you have plenty of time, sunshine."

"She didn't kick me out; she needed some space," he says on another yawn.

"She kicked you out," John reaffirms until Sloan concedes the point.

"Fine, she kicked me out! Called me overbearing! I'm not overbearing!" I put my hand over my mouth. He's overbearing personified. "However, note that irrespective of what happens going forward with this steaming pile of shit, I refuse to allow it to affect my home and my family. Dom, you do whatever it takes, but I will not lose what I have waited years for." Sloan then turns to me, and his eyes soften. "Likewise, you finally have something to live for, too. Understand?" I acknowledge, showing my respect for his honesty. Although, I might as well start digging my grave now – unless it's already been dug for the last decade, waiting for me to fill it, which is probably closer to reality than I'm comfortable with.

I train my eyes on the window. The rain lightly pelts the glass while my mind rewinds a decade to the day my path first crossed with Edward Shaw.

MY EYES SNAP open, and the ceiling gains clarity. As my focus sharpens, the dull throb at my temples deepens. My head feels heavy, almost akin to the sensation of being submerged in water. I'd like to say I had a crazy night, but sadly I have not. This feeling is a side effect of attempting to rid myself of my demons to please an angel.

My hand automatically drifts to the other side of the bed, confirming I'll be leaving it alone. Only, I didn't enter it alone.

I throw off the duvet and drag myself to the other side of the room and pick up the note Em has left. This is one of her most recently discovered quirks. Notes. Love notes. Reminder notes. To-do notes. Notes for everything.

I smile en route to the bathroom, astounded that she has actually managed to get up on time for her uni lecture after another ill-timed, impromptu party Deacon decided to host last night. A party in which I drank my body weight in Coke and picked at my nails while temptation called like a siren.

I flick on the light while balling the paper in my hand. I toss it into the small bin under the sink, then take care of some pressing bodily business.

A few minutes later, drying my hands, I study the reflection of the man staring back at me in the mirror. For once, I don't look zoned out. My eyes are normal, as opposed to permanently glazed, and my skin has a healthy glow and is no longer sallow and grey. Nonetheless, I'd be lying if I said I wouldn't give my right bollock for a hit right now, especially after last night.

I've been fighting hard to stay clean ever since Em sprang tonight's surprise on me last week. So, in essence, I've currently got six days of sobriety under my belt. Still, it's not very appealing at present. The withdrawals, the headaches, the waking up feeling like I've been hit by an HGV... It's always the dream, isn't it? Get clean, live healthily, choose life and all that. And honestly, I do. I want to live like that, but not like this. This enforced cleansing of my tarnished and immorally reprehensible soul is because she feels it necessary for me to get acquainted with her parents - which wouldn't have bothered me if she had given me more than a week's notice. 'Stop looking so fretful and worried', she said. 'They're going to love you as much as I do,' she added further, full of genuine belief and gullible, misguided teenage wisdom.

At the time, she was releasing around me, and I was so deep inside her I didn't stand a chance to refuse in the heat of the moment.

I stretch my hand over my face and run my finger and thumb over my jaw, debating if it's time to shave. As I open the vanity doors under the basin for my razor and gel, a glimmer of something catches my eye from the floor. I crouch down and pick up the object of my attention.

Clutching the carelessly discarded syringe, a grave sensation fills me: a truth, a secret, because this isn't mine. I grip it tight enough to snap it. I'm fuming. Absolutely fuming. I might be an addict, but I'm exceptionally careful never to share needles. Ever. Thus, reducing my risk of contracting hepatitis, or God forbid, HIV or AIDS. I might be a slave to dependency, but I don't want to die. Some may say they go hand in hand, and there's an unspoken truth to that because when you dance with the devil, you run the risk of being welcomed by the reaper every time you flick an air bubble. In my heart-

"Sorry, man, I need to piss!" Deacon barges in, already unzipping himself. I pay him no attention as the trickle of urine masks the rage ready to tear me apart. He flushes the toilet, zips up his jeans, then slaps my shoulder.

"I'm guessing she hasn't told you like she said she would," he says snidely, aware this is the first I'm hearing of it.

Aside from the night I found her high with him and the needle in her bag, the morning after, she swore to me then and many times since, that she wasn't using anything harder than a bit of weed occasionally and that Deacon gave it to her to try - if she needed it. She's even encouraged me to get clean, which I was actually on board with. But now I'm damned if I do and damned if I don't, because two users – and let's be realistic if she isn't already hooked, she's not far off – will only enable each other.

Deacon doesn't comment further as he snorts to himself and leaves the room. Over the past few months, I've often wondered how she manages to party hard, burning the candle at both ends, and now I know.

I toss the syringe into the bin as Deek reappears in the doorway. "I'm off. Business." He pats his chest pocket where he stashes his pills and powders.

"When are you coming back?" I turn off the light and snatch a t-shirt from the top of the wash basket on the landing.

"Who knows!" he replies. "Sorry about the mess!"

The door slams shut as I jog down the last step. Mindful of the dirty glasses and lager bottles dotted here and there, I open the living room door - the scene of the last night's crime.

My heart sinks, even more so than it already has this morning, and I close my eyes in forbearance. The house is a shithole. Some might consider me the lowest of the low, but I'm not a dirty slob who lives in squalor.

I pick up a half-full bottle of wine off the coffee table - which is littered with cig ends and various other nefarious bits of shit and sticky patches that even I dare not touch - ready to throw it at the wall and feel the satisfaction of watching it shatter. Only if I do, I'll still have to clean it up. Instead, I collect as many bottles as I can in my arms and take them outside.

I slam the back door behind me after lobbing the last bag into the bin. I load the remaining dirty glasses into the dishwasher and run the cycle. Opening the sink unit, I grab the furniture polish and dusters. They've seen better days, but if I'm going to do it, I might as well do it right.

Three hours, two full bin bags, and one dangerously full dishwasher cycle later, I turn on the vacuum. Moving around the room, a certain sense of pride fills me. In the few hours following Deacon's departure, I've managed to not only vanquish the shit left behind, but I've managed to tidy the entire downstairs of the house.

Reluctantly for me, this morning has served two purposes. One, to take my mind off the unspoken elephant in the room; and two, to keep myself entertained. It's also satisfied my OCD to no end. Although I know it won't last. Deacon will be back at some point, and the cycle will continue because while he likes to live in clean conditions, he doesn't want to be the one to do it.

I turn off the vacuum and observe my handiwork, wondering where to start next to ensure my idle hands, which usually are the devil's playthings, have something to occupy them when the doorbell rings. The strangled sound gets worse by the day since the batteries are in dire need of replacing.

I stroll towards the hallway. It's probably one of Deek's flunkies or some kid from the estate looking for a fix. It pisses me off, and today I'm not in the mood to deal with them. Hopefully, whoever it is will tire of waiting the longer I take to answer.

Or maybe not, as the bell produces another painful chime, accompanied by a knock.

"One minute," I call out and open the door. My eyes narrow inquisitively the moment I come face to face with the caller. The man appraises me from head to toe, and my brow furrows in question.

"Jeremy James?" He steps forward and smiles.

I mentally query how to answer since I don't know if this man is friend or foe. My forehead creases further because he knows me, but I don't know him.

"Depends who's asking."

The man chuckles, taking another step forward. "I can see why she likes you. I'm Edward Shaw, Emma's dad. Nice to meet you, Jeremy. I can call you Jeremy, can't I?" he asks cautiously, without a hint of caution.

The tension inside eases, and I extend my hand. "Of course. It's nice to meet you, Mr Shaw. Please come inside," I offer. Shaking his hand, I'm suddenly thankful for tidying up this morning. I close the door and motion towards the living room. "I wasn't expecting to meet you until tonight. Would you like something to drink, Mr Shaw?"

"No, Jeremy, and please call me Ed. Forgive my intrusion, I was just on the estate dealing with a line of enquiry, and I remember Emmy saying you lived here, so I thought I'd pop by and make you less nervous for tonight."

I smile, but if anything, his introduction has now made me extremely nervous because someone doesn't just 'pop by'. He's here for a reason. Plus, what does 'line of enquiry' mean? A fearful revelation gains traction in my stomach, and I hide the subtle recoil running through me because Em always changes the subject as far as her dad is concerned.

I study him discreetly. Tall, slightly thinning, mousy brown hair, typical age lines of a man in his early fifties, to hazard a guess. Broad, built, with an air of authority of someone used to being in charge and giving orders. He conducts a loop around the living room, observing his surroundings like a pro. But how pro?

"Well, thank you for your consideration, but really I'm-"

"There's been talk...rumours about this house," he says, halting my response dead. He stops in front of the chimney breast and pins me with an all-knowing, all-seeing stare in the mirror. "Talk and rumours that make me very concerned for my little girl's welfare." He pivots sharply and strides forward. "Now, make no mistake," he continues, his tone turning lethal. "She might be a grown woman, but she'll always be my little girl. I'm aware I can't dictate her life or tell her who to be with, but I can ensure she stays safe and well. So, let's just get something clear between us. Provided she stays in uni and achieves her full potential and graduates with flying colours, we won't have a problem. Understand?"

I nod, wanting him to be done since I fear we may already have a problem. Except, I don't dare voice that I doubt his daughter is safe and well. Because with me, in this house, with Deacon and his bottomless supply of illegal drugs and chemical highs, she probably never will be.

Right now, my biggest fear is that one day she will walk through the door, but she will never walk back out.

"In the future, should her life be affected by yours, we're going to find ourselves with a very serious situation, lad. I can, and do, overlook many things in my profession, but never where my daughter is concerned-" Static *crackle interrupts his speech, and I squint, wondering what the hell that is. He then produces a radio from inside his suit jacket and lifts his finger to request a minute. "Shaw?" he answers.*

"Sorry to disturb you, detective, but our informant is waiting."

Detective… Informant…

I drop my head slightly, nauseated, while my stomach lining eviscerates into a pit of acid, observing Detective Shaw walk to the window and adjust the volume.

"Well, inform the little bastard he'll have to wait. It's not like he has a life to go to since he now lives in my pocket." He exhales a happy sigh. "Tell him I'll be there in thirty, forty minutes. I need something to make me smile today." He turns around, wearing anything but a smile. His expression is curious. He flips the radio in his hand, making a show of who he really is, which is a potentially dirty cop who possibly straddles both sides of the law - if his comment of overlooking things contains an ounce of truth.

"Em never mentioned you were a detective," I say casually.

Edward smirks. "No, I can't imagine she did. Daddy, the bobby, isn't popular with her friends or the lives they live. As I said," he heads to the door, "I can and do overlook most things, even your suspected drug dealing in my city, because if it's true, one of my boys will eventually catch you, but I won't overlook any harm that befalls my daughter." He opens the door but pauses. "Let's not pussyfoot around, Jeremy. If anything happens to my Emmy, I promise I'll slit your throat, lad." His grave expression suddenly flips into a smile, revealing a split personality. "Oh, and if you want to impress Mrs S tonight, bring a bottle of Riesling. It's her favourite." He then strides out of the house towards his car. I refuse to turn away with my guilt until he has gone.

I slam the door behind me and kick the back of it. Resting my forehead against it, I'm livid for an entirely different reason. They say it comes in threes. First Em's surprise dinner tonight, then her suspected drug use, and now finding out her dad is a fairly high-ranking copper in the Manchester Met who could bang my arse up anytime he wants.

I squeeze my eyes tight in anger. I'm ready to rip the house apart to find a desperate fix. Sadly, I cannot because I still have to face the man again tonight. I highly doubt he will be pleased if I turn up intoxicated, swaying from side to side, with his wife's favourite bottle of vino under my arm. That might be the limit of what he can overlook.

But the one thing I can't overlook, especially given Em's unconfirmed potential dependency, is that playing house could be the ruin of us.

FIVE MONTHS LATER…

THE CALM SILENCE is deafening after the storm has passed.

"I'm sorry, I'm sorry, I'm sorry," I mumble over and over, praying the heavens can hear me and will forgive me.

The lights atop the numerous emergency vehicles flash continuously, bathing the area blue. I sit on the pavement alone, my knees to my chest. My body is subconsciously rocking, seeking comfort, failing to find joy. The last hour or so has been a blur, and the defining moment was when the paramedics forcibly removed Em from my embrace in the bedroom and brought her out into the cold.

The coroner's van finally pulls up, and my sight is still trained on Em, laid out on a stretcher, her body covered by a sheet to maintain her dignity and identity in this fucked-up frenzy that shouldn't be happening.

Movement catches my eye from the houses across the street. No one has materialised from those residences, but it hasn't stopped the curtains from twitching.

"Mr James?"

I lift my head to the person formally addressing me. "Yes?" My reply is barely a whisper.

"I'd like you to come down to the station to answer a few questions."

"Am I under arrest?" I ask, suddenly sober, but really, they need to lock me up and throw away the key.

"Not yet," the officer replies. "But considering the circumstances surrounding Miss Shaw's death, we are in the process of obtaining a search warrant. So, is there anything you'd like to confess before we start the search?"

I shake my head. If I don't say anything and don't do anything, I can't incriminate myself further. "No, sir," I reply as tyres screech to a halt, and car doors slam open and shut.

"Emmy? EMMY!" Edward Shaw's pained anguish is heightened by the silence shrouding the area.

A tear runs down my cheek as I watch him run towards the coroner's vehicle. A deathly hush ascends the scene when the sheet is lifted from his daughter's body. A piercing wail resonates in the void, and he lets out a strangled scream. He turns around, his eyes wide, his expression wild, and his fists clenched, ready to beat something to death. He continues to scan the scene like a madman, undoubtedly searching for me. I push myself up from the kerb and wait for retribution to arrive.

It doesn't take long.

He sprints towards me, and I wait motionless because I deserve everything he's going to throw at me.

"I warned you, you son of a bitch!" he screams in my face. He punches my cheek, swinging my head back on impact. His colleagues enter the one-sided melee, yanking him back, but he's too strong, and adrenaline is powering him on. With my hand on my face, I right myself and wait for the next blow.

"I fucking warned you! You killed my girl, you bastard!" He then falls apart completely. "He killed my daughter!" he shouts, and another suited cop consoles him. Eventually, he pulls back, his expression evil. "I want this house ripped apart, top to bottom! I want evidence, and I want this murdering cunt locked up indefinitely!"

His colleague comforting him looks up to the sky. "Ed, there's procedure tha-"

"Fuck procedure, Greg!" he replies. He gets up in my face and grabs me by the scruff of the neck. "I trusted you with the most precious thing in my life. I told you if anything happened to her... Well, we've got a serious fucking problem, and know this, there's a mark on your back and a price on your head. You're a dead man walking until you cease to breathe! You were right about one thing. Remember when you once asked me if I was a dirty cop?" I do. It was at the disastrous dinner after he turned up that first afternoon. He drops his head with intent. "Unfortunately for you, you're going to find out just how dirty I can be. Remember what I promised?"

I grimace and run my hand over my throat, which feels tight and scratchy.

He leans in close, his lips almost touching my ear. "I know you and the other drugged up cunt you live with aren't stupid. I know they won't find anything inside. I also know Franklin Black's behind all of it, but he'll get what's coming to him one day, and so will you," he hisses and pulls back. "Get him in cuffs. I want this bastard questioned until he breaks!"

The cold metal snaps tight around my wrists, and I let out a grunt as Ed strikes me hard in the side of the head. My body slumps to the ground before his prick colleague Davies gets in a few good kicks to my stomach. He then drags me to the car for the night's impending interrogation.

Not so long ago, I knew in my gut that playing house would be the ruin of us. Like I know now that this entire, colossally fucked up situation could be the death of me.

"REMY? REMY!"

A continuous shaking vibrates through me, and I vault out of the chair. My face is perspired, and a trickle of sweat drips from my nape down my spine. Dom holds his hands up in appeasement, but it's no use. Certain things can't be unseen, unheard, or unremembered, and that night offered all three.

"I'm fine!" I wipe my clammy brow, clutching hard at that mental fear chipping away at my heart and soul. I stride towards the cupboard concealing the fridge, and remove a bottle of water. Three sets of eyes watch with acute alarm as I toss the cap on the table and finish half the bottle in one long mouthful. I move in front of the long wall of windows, rest my head on the glass and gaze down at the quiet street below. My hand instinctively rubs my throat, wondering. It feels like an eternity passes until my breathing returns to normal. I listen without engaging as the conversation plays on behind me, by men who are ready to release the dogs of war on an old enemy.

"Shaw's always been dirty, and a leopard never changes its spots," Dom says nonchalantly.

"How dirty is *dirty?*" Sloan enquiries, somewhat aware of Edward Shaw's character and dealings within the Manchester force. "Dirtier than you?"

Dom scoffs in disgust. "That's insulting! I will *never* be dirty like him! I play both sides. I don't murder, maim, or falsely accuse to fatten my pockets or inflate my bonus!"

"Well, between enemies of old and potentially present, it seems we won't have a choice on what we do moving forward. Regardless, we can't just go off half-cocked." John leans back in his chair, deep in thought.

Their conversation becomes white noise in my ears. It's all should've, could've, would've, but nothing changes. Sloan will go to war because he fights from his heart, but John and Dominic? They will go to war because they're army men. They're institutionalised - to a certain degree. They've toured war-torn countries, but they've never seen the drugs war being fought tooth and nail on home soil. They've never been on the streets, touting shit to survive. Yet regardless of how many of their battalion sadly didn't make it home, they've never watched someone die from an overdose as paramedics battled in vain to save them in a dingy alley, surrounded by used needles, soiled condoms, and pimps and whores. And they've certainly never held the women they love when she's already been dead for hours and rigor mortis has started to take effect. The reality is we've all seen war, just in different settings and concepts.

I touch my neck again, but that reality is far too real and painful. "Dom, have you heard anything to the contrary other than what we talked about last year?"

"No, but don't get any ideas. I can't imagine K's rudimentary stitching skills stretch to necks, lad."

I inadvertently catch Sloan's shocked expression. "I'm sorry, am I missing something?"

I inhale audibly and hold his gaze. "Shaw threatened to slit my throat if anything happened to his daughter. He insinuated it again the night she died." I pinch my nose, feeling the tension headache deepen in the depths of my skull. "Look, for all intents and purposes, he doesn't even know where I am, so until we get wind of his movements, or he sneaks under radar and turns up outside my door... Well, then we have a problem. Besides, not to be flippant or uncaring since I've lived with this for a decade, remember I wasn't charged. The coroner recorded a verdict of misadventure, and you can't get blood out of a stone." I exhale, fed up of going over this.

"No, but he can get blood out of you, and something tells me he won't be happy until he's spilt every last drop. Not to mention, Andrew fucking Blake knows his name when he couldn't possibly." John's worried, but he's not wrong. I'll never tell them, but I'm worried, too. In fact, I'm terrified because I believe Shaw *does* know where I am. He's just biding his time.

I push up from the chair and stare at them. "I know. I'll be careful." I throw open the boardroom door and stride back the way I came. My head is running riot, dreaming of a future that I've always known has never been mine. Now I'm trapped between two worlds – the past and the present - that were always destined to collide, and the fallout will be catastrophic.

And potentially fatal.

Chapter 23

"WHERE ARE WE going?" Evie asks again, delicately brushing her fingers over the head of a carnation, before sniffing the rest of the bouquet. I make a mental note to buy her some flowers regularly, even if it's just a bunch of five quid tulips from the supermarket.

I study her intermittently while she gazes out of the window at the majestic beauty of the English countryside in winter. The frost tipped farmers' fields, bordered by hedgerows and dry-stone walling, guide our way. I press harder on the accelerator. The car eats up the distance to our destination - which is less than two miles from the village I grew up in, and also somewhere else I need to take her imminently.

"Consider it a surprise."

"Fine, keep your secrets!" She harrumphs, tugs her beanie further down her ears and fiddles with the radio as the transmission begins to lose signal. I side-eye her and smirk at her vulnerability. She thinks I'm taking her somewhere nefarious. Depending on your view, I probably am, but this visit is long overdue. I've been putting it off for the last week, but I can't put it off any longer, not unless I want Sloan at my door, chomping at the bit. Besides, this last week has proven the wheel can and does eventually stop turning. If someone had told me a few years ago that Sloan would be married and a father, I would've laughed. He was the biggest tart walking for a long time. Now with the woman he has loved for a decade, finally his, he's a saint, a perfect husband, and will probably be a perfect father too. It's something to aspire to.

Ten minutes later, I indicate pointlessly on the deserted road and turn into the private lane that ends at the mansion. Good memories of yesteryear flood back, rewinding the days when Sloan and I would pedal our bikes over this dirt path, enjoying the rare, long hot summer days. Or other days, we would sprint up and down, practising for school sports day. Or the days when Charlie was little, learning to balance on her roller skates and she would sit crying in the middle, clutching her scraped knees after toppling over.

But with the good is always the bad, and the memories of when Julia would put me up for the night after fighting with my mum are prevalent. As are the memories of my being drunk and high, staggering, swaying, yet surprisingly still able to walk a straight line, but powerless to stop from slumping into the hedges, wondering where my young life had gone very wrong.

I pull up at the defunct security booth and climb out. I press the intercom buzzer and rub my hands together. The morning air is biting. I press the button again, and the electrical buzz of the camera overhead rotates and points down. The gates finally open, and I quickly climb back into the car. Moving at a snail's pace, I watch the gates close securely in my rearview.

My eyes glance over the side of the house at the row of high-end motors and the bikes we all sometimes go for a legal joy ride on. Parking my car beside the Aston, I walk around to the passenger side and offer Evie my hand. She grips it tight, looking around in awe and wonder, clutching the bouquet in the other.

"Whose house is this?" She gazes in awe at the long-curved driveway, the manicured garden, and the grand façade.

I figure I've left her in the dark long enough, and I'm about to answer when the door opens, and Sloan slouches beside the frame, yawning as the sound of a very unhappy baby leaks from inside. I grin. Gone is the high-powered CEO. Before me stands a man, unkempt and dishevelled. A man undeniably knackered, who probably hasn't slept in a week and is currently being dictated to by a one-week-old.

I feel its arrival before it hits, and my mouth opens after his does. "I'm going to kill you!" I say on a yawn, and if I wasn't feeling tired before, I am now.

"Get in line behind my son!" he replies, yawning again, then ambles forward. "It's about time! Were you waiting for a twenty-four-carat gold embossed invite?" he asks sarcastically, throwing his arms around me.

I hold him close. "No, just a horse-drawn carriage to escort me!" I laugh and slap his back. "Besides, I also have someone you both need to officially meet, too." I let him go and hold my hand out for Evie, who steps forward. "Sweetheart, I know you already know him, sort of, but meet Sloan Foster."

"Evie, it's lovely to meet you," he says genuinely, tipping his head and kissing the back of her hand.

She smiles and straightens her shoulders. "It's nice to meet you, too, Mr Foster."

He chuckles. "Sloan, please. Mr Foster was my father, and since I'm not that much older than you, it feels weird."

A gurgle seeps from inside again, and we all turn as Kara appears with Oliver bundled up in her arms.

"And this is my beloved, Kara."

For a moment, it's all peace and light, then Oliver's face scrunches up. He opens his little mouth, and an almighty baby wail scares the birds from the trees.

"A murder of crows," I mutter, mesmerised by the birds ascending skyward. I look back at Sloan and Kara, who both look ready to cry, and I cringe, observing Kara attempting to soothe their son to no avail. Sloan is beside himself with concern for his wife's mental welfare, and I realise there will be a murder of something – possibly me – if I dare open my mouth and say something sarcastic.

I exchange a look with Evie, but neither of us has any experience with babies, so there isn't much we can do to assist.

When it becomes apparent Oliver isn't going to quieten down, Evie steps forward. "Hi," she greets Kara, who smiles, equal amounts of surprised and happy to finally meet her and exhausted from being a new mum. "These are for you. Congratulations." Evie holds the flowers. "Hello, Oliver, nice to meet you!" she says, but he just starts to squirm again.

"Oh, they're lovely. Thank you." Kara glances between Evie and me. "As is finally meeting you. Come inside; it's cold."

Evie enters after Kara, removing her scarf, gloves, and beanie as she goes. I step into the foyer, listening to the female chatter fade into the house. Sloan locks the door, and I drop my car keys on the table and take off my jacket. I pad behind him down the hallway, to where the sounds of our women and his son are coming from. We pause outside the living room door, and I smile involuntarily, knowing I made the right choice this morning.

Watching Evie converse with Kara, I don't know what I thought would happen when they eventually met. I certainly didn't expect them to suddenly become best friends, but this is a good start. It's also blatantly obvious that Evie needs a friend independent from her current circle. Someone her dad wouldn't dare call to check up on her, and someone who knows nothing of her family. Likewise, Kara also needs someone far removed from the familial group who still try to coddle her these days. Someone who will be an independent voice and someone who knows nothing about her past.

Yet.

"I have a niggling feeling we might have another regular visitor going forward," Sloan comments, observing his wife and Evie set the foundation for a new friendship. "At least this one isn't going to cost me an arm and a leg, and she won't backchat!" I snicker, and he reciprocates, but his face drops a little. "Let's talk," he says, his eyes indicating elsewhere.

I follow him perfunctory into the kitchen. Closing the door, I pull out a seat at the island, my usual spot as a child. Just like the rest of the house, it has undergone numerous transformations over the years. First, when Franklin Black redesigned the style that Oliver Foster Senior, Sloan's father, had chosen when he bought this place for his new wife and family. Later, having survived the mental and physical abuse Jules, Sloan, and Charlie suffered at the hands of Franklin, Jules then ripped out everything he installed and made it hers. Since then, Sloan has put his own stamp on the place, which is only a modern update of the kitchen and bathrooms as it was never his intention to live here. But love conquers all, including the memories of ghosts roaming the halls of years gone by.

Sloan begins to make some coffee, and I look from left to right. The clean, pristine, contemporary minimal appearance is gone. Now the worktops are sufficiently occupied by a steriliser, a bottle rack not designed for expensive wine, and various other bits of baby equipment here and there.

He slides a couple of mugs over the top and takes a seat on the other side. "So, has anything interesting happened since last week?" He holds my eyes, referring to our covert meeting on New Year's Day.

"Well, you'll be happy to see that my neck is still intact, if that's what your query pertains to," I reply flippantly, my hand gracing my throat.

"That's not funny!"

I chortle and lift the mug. "I'm not laughing." I swallow a mouthful of scorching coffee, convinced my palette is going to melt. Another unhappy baby cry seeps in, and I give Sloan an apologetic smile.

"How's the first week of fatherhood treating you?"

He grins. "Terrific. I've never felt so exhausted in my life. Thanks for coming over." He raises his own mug, but before he can consume it, he yawns loudly again. "Thanks for bringing Evie, too. Do you know if her dad has said anything further?"

I shake my head. "No, he's too smart for that. Instead, he's just slowly poisoning her mind."

"Slowly?" Sloan repeats incredulously. "I think he's already done that."

"True," I reply over the distressed sounds leaking into the room more frequently. "Anyway, he's planning something. Look, today is meant to be a good day, and I don't want it consumed with talk of Andrew Blake. Come on, Dad, your son sounds upset."

"No, that's normal. When he's happy and hasn't cried in five minutes, that's when I'll start to worry."

I rise from the stool, indicating for him to move. "It's a brave new world for him."

"He's not the only one," Sloan grumbles behind me, and I halt, causing him to walk into my back. I turn around just outside the living room door and grip his shoulder.

"It'll get better, but she needs you. She's strung out and exhausted, you both are, but at some point, you get to go to work, and she'll be alone experiencing everything without you, meaning there'll be some things you'll miss, and she'll remember forever. Don't take the time you have for granted, even if he is incredibly vocal right now."

Sloan nods absentmindedly, pensive, deep in thought. "When did you become so philosophical?"

I lift my hands in a 'I don't know' kind of way and grin. "Since I spent the best part of fifteen years flitting between here and Yorkshire. Between Dom and Kieran, I've had daily doses of Loiner and Liverpudlian pearls of wisdom to last me a lifetime. Come on, introduce me to your boy."

He pushes the door open, and Evie instantly turns to me. There's a new look in her eyes that I can't say I've witnessed before. It's a mixture of fear and longing. Kara smiles at me in that overstressed, overworked new mother way and cradles her son.

"Hey," Evie whispers as I take a seat next to her and squeeze her hand in comfort.

"Evie, would you like to hold him?" Kara asks, a hopeful expression on her face. Evie immediately glances my way for moral support, but I just purse my lips. Only she knows if she wants to hold him or not.

"I do, but I'm scared I might hurt him," she confesses.

"Oh, me too," Kara replies, rising with Oliver, easing Evie's fear considering the lessening tension in her body. "Up until a week ago, I'd never held a baby before either. Good job his father has." She gazes lovingly at her husband.

"But you're his mum. It's instinctual, ingrained on a base level."

"True, but instinctual or not, he didn't come with an instruction manual. Besides, you probably have the same ingrained instinct too." She then passes the baby into the arms of my blushing young lover. Evie's back is ramrod straight, staring at him like he has two alien heads. She attempts to rock him, but I think that motherly instinct is yet to kick in. Oliver, sensing Evie's fear in his newborn wisdom, opens his mouth again. I swear, the kid will have a sore throat with all his crying and carrying on.

"Kara!" Evie calls softly, panicked.

Sloan bends down and kisses his beloved, then carefully lifts his son from Evie's embrace, much to her relief, and sits next to me. He motions his head and transfers Oliver from his arms to mine. The boy quietens as his eyes focus, absorbing this new *thing*.

"Jeremy," Sloan calls me by my actual name for the first time in years. "Meet Oliver John Foster. Oliver, meet Daddy's oldest friend in the entire world, Uncle Jeremy." Oliver's eyes expand, revealing his beautiful dark pools so full of learning and intrigue. It makes me wonder how amazing it must be to see the world through new, uncorrupted eyes. With him settled and content in my arms, he grips my thumb, and I'm going to translate that as we're buddies now. Holding him close to my chest for the first time in a long time, I feel a renewed peace in my soul. One that is the protective kind, the fatherly kind, and I have to say this enlightenment is amazing.

I hold him up, eye to eye, man to man. "What's with all the noise, kid? You even managed to murder the crows outside, and that's a mean feat, sunshine." Oliver's mouth pouts, but he has no clue what I'm talking about. "I'm guessing Mummy and Daddy are annoying you already? Yeah, I know, but it's only been a week. You've got to give them time." I glance between Evie and Kara, both wearing amused expressions but failing to hide their surprise at my interaction with him. I wink at Kara and move Oliver to my ear, pretending, playing. "It's always Daddy, isn't it? Well, when Daddy annoys you, you call Uncle Jeremy, and we can arrange a weekly chat about him."

The muffled sounds of Kara's laughter piques my attention, and she's beaming with her hand over her mouth. In the periphery, Evie is also giggling while Oliver gurgles.

"Don't encourage him!" Sloan grumbles with a smile.

Oliver's hand then touches my cheek, and very specifically, my scar. With his eyes so dark, so very reminiscent of his father's, I swear they are seeking, searching. Penetrating deep into my soul, claiming a piece of my heart.

I glance around the quiet room. Kara now has her hand on her chest, watching with love as her son interacts with me. Evie beams, and I debate if it's ingrained in women to love a man holding a baby, playing the family protector. Her hand touches my face, and she remains quiet. She then gets up and moves to the opposite sofa to sit with Kara.

I make a mental note to bring the condoms back into our relationship because her longing look is back again.

"Broody?" Sloan whispers perceptively. My eyes drift back to Evie, but God, if the idea of being the protector isn't gaining prominence inside me, condoms be damned.

"No," I fib and hold my new baby chum closer.

"Liar!" he grins. "Remember, you've got until August to get committed."

TIME PASSES SLOWLY, we've spent the morning and afternoon here. Kara has made the most of having someone else entertain her son and give her some time for herself. She even kindly made us lunch, while Sloan has ensured Evie has been made to feel welcome. He's even talked shop with her, found out her likes and dislikes of her uni course, and advised which areas she should concentrate on for the different fields she's interested in for her future career.

"What is that?" Evie asks, her eyes lighting up in excitement as Sloan puts down some papers. Unfortunately, this look isn't good, because it's a look that's going to get me in trouble.

"It's what it sounds like - a trainee scheme run over the summer. You should apply. I'm sure you'll find some elements incredibly valuable. Not to mention, you'll work with the individual sector heads over your two-week period and learn how they do things. Also, it looks good on a CV. Dedicated, willing to learn."

Evie slides over the papers and starts to read them. "I'll consider it," she says, which means she needs to run it past Andy first.

The living room door creaks, and Kara elbows her way in with some fresh drinks. I cradle Oliver in my arm, giving him his feed. His little face is full of determination as he consumes his lunch with vigour.

Kara smiles, puts a bottle of water and a glass on the table for me, and then slides in next to Sloan. "Did you ask him?" She nudges her husband.

My eyes shift between them. "Ask me what?"

Sloan grins – the same one he wears when he wants a favour. "Jeremy James, would you do us the honour of being Oliver's first godfather?"

I baulk, completely taken aback. Their request is magnanimous in scale and huge in gratitude. "Really?" I ask, unable to keep the surprise from my tone or my face from curving into a smile.

"Yes, really. Rem, I've told you before, I trust you with everything, that includes my life, my wife's, and now my son's."

"Honestly, I feel like a fraud since we don't go to church, but Gloria said we should get him christened. I've got a meeting with the vicar soon, and we're thinking of arranging it for May," Kara confirms while I continue to ruminate over the request.

Again, enlightenment is wonderful, proving it isn't Kara's redemption I need; it's my own. And more recently, Evie's. Eventually.

My back twitches and I push up from the sofa and walk to the fire surround. My eyes fix on the wedding picture of Sloan and Kara at the church entrance after affirming their vows.

"Rem?" Sloan calls.

I rotate, my eyes fixed on my baby chum. "I'd be privileged, truly. Of course, I accept." I grin wildly. I'm excited, terrified, unsure of what the role entails, but holding Oliver close to my chest, feeling his heart pulse near my arm, I vow to lay down my life for him.

Chapter 24

I TURN OFF the water, run my hands over my hair and nudge the cubicle door open. Wrapping a towel around my hips, I listen for any signs of life stirring. As expected, it's still deathly quiet.

Roughly drying my hair, I stride the ten feet from the bathroom to the bedroom and push back the door. I lean against the architrave and stare at the naked body sprawled over the bed, face down, arse up. It's pretty much the same way I left it thirty minutes ago after its owner's wandering hand found me hard and inviting, and I knew only a cold shower would suppress it. Although the twinge currently gaining momentum south tells me it hasn't worked.

I close the distance, sit on the edge of the bed, and study the smooth, curved skin in all its unclothed glory, debating whether to wake its irrefutably sexy owner with some slapping or rubbing.

Or both.

Resting on my side, I pull the duvet away, wrap my arm around the back of her thighs and descend. She murmurs incoherently when I tongue down the arc of her lower back.

"Too tired," she grumbles, causing my eyes to flicker in surprise.

Although it's not surprising, considering she found new ways to play with me last night. Like any young woman just out of her teens, she has more stamina than a prized thoroughbred. Something that has kept me entertained and extremely satisfied daily these last few months.

"Wake up, beautiful. You're going to be late." I firmly pat her backside.

"No!" She protests further and attempts to drag the duvet back over herself - to no avail with my fist tight around the material. Mouthing her delectable, rotund cheek, she sighs the same sigh she makes when she's turned on. I glance up the length of her in time to see her fingers dig into the sheet while her back bows impulsively in anticipation.

I grin and kiss her again, this time more forceful, giving a cheek a hard suck, digging in my teeth, marking her as mine.

"Oh, that's good!" she moans. "Keep going." Her leg moves against my arm, and she spreads it out. Teasing my finger from the front to back over her sensitive flesh, I reluctantly withdraw, doing the complete opposite of what my groin is craving.

"You're going to be late," I repeat with more authority because I refuse to have her father breaking down the door when his little princess fails uni. God knows his visit yesterday - when he brought her home after demanding her presence at Sunday lunch, of which I wasn't invited - was entertaining enough. Especially when the penny finally dropped that she had moved herself in a pair of shoes, an item of clothing, and a handbag at a time. It speaks volumes about him since he hasn't even realised it until now.

"Please, just a quick touch," she begs innocently.

I chuckle because I'm not falling for it. "Sweetheart, it's never quick, and it's never just a touch. Come on, up. Now."

"Please, Jeremy," she pleads, ensuring my resistance snaps instantly.

I ease her closer and manoeuvre her leg higher, titling her arse up, opening her before me. She glistens in anticipation, making me painfully hard at the luscious sight, imploring me to go for another test drive this morning. She happily exhales the moment I gently cup her sex. My fingers probe her hot flesh before I slide two deep into her heat. She lifts wantonly, rendering my entry effortless. I pull her against me, her back to my front, and influence her position to continue my ministration of her core. She rides my hand perfectly, her hips thrusting back and forth while my thumb repeatedly strokes her swollen skin.

"Oh, God!" Her hips grind faster as her hand joins mine at her centre. "Slide another inside me."

I bite the inside of my cheek because my dick is the only thing I want inside her when she's hot, demanding, and ready to explode like this. Instead, I do as ordered. I withdraw my hand, then glide three fingers into her pulsating heat. The heel of my hand presses against hers as she continues to stimulate herself. All the while, her breathing turns harder, her words dirtier.

I slide her mass of hair to one side, cradle her jaw in my hand, and run my lips up the column of her neck. The tip of my tongue moves along her jugular vein, which is throbbing faster with each passing second.

"You're really going to be late," I whisper in her ear. Capturing her lobe between my teeth, giving it a firm nip, my fingers thrust in and out of her core with abandon.

"Yes...but I'm going to come first. Oh, that's amazing..."

Her skin slowly begins to perspire, and I glide my other hand down her neck until I palm her tit. Squeezing and circling her nipple, her breathing grows more laboured and uneven. Eventually, her centre clamps vicelike around my fingers, and she unravels beautifully.

The sound of her crying out over and over is one of the most amazing things I've ever heard, as is witnessing her come spectacularly. Ever since that first time on my desk and then the magnificent shower we shared later that evening, I knew I'd never let her go. She has always made me feel normal, less damaged and tainted, and more like the man I strive to be daily. Just to be good enough for her, to be the man she deserves.

When her body finally ceases shuddering, she lifts off my fingers and twists in my arms. With her hands stroking my nape, her nose almost touching mine, I gaze in awe at the perfect features that form her beauty and gather the mass of dark hair she occasionally uses as a shield to hide from the world in my hand.

"I like waking up like that in the morning."

"So do I, but I'd like it even better if we both didn't have somewhere else to be." I suck my fingers before pillaging her mouth.

"We have time." She wiggles on my lap and palms my stiff dick. "I want you inside me."

"You're playing with fire."

"Good, I want to be burnt." I push her probing palms away, truly amazing myself. Honestly, I have no idea how I manage to harness my constant desire and preserve my control, not when she's offering herself on the proverbial platter to allow me to do whatever I like.

"Later, I'll let you *burn* as much as you want, but right now, shower, dressed. You've got a presentation, and I doubt your parents will be impressed if you fail to attend. Not to mention your interview beforehand. Let's not give your dad any more reason to put a price on my head." I'm half joking, but it wouldn't be a first. "Frankly, I expected a lecture regarding it from him yesterday. No doubt he blames me for that, too."

"He said it was fine," she mutters with an undeniable grimace. Granted, she endeavours to hide it, but I can read her expressive features effortlessly. She climbs off the bed, sashays her luscious arse out of the door, but then pops her head back around it. "Who's going to wash my back?"

"The invisible man! I'll make you a coffee for the journey."

She bestows me a sulky pout, and I conceal my sigh until the door closes. Every now and again, I forget the age difference, but on mornings like this, she does something that makes me remember.

I pull on my shorts and jeans, drop a t-shirt on the bed, and grab my phone. An unidentified number displays as a missed call - probably a potential client - but since there's no message left, I clear the screen and shove it in my back pocket.

I slip the t-shirt over my head as I pad into the kitchen and turn on the kettle. I listen intently to the water still running as I stride into the living room. Titling my head, assured I won't be disturbed, I drop to my haunches, pull out the bottom drawer of the sideboard and extract the contents from underneath.

If there is one thing in life that John has taught us, it is to know who we are with. It's almost vulgar, in a sense, but he's right, and considering Evie now practically lives here, much to her father's dismay, the potentially incriminating contents of this file now need to live somewhere else.

The water shuts off, and I quickly roll the file up and stick it inside my jacket. The hairdryer then blares, and I move back into the kitchen and hang my jacket on the chair. As I make myself a coffee and fill Evie's travel mug, a faint beep resounds from one of her bags on the table. I ignore it, but the beep eventually morphs into ringing and continues, leaving me no choice but to see who it is.

'Dad' appears on the screen, but there is no way I'm speaking to him at this time of the morning. He's probably calling to see if his princess is on her way to uni and not currently naked in my bedroom, drying her hair after a night and morning of rampant passion. No, that won't go down well at all.

It's absurd, but even after all this time, I think a part of him still believes I'm a phase that will pass. She has laughed it off on more than one occasion, genuinely believing he will warm to our relationship. He makes no secret what he thinks of me, and trust me, he will never be tepid, let alone warm and fuzzy.

As I've already said to his face, it isn't my *thuggish* appearance he despises. It's my unlined pockets that are less than desirable. If it isn't advantageous to his interests, it's surplus to requirements.

"Oh, coffee! Lovely." Evie's enthusiasm breaks me from my dire thoughts. She carefully takes the hot mug from my hands and swallows a large mouthful. My eyes scan her from top to toe in her newly purchased navy two-piece suit and crisp pale pink blouse.

"You look nice. Very professional."

"Why, thank you, kind sir!" She blushes a little and juts her hip out. "Did someone call?" She looks down at my hand.

"Your dad. I didn't answer." I gauge her expression.

"Probably for the best, you're not his favourite person right now. You're corrupting me, apparently." She slides her arms around my neck and caresses my lips with hers. "Good job I like being corrupted." Her eyes flick to her watch, and she hastily gathers up her bags. "Oh, Gosh. We need to hurry. I'm going to be late!"

EVIE JABBERS AWAY to whoever called her ten minutes ago as we crawl through the morning traffic. Half listening to the conversation, I wish I could relate. When I was her age, I was living the life of a reprobate, walking the streets of Manchester, slipping small bags of heroin, E's and speed to anyone who would pay me the right price.

"I don't know. I'll think about it. Okay, I'll see you at lunch. Wish me luck!" She giggles and hangs up. Her knee is bouncing up and down, and she lets out an agitated sigh.

I tap my hand on the steering wheel in time with the radio while she constantly flips her mobile in her palm. She stops momentarily to glance at the screen.

"Stop worrying. You'll be fine."

"I'm not worried about the interview." She holds up her phone to show her dad calling again before she tosses it into her bag.

"Sweetheart, what's going on?" I query, considering this is the second time she has ignored him. In our relationship's infancy, if he called, she jumped. Lately, that has changed, like she's finally finding her wings and using them.

"I don't want to talk about it." She turns away nervously when I stop on double yellows outside Emerson and Foster and put on the hazards. I'm conscious she hasn't broached this morning's interview with him. I'm not about to call her out, but it isn't going to be pretty when she has to confess later.

"Hey, what's happened?" I grip her chin, coaxing her to look at me. Her beautiful eyes flick over my scars, and for the first time ever, this look is new and gives me a reason to be fearful. "What's he said?"

"Nothing." She attempts to shrug out of my hold and huffs in defeat. "Fine! He keeps saying you're an addict-"

"Ex-addict," I correct her. "And you already know that." Although what she knows is pointless, because if - or when - Andy Blake finally reveals whatever truth *he* knows, my political correctness will not matter. She will make her own assumptions - assumptions that will be correct and valid - and I shall lose her. It's a thought that has consumed me since it became clear this wilful, spirited young woman entered my life. And even more transparent since her vindictive father has brazenly intimated he wants me gone from hers.

"I know, but once he has an idea in his head, he's like a dog with a bone. For some reason, he seems to think you've hurt people, which is ridiculous! I guess you could say we had a *disagreement* about it yesterday, and I made him bring me home early. I've ignored his calls since."

I blanch but guard it well. "*A disagreement?* Nonetheless, he's still your dad, and you need to apologise." As much as it pains me to say it, I have to. One day, when she realises he was incompletely correct, it will be in his arms that she seeks relief from her pain.

"I'll consider it." Her tone is indicative she isn't going to do anything of the sort. "Wish me luck?"

"Good luck." I lean over and bequeath her a lingering kiss. "Do you want me to pick you up later?"

She shakes her head. "No, I'll get the bus. I'm going out for coffee with the girls after my lecture."

"Okay, but ring if you change your mind." I affix a half-hearted smile on my face as she gathers up her bags and gets out of the car. Straightening her jacket and skirt, she walks confidently into the building.

My smile is immediately replaced with a frown, and I turn off the hazards and pull out into traffic. Catching my eyes in the mirror, I recognise the affliction plaguing them instantly because the thorn in my side is starting to become prickly.

Chapter 25

"COME ON THEN, out with it!" John demands, slamming his foot on the brake as we enter the yard, purposely throwing me into the dashboard.

"Out with what?" He's been asking the same question all morning, and I'm currently winning the battle of wills, but I doubt I will for much longer if he doesn't stop.

"You've been a moody little sod all day. You haven't uttered two words other than yes or no, and you asked me to *look after* that file this morning. So, out with it!"

Bollocks to that!

I hastily open the door of the transit van and stride across the uneven tarmac towards the sandwich van parked outside the gates.

"Hi, love," I greet the girl serving today, my adopted Yorkshire lingo coming out. "Beef and mustard on white, a bag of ready salted and a Coke, please."

"Do you want any salad?"

"Just some onion, thanks."

"Can you also add a cheese and tomato on wholemeal, no salad, a packet of salt and vinegar and a bottle of water?" John requests behind me.

"Sure," she replies with a smile. "Butter?"

"Please," we confirm simultaneously.

I move from foot to foot in uncomfortable silence until she bags up the sandwiches and slides them over the counter.

"Eight pounds forty, please."

"Thanks, love," I reply and pull out a tenner as John nudges my elbow and shakes his head.

"On me. Thanks, sweetheart, keep the change," he says and picks up the two sandwiches and crisps while I carry the drinks.

I put the drinks on the picnic table in the yard and reach into my inner pocket as my chest starts to vibrate. "Walker Security, Jeremy speaking," I answer since any unknown numbers are usually clients, and these days my office phone is on permanent divert to my mobile. "Hello?" I shake my head and hang up. Then my phone immediately rings again. I scrunch my nose and reject Andy Blake's not entirely unexpected call. I lock eyes with John, who passes my lunch over the table.

"Blake?" he asks, then takes a bite of his sandwich.

I roll my eyes. "Alas, he's probably enquiring after his daughter's interview. I swear he tracks her phone and uses it as an invisible fucking leash to keep tabs on her."

John nods repeatedly. "And what about little miss? How's she been?" I shift uncomfortably, piquing J's attention.

"I've seen part of her fade further since New Year's Eve. This weekend being the most detrimental of all since she asked Sloan if there were any places on the summer training scheme after Andy falsely advised it was full. She went to lunch yesterday, and it appears Daddy has been filling her head with stories which means my theory is correct – someone's keeping him informed."

"Define *stories?*"

I grind my jaw. "He told her I'm an addict who hurts people. She already knows I was dependent, but she was shaken by it this morning. I'd love to say my relationship with him has improved, but if anything, it's more volatile than ever. And his snide, reoccurring comment of 'don't you want one more?' is grating on my last nerve and mentality. Yet I'm determined to tolerate it, John, because I'm in love with his daughter, and sadly, I can't cherry-pick which elements of her life I want entangled with mine. But even I can see he's got an agenda, and that is to take me out of the picture completely." I breathe heavily. "These last six weeks, I haven't even bothered to hide my disdain. Whenever I've raised it, Evie refuses to indulge in conversation. Still, it's clear the only career Andrew Blake wants his daughter to have is one of being an ignored and used wife for Piers double-barrel twat, with no way out of a life that she, very demonstrably, doesn't want."

"Don't take it personally." J puts down his water and stares at me with his all-seeing eyes. "All dads want their kids to marry well."

"Really? So, the prospect of being constantly pregnant and tied down to a bastard is what you'd want for your nieces or any daughters you might have?"

He frowns, and his eyes sadden. "I don't think kids are ever going to be in my future, but no, I wouldn't want that for anyone."

"Besides, how the hell is it not personal when he's talking about a past he should know nothing about? John, I-" My phone rings, halting my words of reason and sympathy. "For fuck sake! Hello, Andrew," I answer and put him on speakerphone.

"Why was my daughter at Emerson and Foster this morning, Jason?"

John mouths *'Jason?'*, and I shake my head, holding his unimpressed stare. "I think that's your daughter's business."

"Well, until I stop paying for her education and lifestyle, it is *my* business, Jeffery. I know Foster and that idiot HR woman gave her an interview, but I told her no for a reason!"

I scowl. "Maybe you should've been honest rather than lying then. Did you think she wouldn't find out?"

Andrew curses down the line. "I don't want her any more involved with you than necessary."

"I think it's gone past that by now, don't you? But why don't you call and tell her that? I'm sure it will go down well after yesterday's lunch."

"I would if she would answer her phone!"

"Wait, if she isn't answering, how do you know where she is?" I ask with indifference, but I've been apprehensive for months that he's tracking her whereabouts.

The line remains silent for a beat, and then he inhales. "You think you're untouchable with Foster at your side, but you're just a piece of shit! Rather than worrying about her finding out *I* lied to her, maybe you should be worried when she finds out that *you've* done more than lie! Shall we talk about the girl you killed in Manchester? Or better still, shall we talk about Foster's wife?" The connection quickly dies, and John fists the table.

"Son of a bitch! Someone *is* keeping him informed." John pulls out his phone. "Does she know he's tracking her?"

"Probably not, but if I raise it and she calls him out on it, it's bound to set him off again. Right now, I'm more concerned about where he's getting chapter and verse from. I'd also like to know how he knows about Kara. If Shaw's feeding him information, he didn't know about Kara, so who's telling those tales?"

John's pensive expression furrows into his brow as he taps away, probably to Dom. "Out of interest," he asks, not looking at me. "What's with the random J names?"

"He thinks he's a funny cunt claiming not to remember my name, but he's just a malevolent wanker."

And he's proving to be pricklier this afternoon than he did this morning.

I PACE FROM one side of the small balcony to the other. My fingers twitch; my hands are restless. Usually, when I come out here to think, I come out here to smoke. And while I do have a stash, I'm determined not to burn them up. For me, it's the hand to mouth action that needs to be replicated with something else. Something to keep my idle hands active and something that doesn't involve the other two of my three evils.

My phone beeps singularly, and I lean over the table and swipe the screen. I skim the text, along with another containing only a series of emojis I can't make head or tail of.

I'm on my way home

I leave it on the table, pick up my tea and cradle the mug between my hands, desperate to ward off the persistent nip of winter still dominating the spring air.

I lean on the railing. My mind is in overdrive from Evie's admission this morning, to her father's unvarnished threat this afternoon. A lesser man may feel it's time to end it now - eight floors up being the perfect opportunity.

But I'm not a lesser man. I've fought invisible demons inside my own head. I've fought the controlling power of addiction. I've watched people die from overdoses, and yet I'm still standing. I won't lie; his current obsession with my past is causing me some sleepless nights, but I've already battled for my right to live and breathe in this world, and I refuse to allow anyone to arbitrarily take it away from me.

My phone pings again, and I reach for it behind me. I glide my thumb over the screen, then glance down the street, capturing Evie's smiling face, tapping out my response.

I can see you

From the minute uni finished this afternoon, she has kept me informed as to where she is, who she's with, and how long she will be. I guess I should be happy I have a good girl in my life. One whose father has mentally trampled her into submission and obedience, ensuring one day she will adapt to be the perfect trophy wife; there to be seen and not heard, there to look pretty but never to use her voice. But there's only one type of man who wants a brain-dead doll. There's a side of me that wants her to step out of her comfort zone, just once, and say 'to hell with it' and to live without being under his thumb. But regardless that I've possibly pulled her half out, she's still half in.

The sound of the key twists in the lock, and the door chime resounds. I glance over my shoulder as she runs in and flings her bag, her portfolio, and the canvas bag she uses for her uni stuff on the sofa.

"How was your day?" I ask, and she smiles in a way that cannot be contained.

"Depends on which part."

"Your presentation?" I query the most important aspect – in my eyes, anyway - because notwithstanding the summer placement, if she fails her exams, there will be a secondary target on my head - if there isn't already.

She breathes a sigh of relief, and that beaming smile enhances further. "I think I did very well! At least I hope I did!"

"Of course, you did!" I say supportively and sweep her up in my arms. My palms drift down her back, and she relinquishes further. "And the interview?"

"The interview was okay, I think. I think I demonstrated enough to satisfy HR's requirements." Her eyes drift to the floor, and she nods subconsciously, convincing herself.

"I wouldn't expect anything less, sweetheart," What I fail to add is that this is Sloan we're talking about, which means she's already got a place. Her interview was just a paper exercise to dot the i's and cross the t's. I comprehend her apprehension. She doesn't want anyone to think she's getting special treatment because her dad is on the board. It's a crude truth, but it's probably a more accurate assumption that Sloan has already given her a position because she's in my bed.

I turn her in my arms and press my lips to hers. She submits instantly, and the urge to devour her again is my only mission. Running my hands through her hair, the waves of dark satin slip between my fingers, adding to the sensory explosion gaining prominence.

"Jeremy," she moans delicately into my mouth, and her hands move up and under my t-shirt. With her legs tight around my back, I push open the bedroom door and kick it shut behind us.

THE AFTERNOON SUN fades with each passing minute. My fingertips drift up and down Evie's spine while my mind formulates outrageous scenarios.

"Jeremy?" Evie's timid tone breaks the silence in the impending darkness. "Are you awake?"

"Hmm?" I reply, rolling her onto my front. She's been awake for a while. She likes to think she has me fooled, but considering how often we've shared a bed, I'm aware of the sounds she makes in various stages of sleep. "Sweetheart?" I brush the hair from her face, revealing her concern.

"I lied this morning. I didn't tell him I was still attending the interview."

I softly stroke her back. "I know."

"You're not mad?" I shake my head. "During lunch yesterday, I told him about the interview."

I continue to slide my hands down the length of her soft, supple skin until I caress her backside. "And?"

"He demanded I cancel it." She's sheepish and embarrassed and fixes her eyes on my chest. "When I refused, he started saying all those terrible things. He said you were turning me against him." I continue to hold her close, basking in her presence and the warmth of her body.

After a few speechless minutes, I carefully lift her chin and stare into her eyes. "So he wasn't aware you still attended this morning?" I ask softly, redundantly.

She shakes her head and whispers, "No."

I subtly grind my jaw, but I cannot fault her, not when I consider how the man treats her. "Well, that's one more thing he can hate me for," I mutter rhetorically, causing her to shift away. "Sweetheart, don't. This isn't your fault, but there is something you need to know. He called me this afternoon, asking about the interview. He pays for your phone contract, doesn't he?" She nods, her nose scrunching up in confusion. "Well, I think he's got a tracking app on it. It would certainly explain how he knows you were there this morning."

I glide my fingers over her cheeks as her tears begin to tumble over her cheeks. "Shush, darling, it's not worth your tears. And I have big enough shoulders, okay?"

She snuggles closer, but history feels like it is starting to repeat itself.

Chapter 26

I STRETCH MY neck from side to side and tug the stiff collar once more. Yanking the front, the sound of tearing resounds in the limo. My horrified expression ascends the moment the slackening around my neck confirms the bowtie is done for.

I dare a glance at Evie. She's a magnificent sight in her deep purple gown with an elongated boat neck – whatever that is - framing her delicate collarbones and creamy skin and the pretty cap sleeves and cinched in waist.

"Come here!" she commands with a pointed glare, and I comply immediately. I was brought up by a single mother. I know better than to fight against a strong woman when ordered.

A thought suddenly lodges itself in my wayward brain. "Come...where?" I meet her intrigued eyes as she affixes the bowtie back in place. She leans over, wide-eyed, mouth parted, and drags her lips the length of my right scar from mouth to temple.

"Wherever you want," she whispers, sultry. "Just don't ruin the dress."

I manipulate her chin and suck on her bottom lip, simultaneously sliding my hand under the mass of flouncy material. I could go all the way, but instead, I settle on rubbing the inside of her thigh. It's definitely a bad choice, considering the pathetic prick is now paying attention. Letting go of her lip, I trace the tip of my tongue over her cheek, tasting and tormenting her. "Does screwing you in it constitute ruining it?"

She pulls back, her lips naturally crimson through kissing and her cheeks rosy through sexual innuendo. She grasps my hand and attempts to move it higher.

"Possibly." She bites down on her lip and presses her chest to mine, ensuring she rubs in a way that guarantees I feel her hard nipples through my shirt. "Although it depends." She looks at me innocently, and it's indicative she's going to say something to the contrary. Her hand suddenly caresses my groin, and she digs her fingers in, adding pain to my already growing pleasure. "Good girls get hearts and flowers-"

"And bad girls get fucked unrelentingly in sumptuous hotel suites."

I'm aware she's booked the spare suite at The Emerson tonight and has already dropped off an overnight bag for us both earlier today. I grab her shoulders hard and take what I need. She laughs into my mouth and forces the separation.

"That's what I thought, and Sloan's PA kindly booked the penthouse suite for us!" With that, she starts to reapply her lip gloss. When the car door opens, she closes her eyes as the evening chill fills the interior, cooling her heated skin. I stare at her, amazed, astounded, absolutely hook, line, and sinker in love with her.

I inhale deeply, mentally counsel my appendage to behave, and climb out of the car. I stride around to the other side and hold out my hand, proving I'm still an unlikely gentleman. She takes my arm and stares up at me. Her entire countenance is breathtaking, while her eyes twinkle under the exterior lighting.

"You look insanely handsome, Jeremy James of the sad eyes."

I laugh and bring her hand to my chest. "And you look good enough to eat, Evelyn Blake. And I'm going to enjoy feasting on you before this night is through." I'm so caught up in the moment I don't realise she's stopped us until she tugs on my arm.

"This is where we got our second chance." I glance around as recognition develops as to what she's doing. A wicked smile appears, and she positions herself on the step above me, an apparent re-enactment of the night we reconciled, and she pouts. "I'm *Evie* to you."

I gently grasp her shoulders and pull her closer. "Yes. Tonight has proven you're everything to me. You'll never be another man's woman, and I'll never have to break up a relationship... Or take other men's women." I press her closer and touch my lips to her ear. "But tonight, *Evie*, you are also Evelyn. Because Evelyn is the good girl personified, whereas Evie is the good girl who wants to be bad and hires expensive hotel suites to enact her fantasies in." And that's a fact I've never been ignorant of. "But tonight, I want to screw my good girl and make love to my bad," I whisper.

She parts her lips, but only a short, sharp breath comes out. I smile, proud of my ingeniousness and her loss of words, until her lips purse.

"Whatever! Anyway, I think I'm supposed to tell you not to walk away from me, but this isn't how it went that night!" She links her arm in mine, and we head towards the entrance.

"Yes, you are, and no, this is the improvised version. Still doesn't change anything, *Evelyn*." She looks at me expectantly. "You're still-" I halt my train of thought as my least favourite person in the world lodges himself in my line of sight.

The belligerent little aristocrat.
Piers Maxwell-Clarke.

"Ah, Evelyn!" he calls out, causing Evie to squirm as he bustles his way through the crowd towards us, dragging his unimpressed date behind him.

"Piers." Her greeting is short and emotionless. "It's nice to see you. Please excuse us," she says icily and faces forward.

"Is that all you have to say to me?" he demands, taken aback by her cold dismissal of him.

I wrap my arms around her front and press my chin to her shoulder. "Ignore him."

"Easier said than done," she mumbles and entwines her arms with mine, holding me close.

"Do you not remember what happened the last time we were here? Do you not remember the great night we had? How you begged and pleaded?"

Evie's arms tighten because it was the night he endeavoured to rape her. It's selfish, but the only thing assuaging me right now is, by her own admission, she has never been sexually involved with him, and that is priceless. Still, his words feel like a knife slicing through my flesh again.

"You're just a dirty little fucking slut! I waited years for you, and all you wanted was...was..."

I feel a warm burst of air drift over my nape, and I disentangle Evie's arms from mine and pivot to find Piers mere inches from me.

"Jeremy, don't," she whispers.

"Was him...whatever his fucking name is!" Piers addresses me, waving his hand. I study him closely. I recognise the signs of addiction from afar. From the prominent glassy eyes and slurred speech to the unobvious jittery demeanour. The inability to stay still, and the constant touching, trying to scratch the invisible demons under your skin.

There are plenty of things I could say, but they would be wasted on someone who thinks so highly of himself that anyone less fortunate is beneath him.

I puff out my chest, straighten my spine and glower down at him. "My name is Jeremy, *Peter Maxwell-Twat!*" I take a leaf out of Andy Blake's book on how to press someone's buttons.

"I beg your pardon?" The toff is offended.

"Oh, sorry!" I laugh dramatically. "Pardon my French, Piers!"

He scoffs incredulously. "I doubt a degenerate like you would know any French!"

He's right; I don't, but I don't lack enthusiasm either. Capturing my chin between my finger and thumb, I rewind back to my school years. "Erm? C'est le...le... *Le twat!*" I put on a thick French accent, waving my hand in the air dramatically. Piers' eyes narrow in anger while his mates laugh behind him. And, very notably, at him. "Have a nice night," I offer cordially to his date, not him. The woman purses her lips, somewhat entertained, but it's apparent she's not comfortable.

"Darling." Evie beams with pride and admiration. "I'm sorry. I shouldn't have let him bait me."

"Don't worry, I only recognised *twat*. Besides, you were far nicer than he deserves!" she responds loudly, ensuring he hears it.

A pained gasp subsequently carries over the atmosphere, followed by a sharp hiss, and I turn around to see his date holding her side.

"Are you okay, sweetheart?" I ask, and she gives me a glimmer of a smile, but it vanishes just as quickly when Piers pulls her towards him.

"I'm fine," she whispers in capitulation.

I narrow my eyes at Piers. One day, he's going to get what's coming to him, and I hope I'm there to see it. All money and power, but he beats women to make himself feel like a man, the pathetic little bastard.

"Evening!" I rotate from Piers to Sloan, who has one brow raised at the show while his accompanying security observes with concern. Or possibly glee, since if Piers does act up, they will torpedo him out of the door headfirst. Always a sight to behold.

"Hi." Curling my arm around Evie's waist, we follow Sloan and his security to the entrance. "Where's Kara?" I ask since it's rare whenever they are not together at these things.

"She *was* with Marie," Sloan confirms, opening the door. "But who knows who is monopolising my beloved now."

"Thank you," Evie replies. We enter the busy foyer, and I wonder if I'll be able to manage avoidance of certain parties tonight. "Oh, there's Sophie!" She pecks my cheek and rushes towards gobshite Morgan.

"So…" Sloan passes me a glass of something sparkling while we walk towards the table. "It's water with lime. So, a little birdy tells me a certain little miss has booked the spare suite tonight."

I chortle, shaking my head. The pesky little bird is him. He wants everyone happy, irrespective of how everyone gets there.

"It's true, isn't it?" I bestow him with my best bored expression. John, Tommy, Simon and Stuart all perk up. Sloan's brow furrows, confused. "I never really believed it before, but since you offloaded Oblivion to the first and cheapest buyer, effectively making me redundant and forcing me to work for a different type of arsehole-" I tilt my head to J who gives me the finger "–I see it daily. Doc, I understand; he's surrounded by it, but the rest of you?" I shake my head as Doc furrows his forehead, still as clueless as the rest of them.

"Are you high?" Sloan asks sarcastically.

"No, this instantaneous delirium is borne from every chap in my inner circle being prone to gossip worse than a woman!"

"Hey!" a collective chorus of discontent starts, but I stride to the dance floor, an added swagger in my gait, heading straight to where Evie is now chatting with Kara.

"Good evening, you look lovely," I tell Kara, who still finds it hard to accept compliments and returns a polite 'thank you'. "Who's babysitting?"

"Charlie and Jake. They need practice, or so they said."

"And Jacob already knows there will be no practising, my love." Sloan slips his arm around his wife's waist.

"Poor Jake," I mutter sarcastically, causing Kara to give me a sympathetic smile. She mumbles something about an overbearing hypocrite before her husband twists her around and occupies her smart mouth with a prolonged kiss.

Downing the last of my drink, Evie escorts me towards the bar and requests two glasses of alcohol-free wine from the bartender. I quirk my brow, and she smiles shyly.

"It pales in comparison to the real thing."

"True, but I love and respect you, and so if you don't want to drink, I need to be the supportive spouse. Besides, if I want one, I know you won't mind, but this is the right thing to do."

A fullness I can't explain overwhelms my heart, and I cradle her cheeks. "I love you too, sweetheart, and thank you, however unnecessary." Our lips touch, heating the moment when I glimpse Marie coming this way. This is the first time I've seen her since a very unfortunate afternoon at WS when she and John were testing out the durability of his desk. She's been acting weird ever since, although I'm relatively certain my interruption isn't the entire crux of it.

"What's wrong?" Evie queries, looking between me and M.

"Nothing!" I rush out and tug her away.

Her eyes narrow, and she moves around in front of me, passes me her drink, rendering my hands full and void and twists my jaw. "Are you avoiding Marie?"

"No." I squirm.

"No?" she repeats distrustfully. "You're lying!" She presses her lips together, identifying my refusal to yield. "Fine. Bad boys who lie go home alone. Good boys who tell the truth get screwed senseless in hotel suites!" She takes back her glass of fizz and studies me as I weigh up which type of boy I plan to be later this evening.

"Fine! I kind of walked in on something I shouldn't have."

She pulls a face. "Like what?"

"Like use your imagination!"

Her mouth opens while she uses her imagination. "Oh...*Oh!* Oh, don't be stupid! Come on!" She drags me back to the bar and positions herself so that I have no choice but to get chatty with M.

"Evening," I greet. Marie looks at me cautiously, and it's clear as day she's as uncomfortable with this first meeting after the *event* as I am. "I'm sorry about the other week."

Her cheeks redden, but she shrugs. "Notwithstanding I'm old enough to be your mother and embarrassed you had to see me like that-"

"I didn't see anything."

"True, but imagination is a powerful tool. You're a good man, Jeremy. Let's pretend it never happened and never talk about it again. Can I convince you to come for dinner one evening?"

"We'd love to!" Evie says, shocking me since she's usually as distant with my ragtag family as I am with her dysfunctional one.

"Now, if you don't mind, Marie, I'm going to drag my *good man* onto the dance floor. He said he had smooth moves to woo me with!"

Marie presses her hand to her chest. Her disbelieving expression turns into a belly laugh. "Now this I have to see, but luckily for you, Nicki is off tonight with Devlin, and there's a calamity in the kitchen I need to deal with. Have a great night, you two!"

"*'Smooth moves to woo you with?'*" I repeat. "When did we decide I had smooth moves?"

Evie laughs, takes my hands in hers and walks backwards onto the dance floor, leading me like a lamb to slaughter again. Everything about her tonight is playful, and I can't help but wonder if it's because Daddy isn't here to tell her to rein it in.

"I decided a long time ago when you proved to have the ability to release me from a controlled, tedious existence." She cocks her head to the side, rolls her eyes dramatically, and stretches up on her heels to my ear. "And being able to give me multiple orgasms helps, too!"

"Well, thank goodness I'm smooth at that!"

The big band begin to play the crooners, as usual, and Evie steps in time to the opening chords, twirling around and crooking her finger. I saunter towards her as the first line starts, clamp my hands in hers, and press her front tight to mine.

"I've got you under my skin," she sings along with the lyrics. I glide my arm around her, and my fingers lightly tap her waist. I twirl her out in synchronisation with the music. She sways from side to side and tilts her head in exaggeration, her dress and hair moving in opposite directions.

And in this moment, the penny finally drops that I have perfection in all its astounding glory.

My eyes inadvertently glance around the floor, noticing the appreciative looks as my ravishing beauty grows more carefree by the second. She twirls around, ensuring every man who still has a pulse in his favourite body part looks on.

The songs change seamlessly, and she slows down, breathing heavily. "I think I need a drink. You know, I was only joking about the *smooth moves*, but you've got them in abundance."

I chuckle and guide her off the dance floor towards Sloan's preferred table, which gives him a clear view of everyone. I push a few bottles aside, happy when a low alcohol lager is pushed under my nose by Tommy.

"Thanks," I reply, watching Evie pick up a bottle of real ale, forgoing a glass, and she pretty much downs it in one.

She lowers the bottle when she realises we're all watching with curious fascination. "What?"

"Nothing!" everyone answers in unison, averting their eyes elsewhere.

Evie slinks into my side and reaches her arm up the rear of my jacket. Gliding her fingers up and down my back, she yawns. I don't blame her. For the last few weeks, she's had a stack of uni dissertations and research, and she's also accepted a place on the summer scheme at Emerson and Foster. She's even advised me to get my fill of her while I can since she won't be in any fit state to stay awake until summer arrives.

"No! Sleeping is cheating!" Sophie says, throwing her arm around Kara's shoulders, who shrugs her off. "We all need another drink and a boogie!" She picks up another bottle, passes it to Evie, and hands another to Kara.

"I'm breastfeeding, Soph." Kara puts the drink down and reaches for the carafe of water instead.

"I know, but you always use that as an excuse," she mutters, having disconnected the filter between her brain and mouth again, ensuring Kara gives her a venomous glare.

The carafe slams down on the table. "Sophie, as already previously discussed, my son is not an excuse. You should be grateful I'm even here tonight! Trust me, if it wasn't for your insistence, I wouldn't be. Now, if you don't mind, I'm going to check on my child's wellbeing!" Kara blusters past Sophie, and the uncomfortable silence thickens. Soph mumbles sorry to everyone before running out of the ballroom - probably to dig herself out of the sticky spot with her best friend, which seems to be their forte these days.

"Well," Simon flips the conversation. "Who knew Remy had such slick moves, gents? I guess getting high and off his-" Si's eyes turn into saucers, realising what he's just announced.

Evie gives me a cunning wink, and she slowly drops her mouth open. Simon's eyes expand, and a fearful mien consumes his features. His head darts between Sloan and John, whose frown slowly upturns into a smile while Evie's stance of shock lessens, and she laughs uncontrollably.

"I'm only joking, Simon. I know about his past," she says, causing all eyes to promptly look at me. The snippet of what she knows is only the beginning, and it's the end she really needs to be aware of. The end that is still to come. However, it may transpire.

"Right then, since Rem has made us all look bad, I'm going to polish up my skills!" Si knocks back the last of his wine, relaxing the tense atmosphere.

"Si, we've talked about this – who told you you had discernible skills? Although if your dancing skills are anything like your charm skills, get out there. I haven't had a good laugh in ages," John says, propping his feet up on a spare chair as Sloan's head darts between the ballroom and the door.

"As always, boss, these chats are inspiring! Evie, care to dance?" He offers her his hand. I smile as she puts on a bold display of consideration.

"I'd love to, but I fear you may make me look bad. I remember your *moves* from the nightclub last year."

Simon laughs as he guides her to the floor. "Don't worry, darling, my moves haven't got any better with age."

"This should be the best entertainment we've seen all night!" Tommy exclaims. He sits down with a fresh drink, ready for the show. I put my hand over my mouth and snigger.

"What's going on?" Stuart asks, pulling over Sophie as she returns. He rests his chin on her shoulder as she affectionately links her arms at her front with his, looking glum.

"Park is going to delight us with his version of the Strictly Charleston." John leans over the table for the wine.

"Seriously?" Stuart looks worried, whereas the rest of us just laugh.

"Oh, I love Strictly!" Soph exclaims, clapping her hands enthusiastically. "Can he dance?"

I wipe the tears of laughter from my eyes. I meet Tommy's amused expression and crack up further. "Well, let's put it this way, Kie–" John's brow quirks, and I halt my loose tongue, aware some of our group have no idea the man even exists – and for good reason. "The last time, *someone* thought he was having a seizure... Or auditioning for Grease!"

Luckily, the band always refuse to play anything other than the crooners, which thankfully has saved us all from being subjected to Simon's other *smooth moves*.

I lean back in the seat and gaze in awe at Evie gliding around the dance floor with Si. To be fair to the chap, his modern moves might lack a certain something, but he can foxtrot with the best of them.

"He's good at ballroom. Why have we never known this?" I ask anyone listening.

John chuckles. "It's one of the many discernible talents his nan made him learn. Pity she didn't force him to learn how to bloody tarmac!"

I snigger and study them again, or more specifically Evie, and the way her hair glimmers under the lights. How her stunning dress accentuates her slender frame, cinching in at her waist and flaring over her hips, creating the perfect hourglass. Then there's the delicate doll-like features that drew me in in the first place. She's perfection, and I haven't earned her, but by God, she's mine, and I'll fight to keep her, even die to.

"It's a good feeling, isn't it?" Sloan sits next to me, perching his wife on his lap.

"What is?"

"Being in love and someone being in love with you," he replies sincerely. In the corner of my eye, I watch him caress Kara's face, tenderly bestowing her a kiss.

"It certainly is." I look back at the dance floor, just in time to see Evie twirl the length of Simon's arm again, charming all present, and I stride towards them.

"May I?" I ask my friend.

"Of course," Si replies, carefully moving my woman from his arms to mine.

Evie presses her cheek to my chest and wraps her arm around my waist. I glance up and inadvertently lock eyes with Piers, who has, surprisingly, managed to keep a distance between us tonight. I nod in acknowledgement, and he scowls and downs the drink in his hand and replaces it with a fresh one.

The rest of the evening passes slowly as we move around the perimeter of the dance floor, stopping intermittently to chat to other guests or to have a drink until it's time to call it a night.

"Do you want a lift?" Sophie slurs as Stuart practically carries her down the stairs to the waiting limo. I open the door as Evie helps Stuart to get her inside.

"No," Evie replies. "We've got one of the suites upstairs tonight."

Sophie suddenly crackles to life in her drunken state. "I bet you have!" I narrow my eyes as Evie emits a resigned noise, indicates a moment, and gets into the car. I wait with Doc, making small talk about life and love when movement catches my eye at the end of the building, and a ruckus seeps into the subdued night atmosphere.

"I told you to be quiet!" Piers hisses at his date, who is following sheepishly behind him and his mates. She looks somewhat dishevelled, fixing her clothes. "You wanted it, so shut up!"

The hairs on the back of my neck stand on end because, in my life, I've seen it all. From intentional and unintentional overdoses and suicides to pimps whoring out their girls to johns, to prostitutes being assaulted by punters, to group sex from both willing and unwilling participants, and sadly, gang rapes in dark alleys. Nothing shocks me anymore.

Stuart and I share a glance. "I've got it, don't worry."

"Are you sure?"

"Redemption, remember?"

Stuart slaps my back in a goodwill gesture as the voices gain clarity above all others.

The car door opens, and a murmured 'thank you' piques my attention as Stuart grudgingly climbs in. Evie then fills my peripheral vision as the limo pulls away. "Soph said-" I lift my hand to stop her, and she turns just in time to see Piers backhand his date.

"I see the grand prize isn't so grand anymore. Sooner or later, we all learn," she whispers. The context of her statement should be fun, but her tone leaves a lot to be desired. Staring at her, everything falls into place - she's painfully recalling the night he tried to rape her.

"Stay here, sweetheart." I tenderly stroke her cheek and claim her lips. "I won't be long. Get security."

I stride with fortitude towards the commotion as Piers hits the woman again. Like any rich arsehole who thinks he can use his connections in life and treat others without due care, not one fucking person does anything to help her.

"You want her?" Piers asks his mate, who is downing a can of something, already pissed to high heaven. "Have her. She's a good fuck, but not much else! You'll play nice with him, won't you?" Piers presses his fingers into her terrified face.

My vision is red as he shoves her back, and she hits the ground unforgivingly, clearly hurting her rear and hip. I shoulder one of his drunk mates out of the way and go nose to nose with the little bastard. I'm a good half a foot taller than him and at least three stone heavier in muscle. I don't usually fight, but fuck, if he isn't enabling me right now.

"Do you want to push me to the ground, Piers? Go up against someone your own size, see how you fare?" I grind my jaw and scowl.

He doesn't reply, just slinks back one step at a time.

"Are you okay, honey?" I stretch my hand, offering her a lifeline. The woman looks between us, and that pisses me off. "Not all appearances are equal." I touch my scar. "Come on, I'll make sure you get home safely. You don't have to be frightened of these pricks."

She takes my hand, and I pull her up, not failing to notice her torn dress, broken nails, and the faint smattering of blood on her leg.

"But she should be frightened of you, shouldn't she?" Piers goads, showing off in front of his feeble friends. The woman quickly shadows herself behind me, genuinely terrified.

I move her aside and step back in front of him. "Really? From the man who abuses women to feel masculine. A man who puts a woman down in the street like a dog to belittle her. And a man – or men – who rape women because no woman in her right mind would willingly touch any of you!"

Piers' face reddens, absorbing my statement. His scowl deepens, and he turns to his friends, who are all spurring each on. I wait for it because I know what's coming. I know what he's going to use as a weapon.

"Says the man with the scars!"

I drag my fingers down either side from temple to mouth. "These are a visual testament of what I will do to protect defenceless women from arseholes, bastards, wife beaters, and rapists like you. All of you."

Piers suddenly gains a second wind, and he throws himself at me. "You son of a bitch!" I easily block the punch he throws, but his friends step in and hold him back.

The soft touch to my arm calms me instantly. I don't need to look to know it's her. "Let's go inside. Security will deal with them." I glance behind her to see the woman now being consoled by Sloan's security team.

"Ah! Evie! Still slumming it, I see? Did you tell him? Did you?" When Evie doesn't respond, he breaks free from his friends, smirks cruelly and rubs his groin. "Fuck, it gets me hard just thinking about it! And *her*. Thinking about her begging and pleading for me to take her. Did she tell you about how she flaunted that dirty, polluted pussy of hers for me? How she spread those dirty legs for all of us?" Piers is inciting, laughing with his friends, but I'm not. "No? What about that sexy red dress I bought to fuck her in-"

My fingers wrap around his throat in a split second. His hands come over mine, desperate to prise my fingers apart. I have no intention of suffocating him, but I am going to ensure he leaves here with fear in his heart.

"I burnt that cheap, nasty fucking dress. It went up in a fireball of petrol. Now, as much as I'd love to set you alight, the best I can offer is what you're going to have to live with."

Piers' eyes increase in fear, and rather than overthink it, I do what I must. My fist slams hard into his face. One solitary punch is all it takes, and he slumps to the pavement. I gaze down at my fist, now bloody but surprisingly painless. I crouch down and pull him forward, ensuring he's still breathing. He stares at me with glazed, disorientated eyes, his nose emitting a steady stream of blood, indicating it's probably broken, plus the split skin is likely to scar. A part of me feels guilty. Of all my former delinquencies, I've never readily hit someone and caused them physical harm.

I wrap my hand around the back of his neck, steadying him as his friends just watch.

"Addiction is a lonely, unforgiving path, isn't it?" I confess, remembering my prior experiences.

"Fuck you!" he hisses and groans, pinching his nose. "I'll have you arrested!"

"God, you are a poncey, self-righteous prick. It's a shame your morals are not as high as that invisible horse you've got yourself elevated upon." I shake my head and push him back down. "Go ahead, call them, and when I'm being questioned, I'll inform that about the poor woman you all gang raped tonight. I'm sure they'll find enough DNA, blood, and semen to convict all of you."

A small hand touches mine, and I straighten up. Removing my dinner jacket, I wrap it tight around Evie's shoulders. "Let's go inside," she whispers. Her palm slips tight against mine, and I don't miss the disgusted glare she levels at Piers.

"I'm sorry," I apologise, holding the foyer door open.

"Don't." She strokes my cheek.

319

"I lost control. You shouldn't have had to witness that." Inside, I'm distraught, fearful she may now fear me.

She pulls me into a shaded corner, hidden from view under the foot of the grand staircase. She studies me intently, both hands caressing my cheeks, her body pressed so tight to mine, her heat warms me.

"Don't apologise for something he deserved. I appreciate you were protecting that poor girl, but the true motive beneath it was that you did it to defend my honour, and I will never hate or fear you for that."

I rub her shoulders, my eyes roaming the foyer before us. "Do you ever wonder?" I murmur, and her brow furrows. "I can't give you what he can, probably never will. A fancy dinner in a Michelin starred restaurant is too rich for my blood. Even a table here at mates' rates is pushing the boat out."

Her hands tighten around my head, and she pulls me forward. "I don't care about that stuff."

I chortle unamused. "But this is your life. Growing up, luxury is all you've known."

Her lips purse. "True, but there's a cost to that lifestyle. That so-called luxury doesn't come for free. You pay for it with everything you have in your soul."

"But look at what you could have won." I sigh. She can be a stubborn little thing when she insists on it.

"Jeremy, stop. Please!" she begs, touching her nose to mine. "As far as I'm concerned, I've already hit the jackpot." She inhales and swipes the tip of her tongue over the seam of my mouth, finishing with a simple kiss. "Now, we've drank, we've danced, you've affirmed your love for me with violence, and I've condoned said violence-"

"Flipping heck, you make tonight sound scandalous!"

"Oh, it's scandalous all right!" She trails her hand over my lap, allowing it to linger tentatively at my groin. "So scandalous, in fact, we're booked into a plush hotel room that isn't nicknamed the shagging suite for nothing!"

I rotate my hips against her hand, thoroughly turned on by her evening recap. "How do you know that's what we call it?"

She shrugs a shoulder and stands up, bringing me with her. "Sophie told me." She shrugs nonchalantly.

"Did she now?"

Tugging me to the lift, we board the next one, and she surprises me when she pushes me into the side. Her mouth devours mine as she hooks her leg around my hip, pressing her heat to my hardness.

"She's got a big mouth," I mumble between hot kisses.

"Hmm hmm..." Her hand breaches my waistband, and cold fingers toy with my dick, hardening it further. "She also told me to tell you that you have to fuck me like a good boyfriend should!"

She slaps her hand on my nape and tugs me down to her level as we reach the penthouse floor. The bell dings and the doors slide aside. Evie grins mischievously and slides her hand into the bust of her dress to reveal the old brass key.

"Really? What else have you got in there, *Evelyn?*" I ask with insinuation. Her eyes glint, and she purses her lips.

"A good girl will never tell, *Remy!*" she says seductively. "But why don't you come in and find out?" She walks off into the suite, reaching back to unzip her dress as I lock the door.

"Come in...*where?*" I chuckle and remove my jacket. "And I think we've already concurred that you, Evelyn Blake, are no good girl!"

"True, but I'm waiting!" She calls out from the top of the stairs in the split-level suite. I jog up two at a time until I'm face to face with her. Without caution, I lift her around my waist. Palming her arse until she finds the right position, she clenches her thighs at my hips for ballast. Opening the bedroom door with my elbow, she flicks on the light, and her face delights with the extravagance on display.

"Oh my! I didn't realise it was this plush!"

I grin as she absorbs the surroundings. "You were wrong earlier."

She shakes her head. "About what?"

"Good girls don't only get hearts and flowers. They get fucked unrelentingly in sumptuous hotel suites, too."

Chapter 27

THE CONSTANT MOANS of insatiable rapture, unequivocal demands, and variants of my name ripple around the luxurious bedroom. The moonlight shines through the large window, highlighting the adjacent wall, bathing my beauty with light. On my knees, with Evie on all fours in front of me, I glance at our entwined image reflecting on the pane. I lunge in and out, and she cranes her head back. Her back bows down, pushing her arse up. Clutching her hips, I drive forward, harder than before, resolute in giving her want she wants – fucking her like a good boyfriend should.

"Oh, God, that's incredible. More, more!"

I indulge her immediately, rocking myself back and forth out of her heat. Leaving one hand on her hip, I slide the other under her belly, manipulate her closer and then toy with her hot flesh. Spreading my fingers over her sex, she judders the instant I tease her folds.

"Harder, Jeremy. Harder."

"Turn around, sweetheart," I ask gently, and she glances over her shoulder. "Suck." I stretch my arm forward. The movement ensures I push further inside, thus assisting her in lowering down onto the duvet. Her hot lips wrap around my fingers, and she obliges with a sultry glint in her eye, silently showing me what else I might be missing right now.

I slowly slide my fingers from her mouth, not missing the dirty insinuation when she grips them in her teeth and bites hard.

"Naughty girl," I mutter with a smile, ease back, and slide my fingers over her nub. I work her into a rhythm, enjoying the ripples of lean muscle in her back each time she rocks on my shaft, chasing ecstasy and the euphoria soon to follow.

"More, more, more!" she demands, and I feel her fingers join mine again. She slides my hand back to her hip and sits up. "I've got this."

Her head leans back on my shoulder, and she wiggles her backside into my thighs, pressing herself deeper onto me. I curl one hand around her hip bone as I power up and down while my other cups her breast, my thumb rubbing her hard peak. Her hand comes around the back of my head, and she manipulates me to kiss her. Her breathing is laboured, and I glance at the window, mesmerised as she turns, and a glance down confirms she's stroking herself to fruition.

"God, I'd love to watch you touch yourself." I'm so turned on I can't think straight. With her sliding up and down on my dick, the feel of her hard nipples gracing her tender tits, to the fingers currently playing with herself, it's all too much to withstand.

"So would I," she says, strained and breathy.

"Tell me I can."

"Hmm, I want you to watch when I make myself come, but right now, I want you to do me so hard, I can't walk tomorrow. Don't hold back." She gives me a determined look, frees my nape, and falls forward on her hands and knees again. She rests her forehead on one arm, the other disappearing beneath her, clearly assisting again. I lick my lips when she moans and sticks her inviting backside in the air.

"Fuck," I mutter and slam into her, each thrust tougher than before, and her probing fingers rub against me with each slap of my balls against her skin. The action is rough, dirty, and fuck if I don't just want to do her until she begs me to stop.

"Yes...yes..." Evie's muffled voice seeps into my ears. Seconds later, her core constricts my shaft. She lifts up, her back curved deeply, her head to the ceiling, and she cries out my name.

The sound of my substantial breathing fills the room. It's harsh and unforgiving as the release in my groin takes me over the edge.

"Fuck, beautiful!" I rut into her but quickly pull out, flip her over and slam back inside. Evie's arms draw me down, and she wraps her legs around my hips as I release. "Evie!" My body is thrumming, my orgasm rolling on and on.

"I love you, Jeremy," she says, reaching completion, and her core tightens around me again. Her face perspires, her skin is silken under the moisture, and she digs her nails into my arse. "Deeper, deeper!" Her entire body shudders with the force of her release.

I roar out and collapse on top of her. Her breasts rise and fall against my chest, and she exhales, causing my hair to waft up.

Minutes pass, and her shudders turn into trembles. I brush the damp hair from the side of her face and cradle her cheeks. "God, I love you, you crazy, demanding woman."

"And you, you thoughtful, calming man. I was right back in August; we fit. Square peg, round hole."

I smile and claim that quick mouth of hers. "Speak of round holes..." I ease my hand down her front and gently stroke her entrance. "Was I too rough?"

"Jeremy." She exhales, her eyelids fluttering. I stop touching because it's a sure-fire way to get her aroused for a third run.

"Was I?"

Her cheeks flush darker. "I asked you to do me hard, and you did. I love what we do. I don't want you to treat me like a fragile doll, too afraid to put any physical pressure on me."

"I'm glad, but you didn't answer my question."

"I feel sore, but it's an amazing sore," she quickly adds, and her legs rub together voluntarily.

"I'll kiss it better," I say, causing her to blush further at my implication. "I'd like to say I'm just being kind, and I am, sweetheart, but know I have every intention of getting my mouth on you before we check out tomorrow."

"I STILL THINK I've gotten the short straw!"

Entering the bedroom, a towel around my hips, water trickling down my torso, I scrunch my face in question. "How so?" I query, considering I've just given her two further orgasms in the shower and not expected or requested anything in return. She undoes the knot at my abdomen and drags the towel away.

"You wouldn't let me play." She delicately squeezes my bulbous head, and the blood rushes back south. I tap her wayward hand and back away.

"I let you play enough. Besides, we've still got ten hours to play, and I intend on making the most of it." I untangle the towel from her head, indicating for her to sit on the bed and begin to dry her hair.

"This is nice. Romantic." She smiles broadly.

I kiss the side of her neck. "I'm Mr Romantic through and through, sweetheart."

She leans back into me, and I continue my tender care of her. The silence is comfortable and welcoming, a true moment of reflection for what we've done and the love we share when a pinging noise fills the room. Evie's back straightens, and her demeanour changes before she has even picked up the phone.

"Two guesses?" She shakes her head.

"I only need one."

"Two guesses why, then?"

"Again, I only need one." I roll my eyes while she continues to scowl at her phone. "I'm sorry, I shouldn't have said or done anything to the prick."

"Stop saying that. You were defending mine and another woman's honour. You have nothing to be sorry for. If anything, I'm mortified that my father thinks *Piers twat* walks on water."

I smile but still admonish. "Don't call him that. Regardless, your dad wants you with him. It could make your life hard." She unravels the towel, drops it on the floor, and in all her beautiful nakedness, she pushes me down on the bed and curls into my side.

"My life is already hard, and we don't always get what we want, do we?"

"No. No, we don't," I confirm. My fingers tangle in her hair while her long, relaxing breaths swathe my torso and tickle my chest hair.

"Jeremy?" I glance down, capturing her inquisitive eyes. "Why did you do it? Defend her?"

My arm instinctively tightens around her, needing her closer, needing her skin as one with mine. "Because sometimes we all need a protector, someone to fall on, someone to depend on when we're at our lowest. It brought back memories. I know someone who has been a victim of unimaginable acts, and I guess I felt the need to attain reparation. But more than that, I was defending you against every vile, hurtful, dirty word that left the bastard's mouth."

She quietens, and her chest rises and falls against mine as she snuggles closer. Her fingers draw patterns over my chest, and she presses subtle kisses to my arm and shoulder.

"The person who was the victim... Was that an ex or a friend?"

"Neither. Where are you going with this?" I roll her onto my front. Her taut nipples press into my chest, while the delicious soft friction of her warm centre, straddling my thigh, creates a consciousness I don't know if I can endure.

"Have you ever been in love?" she eventually asks, resting her forearm on my chest.

"Yes," I reply with a smile, smoothing the hair from her face. "Twice. The first time was new and experimental. The second was – *is* - life-changing."

She lowers her chin onto the back of her hand. I slide my arm under my head, elevating myself so we can have this conversation eye to eye.

"Am I the second?"

Her tentative query incites a smile to curve my lips. The longest relationship I've ever had in my life had been with dependency. I could play around and tell her she's the latest in a long line, but that just isn't true, and for all my faults and issues, I don't play games like that.

"Yeah, you are."

Her hand slides up my neck the same instant her front slides up mine, adding further sensual friction, and she bestows my scars with kisses. "And the first?"

I subtly drop my head to the side, enjoying her mouth on my cheek, weighing up the situation. The fact is she's probably going to be annoyed at hearing about my relationship with Emma – the good parts, anyway. However, when the time comes and whatever happens going forward, I don't want her to be blindsided when my secrets are spilt. I don't want her to look any more foolish than her father already perceives her to be when the unvarnished truth and every sordid fact in-between comes out – because it will come out if he has anything to do with.

"The first was a girl called Emma Shaw."

Evie's face suddenly gains a look of understanding, and she shakes her head in thought. "She was the name you called out the first night we spent together. Apparently, she promised something?"

I purse my lips together and grimace. I didn't think she heard me that night. After I woke up, I was worried about trying to explain how she had nothing to worry about, but obviously, fate has other ideas.

"Was she abused? You don't have to tell me. I'm just trying to understand."

"No." I grimace.

"But someone close to you was?"

I nod, numerous someone's close to me, but I dare not air that because I doubt Kara or Charlie would appreciate me disclosing their darkest, most private secrets to anyone.

"What happened? Why did you split up?"

I inhale deeply. "We didn't... She died."

"Oh God, Jeremy, I'm so sorry. I didn't-"

"Of course, you didn't know, and thank you but it's unnecessary."

"You don't have to tell me any of this if it's too painful."

"No, I do because you *need* to know," I tell her. "However, I want to caveat this entire conversation. Firstly, I think we're both aware

327

you can't compete with the dead, and secondly, whatever I say is just a memory now."

She shakes her head again, understanding what I'm saying. I allow long minutes to pass and take a breath.

"When Emma and I first started seeing each other, my life was vastly different. Up until I met her, I was a one-night stand guy. I had nothing to offer, and I didn't need a relationship to find someone willing to share themselves with me for a night or two. You'd be surprised at what people will overlook in exchange for a pretty face and a nice body.

"What do you mean?"

"Well, at the time, I was already in the steely grip of addiction. Would you pursue sex with someone who was high?" I query, and she shrugs, uncertain. "Anyway, I was down on my luck, trying to get clean, trying to overcome the power that had hold of me, and then she entered my life."

"Was she also an addict?"

My Adam's apple bobbles painfully in my throat, and I swallow, but my saliva might as well be shards of glass. Of all the questions she could've asked, she asks the most turbulent and complicated of them all. Now do I say no – it isn't a complete fabrication, Emma wasn't an addict when we first met – or do I harness honesty, be forthright, and confirm she was? The truth is always best, but either reply brings another set of questions I don't know if I'll be able to answer efficiently.

"Jeremy?"

I tenderly stroke the back of her head. "Yes, she was." I lay one of many secrets bare and await her reaction. Time passes worryingly without so much as a peep from her. The tears slowly fill my eyes, and I carefully slide her off me. I swing my legs off the bed, drag on my shorts and leave the room. At the top of the staircase, I gaze skyward, praying for divine intervention to give me the right answers.

I jog down the stairs into the opulent living area. After pacing for a few minutes, I straddle the end of the chaise longue and drop my head in my hands. In the corner of my eye, the city lights twinkle, prettifying the grim city streets. Even in this part of town, shit lingers below the surface if you look hard enough for it.

The soft creak of a door and Evie's delicate steps descend the stairs. I temple my hands together at my chin, my eyes fixed on the glass, on the tentative reflection of the woman I love. She steps closer and hesitates, fidgeting with the robe she's now wearing. She repeats this again and again, showing her uncertainty until she's beside me. I slide my arm around her waist, much to her surprise, and I sweep her off her feet and onto the small space in front of me. She sits side-saddle on the end, crossing one knee over the other. The robe exposes her shapely legs, and she rubs her toes up and down my calf.

She cradles my face between her palms and kisses my forehead. "I'm sorry," she whispers.

I place my hand over hers, stroking her fingers. "Don't be. It's just so hard to talk about."

"I can imagine. You don't have to talk about it if you don't want to."

I squeeze my eyes closed. "No, I do. You need to know, but I just... I don't..." *I don't want you to hate me.* The unspoken words rattle around my head, giving weight and merit to the truth I never wanted to confess or own again.

She rises abruptly. Her fingertips trail along my collarbone, over the top of my arm and around my upper back. She places her hands on my shoulders behind me, caressing the curve where they meet my neck. She then slides down, her skin grazing mine, and straddles the space behind me. Her thighs compress the sides of my hips, cradling me tightly in her embrace. Tender kisses line my spine. She rests her cheek on my shoulder blade and teases her hands around my stomach.

"Whenever you're ready to talk, I'll always listen. Or we could sit like this until the sun rises," she says quietly. I rub my hand over hers, seeking her comfort and warmth.

I stare at my reflection in the glass once more. Some days, in amazing moments like these where she sees past the exterior, I'm unable to reconcile myself with the man I used to be. However, I still see him whenever I brush my hair or teeth or when I shave. If my memory wasn't so clear cut of the three events that have mentally scarred me, I'd swear I was just telling someone else's story whenever I relive them.

I close my eyes and curl my fingers around hers. "I was nineteen when I met Emma. She was eighteen and in her first year of uni. She was a sweet girl, very much like you. And she was a good girl. Again, very much like you."

Evie scoffs playfully behind me and teases her fingers over my stomach muscles. "I'm not a sweet or a good girl."

I murmur in agreement. "I guess that's subjective upon which persona you choose, but they're both one in the same." She tuts, unhappy with my observation. "As discussed, Evelyn is the good girl who toes the line, while Evie is the wannabe bad girl who enjoys multiple orgasms in extortionately priced hotel suites."

"Yes, and I'm worth every penny! Or I would be if you had paid. Or I, for that matter!" Her amused chuckles mingle with mine, and then the silence ascends again. A drawn-out breath plays on my skin, and the heat at my back intensifies.

"So what did Emma look like?" she asks, barely audible, making me wonder.

"Does it matter?" I counter. "She's been dead for a decade. You can't compete with the dead, darling." My reiterated response isn't to cause animosity, it's because it is irrelevant now, but I appreciate looks are very much a girl thing.

"I know. Jeremy, I'm not jealous." Her tone confirms she isn't and that it's probably more curiosity. "I'm just trying to paint a picture in my head. Was she tall, short, fat, thin, blonde, brunette? Wore specs or perfect eyesight? That kind of thing."

I drop my hand to her exposed thigh and trail my finger up and down her skin, causing goosebumps to form. "She was a bit taller than you, blonde, roughly your size. I don't know. I'm not good with descriptions," I tell her uncomfortably. "She was my first real relationship. I was in a bar in Manchester when she approached me. Again, much like you did." Evie's cheek moves against my shoulder blade, indicating she's smiling. *I hope.*

"We spent the rest of the afternoon and evening together and-" I gasp because whoever coined the phrase *the truth hurts* weren't lying.

"Jeremy?" Evie's hand moves up my chest, resting over my heart. It's symbolic, beautifully poetic and heart-breaking, in that she's coveting to protect mine when ultimately, one day, I'm going to break hers.

"After that, we rarely spent a day apart. She was a ray of hope in the misery that surrounded me. She saw through the bullshit I carried around daily. She saw the broken soul that was desperately in need of something that it had never really had before... Love. And love me, she did. And I returned it tenfold, right to the day she died."

"Oh, Jer-"

"Shush," I interrupt her soft, hurt tone. "Remember when *we* got back together, and I said someone died and that in tragedy I was reborn?"

"I remember," she murmurs. "I remember everything."

"Emma was the someone who died. At the time of her death, she was just nineteen, and we'd been together for just over a year." I inhale, braced for despair. "She died on our bedroom floor, less than two feet from the bed I was sleeping in, curled up in a ball, clutching her arm after accidentally overdosing on heroin."

She gasps, shocked. "Oh, my God!" The sound of her sadness fills the quiet space. Her palm unexpectedly cups my cheek, and she manipulates me to face her. I twist my neck to the point of pain and stare at her over my shoulder.

I hold her upset gaze. Hot tears sting my eyes, leaving a solitary trail over my cheeks. "I held her in my arms until the coroner took her away from me."

She softly strokes her thumb, capturing my fallen tears. "When did she become addicted?"

I sniff back and shake my head. "Honestly, I don't know, but it didn't take long. She was clean when we first met, and then she started smoking weed at parties. She promised me she wouldn't start using the hard stuff, and I trusted her. Then one day, I found a used needle."

Evie nods. "The promise she made you... The nightmare. Did you encourage her?"

I shake my head vehemently. "No, never! Being an addict is akin to a life sentence. I wouldn't wish it on my worst enemy. The highs, the lows, praying for life, praying for death. Desperate to get clean, desperate to stay high. It's a mental battle. A personal conflict where the drugs always win because even when you get clean, you always remember what it felt like to get high. And that's the biggest battle of them all, remembering that feeling but never succumbing to it again."

I place my hand over hers, leaning into her touch. Staring intensely into her sad eyes, if I allow the following confession to omit my lips, there's a chance she's going to hate me shortly, but it's a chance I have to take.

"What's wrong?"

"There's no easy way to say this, but Emma died taking my drugs." I study her eyes, watching the cruel truth embed itself in her head. "It's a harsh truth, but if it wasn't for me, she'd still be alive today."

She slowly moves her head from side to side. "No, no. Please don't do this!"

"I told you last summer that you should leave and never come back."

"No! Stop this and look at me!"

"I am!"

"No, you're not. You turn around and look at me!" she orders, exposing her hidden fire.

I shuffle around, and she holds my jaw firmly, allowing no room for me to move or deviate from this course of questioning.

"Did you put the drugs in the needle, or did she?"

"She did."

"And did you inject it into her vein, or did she?"

"She did," I repeat. "But they were drugs *I* was selling! I may not have been the one to pierce the needle into her vein, but it was *my* lifestyle that gave her the impetus and desire to do it. My own addiction at the time infested her like the plague, and the word *no* became ineffective!" I'm shouting, frantic, unable to run away.

Evie's finger covers my lips, and she makes a soothing sound. She presses her forehead to mine and strokes my temple. "Shush, it's okay. I know you loved her. I appreciate you had to lay witness to her heart-breaking death, but you didn't kill her. It was an accident. I know you want me to see the bad, but I can't. Do people not deserve a second chance anymore? Does a good man who clearly got mixed up with the wrong people deserve to be reviled over an action that wasn't his fault?"

"Sweetheart..." I attempt emancipation from her grasp, resentful that she's being so calm and considerate.

"No! You've spent a decade blaming yourself for her death, but it's called free will, and she made her choice. I can't imagine she would have wanted to die, but she chose to take drugs, and she chose to inject that needle. She had free will, and she used it. And I *envy* her that," she whispers firmly. A flicker of light glimmers in the corner of her eye, and I pull back as her tears fall.

"Don't cry, sweetheart," I tell her, but it's an unspoken truth that she envies Emma's free will, irrespective that fate turned out of her favour because Evie's free will is ninety per cent dictated by another. "Let's get you dressed. I'll take you home."

She tugs my hand when I attempt to move. "I know you now want to push me away, but it won't work. Yes, I admit, I'm shocked, but I think living with it is more than enough punishment. I know you'll never let it go – I can't imagine anybody would – but please stop blaming yourself. And just so you know, I'm not going home unless it's with you."

"Darling, please," I urge, not quite sure what to say. I should be punching the air and beating my chest that she isn't holding me accountable for my actions.

"The dead can't hurt you. Only the living can," she unknowingly speaks a silent truth. The final truth I've carried with me for also as long.

"Evie," I say, resigned, and she puts her finger over my mouth.

"I'm going to make you forget. Just for tonight, I want you to forget your past and just concentrate on the here and now. Concentrate on me and you and the love we share. Seeing is believing, as is forgiving. I forgive you the blame and guilt that you carry."

She presses her lips to mine, tentative at first, finally apprehending that I'm not going to stop her, then she influences the kiss. I allow her to set the pace because she needs this. This is also a small part of her life that her father can't control. Her arms glide around my neck, and she shuffles further away. When her shoulders touch the backrest, I crawl forward and support her neck in one hand.

"Jeremy," she breathes. "I want your mouth on me."

My lips move with fervour, each brush more demanding than the last. My hand moves down her chest, slipping inside the robe. She makes a noise of satisfaction but pushes me away. "Kiss me!"

"I am!" I retort sharply, misunderstanding.

Her skin is flushed, her mouth dark and puffy, and she adjusts the cushion behind her. Her hand then tracks down the robe, and she tugs at the belt. The fabric parts and falls to the sides, exposing the full length of her bare skin.

"I want you to kiss me...*here*." Her hand moves down her stomach, lower and lower. "I want your mouth on me." She bites her lip in embarrassment, and I grip her hips and kiss her. Her tongue breaches my lips, and she raises her pelvis impulsively.

"Thank you," I whisper, brushing my thumb over her lips, earning it a lick and nip.

"For what?"

333

"For listening. For not judging my past transgressions. For still loving me...I think?" She nods in confirmation. "But most of all, for trusting me. I know this isn't your favourite thing, but I love to taste you and the intimacy of this." Kissing down her stomach, I drag my tongue over her pubic bone. I finally reach her centre and slide my fingers between her skin. She hisses and jerks, and her legs fall wider apart.

I grab an ankle and adjust it higher. "Rest your feet on my back, sweetheart." She complies immediately, and I assist in moving her limbs to rest comfortably behind my shoulders.

I shift back, one knee on the chair, my other leg planted firmly on the ground, and with my hands behind her hips, I finally devour. My mouth varies between licking and sucking as I glide my finger up and down, determining how turned on she is. Slowly parting her flesh, I swirl around her opening and gently press it inside.

Her body vaults upright, and her legs tighten. Her hand presses down on the back of my head, guiding me, losing herself in this moment. Familiar sounds of rhapsody bleed into the room in time with the rhythmic, undulating twist of her hips, giving me one of the most intimate gifts she can.

I gaze up her body, hungry for her, never stopping my ministration, to see her completely lost. One arm is thrown back on the headrest. The other is still at the back of my crown, controlling the action.

I close my eyes and suck harder, deeper. For all my earlier bravado of getting my mouth on her, after hearing one of my evil deeds, she's given me this, this amazing gift she isn't particularly fond of.

"Beautiful...amazing...life-changing," I murmur into her flesh, causing her to rotate harder, chasing my mouth. "And I'm never going to let you go."

Chapter 28

"JEREMY, YOUR PHONE!" Evie calls out as I drag the WS branded polo shirt over my head and pad into the living room. She smiles, my phone to her ear, and motions for another minute.

"Really! OMG! Sorry, I mean, thank you, Mr Foster. I'm so excited and very grateful!" She pauses, and a look of panic overtakes her overjoyed features. "Are HR able to send them by email?" She pauses again. "Mr Foster... Sloan... Please can you send them to Jeremy's?" I loiter in the doorway, uncomfortable at the lengths she's going to in order to ensure her father doesn't intercept her official offer on the summer placement scheme. Thinking back to when Sloan told me weeks ago that she had a place but said he would wait to tell her until all the applicants had been interviewed to ensure fairness – although there was no fairness involved here – I should've asked him them to send everything here.

My attention draws back to Evie, who bites her lip, forcing a smile. It's cold and desperate, but eventually, she thanks him graciously and passes me the phone on her way back down the hallway. I don't speak until the door slams shut.

"Sloan?"

"Hey, I need to talk to-"

"Sloan, if you send those documents to her dad's, she won't get them. He'll make her life hard, and in turn, a further target gets added to my back. Please send them here. I've never asked you for anything, but I'm asking for this. I'll beg if I have to. Please make it happen," I request desperately.

"I'll call Lisa in HR, but that's not why I'm calling. I'm just killing two birds with one stone." The grumbling sound of Oliver seeps down the line, followed by Sloan trying to corral his boisterous boy. "Shush," Sloan says, attempting to soothe him. It obviously works when Oliver screeches happily, and the noise echoes.

"Where are you?" I ask, screwing up my forehead, wondering.

"Work. Look, never mind that. John and Marie had an argument last night, which resulted in John spending the night at mine testing out my gin collection."

I huff out. "Fucking hell. Maybe I should phone in sick!" I ruminate rhetorically, but the prospect is attractive. "Do you know what happened?"

"No, he refused to talk about it, and I've just had a mouthful from Marie when I asked her," he says sheepishly, silently confirming he didn't ask; he ordered.

I close my eyes in resignation and grit my teeth. "What did you say to her, Foster?"

"Nothing! She made a few threats and, well, so did I! She threatened to take away my beloved!" he says in his defence.

With my eyes still close, I pinch the bridge of my nose. "God give me strength!" I inhale raggedly. "You need to apologise! Right now! Argument or not, if John finds out you've spoken to *his beloved* like shit, he'll reacquaint you with his fist. Repeatedly! So, you better apologise. And contritely!"

"I already have! Christ, Rem, I love that woman, but I love John more. Look, just find out what's going on, then call me!" He hangs up, and I shake my head. I have enough of my own issues, and he expects me to play agony uncle to everyone else!

"You're chuntering, Jeremy James of the sad eyes," Evie says behind me. I turn around, slip my mobile into my pocket and approach my girl.

I delicately place my hands on her cheeks, cradling her. I coax her closer and manipulate her face higher and pilfer her lips, stealing her kisses, reclaiming her as mine.

Her arms slip around my middle, lingering at the top of my backside. She presses her chest into my torso, her heat emanating through the layers of fabric. I reluctantly pull away and glide my nose alongside hers, from her mouth to her eye.

"You make it hard to leave."

"So stay," she whispers. I kiss her nose and press our foreheads together.

"That offer is far more tempting than you can even imagine right now. What are your plans for the day?"

She leaves her hand around my waist on my hip and strolls with me down the hallway. "Studying, possibly some TV binge-watching." She indicates with her finger and thumb. "I was thinking I might call Mum and see if she wants to meet for lunch."

"That sounds nice. She'll be happy to hear from you." I encourage the idea for her benefit as much as mine.

"What time are you finishing?" she asks as I slide into my jacket and pick up my keys. "Around four, or earlier if John's being an arse." Evie furrows her brow. "He and Marie had a fight last night."

"Really? That's sad. They seem so in love and together. I guess it happens to us all at some point." Her words and manner turn dejected, no doubt remembering our fight, but she snaps out of it. "Oh, can you ensure Sloan-"

I put my finger over her lips. "Don't worry, I'll speak to him again." I cup her chin and kiss her goodbye at the door.

I PARK IN my reserved bay, climb out and stride towards the sandwich van parked outside the gate on the industrial estate.

"Hi, Suzy," I greet the usual woman behind the counter.

"Hi, Jer. The usual?"

"Please, and the guys' usuals, as well. Thanks." I glance back at the yard and spy the convertible BMW parked between Si and Tom's Range Rovers. "Suzy, stick a cappuccino on there, too."

"Sure thing."

Just under ten minutes later, with two trays of scalding hot beverages stacked on top of each other, I wrangle the security card from my pocket and make my way into the building. Elbowing through the last security door, I swing my head around the architrave of the mess room.

"Did someone order coffee?"

"Oh, nice! Feeling generous this morning?" Jake asks.

I scoff. "I'm just a nice guy, Evans."

"Yeah, well, wish I could say the same for some. Just throw John's in his eyes, it'll work faster and hopefully wash away his foul mood this morning." He rotates the disposable cups to find his usual.

Soft feet tap along the corridor outside, and I turn to find Kara in the doorway. "Hi," she says.

"Hi, honey." I smile, completely at ease.

We've come a long way in the last four months, Oliver's birth being the turning point, I think, along with their request that I be one of his godparents. These days, she's no longer uncomfortable around me, and I'm no longer awkward around her. I turn back and locate the drink I got for her.

"I didn't know what you liked, so it's just a standard cap."

"Oh, lovely. Thank you." She takes a sip and nudges her head out of the door for privacy. "Did Sloan call you about John and Marie?" she asks the second I'm out of the room.

I nod and glance at the guys. "I presume they don't know what's gone on?"

"No, but he's been biting everyone's head off this morning. I'm only here because Sloan's worried about him. Please can you talk to him?"

I force a smile. "I'll try."

I move back into the mess room, pick out the flat white and tentatively head to John's office. I knock and open the door uninvited. John is sitting at his desk, his head in his hands.

"If I'd have known you were this bad, I'd have got you a triple espresso."

His head lifts, and he leans back in the chair. His eyes are red, and he looks exhausted, but that's what drowning your sorrows in gin will do for you.

"So you don't feel left out, I'll tell you exactly what I told them this morning." He scowls and jerks his head to the door. "I don't need your advice, so get out!"

I put on an unconcerned expression, absorbing and subsequently ignoring. "John, don't. You forget who you're talking to. Your empty threats don't work on me, *sunshine.*"

He slams his hand down on the desk, and his scowl lessens, but it's still there. I sip my coffee with my eyes trained on him. If there's one thing my OCD has granted me, it's stamina and patience. While some people are fidgety, I'm a procrastinator. I can ruminate and dwell with the best of them. Likewise, I can hold a steely gaze and a lasting silence for longer than most, too.

I turn my cup on the desk, the silence tolerable, and I debate how long I can make the last few mouthfuls last for.

"Have you ever loved someone so much that you fear one day they're going to do or say something that will make you hate them?"

I lift my cup, furrow my brow and give him a dubious look. "You're preaching to the choir, J. What's happened?" He shifts in discomfort. "Look, Kara sent me in here, and I've already spoken to Sloan this morning. So what's going on?"

"Marie's hiding shit. Everything that we talked about on New Year's Eve? It's got progressively worse, and then when I got home yesterday, she was laying on the kitchen floor, her feet scalded and cut to ribbons, blood and coffee all over, clutching a battered teddy bear. When I asked what happened, she refused to talk!"

I purse my lips. I could comment that it sounds familiar because I doubt he's told Marie about his disastrous marriage, but now isn't the time for flippancy. "John, you've just got to give-"

"Don't you dare tell me to give her time! She's had three years!"

I scoff, kick the chair back and stand. "The past can be a hard limit, John. Considering how protective she is of Kara, I'd hazard a guess and say something of such monumental significance has happened that she can't bring herself to discuss it."

He stares at me unequivocally. "Well, you would know, wouldn't you?"

I laugh, unimpressed. His face drops, and he now appears ashamed. And he should. He knows I'm going through the same thing with Evie since my past is also a hard limit. "Fuck you, arsehole! And if this is how you spoke to her, I don't blame her, and you don't deserve her!" On that, I stride out of the office, slamming the door so hard it's lucky the glass doesn't shatter.

"Hey, are you okay?" Simon asks when I re-enter the mess room.

"Fine!" I reply, my eyes finding Kara. I subtly shake my head, and her forlorn look deepens. Having done all I can, I pick up the stack of overdue demands on my desk, pop in my earbuds and lose myself for a few hours.

I SCAN EVIE'S text confirming she's meeting her mum for lunch, then put my phone back on the table and turn up the radio. *Sympathy for the Devil* is playing – it's fitting because we could all use some of that this morning. I lean over the desk as Tommy continues to sketch out the installation and modification requirements for a job next week on a new office construction on the other side of the estate.

"How much is the company coughing up for this?" I ask as Kara brings some fresh drinks in. "Thanks, honey."

"Cheers, Girl Friday!" Simon quips behind me, and Kara threatens him with physical bodily harm.

"I quoted five thousand, but it will probably come in around four with profit," Tommy replies over them. "But it means I can knock off a decent chunk for Mrs Barnes. Kara? Would you mind drafting me an invoice for Gladys for two hundred?"

"Wait, do you mean all these stupidly cheap invoices I used to raise for the little old dears were false?"

Tommy smirks. "Not false, just greatly adjusted. We accurately charge the rich and heavily discount the poor. Besides, you can't put a price on security, especially for those less able to defend themselves." I glance at him. His statement is appropriate, reflective, even.

Dev's mouth opens, but the door is then thrown back, and we all share the same hesitation as John strides inside, slaps a court order in front of me for service today and thuds back out.

"Are you shocked?" Dev asks Kara, ignoring John's intrusion as the security door reverberates.

"Yes, because Robin Hood and his Merry Men have nothing on you guys."

Simon chuckles and grips his chin. "Just get us some tights and a skirt!"

"Doc might be able to source us some dresses," Tommy replies, flicking his pen.

"I don't recommend it. Open back and scratchy," Dev adds, pretending to close the open back of his invisible NHS gown while Kara points him – even she can't hide her amusement.

The door creaks outside, and my good mood vanishes again, ready for John to rip me a new one - or a new third or fourth one at this rate. "God, I should've phoned in sick. I'm losing the will to live," I express despondently.

Jake slaps his hand down. "My will to live vanished the moment I walked through the door. It's probably still sat in the car, waiting for me to return."

"Hi, everyone."

We all turn simultaneously as Marie's surprisingly pleasant tone fills the room. Kara turns ever so subtly, and her lips purse together.

Dev looks ready to cry with joy. "Thank Christ, you're here! You need to speak to Uncle J. There's something seriously up his arse this morning. We've lost three clients because of him. I don't know what's going on, but he'll be happy to see you."

Marie smiles awkwardly and then catches Kara's concerned eye. "What are you doing here?" Marie asks her.

"Volunteering. They needed a skivvy."

"That's Girl Friday, little lady." Tommy grins as she glares at him.

"Skivvy, Girl Friday, tea lady… What's the difference?"

"Plenty. And it's in your financial interest to be here."

Kara's forehead furrows. "True, but you boys forget this is the reason why I quit last time."

I begin to read the order John slapped in front of me as Kara and Marie move to the door to talk. I keep one ear on the conversation as Marie queries what Sloan is up to today with Oliver.

"He's taking him to the office to meet everyone. He's been wanting to show him off for months." Kara wears a hundred-watt smile.

Dev's head whips up, and he gives them a repugnant glare. "Taking him to the office?"

I grin but can't resist. "And what type of father takes his kid to work for a meet and greet with the minions?" I offer up for the best answer.

"The devil!" Tommy and Simon high-five, while Marie covers her mouth, dying to laugh.

With a can of pop in his hand, Simon saunters over to Kara. "Just think, little lady, you could be getting replaced as we speak. They both have that dark, handsome broodiness going on. And God knows the women in that office love Sloan. Many a woman has splashed out on expensive knickers in the hope he will remove them."

The room falls silent except for the music still playing. I share a look with the others, while Kara gives Simon a look that, if it could, would annihilate him on the spot.

"Fine line, Si, and you're at risk of crossing it." Dev immediate looks at Kara, his tone confirming the comment has just pissed him off.

The door is abruptly thrown back, and John strides in. He looks ready to commit murder and points at Si. "That wasn't a fine fucking line, sunshine, that was a liberty, and she allowed you take it. The next time I hear that shit, I won't. You two have got papers to serve." He points between Dev and me. "They're not going to serve themselves, are they?"

I huff and shake my head. "For fuck sake!" I throw my pen on the desk and locate the rest of today's deeds, and motion to Dev. "Let's go. John, do us a favour? Stop being a bastard! It's not becoming."

John's face emits an element of surprise, and he scowls. "Really? Is employment becoming, Jeremy?"

"Twat!" I hiss and grab my jacket as Dev says bye to Marie. I lift my hand and stick my finger up at John until I'm out of the office.

"He's got a serious fucking problem this morning!" Dev says as we jog down the stairs. I hold open the security door for him and turn him around when it slams behind us.

"He had an argument with Marie last night." Dev immediately starts to turn, but I stop him. "No, they need to sort it out between themselves. Right then, how many people are we going to upset today?"

Chapter 29

"I'VE ALREADY TOLD you, he doesn't live here!" the woman cries, repeating herself unnecessarily. I'm aware he doesn't live here - she's screamed it at me fifty different ways since I knocked on the door ten minutes ago. But she's his mother, and it's her job to protect her child against threat, even lie, if need be.

"Madam, you're wasting your breath. I'm just here to confirm service." I move back towards her rather than air her son's poor financial intelligence on the street. I hold my hand up in yield. "I suggest you call the court and arrange a payment plan with them. It's hard times, and he's not the only one, but tell your son to get his head out of the sand and do something. It isn't going to go away because he ignores it. Okay?"

The woman nods and sighs. "Thanks. Hey, sorry I called you a bastard."

I laugh. "I've been called worse. Just tell him to ring the court and sort out his life." On that, I stride back to the car and get in.

"You look like a big, mean bastard, but you're just a soft, cuddly kitten underneath the hard arse exterior!" Jake quips. "You're far too nice to them."

I don't take the bait as I start the car. It's not that I'm nice or that I feel sorry for them, it's because I know all it takes is just one stupid mistake, and your entire life can spiral out of control in the blink of an eye. *I know.*

Jake thumbs his phone screen, and I subtly shake my head. For the last week, serving orders and court documents has been my punishment for mouthing back at John and calling him a twat. God knows what Jake's done to deserve such abominable current working conditions, although knowing him, he probably offered just to get away from John's overbearing broodiness. Dev, on the other hand, kissed his uncle's arse spectacularly and got the cushy number of quotations. Except I don't know if that's any better. I'd rather be called names than argue with potential clients in a race to the bottom.

Jake chuckles to himself, then swings his head to me. "Fancy a pint, bastard?" he asks on a laugh, using the name I've been called most today.

"Why not, cunt!" I reply, using his new name for today.

"HEY, WHAT CAN I get you?" the bloke behind the bar asks.

"Two pints of coke, please. Can I also order a couple of sandwiches?" I give him our usual choices, and he passes me a number and rings it up.

"That's twelve eighty, mate."

I pass Jake the numbered card and a pint of coke. He holds up the glass, studying it in disbelief. "When I suggested a pint, I did expect a little alcohol to pass my parched lips," he mutters, then grins at his phone

I shrug. "In that case, you should have paid, and then you could've ordered whatever you wanted. Besides, this is just a convenient excuse to see your missus."

He gasps, pretending to be offended. "It is not!"

"Oh, really?" I pick up my drink and stroll outside to the beer garden. I slide my legs over the bench, pluck my sunglasses from the neck of my polo shirt and get comfy. Retrieving my phone from my pocket, I find Charlie's number. "So, if I call her, she won't say she's on her way over?"

Jake squirms opposite, grinning broadly. "Okay, fine, she's coming over in an hour or so." His smile falters, and I narrow my eyes. "And she's bringing a friend."

I chuckle, but really, I should be cringing. However, contrary to the nickname I've secretly bestowed upon her, I do love gobshite Morgan. Her world is bright and airy, full of goodness and light, and I could use some of that. We all could.

"How are things with Evie?" Jake asks, distracting me from my tumbleweed of thoughts.

"Great," I give him a clipped, one-word answer. His brows raise, and I concede. "She's busy with uni and summer prep."

He nods and sips his coke. "But things are better between you?" I give him what must be a scowl because he immediately goes on the defensive. "Hey, I'm just concerned for your welfare, so don't give me that look."

I acquiesce. "We're great. We're fine." The waitress puts our food on the table, and I pick up my sandwich in a bid to avoid further conversation. The silence is enjoyable but diminished when our guests arrive.

344

An hour later, the strength of the sun beats down overhead as Sophie places a fresh Coke in front of me. I pull a twenty from my wallet for the round she's just bought and hand it over to her.

"No, it's fine," she says, and I shake my head as Charlie sits beside Jake.

"No, take it, or I'll just give it to Doc when I see him next." I hold the note with determination. She's going to take it if it's the last thing I do this afternoon. After a short standoff, she accepts and takes the cash.

"Thanks, but it's on me next time!"

I agree for good measure, but it isn't, although she doesn't need to know that.

With a vigilant ear on the conversation around me, Soph regales the three of us with her take on her last disastrous date night with Doc. I grin to myself, thankful I'm not looking at her since I still can't look at her and not recall Stuart's comment regarding her beautiful mouth.

My phone buzzes, and I swipe the screen. I squint behind my aviators at the text Evie has sent confirming she's going to have lunch with the girls, and she'll see me later. I grin, send her a snappy reply with a kiss on the end and put my phone down.

"Oh, look at you with the Cheshire cat smile, mister!" Soph comments with a smirk. She lowers her sunglasses and tosses her hair back. "Evie?" She waggles her perfect brows. "Care to share?"

"Never in a million years!" I laugh, causing everyone else to too. However, it's short-lived when Charlie abruptly rises.

"Finally!" she says, looking over my shoulder. I turn around as Kara pushes Oliver into the beer garden with Marie following behind them.

As they take their seats, I wheel the pushchair over and unbuckle my happy little man. "Hey, sunshine!" Baby boy bounces on my knees with exuberance, making me realise just how big he's growing now. I tuck him into my chest and reach behind his wheels for his mum's bag of tricks. I pull out his bottle first, but his little hand hits it away.

"No? How about this?" I wiggle a jar of pudding, and he emits a happy reply. "Oh, good choice, Mum!" Kara passes me his spoon, and I wink and unscrew the jar. Cradling him in my arm, I make looping movements with the spoon. He opens his little mouth in eagerness, his dark eyes resolute in getting what he wants. I inadvertently glance around the beer garden, and a woman a couple of tables over smiles. I don't encourage, nor do I acknowledge her. Instead, I continue to concentrate on Oliver and the conversation in full flow around me again.

"A suit?" Sophie repeats with disgust at something Marie has just said. "You always buy a flaming suit!"

I lift my head to M, and my eyes cross when she downs a couple of tablets. She puts down her glass and glares at Sophie.

"What do you expect me to buy? A thigh-high, crotch-skimming, clubbing number?" Everyone laughs, but I don't miss the discomfort she's desperately trying to hide.

"Don't be so defensive! I just thought you might go a little daring for once. You always wear a suit. It's boring!" Soph replies.

"Sophie, I'm forty-three, not twenty-three!"

"Forty-three *is* the new twenty-three!"

"Hmm, and twenty-six is clearly the new six!" Marie finally shuts her up.

"Soph, I'll have you know I'm wearing a suit, too. Urgh!" Charlie's grumbling manages to filter through.

"What is it?" Jake asks, and I tip my head up and immediately drop it back down when it's clear she's just moaning about big brother.

The cacophony of voices fade in my selective hearing, and I fix my attention back on the baby yawning in my arm. I smile and rock him gently, loving how his podgy finger grips mine. I stare at him, wondering if this will ever be my future. A family, a son...a wife.

"Understatement of the century!" Jake's voice rises, forcing me to pay attention. "Soph, are you and Doc coming to the bash at the hotel at the end of the month?"

"No. We're having a romantic weekend in the Cotswolds." She grins and lifts her drink.

Jake rubs his hand over his head. "God, I'm in the wrong profession! He's making money hand over fist, while me and you," he waves his hand, "are scraping the fucking barrel, installing systems, arguing the toss with tight bastards, issuing process demands and tracking down degenerates!"

"Language!" Kara interposes.

"It's not his fault he's a doctor!" Sophie replies, ignoring Kara.

"And you love to be his nurse!" Jake counters.

"That's right, I do! How many emails, Char?"

"Ten. No, make that eleven." Charlie looks ashen. I'm about to ask when Oliver fusses in my arms, and I lift the plastic spoon again.

"What's he said?" Sophie asks her.

"'Get your arses back here now, or you're both fired! Right…'" Charlie appears confused. "'Right' what? Oh, no, make that twelve. Now! 'Right now!'. We better go."

"He's such an unreasonable arse!" Sophie says, and I see red.

"Hey, baby boy present, and that's his father, remember?" I point the spoon at her.

"And that's my husband, remember?" Kara adds, and I smile. She truly is perfect for him. Notwithstanding she thinks he can be domineering; she'll be damned if she allows anyone else to state the obvious.

"I didn't mean it like that, chick. You know I love him, really." Sophie smiles at Kara.

"Well, I'm glad to hear it. Because if it wasn't for him, you'd still be at a firm you despise, dating men who aren't worth your time." Kara makes a fair point while Soph moves towards me and bends down to hug Oliver, who emits some unhappy grumbling that the crazy woman is interrupting his food.

"I know; I owe him a lot. Marie, I'll call you, and we can go shopping for a dress for girls' night!"

Marie smiles broadly, but I don't miss her quiet cursing.

"No crying off now. I've got it all planned. I can't wait!" Soph claps her hands and says her goodbyes. I avert my eyes as Jake mauls his girlfriend, then watches with satisfaction as she runs through the garden. He sits back down with a thoughtful expression and downs the rest of his pint.

"I think you might get that thigh-high, crotch-skimming number, after all, Marie," he says, and she gives him a stern 'don't'. "Just making an accurate observation. John will love it." He reaches for Oliver, and I reluctantly pass him over.

My phone buzzes, and I flick the screen leisurely. Scrolling through the junk emails, I spy Marie making faces at Oliver, who giggles infectiously. I rest my chin on my hand and watch him stretch his arms out to her, and she reaches over. Abruptly, she slams her hand on the table, and I'm up before the bag of crisps hits the ground.

"Are you okay?" Kara asks, concerned as I hold Marie steady.

Marie smiles in discomfort. "I'm fine, honey, but I think I need to go home. I suddenly don't feel well."

I reach down for her bag and jacket and secure my arm around her. "I'll drop M home and see you back at work," I tell Jake. "Kara, I'll see you later. Take care of my sunshine."

"Call and let me know you're okay," Kara requests of Marie.

"I will, honey."

I hold Marie tight until I have her safely seated in the car. I get into the driver's side and start the engine.

The drive is quiet, comfortable, and contemplative until Marie breaks the silence. "How's John been this last week?"

"Fine." I look at her.

"I'm sorry he spoke to you the way he did."

I purse my lips together, uncomfortable that she feels the need to apologise for what happened. Granted, something transpired between them that put J in a foul mood, but it wasn't her fault. "We all have bad days, Marie. John's are few and far between, but he has them."

"True. How are you and Evie?" she asks tentatively.

"Good." My reply is short and snappy, and I hope she doesn't take offence and give John something else to find fault with me again.

"Jeremy…"

"We're good, really," I cut her off because she has that sympathy tone going on.

"Really? I don't believe you."

I sigh discernibly and clench the steering wheel. "Marie, I know you care, but we're fine. I'm even learning to tolerate Andy Blake," I lie, since she has her own issues, and if she learns the truth, she'll mother me.

"Yes, but is he learning to tolerate you?" she asks with a hint of mischief.

I laugh and falsify further. "It's a work in progress."

The traffic picks up again, and it seems to be stop-start for the rest of the journey. Outside John's house, I reach into the back for her bag as she unbuckles her belt.

"Thanks, darling. I'll see you later," she says, and I nod and start the car as she is accosted by her neighbour.

"HEY, SORRY I left you." I pass Jake a mug of coffee back in the mess room of WS. "Did Kara drop you off?" My phone buzzes in my pocket, and I ignore it since it's probably a stupid news notification or an email about fifty per cent off shoes and fragrances.

"Yeah, don't worry about it. Is Marie okay?"

I shrug. "Seems to be, but who knows with her and John. If you try to interfere, you get a mouthful from both sides."

Jake nods repeatedly. "Isn't that the truth!"

"Where is everyone?" I ask, observing the notable peace and quiet.

"John's gone to see a man about a dog, Dev's still out quoting, and Simon's trying to get the idiot who laid the yard to fix it," Tommy answers, walking through the door, removing his jacket.

The buzzing in my pocket starts again, but unlike before, this time, it doesn't stop. I shift uncomfortably. I swipe the screen, and the alarm app pops up, displaying a red warning bell.

"Tommy?"

"Which room?" He's looking over my shoulder, iPad in hand.

"Hallway one."

"It's probably just a fly on the sensor – your door contact alarm is still silent. Just turn it off."

I glance back at him as *Hallway Two* kicks in. "There isn't a sensor attached to the door." I share a look with him as the living room sensor now indicates movement in the flat. "Evie!" I'm up out of my seat and sprinting out of the building with Tommy and Jake running behind.

"I'll call Dev and Si! Ask them to meet us there," Jake says, throwing himself into his car.

Driving above the speed limit, I constantly call her to no avail and resort to leaving a message. "Ring me back ASAP, sweetheart! If you're on your way home, stay outside. Do not go into the building!" I hang up, realising when she hears this, it's probably going to put the fear of God in her, but good, she needs to be worried. Most of the time, she doesn't even lock the door when she's home alone.

"The kitchen just triggered," Tommy says next to me. I slam my hand on the wheel. I don't give a shit about the flat. They can take the TV and laptop; it's Evie I care about. The thought of her stepping inside and someone being there... I press harder on the accelerator and indicate right, using every shortcut to avoid traffic.

Half an hour later, I slam the car to a stop outside the building as Jake, Dev, and Simon pull up in a three-vehicle convoy behind me. Jake climbs out of his Range Rover, opens the boot and nods at the black holdall. The boys all don gloves and grab a weapon, of which I shake my head because I don't agree with it. There's a reason the police don't carry guns here. However, I leave them to get on with it because voicing my pointless sentiments will go through one and out of the other.

I calmly enter the building and press the lift for the eighth floor. Jake and Dev take the stairs while Tommy waits for the second lift, and Simon stays in the foyer. I tap my foot as the numbers ascend on the panel. Within a minute, the doors open, and the four flat doors are in view. There is nothing nefarious or anything to indicate there's a break-in going on, which makes me believe whoever was inside has now gone.

The faint beeping originating from my flat is still alarming out, but it's negligible. To others, it could just be an alarm clock or a smoke detector, which in itself should be a worry. Unfortunately, an internal, lower than standard siren is the only protection the building owner permits. Their reasoning being the main foyer is manned, which these days is sporadic at best, as confirmed today.

I depress the handle, and the door opens effortlessly. I kick the bottom, and it hits the wall behind it with a thud, ensuring anyone still inside will be alerted to an incoming presence.

"Evie?" I call out. I need to ensure she hasn't come back. The lift bell dings again, and Tommy steps out of the other lift. He looks up at the building security cameras and hides the gun beside his opposite thigh. The door to the stairs opens, and Dev and Jake stride towards us, again looking up and around for the cameras.

"Do they work?" Jake asks.

"According to the freehold charge, they do. Right after the clause confirming a staffed security desk twenty-four-seven," I add flippantly. "After you." I eyeball the three of them since they've got the weapons.

Entering the flat, Tommy disarms the siren and resets each room. Jake bends down and studies the lock on all three sides. "No damage. Doesn't even look like it's been shimmied." He squints through the keyhole. "Do you have some screwdrivers?"

"Somewhere," I offer vaguely as he closes the door.

I continue to walk through the flat with Tommy leading. The rooms are clear, confirming whoever was here has now gone. The only thing leaving a bad taste in my mouth is that nothing has been touched. The TV and CD player are still here. Even mine and Evie's laptops are still sitting on the coffee table. None of this makes any sense.

"Thoughts?" Tommy queries, tapping my arm. I shrug because who knows.

"Rem?" Jake calls out from down the hallway. I follow his voice, but he's no longer at the door. Instead, I find him in my bedroom. Or, more accurately, what was my bedroom prior to this afternoon's ransacking.

Clothes and shoes have been dragged from the drawers and wardrobes, while the pillows and the duvet are all over the place. My alarm clock has been smashed, and the mirror is cracked. I guess it could be much worse, but again, nothing seems to be missing. A thought occurs to me, and I politely shove Dev out of the way, stride to the wardrobe and open the safe inside. Thankfully, my passport and a small wad of cash are still inside. I stand up, my hands on my hips, misunderstanding.

The front door opens, and the atmosphere turns tense as three guns are raised.

"It's just me!" Simon announces, sounding serious for once in his life. "No one's been in or out in the last fifteen. Whoever did it had gone before we arrived."

I move back into the bedroom and pick up Evie's things from the floor and place them on the bed.

"What type of person breaks in, takes nothing of value, but trashes the bedroom?" Jake asks.

"The type who wants to send a message," Dev answers.

A glimmer catches my eye at the corner of the bed, and I recognise the watch Evie's mum bought for her eighteen on the floor, which I hope to God isn't damaged.

As I move around the side of the bed, a piece of glass cracks under my foot. I bend down and move the duvet from the floor, and Emma's picture – the one I normally keep in the drawer – is hidden beneath it. I step back and stare at it. My eyes flit from the picture to the bed, remembering. I exhale loud enough for everyone else to hear, then bend down. Picking up the picture, I disturb a small bag of powder aptly placed underneath it. This entire set-up has been orchestrated in the hope I would probably call the police, and they would sweep the place and find this.

"Rem?" Tommy's boot taps my thigh. I rise and hold up the picture in one hand. "Pretty girl," he says as I lift the bag of H in my other.

"A pretty girl who died of an overdose, a foot or so from the bed. How very fucking convenient!" I hiss and stride out of the bedroom into the bathroom. Lifting the toilet seat, I rip open the bag of dope and flush it. I leave the bathroom and head into the kitchen. Returning with my toolbox, I open the door and begin to unscrew the handles.

"What are you doing?" Jake asks as I drop them on the floor.

"The answer to your question, Jacob, is someone who has nothing to lose. That's what type of person breaks in. I know exactly who coordinated this. I can't prove it, and he would deny it, but *I know*. And just to confirm my suspicions, I want a new lock put in ASAP." I toss the barrel mechanism to Tommy. "There's no damage to it because the intruder had a key."

"Well, who has a key to this place?" Simon asks.

"Outside of us? Evie."

Dev begins to shake his head. "Rem, no she-"

"No, she didn't," I cut him off. "Her dad did. He's obviously taken her keys and had another cut at some point, and he knows *something* regarding Edward Shaw. This isn't a break-in. It's a warning. Or maybe today was my lucky escape," I add under my breath.

"We need to tell John," Jake says.

I shake my head. "No, he's got enough on his plate right now. I'll call Sloan and Dom, but this stays between us. Just put me a new lock in, one with the keys that can't be cut and register it to me."

Si nods. "Will do. I'll be back soon." He exits the flat, leaving his gun with Jake.

I head into the kitchen and grab a bottle of light ale from the fridge, thankful Evie picked up the wrong thing in the supermarket last week, much to her humiliation that she was 'tempting the devil'. Knocking back a mouthful, I gaze at nothing of significance and let my mind ramble.

"You need a better alarm system," Tommy says from the doorway, disturbing my solitude. "I'll speak with the freeholder and discuss what we can install. Either way, I'll be by during the week to set up some internal security cameras. Do you want us to stay until Simon gets back?"

"No, I need to call Dom and Evie. No one's going to come back. The message has been delivered."

Jake, Dev, and Tommy shuffle hesitantly, but they eventually leave with explicit instructions to call if anything looks odd tonight.

Alone with my thoughts and fears, I turn my mobile in my hand, suspending my finger over Dom's name, when the front door opens, and Evie comes rushing in.

"Oh, my God, I got your message. I was so worried!" She flings herself around me and holds on for dear life. I pull her back and smile.

"I'm okay, but I told you to stay downstairs."

"I know, but I was frightened something had happened to you!" She glances down, visibly upset.

I cradle her jaw. "I'm not angry, but the thought of you being here alone and someone coming in... Your safety means more to me than anything else." I press my lips to hers, and she grips my face, intensifying the kiss.

The front door opens again, and Simon stops dead in his tracks. "Sorry, I didn't mean to..." he trails off as I cock my head in disbelief. "Hi, Evie," he greets, and she gives him a small smile. "I'll be ten minutes." He then closes the living room door to give us privacy.

"Have you called the police?" Evie asks as we sit on the sofa, and she curls into my side. I stroke up and down her arm, needing to keep her safe, pacified yet unaware.

"No, because nothing was taken. Probably just kids who sneaked in when the downstairs door was open," I say, lying to keep her sane. "Simon's going to fit a new lock, and Tommy and Jake are going to install some internal cameras during the week and a new alarm."

"Okay," she murmurs, her fingers drift under my shirt, drawing patterns on my stomach.

As I kiss and wrap my arm around her, a thought that has plagued my conscience once before comes back to haunt because sometimes history repeats itself, and playing house may also be the ruin of us.

Chapter 30

EVIE'S SOFT MURMURING rouses me from my sleep. I drop my head to the side and admire her sleeping form before I carefully shift over.

I reach across and slide her hair from the side of her face. The urge to touch her, to kiss, and ultimately, to love her, is so powerful, so all-consuming, it's almost like she's under my skin, weaving that invisible magic she's already bewitched me with.

A few weeks ago, I dared to imagine that one day I might have everything I wanted, a family, a wife, but those ideas crystallised at Oliver's christening last week when she made a random comment which both intrigued and terrified me but reaffirmed that one day, she wanted the same thing.

With me...hopefully.

I GRAB THE glass of white wine and the non-alcoholic ale from the bar top and move around the other guests. Putting them down on the table, my eyes automatically find Evie's, but hers are concentrated on Oliver, who is smiling and giggling, enchanting the guests in his white christening dress.

"That's an extremely contemplative expression you're wearing, sweetheart."

Her head snaps up. "I'm a very contemplative kind of girl." Her lips curve into a smile, enhancing the natural blush on her cheeks. She reaches for the glass of wine and downs half. "What are your thoughts on children?"

I peak my brow and side-eye Oliver. A potentially fatal thought gains prominence, and I stare at Evie's front. She suddenly gasps and puts her hand on her stomach.

"Oh, my goodness, Jeremy! I'm not pregnant! I'm only twenty, for crying out loud!" she says, keeping her shocked voice down. Elation and deflation battle simultaneously inside me at her exclamation, leaving me conflicted and content. "I just wanted to know your stance, that's all." She sips her wine again. Her disappointment and annoyance at my presumption are clear.

"Come here, sweetheart." I grip her hand and lead her into the hotel foyer. Sitting in the little nook under the main staircase, I drag her chair closer, so her knees are between mine, and my hands are massaging her thighs. "I like kids. I'd even like a couple of my own in the future, but please,

promise me you will not build some romanticised idea in your head and neglect your pill. You're a smart, beautiful young woman, and that's something that has always attracted me, but I can't have you ruining a brilliant, bright future for a current, impractical dream."

She huffs and shuffles closer. Her hands reach up to my nape, and she rakes her fingers through my messy hair. "Jeremy," she begins, softly shaking her head, making me fall further, harder. "I'm not planning on getting pregnant or neglecting my pill. Except, we need to be realistic. Every time we make love, we accept the risk. I was just wondering what your thoughts were because if it ever happened, I'd need you." A lone tear fills her eye, and I tip up her chin.

"And I would be there every step of the way, whether you wanted me to be or not. I'm not going anywhere. And especially not if you were carrying my child."

She nods, but her eyes narrow. "But?" she queries, reading me perfectly.

"But you make a very tangible point. We are running that risk, and maybe until you've finished uni and achieved everything you want to, we need to add further protection."

Her mouth opens, and she purses her lips and shakes her head. "No, I don't want to use condoms again," she whispers, her eyes darting to the foyer. "I never forget to take my pill, and I refuse to have anything between us. You just said you would accept the risk if I got pregnant, and so do I."

I cup the back of her head and coax her closer until our lips are touching. I sink into the kiss, fully accepting every action and consequence in terms of our intimacy. However, fear still exists because one day, if she does announce she's prematurely pregnant, it won't be condoms I wished were still between us. Her father will ensure I am removed from the picture permanently.

I BLOW OUT my breath and shove that particularly oppressive thought to the back of my mind. I softly slide my finger over her cheek, along the length of her neck and down the side of her breasts. She murmurs, and her eyes slowly open.

"Hi," she whispers sleepily. In a fluid movement, I quickly roll us over. She wiggles beneath me and runs her hands up and down my shoulders and back. She then arches up and takes my mouth in hers.

I balance my weight on one arm beside her pillow, and my other hand cradles the side of her head. Pillaging her mouth as urgently as she is mine, her leg hooks over my hip, and she presses her pelvis up. I move my hand from her face to her chest, shift her bra aside and cup her breast. I swipe my tongue over her firm nipple, and her immediate response is perfection, bowing further, moaning beautifully. I quickly strip her of her bra and continue my gentle assault. She moves her hand between us and slowly strokes me until I'm hard as granite.

"Make love to me," she begs, turning me on something fierce. I release her tit and snake my hand between her legs. I tentatively stroke her covered flesh, pinpointing my thumb at her apex, leisurely taking my time, relishing how receptive she is under the flimsy material.

"Jeremy..."

"Shush." I bend my head and recommence loving her nipple, alternating between the two. My fingers eventually breach the fabric and find her hot, tight centre. Her breathing increases and her body moves in harmony. Working her harder, showing perseverance, I graze her soft, hard peaks and part her swollen folds.

I grin to myself while she attempts to prevent the inevitable, but my circling at her centre proves too much, and she begins to pant uncontrollably. I pull back quickly and drag those very attractive but very pesky shorts down her legs. She gazes at me with aroused eyes and shifts her legs aside. I lovingly stroke her cheek, position myself at her entrance, and slowly enter her, just in time for her walls to clench around me.

"Jeremy!" she cries out, reaching fruition. I get comfortable, then push deeper, higher. "Oh, that's amazing! You feel outstanding. So thick and deep inside me." I thrust again, and she rocks up. "Oh my, don't stop. Don't stop." She moans and continues to mutter incoherently. Her tight core squeezes my delighted dick impeccably as she unravels and releases.

I plunge in and out while she digs her nails into my arse. Her teeth find my neck, and she grazes them along my skin before she licks the abated area lovingly.

"I want you under me!" she demands breathlessly. "Then I'm going to screw you like a good girlfriend should."

I grin, having something else to thank gobshite Morgan for, then put her out of my mind as I roll my woman over effortlessly.

She sits tall astride my groin, her hot core faintly thrumming around me. I place my hands on the top of her thighs, my thumbs just above her apex, rubbing her pubic bone, and I grasp her hips. She bends down, gives me a mischievous kiss and pulls back. Placing her hands on my chest, she strokes my nipples, returning the teasing. She walks them down my stomach and presses her fingertips into my abdomen, and lifts her body up.

"How do you want me?" I ask playfully and throw one arm above my head, very relaxed.

She blushes and drags her teeth over her bottom lip. Her uncertainty disperses, and she lowers herself down on my shaft and brushes her lips over my left scar. "I want you deep inside me. I want you to fill me. I want you begging me not to stop."

I breathe heavily. "I think that's a foregone conclusion because I'll never stop, sweetheart, ever." I palm her hip, and she rotates forward and back in long strokes. Her breathing begins to deepen again with each rotation, and she parts her lips and her tongue darts out to moisten them. Digging her hands into my front, her action intensifies until she's granted her wish.

"Fuck, sweetheart!" I hiss, my body reacting. Inside her, my shaft is cocooned by the most incredible constriction. Combined with her heat, her wetness, and the way her muscles hold me, it's maddening and amazing, and I never want to be anywhere but here.

I stare into her eyes, studying her, watching every little flicker and enjoying every feeling while she continues to work her body on mine. She gazes up at the ceiling, circling her hips, trusting instinct. My abdomen begins to throb slowly, and I lick my lips when her hands leave my stomach, and she presses them to hers and moves them up her front. She pauses at her breasts and touches them as a lover would – as I would – then she commences the movement up her clavicle, to the back of her neck, until she gathers up her hair. I arch up beneath her, and she groans.

"Again."

I vault up, bend my knees, and press her into me. Her tits rub my chest, and I shift my legs to manipulate her groin closer to mine. She smirks and performs a perfect pelvic roll that consumes me. Turned on beyond belief, my release building ardently, I tangle my hand in her hair and pull her head to the side. She smiles with satisfaction and gives me a sultry, smoky look.

"You like that?" Only I don't need to ask. I'm already aware she sometimes does like it a little rough and ready.

"I like *you* doing that." Her eyelids droop further, and she tilts her head to expose more of her neck. "I love what you do to me, but I'd like you to do even more." Her eyes flick down to her rear. Hearing her say that ignites something primal inside. I tighten my hand in her hair, observe her closely and grip her hip hard.

"Fuck me, sweetheart. Make me come inside you." Encouraged, she moves harder, faster, more determined than ever. With my impending orgasm building, I shift my hand from her hip and slide my finger between her cheeks. She tenses as anticipated, then relaxes when all I do is stroke. But make no mistake, one day, this part of her is mine and only mine. And I'll be inside her, pulling her hair back, holding her secure, while she screams my name.

The thought of her in such a submissive fashion prompts my length to pulsate, and I growl in victory. Her legs tighten around my hips, and her core throbs as she cries out, chasing amazing, and she comes around me. Staring into each other's eyes, we finally succumb to the hedonistic high.

"God, Evie!" I manage to get out. "Christ, I love you, you amazing woman."

"I love you, too. You sexy, addictive man," she replies, her expression euphoric while her heat squeezes me deep within.

Gradually, my thighs flop to the sides, and Evie flops onto my torso. She lifts her head, smiles and exhales, satisfied. I stroke her skin, feeling myself start to soften inside her.

"That always feels funny." She carefully pushes herself up and off. I puff out, objecting to her loss. "Come on, my sexy, addictive man," she orders, tugging my hand. "Before I leave you this evening, I think we need to test the shower." I'm up in a shot but stop dead when she wiggles her hips with a wink. "Then maybe the sofa, the balcony, possibly the kitchen worktops, but most definitely this bed again."

I grin and allow her to lead me into temptation. But if this is the reward, I'll gladly obey.

Always.

"SO, WHAT ARE you all planning on doing tonight?" Evie asks, tying her trainers.

"Poker, pizza, and pop, I'm told." I gauge her amused expression.

"Pop?"

I shrug. "Well, there's my abstinence, obviously, but Oliver will be there, and Sloan will murder anyone who gets pissed and puts his son at risk. Plus, the guys might pick up their women later depending on the time, so we're having pop."

"Makes sense."

"Are you sure you don't want to join them?" I press her again. "I know they'd love to see you."

For the last few days, I've had both Charlie and Kara on my case regarding why Evie declined their invitation to girls' night. I'd love to be able to say I'm aware of her reasons why, but I'm not. Yet again, her reticence has proved prevalent, further confirming she doesn't want to get too close to them for whatever reason. And I'm desperate to understand why.

Evie rises and puts on her denim jacket. "No, I promised Mum I would spend the night with her since I'm hardly home these days. My dad is meeting some friends, so she asked for us to have our own kind of girls' night in."

I nod, feeling my eyes narrow slightly. "Okay, but if you change your mind, you can still join them later."

"I'll consider it," she lies. Reaching up on her toes, she presses a lingering kiss to my lips, then shoulders her overnight bag. "I'll see you tomorrow after uni. I love you."

"I love you, too," I reply, watching her leave.

Chapter 31

I PULL UP on the street in front of John and Marie's house since the driveway is unmistakably full with more cars than you can shake a stick at. I click the remote locking and stride up the garden path, and ring the bell.

The door opens, and Sloan appears on the other side, rocking Oliver on his hip, his mobile to his ear. I automatically take his son and tuck him into my chest. "Evening, sunshine. Ready to party hard with the big boys?" Oliver laughs, probably at me rather than with me, considering he has no clue what I'm talking about, but at least he doesn't answer back. *Yet.*

"I think the big boys might be a bad influence on him." Kara strolls towards me, dressed and ready to go. "But at least you don't use him to pull like Parker and Tommy do," she adds thoughtfully.

I offer Oliver my finger, which he grips as per usual. "No, my future teachings will be more educational."

Kara smiles. "Just say no?" she queries good-humouredly.

"Something like that," I murmur, but the answer entirely depends on the question. "You look great, by the way." I motion my head at her dress.

"Thanks. Everyone's in the kitchen. I think I should warn you that John's being a bit...funny," she confesses, and I don't think she means in a *ha-ha* kind of way either.

"Cheers for the warning. Have they had another argument?" I lower my voice.

She shrugs and plucks her yawning son from my arms. "Not exactly. Let's just say he thinks Marie's dress should be for his eyes only." She purses her lips and sneaks back into the living room, where her husband is camped out as I head into the kitchen.

"Hi," I greet. John is the first to turn, and he grunts while everyone else manages a cordial 'hello'. "My, my, who knew a dress had the ability to render him speechless!" I wink at John, who gives me the finger. "Stroppy, too!"

Everyone laughs, but John just continues to grunt. "I'll show you stroppy, you little arsehole!"

"Actually, I'm a sulky, obstinate, contradictory twat, remember? But clearly not as sulky as you, though!" I tell him as he stomps out.

Tommy chuckles and slaps me on the shoulder. "Pizza's on the way, and there's some alcohol-free ale in the fridge, if you want one."

I shake my head. "Coke's fine." The kitchen door opens, and I expect John to come back in. Instead, Sloan appears looking aggrieved and exhausted. He grabs a bottle of water, shakes his head, and leaves again. As I've said before, it's tough when you're king.

"Right, gentlemen, let's begin our inaugural booze-free poker night!" Simon announces as Jake puts a tray of pop on the table.

"No Doc?" I glance around, noting his absence.

"Nah, he's been called to cover sickness," Si says, opening a can.

Tommy puts down his phone and grabs a drink. "He's always covering bleeding sickness these days."

"He's dedicated, which is more than we can say for some. So if you want him here next time, you better make sure you don't need A and E and not add to his workload." I wink, and he blows me a kiss.

"Save the bromance, gents, let's play!" Dev deals the deck.

The first hand is drawn, the cash is thrown on the middle of the table, and calamity commences.

I glance at the clock. It's been almost half an hour since John stomped out. A repetitive thud echoes from upstairs the moment I slap down my cards and chuckle wickedly.

"You're cheating, you tight git!" Dev shouts at me, and I grin maniacally.

"Better luck next time, sunshine!" I pick up my cards and can and take a sip.

Tommy enters with the pizzas that have just arrived and rolls his eyes where Dev can't see. "Yeah, pipe down, Dev. Less complaining, more playing." He stops as Marie and John loiter behind him. "You look nice," he tells her admiringly. Marie thanks him, but it's an uncomfortable appreciation.

"At least it isn't thigh-high and crotch-skimming," Jake states, much to Marie's dismay. I shake my head at him because that's something she wouldn't want everyone to know.

"I see you gents have a hard-core night planned." She looks ready to laugh as she eyes the pop.

"Yep." Jake grins. "After we've cleaned out the soft stuff, we're going to start on the hard stuff – the baby's milk."

"I heard that!" Sloan calls out from the living room.

"Well, have fun," She says, shutting the door as we all say 'goodbye', 'have nice night', so on and so forth.

The second hand of cards fly over the table as Dev deals proficiently again. I pick up mine and arrange them as the door flies back, and John glares at Jake.

"Right, then, Jacob." He moves to the fridge and grabs two bottles of water, and puts them on the table. "Talk to me about thigh high and crotch-skimming." He plunks down into a chair, and Dev deals him a hand. Jake smirks, ready to divulge when footsteps patter down the hallway.

Sloan sits the baby monitor next to the pile of cash, pulls up a chair and unscrews a bottle. "He's asleep in the travel cot, so keep the noise down. Otherwise, Marie has already offered to dig up the patio in her heels after John murders you."

Jake's smirk vanishes, and he squirms when John presses him on thigh high and crotch-skimming again. "I will, on the proviso you don't bury me under the patio the next time I piss you off, or God forbid, wake the baby. Now that I know you've got a woman who's willing and able to assist, I need that security, boss." He gives him a pitiful expression, and we all take the piss as he piles it on it.

I shake my head in amusement, slide over the box of pizza and take half. "Someone order more takeaway." I dig into my pocket and chuck my wallet over the table, then pick up my hand.

"Now tell!" John urges, and Jake conveys the tale from lunch the other day. John relaxes back in his chair and looks thoughtful. "I think I need to have words with Sophie and ask her why I didn't get thigh high and crotch-skimming! Better yet, maybe I'll just take her shopping."

Sloan snorts. "If you do, sunshine, I think you'll find heavy lifting won't be an issue, and *you* will be under the patio."

"Wishful flaming thinking is what it is! But a man can dream... And shop online with next day delivery." He grins, pulling out his phone.

Dev deals Sloan some cards while Jake orders more pizza. "What state do we think they're all going to be in when they get home tonight?" he queries.

"With Soph leading the festivities? Paralytic, but I've got eyes on them," John replies, and I exchange a wary look with Sloan.

"That's a dangerous game you're playing, J," I tell him, not giving a shit if he doesn't like the truth.

"You have no room to talk, sunshine."

"Touché, but you have more to lose."

John sighs. "So do you." Sloan and I, aware it's an argument we cannot win, avert our eyes and concentration on our cards.

The evening passes quickly until morning eventually follows night. Sloan was the first to bow out around half past nine after it became obvious Oliver wasn't going to sleep anywhere but in his bed tonight. Simon and Tommy were next and called it a night around eleven, both a few hundred quid poorer but ensuring I was slightly richer. Dev followed after he got a call from Nicki to say she was done and on her way home. And Jake left with me about ten minutes ago to pick up Charlie and Kara.

The apartment security barrier lowers behind me, and I drive through the car park. I slow down when I see Dominic sitting on the bonnet of his Maserati.

"Well, fuck," I mutter rhetorically, but I should've known. I reverse into my free space and get out. "To what do I owe the honour of such a dubious, impromptu, early morning visit?" I round the front of my car.

"Is your woman home tonight?" he asks, his eyes scanning the surrounding grey concrete.

"No."

"Good." He strides to the lift. "Come on, lad, we need to talk."

I huff quietly but keep my expression neutral. A visit at any time is never good from Dom, but at silly o'clock in the morning, after asking if my woman is home? This has disaster written all over it.

I slouch against one side of the lift and glare at him. A tension I've never experienced in his company washes over me. The lift judders to a stop, and I exit.

"New alarm?" Dom queries, giving me a curious look while I open the door.

"Yeah, something happened." I lock the door behind us and rearm the senor now fitted to it. "So, I'm guessing you were John's eyes tonight?" I walk down the hallway into the kitchen. A bit of huffing and puffing rumbles from the living room, and I stretch around the door frame. "I'm not stupid. I know you were out tonight. I can smell the booze on you. So, were you?"

He removes his jacket and flings it on the sofa. "Fine! Yeah, I was watching them, but I wish to God I wasn't!" And judging by his tone, something went down tonight, something I'm not sure I want to be privy to.

"How long are you staying?" I ask. I put the milk back in the fridge and grab the mugs.

"I don't yet. As long as it takes."

Now that grabs my flailing attention fast. I don't know if I dare ask the next question because if I do, I have a strong sense of foreboding of what the answer will be.

"*Where* are you staying?" I ask in substitute.

Dom's eyes lazily take in the living room, and he grins, which is positively evil on him.

"I don't fucking think so, sunshine! If Evie sees you here, she'll have a fit. She's still touchy after the...incident."

He cracks up laughing and smacks his hand on the sofa. "I'm just playing with you, lad. I'm at the hotel."

"Dare I ask why you aren't there right now?"

"Too much temptation."

I bite my lip to stop my wayward tongue because the temptation is currently living in Sloan's old penthouse suite, pending completion of her house purchase. Temptation has never been as close and attainable as it is right now. I'm also confident it isn't lost on Dom that if he was to knock on her door in what I presume is her current inebriated state, she may suddenly find a one-night stand very appealing.

"Do you not think Sloan is going to find out? That suite is rarely booked, and if it is, he personally vets whose next door, so they won't disturb his privacy if he and Kara go there. Not to mention Jules is living there at the moment."

"Oh, *I know* she's there." His eyes turn dark and brooding. "I booked in under a false name."

"Please, for the love of Christ, do not involve me in whatever shit you've got going on down here. I don't want to know! I've got my own problems right now."

"Hmm, as I'm just hearing. Care to discuss this *incident* your woman is touchy about?"

I grind my jaw. "No," I tell him insubordinately.

His expression is unreadable, but his eyes work over the room. "Okay, you don't want to tell me, but does John know?"

"No, only the guys and now you, kind of. I haven't even told Sloan. If anything happened to them because of me..." I shake my head. I'd be devastated to the point that death would be an easy choice.

"Double standards, but unfortunately for you, you contradictory little git, you've got no choice but to know why *I'm* here. I want to know John's movements for the next few days. Where he's going, who he's got meetings with. Also, I need you to make excuses not to leave the office and let me know if any walk-ins drop by."

I scrub my hand over my face, emitting a pained groan. This is obviously something about Marie. In all honesty, as much as I hate to say it, whatever is about to go down, I'm already involved in. I know it's something that's going to change the turning of the tide, and I probably should side with John whenever *it* happens, but I can't. Marie has been good to me. In the six weeks I spent living with her when John personally repatriated my arse, she never once looked at me as the man who assisted in heinous acts all those years ago. She never once sat me down and attempted to psychoanalyse me. She just cared, and right now, if this is going to be as bad as I anticipate, she needs someone who is going to do the same. And I'm going to ensure it's me.

"Dom, as much as I don't want to get involved, I owe Marie, so what the hell is going on?"

"I think her shit is about to hit the fan," he says, resigned.

"Well, that makes two of us because I don't think my unresolved issues are going to stay dormant for much longer either."

He grinds his teeth. "What the hell has happened that you haven't told me about?"

Chapter 32

FOR THE THIRD night in a row, Evie stirs beside me, subconsciously disturbed by my restlessness. During the last few days, ever since I spoke to Dom about the *opportunist break-in*, sleep has eluded me for fear of the unknown. I've tossed and turned, my morality duelling once again with my immorality over what's right and wrong.

I carefully slip out of bed and close the door. The lock clicks softly shut, and I deactivate the alarm. The display panel reads a little after four in the morning, and I rub the sleep from my eyes with a subsequent yawn. Aware I won't be able to drop back off again, I grab my phone from the sideboard, a bottle of water from the fridge, and sit outside on the balcony. Lighting up a cigarette, I inhale deeply.

Since I left work yesterday afternoon, I've been at war with myself. Only this personal war was just simmering but re-emerged full throttle when Evie entered my life and brought her spark and radiance. Since then, it has been growing stronger with each passing day I've spent with her. Now, in the wake of Marie's long-buried secrets finally being brought out into the open, it's reached boiling point and reaffirmed the need for unvarnished truth.

I take another drag of the cig and blow it out. I rub my forehead with my fingertips, still caught up in the mental crossfire that was Marie's plight to get through to John yesterday afternoon.

As Dom predicted some seventy-two hours ago, Marie's shit really hit the fan. Sides were taken, invisible lines were drawn in the sand, and Sloan repaid John for all the times the man punched him when he was being an arse in his own pursuit of happiness with Kara.

My phone lights up with a text from Dom, who, unfortunately for him and us, is still here regardless of his aversion to London in general. I debate whether or not to open it. Opening it means bad things. Nothing good has come from opening texts these last three days, and more so the last sixteen hours, which has witnessed a strong relationship torn apart, a brotherly connection obliterated, and a familial bond practically shattered.

The pain was real as the rest of us stood on the proverbial sidelines and watched, conflicted, as to whether to stand beside a man who has guided each of us through life in some shape or form. Or beside a woman who has taken each of us into her heart, irrespective of the disguised actualities behind the way we all first met. And it's all due to a decades old secret, An horrific, inconceivable truth, one hidden to save the sanity of a woman who couldn't dare to speak of the brutality suffered due to the failure of remorse of the perpetrator.

When fate forced us to watch Marie fall apart, it was a revelation. It makes me wonder if – *when* – I confess my own sordid, horrific, inconceivable truth to Evie, if I will appear the same.

My phone pings again, and I curse myself for my weakness as I finally open the messages. The first is from Dom confirming he's at the hotel, the second is from Dev, with a short one-liner of *call me now!*

I grind my teeth in agitation. I seriously don't want to call him now - or at all - if I can help it, but I'm aware that that perfect ideal isn't viable. With a sigh, I press call, and the dialling tone rings in my ear. "You've got to be fucking kidding me!"

"Thank Christ! You need to get over to John's now!"

I scoff. "Good morning to you too, sunshine. It's four-thirty, in case you didn't know! The reason why you're calling better be bleeding amazing!"

Dev huffs. "Oh, it is! Uncle J's-"

"No!" I stop him.

"Rem, please, for fuck sake! He slammed the door in Dom's face last night after he confirmed he knew about Marie's past and that he had told me a few days ago." I lift my brows; Dom didn't tell me that. "Now, he's kicked me and Sloan out, too. We're currently loitering with intent on his front lawn. I'm expecting the police to arrive any second to arrest us for something or other." He huffs into the phone, and I can hear Sloan talking quickly, incoherently in the background. "He's not slept all night. He's downed a bottle of gin, and when he tried to kick Marie out, she walked! So please, just get over here. I'm fucking begging you!"

"Okay, okay," I tell him. "I'll be there as quick as I can. Just don't leave him." I hang up and lock the balcony doors behind me. I carefully open the bedroom door, and relief spreads through me that Evie is still sleeping soundly. I grab a pair of jeans and a shirt from the wardrobe and quickly get dressed.

On my way out, I set the alarm and drop Evie a text explaining where I am in a roundabout kind of way, but who knows how long I'm going to be.

A little after twenty past five, I round the corner onto John's street and park behind Dev's BMW. I grin at him and Sloan sitting crossed legged on the front lawn, fed up and pissed off.

I climb out, click the locks, and stride up the garden path. I look down as glass from a broken gin bottle crunches under my boot.

"Shit," I mutter, not having appreciated just how critical this particular crisis actually is. Dev's mouth starts to open as his body begins to rise, but I lift my hand to stop him. "Please tell me that bottle isn't his second?" I point at the broken glass.

"Nah," Dev replies. "He launched that at us to get us out of the house."

Bastard, fuck. I really don't want to be here. The sound of movement comes from the other side of the door. I'm about to knock, but it opens abruptly, and John grabs me by the shoulder and yanks me inside.

Immediate banging resounds from outside, and I cock my head at him. "Why did you kick them out?"

He shakes his head. "I got fed up of seeing their ugly mugs." I reach for the door. "You open that door, and I'm going to-"

"What?" I shout in his face. "What exactly are you going to do? Hit me? Go on. It wouldn't be the first time. You've given me more advice than I knew what to do with, and this morning, it's time for yours." I open the door, fully expecting a smack or punch, but nothing comes.

"This is called an intervention, Uncle J," Dev says as he strides inside, grabs John's arm, and drags him into the kitchen.

Sloan locks the door and gives me a grim look. "You're aware you're back on his shit list now, aren't you?"

"I'd be surprised if I wasn't. Besides, I don't think I'm going to be on that list for very long."

"What are you talking about?"

"I'll tell you later." I head into the kitchen, where Dev is now heaping numerous teaspoons of coffee into a few mugs.

The tension is profound, growing thicker with each passing minute. Dev passes me a steaming mug, and I blow over the surface and take a sip. I glance around, occasionally meeting their eyes, but in all honestly, I'm checking to ensure nothing is out of place or broken.

Thus, confirming nothing was physically hurt last night, but mentally and emotionally, however, it's probably a very different story.

"Have you spoken to Marie yet?" I probe J, who glowers in disgust and slams his fist on the table.

"I never want to speak to *her* again!"

God give me fricking strength!

I nod, but really, I feel like rolling my eyes. Then wringing his neck. This morning's theatrics are thoroughly depressing, and I've been here all of ten minutes. I catch sight of Dev and Sloan, who *are* rolling their eyes, probably having heard this bullshit speech all night.

"J, if that woman was to leave, you would scour the planet looking for her. So let's not pretend otherwise, shall we?" My tone is harsh, but he needs this.

"She lied to me!" He slams his fist on the table again.

"So what?" I scream at him. "Sloan lied to Kara. *I'm* lying to Evie. We're all holding something of ourselves back!" I stand and grab the back of my head in frustration and pace around the table. "John, I swear to God…" I shake my fist. "You need to stop being a stroppy, sulky sod and get over to the mansion and sort this out because if you keep treating her like shit, she'll walk. It's clear she's already been to hell and back once in this lifetime, and considering the origins of it, a second time will be a piece of cake!"

"She was married and had a fucking kid!" he shouts and stands. I've had enough. I march over to him and smash my fist across his face. He stumbles back in shock, but sometimes he's so pig-headed he can't see what's in front of him. I can see it, anyone with a brain can, but he can't because he hates being wrong.

"And where do you think that kid is, hmm? You've seen how protective she is of Kara. She's not a reckless mother, John." I keep my hands on his face, holding him, watching reality reclaim his gin-infused brain. "Keep thinking!" I add while the scent of noxious spirits washes over me with each vexatious huff and puff.

John's face drops, losing all colour as the consequences of his actions finally sinks in. "No, no, no! Fuck, what have I done?" He grabs his phone and holds it to his ear. "She's not answering!" He then starts thumbing the screen.

"Of course, she isn't answering, you lunatic, it's not even six o'clock!" Dev shouts as John keeps calling, leaving her messages to call him back in between sending text messages.

Time passes by slowly. John is still on the brink, going from concerned to pissed off and back again. I'd like to say that the man has sobered up, but he hasn't, and it's making him irrational. One minute she's the love of his life, and he can't live without her. The next, he hates her for what she's done, and he wants her gone.

And me? I just want to put my fist down his throat to shut him up because he's making this worse. Plus, I'm tired because of all this drama, and I'd like to close my eyes just for a little while before the merry-go-round starts again.

"What the hell?" John shouts, and I jerk from where I'm catching forty winks on the sofa. I yawn and stretch the same instant something hard lands on my chest. "She's in Kara's BMW, track it!"

"Give me a minute," I say, tapping in the passcode and swiping the app on his phone.

John gives me a pointed glare. "Now!"

I shake my head in disbelief. "I swear, you're going to get my fist in your face again if you don't shut up!" The app loads and I find the device connected with the car and hit locate. Minutes feel like hours with John glaring at me. Eventually, it pinpoints her current location. "She's in Peterborough."

John exhales like a raging bull and starts tapping away at a text.

"For Christ's sake, what have you just sent?" I demand because he's seething, and that can't be good.

"It doesn't matter," he says and throws the car keys at me. "You're driving."

"I can't just-"

"Get in the car, Jeremy, otherwise you'll find my foot up your arse!" He grudgingly drags me out of the door. I quickly turn to Sloan and mouth *call Kara*, but he's already got his phone to his ear. I get into the driver's seat, buckle up and drive away under duress.

MAINTAINING SPEED JUST under the limit, I fly up the motorway, cutting the distance between Marie and us. John has been agitated the whole journey, and I've already warned him that if I get caught speeding, I'm going to shove my foot up his arse and ensure he becomes my personal chauffeur.

A short time later, the tracking dot stops on the app and John scrubs his hand over his face. He removes the phone from the dash and brings it to his ear. "Hi."

Well, at least he's being affable – for now.

"Rem, how long?"

I screw up my face and take a punt. "Forty minutes, give or take."

"Did you get that?" John asks Marie. "Shit, angel. Why didn't you tell me?"

The conversation carries on in my ear. I feel like an intruder as they begin to hash out the shit storm they're battling through.

"Look, I'll be there as soon as I can, darling. I'm sorry, please forgive me," John says, showing the first sign of contrition I've witnessed all morning. "Remy, put your foot on it." He slips the phone back onto the holder.

"How is she?"

"I've fucked up." He scrubs his hand across his face again. "Why didn't she tell me she was dead?"

I let out a sigh. God, how I hate being right. "Could be a number of things, but I'm betting shame and fear are at the top of the list." I spy J in my peripheral vision, studying me closely. He knows I said those things because they're at the top of mine. I have empathy with Marie because, in her situation, I'd have done the same.

"I'm sorry, Rem. I'm sorry for the insinuations, the attitude, for all the things I've said to you over the last few days, especially yesterday."

I shake my head and raise my fingers from the steering wheel to stop him. "Look, I don't want your apologies, I understand. Just promise me something?" My eyes meet his. "If I ever call and tell you to come ASAP, you will."

John's eyes, still red and inebriated, widen. "Rem?"

"We'll talk about it later, but I just need your reassurance."

"I will. I promise."

I DRIVE SLOWLY into the cemetery and pull up near Kara's BMW. John has reverted back to being partially drunk but not particularly disorderly on the last leg of the journey. I crane my neck and look around the graveyard, but I can't see Marie.

"Come on," I tell him and start to pass over the gravel paths. I turn onto a path near the rear of the church, and Marie's hair glimmers in the distance as she chats with an older man. I hold my arm and stop John from barrelling over there like a bull in a China shop. "Let her talk in her own time." He gives me a death glare but acquiesces.

I grimace when the path stops, and I now have to walk on the grass. I'm walking over the dead, literally, trying as hard as I can not to. A twig snaps under my foot, and Marie's head darts up from where she's kneeling a few graves away. I smile and head towards her.

At the grave, my eyes flash over the stone, realising this is her daughter's resting place. I crouch down and kiss her forehead, shifting some stray hair. "In this life, four women have inspired me to be a better man. My mother - obviously; Kara - a determined woman whose life was torn from her for so long; the woman I love – whose father would rather see me under a bus; and you. A strong woman with a heart that's big enough to put her own pain aside to do what's right." I gaze at the gravestone. "To do this. To come back here and face this, proves you are all those things, Marie."

She nods. "Does he hate me?"

I shake my head as her tears arrive, and I wrap her in my arms. "No, of course not." I cup her cheeks firmly, ensuring she's focussed, because she's just as stubborn as he is. "Marie, look at me. I'm not supposed to tell you this, but that man has loved you for almost as long as Sloan has loved Kara."

"What do you mean?"

I shouldn't, but it's time she knew. "I mean she wasn't the only one being followed. Just talk to him, explain, but don't grovel. This was your life long before he found a way in. And you did that – you let him in." I glance back at John, who still looks pissed. "And he's aware you can just as easily let him back out. You lived without him once, he knows you could do it again."

"I didn't know how to tell him. How could I?"

"I know exactly what you mean. I still need to sit down with Evie and explain the truth. Like you, I'm putting it off as long as possible because when she finally hears it, she will have to decide if she lets me stay in, or if she lets me back out. Trust me, *I know.*"

"Thank you, sweetheart. I mean that." She wipes her eyes. I press my lips to the back of her hand and reluctantly motion for John.

"I need to get back. Evie will be wondering where I am. Marie? Can I take the beamer?"

"Sure."

I exchange the BMW keys for the Range Rover keys. "Here. He's probably still ten times over the limit, so don't let him drive."

"You're a good man, Jeremy James."

My forehead creases. She's told me what she thinks of me many times, but it always catches me off guard. "I'm glad you think so. One day I might be calling on you when I need a character reference." I let her go and stand in front of John. "I'm going to leave you to it, but for once in your life, listen. Allow her to tell you, don't just go off like a firework with no aim or direction!"

"Finished?"

"No, I could go on and on, but I have my own woman to get back to. Remember, listen. I'll see you later, M," I say with a wink and move back through the gravestones.

Climbing into the car, I pull out my phone and call the Foster residence. "Hey," I greet as soon as someone picks up.

"Hi, did you find her?" Kara asks with worry.

I start up the car and adjust the seat. "Yeah, she's fine. I've left her with John with strict instructions for him to behave himself, but if she calls you, will you let me know?"

"Sure," Kara replies. "Where are you now?"

"I'm about to set off with your car." I hesitate. It's now or never. "Kara, these last few days have proven once again that the truth cannot remain hidden, that we need to be honest."

"Go on," she whispers, already knowing what I'm going to ask.

"I need to tell Evie about what I did. She already knows the story about my ex who passed, but I need to tell her about that night, what I did to you. But I need your approval before I do."

She grumbles down the line. "Jeremy, you need to let it go. Does it make any difference if she knows or not? Can't we just forget about it after all these years?"

I grind my teeth because she doesn't get it. "I know it's hard, but yes, it *does* make a difference, and no, *I* can't." I inhale intensely. "And deep down, I don't think *you* can either."

I sit in the car park and gaze at the sky as quiet fills my ear. The line remains silent, and on a wing and a prayer, I wait with hope in my heart.

Chapter 33

"SWEETHEART, I'LL BE back in a minute," I call out, closing the door behind me.

I jog down the sixteen flights of stairs and push through the foyer door. Unlocking my post box on the wall of many, I remove today's offerings. A few bills, some promotional crap - including a flyer for garden landscaping which makes me snort.

My phone pings in my pocket, and I remove it with the urgency of a man on the edge. Except, my act of desperation doesn't alter the fact that I am.

Almost a month has passed since I sat in a Peterborough cemetery and requested Kara's permission to air her - and my - deepest, darkest secret. In the weeks that have proceeded, I'm still waiting for her answer. I haven't pushed her, nor have I called incessantly, because it's a decision she can't just make with the click of her fingers. To allow me to tell Evie is to give someone outside our immediate circle an unprecedented amount of power, entrusting such sensitive information in someone she doesn't know very well. Someone who has a father who would rub his hands in glee with such knowledge that he could weaponise and use against not only me but Sloan, too. Still, the desire to call her is my newest, temporary addiction, and only one answer will cure it.

I stuff the post into my pocket and press the standby button. The screen illuminates with a weather update - thunderstorms today, apparently. Typical. Although I guess I should be happy if there's a possibility this afternoon's unfortunate event may get rained off. I'll never admit that out loud, of course.

With a lacklustre sensation filling my unimpressed thoughts, I press the lift button and wait for it to arrive. *I could've taken the stairs,* I think when the doors slide shut. Except I fear my lungs aren't up to scratch, and I don't want to arrive at today's shindig with perspiration stains and smelling less than fresh. Now that would be criminal.

As I exit, my neighbour, who I think I've maybe seen twice in the last few years - a guy about my age who, judging by his many loud phone calls I've heard in passing, works in investment banking -

greets me. I don't know his name, but I acknowledgement him as he boards.

I open my door, remove the post from my pocket and slide my thumb under the flap. I move into the living room, bracing myself for the exorbitant cost of this quarter's utilities.

"What do you think?" Evie asks behind me. I glance over my shoulder and watch her tiptoe towards me in absolute awe. I spin around from my stance by the balcony doors and smile, yet again wondering how I got so lucky in life.

Dressed in a knee-length, cream flowered dress – a tea dress, whatever that is – she is both demure and conservative in countenance but gorgeous and graceful in appearance. She's beautiful. Breathtakingly so. And every magnificent inch of her is mine to honour, worship and cherish.

She grips the inside of her cheek with her teeth – a rare nervous tell. "Say something," she requests, worried. She consciously touches her intricately curled and styled hair.

I toss the post aside, uncaring where it lands. I remain mute on my slow, calculated approach. When she's within reach, I place my hands under her arms and clamp them on her upper back. My fingers curl over the top of her shoulders, and I stroke my nose over her cheek, making her look at me.

"You're phenomenal," I tell her, causing her to blush and compress her lips shyly. I brush my mouth against hers, softly caressing my tongue over her closed seam, encouraging her to open. My action is slow, deliberate, taking my time, savouring her. My hands move of their own volition, sliding further down her back, teasing the zip.

She murmurs and, surprisingly, pushes me away. "As much as I would love for you to strip me out of this and make love to me all afternoon, we're going to be late." She cups my jaw and kisses my cheek before gliding back down the hallway into the bedroom.

I groan and shift the fly of my beige trousers, desperate to lose the semi-hard state beneath the fabric. Thinking of the most mundane things; security quotes, wires, chasing debts… John, I turn back to the balcony doors and ensure they are locked. A gathering of dark grey ominous clouds blots out the sun, making me wonder if today's downpour will rain us off earlier than predicted.

One can hope.

This afternoon, it's the Blakes' annual summer garden party – they have an annual party for everything. In true, historical Evie fashion, she didn't spring this unfortunate surprise on me until yesterday morning, after querying, very delicately, if I had any plans today. My reply, a mumble of pretend excuses since I was still nestled deep inside her, her legs coiled around my hips like a snake, squeezing beautifully, constricting its prey, bending it to its will – bending *me* to *her* will – were all pathetically contrived until I confirmed I was.

Honestly, given a choice, I'd rather stay here like an unsocial hermit. I think she senses that, but I don't have any other viable options. John is out tonight, supporting Marie at her first – and only – catering gig at the very plush Roseby hotel. Sloan has also been invited, so no doubt Kara will be on his arm, and God knows what everyone else is up to. I could've set up something with Doc or Jake or organised another poker game with Si and Tommy, but, as I've said before, I can't cherry-pick what parts of her life I want to be associated with. And I refuse to give Andy the satisfaction of seeing me gone.

"I'm rea-" Evie stops. "Oh, no, he's serious and pensive," she adds in a deeper tone. I reach out my hand to hers. The moment she takes it, I tug her close, flop us onto the sofa and arrange her on my lap.

"I'm just thinking." I graze my hands up and down her thighs, occasionally sneaking them under the skirt of her dress. She shuffles, wraps her arms around my neck and rubs her cheek alongside mine, tentatively kissing my temple.

"About this afternoon?" she probes quietly, linking our fingers.

I smile and shake my head. "No, about John and Marie," I partially lie. I lean back as her expression mutates into marginally upset.

"Are they okay? Have they had another fight?"

I stroke her neck and breathe in her unique scent. "No, they're fine, but I think we all forget that love is fragile. You need to treat it with care, otherwise, it will shatter." Her eyes widen, and I sweep my thumb over her cheekbone repeatedly.

"Jeremy James...who knew you were a closet romantic!"

I chuckle, the pad of my thumb still on her cheek, my fingers under her jaw. "I'm Mr Romance personified, baby." I secure my arm around her middle and my other under her legs as I lift us up from the sofa. She crosses her ankles and appears completely at ease with my action.

"Well, then, Mr Romance personified, I think we need to test your high opinion later." She stretches over to the security panel and taps in the code. She locks the door behind us, and we leave for what I presume will be a very English party consisting of a champagne afternoon tea.

Although I fear if Andrew Blake is allowed free rein of the booze again, which is a given, I may need to add sympathy to the menu.

I BLOW OUT a vexed breath and stare through the windscreen at the house, still wondering what I'm doing here again and how I'm going to survive this very sophisticated form of torture.

Evie's hand finds mine, and I gaze into her concerned eyes. "It'll be fine," she says, reading me better than I give her credit for. "An amazing gentleman told me that love is fragile, and it needs to be treated with care, but ours is strong, and I believe it can survive anything. Even this. Besides, there's someone incredibly important I need you to meet. Consider it another surprise!" She winks and purses her lips, aware I'm not impressed. I confess I'm growing quite tired of these *surprises* to the point that one day, I'm going to refuse.

I make no comment, even though it's darkened my mood. I climb out of the car and round the bonnet. I open the door, offer Evie my hand and assist her out. She straightens up whilst I adjust my white linen shirt and trousers, hoping I fit in. Hell, I'm even wearing the boat shoes that I specifically purchased yesterday afternoon.

Evie exhales beside me. The sound is troubled and disheartened. "I'm sorry. I shouldn't keep doing this to you, but I'm frightened one day you'll refuse. I'm not stupid. I know you don't like my dad. Sometimes I don't either, but-"

I bend down and lift her up. "I was just thinking that one day *I am* going to refuse you. Then I remember how much I love you and know that I'll never refuse you anything. That's how invested I am in this, *in us*, that I'll endure him until the end of time because our love is strong and unbreakable." Her arms wrap around my neck, and she kisses me passionately, almost indecently, adding some colour to her English rose skin.

Movement inside the house grabs my attention. With my hand still on her nape, an older man is blatantly watching us from the living room window, and I wonder if this is the elusive *interesting* aspect I'm finally going to be acquainted with.

"I don't suppose this incredibly important someone is around seventy with greying hair, round cheeks, and looks like he wants to kill me?"

She laughs and spins around. The man in the window waves and she grabs my hand and literally drags me up the garden path. Entering the house, familiar faces from other parties I've attended smile at me. Some even remember my name and address me eye to eye as opposed to eye to cheek. I mutter a quick *hello* or *nice to see you again* as Evie continues to march me down the hallway towards the kitchen.

"Christ, I'm unimpressed the majority of the time, not unapproachable! *He's* made me this way," Evie's mother, Cathy, says to someone, causing Evie to freeze just before the door. "Him and his tarts! And he wonders why I'm so unenthusiastic, the reason why I drink copiously? When he flaunts his *indiscretions* in my face and brings his current bitch into my home!"

"I told you years ago to leave him. You don't need him. You certainly don't need his money, darling!" a man answers her, his tone full of insinuation.

"Evelyn needs her dad."

"Admirable, but a shame he doesn't need his daughter. Have you ever told her?"

"No, Dad, it would destroy her."

"She's not a little girl anymore, darling. She may even know already."

Evie's jaw tightens, and I suddenly realise why she refuses to become too attached. It's a trusted reaction to what is clearly her father's infidelity. I look over my shoulder. The dining room is empty, and tug her into it and close the door.

"Is your father cheating on your mother?" She nods, chewing her lip. "For a long time?" She turns away, and I force her to face me. "More than once?"

"Yes, and yes," she whispers.

"And that's why you can't be yourself with Kara, Marie, et al., because of what he's done?" Her mouth tightens, the same instant her eyes begin to glisten. I pull her into me. "Look at me. There are still things I need to tell you, one thing in particular, but I would never, *ever* cheat. Please know in your heart that I would never leave you sitting up at night wondering where I am. Or say I have a meeting or need to work late. I would never do to you what he has inadvertently done to you. His adultery has caused your distrust, and I fucking hate him for it! I won't lie, darling, I don't like your father. I can barely abide by him."

She curls further against me. "I know. I've known since that day in Sloan's office at the board meeting when he took my phone by mistake."

Clarity washes over me like a bucket of water. The pieces have just fallen into place. He didn't take her phone by mistake. He took it so he could tinker with the settings and use it to track her because, let's be honest, what teenage girl or young woman would give up her phone freely for a few hours if a parent asked?

Son of a bitch!

I kiss the top of her head and push her back. "Dry your eyes, sweetheart. He's not worth it. Now, tell me who this important someone is. I need to impress at least one man in your life, and I'm thinking he's the one you care the most about."

She grins, almost childlike. "My grandpy. I adore him, and so will you. Really, you'll like him."

"That's what you said about your dad!"

She laughs sadly, then her compose snaps back into place, leaving me worried. "I know I keep springing these surprises on you, and I promise I'll stop, but I have another *huge* favour to ask. Please." I lift a brow, wiping my fingers under her eyes. "If I happen to *accidentally* throw – sorry, *spill* - my drink over a random woman, would you play along?"

I smirk, nodding repeatedly. "I'll even bring you the offending drink."

She beams in delight. "You're a keeper, Jeremy James."

"I'll hold you to that." With that, I open the door. "Deep breath, sweetheart. We've just arrived, you were accosted by *whoever*, and I have no clue who grandpy is, okay?"

She agrees and pulls me back to the kitchen. "Hey!" she greets, her tone weird and fake.

"Hello, darling!" Cathy replies, setting down her glass of fizz. I smile as she clenches her daughter tight. I move deeper into the room and acknowledge Evie's cherished grandad, who is sitting at the island with a glass of what appears to be orange juice.

"Jeremy, it's lovely to see you again!" Cathy says, more natural than she has before, and it's apparent she's a million times better without her husband present.

"Afternoon, Mrs Blake." I approach with ease. She unexpectedly gathers me in her embrace, and I reciprocate.

"One day, you will call me Cathy. This is definitely healing, isn't it?" I nod at her abashed expression. "Sorry, you must get fed up of people looking at them, speaking about them, but they're just…"

"Just there? Hard to avoid? Don't worry, I'm used to it. And yes, it's healing well."

"Grandpy," Evie exclaims, her voice ringing through the large kitchen. I drop my arms from around Cathy's back and watch Evie rush to the older man. I cringe when she flings herself at him, pondering if he will survive the impact or possibly fall and break a hip.

He proves to be more robust and dexterous than he appears, and he hugs her with a fierce protectiveness. "You're too big to sit on my lap, Evie pie!" he says, then blatantly stares at me. "Someone you need to introduce to your old geezer?"

Evie motions me over to the island. "Jeremy, this is Terry Cosgrove, my grandpa. Grandpy, this is Jeremy James, my…my…"

"Boyfriend?" Grandpy finishes for her, and she bites her top lip. "He looks a bit too old to be classed as a boyfriend." His brows lift questionably.

"My sentiments exactly, sir, but unfortunately, I am the boyfriend. Nice to meet you, Mr Cosgrove." I keep my greeting light as I'm well versed in who her Grandpy is, although I didn't think I'd ever get meet him.

"You too, Mr James." He looks between Evie and Cathy, who picks up her glass, and pours one for Evie.

"Jeremy, do you want pop or juice?" she asks, now conversant that I will decline alcohol.

"Pop's fine, thank you," I say, catching Terry's suspicious eye.

"To family. Old and new," Cathy says, and we all clink glasses.

I knock back a mouthful of fizz, trying my hardest not to make unnecessary, lengthy eye contact with Terry because this is the *interesting* side of Evie's family. Not many people know who her grandfather is – or was, I guess, who knows - unless you move in those circles. The man went to great lengths to protect his family from his dishonourable, questionable lifestyle, but lucky for me, I'm aware of some of the *hidden* aspects. Such as Grandpa Cosgrove here, a true east end cockney, wide boy geezer, whom I now have unequivocal information regarding. And his daughter, the wealthy Cathy Blake nee Cosgrove, who can't account for where her personal fortune came from, but traded the east end for the west end, and married a man who would give her a respectable name that isn't associated with organised crime.

The tension lessens while we all make small talk. Terry excuses himself, and Cathy insists Evie shows me the wonder of the garden in full bloom and decoration.

The sun blazes down, hot and sticky, but settling into a beautiful summer's day. We walk through the garden, and Evie politely acknowledges the guests she knows and makes conversation with the ones she doesn't. The garden itself is divided into four defined sections. I'm not a gardener, but what I wouldn't give to sit out here on an evening, observing a beautiful sunset with the scent of flora enveloping my nostrils. As opposed to sitting on my balcony, eight floors up, being serenaded with nothing but the sounds of sirens and the smell of a city which is less than fresh.

"And this is Mum's orchard, or 'The Avenue' as she likes to call it." She eases her hand under a branch, caressing the fruits currently growing. We then stroll along the tree-lined path, the same way a lord and his lady would in centuries' gone by. She leads me into the flower garden, then the veg garden, and finally, back to the main lawned area, which currently houses a wrought iron gazebo, numerous tables, a makeshift bar, and a small dance floor. Fairy lights are strung around the space, and I hope we're still here when dusk draws near because it will look spectacular.

As always, Cathy has gone all out. Sadly, it's telling. She fills her life and home with pretty things, things that make her smile and give her joy in a way her husband cannot. Or will not since he doesn't even try.

"Drink?" Evie asks as a waiter approaches, his tray loaded with champagne and water, of which she takes two of the latter. "I don't suppose you have any non-alcoholic champers?"

"Yes, of course," he replies. Evie requests two glasses and thanks him.

"You don't have to not drink on my acc-" She puts her finger over my lips, quashing my verbal thoughts.

"I need to keep a clear head for the entertainment." Her eyes focus behind me. I subtly bend to pick up the invisible object at my feet and glance over my shoulder at her dad and his supposed mistress. He's flaunting her for all to see. He isn't even hiding it, and the men surrounding him - his friends - are very much at ease with it, so they're aware he's openly cheating on his wife. *Bastard!*

I swear if Sloan or John ever did that to Kara or Marie, I sure as fuck wouldn't be laughing and joking with them the way those dickheads are.

"Don't look at him, sweetheart," I tell her, but she's ready to cry, and it fucking kills me to witness her pained eyes and distressed demeanour. I stand and lift her up, forcing her to swap seats. When she sits back down, she constantly looks over her shoulder. Andy has now noticed, and he subtly moves away from his dirty bit of fluff. His hateful gaze ensnares mine, and I stare off with him. Finally, he breaks and turns.

"How can he do that to my mother?" Evie asks, pursing her lips. "She knows, and she still stays. I don't understand why."

What do I say? I know what I want to say. Instead, I go with facts. "I'm sure she has her reasons, but he's a coward, sweetheart. If you don't want to be with someone any longer, you leave them. You don't cheat."

"Wise words." I jolt around and meet Terry's infuriated gaze. He pulls up a chair between Evie and me, giving him a perfect, unrestricted view of his son-in-law. "Maybe having an older man might be acceptable, after all." He gives me a pointed look, but I'm not foolish. I know when I need to make amends.

"I feel I should apologise. My comments were merely observations. They were not meant to be disparaging about your daughter, sir."

Terry puts down his orange juice and grips my shoulder. "It's Terry, Jeremy, and it's nothing I haven't said to her before."

The waiter returns with a bottle of booze-free fizz and two glasses. Terry gives me a coy look but stays silent. He clears his throat and then begins to interrogate Evie about uni, subtly dropping hints about what will happen to me if she fails and or drops out. The chat moves from now to then, and much to her humiliation, Terry entertains me with stories of his *Evie pie*. Eventually, I excuse myself for a visit to the gents.

Inside the house, the sound of glass smashing and the raised voices of Andy and Cathy leak from the dining room. "Oh, why don't you just fucking leave, Andy? That way, you can fuck your little bitch as much as you like! I'll even send you off with our good bed sheets since I found her hair and fake tan on them!"

"God, you're nothing but a fucking drunk!"

I'd love to go in there and defend her, but I force myself to walk away. This isn't my fight.

After taking longer than I need, I dry my hands and straighten up my appearance. Closing the bathroom door, my mouth curves when I see Evie's bedroom is opposite. Her name on the wall in lights kind of gives it away. Since I'm a gent and she hasn't invited me in, I linger in the doorway and look over the parts I can see.

Footsteps and giggling grow louder, and I give Andy a disgusted look as he stumbles at the top of the stairs, his other woman just behind him, the straps of her dress already down.

"The toilet is right here, Amanda," he says, making a big show.

I cross my arms over my chest and scoff in disbelief. "You're not a very good liar, are you? Considering your wife has already found *her* fake tan in your bed, why don't you just throw *it* on your daughter's bed and have done with it?"

"How dare you?!"

I ignore him. "I mean, you've already obliterated Evie's dream of a perfect family this afternoon, so the bedroom she rarely uses anymore should be a doddle." I scowl, but I can't condone cheating. I guess deep down, I suspect the reason my dad left us is because maybe he found someone else. I don't know.

"Now, you listen to me, you little cunt!" Andy gets in my face and subconsciously twists his ring.

"No, you condescending prick!" I reply as his bit of fluff lingers.

Andy snorts in anger through his nose. "Go on, darling, I won't be long." The woman slinks down the hallway landing to the door at the end, and closes it behind her. "You act so high and mighty, but I wonder how Evie will ever forgive you when she finds out. Maybe... Maybe I should just ask Foster and his wife how they've managed to forgive you considering her virtuous downfall." He grins. "You see, I've been making new friends. New, influential friends, and let's just say, it's amazing what the right incentive will do when you threaten someone's liberty or give them the one thing in the world they can't stop thinking about."

"What the hell is that supposed to mean?"

"You'll see. Eventually." He pats my chest and turns down the landing. The door slamming rings in my ears as their stupid giggling resounds. Dazed, I grab the bannister as I stumble down the stairs.

"Jeremy? Are you okay?" Cathy asks, halfway up. I sober up and glance back, totally at odds.

"I'm fine, but please don't go up there." I give her a sympathetic look.

She shakes her head, hardening her resolve. "He's up there with *her*, isn't he?" I don't respond because my silence is answer enough. "I know you don't drink, Jeremy, very admirable, but I intend on getting sloshed, and I want a handsome, dedicated man on my arm while I do!" She links her arm in mine and leads me downstairs.

It's a good thing because I doubt my legs will carry me after the implications of his potential threat.

I WATCH FROM under the pergola, entwined with vines and flowers, as Evie dances with one of her mum's friends. The night draws in, and the lights add a majestic touch to the evening. There's a nip in the air, and a delicate hint of sulphur lingers on the atmosphere.

"I think we need to talk." I turn to find Terry behind me, two pints of orange juice in his hands. He offers me one, and I study it. "If I wanted to bump you off, son, it wouldn't be with poison, and those scars wouldn't be the only marks decorating your temples." I frown, causing him to laugh. "Evie pie hasn't told you anything about this family, has she?"

"I have a vague idea," I say, one smirk to another.

"Walk with me," he says, and I follow him deeper into the avenue of trees. "You don't drink, do you?"

"Not really. It's one of my three evils," I tell him. There's no point in circumventing it when Evie already knows. If he doesn't get the answers he wants from me, he'll just ask her, and I don't want her caught up in any misgivings he may potentially have regarding my past choices.

"I'm a recovering alcoholic. Sixteen years now." He gives me a hard look. "It takes a real man to admit his faults and take responsibility. My wife left and took my Cathy with her because of it. It took me a long time, but I eventually turned it around. Just like you did."

I quirk my brows in surprise. How much does this man actually know about me?

"So, what do you do for a living?"

I swallow a mouthful of juice and clear my throat. "I work in security, fitting systems, serving papers, but you already know that." He nods, confirming he does. "Just like I know that you're a former east end gangland boss, London mafia, mob... I don't even know what you guys call yourselves because it's not something I've ever been involved in."

Terry is quietly impressed with my observation. "No, I guess a former, petty drug dealer like you wouldn't, would you?" He picks an underdeveloped apple off one of the trees and passes it to me. "But as you can see, I like a man who does his homework, like I do."

"Touché," I say with a genuine smile, and for some reason, I like him.

We've had a few chats over the afternoon. Namely about the age gap between myself and his cherished granddaughter. Needless to say, he wasn't shocked when I run him through the short, simplified version of mine and Evie's tumultuous relationship. He also wasn't shocked when I confirmed she chased after me, much to my misgivings over her age. He was very shocked, however, when I said I encourage her to follow her dreams and to take chances.

"In my defence, I've lived a respectable life for the last decade. I admit I've made mistakes and hurt people, but just like you, I'm not that man anymore."

"Jeremy, stop talking," he says gruffly. "This isn't an interrogation. I can't play the martyr when I'm no saint myself. Everything you can imagine, I've probably done. However, I want my Evie pie happy, and it's clear you give her that. Granted, if there ever comes a time when she's unhappy..." He shakes his head dramatically. "Well, that's when the real interrogation will begin, and it won't be pretty."

I frown, wondering what an ex-gangland boss uses in an interrogation. Words, weapons, tools of torture...

"Stop thinking, son. And before you ask, no, I don't own a pig farm." He smirks as I pick apart his unexpected endearment. The tension dissipates quickly, and we talk sports, of which I don't support any particular team or watch any one thing. Music is a topic of good similarities and interest, as are films and cars.

"So, what does your mother do?"

"She's a district nurse in the local community where she lives. She has been for as long as I can remember."

"And your father?"

I shrug. "He walked out when I was young. We've never seen him since."

"You were lucky then," he says, watching Andy and his tart. The poor tart who is currently walking around with a dark crimson stain on the front of her pale dress, courtesy of Evie's hatred that she let loose around an hour ago when she feigned fainting and fell with a full glass of merlot. "She got her good." Terry grins and slaps my knee. "That's my girl."

I snicker, but my misplaced pride and approval are stamped on my face. "She did, but maybe you shouldn't encourage her." He gives me a hard stare. "I'm just saying. I'm too old for petulant games, but it makes sense why she's so introverted when it comes to making new friends – she's terrified he'll ruin it."

"Well, you're a good lad, even with all the baggage you carry." He quirks his brow. "Oh, come on, you think I don't know about you? Your past, the drugs, the dead girl, your best friend's wife?"

My mouth falls open and closed. I expected he did, but thinking it and hearing him say it…

"Shut your mouth; you're not catching flies. You've obviously pocketed some coin from it. That's a nice Lexus you've got, son."

I laugh. "I'll tell its owner you like it." He gives me a surprised look. "It was gifted to me, along with my flat. Believe it or not, I didn't pocket anything. After my girlfriend died, I left with whatever little money I had at that time. I'm not rich. I'll probably never live in a house like this, and I won't have a convertible Bentley in the driveway either."

Terry chuckles. "Keeping up appearances. This is the illusion of grandeur, but I respect your honesty. It will be comforting to know that on paper, I live in a four-bed, nineteen-forties semi, yet in reality, I also own a six-bed, mock Tudor mansion and a convertible Bentley." He lifts his glass to mine, and I tap the top.

Holy fuck! I need to stay on the right side of this man. But that may prove impossible in the foreseeable future.

"Does my Evie know about the dead girl?" he asks quietly.

"Yeah, I told her. I wanted her to hate me, but she doesn't. 'Free will', she called it."

Terry inhales, satisfied. "Figures. She'll always envy anyone who has that. She's a good girl though, caring, empathetic."

"She's too good for me."

Terry eyeballs me and shrugs. "Maybe, maybe not. It doesn't matter what you think, she chose you, and that means you don't get a choice. Women rule the roost. The sooner you learn that, the easier your life will be."

A streak of colour is magnificent on the dark horizon, and a slow rumble of thunder echoes from the heavens. A tepid droplet of rain lands on my forehead, evaporating almost instantly before further begin to fall.

The collective sounds of people running for cover fills the night, but I stay put, enjoying the solitude as does Terry.

"You're a man after my own heart," he comments. He's ready to say something further when commotion from behind us disturbs the peaceful serenity of our hiding place.

I angle my body, identical to Terry's, to find Andy Blake lurking in the darkness at the back of the house where they store the bins.

"I told you not to come here!" Andy says to whoever is out there with him.

"And I told you that we do not care!" a man responds, his voice familiar. It's vague, and I've heard it before, but where? "Follow me."

Andy sheepishly paces behind the man with a subdued demeanour that speaks volumes. They stop alongside a distinctive black and burgundy convertible BMW, idling under the streetlight, its exhaust discharging a steady stream of vapour.

I jerk when Terry taps my shoulder. He squeezes himself through a gap in the tree line and furtively moves past the bins, and proceeds down the driveway. I want to ask if he's done this before, but I fear the answer will probably be yes.

"You're stealthy for an old guy." I laugh quietly.

"You have no idea." He winks, unoffended.

He stops just before the privet ends. In an ideal world, this would expose us, but the rain is coming down heavier now, drenching us both to our skin, making our hiding spot more than ideal.

"All the crims together," Terry mutters. I quirk my brow, feeling his eyes on me. "What? It takes one to know one, and you were one too, so you know I'm right." He shakes his head. "At least we don't wear a designer suit like a flashy bastard, trying to disguise what we are."

The car door opens, and Andy edges back. An action that demonstrates his fear. Two men get out and surround him. My breath catches in my throat as the first man steps under the light.

Detective Davies. Ed Shaw's number two.

"What the fuck?" I mutter, disbelieving my eyes.

"You know him?"

I grind my jaw in frustration. "He is - or maybe now was - a copper up in Manchester," I reply.

"Dirty?" Terry asks casually.

"Unquestionably," I reply flatly, remembering the beating he gave me in the cell the night of Em's death.

"And him?" he queries as the second man passes something to Andy, clamps his hand on his shoulder in a clear sign of warning, then he levels his gaze into Blake's eyes.

I stare as he turns, and the light illuminates his face, finally revealing his identity. A sickness rises from the pit of my stomach, staring at the face that has plagued my conscience like the black death for years. I expected his arrival one day, but I never thought Andy Blake would get into bed with him just to see me gone. But I was wrong. His penchant for money, power and status, and the chance to address *Piers Baron Twat* as his son-in-law is, to him, worth the risk. I've underestimated him. I took his threat of making friends and the right incentives today too lightly.

My thoughts are scattered the moment Terry drags me back by my shoulders and grips my nape. "Who is he?"

"Edward Shaw. The dirtiest copper of them all."

I shrug Terry off and pad back to the house. I'm truly soaked to the bone, but my mind is awash with what may or may not come to pass. But of all the uncertainty, I know this: I wasn't wrong when I told Sloan I wouldn't be committed to Evie by August because there's now a very genuine possibility that in a month's time, I might indeed be dead.

Chapter 34

"MORNING, PAUL," I greet today's doorman. He salutes, as per his usual greeting, and holds his palm out. I pass him my car keys and enter the hotel foyer. My purpose here today is logistical, but it also means I can kill two birds with one stone.

"Thank you for staying at The Emerson. Have a safe journey home. Bye-bye," Laura imparts to a guest checking out. I loiter at the end of the reception desk and slide towards her when the coast is clear.

"Morning, Laura," I say with a smile.

She glances up from where she is stowing the key card under the desk. "Hey, Jeremy. Mr Archer is in the restaurant. He's expecting you." She straightens her waistcoat and cravat. "Feel free to indulge in breakfast."

"Lovely, thank you. So, how's life?" I make light conversation. Without warning, she stops abruptly, causing me to walk into her back, and she turns. Her cheeks are bright red – almost as red as Foxy's hair. "Are you okay?"

She mumbles something akin to sorry, and I continue to follow her into the restaurant. The clinking of cutlery, low chatter, and table service completes the background noise. At the far end of the lavish space, Dom is flicking through a newspaper. His usual contacts have been replaced by thick black-framed glasses, which he rarely wears.

"Thanks, Laura. I'll announce myself." I wink at her. "Oh, can you also give us a shout when Kara arrives?"

She nods. "Is Mrs Foster going to be joining you?"

"No, just keep her in the foyer. Thanks." Although if this morning turns out as anticipated, I have no doubt I may finally be exposing Dominic's true identity to her. Especially if she takes offence at being told she has to wait in the foyer of the hotel she now technically owns through marriage.

Today could be a revelation for all of us.

"Sure, Jeremy. Enjoy."

I watch her walk away, then acknowledge Dom, who is tilting his glasses further down his nose, watching with interest, seeing everything in those eye expanding specs. He cocks his head, and I shrug playfully. As I walk towards the breakfast buffet, my mouth waters the closer I get. It isn't every day I can indulge in a five-star breakfast cooked to perfection by a Michelin starred chef. Not that there's anything wrong with the bacon butties from the sandwich van outside WS, of course, since we're the most frequent customers.

"See something you fancy?" Dom queries suggestively behind me. I rotate and meet his gaze as Laura shows another couple into the restaurant.

"Laura?" I shake my head. "She's Foxy's squeeze, but he'll never admit it. I'm perfectly happy with my woman. Well, *branches* of her, anyway."

"Really? Branches? *Interesting.*"

I chortle. "You have no idea." I tong up two sausages and debate a third. "Or maybe you do," I add gleefully and grab some bacon, my mouth salivating in anticipation. "I need to come here for breakfast more often."

Dom grins knowingly and loads his plate up. "Hmm, I think I might have to encourage K to cook when I get back to the office."

"You better make sure you have a cast-iron stomach, son," I retort on a snigger.

We make our way back to the table, and I lay the jacquard cloth napkin over my lap. I am in civilised, wealthy company, after all, and I refuse to let the side down.

"Now, tell me about what's been happening," Dom requests, stirring his tea. I wipe my mouth and put my fork down.

"Do you want the short and sweet or the long and depressing?"

"Amuse me," he replies, glancing at his watch. "I'm not meeting John and Marie until eleven."

I lean back in my chair and gaze over the top of his head. My mouth opens, finally giving him a detailed rundown of everything that has happened these last few months. From Evie being attacked by Piers and the unrepentant retribution I served upon him, to the taunts and threats from Andy, to meeting Evie's beloved grandpy, Terry Cosgrove, the ex-gangland boss. Although, I get the sneaking suspicion that he's not quite as *ex* as I've been led to believe.

"How did you find him?"

I smile automatically. "I like him. He knew all about me, about Em, her death, even my erstwhile drug dealing exploits. Called it doing his homework. He was there when Andy consorted with Ed Shaw and Greg Davies. He even asked me who he was."

"Did he threaten you?"

"No. Believe it or not, he was the perfect gentleman. Just before I took Evie home, he told me if I needed anything..." I leave it hanging between us. Never in a million years did I ever expect to fall into the good graces of a former London crime boss. Especially not with my past and how much he loves his *Evie pie*.

I clasp my palms together, steepling them in front of my mouth. Dom is deep in thought, his eyes saying all the things his mouth isn't.

"And John doesn't know any of it?" he asks sceptically.

I shake my head. "No, and I'd rather keep it that way. He's been so distracted lately; it just didn't feel right to burden him with all my problems on top of his own."

"He won't see it like that. You know I have to tell him, lad," he says, shaking his head.

"I know."

"Have you seen anything of Shaw since?"

"No, but a few days after the party, these were in my post box." I remove the small jiffy envelope from my pocket and put it on the table.

Dom slides it over and removes the cable ties. His brows pitch together further, deepening his frown lines, and he shakes out another napkin and tips the envelope over it. The used syringe containing traces of blood falls to the table, and his frown turns murderous.

"Shaw," he hisses, his jaw grinding from side to side in disgust. He pinches the edges of the fabric and folds up the nefarious objects into a parcel, hiding its contents.

I pick up my fork again, allowing him to process this new information and what, exactly, he plans to do with it. Except, he better expedite it because I fear whatever is brewing in the unknown won't take long to come to fruition.

"Jeremy?" I turn around to find Laura at my back. "Sorry, but Mrs Foster is here." She turns to the doorway, where Kara is waiting with Oliver in her arms and Jules by her side. I stare at Dom, who carefully places the bulging napkin inside his jacket pocket.

"Thanks, Laura." I motion the women over. "Text Sloan and John, let them know Kara and Jules have met you. It'll be easier to smooth over later." Dom pulls out his phone and starts tapping away at the screen.

I rise from my seat, my belly considerably fuller than it was when I first walked in. Whether or not confessing my sins on a full stomach is sensible, however, remains to be seen.

"Good morning, ladies," I greet.

Kara's eyes narrow on Dom, who gets up and moves around the table. She instinctively hugs Oliver to her chest, wary of who this man is, but little does she know she will never find a greater protector or confidante.

"It's nice to finally meet you, Mrs Foster. I'm Dominic Archer. I've been friends with John for nearly twenty years." He holds out his hand, his eyes studying her. Kara looks at his hand, and she drops her arm from around Oliver's back and shakes it reluctantly.

"You too, Mr Archer. This is my son, Oliver." She turns so he can see baby boy's handsome chubby chops. "And this is my mother-in-law, Julia Emerson."

I stand back as Jules comes face to face with the man who faked her death all those years ago. Dom takes an eager step towards her. Jules's cheeks turn a darker shade of pink with each centimetre closing between them.

Dom grins and holds out his hand. "It's nice to meet you, Ms Emerson." He grips her fingers and kisses the back of them.

Jules purses her lips together. "And you, Mr Archer," she replies, sounding weird. "Are you staying in the hotel?"

Dom nods. "I'm in the second penthouse suite."

"Oh, I'm in the first."

"Convenient," he replies lowly, ensnaring her eyes, never releasing them from his gaze.

He leans forward, and I squint, wondering what he's up to. A nudge at my side draws my attention. I glance at Kara, who observes the interaction with interest. He's looking at Jules the way Sloan looks at Kara and the way I look at Evie. Honestly, I might be a man, but even I can feel the attraction simmering between them. It's raw and primal, creating enough smouldering embers that they may eventually spark to life and scorch everyone in the immediate vicinity with the force and intensity of their mutual heat.

Kara clears her throat, ensuring Jules becomes aware of her surroundings again, and she drops her head down. "Jeremy, if you want to spend more time with Mr Archer, we'll be upstairs whenever you're ready."

I share a look with Dom. Even though meeting with him is important, so is this. More so, considering my future is pivotal upon the choice she has finally made and come to terms with.

"Actually, Mrs Foster, I have another meeting scheduled shortly," Dom lies, "so he's all yours. Ladies, it's been lovely to meet you." He smiles at them both but cleverly angles his stance towards Jules. "Hopefully, we will meet again soon. Very soon, indeed." He kisses their hands before sliding his jacket on, and he leaves the restaurant. I make a mental note to call him and reiterate our many conversations about why he cannot conduct a relationship with her.

"So, that's Dominic Archer, then?" Kara comments rhetorically, wearing a sly smile, looking between Jules and me. "He doesn't lack confidence. Then again, none of you do." I raise my brow, wondering where she might have heard his name before. She gives me a shrewd grin, then moves behind Jules. "He's very attractive for an older man, isn't he?" She nudges her mother-in-law, finally snapping her out of the trance she's found herself in. I aim to appear solemn, but I can't stop my smirk from forming.

"What? Oh, sorry, I didn't notice," Jules says, still watching the door with a longing expression. Maybe Dom isn't the only one I need to have a chat with regarding pursuing a relationship that may be doomed from the start.

"No," Kara breathes out, "of course, you didn't. Just don't let Sloan see you like this if he's sticking around. He's overbearing already, and the last thing I want is to hear his *views* again. Once was enough, thanks."

Jules' mouth opens like a fish, but she can't defend that. Kara's right: Sloan is overbearing when things don't go his way. Such as when Jules decided she was going to start dating again. He threw a fit that Oliver would have been ashamed of. He won't be anything less if he gets any misguided image of his mother and Dom in any kind of non-platonic relationship.

"Come here, little man." I change the subject and ease Oliver from his mother's arms as we all board the lift to the penthouse. His little fingers stroke over my beard, and he giggles. "Is that funny?" I ask, pulling a surprised face, then proceed to test out his responses by tickling under his chin. He continues to laugh like a little maniac, distracting his mum, who looks typically uncomfortable, until she turns to me, her eyes curious.

"Did he fake my ID?"

"Which one?" I ask - she did have two, after all.

"Kara Dawson." She looks hopeful that maybe another piece of her life puzzle has just been placed.

I shake my head. "Sorry, you need to ask Marie about that. Dom did the Emma Shaw ID."

"I thought Jake did it?"

I lift my brow and shake my head. "He took the credit for it."

"I see," she whispers. "It makes sense now." She looks at Jules, possibly aware the man faked the woman's death.

The lift stops in the private foyer, and we all step out. Jules opens the penthouse door, but I don't miss her tiny glance at the second door. We enter the suite, that apart from some recent redecoration, is the same as it has always been.

"I'll pop the kettle on." Jules hurries into the kitchen to busy herself.

Kara carefully eases her son from my arms and walks with him towards the large glass window that makes up one wall of the suite.

"You know, I never expected the first time I walked into this suite that all these years later, I would still be here. It was meant to be a one-night stand!" A scoff comes from the kitchen, and I'm also ready to burst out laughing. She gazes down at Oliver, facially identical to his dad, and smiles. "Sloan had other plans, of course. Plans I never thought could – or would - be mine." She turns around and looks at me. "But he gave me life again. For years I was barely breathing, living in a world where no one knew I existed. Now, when I think back to the old me, I can't help but think of you because for years, you've just been breathing, also living in a world where no one outside of our immediate circle knows you exist. Until her. Evie gave you back your life." She turns back to the window, and I absorb her assessment, desperate to tell her it's more accurate than she realises.

I catch Jules in the corner of my eye as she places down three steaming mugs. I didn't request a drink, so it's potluck as to what I'm going to get. Luckily, she slides over a strong coffee.

"After everything that has happened these last few months, it's galvanised the need to be honest with those we love." Kara moves away from the window and sits Oliver in the travel cot. Jules pats the sofa on her opposite side, ensuring she's seated in the middle of us, then she takes both our hands.

Kara picks up the mug, hesitates, and puts it back down. She then takes a breath. "This has been one of the hardest decisions I've ever had to make, and I've gone back and forth with my answer for the last six weeks," she says quietly. "But you have my permission to tell Evie about the night Deacon raped me for the last time and made not only me but also you, the true victims of his depravity." And she's finally just put me out of my misery. "If she doesn't take it well, you also have my permission to tell her to call me, and I will explain."

A lone tear runs down my cheek because the control she's giving me is monumental. She's willingly giving up a piece of herself, so I can finally fix a piece of myself. She is allowing a detrimental and private part of her life to be aired so one day I can sleep easy at night. Ultimately, she's trying to mend my tortured soul. My thoughts are running wild. *Thank you* is on the tip of my tongue, and my mouth opens-

"Jeremy?" Kara asks quietly, tentatively. "The fake ID in the name of Emma Shaw?" My eyes meet hers. "I'd like to hear about the real girl in question. I know she died of an overdose, and I know it's hard, but please."

"Kara," I say, resigned, proving I'm a hypocrite of the worst kind. Not less than five minutes ago, she gave me the green light to divulge her past, but still, I'm sitting here refusing to divulge mine. It's not because I'm being evasive, it's because I don't want her sympathy. I know if I tell her there will be tears and crying, and I can't handle that.

"No!" She grabs my hand when I attempt to turn away. "You always say you need redemption, my forgiveness, but really, that cuts both ways. There isn't anything you don't know about me. Now it's your turn," she orders, constricting my hand in hers.

I stand and pace in front of the travel cot. I gaze down at Oliver, hoping I don't wake him, but I then stop, positive his dad will hit me if he doesn't get his daily nap and is cranky later on. Instead, I edge to the window and press my palm to the glass above my head. I gaze down at the street below.

"I don't know if you know, but I didn't live too far from you in Manchester. Deacon and I had a really shitty place." I glimpse over my shoulder. Kara looks uncomfortable, probably because I've said the devil's name aloud.

"About nine months before *that* night, Emma died of an overdose." I sigh, aware I can't start my psychological purging here. "But in order to understand properly, I need to take you back to the first time I ever saw her." Sitting back down, I pick up the mug and nurse it in my hands, needing something to control their idleness for the next hour or so. Or for however long it takes until forgiveness finally releases me from this invisible prison I've built around myself for the last decade.

I INHALE AND slowly exhale, wondering where I now stand, considering I've just verbally cleansed my soul.

"How do you come back from something like that?" Kara queries softly, her tone pained.

A muffled sob from the fireplace, where Jules is rocking Oliver in her arms – after confessing that she needed to hold him – accompanies the returning silence.

"You don't," I eventually tell her. "You can't. When we first met, Kara, that day in your flat with Sam, I couldn't look you in the eye because I was positive you would remember me. Dea-" I stop myself. "*He* assured me that you wouldn't. Even Sloan had said the same, but as much as I wanted to believe it, I couldn't put my faith in that. And I was right because the way you looked at us... A part of you did remember. It was faint, a vague recollection, a subconscious memory. All it would have taken was a few appropriately timed innuendoes, and it would've transported you back to that time. It's the same with Emma. For years, I never dreamed of her. But the day I returned here last year, months after the final assault, I was sitting on my balcony looking at her picture, and it all came flooding back."

"Does Evie know about Emma?" Jules asks as she moves towards the window with Oliver, now wide-awake and grumbling.

I breathe heavily. "Yes," I whisper. I don't want them to feel put out that I told her and not them. "She told me it wasn't my fault."

"She's right; it wasn't," Jules replies. "How did she take it?" She passes Oliver to his mum and sits back down next to me, leaving the gap between Kara and me empty.

"She was shocked, naturally, but she said Emma had a choice and-" I'm cut off by three mobiles and the penthouse landline all ringing simultaneously.

"What the heck?" Kara mutters, pulling out her phone the same moment Jules does.

A constant knocking erupts on the door, and I bring my phone to my ear as I stride towards it. "Hello?" I answer, not recognising the number.

"Jer, it's me," Doc replies, sounding shocked, yet subdued. "John asked me to call you. Marie's in hospital. She was attacked by her ex-husband this afternoon."

"What?" I reply, lost for words, opening the door. In my peripheral hearing, Jules and Kara are having the same conversations separately.

"Dead! Who's dead?" Jules asks urgently, already getting her coat on.

"Oh, my God, I can't breathe! Is she alive?" Kara is distraught at whoever is calling her.

James and Laura are still waiting in the foyer, their expressions devastated, obviously here to impart the same news. No doubt John, or possibly Dom, made one call to the office and said to pass it on.

"Hang on, Doc," I say and step to the duo. "We've just heard."

Laura's eyes water, and James wraps his arm around her. "Will you let us know when you hear anything further?"

I nod, impart thanks, and close the door. "Sorry, Stu. How's it looking?" I turn away, daring to ask the question that no one else will probably have the courage to. "Is she alive?"

"Yeah, but it doesn't look good, Jer. She went down a full flight of stairs holding on to her ex. Before she lost conciseness, she said she couldn't feel her legs. She's currently in surgery."

"Fucking hell! Where's her ex now?" I ask because if he's in the hospital also getting treatment, I can guarantee he won't be breathing for much longer if John gets his hands on him.

"He's dead," Doc replies in a whisper, breaching data protection and every other privacy rule and regulation in effect within the NHS.

"Fuck! How's John? Have you seen him?"

"He's ready to end the world. The police have already said they'll arrest him if he starts creating. Dom's here with him. I'm calling you because you can't let Kara come here. I know she'll want to, but M's still out of it, and she won't be able to see her anyway. The last thing anyone needs is both her and John here working each other into a frenzy. I've already called Sloan. Just keep her away, okay?"

"Sure. Keep me informed," I whisper and hang up, unsure how I'm going to hold her back.

Kara dashes towards me and grabs my jacket. "Sloan's on his way over from the office. Marie's ex-husband attacked her in our old house. She could be paralysed! She could be dying! I need to go to her! I need to be there! Jules, would you look after Oliver?" She's flinging on her jacket and gathering up her bag and belongings.

"Honey, you can't go. Doc just said they won't let you see her." Kara struggles out of my arms, and I drag her back. "No! You can't see her yet." Kara's eyes glisten, the whites now sore and red. Her tears, now fully-fledged, begin to fall faster, and she drops to her knees in front of me, her bag hitting the floor with a thud. I pull her back up. She needs to hold it together, if not for her, but for her boy.

"I'm sorry for shouting at you, but you can't go."

"But I need to. If anything happens, and I don't get a chance... What will I do if she doesn't make it?"

"She'll make it, honey," I say, smoothing her hair, holding her close. "She's strong. She's going to pull through." I'm lying to her because I don't know what's going to happen. Still, I have to say something. That woman is her rock, and if she doesn't make it... I can't even begin to comprehend the fallout. Marie has to survive. She has to.

Jules approaches with Oliver, and the four of us huddle together until the door opens and Sloan walks in. He gives me an ominous look that speaks volumes. Then he embraces his wife and son with one arm and his mother with the other.

I loiter in front of the window, blocking out the tears and heartbreak behind me. My phone buzzes in my pocket, and I swipe the screen. Two texts are waiting. One from Evie, and another from my mother, who I haven't seen in a couple of months. I leave Evie's message unread for now and reply to my mother, asking if she has some free time today for a coffee and a catch-up. Her reply to come over is almost instant, and as soon as I know Marie is going to be okay, I'll be checking on my own rock. Because if today has proven anything, it's how precious life is.

And how quickly our past misdemeanours can ensure our futures are flawed and uncertain.

Chapter 35

I RAISE THE mug to my lips, mesmerised by the light patter of rain splattering against the windowpane. The clouds move slowly overhead, exposing the sun, confirming today's forecast of sunny and warm may indeed materialise, compelling me to sit and stare. Not that I have anywhere else to be since I dropped Evie off to meet her friends for brunch and shopping this morning, *and* it's also a workday.

Pressing the rim to my lips in contemplation, my grey matter is working overtime. These last few days have been hard, and some of us are still feeling the effects worse than others. Marie is still in hospital, but Stuart has personally informed me she's no longer ready to rip him a new one. I chuckle rhetorically. I would've loved to have been a fly on the wall when she discovered she was all tubed up with nowhere to go. I continue to ruminate in deliberation, aware I need to put in an appearance. If not, Stuart won't be the only one on her shit list. However, according to Jules, today is ladies' day, so I'll probably grace M with my presence this evening or tomorrow.

I swallow another mouthful of tea when the door opens, and John's utterly focused entrance abates. His expression is one of disbelief - his mouth unable to express his surprise, considering it's stuffed with half a croissant.

"Last time I checked, this was my office," he says around the mouthful of masticated pastry.

I shrug, having long ago failed to be afraid of his half-arsed threats. "Last time I checked, life was simple."

He snorts and sits in the seat opposite his usual. "Wishful thinking. Although history has proven time and time again that our lives are never simple. Yours especially." He points his mug at me, and I have to agree there's a certain truth to that statement.

"I thought you'd be at the hospital?" I ask not to divert any conversation that may arise from the burgeoning tension, but just in simple query.

"No, the women are going over," he grimaces, "so I thought I'd have a breather. Besides, I've got something coming." He throws his feet atop his desk and lounges back. His stance is relaxed, but I'm not an idiot. I'm aware Dom's probably already filled him in, but John – just like Dom – likes to hear it first-hand. He likes a man to confess his sins and respects him when he accepts ownership.

I spin the chair around from the window, so he's no longer in my marginal vision. With my elbows on the desk, my forearms aligned, and my hands clasped, he finally breaks the tension. "Dom and I had a fairly lengthy chat before he left yesterday."

Well, that was as expected, and now it's my turn. "John, I've not been entirely truthful, and I owe you that courtesy now. There was so much was going on with you and Marie, I just didn't want to heap more shit on your plate," I confess, my eyes lazily cataloguing the room I've spent countless hours in.

In this room, I've been judge, jury, and executioner. I've listened. I've learned. I've argued and debated, and I've sat in the chair opposite while the man occupying it has lectured me on how I'm living – or wasting – my life. Now I'm sitting here as master and commander of my fate, and this morning I shall be the confessor of my sins.

I open my mouth, but it closes when the slam of the security doors echoes, then it is almost drowned out by the thudding and stomping of feet.

John rolls his eyes, and his brow furrows. He pushes up from his seat, strides across the room and opens the door. Voices rise and lower as he addresses whoever is, unfortunately, first in the assembly outside, and he closes the door again. Reclaiming his seat, he commences his laid-back pose, picks up his coffee, and waits for me to purge.

The atmosphere between us is heavy, but stalling won't save me. I've already spoken the hard part, but my heartache will not be vanquished until I release myself completely.

"I need to tell you what's been happening these last six weeks. Well, months, really." The words leaving my mouth ensure I'm experiencing déjà vu. The setting might be different, but the content of my confession is not. It will also be the second time in as many days that my lips have spilt these words. Unravelling my truth once more, I offer him an identical confession to that I bestowed upon Dom. "It all started months ago when my flat was broken into. Nothing was taken, but the place was ransacked, and then I found Emma's picture on the floor with a bag of heroin stashed beneath it." John's lids raise, and his mouth opens in shock. I continue rather than allow him to placate me. "I thought it was kids, possibly an opportunist burglary, but-"

"When?" He derails my train of thought.

I inhale deeply and prepare for the fallout. "Just before Oliver's christening."

His face drops, and I wait for the fireworks to explode. "Are you fucking kidding me?" he shouts. "That was months ago! Please explain why I'm only hearing about this now?"

"Because you had your own shit to deal with! Because I asked the guys not to say anything!" I shout back but realise the error of my ways.

He leans forward, both hands on his desk, his face a picture of furious disappointment. "They all knew?" I nod. "Even Park?" I nod again. "Well, I guess I must thank him for showing restraint and respect for your wishes. Usually, that lad can't hold his own piss! But you?" He thumps the desk with the side of his fist. "You, I expected better from. Over the years, I've bent over backwards to accommodate you and your predicaments, and this is how you repay me? By lying to me?" He pushes up from the desk.

"I didn't lie!" I also rise up, now nose to nose with him.

He growls. "But you didn't *not* lie, either!"

I huff and shift to the window. I lay my forearm across the glass and lean in to it, the cool pane chilling my skin. "For as long as I've known you, you've run after us, picked up our shit, and dealt with the consequences of our actions." I sigh. "For once in my troubled life, I didn't want to burden you, especially with something that may bring unwanted attention to your door."

John's chair creaks, and his formidable presence fills my personal space. I rotate and sit on the wide windowsill, my body half angled to observe the concrete landscape, peppered with green spaces, spreading into the distance.

He sits and wraps his hand around the back of my neck, manipulating me closer. "I commend your act of altruism, but I think with a friend in high places and another scraping the barrel at times," he says, amused, referring to Sloan and Dominic, "I think there may already be unwanted attention watching my door. And if there isn't, well, my wife's ex-father-in-law is a judge who is out for blood for his bastard son, so I'm positive my door is already marked and on someone's radar." He plucks his phone from his pocket, taps the screen, and brings it to his ear. "Park, coffee times two, now!" he orders and puts it back down. I grin as the sound of Park huffing and puffing a few choice words a couple of rooms over seeps through the dilapidated walls.

"No wonder he's lacking confidence," I mutter, unable to suppress my laugh. John gives me a broad smile. "But he won't be lacking anything with your size eleven up his arse!"

"Absolutely. Now," he says, "start at the beginning."

My deep inhalation floats over the tension. J pats my knee, giving me encouraging comfort. I start as requested, elaborating more about the burglary. I reach into my pocket and pass him one of the spare keys I ordered. I then lodge my head against the glass and recant the garden party, Terry Cosgrove, Andy Blake's snide comments, and finally, the real issue – the re-emergence of Edward Shaw.

"Did he see you?" he asks, sipping the coffee that Park brought in somewhere between the garden party and Terry Cosgrove.

I shrug. "I don't know, but a few days later, a used syringe and a packet of cable ties virtually identical to the one's Deacon-" My voice falters, and I shudder. "They were in my post box."

John's head repeatedly bounces, his wheels turning behind his eyes. "I appreciate Dom's legged it back up the M1 to his precious Yorkshire, but we need to discuss this, maybe even get Kieran down here to keep an eye on you."

I scoff in indignation. "I don't need the scally scouse to babysit me."

"No, but *I* need him to, because if anything ever happened to you-" He touches his heart. "It would kill me, Rem. My world may be a frequently complicated place with you in it, but I refuse to imagine one where you're *not* in it. So, if that means our Viking Scouse has to drive his arse south and sleeps in the same bed as you, you will tolerate it."

I'm about to backchat about three in a bed, Evie's possessive nature, and how she won't share when the landline rings.

"Perfect timing!" John reaches over to pick up the handset. "Good morning, Reverend," he says, and I furrow my brow. Why a Reverend would be calling here, I have no idea. This place is as far removed from holy as one can get – just ask Kara about the ungodly conversations over blueprints and invoices. Not to mention, John is so far from pious, it might as well exist in an alternative universe. "I can pick you up when you arrive." He offers, rattling off the address.

The jovial chat continues, and I screw my face up. I'm not noisy, but I want to know what I'm missing. John then shows me his back, and the call becomes vaguer, although I don't miss him asking something about a Victoria sponge cake and the Women's Institute.

"If you do, I swear I'll say grace in return." He then grins like a Cheshire cat. "God bless you, Maggie. I'll see you soon."

I shift on the sill, popping my ankle over my knee and cross my arms. "Who was that?" I ask the moment the handset hits the base.

"Nobody!" he replies quickly. "And you're changing the subject."

I tut. "Says the man talking to *Maggie* about cakes, the Women's Institute, and saying grace. And I'll have you know the phone changed the subject, you evasive sod!"

"Fine!" He grins. "You'll find out soon enough. Let's just say she's a gift from God." He smiles gloriously, and I wonder what he's up to. He strides to the door and shouts for someone to buy some fresh milk and good biscuits ASAP. He turns back around, and his smirk widens. "Oh, and between you and me, you won't be seeing double!"

"What do you mean?" I query as he leaves the room, leaving his mystifying comment to hang in the ether, ready to be solved.

Not that the challenge isn't worth a good biscuit or two, of course.

THE RADIO PLAYS to itself in the background as I shade in the plans Tommy's been working on this morning. After my awkward chat with John, I've indulged myself in work, and he's shut himself in his office, awaiting his gift from God.

"Tea?" Tommy asks.

"Sure, but Park still hasn't returned yet," I say, noting the corner shop is a five-minute walk around the corner at the petrol station.

Tommy chuckles as the security doors bang and Dev and Jake enter, having done an hour-long sandwich run – to the sandwich van within spitting distance outside.

"Did you get John's, plus one?" I ask, still eager to find out what's going on. Cakes, Women's Institute, Reverends, fresh milk, and an extra sandwich?

"Yep, has he come clean yet?"

I shake my head. "Nope, but I have a gut feeling that whatever we're waiting on will be a game-changer."

"That might just be a water infection. Or the phantom sensation of John's size eleven up your arse!" Park says as he enters.

405

"Finally! Did you have to milk the bloody cow, son?" I ask sarcastically as the landline begins to ring, accompanied by the doorbell chiming through the building.

"Expecting someone?" Tommy puts three mugs of black tea and coffee on the plans, and I afford him a death glare.

"No, but if you've got tea rings on these, you're going to need a vicar!"

"Park, make yourself useful, answer the door!" I jerk my head.

"No, that's for me! Park, fresh tea, now!" John takes off at speed, the heavy fire doors slamming in his wake as the bell resounds again.

Park scoffs. "Is it pick on Si day? I'm not the bloody tea lady! Someone get on the blower and call Girl Friday."

"That's misogyny." Tommy shares a look of disbelief with us. "Is J going to personally answer the door?"

"Apparently so." I eyeball each; their suspicious squints fixed on me. "Don't look at me like that. I don't know what's going on. He's been acting funny all morning," I mutter, but I think we're going to find out why imminently.

The distinctive sound of the rickety elevator kicks in, and I wait with undisguised anticipation to see what's about to be revealed. I'm guessing 'Maggie', whoever she is, will be the epicentre.

The lift groans to a stop, and John's voice fills the corridor as he explains to our unknown visitor what we do here. The air is full of concern and expectation. Finally, the door opens, and the guys all turn. The tension dissipates when they realise it's just Marie.

Only, this isn't M.

A chorus of 'Hi, Marie', 'why aren't you still in the hospital?', 'when did Doc release you from prison?', all ask over each other. I meet John's eyes above the clamour and share a knowing nod. I'm not seeing double, and it's undeniably clear this lady and Marie are more than related – they're one in the same person.

Maggie smiles, looking between Tommy, Dev and Jake, but she doesn't correct them. Instead, she removes her coat and scarf, unveiling the clerical collar, causing all three to baulk. The penny slowly drops, and Maggie introduces herself to each subdued man in turn. The trio all step back when Park returns carrying a tray of tea, including a teapot, sugar bowl and milk jug, and the elusive good biscuits. His eyes flick up as he breezes past, not seeing the varied expressions or John's very satisfied grin.

"Did someone arrange doorstop confession?" He puts the tray down." You could be here a while as we purge our sins, especially his!" He empties the tray, inclining his head towards me. He rights himself and gives me a broad grin. "Right?"

John clamps his hand on Park's shoulder. "Right. And this lady may be interring you under the shoddy tarmac outside if you piss me off further!"

A feminine sigh floats over us. "It's fine, John. Really," she says. And not only does she look identical to Marie, but she also sounds identical too. "But is that what you do to insubordinate boys here?"

Park chuckles. "Oh, Marie! When did you get here? And what's with the get-up?" His eyes flick to John, and he leans closer to him. "Is this some kind of kinky Walker fantasy?"

John tightens his hold on the scruff of his neck. "Parker! Apologise to Reverend Booth, now!"

She shakes her head with a smile and digs into her overnight bag as Park's awareness comes to fruition, and he stares in shock. "Holy shit, someone must really hate me!"

John cuffs him on the head. "Language!"

"But there's two of them! Someone up there is conspiring against me!"

"Just someone?" J mutters sarcastically, and we all snigger.

"Persona non grata!" he says. Maggie turns around and holds a Tupperware box containing what looks like Victoria Sponge Cake. Park's eyes widen, and we all take a step forward.

"Anyone touches that, and we'll be having an afternoon burial!" John states, reaching across for the box and places it on the desk away from everyone else. Maggie grins and reaches back into the bag, and reveals a box of brownies. She holds them out to Park.

"So, would you like a brownie while you confess your sins and tell me why you feel so unappreciated?" She takes his hand in hers.

Park gives John a victorious, gleeful look. "Why, yes, I think I would, Reverend Booth. And it's not so much that I feel unappreciated; I feel unloved." His face then saddens in self sympathy, really milking it for all its worth. I silently scoff and laugh, but Maggie has him figured out.

"Call me Magdalene or Maggie. If you haven't twigged, Marianne and I are twins." Park nods, his woeful expression indicating he's most definitely twigged that there's two of them to put the fear of God into him now. One more literal than the other, I might add.

Hence why he's aiming to get her on side. However, if there's one thing he's definitely twigged, it's that at least this one won't put him in a penguin suit. Now, a dress in the front of the choir is a possibility he hasn't quite grasped. *Yet.*

"This is a good brownie, Rev," Jake says, stuffing his second into his mouth.

Maggie stirs the cup of tea she's just poured for herself. "I'll inform the WI ladies they were highly praised. They may even bake you some more." A chorus of approval sings out around her. At some point, she'll stop promising the greedy gits cakes and treats when she figures out they don't last longer than thirty minutes in this office. She looks at John, who is still hiding the box of Victoria Sponge – his favourite – and tilts her brow, identical to Marie. Poor J. He looks admonished enough to pass it over. *Grudgingly.*

"Christ, that's fuc- flipping freaky!" Tommy says. Maggie gives him a calculating smile identical to the one Marie usually gives him and Park before she puts them in suits and tells them to serve the petit fours.

"Thomas, I'll forgive you for taking the Lord's name in vain." She crosses herself with a resigned sigh, then her lips curve, and she grins. "John? Earlier you mentioned lunch? I always believe interring and burials are better performed on full stomachs. Depending on how you're participating, of course." With a straight face, she takes another sip of tea, failing to recognise – or blatantly ignoring – the shocked expressions of all present, except John, who is ready to roll around on the floor laughing.

"She has a unique sense of humour which doesn't compliment the profession. Maggie, we've only got sandwiches from the deli van outside, but-"

"That would be lovely. Gentlemen?" All eyes give her their full attention. "I was only joking about the interring and burials. However, as I told John when we first met, you need not fear; I won't indoctrinate you all until the next visit."

A chunk of brownie flies in front of my face. Jake begins to cough and splutter in shock, his hands at his throat, while Maggie recommences sipping her tea, very prim and proper.

"Don't choke, Jacob," she says, passing him some napkins and a bottle of water from the desk. "I already have a busy afternoon scheduled."

I laugh, push up from the desk due to my arse being numb, and subtly tip my head at John. His recognisable gait follows me along the corridor and into the kitchen. I remove the sandwiches from the fridge and proceed to grab the plates to make us all appear civilised.

"Well, your gift from God is…interesting."

"Hmm, isn't she just."

"So, how long have you known about her?"

"Since the day after you left us in Peterborough."

My mouth falls open. I rotate and grind my jaw. "And you didn't think to tell us? Does Kara know?"

He shakes his head. "No, she'll find out shortly." He takes the cheese and onion sandwich he requested for Maggie, along with a bottle of chilled water. "Don't bother with the plates, she's not precious, and she's going to see Marie shortly. She's also going to stay for a few days, and I said we'd all have dinner, so make sure you bring little miss."

"We'll be there," I say, also finally twigging. "Will you be saying *grace* at dinner?" I ask sarcastically. He rewards me with a pouty smirk, reminding me of something else. "On a different note, you're going to give Park a complex if you don't ease up." John's head jerks. "You were harder on him today than usual. I know he's your favourite, but he doesn't, so just ease up, okay?"

His jaw grinds thoughtfully. "He keeps me on my toes, makes me smile, warms my heart, but I don't have favourites." My forehead lifts into my hairline; he's a lying sod. "I'm unnecessarily hard on you all sometimes, but it's because I love you. All of you, and if that means I have to be hard to keep you in line, so be it. I'm an equal opportunities hard arse, after all."

I chuckle and shake my head. I put Maggie's sandwich and a bottle of water into one of the many paper bags we have spare from the van outside, ready for her to take away.

"Anyway, you've got no room to talk. We all know you're Dom's favourite."

I push open the door, my lunch in one hand, Maggie's in the other. "Yeah, but maybe that's because I'm the only idiot who sticks around Yorkshire long enough to tolerate him. It isn't favouritism; it's convenience and lack of options."

"Call it whatever you like, sunshine, but you'll have more than enough time to debate this with *he* who knows you both best."

I halt and turn back to John, sauntering behind me, looking smug. I slam my hand on the wall to impede his journey. "What have you done?" I ask with accusatory calm. He's trying my last nerve today.

He shrugs and pats my chest. "Let's just say, this morning has been informative, and you'll have plenty of time to discuss the finer points of that particular conversation with a certain scally scouse in the foreseeable." He rubs his chin between his finger and thumb, and I narrow my eyes. He's a meddlesome sod. "As a matter of fact, if Andy Blake was worried about his little precious being corrupted, he's going to have a heart attack when he finds out you're not the only man in the house. I think it could get very cosy with you, Evie, and Kieran. Unless one rolls over, and little miss falls out!" He ducks under my arm and starts to hum the nursery rhyme as he takes Maggie's lunch and strides back into the mess room.

I shake my head with a mixture of dismay, amusement and horror. Evie's already met Kieran, but how I'm going to explain his extended stay - especially if he's intending on staying at the flat - is another obstacle I'm going to have to navigate with her.

Except a part of me is relieved. At least there's a small chance I'll have the man-mountain at my back whenever Andy Blake decides he's had enough and finally starts to twist the knife in it.

Chapter 36

THE TOILET FLUSHING resonates through the bedroom wall, followed by whistling. The jolly, infernal whistling I had all but forgotten about. Or maybe I've just developed a selective memory over the course of the last year that I've not had to deal with him on a daily basis.

The shower then turns on, and humming replaces the whistling. Again, my selective memory has scrubbed away the time we once lived together from the recesses of my brain.

I stare at the ceiling unimpressed, grinding my jaw. The desire to put my fist in his face is obscene, but that would mean I actually have to get up, and quite frankly, after weeks of his presence lingering like an unwanted smell, my objective will be futile.

The water shuts off, and movement commences. Evie stirs beside me, and I pull her closer.

"What time is it?" she mumbles, yawning. She stretches her arm out, arches her back and presses her chest up.

"It's just gone half six," I tell her as the bathroom light pull clicks off and a heavy stature treads from the bathroom and stops outside the door.

"Wakey, wakey, little lovers!" Kieran laughs as he proceeds into the other bedroom and closes the door.

Evie leans over and turns on the bedside light. She gives me a sly grin, then pins me down and straddles my hips. I smooth my hands over her tiny crop top, stalling them at the sides of her breasts, my thumbs grazing the hard tips lightly. She sighs beautifully.

"Oh, that always feels good!" she moans, but the moment is lost as Kieran starts to sing *The Beatles' I Am the Walrus.*

"I know he's one of your closest friends, and as much as I enjoy learning the finer and filthier, words our Liverpudlian guest can teach me, how long he is staying?"

I flip her over. "No idea, but I'll see if I can get John or someone to put him up for a night or two, if you want?" My suggestion is in good faith, but I have a feeling nothing with come of it since I can't imagine the others will be forthcoming in agreeing.

In the few weeks Kieran's been here, he's done the rounds around the houses, quite literally, although he's already said his preference is to stay here or at the hotel. He did try for a few nights at the mansion since it has a pool, gym, stunning gardens, and surrounding countryside, but Sloan vetoed it. He reasoned his wife is still very fragile due to Marie's assault, claiming it brought back memories. Truthfully, he didn't want to address K's identity and why Evie has already met him when Kara hasn't. I can easily say I wouldn't like to be in his shoes when Kara finds out she's being kept in the dark again.

Evie smiles, but it disintegrates almost as quickly. "It's fine. Besides, Marie is still recovering. I'm sure her and John are in more need of their personal space than I'm in need of a body shattering orgasm."

I slide my hand under her pyjama shorts. "True, but now you've said it, *I* need to see you have a body shattering orgasm." I ease my finger beneath the flimsy material and find her already wet and wanting.

"But Kie-"

"Don't think about him, but think of this as an appetiser. I'm sure I can find him a temporary home this afternoon so we can have our flat back. Just ensure you're ready when I call."

"Our flat? That's the first time you've ever referred to it as my home as well as yours."

I smile but don't take the bait. I claim her lips as I stroke my fingers over her swollen flesh, simultaneously teasing her clit. I slide my tongue against hers before licking the inside of her cheek. My fingers rim her opening, replicating what I'm doing to her mouth before I work them inside her heat. Thrusting them into the tightness, continuing to tease her hard nub, her distended nipples point at my chest. I swipe my tongue again then move down to her breast. Kissing her through the vest, I pull it down to capture her perky tit in my palm. Reverently sucking her nipple, she moans low, and I grin, loving the build-up. I alternate my care and attention, tasting the other. My fingers play harder while my groin begins to advance beyond uncomfortable. Inside, I'm desperate for release.

She gives me a turned on, sultry look, and I gasp when her tormenting hand encompasses my hard shaft. Her fingertip circles the head, and she pumps from base to tip. Over and over, making me want more and more. "Your fingers are good, but I'd rather have this inside me."

I groan. "So are yours, and so would I," I agree as noise emanates from next door.

"Do you think he can hear us?" she asks in a panicked whisper.

I laugh. "I think so!" I reply in the same tone. She attempts to move my hand, but I stop and stroke her face. "Do you really want me to stop? I will, but I-"

She puts her finger over my lip, pushing it inside, and I suck it.

"Maybe just a quick touch. I promise I'll come quietly," she whispers. I chuckle as her centre twitches in silent response and approval.

"Sweetheart, we've had this conversation before, it's never quick, and it's never just a touch. And you couldn't come quietly if you tried!" And to prove it, I extract then reinsert my fingers deeper and harder into her heat while her moans grow louder. I seal my mouth over hers again to quell her enthusiasm.

Evie's eyes remain on mine as she gives herself to me, allowing me to do what I like. Her hair is spread out over the pillow, her skin is slick with perspiration, and her eyes are sparkling, the only way they can when she's turned on.

My fingers stimulate her to perfection until, eventually, her core clenches and pulsates, and she writhes with unadulterated gratification. It's a sight to behold, but I never want her to be ashamed to let go like this. Her hand gently plays with my very happy dick, which is desperate for release, but I won't until she does. As painful as it is to wait, the end result is always spectacular.

"I love you." She bites her lip, and her eyes turn smoky.

"I love you too, sweetheart. Always. I don't think I could stop if I tried. I don't think I'd even know how to."

Her eyes begin to water, and she grips my cheek with her free hand and pulls me to her for a kiss. Her core is throbbing wickedly, and she releases my mouth and touches hers to my ear. "Come with me."

I grin and allow myself to release simultaneously with her. Her beautiful, breathless mixture of muted cries, low moans, and further declaration of love fills my ear as I come apart and, unfortunately, on her hand.

Time stands still as we come down from the afterglow of the quietest lovemaking she's ever managed to participate in, and I pull her over my front. I grip her sticky hand and rub it over my boxers. She kisses me passionately, giggling between kisses, continuing her teasing. She leans back with a mischievous grin and places my hands back on her tits.

Honestly, it's like I've died and gone to heaven, but I know that my venture into paradise is going to be cut off prematurely.

"Breakfast!" Kieran bangs on the door, causing us both to jolt in shock. I laugh as Evie attempts to throw herself over the side of the bed along with the duvet.

"He's not going to come in. He knows better than that." I circle her nipples, earning myself another lazy, smoky-eyed expression.

"Do you really think you can get him adopted out? Even just for a night?"

I nod. "Even if I have to pay for a hotel."

"Good, because I don't want another quick touch. I want to rediscover every inch of you. I want us to be messy and dirty, and I want to tell you how much I love you while you do it all to me."

"Come up for air! Breakfast is burning!" Kieran calls again, and I gently ease her off me and swing my legs over the bed.

She writhes her lush body up and down like a cat, tempting me with all her skimpy clothed but tits-still-out glory. I pull her up and cradle her face. "Considering you look like a woman who's just done very naughty things-" the unique scent of her skin stalls my statement, "and you smell divine with it, I would suggest a shower then clothes."

"Join me?" she pleads as I cover up her breasts.

"Not unless you want him banging on the door again."

"Fine, but you owe me," she grumbles, sliding on her robe. "You were right, by the way." She gives me an innocent, pouty look. "I can't come quietly."

I chuckle. "I know, and trust me, I love hearing you loud and proud."

"Well, thank goodness for that," she replies, opening the door. "Because being quiet almost flipping killed me!"

THE SMACK OF flesh on the leather jab mitt adds to the sounds of the cars passing by and the crusher being operated at the scrappers around the corner. The morning has brightened significantly and has developed into the perfect August day. The sun is bright and warm, and the sky is a splendid azure blue.

"Again, Remy lad!" Kieran grits his teeth as I put my full weight into the hit, forcing him to stumble. "Nice!" He steps back and picks up his bottle of water from the picnic table in the yard. "I've got to say, if this is what a little morning loving with little miss does, you need to get your leg over more often!"

I growl and swing my clenched hand out, not stopping until the sound fills the atmosphere, and Kieran is falling backwards for the second time in as many minutes.

"Don't talk about her like that. I don't like it. As a matter of fact, I absolutely detest it!"

"Touchy, but I have to live vicariously through someone. Dom's dolly birds aren't up to much, and these days he's either turning up with a different one every other day or, get this, some weeks it's almost like he's suffering an attack of conscience and doesn't go anywhere! That's a good hit, lad!" he compliments, his hand to his cheek, working his jaw from side to side. "Just so you know, I don't think of little miss like that, and I never have. I like the girl. She's good for you. Loosens you up, gives you a reason to live. Besides, you'll both be happy to know I've got a date tonight with a certain other little miss, Holly, Evie's mate. I'd like to say I might be home late, but in truth, I won't be home at all. Sloan's booked me into the hotel for the night. I figured I might get lucky, but also that you two need some alone time." I'm about to lie and refute it, but he cocks his head, challenging me to.

My phone buzzes on the table, and I flick the screen while swigging my water, debating whether it's safe to read the delights that Sloan has to impart this morning. "Fancy a trip to E&F?"

"The king having problems?" K queries knowingly.

"Not necessarily," I confirm, re-reading the message again. "But he might if he sticks me in a tight spot again."

"Hmm, you're well-acquainted with those this morning." He winks, and I scowl at his back as he throws me a towel and my t-shirt. "Let's go, lad."

"JESUS! THERE ARE some right shitholes up north, but this takes the cake!" Kieran exclaims, his eyes taking a respite from scrutinising the wing mirror long enough to observe the current panorama as we drive through some of the more rough and ready parts of the city.

"It's not all multi-million-pound mansions, high-powered sports cars and fancy restaurants. Most are barely living above the breadline," I clarify, but he doesn't need to tell me about shitholes. In every city, in every country, there are less than desirable places – some more than others.

I depress the brake pedal and shift gears as the traffic slows ahead. I stretch my neck and catch K tapping the mirror with further interest again.

"Have you guys ever heard anything from Black?"

"No," I reply. "He took Sloan's payoff and disappeared. He didn't even return when Deacon was dropped into an unmarked grave." I slowly inch the car forward.

"Not surprising." He pauses for a beat. "Do you think he'll come back?"

I shrug. "Possibly. I guess it depends how long it takes for the money to run dry. Why do you ask?"

"Just wondering," he replies. I give him a subtle glance, but I don't miss his suspicious tone before he returns to staring into the mirror again.

When the traffic stops, I adjust my mirrors. Scanning the cars behind, I notice a distinctive convertible BMW. I grind my jaw, but I knew it was only a matter of time. But while there may be thousands of convertible Beamer's in this city, I don't believe in coincidences.

I maintain a steady speed, and although the journey is only ten minutes longer than usual, it allows me the unsolicited luxury of knowing the occupants of the car are following us. Eventually, Emerson and Foster comes into view, and I drive down the ramp to the underground car park and wait for the barrier to lift. I train my eyes on the rear-view mirror as the suspect car also manoeuvres down the ramp. It's so close; its front is almost touching my back. I drive through, then brake hard, leaving just enough room for the barrier to drop behind us.

"What are you doing?" Kieran asks, confused.

"I'm ensuring our *friend* can't follow us." I glance over my shoulder.

K's expression darkens, and he climbs out and slams the door. He starts to walk towards the car, but the driver reverses back up the ramp and skids onto the street before speeding away.

I manoeuvre forward and reverse into one of the reserved spaces. Climbing out, Kieran is already waiting, giving Sloan's Aston an appreciative once over. I stride to the lift and press the button. Stepping inside - almost as if I'm on autopilot - I stare ahead.

A hand moves in front of my face, and fingers snap repeatedly. "You okay?" K's brows furrow and he motions his hand to the open door.

"Fine," I mutter.

"Sure? You look like you've seen a ghost," he says, entering the foyer.

"Yeah," I whisper as the glass door swings shut behind him. "Ghosts of Moss Side." Following him a minute later, the first thing I see is Sophie is standing behind the desk, phone in her hand, glaring at Kieran. "What have you said?"

"Me?" Soph retorts aghast, while Kieran simultaneously says "nothing!" They both glare at each other, then at me, unsure to whom I'm referring. Although both is probably legitimate right now.

I roll my eyes, exasperated. "Sophie, meet Kieran Hyde, a good friend of the family. K, meet Sophie Morgan, Sloan's PA, also a good friend of the family."

Sophie lets out a dramatic breath. "It's a bloody good job you know him!" She places the phone down. "I was about to call security."

Kieran steps back, horrified. "You cheeky cow!"

Sophie flips her highlighted hair back, disregarding him. "Sloan's in the boardroom, Jeremy."

"Thanks, Soph." I stifle a laugh and turn on my heel.

"You know, sweetheart, if you ever take that stick out of your arse and fancy a good-"

"Goodbye!" Sophie barks out, shutting him down completely just before a stapler flies past his head. Sadly, it misses.

Kieran strides towards me as I knock and open the door. "Oh, I like the feisty ones," he says, entering the boardroom behind me.

With a smile, I turn and pat his chest, and he flutters his lashes in faux flirtation. "I hate to break it to you, darling, but she's Stuart's."

The eye fluttering ceases, and he grabs my hand. "Stuart's?" He shakes his head. "Bleeding typical! Couldn't you let a guy down gently? You jammy gits have got all the good ones!"

"I'd recognise that scouse twang anywhere!" Sloan announces, rushing from the head of the room to embrace him.

"Long time no see, you handsome son of a b-"

"If you value your life, do not finish that sentence!" Sloan warns as K lifts him off the floor.

A knock raps on the door, and Sophie enters backwards, carrying a tray of drinks and biscuits. "Thanks, Soph. I should've told you we were coming over."

Her head bobs up and down, but she isn't looking at me, she's looking at the scene behind me. "It's fine," she says, her attention piqued by the large loudmouth Viking hugging her boss like old friends. "Is he a good friend of Sloan's, too?"

I keep my smile neutral but place my hands on her shoulders and gently manoeuvre her out of the room. "Thanks for the tea. I'll come out if we need anything else."

"But-" Her hand raises, but I close the door and twist the lock.

I exhale deeply - a storm is coming. "Sloan, as much as I hate to break up the bromance-"

"You're just jealous that he loves me more than you!" Sloan says, now batting his lashes with K reciprocating. They look like they're having a collective seizure.

"Absolutely, and I feel aggrieved you give him the same treatment you do me. However, your wife is about to be imminently educated regarding our fine friend here if your PA has anything to do with it. Forewarned is forearmed, as you have previously mentioned."

Sloan's grin withers, and he grimaces. Kieran looks between us, his expression puzzled. I tilt my head to him. "Sophie is Kara's best friend. She has been for years, long before his highness here appeared back on the scene. Or came on the scene, I guess, whichever way you look at it," I mutter.

"Jesus Christ! It's like incest anonymous down here!" Kieran exclaims. I chuckle loudly and pour myself a drink. Walking to the window, I gaze over the vista of the wealthier part of the city. The hustle and bustle, the money working its magic, and the requisite wide boys looking to make a few bob to retire early in the Med.

"Dare I ask why I've been summoned?" I glance over my shoulder. Sloan slips his hands into his pockets and casually pads to the table. I have an inkling of what he's going to ask of me - I've been expecting it for months – but I just want to hear it from the horse's mouth.

Sloan starts to open various folders. "I have a proposition. Ever since I sold Oblivion, I've been approached with numerous opportunities to buy out businesses currently on the brink. None were profitable and, quite frankly, nor were they appealing. However, a few months ago, I had a meeting with the CEO of a chain of restaurants who is looking to sell before he's forced into administration."

Sloan passes a file to me, and I flip through. I admit I don't have business acumen or a degree like he does, but even I know when the figures are attractive. Kieran moves beside me, turning pages, nodding at the pictures of the various locations.

"Will you be buying the full portfolio?" I query.

Sloan nods. "All ninety-one premises, including assets, with a full rebrand. We completed this morning." I quirk my brow. He can't replicate the monetary profit of Oblivion, no matter how hard he tries.

"Current staff?"

"Transferring over."

"Rebrand name?" I look up from the file.

Sloan's smile increases, and his shoulders straighten. "Oliver's," he replies with pride, his smile adding to his conviction.

My lips curve. I want to say something he won't approve of, but I don't because baby boy will always be in my heart, and if his father wants to name restaurants after him, so be it.

"And I want you to manage the flagship premises," he says adamantly. "Before you decide, come and have a look at the place." I furrow my brow, and he slaps my shoulder. "It's just down the street, which means you won't have to torpedo the pissed kids out of the door at three in the morning."

I shake my head as Kieran chuckles. "No, just the cocky wankers in the suits! Besides, that was Craig and Paul, and no one managed crowd control like they did.

Sloan strides to the back of the room to retrieve his suit jacket from the chair it is draped over. "Very true. So you'll be happy to know if you do take the job, the full team will be back together. Craig and Paul have already agreed to return along with their crazy boys. And there's someone else who's coming back, too."

"Who?" I query because the bar staff were all part-time and working their way through uni. I can't imagine they will want to pull pints for the rabble again. Sloan strides out of the room, and I follow behind with Kieran, who scowls at Sophie as Sloan tells her to divert any calls to his mobile and enters the lift. "Who, Foster?"

"You'll find out soon enough," he says, and the doors close. Sloan's phone buzzes, and he smiles mischievously, lifting it to his ear. "He's still undecided, but I've not told him yet." He hangs up as the lift doors open.

Striding over the marble foyer floor, I stop dead in my tracks when I see Andy Blake near the entrance, deep in conversation with bent cop, Greg Davies.

A hand on my shoulder shocks me, and I turn as Kieran bends to my level. "Is that who I think it is?" I nod, and he starts cursing and pulls out his phone.

"What's going on?" Sloan queries. I position myself so I can see Andy and his *friend* clearly.

"The man with Blake is an ex-detective from Manchester. He was Ed Shaw's number two back in the day. He used every dirty trick in the book to line his pockets and incarcerate those who were innocent." I glance over at Kieran, who looks ready to explode. "One of them is his cousin, Chris, who was just a kid when they fixed him up. He was befriended by the wrong people. He was in the wrong place at the wrong time. He's now serving fourteen years for a crime he didn't commit with no chance of early parole."

"How's that possible?" Sloan replies, practically bewildered.

I give him an incredulous look. "Money talks, Sloan. *You* know that," I tell him with more venom than intended. Albeit, we fly close to the wind, but Emerson and Foster isn't dirty. One of the main aspects of his leadership all these years has been financial integrity and moral scruples. He refuses to deal in the darker side that could ruin the business his father built, that he hopes his son will take over one day.

"Maybe his money needs to stop talking," Sloan says to himself, looking conflicted. "And maybe that time is now."

I barely have time to acknowledge the implications of Sloan's statement before Kieran drags me towards Blake and dodgy Davies.

"Come with, lad!" he says as Sloan quickly strides beside us, wondering, just like me, what the man-mountain is planning to do.

"Detective Gregory Davies!" K hollers out.

I glance at Sloan, but in my peripheral vision, the building security casually stride towards us, and Sloan discreetly waves his hand to stand them down.

"What's a bent bastard like you doing down here?" Kieran shows his teeth in a fake smile and leans in closer. "Making friends and influencing people? Hmm? Or maybe you're just slumming!" K flutters his lashes and rotates to Blake. "Hello, Andy. You don't know me, but I know you, and that makes me wonder how you," he points at Andy, "know him," he then points at Davies. "Buying friends and paying people, in your case, I think."

Andy squirms and twists his ring, his eyes rotating all over until he manages to compose himself. Going toe to toe with Kieran, he pushes out his chest, making a show in front of his new pal. "I'm sorry, but who are you?"

Kieran grips his chin with his finger and thumb and gives me a grin. I shake my head, but he just ignores me. "I'm wounded she hasn't told you about me. We've spent three long, intimate weeks together, and she hasn't seen fit to tell you!" He lowers his head, appearing in despair, but the sly smirk he's wearing at the rage consuming Blake's face is indicative he's done what he set out to, and that is to piss off my nemesis.

And right now, I could kill him for it!

Davies eyeballs Andy before turning his steadfast gaze back on us. "Be careful, Hyde. You don't want to end up like your Christopher. Not even your rich, corrupt friend could save him." He then turns and gives me a calculating glare. "But you? Your time's coming, and when it does, you'll suffer the way *she* did."

I step forward. "Are you threatening me? Or is that Shaw talking?" I ask through gritted teeth, looking between the two.

Davies smiles coldly. "Neither." He splays his arms out, walking backwards. He shares a knowingly look with Andy before he reaches the main doors and exits with a salute.

Andy begins to follow, but Sloan grabs his elbow. With a subtle nod, he silently beckons the guards over, and they take a menacing stance behind him.

"Please escort Mr Blake to the office and stay with him while he collects any personal belongings. He isn't to access his computer, nor is he to take any files, documents, or company property." Sloan then addresses Andy, who is undeniably furious, but inexplicably also looks somewhat relieved.

"What the hell are you doing? What is this?" he shouts, drawing attention our way.

"I'm doing what I should have done a long time ago. There have been misgivings on the board regarding your professional conduct for a while. Granted, I could pardon it – to a certain extent – if I really wanted to. What I won't pardon, however, is your blatant colluding with certain individuals who mean my business harm." Sloan looks at me, and Andy turns bright red in anger, knowing he's been well and truly caught with the crims. But this has nothing to do with the business and everything to do with me. "So there is no misunderstanding, Andrew. You are officially suspended, pending investigation. Now, let's make this quick and painless. Your company mobile, please?" Andy grinds his teeth, reluctantly handing over the phone. "Your laptop and security pass, too." Again, he passes Sloan the bag and slaps the door pass into his hand. "My PA will contact you this afternoon with details of a disciplinary meeting. Ensure you are able to attend tomorrow. If not, the consequences may be dire." Sloan turns on his heels as the guards motion for Andy to move.

"Sloan, you can't do this!" Andy pleads indignantly, reaching for his arm. Sloan shakes him off, wearing a rare, incensed expression.

"I can, and I have. My only wish is that I had done it a long time ago." Sloan then glances at me then back again. "And if you so much as conspire against my friend, note I also have acquittances who are willing to sink lower than yours to ensure your life will be ruined. Bear that in mind."

Sloan strides confidently out of the building, and I quickly move after him with Kieran hot on my heels. Outside, I grab his arm. "Please tell me that little scene in there is something you've been planning for a while?" Sloan maintains his unwavering stance but neither confirms nor denies. I close my eyes in provocation. "Look, if you've got something on him - something above board and legal - you need to make it stick because if he thinks I'm behind it, my life just got very fucking hard!"

"Relax, Remy lad," Kieran says. "Do you honestly think the king here would do something to put you in danger?"

My mouth gapes because it wouldn't be the first time. He made me get back into the proverbial bed with the Blacks for his own benefit, and look where that got me. But in truth, I have to believe he has my best interests at heart.

Sloan's expression softens. "Honestly, it's been a long time coming. I won't lie; your situation has *some* bearing, but not much. Now, let's just forget Andy arsehole for now, and let me show you the new premises you'll be managing."

"I haven't said yes," I mutter as he walks off in front with Kieran.

I follow the two overbearing gits down the street, debating what the upshot will be in light of today's unexpected turn of events.

Considering his association with Davies and Shaw, I'm not willing to find out just how low Andy will stoop to gain vengeance.

However, if there is one thing I am sure of, it's not only Andy's impending disciplinary meeting that shall be dire tomorrow. I have a feeling my life is also about to take a sharp turn down shit street, too.

Chapter 37

WITH ONE EYE on the pavement, the other on my phone, I tap out a text to Evie. Its purpose is dual serving. One, to find out what time she anticipates being home later, and two, to get the lay of the land. There's no doubt in my mind that Andy will likely spin his current garden leave status to his advantage, ensuring it causes cataclysmic ructions between us. The man is far from innocent, but the brazen sod will proclaim it profusely to anyone who gives a toss.

"We're here!" Sloan exclaims, derailing my train of thought.

I put my phone on standby and lift my head as I slip it into my pocket. I crease my brow. He wasn't lying when he said it was just down the street. Less than five minutes from leaving Emerson and Foster, we're now outside the new premises.

"Just to think, I can wave at you from the boardroom window!" he tells me gleefully.

I glance over my shoulder, gauging the distance between the two buildings. "Hmm," I grunt. "And I can give you the finger from the front door!" I love the man, but I'm not kidding, the daily royal wave may prove too much.

Sloan chortles and holds the door open. Stepping inside, Kieran whistles low as he ambles in the opposite direction, looking around.

I stroll through the dining areas and approach the bar. Running my fingers over the top, they chill under the gleaming grey marble. An Italian aroma infuses the atmosphere. It permeates my nostrils, masking the faint, lingering smell of fresh paint, indicating Sloan has already had the decorators in. It's ornate and plush, exuding class and wealth in a bizarre yet exquisite combination of classical and steampunk.

"When's opening night?" I ask.

"Next Friday."

I nod; that gives me eight days to finalise my life at WS.

If I accept.

"So, what do you think?" He nudges my side.

"I'll think about it," I reply flippantly, fifty per cent sure I'm going to be managing opening night.

He scoffs indignantly and throws his hands up. "What's to think about?"

"Oh, I don't know," I reply blasé. "At WS, there are no unsocial hours, no nights, no fights, no idiots, drunks, druggies, degenerates, or arseholed wankers shaking the place up." I scrunch my face thoughtfully. "Or at least there isn't until John consumes a bottle of gin! Plus, at WS, I get to see my woman during waking hours, and I have relative job security."

Sloan's mouth drops open, completely appalled. "I can guarantee job security!"

I shake my head. "Pubs and bars are closing at exponential rates on a weekly basis. No business is infallible, not even yours. And whereas social drinking is on the downward spiral, people always need security systems."

"What if I said there's an incredibly plush, newly renovated flat upstairs?"

I tilt my head. "I'd say I don't want to sleep in a plush flat upstairs. I want to sleep in my own bed beside the woman I love."

My phone buzzes in my pocket, and I quickly pull it out, hoping it's Evie. Unfortunately, it's just a news notification. I place it on the bar and turn to Sloan, who eyes it gravely. We both know what's coming, probably imminently, and when it does, it isn't going to be pretty.

Silence is truly golden, that is until the kitchen door at the far side of the premises opens. We rotate simultaneously, and my mouth drops in surprise, whereas Sloan's curves in accomplishment.

"Just in time! I was about to call and see if you wanted to sample the new menu," Ethan Lewis, the former head chef of The Emerson, says, wiping his hands on a tea towel as he walks towards us. He halts midway, grinning when he sees me. "Jeremy James in the flesh, you handsome devil!" He slings the towel over his shoulder and runs at me in his sauce splattered chef's whites.

"It's been a while," I say as he leans back. As expected, his eyes automatically find my scars. "It's been eventful."

He baulks at my nonchalance. "I can see." Silence turns golden again, and he exchanges glances with Sloan and clears his throat. "Have you convinced him yet?"

"I'm working on it," Sloan replies tightly, knowing my opposing reasons are all valid, and he needs to work harder.

"We only have a week," Ethan states the obvious.

"Stop panicking. It's a given."

"I'm right here, you know!"

"So am I, and I'm hungry. Is that steak? Arrabbiata?" Kieran asks, sniffing the air, shifting his head towards the kitchen. "Kieran Hyde." He offers his hand to Ethan, who shakes it, then appears thoughtful.

"Foster, we might need to raise the staff catering budget if he's going to be one of security. He looks like he could eat us out of house, home, hotel *and* restaurant!"

Kieran's return expression is comical. "Cheeky cockney git! I'm not scraping the barrel doing security again!"

Sloan scoffs. "But, darling," he bats his lashes, "you already are." He slants his head towards me.

"Semantics, but I guess there's a certain truth in that," Kieran replies as I huff out in vexation.

"I've told you, repeatedly, I don't need a babysitter."

Kieran smirks, sniffing the air again as the fragrant aroma thickens on the atmosphere. "True, but who's going to warm your bed, baby?"

"Evie! And speaking of which, you need to disappear for the rest of the day." I point at him.

"Why?" he asks innocently.

My mouth gapes. "Because we want our flat back!"

He inhales and exhales dramatically. "No, you just want to get your end away! It almost feels like you're cheating on me. Did all those years we spent together in Yorkshire mean nothing to you?" He touches his eyelash, milking it beyond belief. Sniggers float between us, and I turn to Sloan and Ethan.

"Don't encourage him! And you," I turn back to K, "I swear to God, you're going to get my fist in your face. But yes, actually, I do, preferably without the whistling, the singing, and the banging on the door to enhance the ambience!"

"Fine! Sloan, I would like a room for the night, please. Preferably that sweet, cushy penthouse."

Sloan shrugs, uncaring. "So pay for one. I'm not running a charity." He winks at me. Of course, he's going to give him a room so I can have some privacy in mine.

Kieran whips around and bares his teeth. "You tight-fisted little wanker!"

"Gentlemen, as entertaining as this is, shall we discuss the finer points over lunch?" Ethan queries and strides to the kitchen. Kieran and Sloan stop smirking at each other and confirm their agreement.

"Oh, and for your information, *scouser*, I'm not cockney. I'm from the West Country." And the door swings shut behind him.

"Yeah? Well, I'm from the Wirral!"

"REM, GRAB THAT dish," Ethan orders, throwing an oven mitt at me. I push backwards through the kitchen door and stride to the table and place the red-hot dish in the middle. I furrow my brow and watch K set the table, complete with jacquard cloth napkins and lead crystal glasses, while Sloan polishes the silverware with a tea towel.

"What?" K queries. "My ma taught me to be civilised... And my dad taught me everything else!" he says, and I chuckle.

Taking my seat, I pour a glass of water. "If you don't mind, what happened to your bistro?" I ask Ethan as he serves me a rather generous portion of lasagne.

"No, I don't mind." He sits down. "It went to the wall. Too much competition, numbers dropped, no shows, increased business rates. When you start making a loss, it's time to cut those losses. Fortunately for me, Sloan and Kara came in a few months back, and I swallowed my pride and asked him to consider me if he needed a chef. Some may think it's embarrassing to admit defeat, but it's a guaranteed wage at the end of the month, and we all work for money."

Sloan clears his throat. "Nothing to be ashamed of. Businesses fold all the time. I consider myself exceptionally fortunate to have you back on my team. If you remember, I didn't want you to leave in the first place."

"And just to think, it also guarantees you a second arsehole!" I tell Ethan, then tuck into the amazing lunch he's prepared.

I grin triumphantly at Sloan's insulted glare, and Kieran sniggers. "Says the man who's got-" he starts counting off on his fingers "-four, including his own!" An undisputed reference to Sloan, John, and Dom.

Sloan dabs the corner of his mouth with the napkin and puts it down. "Right, let's get back to business. Have you made your mind up yet?" I pick up a slice of garlic bread and pretend to mull over my options. "Jeremy?" he pushes.

"Fine, but I have a few stipulations."

"Such as?"

"Such as preferably two days off together and a good variety of shifts. I have a life outside of work these days, remember?"

He grins jubilantly. "All acceptable."

"Good, and I need to tell John."

He shakes his head. "Don't worry, he already knows you're on the way out." He picks up his knife and fork.

"Jesus, Sloan! You make me sound like I'm dying!" I pick up another slice of bread, and he throws a clean napkin at me and another at Kieran.

"I thought your ma taught you civilised manners?" Sloan asks K as he cuts his garlic bread into small bitesize pieces.

Kieran shrugs and stuffs a slice into his mouth. "She did, but you're just a stuck-up swine in a three-piece suit."

Ethan laughs, licking his fingers. "Come on, Foster. Come down into the gutter with us!"

Our collective laughing echoes in the empty premises. Sloan then pops the top off a bottle of champagne and pours four glasses. I motion for him to stop when mine is only a fifth full. "To old friends and new beginnings."

We all raise our glasses, and I take a small sip as my mobile vibrates. The prospect of opening the text that has just arrived fills me with dread.

"Do you think Daddy's arrived home yet?" Kieran queries gently.

I pull a face. "Well, she isn't answering my texts, which isn't like her, so yeah, I'll safety take a punt that he's probably filling her head with lies as we speak."

"What's going on?" Ethan asks.

Sloan's about to answer, but Kieran beats him to it. "Remy's girl's dad is a dodgy bastard who hates him, and Sloan's just fucked his life up."

"Which means he's going to fuck my life up."

Sloan's head swings, and he rolls his eyes. "Like it or not, I needed to remove him from the board. I don't trust him, and I haven't for a long time. I'm fed up of being pulled aside after each meeting and listening to criticisms from other members. The disciplinary is just following procedure. However, we have to vote, and he's still got friends on the board, so it's likely I can't oust him as soon as I'd like, but this is just the start."

"But what does confiscating his mobile and laptop do if you're going to have to give them back tomorrow?" Kieran queries.

"It means," Sloan begins, "my IT guys can image them and install monitoring and blocking software before he gets them back. It also means he has less immediate contact with our enemies."

"For now," I murmur as my phone rings, and Evie's name flashes over the screen. Sloan and Kieran both sit up straighter and crane their necks. With my eyes fixed on Sloan's steadfast gaze, I answer and put her on speakerphone.

"Hey-"

"My dad's just been sacked because of you!" is her opening gambit. "Are you happy?" she shouts.

"Sweetheart, calm down," I reply softly as Sloan shakes his head, but we both knew this was inevitable.

"Don't, *sweetheart*, me!"

I huff out; this isn't her. "Fine!" I snap. "Your dad has been temporarily placed on garden leave pending investigation." Sloan nods at me as he furiously taps away on his phone.

"Why?" she asks, calmer now but still pissed off.

"Why?" I reply. Sloan slides his phone to me and mouths for me to relay what he has typed. "Because there are internal reservations regarding his integrity."

A chortle pierces my hearing. "Integrity!" she hisses. "You'd know all about that, wouldn't you?" Her statement is scathing, and I know what's coming. "All this time, I trusted you. I trusted you to protect me and to look after me. And you did. You looked after me when my dad attempted to whore me out, and you protected me when Piers tried…" her voice breaks. "I didn't just trust you; I loved you. I *worshipped* you. Now I don't know what to think. But you can finally stop lying to me, Jeremy, because *I know!*"

I feel my face drain of all colour, and my subsequent expression speaks volumes considering the three men at the table are all leaning closer, their expressions grim.

"You know what?" I finally find my voice, but it's futile. I snatch up my phone, take her off speakerphone and put it to my ear.

"I know about you," she repeats, then the barrier breaks. Her tears flow freely, amplified through the receiver. "You raped a girl!"

Her erroneous assertion rings in my ears. I stand abruptly, my body swaying, threatening to take me down. I slam my hand on the table in anger. My thoughts tumble through my head. I should be screaming, shouting, protesting my innocence, but the only words penetrating are that *I raped a girl*. Her claim is portentous, but clearly, she doesn't know which girl – not that there actually was one – which means Andy is cautious of trifling with Sloan further. So instead, he plants the seed and then allows her to work herself up like this.

My God, he's a first-class cunt!

"Evie, please. We need to talk about this."

"No, we don't. You lied to me. You had ample opportunity to tell me, but you didn't. Please, Jeremy, tell me he's lying. Tell me you didn't do it. Tell me that you didn't hurt someone like that!"

"Sweetheart, please!" I shout pitifully. "He *is* lying."

"I don't believe you!" she shouts back. "Well, know this, Jeremy James. You've shattered me! You've destroyed a part of me I never thought you would. You've broken my heart, and I hate you for it! And I'll hate you every single day until the day I die because I allowed you to have me when you cruelly allowed yourself to have someone else against their will. *I fucking know!*" she screams and hangs up.

"Rem?" Sloan urges as I slide on my jacket and push back the chair. "Rem?"

I stop and turn back. "She knows."

A sickness swells in the pit of my stomach because regardless of what she thinks she knows, *I know*, too.

Chapter 38

I ALTERNATE BETWEEN intermittently bashing my fist on the steering wheel or gripping it as though my life depends on it the closer I get to home. Ever since Evie hung up on me not less than forty minutes ago, my mood has vacillated from volcanic and vibrating to soothing and subdued, until finally, to horrified and heartbroken.

Turning onto my street, Evie's Fiat is parked alongside the kerb, as opposed to occupying its designated space downstairs. Pissed off at her unconfirmed assumption, I brake harshly and reverse until there is less than an inch spare and my boot is practically caressing her bonnet in a futile attempt to impede her impending escape.

I slam the door and engage the locks as I jog towards the communal entrance. As expected, the security desk is unmanned and bears its usual sign of who to call in an emergency. Well, I guess that's one less person to see her leave devastated, I mentally muse as I step into the lift.

A minute later, the doors part, and I rush out, almost knocking over my neighbour in my haste. "Sorry, mate."

He raises his hands in surrender. "Don't worry, I'm having one of those days, too," he replies and boards the lift I've just vacated. Again, I'm grateful he's also one less to hear the catastrophic blast that is possibly going to erupt imminently.

I pause outside my flat, take a breath, then depress the handle. The door swings back effortlessly. I grind my jaw, even more pissed off that she's not even locked it. I appreciate she hates my fucking guts right now, but to be so reckless with her own safety is just adding to my stormy temperament.

The flat is quiet, and I furrow my brow as faint tears drift from the bedroom. I loiter outside the door. The urge to enter is overwhelming, but instead, I pace into the living room. I glance around. There's a suitcase – which wasn't here this morning - stuffed to the seams. Her car keys and phone are on the coffee table, which means she's going to be collecting them before she leaves for the last time.

I clench my hands, debating the next course of action since my tumultuous thoughts are creating a perfect storm inside my head. I could sit and wait but considering that will only allow me time to grieve the loss of something I've yet to lose physically - notwithstanding emotionally it's already gone - I venture onto the balcony and remove my stash from under the plant pot.

The hit of nicotine at the back of my throat is perfect, if not potent, having not indulged for a while. I grip one hand on the door frame above me and inhale deeply, enjoying the vile vulgarity of smoking, when steps approach.

I turn and eyeball Evie. Her eyes are red from crying and smudged mascara shadows beneath them. Her cheeks are tear-stained, and the tell-tale lines she has tried to cover are visible under her makeup. I shake my head softly and reach out for her. *My mistake.* However, well-meant my intention is, it's still an error of judgement when she edges back towards the hallway.

"I didn't hear you come in," she says, cautiously moving as far away from me as possible. "What are you doing here?"

The gall of her asking such a question has now become her mistake. I appreciate she's angry, and her emotions are running high, but *what am I doing here?*

"I live here!" My response is evidently harsher than she expects, and she starts to mumble. "And in case you've acquired sudden amnesia in the last few hours, you live here, too! So, tell me why your things are in a suitcase that has magically appeared in our flat?"

She gasps, taken aback. Her hands fist at her sides, and her cheeks redden, more so than they are already. "*I've* got amnesia? How fucking dare you?!" she shouts, and for once, I couldn't give a shit if my neighbours hear through the tissue paper walls. "How dare you think you have any right to tell me what to do. Not after what you've done!"

I gasp mechanically. Oh, I bet Andy laid it on real thick for her to be this worked up. I take a final drag on the fag and lob it over the balcony. "What *I've* done?" I toss back, and she scowls. "Whatever happened to innocent until proven guilty, Evelyn? Instead, you throw these recriminations around and don't allow me the opportunity to defend myself." Her mouths parts, but I don't let her get a word in. "You haven't even asked me. You've just screamed and shouted about things you have no comprehension of!"

"I did ask you, and you didn't deny it!" she fires back. She rushes towards me in all her undisguised fury and hits my chest. Once. Twice.

"No, you're right, but I didn't confirm it either, and there's a damn good reason why! God, your dad's a piece of fucking work!" I hiss and throw my hands on my hips.

"But he hasn't lied to me!" she volleys back, recommencing the fight. She finally gains momentum and beats my chest as hard as she can. I grit my teeth and allow her to vent her anger and betrayal. Irrespective of whether she hurts me or not, I'd never retaliate. I did once when Kara was out of control, and it's something I'll never do again. "He hasn't lied to me!" she repeats, and I grab her wrists.

I could say that he has. I could say he's been lying to her about everything from the day she was born, but the fact of the matter is I *was* there *that night,* but I sure as hell didn't do what I'm currently being accused of. Instead, I let her go in an attempt to regain control of the situation.

"It isn't a lie. It's an omission. One I had already planned to tell you about."

"It doesn't matter." She grabs the suitcase.

"You're not taking your stuff. We're going to sit down and talk about this calmly and rationally."

"No, we're not because I'm leaving, and I'm not coming back!" she says, practically rote.

"No, you're not!" I rip the suitcase from her hand and throw it across the room.

The sting on my cheek radiates as she slaps me hard, shocking herself at such another forward response. She presses her lips together while tears stream down her face. "Like I said, it's over, so it doesn't matter anymore!" Her words are powerful, but they lack conviction when she allows herself to break in front of me. I want to comfort her, but I cannot because she needs to understand. We must wade through this shit in order to come out stronger.

And we will. I'll make sure of it.

"Really? If it doesn't matter, why has he only told you now?" Her mouth tightens, and I step closer again. "He has the audacity to put you in a situation where you question my integrity, but you really should be questioning his because he's known for a while, sweetheart. The only reason he finally told you is because he got caught out today. Ask him. Ask him why he was colluding and conspiring in the shadows with the father of my dead girlfriend at your summer party. Ask him about his relationship with corrupt ex-coppers. Better still, ask your grandfather. He was there. He saw your dad with them. He knows all about my past, too. Do you honestly think he would still allow me to even breathe near his beloved *Evie pie* if he thought for one second that I did what I'm being accused of?" I'm thoroughly fed up of wasting my breath on an argument I can't win. I turn around reluctantly as the truth starts to penetrate as I can't bear to watch her fall apart when I know she won't allow me to comfort her.

"What?" her belated soft reply surprises me.

I sigh and rotate. "You heard me." My reply sounds defeated. "Ask him why Edward Shaw was hiding in the back alley behind your house, then ask him about his meeting with Greg Davies today. Because that's who he was with just before Sloan put him in the garden this afternoon. Did Daddy tell you that too while he was filling your head with everything else?"

She steps towards the suitcase, but I rush towards her and grab her hand. She baulks under my touch, and her lip quivers. "Don't. You know I would *never* hurt you like that." She acquiesces and nods because even in all her anger, she knows I would never raise a hand to her. I let go of her wrist and move to the other side of the living room.

"Look, it's pretty damn obvious it's going to take more than one night and one fight to work through this, and I know I can't lock you in the bedroom and make you stay." The tears of loss well in my eyes, and I steel myself to keep them contained. I'm meant to stay strong, but my defences are presently weakened. "All this time, I've bit my tongue as far as your dad is concerned, but he's not a good man. Some may say the same about me, but I've spent the last decade aiming to redeem myself for the horrors I've committed. Your father, on the other hand, he's ruthless and hateful, and he cares about no one but himself. Not your mother, not you, not anyone. But I think you already know that."

Her demeanour softens, and she's about to respond, but I lift my hand. I don't want her saying things to settle scores or to stop the pain.

"No, don't." I wheel the suitcase towards her. "Before you walk out of here, I want you to know the truth. Months ago, I told you there was more to my story, but it involved someone else." I inhale, finally willing and able to speak to the truth. "After Emma died, I went off the rails. I didn't have a reason to live anymore. These days, I can't even bring myself to think about those dark times. Sometimes I didn't leave the house for days, weeks. Then around nine months after her death, I was dragged to a party where a teenage girl was raped. That girl is now Sloan's wife."

Evie's mouth drops open in shock, but I shake my head. "She was beaten and drugged by Deacon – he wasn't only my best friend, but he was also Sloan's stepbrother - and my part was truly atrocious. I did something unintentionally evil in my heavily drugged up state." My tears fall down my cheeks. I'll never be able to forgive myself those irreprehensible actions. "I fastened her wrists to the bed, and I left her with him."

"Oh God, Jeremy." Evie's soft sympathy invades my memories. "You need to give me more than that right now. You can't tell me that and leave the rest unsaid!"

"I want to, I really do, but you need to hear it directly from Kara. She deserves to be heard. To voice her memories and have justice. Whether you believe me or not, I'll carry the guilt of what I did to her with me until the grave. I'm many things, but I'm *not* a rapist."

Evie wipes her tears and slumps against the wall. "How do I know you're not lying?" she asks, almost inaudibly and throws her hands up in desperation. She's internally fighting with her own morality.

"Sweetheart, I swear I'm telling you the truth. I've never lied to you. Omitted, yes, but lied? No. And in your heart, you know that's true. Look, I've left you with a lot to consider again." I pull out my phone and swipe the screen, unsure whom I'm going to call. "I don't want you driving in this state, but I don't want you going back to your parents tonight either."

She shrugs. "I'll be fine driving, and there's nothing further Dad can say to me because he's already put a chasm between us. Going back tonight isn't going to change anything. The damage has already been done."

"True." I tentatively stroke her cheek. I'm thankful she allows me to before she pulls away, remembering she's meant to hate me right now. "But I have to believe he hasn't damaged us beyond repair."

She puts her keys in her pocket and grabs her phone. I watch as she calls her grandad and asks if she can stay for a few days. She hangs up and wheels her suitcase down the small hallway. I follow behind, desperately hoping she'll change her mind and stay. But she won't. I already know that.

"I want you to sleep on it, give it a few days - a few weeks, if need be - but don't end us because of hateful vengeance and lies. Not before you hear the facts from the person who actually lived through and survived it." I pull out my phone and text her Kara's number. "Kara's expecting your call. She has been for a while."

"How long?" Evie queries, as though the length of time that Kara has been planning to talk to her will play a part in whether or not she forgives me.

"I first broached the subject with her around eight weeks ago. She finally confirmed I could tell you a fortnight ago, but so much has happened with Marie in the last few weeks that it slipped my mind."

She stops and pivots. "It's okay. I understand. I just need time to think about everything that's happened today."

I bite the inside of my cheek. I can feel the tears flooding behind my eyes, and the longer it takes for her to walk away, the harder it's going to be to keep my composure. "Don't hate me," I whisper because I'd rather be dead than have her live in the world deriding my existence.

"Jeremy..." I hold my hand up because I also cannot live with false hope. She purses her lips as her phone vibrates. "Grandpy's almost here. It might be better if you stay here until we're gone."

I scoff. I'm nothing if not consistent, and God loves a glutton for punishment as much as he loves a trier. "I'm walking you down, sweetheart. I'll take whatever he throws at me." I grab the suitcase and hold the door open for her.

She inhales, and her bottom lip quivers again as we enter the lift. "Here." She hands me her car keys. "Can you put her back downstairs?"

I hold her gaze. A moment of significance passes between us, not to mention the ever-present chemistry. "Sure," I reply because it means she has to come back and talk to me to retrieve her keys. She doesn't want this to be over any more than I do. It feels like forever until we reach the foyer, and the doors slide aside. She attempts to reclaim her suitcase, but I hold tight. I might be an arsehole prick with a poor past and even poorer judgement, but I can still be an unlikely gentleman.

The flash of headlights beams through the glass as Evie exits the building. "Fuck!" I murmur rhetorically. Terry Cosgrove is a hard man, and considering the screeching halt he's just come to, he's probably not going to be very forgiving, either.

"Evie, in the car!" he orders the moment he strides into the communal garden. Evie turns around and takes her case from me. "Now, darling!" With her nose screwed up, she meets him in the middle.

"Grandpy, please don't hurt him," she pleads, her hand on his chest. And fuck me if it doesn't work when his eyes soften a little. "I love him. I love him today. I'll love him tomorrow, next week, next year. He made a mistake."

"A mistake!" Terry roars and puts his arm around her. He points at me as he guides her to the car. "Don't get too fucking comfortable. I'll be back for you!" I wait with bated breath, but I'm hardly comfortable. A part of me wishes he would just put a gun to my head and have done with it. Although, I think he prefers the long, drawn-out, torturous method as opposed to quick and easy. I really should have probed Evie more to find out how *involved* he still is.

The soft, reverberating thump of Evie's fists against the inside of the car window punctures the suburban quiet. Ready for the repercussions, I straighten up. Terry ambles back to me, a man on a mission, his face full of thunder. He swings his arm out, smashing his boulder of a fist against my cheek. I stumble back and catch sight of Evie, silently screaming inside the car. I hold up my hand because I deserve this, and he's the only one who will dare do it. Sloan should have done this to me years ago, but he never would.

"I fucking trusted you!" Terry bellows in my face as I flounder over the path in the aftermath of his fire. "That bastard son-in-law of mine called, saying you've raped multiple girls!" I raise my head as his words sink in, *multiple*. I start to shake it, but he levies another punch at me. "I know you're no beacon of light and virtue, but I trusted you with my Evie!" Another hit floors me completely, and I groan, aware my face is going to be purple in the morning. A car door slams, and in my peripheral vision, Evie is running back through the garden. She slides on her knees in front of me to shield me from her irate, impassioned grandad.

"Get back in the car, sweetheart. It's fine, we're just working out our differences," I say flippantly, aiming to smile through the blood filling my mouth.

She gives me a disbelieving stare and shakes her head. "Grandpy, please!" she begs, tenderly touching my face. I brush her hand away because I need to withstand this. Terry huffs, shakes his head and picks her up with his arm around her waist. "Please, for me. Don't hurt him any further!" she appeals to his tender side again. "Please, Grandpy. Please."

"Fine!" Terry growls reluctantly and drops her on her feet.

"Promise me!" she orders.

Terry rolls his eyes. "Fine, I promise. Now get back in the car." She gives me a longing look, clearly at odds with everything that has happened in the last few hours, but does as she's told. Still, it doesn't stop her from peeking back to ensure he's keeping his word.

Terry subtly glances over his shoulder, and he bends down. "I'm going to take my granddaughter home, and after she's told me everything that's been said between you both today, I'm then going to call that arsehole father of hers and see what his reaction is. However, if she tells me things that I find unappealing, well, you and I are going to have further, heated discussions. Understand?" I nod, breathing a sigh of relief until his arm rears back, and he leaves me with a parting shot. My head jerks to the side, jarring my neck, ensuring the pain spreads like liquid fire.

Terry strides away in my fringe vision, and the sound of the door slamming and the car driving away are last things I hear as my body attempts to shut down in order to begin the healing processing.

I fight against the inevitable and lift myself up from the pavement. I manage to manoeuvre from the garden to the lift and then into my flat. I slump on the sofa, pick up my phone and squint as I scroll through the phonebook.

"Walker," John answers on the first ring. I'm at odds to divulge because he's got his own issues with Marie and her former in-laws making waves, but I can't keep it from him since Sloan will spill anyway.

"Evie knows about that night." My confession is precise and to the point. My head is fuzzy, and John's response that he's coming over ASAP withers inside my head as the darkness slowly approaches.

I curl up on the sofa, suddenly cold and shivering. I'm wrapped tight in my grief, fully consumed in my misery. The phone gently slips from my hand, and I close my eyes, hoping tomorrow comes swiftly.

In all honesty, I knew the reality from the fallout was going to be catastrophic. However, if I'd have known the truth was going to be this painful, then I would have realised that the lie that has been weaved is going to be far, far worse.

Chapter 39

IT'S DONE JEREMY.

Kara's week old, three-word text confirmation sears my irises for the millionth time. I grind my jaw and grunt in frustration as I toss my mobile onto the picnic table.

I gaze up to the sky, praying for divine intervention to assist in untangling my complex web of a life. The sun is slowly burning through the morning mist that has blanketed the city in a hazy ambience. The gentle breeze teases the diminishing thermals and wraps around me while I continue to pace.

As I kick my toe against the cracked tarmac, my phone beeps. I dash towards it, hoping against hope it's Evie. It's been nearly two weeks since she left our flat, one week since Kara confirmed they had spoken, and yet I'm still waiting for her to call. Heck, even her car is still sitting pretty in her parking space, also awaiting her return.

My prayers are dashed when it's only my mother. I let it go to voicemail because she's probably only calling to find out what I fancy for dinner tonight. And my answer will be the same as it has been for the last week or so since I dragged my arse back there: don't go to any trouble. She hasn't said, but I think she's just happy I'm finally allowing her to mother me, regardless of my age.

Fed up of my own company, pissed off with Evie's radio silence and annoyed with anyone offering advice and reflection on my situation, I clamber onto the table, slam my feet on the bench and light up a cig. Inhaling, my body relaxes while the toxins fill my lungs, coating them in chemicals. I need to stop once and for all, but really, is there any point if I live or die anymore?

My gloomy disposition darkens further, eliminating the remaining bright spots that have yet to be extinguished this last fortnight. I guess today is finally the day my hope flies – I wouldn't blame it.

I take another drag of the cigarette and exhale. The heavy metal clang of the warehouse door closing behind me accompanies the fraught atmosphere, and the smoke rings I'm expelling into the air.

"I'll get him to call you back, April," John says. I glance over my shoulder and fist my hand as he, accompanied by Dom and Kieran, casually ambles towards me. I keep my expression neutral, but their constant pandering has finally severed the internal threads of my frayed sanity. This is the real reason why I was summoned back to work this morning. Personally, I'd have preferred to stay away and served the idiots and dickheads their court papers and orders on my own.

"Here you go, lad." Kieran hands me a mug of tea and loiters in front of the table, drinking his own. He may be acting relaxed and unperturbed, but his demeanour confirms he has one ear on the current undisclosed intervention.

John climbs onto the table next to me, and Dom boxes me in on the other side. "That was your mother," John states the obvious.

I swallow a mouthful of hot tea. "I gathered."

"She still doesn't like me."

"Nor me," Dom adds.

"Or I," Kieran finishes.

I smile reluctantly. "She holds a mean grudge."

"Hmm, against the wrong people," John replies.

I take the last drag on the cig and flick it in front of me, missing Kieran by millimetres. His brow perks in annoyance, and I dare him to retort.

"John, I allow her to embrace her hatred, whether it's aimed at the wrong people or not because it means she temporarily forgets her own unfounded guilt. And trust me, it's all I've heard these last ten days."

Kieran chuckles gleefully. "That's what happens when you move back in with Mummy!"

"I guess it's a good thing I'm going back home tonight, then."

"Have you informed Mummy of that decision yet?" K retorts.

I shrug. "Not yet." My reply is sheepish as the roar of a familiar supercar rolls into the yard. Sloan brakes smoothly, climbs out, moves to unbuckle his son from his baby seat and strides towards us.

"Meeting of the minds?" he queries, whereas Oliver grumbles loudly, clearly unhappy about something in his little life. Sloan and I share a brief look, and he thrusts his temperamental tot into my chest.

"I've been smoking," I tell him, tugging on my shirt to sniff it. Hmm, it's definitely lingering.

"I'll let you off this once, but you need to quit that."

I acquiesce and reach for baby boy, deliberately holding him, so he faces forward. Oliver, on the other hand, has his own ideas. He wiggles on my thighs, turns around and smashes his small hands to my cheeks. It's almost like he knows his touch can soothe me right now, and he shuffles closer.

"I've been smoking, son. You don't want to do that." As expected, little man ignores me, squishes my cheeks in his palms and places a sloppy kiss on my lips, making a kissy noise. I automatically smile. "I love you too, kid." I cuddle him close to my heart, revelling in his warmth and innocent affection.

"And dare we ask why you're slumming it here today?" K queries.

Sloan grins. "I was promised free babysitting and adventure," he announces. I crease my brow in request for elaboration. "Kara's spending the day with Marie and Maggie. Which means she's going to come home with an even greater sarcastic streak than usual." He gives John a pointed look, who returns it with a proud smile. He can't protest; he knows his woman can be wicked when necessary.

"And this intriguing adventure you speak of?" I look between him and John, but I have a good idea.

He pats his suit. "I get to serve papers with you today."

I grunt and press Oliver's head to my chest, safeguarding his innocent ears. "Shouldn't be too taxing. A seasoned professional like you has been called a cunt and a bastard before."

Kieran and Dom snort simultaneously while Sloan edges closer, his grin morphing into a scowl. I ignore him and lift up his boy and coo. "Have you heard from little miss yet? I thought she would have called you by now," he queries, knowing right where to stick it. My upper hand on the conversation is short-lived. I'm about to reply when a glimmer of sun reflecting off a shiny surface flashes over the building, and a car slowly enters the yard. We all move in sync, and I pass Oliver back to his dad and consciously stand in front of them. The car turns, and the sickness that has laid heavy in my stomach since Evie found out roils. I've been expecting this reunion since the man decked me on my doorstep.

"Who is that?" Sloan asks.

I exhale. Irrespective that the car's occupants are yet to reveal themselves, *I know*. "Terry Cosgrove." I subtly indicate for them to stay back, and I approach the car, sympathy pain already emanating in my chest of what he might do. I wouldn't mind, but the bruises from the last time we met are only just fading. I suppose these are the further, heated discussions I've been waiting for.

"Terry," I greet flatly as he exits the car. The driver backs it into the free space next to Dom's Maserati and remains inside.

"Jeremy," he replies, taking in my face, then the men standing sentry behind us. "Is there somewhere we can talk?" I nod and lead him towards the entrance. As I open the door, my quartet of defenders follow, refusing to leave me alone with him. Terry, totally astute, senses their reluctance. "You can all relax. I just want to have a chat with him. If it makes you more comfortable, you can all sit and listen."

"That won't be necessary," I confirm, ensuring they stop in their tracks. Jesus, even in the face of my turmoil, they're still eager beavers.

I hold the door open, but Terry turns to Sloan unexpectedly. "Your son?" Sloan's head moves suspiciously. "Any chance you will part with him for a while? I do like the little ones with chubby, cheeky chops!" He tickles Oliver's cheek, and baby boy laughs. *Traitor* – or possibly a good judge of character. Sloan's brow quirks in surprise. "May I hold him, Mr Foster?" Terry asks Sloan, who steps closer, Oliver nestled securely in his arms.

"Mr Cosgrove, I may not be familiar with the laws of *your* world, but if anything happens to my son or my best friend, I'll hunt you down, and I'll watch while someone guts you."

Terry nods with respect and gratitude. "Understood. Look, I just want to talk to Jeremy, and your boy seems to be very content with him, so lets us not deny the little lad... Or the grumpy old geezer, for that matter."

A chortle resounds, and Sloan reluctantly hands his boy back to me. Another look of unspoken truth passes between us. He knows I would lay down my life for his son, but I can't disregard his concern of a man whose reputation is known far and wide in various circles.

"We won't be long." I curl Oliver into my chest and enter the building.

Motioning Terry to the lift, when inside, he fusses over Oliver, ensuring the seconds in such a confined space are pleasant. The door creaks open, and I step out and enter the code for the security doors, and he follows me into the kitchen.

"Tea, coffee?" I ask, wondering how I'm going to hold baby boy, retrieve the mugs, and fill the kettle.

"Here." Terry holds out his arms for Oliver, who gives me a pouty look but soon regains his usual charm and mischief with the new shiny grandad figure he's never actually had. Maybe I'm clutching at straws, but maybe this might be a good thing for both of them. "You're a handsome little chap, aren't you?" Terry coos. "I remember when my Evie pie was your age; bundle of fun but always in trouble!" Oliver laughs at him when he tickles under his chin, and as much as I want to remain pissed off at the man, I can't. I can't because he's doing what every loving parent does - he's protecting his child. And let's be honest, he's more of a father to Evie than her own is.

"I'll have a weak tea, son, and put a couple of sugars in it," he says and laughs at Oliver. "I'm not supposed to have it, but what Evie pie doesn't know won't hurt her!"

I pause, the loaded teaspoon suspended above the mug. "Are you diabetic?" Terry shrugs innocently, pulling faces at Oliver. I shake my head because he's going to get me in trouble. *Again.* "I'll give you one sugar, but if you keel over on me..."

"She won't know, son!"

"She will if you drop down dead! And besides, *I'll* know."

"Don't be so melodramatic. It'll take more than a sprinkling of the good stuff to get rid of me. I've been shot, stab-" he stops when I glower at him. I hold his gaze as he repeatedly jerks his head for me to tilt the spoon, and I repeatedly shake mine for him to zip his mouth shut. "I promise I won't say another word to give the little lad nightmares. Or you, for that matter."

"Fine." I stir the spoon in. Grabbing both mugs, I lead the way into the mess room.

"So, what do you boys do here?" he queries, looking around, curious.

I make myself comfortable for the interrogation. "Security systems, CCTV, residential and commercial. We also run a process server, and occasionally, we offer some protection services, but that's fallen by the wayside in recent years due to lack of interest. I guess you could say we do a bit of this and that, but not your kind of *this and that*, that's for sure," I add for clarity.

"I guess not. You boys are definitely more above board," he says, pointing to one of the cameras. I pull out my phone, log into the app, and turn them off. "Thanks."

"We walk a fine line, but you didn't come here to talk about how fine that line is, did you?"

"No, I didn't. I came to apologise." He carefully sits down and takes a sip of his tea, mindful to keep the mug away from the curious little hands trying to grab it. "That afternoon, when he called to gloat, saying you'd raped girls, using it as a weapon to get one over on me because I approve of you... You see, that's what the basta-" He quickly controls himself. "That's what he does; he plays games. There's nothing he won't manipulate until he gets the outcome he wants. You've already seen that with Evie."

Oliver shuffles in his arm and stands on his legs. Baby boy then puts his hand over Terry's mouth and makes a loud shushing noise, his little lips reverberating and spitting at him in his baby attempt to get it right.

Terry wipes the spittle from his face and chuckles. "You're absolutely a cheeky boy!" He bounces him on his knees; the actual reason behind his visit is being overshadowed by said cheeky boy. I bring my mug to my lips, wondering. "I might be getting ahead of myself and the current situation, but one day, maybe you and Evie might give me another one of these to cherish."

I practically choke on my tea and slap my hand to my chest. "I think you're definitely getting ahead of yourself! But one day, possibly. Preferably when she's full grown-up, forty, and not throwing wine over women she abhors with her grandpy egging her on!"

Terry grins. "Good answer, son. I knew I liked you." His smile gradually fades, and I wait for it. "You know, Evie spoke to the girl who was attacked." He swipes his hand gently over Oliver's cheek and studies him. "She's his mother, isn't she?"

"Yeah," I confirm as shadows move outside the glass door. "There have been times when I've wanted Sloan to beat me for what I did, to seek vengeance for his wife's honour, but he won't. I guess you could say it's complicated."

He inhales, appearing thoughtful. "The best, and usually the most important relationships always are."

The door then opens, and Sloan strides inside. "Since we're all now fully acquainted on past, painful recriminations on both sides," he says, clearly using a trick from his wife's book on eavesdropping. "We have more pressing issues to resolve." Terry eyes him with both surprise and respect and offers Oliver back to him. "No, it seems he likes you, and I was guaranteed free babysitting. Now, I think we need to discuss the potentially explosive situation your son-in-law is bringing, not only on himself and us but possibly on you, too. We need to work together to divest ourselves of this problem. You see, unlike him, we don't use our family against our friends," he finishes, sounding like Dominic.

Christ!

"Or our enemies," John adds, entering the room with Dom. Terry once again weighs them up keenly.

"No, we just use them on lying arseholes who listen to lying cunts who are currently in the garden." Kieran leans against the wall beside the door. "But unfortunately, you will have to deal with him for far longer than we will."

"Touché," Terry says unoffended. "Look, first and foremost, I owe you an apology." He studies my face, searching for bruises. "I'm sorry about-" I stop him. I don't want him to be sorry. The truth of the matter is, taking his fist to my face, man to man has inadvertently cleared the air. "I'd always trusted my instincts, but hearing him... I know he's a lying, nasty piece of work because he also made inferences about-" he pauses and turns to Sloan. "I know about your wife. Your mother and sister, too." Sloan starts to move, but Terry raises his palm. "I was told those truths in confidence."

Sloan glares at me. "Don't look at me like that. I wouldn't dare say anything!"

"No, he didn't," Terry confirms. "How I know is unimportant. My source will take it to the grave, as will I. Their secrets are safe with me. Now, let's get back to where we were," he says, gazing at Oliver, who's yawning. "That day at your flat, I had to vent my fury. I needed to hit something!"

I press my lips together. "Terry, it's fine, it's done. My face has healed. Everything else, however, is still up for debate."

He shakes his head, a sheepish expression taking over. "Like I said before, son, I can't exactly play the martyr. I just wish you'd have said something sooner."

"I hoped I'd never have to," I say in resignation, taking in the other men's expressions of sorrow.

"I've spoken to Evie at length, and she told me what you said that day. If I thought for a second that what that arsehole's saying is true, my friend outside would've taken care of you already."

I grimace. "I respect that, but I swear I didn't do-"

He holds up his hand to halt my pleading. "I believe you, and more so, so does Evie. And if you're wondering why she hasn't contacted you for a fortnight, well, that's on me. I made her give up her phone. She had to be sure you were the one for her because there's a very real possibility she's going to walk away from her dad and everything he's ever given her for you."

A low whistle emanates. I look between the bystanders, all wearing a weird mix of pride and intrigue.

"I have no doubt you'll be the first person she calls when I give her her phone back later. She's talked about nothing else for the last week or so since she spoke to your wife." He acknowledges Sloan. "Just make sure you make it right. I want her happy, and right now, without you, she's miserable."

A spark of hope flourishes in my chest. "Why are you encouraging this?"

"Because I like you, lad. We're all entitled to make mistakes in life, but it's what we learn from them that's really important. I'd say you've learnt those lessons harder than most," he says, rising from the chair. "Well, it's been nice to meet you all, gentlemen. If you ever need anything that your services cannot provide, Jeremy has my number." He reluctantly passes a sleepy Oliver back to his dad. "I'll see you again, cheeky boy. Jeremy?" He turns back to me. "Call me when this little guy comes back for a visit." I smile and accompany him outside. "I'll see you later, son."

Ten minutes later, the five of us loiter in the yard as Terry is driven away from the building.

John releases a long-suffering sigh. "Considering all the shit I'm going through with Marie and that bastard of an ex-father-in-law of hers, I don't know how I feel about having a former gangland hard arse not only gracing my building and pristine tarmac but the fact he's just offered us some of his more nefarious services!"

I give him an incredulous look because if I make this work with Evie, I have a feeling Terry may just turn up on the off chance to feel part of a team again. Even more so if there's a baby to pamper.

"Don't look a gift horse in the mouth," Dom starts. "His type of services might be just what you need to *bargain* with good old Judge Beresford." He shares a thoughtful look with John.

Sloan huffs. "Well, screw your tarmac and your gift horse. It's not your son the gangster has taken a liking to. I don't know if I should feel triumphant or terrified!"

Kieran chuckles at today's very strange turn of events. "Sloan, I think it's safe to say that when he's older, if he comes back from Uncle Jeremy and Auntie Evie's house talking about pig farms and a cigar dangling from his mouth, then you should worry!" The foursome laugh behind me, but I'm not finding any of it amusing.

"I don't think any of us have the right to judge, do you? Underneath his reputation, he's a good man. I trust him, and so should you. He practically assisted in raising Evie. He's the one she tells her troubles to. And no disrespect," I turn to Sloan, "but he might be the only grandfather figure your boy ever has."

On that, I stride back into the building. My dark mood has finally dissipated. I put my mobile on charge and wait anxiously for Evie to call. I smile. Inside, I can't contain my happiness because tonight is finally going to change everything for us.

Tonight, I'm finally going to get everything I deserve.

Chapter 40

I GLANCE UP from the draft designs spread over the desk to the clock on the wall and emit a resigned groan. It's been hours since Terry left, and Evie is still exercising radio silence.

"Still not heard from little miss?" Jake asks, and I subtly flick him the finger as my phone finally wakes up.

I grab it before Jake does and he puffs, relieved on my behalf. "At last!" he announces and walks away, thinking it's little miss. *I wish it was!*

"Hi, Mam," I greet, slipping back into northern dialect while trying to steer the dissatisfaction from my tone.

"You didn't call me back earlier. What do you want for dinner tonight?"

I smile. Typical. "Actually, I'm going back home tonight." My announcement is met with silence.

"Oh, has Evie called?" she asks, hopeful.

Honestly, it doesn't matter that Terry pummelled me on my doorstep, all April James cares about is that I make this work. She's never said it, but she wants me settled and happy, and I can't fault her for that. For so many years, I sailed through life rudderless, without a compass, navigating unknown waters, until I finally found land. And landed, I did. In some eyes, what should have been a typical one-night stand turned into a one life stand. I have no intentions of letting Evie go. Even if she doesn't want me, I'll just grow old alone and become further disillusioned with the world than I already am.

"Jeremy?" Mum draws me out of my procrastination.

"Sorry. Terry came over and said she would call me later today, but she hasn't yet."

"She will!" Mum's positivity is enough to convince even me. "Right, I know you're too old for the birds, and the bees chat-"

"Mam!"

"But-" she ignores my protest "-when she calls, invite her over for dinner. You need to wine and dine her. And ensure you actually cook something other than a frozen pizza! You've got to make it romantic. You've got to make her want you again!"

I furrow my brow. "Wanting me was never the problem," I mutter while she waffles on about wine and desserts. Then she shifts the subject to a clean shirt, trousers, boxers, and fresh bedding – just in case!

For fuck sake! I dare not verbalise my vexation, but if this carries on, she's going to be telling me what the best condoms are, and if she does, I'm going to wipe it from my memory as to how she knows.

I let it go through one and out of the other and rub my forehead. I stare, brain dumb, at the desk in front of me, resisting the urge to bang my head against it for momentary relief from her romance tips.

"Jer!" Dom yells, and I lift my head. "Someone's on the blower for you!"

Jesus Christ, there is a God, he's listening, and he's just recognised my distress!

"Ma-"

"I heard. Look, call me tomorrow. I want to know how it goes. I'll be back from baby clinic around two. I love you, kiddo."

"I love you, too. I know I don't say it often enough, but I do. Always have, always will." I speak words that should feel foreign from such little use, but they naturally roll off my tongue.

"I know you do. You're a good boy, really. Always have been, always will be. Remember, call me - tomorrow, not next week! Bye, kiddo."

I smile. "I promise I will. Bye." I quickly hang up and grab the landline handset. "Put it down, Dom!"

The man grumbles. "Spoilsport," he replies as the line clicks, and a gracious giggle I know as well as my own fuels my hope and imagination.

"Evie?"

The giggle switches to a content murmur, and her sultry exhale peaks. "Hi, Jeremy."

"I can't. I can't," I stutter out my words, unperformed and unsure. "I can't believe I'm finally hearing your voice again. It feels like forever. God, I need to see you." I get up and close the door. "I'm desperate to touch you, to hold you and never let go."

She gasps unambiguously and inhales again. "Jeremy, I think we-"

"Sorry, I know we need to-" I stop because I know precisely what we need, and it's to stop lying since that's how we ended up here in the first place. "Actually, sweetheart, I'm not sorry. I want to do all of those things, and I'm not sorry if that makes you feel guilty or uncomfortable."

"You're right. I could play dumb, but that would be insulting to both of us. Honestly, I can't wait to see you either. I've missed you so, so much. I've dreamed of you, but to dream of you isn't the same as the real thing."

My heart beats rapidly, fully prepared to burst from my chest upon hearing her truth. "Come over. I'm sure John will let me do one for the rest of the day."

She groans. "I'd love to, but I can't. I'm helping Holly move house today. How about I come over early this evening? We can talk properly and figure out how to take the second step forward."

I furrow my brow in confusion. "What about the first step?"

She laughs again. "This *is* the first step, and I have no intention of making it the last. I lost you once, and I've almost just lost you twice. I won't risk a third time. I can't let our love and devotion die because of hateful vengeance and lies," she says, repeating my prior statement verbatim.

"Come over around six-thirty. I'll make us dinner."

The silence is thick and unexpected. "Oh," she murmurs, surprised. "So, is this a date?"

I chuckle. "Yeah, the first of many to come. Consider this the reset, sweetheart. I'll let you go, but I'll see you later, yeah?"

"Yeah," she whispers. "Jeremy?"

"Hmm?"

"I lov-" she stops, a part of her still unable to say it.

"I understand, darling. I love you, too. I'll see you tonight."

Evie hangs up first, and I sit on the desk, a smile stretching across my face, causing my cheeks to hurt.

"Little miss?"

I snap my head back. John fills the doorway, then strolls inside with Dom and Kieran jockeying behind him for second place. K's bulk wins the battle of wills, and he pushes past effortlessly. I watch as the three of them sit on whatever will hold them comfortable and wait for me to spill.

"She's coming over tonight."

"Good. So am I," J replies, very matter of fact, as Kieran says, "me too," and Dom throws in, "and I."

"No, you're not. You're all staying away. I need to talk to her alone, John. I don't want her pouring her guts out while you three stooges have your ears to the wall!"

Kieran's features twist, and he's ready to fire something sarcastic back, but Dom presses his hand to K's chest and shakes his head.

John grunts. "Fine! Call me when she leaves. We'll come over, have a drink and discuss where we currently stand."

God, give me fucking strength! I rub my eyes and nonchalantly wave my hand. "Because the issues surrounding Marie haven't already put enough on your plate, you've still got to heap my shit on top of it, too?"

"I'm a glutton for punishment, sunshine!" He winks and crosses his arms behind his head, and leans back to lounge. "The truth? I don't trust anyone or anything outside of our inner circle right now."

I catch the inside of my lip between my teeth, but I don't validate his point. "J, it's going to be fine. You'll see."

He subtly grinds his jaw. "Maybe. Remember years ago, when I said I'd hate to stand by your grave and mourn you?" A cold chill blankets my spine, the memory taking hold. "Still stands, son. I make no apologies for protecting those I love, and that now includes little miss, regardless of how much she tries to emotionally detach herself from us. Although if what Cosgrove said is true, I think we may see changes afoot."

I move to the window and perch my backside on the large sill. "Possibly, because if she's going to acquiesce and come to me willingly, then Andy is going to fight back with every dirty, low-down trick in his arsenal."

No John or Dom pearls of wisdom are imparted, and I gaze into the city vista, prepared to go to war for the woman I love.

I STRIDE FROM the lift and fish the key from my pocket. I transfer the bag of groceries and bunch of white and pink roses from one hand to the other and insert the key the same moment the door opposite opens.

I smile over my shoulder at my neighbour. "Hi, mate." God, I really should find out his name – asking will look pathetic since we've both lived here for a few years.

"Hi," he reciprocates, looking down the corridor, edging closer. "I've not seen you for a while, but there was someone here last week looking for you. He knocked on my door first. I said I didn't know who he was talking about, but he came back later on in the week and again yesterday, too."

My nape bristles. "What did he look like?"

"Tall, a bit stocky. I've never seen him here before, but I might have some footage from the camera." He jerks his head back, indicating the small camera affixed to the door architrave.

"Thanks, I'd appreciate it." I start to turn but then turn back. "I'm Jeremy, by the way."

"Yeah, I'm Aaron. I'll come over later if I find any decent images." I smile and shake his hand, then watch as he boards the lift and the doors ping.

I open my door and kick it shut behind me. My phone buzzes, notifying me of movement from my own cameras, and I turn off the app. Emptying the shopping bag, I place the dead bird on the worktop and flick open Google, because after advising me on how to wine and dine a lady, I'll be damned if my mother has to give me cookery tips, or worst still, an impromptu visit to cook the bloody thing herself.

Two hours later, the smell of roast chicken diffuses through the flat as I pull down the oven door to check on my creation. I waft the tea towel in front of my face, redirecting the immense heat before it singes my eyelashes. Closing the door, my phone beeps from the small dining table I've moved from the kitchen into the living room, and I swipe the screen. Evie's text of *I'm on my way* supersedes John's of *don't forget to call me*. Since we spoke a few hours ago, it's been like waiting to be led to the gallows anticipating her arrival. I put the phone down, toss the tea towel over the back of a chair and move into the bedroom. I open the wardrobe door and dig out some suitable dinner attire.

Folding down my collar, inspecting my appearance – not that I can physically change anything now – the intercom buzzes. I press the entry button, and excitement ripples through me. I straighten myself up again, hoping she approves of my crisp white shirt, navy trousers and shiny belt. I'm even wearing clean underwear – not that I'm expecting her to see them – and sprayed on some cologne, heeding my mother's advice of what women want, or at the very least, the minimum they expect.

I lean against the wall, counting the seconds until a light knock resounds through the hallway. I resist the urge to look through the peephole because I want to see *her*. To know that what I see and feel is flesh and blood. I take a breath and open the door. Evie is on the other side; a fantasy finally realised.

A delicate blush stains her porcelain cheeks, and she smiles, biting the inside of her lip and looks down. "Hi," she whispers, her eyes trained on the bland, grey linoleum beneath her feet.

"Hey," I reply and hold out my hand. "Come on in." Her head lifts, and she slides her palm across mine. The painless burn of the chemistry we share transfers between us, and I tighten my fingers as they automatically entwine with hers. I close the door the moment she crosses the threshold and raise her hand, holding it to my heart.

"Something smells delicious." She subtly sniffs the air. I grin; mothers are always right – and I'll thank her when I call tomorrow.

"Here, let me take this." I carefully take the bag from her hand. She remains quiet, studying my appearance while she removes her jacket.

"I feel underdressed." She touches her black lace top and skinny jeans.

I chuckle. "No, you're perfect, and I'm going to wine and dine you and make the best first impression I possibly can." My body is mere inches from hers, and the warmth of her skin and the scent of her perfume teases and tantalises. I raise my hand to her cheek, and she leans into it.

"Jeremy..." she murmurs, her eyes closing. I cup her cheek with my other hand and cradle her face. Her eyes ensnare mine the same way they always have, and she stretches up on her toes as I lean forward. With our lips practically touching, sanity and realism prevails.

"Evie," I whisper, and lightly touch my forehead to hers. "I can't."

She pulls back abruptly and stares into my eyes, hurt consuming hers. "You don't want me anymore?" she asks the most ludicrous, insulting question of them all.

"'Don't' isn't even in my vocabulary when it comes to you. I'll always want you. I even resigned myself to living the end of my years alone if you wouldn't take me back. I already told you; I want to touch you and feel you. I want to kiss and taste you. I want to wrap myself around you when I slide inside you again and remember what it felt like to experience heaven on earth. Trust me, sweetheart, of course, I want you."

"Oh," she breathes out, her cheeks a darker shade of pink.

"But first, I need to regain your trust because, without it, we don't have anything."

"Okay." She smiles and leads me into the living room. She halts, and I grab her hips to stop myself from body slamming her. She runs her hand over the vase of flowers in the centre and the tealight candles. "For me?" I smile. "Mr romance." She laughs and licks her lip.

"Sweetheart, I think we've already established I'm Mr Romance personified."

"That we did." She reaches for the bottle of wine and the carafe and pours a glass of wine for herself and a glass of water for me. I pick up the glass and tap it against hers.

"To new beginnings, but we still need to discuss old endings."

"I know." Her reply exposes her sadness. "So, what's for dinner?" she asks, changing the subject as easily as flicking a switch.

"Roast chicken," I reply rote as she sits on the sofa. "Have you spoken to your dad recently?" I dare to broach the elephant in the room, or more specifically, I'm asking if she has dared to question him about his new nefarious connections. Evie, curled up with her feet beneath her, gains instant awareness.

"No," she eventually confesses. "I've not really seen him since after he told me about…" *About you*, is what she wants to say.

I sit down, reach over, and rub her knee. "It's okay, you can say it."

"I know I can, but I don't want to." She huffs. "You know, I've spent my entire life doing what he wanted me to. Speaking how he wanted me to, dressing how he wanted me to. Even flirting with Piers Baron twat, the way he wanted me to! And the one and only time I dare to do what *I* want to-" she stares at me "-he destroys it. I really shouldn't have expected anything less. I mean, he tried to whore me off to the highest bidder numerous times until Piers finally started to find me attractive." She lifts her glass up, concentrating on the rim, the receptacle partially veiling her sadness and fury. "All the times you used to say he hated you, I didn't want to believe it, but *I knew*. For the last fortnight, I've been going over and over what he said. He had to have known I would find out the truth from Kara and Sloan. So, why?" she asks heatedly. "Why would he accuse you of such things?"

I shrug, but we both know why. "Because I'm poor, and my reputation does nothing for his social status. He despises me; he even said so. And maybe it's because he has some new friends who also despise me lining his pockets further, especially now Sloan has put him in the garden."

"Regardless." She shifts closer. "To accuse you of rape, *that* I don't-"

"Don't underestimate him," I interrupt her. "You said it yourself. He tried to whore you off to the highest bidder. Why should it be any different in his attempts to get me out of the picture?"

"But that's different! Jeremy, he accused you of ra-"

"Stop saying that word!" I release a frustrated breath then inhale. "Sweetheart, I'm sorry. I just…"

She shuffles towards me on her knees until she's practically straddling my lap. "I understand." She strokes my face and brushes her nose over mine. Her eyes darken and smoulder, and I know what's coming. "Kiss me, Jeremy," she demands. "Make me remember. Make *us* remember."

I gasp in shocked anticipation. I shouldn't allow her to take advantage of the situation, but I can no longer resist. The instant our lips touch, my hands automatically grab the back of her head, angling her where I want her.

Evie, as desperate for this moment as I am, takes the initiative and climbs onto my lap. Her arms wrap around my shoulders while her fingers dip beneath my collar, caressing my skin.

"Oh, God, Evie," I breathe out, amazed this simple little touch can turn me on so quickly. I lower my hands to her hips, and she rocks them back and forth, applying further pressure with each roll, ensuring my deprived dick reacts gratefully. She continues to caress the supple skin at the back of my neck. Each tender touch stokes my awareness, creating a full sensory assault. I grip her hard and devour her mouth. In the heat of the moment, passion is the driving force, and I allow it to shuttle me away from reason.

Long minutes pass, and she tugs up the bottom of her top. "I want you, Jeremy. I want to feel your skin on mine. I want to feel you inside me."

I silently place my hands over hers and manipulate them away from her clothing. The conflict I'm experiencing is very real, and those big, beautiful eyes, pleading with me to take what she's willing to give, are more convincing than she realises. If I allow her to, she will show no inclination or willingness to repel my advances or deject my ministrations. She will happily allow me to strip her bare and take her back to our bed – or on this sofa. But as tempting as that is, my sinner is also a saint, and as alluring as those prospects are, they have also sparked my sense of sanity.

"Evie, Evie, Evie," I pant. Her receptiveness is on key, and she tries to shuffle back. Her mortification at being rejected – in her eyes – is ostensible, but I hold her steady and touch my forehead to hers.

The strangled silence is palpable, and the atmosphere is uncomfortable, thick with her need and mine. But I guess her unspoken ideal is that if we don't talk about the reasons why we're here, then we can pretend the imminent problems we're going to face don't exist. But if we do talk about it, and of course, we will, then the truth is tangible.

We both know there's nothing more real than reality. And this is ours.

"I'm sorry," she whispers.

I cradle her head and press my lips to hers. "Don't be, but I didn't invite you here to get you naked."

She presses her lips together. "Shame, because it was totally my intention of getting *you* naked."

I laugh and curl my hand around her head. Kissing her crown, I sit her back on the sofa, and the return of easy civility is welcome when she sulks dramatically.

"Sweetheart, when I spoke to your grandad yesterday, he said something. Something important, and I'd like to know if it's true." She cranes her head, ensnaring my eyes with hers. "Are you going to give up everything for me?"

"Why do you ask?"

"Because if you are, I need to start planning for the life you deserve. You need more than what I currently have to offer."

"Meaning?" Her brows twitch together.

"Meaning I refuse to raise our future family in an eighth-floor flat. Meaning I need to start working towards a new financial goal and not just squirrelling my cash away because I'm just existing."

She purses her lips in contemplation. "There are numerous ways I could answer that, but there have been enough omissions between us, so the simple answer is yes, I intend on turning my back on my dad, but it's not as dire as it sounds."

She sounds positive, but I can't put my faith in her optimism. Rather than force the subject, I lift her up from the sofa. She wraps her legs around my waist, clinging on for dear life.

"I'd never let you fall, sweetheart."

"I know." She kisses my scar. I cradle the back of her head and claim her lips again. She squeaks in protest into my mouth as I lower her to her feet. I pull out her chair, and she sits and shakes out the cloth napkin.

Five minutes later, I place the plates down and take my seat. She smiles beautifully as I pour the wine. I pick up my glass – a rare treat for me – and tap it to hers.

"To us," she says, and I repeat, silently rejoicing there is still an *us*.

Chapter 41

EVIE YAWNS, FILLING the silent void.

My arm tightens around her, and I trail my fingers up and down her forearm, feeling at peace with myself for the first time in weeks.

It's been an hour, almost two since we finished dinner, and during that time, we've talked, we've laughed, we've kissed and touched, but this? This is perfection I cannot articulate.

But our perfection is diminished when another soft yawn ripples through the calm.

"Tired?"

She turns in my arms. "A little. It's getting late. I should go. Unless you want me to stay?"

I squeeze my eyes tight because she's challenging my resolve. "Of course, I want you to stay, but I have to let you go. For tonight, anyway."

She smiles beautifully. "Don't worry, I'm just testing the waters. Besides, Grandpy is expecting me. I told him not to wait up, but he's protective."

I stroke her rosy cheeks warmed through dinner, alcohol, and passion. "Good. He's protecting your reputation as well as your virtue."

She shakes her head. "Maybe he should have thought of that a few years back," she retorts far too flirty.

I frown. "And maybe we should keep quiet about that in front of him." Especially if I value certain body parts.

"Jeremy, he knows I'm not a virgin, and our relationship is sexual."

"No, he doesn't," I reply. She gives me a *are you thick?* expression, and I concede. Yes, he probably does, but ignorance can be bliss. "Okay, fine, he probably does know, but I have a lot of respect for him, and I want him to like me. I don't want to end up waterboarded and dead at some secluded beauty spot." I finish on a mumble.

"What?" She puts her hand over her amused mouth.

"Nothing, I just-"

"You've just watched too many gangster films." I grin as she takes my hand and pulls me up from the sofa. "Walk me down?"

463

"Sure." I open the sideboard drawer and place the car keys in her hand. The zap of electricity sparks between us again, but it's always there, simmering beneath the surface. I hold open her jacket, and she slips it on and shoulders her bag.

"Can I see you again tomorrow?" she asks. "Date number two?"

"Absolutely," I confess it's hard to watch her leave, even if it is only for a day. I'd love to make her stay, but I respect the boundaries currently between us. I hold her hand as we make our way to the lift.

"Oh, by the way, Grandpy is quite smitten with Oliver, spoke non-stop about him. Calling him his cheeky chap!" I laugh and hold her close as the lift descends the floors. "Sloan is aware his son has found himself a new grandad, isn't he?"

I politely kiss her lips and smooth her hair back. "He knows, but he's still resisting the truth penetrating his thick skull! Don't worry, sweetheart, I'll reiterate."

"Well, make sure you do." She wraps her arms around my waist. "He's already talking about making a special trip to Sloan's office to extort some baby time out of him. He even tried to use my phone as leverage to con me into giving him their address. That's why I didn't call earlier. Really, can you believe him?"

The lift pings and I grasp her hand again. "After seeing him with Oliver today, I really can." We stop beside her car, and I reel her back into me. "This afternoon, he gave me a weird sort of permission to father his grandchildren." She opens her mouth, but I put my finger over it. "Don't panic. I told him no babies until you're grown up."

She slides her arms around my neck. "Until then, he's going to monopolise Oliver. It's a good thing I don't mind sharing." She laughs. "But warn Kara and Sloan that he will use hard-handed tactics to get what he wants."

"I will." I open her door, and she tosses her bag inside. "I love you." I gaze into her eyes and bestow her a lingering kiss.

"Jeremy," she breathes against my mouth then reluctantly pulls away. "If you don't let me go now, I never will."

"Sounds good to me." I press my forehead to hers.

"I'll see you tomorrow." She finally gets in the car, and I walk behind as she drives up the ramp onto the street. Watching her taillights fade, movement a few hundred yards away catches my attention. I squint, unable to make it out, and I walk backwards into the car park and activate the barrier.

A broad smile graces my face. My world is a more balanced and perfect place again with Evie back in it. My phone buzzes in my pocket, and I swipe the screen as I call for the lift.

"Hey, she's just left," I tell John.

"Good, we're coming over."

"Fabulous. I'll leave you the washing up."

"You're wishful thinking, you funny little git! We'll see you soon." He hangs up, and I laugh, boarding the lift.

I dial and press call when the doors open. With the phone to my ear, I pause outside my door.

"How did it go?" Sloan asks the moment he picks up.

"Fine," I reply. "I'm just calling with some friendly advice, which means you may need to set an extra place at the table for Christmas dinner."

"Why?" he asks, sounding thick for a highly intelligent guy.

"Because I've been told your son has adopted himself a new grandpa! I've also been advised that you may receive some unexpected visits of the corruption type, but don't worry, Evie said she doesn't mind sharing him!" I'm eager to laugh as Sloan stays silent before groaning.

"Fucking great! Of all the grandpas in the world, my son had to score himself that one."

"It could be worse, Sloan. A lot worse," I impart, an unspoken inference to the Black years and the dark clouds of Franklin, and God forbid, Ian Petersen.

"Yeah, it could. I think I could arrange a visit or two with the old codger if it puts a smile on his face and keeps you in his good books."

"Appreciated."

"So, you and Evie?"

"Yeah, we're good."

He's silent again, and I wait for it. "I wasn't wrong, was I?" he asks thoughtfully. I narrow my eyes, no clue what he's talking about. "Being in love and someone being in love with you. It's a good feeling, the best in the world."

"It definitely is," I reply.

"When the dust has settled, bring her over to the house. I know my beloved wants to speak to her."

"I will."

"I'll see you later. I love you, man."

"I love you, too." I hang up and baulk at the plates and glasses in need of washing.

Instead, I pour another small glass of wine and open the patio doors. The early night breeze fills the living room, and the sounds of the city accompany my content silence. I sip the wine, grateful my life is turning in the right direction again. I close the door and place the glass on the table. Picking up the dirty plates, the doorbell chimes. I deposit the plates on the worktop and wipe my hands. As I walk to the door, the bell goes again.

"Flipping heck, John, that was quick!" I reach for the key. "Don't you remember what happened the last time you were caught speeding!" My laugh withers when the handle depresses repeatedly, and I step back. For all of John, Dom, and Kieran's bravado, they don't attempt to enter uninvited, even with family. My sunny demeanour evaporates as voices drift inside. I lean into the peephole, and three figures dressed in black are converged in the hallway. I stride back and whip out my phone.

"We'll be there in twenty," Dom answers.

"No, you need to be here now! There are three men outside my door, and I'll bet my life that one of them is Ed Shaw, or the guy scoping the place out for the last few days."

"What?"

"Never mind, just hurry up!" I hiss when a thud is levied against the wood. I move into the kitchen and grab the cricket bat from beside the fridge and hold it prone in front of me. I'm not a fighter, but I'll use whatever it takes. I also have a very good idea who is outside, desperate to get in.

A repetitive banging ensues, accompanied by the continuous melody of the doorbell, until an almighty thud splinters the frame, and the door flies open. I dash to the patio doors and activate the panic alarm button hidden behind the curtains and the siren sounds. My respite is short-lived when one of the intruders rips the internal siren off the wall and stomps on it until the sound turns strangled, then dies completely. The other two now rush inside, and I know all I need to do is hold them off until the calvary arrives.

I swing the bat as hard as I can in front of me, and the end connects with the shoulder of the taller of the two now advancing towards me. He grunts and falls back, and I thrash out at the second assailant. The man shouts but dodges my swing, and the pointless crap atop the sideboard flies through the air. The man continues to goad, stepping back and motioning for me to approach. I accept and continue to swing, my focus transfixed on him, until something silences my stomach. I glance down at the kitchen knife sticking out of my side. I pull it out, although I know I shouldn't, and toss it behind the sofa. Gripping the bat again, my body sways with a light-headedness, and I swing out and lose balance.

In my weakened state, they advance on me. The effects of being repeatedly punched and kicked is too much for my body to take, and as much as I put up a good fight, I drop to the floor. Two crucial memories come back to haunt, remembering the moments Deacon had me in the same position, cutting my face to ensure I'd never forget what it felt like to protect, and months later, to betray. In indescribable pain, I grasp the bat and thrash it in front of me. I fall forward, unable to muster the strength needed to carry on.

Unexpectedly, a punch is levied to my temple, and I grab the side of my head as my ear starts to ring. I lift up and spear the man with a hateful glare. "Come on, you son of a bitch, Shaw. Take off the fucking mask. I know it's you!" I spit out the blood in my mouth while the fire in my side penetrates deeper.

As I'm grabbed from behind, and my head is forced up, a blade is pressed to my throat, immobilising me. The chuckle that has plagued my nightmares resounds from under the mask as the bastard finally reveals himself. A decade older, wiser, and more odious, Edward Shaw is in front of me again after all these years. My eyes track from him to the arsehole behind me, and Shaw flicks his brows, and the second man also removes his mask, revealing Greg Davies, as expected.

Ed crouches in front of me, wearing a cruel smirk. "It's been a long time, James. I've prayed for this day from the moment I buried my Emma. It's not enough that a delinquent cunt like you gets to live and breathe while my girl rots in the ground, but then you have to go and corrupt another good girl." He glares behind him at the third, unidentified intruder nervously fidgeting. I start to shake my head but remember the blade at my jugular. I stop, but it still doesn't change the fact that the unidentified man with the anxious and agitated disposition, now twisting his ring, is Andrew Blake. It makes me wonder if he realised he was signing on as an accomplice to whatever dirty deed Shaw is planning when he made the pact with these two evil bastards.

"We're all acquainted here, Andrew," I say. "So, you might as well remove it!"

The man shakes his head, refusing my request. It's a smart move, but the ferocious shaking of his limbs reveals the fear of a petrified man with no real comprehension of what he's signed up for, just as I presumed.

Shaw forces my chin back with the knife, and his breath wafts across my face. His calm demeanour is deceptive, and something is lighting up his eyes disturbingly.

"Like I said, I've prayed for this moment for a long time. After what you did to my daughter, I'd personally like to see you hung, drawn, and quartered, a purer type of justice, so to speak. However, that's all inconsequential now, and this is the best I can do under current time limitations."

He scowls, then the blade is retracted from my throat, and a plastic bag is suddenly dropped over my head. I fall, my arms out, unable to breathe and take advantage of Davies' distraction and manage to get to my feet. Unrestrained, I manage to rip the bag apart from the mouth. I gasp for air as the knife scrapes past the fresh wound on my stomach. I move back until someone lands a foot to my gut, and I flail, landing hard on the floor, feeling my hip pop and my back crack.

"Hold him up!" Shaw demands, and Davies grabs one arm while anonymous Andy moves to the other.

"Jeremy?" A voice drifts into the flat, and I glance over the hallway to see my terrified neighbour frozen in the doorway. "Holy fuck!" he says before running back into his flat and locking the door. I pray he calls the police - not that they will be able to do much now.

"I guess that intrusion means I can no longer draw this out?" Shaw states, void of emotion, ensuring my hope perishes instantly.

In retrospect, I should have seen this coming, because that bullseye on my back had never faded, only shifted. I always knew my past crimes would eventually catch up and potentially crucify me. But this isn't a simple beating or an act of revenge, this is a premeditated execution.

A sudden, sharp prick is injected into my neck, and the long distant friend I haven't met in so long comes to visit. And sadly, a decade of drug-free sobriety disappears in an instant. Drifting through my veins at warp speed, the sensation I remember from yesteryear smooths the edges and mellows the senses. Somewhere in my head, it tells me that may be a good thing, considering how I may be meeting my maker imminently.

"...and now I hope you rot in hell!" Shaw hisses.

The knife glistens in front of me, but even in my subdued state, I refuse to go down without a fight. As the blade moves closer, I pull back at the last minute and feel the tip puncture my skin. I don't know what I expect, maybe a burning path from the side of my throat, down to my chest, but I feel nothing, just trickling heat. It creates a line of liquid fire that I'm not sure I'm going to be able to survive. I press my hand to my throat, and my palm is heavily smeared red, a sign my life is already draining away.

My haemorrhaging body slumps to the floor in my high, dying state, and my heart beats a thunderous tattoo in my ears. Unidentified Andy, his hands and face spattered with blood, starts to hyperventilate and runs out of the flat in a panic.

Unperturbed by this turn of events, Shaw bends down and gets in my face. "One day, I'll continue this in hell with you!" His words ring in my ears, and I start to lose consciousness as Davies drags him out of the flat.

The moment the stair door thuds, the flat door opposite opens, and Aaron runs in brandishing towels. He pressurises one over my neck, telling me the police and ambulance are on their way. Only they can't help me now. *Nothing can.*

The silence devours, and the faint blare of sirens intensifies. When the pressure being applied to my throat starts to become numb, causing my body to relax against its will - since we're both aware this is the end - a commotion from the hallway emanates, but I'm too far gone, and my failing eyesight confirms it.

My body feels heavy, but I feel like I'm floating. The subsiding pain brings a new realisation as it claws its way deeper and deeper, poisoning my bloodstream, making me remember the good old days and the addict I tried to hide. Back then, it was a chemical evil to take away the pain. A shot in the dark to forget the suffering. Today, however, it's assisting to smooth the way from life into death.

As my world turns black and murky, the dark swallowing the light, my earlier assumption is true. My sinner really is a saint, but my quest for redemption still wasn't enough to alter my path into purgatory.

And inside my dying heart, I realise I was wrong, and maybe hell still holds a special place for men like me.

Author Note

Redemption is the fifth instalment of the Fractured series and is Jeremy and Evie's story. It is a long, slow-burning, all-the-feels romance.

The sixth novel, Reparation, completes the duet and will be released in due course.

Finally, if you enjoyed this novel, please consider sparing a few moments to leave a review.

Follow Elle

If you wish to be notified of future releases, special offers, discounted books, ARC opportunities, and more, please click on the link below.

Subscribe to Elle's mailing list

Alternatively, you can connect with Elle on the following sites:

Website: www.ellecharles.com

Facebook: www.facebook.com/ellecharleswriter

Twitter: www.twitter.com/@ellecharles

Bookbub: www.bookbub.com/authors/elle-charles

Instagram: www.instagram.com/ellecharleswriter

Or by email:

elle.charlesauthor@gmail.com

elle@ellecharles.com

About the Author

Elle was born and raised in Yorkshire, England, where she still resides.

A self-confessed daydreamer, she loves to create strong, diverse characters cocooned in opulent yet realistic settings that draw the reader in with every twist and turn until the very last page.

A voracious reader for as long as she can remember, she is never without her beloved Kindle. When she is not absorbed in the newest release or a trusted classic, she can often be found huddled over her laptop, tapping away new ideas and plots for future works.

In-between other works in progress, she will be continuing the series, and is currently working on book 6, Reparation, and book 7. Release dates will be announced in due course, but please do get in touch if you would like any further information.

www.ellecharles.com

Works by Elle Charles

All titles are available to purchase in ebook, paperback and hardback formats.

The Fractured Series:

Kara and Sloan
Fractured (Book 1)
Tormented (Book 2)
Aftermath (Book 2.5)
Liberated (Book 3)

Marie and John
Faithless (Book 4)

Jeremy and Evie
Redemption (Book 5)

The Fractured Series Box Set:
Box Set 1 (Books 1-3 inclusive) (ebook only)

FUTURE RELEASES:
Release date to be confirmed

Reparation (Book 6)